CRETE

Paola Pugsley

Revised, rewritten and updated from the
previous edition by Pat Cameron

Somerset Books • London

Eighth edition 2010

Published by Blue Guides Limited, a Somerset Books Company
Winchester House, Deane Gate Avenue, Taunton, Somerset TA1 2UH
www.blueguides.com
'Blue Guide' is a registered trademark.

ISBN 978–1–905131–29–7

A CIP catalogue record of this book is available from the British Library.

Distributed in the United States of America by
W.W. Norton & Company, Inc.
500 Fifth Avenue, New York, NY 10110.

The editor and publisher have made reasonable efforts to ensure the accuracy of all the
information in *Blue Guide Crete*; however, they can accept no responsibility for any loss,
injury or inconvenience sustained by any traveller as a result of information or advice
contained in the guide.

Statement of editorial independence: Blue Guides, their authors and editors, are prohibited
from accepting payment from any restaurant, hotel, gallery or other establishment for its
inclusion in this guide, or on www.blueguides.com, or for a more favourable mention than
would otherwise have been made.

All other acknowledgements, photo credits and copyright information
are given on p. 432, which forms part of this copyright page.

Your views on this book would be much appreciated. We welcome not only specific
comments, suggestions or corrections, but any more general views you may have: how this
book enhanced your visit, how it could have been more helpful. Blue Guides authors and
editorial and production team work hard to bring you what we hope are the best-researched
and best-presented cultural, historical and academic guide books in the English language.
Please write to us by email (editorial@blueguides.com), via the comments page on our website
(www.blueguides.com) or at the address given above. We will be happy to acknowledge
useful contributions in the next edition, and to offer a free copy of one of our titles.

CONTENTS

THE GUIDE

MAPS & PLANS

About the author

Paola Pugsley is a professional archaeologist with a particular interest in ancient technologies, particularly woodworking, the subject of her doctorate in 2002. Alongside her own academic research she is keen to foster a deeper understanding of history and its material manifestation (i.e. archaeology) by visitors enjoying a holiday in the sun. This new Blue Guide to Crete has been written very much with that approach in mind, visiting and revisiting the island in its furthest recesses both as an archaeologist and as a tourist. In the summer Paola can be found working on excavations in Greece, Anatolia and Mesopotamia.

Pat Cameron, author of the previous four editions of this guide, studied English at Oxford and obtained a diploma in Archaeology from London University. Following this she worked for five years on Crete, cataloguing material in the British School at Athens' Stratigraphical Museum at Knossos.

Editor's note: transliteration

The transliteration of Greek is no easy task. As John Pendlebury wrote in his *Archaeology of Crete* 70 years ago: 'Orthography and the transcription of modern Greek names is a problem. I confess to inconsistency.' I confess to inconsistency too. The aim has been to find transcriptions that help with pronunciation without stripping words of their character. As the very word 'orthography' shows, the English language is able to accommodate 'Υ', and 'Φ'; in the spirit of 'Greekness' these have often been rendered as 'y' and 'ph': thus Pyrgos not Pirgos and Phourni not Fourni. The diphthong 'αι' has mainly been retained as 'ai'; so, often, has 'ει', as 'ei'. 'Οι' is sounded very differently in English, and for that reason is rendered simply 'i'. The guttural 'Χ', pronounced much softer in Crete than elsewhere in Greece, is rendered 'ch'. The gamma (Γ), which on the mainland is often so soft as to justify the transliteration 'y' (Yeoryios), is not so soft on Crete: we usually render it 'g' or 'gh' (Chania likewise transliterates the name of its airport as 'Daskalogiannis'). Names and place names from the Classical world are spelled in the way most familiar from literature (Daedalus, not Dhaidhalos). The same is true of well-known names from art and history (Damophon; Nicephorus Phocas). Accents indicating the stressed syllables on place names are given in the index.

HISTORY OF CRETE

Situated at the south end of the Aegean Sea, measuring some 250km in length but at its narrowest point, the Ierapetra isthmus, only 14km across, Crete is by far the largest island of the Greek archipelago. Geologically it is part of an arc stretching from the Dinaric Alps through the Peloponnese and Kythera and continuing via Karpathos to Rhodes and southern Turkey. It is bounded to the northeast by a volcanic ridge running roughly from Athens to Cnidos via Santorini. To the south the African plate meets the Eurasian plate in the Hellenic trench, a deep sea depression which over time has given the island it present appearance through a history of tremors and earthquakes which have caused the land alternately to rise and fall. Crete was once covered by the sea, which explains why the limestone mountains that now form its spine (the White Mountains, Ida and the Diktaian massif) have abundant marine fossils.

The first Cretan landmass was not an island at all: it was part of the Aegaiis, an extended area occupying the whole Aegean region and created by a process of orogenesis (mountain formation) some 23 million years ago. Things changed considerably c. 11 million years later when the southern portion of the Aegean underwent a process of fragmentation and subsidence. Crete became not one island but several, a situation which continued for a long time with fluctuating sea levels, significant uplifts and tectonic movements. This long period has left a large quantity of fossil remains, including those of extinct mammals such as the Hipparion, a horse, and the Mastodon, an elephant. Gypsum, which was to play an important part in Minoan Crete, was formed during this period, as the Mediterranean dried up and sedimentary deposits of calcium sulphate in caves underwent a process of evaporation turning into a rock that could be easily cut and finished to an attractive, translucent, if not very resilient, building material.

At the time when the first humans were appearing in Africa, Crete roughly achieved its present form as a single landmass created by extended tectonic uplift. It was a dramatic landscape with a busy topography intersected by numerous gorges where the cracks in the land had deepened through a process of water erosion; that, together with island isolation impacted considerably on animal (*see p. 315*) and plant (*see p. 32*) evolution and speciation.

THE NEOLITHIC PERIOD
(7000–3400 BC)

There is no secure evidence of human occupation in Crete in the Palaeolithic and Mesolithic periods, not even during the glaciations when sea levels were considerably lower: fragments of obsidian and traces of shelters in the Herakleion region are still poorly dated, as is the rock carving of hunting scenes from Asphendou in the Sphakia area. Human presence is attested from the very beginning of the Neolithic period (7000 BC). Evidence of Neolithic occupation has been found all over the island in cave sites, in settlements and also on the nearby islands. Of particular interest is the village of Kastelli Phournis in the Mirabello region east of Neapolis near Dreros (*map p. 431, B1*). It can claim to be the longest uninterrupted settlement in Crete. Here in 1959 Nikolaos Platon was called in to investigate a series of wells, discovered while excavating a modern cistern. From the bottom of the wells he recovered 28 complete pots and numerous sherds belonging to the last phase of the Neolithic period (4400–3400 BC). Remains of plaited cord were also found, but being made of organic material they quickly disintegrated when they dried out.

The oldest site so far known is Knossos, where investigations below the palace levels have shown that the original occupation went back to c. 7000 BC in the aceramic phase of the Neolithic, when farming was practised but fired clay was not used for vessels (it may have been used for figurines).

Sir Arthur Evans had already identified Neolithic levels during his excavations of the Minoan occupation but it was only later, in campaigns carried out in the 1960s, that the period was more thoroughly investigated. The quest was hampered by the fact that the palace at Knossos had been built right on top of the Neolithic deposits. Limited excavations could only be carried out in the central and western courts and in the area surrounding the building. The later Minoan development, destructive as it was when it levelled the hill to build a platform for the palace, was in fact instrumental in sealing and preserving the earlier levels. The investigation has allowed archaeologists to reconstruct the original shape of Kephala Hill as the first settlers saw it. This was a low triangular promontory bounded by two watercourses (the Kairatos and the Vlychia) with an oval knoll to the south and a slightly curved spur running northwest. The earliest evidence shows a small settlement in the region of half an acre with farmers practising a mixed economy with wheat, barley and lentils and the full complement of domesticated animals (sheep, goats, pigs and some cattle). There is no reliance on hunting and no evidence that marine resources were tapped apart from a limited amount of shellfish. Houses were small: single rooms made of mud bricks dried in the sun. A couple of thousand years later the process of flattening, infilling and creating a platform had already started. Building techniques had evolved and walls were made in pisé, a stiff clay mixed with pebbles and rammed between two boards set on stone foundations. Floors were of cobbles or trampled clay. Outside contacts with the Aegean (Milos and its obsidian are 80 miles away) are first attested in the Middle Neolithic, when the pace of change appears to accelerate. By the final phase of the period, spinning and weaving were practised, houses consisted of several rooms and had a fixed hearth. The settlement extended for 11 acres as far as the Royal Road and contact with Phaistos had been established (both the ceramic and the obsidian industries show similarities).

Who were these people originally? At the beginning of the Neolithic, the Aegean islands were not settled, which means that the very first colonists must have come from the mainland. Archaeologists believe they came from Anatolia, where comparable building and pottery styles as well as farming practices, are attested. After a long and perilous voyage across the Aegean, they arrived as fully-fledged Neolithic farmers with their domesticated animals. Estimates put the original settlement at 25 to 100 people.

THE BRONZE AGE
(3400–970 BC)

This is the period of the 'palaces' and commentators have tended to interpret evidence on the ground through assumptions about palatial buildings. This is not always helpful. Though for convenience's sake and by force of habit the buildings are referred to as palaces throughout this book, the purpose of these structures is still not fully understood. There is no firm evidence for royal residential occupancy.

CHRONOLOGY OF THE CRETAN BRONZE AGE

When Evans began digging at Knossos he found himself confronted by a hitherto unsuspected civilisation which he called 'Minoan' after King Minos, the mythical ruler of Crete mentioned by Homer in the 8th century BC. Before Evans, Minos (the name is entirely coincidental) Kalokairinos had already made the connection and had thought, in a three-week excavation in 1879, that he had hit upon Minos's law courts, the royal place and the labyrinth. In 1900 Evans was able to give an absolute date to the Kamares ware he found below the Mycenaean levels, because J.L. Myres had recognised it as the same as the 12th-Dynasty ware that had been excavated by Flinders Petrie in the rubbish heaps at Kahun in Egypt. The rest of Evans's chronology was relative and based on stratigraphy and pottery styles. He devised a tripartite system mirroring, in a way, the Egyptian one, with an old, a middle and a new kingdom. The Early, Middle and Late Minoan periods were then each subdivided into three further phases (e.g. EM I, EM II, and EM III) and sometimes even further (e.g. LM IA and LM IB) to accommodate the evidence on the ground. Evans's framework is still used today, with minor modifications and additions.

More recently the Greek archaeologist Nikolaos Platon proposed a chronology based on the evolution of the Minoan palaces. He divided the Cretan Bronze Age into four periods: Prepalatial, Protopalatial (or Old Palace), Neopalatial (or New Palace) and Postpalatial. Occasionally a different terminology (First Palace, Second Palace, Third Palace) has also been used. To confuse matters further, some excavators working on sites not strictly palatial have devised their own nomenclature, as did Gerald Cadogan with his Pyrgos I–IV to describe the phasing of Myrtos Pyrgos.

The different dating systems are all in current use. The quest for absolute dating has been pursued from the very beginning of Minoan archaeology. It is based on building connections between Minoan Crete and the outside world using foreign artefacts excavated on the island in reliable contexts and Cretan objects found similarly abroad. Egypt is of particular importance in this respect because the ancient Egyptians left written documents which can be read. Dendrochronology and radiocarbon dating techniques are also used.

A chronological table of the Cretan Bronze Age is given on the inside back cover.

The Prepalatial Period (3400–1900 BC; EM I–MM IA)

In the Early Minoan Period, before the emergence of 'palaces', the evidence consistently shows sustained growth in the number of settlements. New arrivals are a distinct possibility: but where from? Evans proposed a Libyan element from Egypt, but nowadays attention is more focused on the Levant and Anatolia. The archaeology shows changes in technology and in society. Apart from the introduction of metalworking, pottery is marked by innovation in techniques and styles. It is still not turned on the wheel but is much more skilfully fired and shows an array of distinctive new designs. The mottled Vasiliki ware, named after the site where it was first found (*map p. 431, B2*), is an instance of this. Socially there is evidence, not so much from the settlements but from burials, of a move towards a stratified society. The Mesara graves date from this period too, a time when the plain (*map p. 430, A3–B3*) was enjoying an economic boom. The graves may still be communal but they show that an elite could be buried in style in specially constructed structures and with rich offerings. These testify to overseas contacts as well as to the emergence of a class of craftsmen skilled in the manufacturing of luxury goods, the emblem of the new elite.

It remains to be seen how this development came about. The current thinking favours an evolution in agricultural practices towards a more complex system, with an increased emphasis on wine and olives, both crops that require a long-term commitment, and in the rearing of sheep for wool—though one must also take into account an environmental component. At the beginning of the Bronze Age, a drier and warmer climate set in. At the same time the emergence of regional peak sanctuaries acted as a focus for the creation of a community identity and it can be argued that rank and prestige would have been acquired through a role in cult activities. This situation is not dissimilar to what had happened in Mesopotamia, where temples as communal foci also preceded palaces.

The Old Palace Period (1900–1700 BC; MM IB–MM II)

This period is characterised by the emergence of huge buildings that appear to combine many functions: religious, administrative, social, cultural and economic. The best known are those at Knossos, Malia, Zakros and Phaistos. Because these first 'palaces' all came to grief and were destroyed and rebuilt, it is not easy to determine whether they had been planned as a single unit or were erected piecemeal (which is more likely). That said, they exhibit a remarkable degree of standardisation, with a central court, a western court, a monumental staircase and an almost identical orientation.

The palaces are also well equipped with storage facilities, an estimated 30 percent of the surface area. In the case of Knossos and Malia these are also located outside the palace, in the western court, suggesting a form of interaction with the surrounding urban area. Storage of staple foodstuffs appears to have played an important role in life of these buildings, either because food would be redistributed in times of shortage or crop failure, or as a way of mobilising manpower. This suggests that an elite was either managing resources for the common good or using them as a way of organising the population into a workforce. Storage on this scale is about controlling the future, and one way or another it implies authority.

Administration coincides with the emergence of writing for the purpose of reckoning, recording, certifying and labelling. Two forms coexisted, known mainly from seals and sealings (seal impressions): Linear A, which is prevalent in the Mesara, and hieroglyphs, more present in the north and in the northeast. Neither has so far been satisfactorily deciphered (*see p. 268*).

Palaces were also cult centres, as shown by the abundance of finds suggesting religious ritual. There are no temples in the surrounding urban areas nor anything to suggest that religious observance was not presided over by a body of male or female hierophants who were removed from daily life. Cave and peak sanctuaries continue in use.

Out in the countryside archaeologists have identified structures that seem too grand to be ordinary houses and have also dubbed them 'palaces'. Monastiraki (*map p. 429, B2–C2*) is a good case in point. It was first investigated by a German team who were looking for a palace in the western part of Crete. That was before one was found in Chania. But as Anastasia Kanta has correctly pointed out, the storage element here is rather meagre. Forty-eight pithoi may sound a lot, but ethnographic research has shown that up until very recently a standard Cretan rural household would easily have had 50 pithoi. (Now of course this is no longer so, because as pithoi break they are replaced by plastic.) However, what it does suggest is that we may be looking here not at a palace, but at a well-to-do farm.

Technologically this is a time of innovation, with Kamares ware (*see p. 30*) and also metalwork, with the mastering of granulation, filigree and the lost wax (*cire perdue*) techniques. At the end of MM II a great catastrophe, probably an earthquake, destroyed everything.

The New Palace Period (1700–1450 BC; MM III–LM IB)

After this destruction, the palaces were rebuilt—with temporary setbacks, such as the earthquake that struck in MM III and hurled huge blocks from the south façade of Knossos onto the House of the Fallen Blocks. Our knowledge of the Minoan civilisation dates mainly from these and other buildings, which sprang up both in the countryside and in the urban landscape around the palaces. These structures were eventually destroyed in their turn in violent events and then abandoned. In most cases they were not subsequently levelled or built over: hence the better preservation.

These were truly elaborate dwellings, with a varying layout thanks to the pier-and-door partition system, and efficient plumbing. Frescoed walls abound: indeed, according to the latest research, true fresco painting was practised in Crete from MM IIA, before it was known in the Middle East. As time progresses storage space decreases (though it is still impressive), making room for an expansion of cult areas and industrial quarters for the production of luxury objects in metal, ivory and stone. Access becomes restricted and, as peak sanctuaries go into slow decline, religion becomes truly concentrated in the palaces, totally in the hands of an elite that appears increasingly detached and which is now dispensing supernatural favours as well as staple commodities. Across the island the number of prosperous residential buildings (villas) increases and it is here that the extra storage capacity is to be found. It is thought that a number of them (especially those in an urban setting) belonged to minor officials connected with the palace.

Foreign contacts are wide ranging. There are a number of sites in the Aegean showing clear Minoan influence and there has been talk of colonies, though nothing is proven in this respect: there is no evidence that the Minoan navy (of which we know next to nothing) held sway in the Aegean (the 'Minoan Thalassocracy'). The evidence points to Minoan ideas, artefacts and perhaps craftsmen reaching Kythera and mainland Greece and leaving their mark on the Mycenaean civilisation. In the Cyclades the most outstanding instance is on the island of Santorini, where exceptionally well-preserved frescoes have been instrumental to our understanding of elements of the Minoan iconography on Crete itself. Judging by the sheer scale of the metal finds, one of the engines behind the expansion must have been the quest for metal. Crete is rather short on metal resources. The manufacture of bronze requires a supply of both copper and tin. Crete got its copper from Cyprus, from Lavrion in Attica and from the Cyclades. Tin is more of a problem. For a while, Minoan smiths used arsenical copper, whose fumes are poisonous, but then they switched to tin, which is safer but not so readily available. Suggested sources range from Bohemia and the Balkans to Mesopotamia and Sinai. Contacts with Egypt are attested not just by the finds (stone vases and scarabs) but by ostraka, papyri and the well-known procession of the *Keftiu* in the tomb of queen Hatshepsut in western Thebes. Here the Cretan envoys are shown as typical Minoans (long wavy locks, no beard, short skirts, rhyton in hand) bearing tributes, submissive and asking for protection. Submissive they may have been in view of later events, but they must also have come for the ivory and the minerals.

The causes of the decline of the Minoan civilisation are still poorly understood. The most dramatic event is the destruction of the palaces and for a while this was linked to the eruption on Santorini, 150km north of Crete, leading to the theory of a general conflagration in the Aegean followed by a devastating tsunami. This hypothesis no longer holds. The Santorini eruption has now been securely dated to LM IA, if not earlier, by dendrochronology and by cores in the ice fields of Greenland and closer to home in Lake Kournas (*map p. 428, D3*). This last core shows no disruption at the time of the eruption. If Santorini created a tsunami it clearly did not hit the north Cretan coast. As for the abundance of pumice stones that has been reported in some sites on the north coast, they were probably brought in by the waves and came in handy as an abrasive.

What, then, did happen? Evidence on the ground shows major widespread destruction by fire across the island in LM IB, preceded by a form of retrenchment from LM IA if not before, suggesting troubled times. Settlement and trade decrease, areas are abandoned and, as insecurity sets in, entrances are blocked and wealthy buildings are downgraded. Religion is also affected, with the desertion of peak sanctuaries and the introduction of cult areas in settlements and in individual mansions. If there had ever been a central government or at least a regional one, it seems now to have failed: the result is a decentralisation or rather fragmentation, leading apparently to chaos. The destruction of LM IB bears the mark of the human agent. Whether it was local or came from overseas (the Mycenaeans are the chief suspects) it is impossible at the moment to tell.

The end of Minoan Knossos (1450–1370 BC; LM II–LM III AI)

Knossos for some reason was less affected by this cataclysm. Damage was soon repaired and the palace reopened 'under new management'. The Mycenaean Greeks, who had either been responsible for its destruction or had taken advantage of the situation, were now in charge, as shown by the adoption of a new script (Linear B, an ancient form of Greek; *see p. 268*) and the change in burial style with the appearance of warrior graves. For a while around the early 14th century, Knossos was the only power in the island and its major administrative centre. There is evidence for yet another destruction in LM IIIA, and while some parts of the palace remained in use into the 13th century, this occupation was subdued.

The Postpalatial Period (1370–1070 BC; LM III)

The widespread destruction of LM IB resulted in the definitive abandonment of a number of high-status sites: it undoubtedly dealt a serious blow to the system based on the palace economy. There are, however, exceptions, and Knossos is not the only one. In the west, Kydonia (Chania) was also resurrected and peaked in LM III, trading widely, as far as Cyprus. In the south, the port of Kommos (*map p. 430, A3*) boomed: this was the time of the gigantic shipsheds. Clearly the harbour had survived the demise of Phaistos. Nearby, Aghia Triada itself was reoccupied with a new building style suggesting Mycenaean influence, though whoever was running the place was still using Linear A. Times were not easy for the Mycenaeans either, as their world imploded towards the end of the 13th century, bringing to an end a short period during which they had successfully ousted Minoan dominance in the Mediterranean. Religion too was undergoing changes, with the appearance of the snake cult and of goddesses with bulging eyes, raised hands and stiff skirts, while in the cemeteries this is the time of the larnakes, the rectangular clay tomb chests.

The Subminoan Period (1070–970 BC)

These were troubled times on the island and safety was sought away from the coast, up in inaccessible mountain refuges. The iconic site of the period is Karphi (*map p. 430, D2*), where the last Minoans held out and were ultimately defeated by a hostile environment. This is an extreme example, but there is evidence of inland defensive sites with a long history ahead of them and able to weather the transition into the Iron Age (Rizenia, to name but one; *map p. 430, B2*). The influence at work here is neither Minoan nor Mycenaean; as new populations from overseas work their way into Crete's destiny, the island's history becomes increasingly tied to the mainland.

THE IRON AGE
(970–630 BC)

The Geometric and Orientalising periods

This is a phase better known through burials than settlements. Funerary practices show a sudden change. The development is particularly apparent in places like Knossos, where Late Minoan chamber tombs were methodically cleared before receiving new burials. Among the goods deposited, iron objects show an increased familiarity with the new metallurgy. Later, around the 10th century, cremation becomes the norm. The prevalent pottery style is also not home-grown: Geometric decoration is shared with mainland Greece, though in some instances, such as in Knossos, the pattern can be more individualistic.

From the 9th century onwards there are signs of intensification of foreign contacts with the Levant and especially with the Phoenicians, who may have come to Crete for the iron, to trade or indeed to settle. This new development sweeps across the Mediterranean as far as Etruria in central Italy and is particularly apparent in the outstanding quality of the metalwork. In Crete it is best exemplified by the votive bronze 'shields' found in the Idaian Cave, with friezes of mythological animals in high relief.

Socially this is a period of population growth with settlement expansion. The standard unit, as on the mainland, is the *polis*, the city-state built in a defensible position with its own water supply and agricultural holdings all around. It is ruled by an elected body of ten or so *kosmoi*, who act as administrators and as war leaders when required. The pattern in Crete is ever closer to that of the mainland, with intense rivalry between the different units. Homer speaks of 90 cities and also gives a rare insight into the composition of the population. He mentions the Dorians from the mainland and the locals (the Eteocretans). These apparently still followed the Minoan traditions, though there is not much evidence of that. They probably spoke a different language, not of Greek origin, as the bilingual inscriptions at Dreros and Praisos suggest.

In the late 7th century archaeologists recognise an abrupt break in the record, with a sudden abandonment of burial chambers and the consequent loss of the information provided by the variety of grave goods. A new script also appears, of Semitic stock adapted for the Greek language. With this come a crop of inscriptions that can now be read.

The Archaic, Classical and Hellenistic periods (630–67 BC)

In mainland Greece, the Archaic period is characterised by the emergence of sculpture. The Daidalic style, named after the legendary architect Daedalus, played an important role in shaping Archaic sculpture. It appears to have originated in Crete and betrays Egyptian influence, being characterised by a rigid posture and wig-like hair. A statue from Eleftherna now displayed in Herakleion Archaeological Museum Temporary Exhibition, and the goddess from the façade of Temple A at Rizenia, are excellent examples of the style.

In the Classical period Crete was politically a backwater compared to the brilliance of Athens but, while the latter was busy laying down the foundations of Classical architecture and art, in Crete the Gortyn Law Code, dated to the 5th century, was doing the same for the legal system. This important document, one of a number scattered across the island, should be viewed as the culmination of a long process dating from as far back as the mythical Minos himself, the first lawgiver.

Crete maintained a prudent neutrality during the Persian Wars and flourished in the Hellenistic period, well represented in the sites of Lato and Trypitos. The latter's shipshed shows a renewed interest in the sea. As overseas markets opened up, a new commodity, namely the Cretan mercenary, found employment—and sometimes a fortune—on the mainland, while at Olympia the Cretan athlete Ergoteles won the men's foot-race in 472. Back home, piracy became a well-documented source of income (*see p. 270*). Crete was enjoying a revival because of its location at the centre of a world that had been made smaller by the conquests of Alexander the Great. Control of the Aegean and of trade routes was important. And these flowed through Crete. Foreign powers took an interest in the island while the different *poleis* jockeyed for position.

Eventually Knossos, Lyttos, Gortyn and Chania emerged as the main contenders for supremacy. Inscriptions commemorating alliances show how the Egyptians had a presence in Itanos, while Rhodes cultivated Olous, and Eumenes of Pergamon was allied with 13 of the city-states. Meanwhile the greatest power of all was looming from the west. Rome had already conquered mainland Greece in 146 but was certainly aware of Crete from earlier on, when Gortyn had offered shelter to Hannibal after he had been defeated in the Second Punic War. There was also the problem of piracy, which Rome could hardly tolerate in the *Mare Nostrum*. After an unsuccessful expedition in 71 BC, the Roman general Quintus Caecilius Metellus invaded with three legions and was able to subdue the island in three years, after which he was allowed to style himself 'Creticus'. With Crete conquered, Rome had control of the major Mediterranean islands.

THE ROMAN & FIRST BYZANTINE PERIODS
(67 BC–AD 824)

As a Roman province Crete was placed together with North Africa in a newly created administrative unit: the province of Crete and Cyrenaica, with its capital at Gortyn. Traditionally Crete had looked north and east for its trading and artistic contacts and had only had limited connections with the land to the immediate south, separated by a two-day voyage across open, treacherous seas.

The organisation of the new province shows that it was deemed to be fully pacified. It had no resident army and the governor was a minor Roman magistrate of civilian rank. As Plutarch relates Brutus, the most famous of Caesar's assassins, was given the job between 44 and 42 BC to keep him out of Rome in gilded exile. He moved out to Macedonia where he raised an army and was defeated at Philippi. Octavian, the future emperor Augustus, used some of the land around Knossos to reward some 3,000 of his veterans, thereby making a number of enemies among the dispossessed locals, but on the whole the island settled down to a period of peace and prosperity which lasted well into the 4th century AD. Settlement expanded, and the population left the defended positions high up in the interior for coastal locations. Hierapytna, modern Ierapetra on the south coast, on the corn route from Egypt to Rome, is a shining example. The countryside became populated too, with rural villas at the centre of agricultural estates. Some places saw settlement for the first time since the Bronze Age.

Crete's main exports were agricultural: cereals, wine, beeswax, salt, herbs, oil and live fish from the coastal fish tanks. People also figured in the list: by the 1st century AD Rome had a professional army which offered a structured military career. The famed Cretan archers and slingers would join the auxiliary troops with the prospect of secure employment, a good rate of pay and Roman citizenship upon retirement, meaning that their children could enrol in the legions. Among the imports building stone (marble and granite) loomed large, as new civic buildings and theatres went up.

The division of the Roman Empire after Theodosius in 395 marks the beginning of the Byzantine period, as Crete came under the influence of Byzantium. The period is characterised by the building of Christian basilicas, as the new religion gained ground. The arrangement of a nave and two aisles separated by rows of columns, with one or three apses acting as a sanctuary, is that of a standard Roman civic building, but in Crete it betrays Syrian influences. There are 70 or so known or suspected Early Christian basilicas in Crete, most of them of huge proportions and with lavish decoration, contrasting with the tiny chapels of later on. Although the building of basilicas is attested until the late 8th century (the date of the basilica of Vizari; *map p. 429, C3*), signs of decline were already apparent before the Arab conquest. Indeed, the comparison of the building technique used at Aghios Titos, Gortyn (ashlar blocks) and at Vizari (stone boulders and brick levelling courses) is telling. These were difficult times. Earthquakes struck frequently. The so-called 'Byzantine Paroxysm' of 21st July 395, graphically described by Ammianus Marcellinus, who saw the tsunami wave that devastated Alexandria, had its epicentre in Crete, and this was not the only one. Late antique Knossos was still a vibrant and prosperous city in the 5th century but by the 7th was in terminal decline, with evidence of disrepair and occupation by squatters. The empire at large had its own problems and Crete was again vulnerable to outside attacks.

THE ARAB OCCUPATION
(824–961)

This is an obscure period in Cretan history. Archaeologically it is vastly under-represented; what we have to go on are written sources. According to the Christian texts, mainly lives of saints, Crete was attacked by a band of Muslim pirates, ravaged and laid waste for 140 years. The Arabic sources tell a different story. With the conquest of Spain in 711, the southern expanse of the Mediterranean was an Arab sea. In Spain the original population had to some extent integrated with the invaders and converted. In the urban areas conflicts arose between the different ethnic groups. Some of the original Romano-Celtic stock, now fully arabised, felt discriminated against by the ruling Muslim authorities. There was also a problem of overpopulation, which prompted groups to leave and look for land to resettle. One of these groups, made up of craftsmen from Toledo and Córdoba, left under the leadership of Abu Hafs and arrived in Alexandria in Egypt in 818. They remained for a while but then had to leave again.

The force that landed in Crete in 824 numbered some 10,000 people, including women and children, carried in 40 ships. There was no Byzantine fleet in Cretan waters at the time (the emperor Michael II had the revolt by Thomas the Slav on his hands), which is probably why the new settlers chose Crete. They could also bank on some local support as the Cretans were at odds with Byzantium over the iconoclastic reform. Crete became the most advanced Muslim outpost in the Mediterranean (the conquest of Sicily only began in 827). It was divided into 40 districts ruled by an emir, nominally answerable to the caliph of Baghdad.

The scant evidence suggests that the newcomers settled in cities (that is where Phocas found the mosques to destroy when he reconquered the island). Coinage points to a stable economy including the export of foodstuffs and metalwork, mainly to Egypt. There is no hard evidence of wholesale destruction of sites and buildings by the newcomers; indeed Orlandos has found signs of renovation and repairs at Aghios Titos, Gortyn, which he dates stylistically to this period. The fabric of the island was already in disrepair and suffering from neglect. The occupation may have been the last straw.

There is no mention in the Arab sources of the slave trade that flourished in Rabdh el-Khandak, the nucleus of modern Herakleion, and which turned it for a while into the largest slave market in the eastern Mediterranean.

THE SECOND BYZANTINE PERIOD
(961–1204)

By the 10th century Byzantium was reasserting its power in the Mediterranean. After landing with 250 ships and conquering the countryside, Nicephorus Phocas, a brilliant general and future emperor, lay siege to Rabdh el-Khandak, conquering it on 7th March 961, with the help of a particularly harsh winter.

With the island restored to Byzantium and much of the Muslim population departed for Egypt, Sicily and Spain, the first task was to bolster the much depleted Christian community. This involved a programme of restoration of damaged ecclesiastical buildings to house the re-established bishoprics, and much preaching of the Gospel to rural communities that might have allowed their allegiance to the Christian creed to lapse during the occupation. Cretan folk history is teeming with legends of monks who scoured the countryside spreading the good word and building chapels. The island also needed a new capital. Gortyn was not suitable (it was too far inland and a dead city by this time) and Khandak was too vulnerable. Byzantium opted for a location overlooking the north coast and in a defensible position. But anyone visiting Temenos (*map p. 430, B2*) can see why it was soon abandoned: the location is just too harsh for anyone to want to live there permanently. The administrative centre was thus moved back to Rabdh el-Khandak, thereafter Khandakas.

In the 12th century it became necessary to strengthen the ruling class. According to tradition, the scions of 12 Byzantine ruling families were sent out by the emperor and allocated tracts of land. Certainly the names of these *archontopouloi* ('sons of leaders'; the Kallergis, the Skordilis and the Chortatzis, for example) loom large in subsequent Cretan history; unfortunately it appears that legally they did not have a leg to stand on. The latest evidence shows that their claims were based on forged title deeds. When the Venetians took over the island there had been no central government for a while, allowing some local families to become well established. The forged documents these families produced to bolster their claims were an attempt at defending their estates.

The Second Byzantine Period saw the beginning of the Crusades, a movement originally intended to rescue Christian holy places from the Muslims but which developed eventually into a political struggle between the different powers. Venice was now the up-and-coming power in the East. It had been a vassal of Byzantium, but as that empire waned, it wrested concession after concession from it to bolster its Eastern trade. In 1182 this came to a head with the Massacre of the Latins in Byzantium, but shortly after Venice was able to hit back. In 1204, directed by Doge Enrico Dandolo, who had been present at the massacre, she was able to divert the Fourth Crusade to Byzantium in order to put Alexius IV on the imperial throne. When the newly-created emperor failed to honour his promises, Venice led a sack of the city and took much booty home, including the famous four gilded copper horses from the hippodrome, which were used to decorate the façade of St Mark's basilica.

THE VENETIAN PERIOD
(1204–1669)

In the subsequent division of the Byzantine spoils, Crete had been given to Boniface of Monferrat, the leader of the Fourth Crusade, while Venice received three eighths of the city of Byzantium. As a maritime power, Venice had a natural interest in Crete and had no difficulty in persuading Boniface (with the help of 1,000 silver marks, some 200kg of silver) to part with it. Unfortunately for Venice, the island had by then been occupied by Enrico Pescatore, a pirate from Genoa, with the help of the people of Chania and Sphakia. By the time Venice arrived to claim her due, Pescatore had already built a number of castles. So he had to be bought out as well. He was paid a sum equivalent to the arming of three Venetian galleys and promised a fair Venetian lady, with dowry, as a bride for his nephew. The Venetian occupation, the newly created Regno di Candia, got off to a famously bad start when in 1211 one of the leading Byzantine families rebelled and the ruler, the Doge of Candia, had to flee to Temenos to await reinforcements.

Crete was Venice's first overseas colony. Before that the Republic had only had trading posts and she as yet possessed little of the hinterland back home. Venice was a maritime power and intended to use Crete as a base to bolster her trading links with the East. It was imperative that the island be self-sufficient and not become a burden on the motherland. Immigration was limited at first: just enough people to run the place. The island was divided along feudal lines with a web of obligations and duties linking the local Venetian noble in his castle, at the centre of a *castellania*, with the local population. This immediately created friction with the local families who had run the island before. Prominent among these were the Kallergis, who claimed connections with the emperor Nicephorus Phocas himself. After a long struggle Venice was able to buy them off with the grant of vast tracts of land and other concessions including the right to marry into Latin families. The *Pax Kallergi* worked, and the family never reneged on it, always siding with Venice. The Kallergis eventually moved to Venice, but not into the Greek quarter. By the 16th century one Vettor Kallergis had his own palace on the Grand Canal. Now known as Palazzo Vendramin Calergi, it is the house where Wagner died in 1883.

Venice was also making huge demands on the local workforce by the imposition of forced labour. As a result, rebellions were frequent: after the *archontopouloi*, the Venetian settlers themselves took the lead, raising the standard of St Titus to replace St Mark in the St Titus Revolt in the 1360s. Faced with continual unrest, Venice decided to deny the rebels the refuge of the natural fortress of the Lasithi plateau. Settlement was banned, houses were demolished, fruit trees uprooted and cultivation forbidden. This state of affairs lasted until 1514 when the plateau was resettled with Venetian families fleeing the Peloponnese, which had fallen to the Turks. They called in hydraulic engineers from Padua University to organise the water management. The move was also linked to agricultural expansion as the island became an exporter of wheat, wine, cheese and cotton.

After the fall of the Byzantine empire to the Ottomans in 1453, Crete played a pivotal role in the Aegean as the only possible stopover where Venetian ships could be refuelled and repaired. A degree of prosperity set in, as relationships between the indigenous population and the occupying force improved. On the whole, the last 150 years were better for both sides. Friction over religious matters abated. The Orthodox and the Latin rites coexisted, sometimes in the same church. Venice showed a remarkable degree of tolerance in the matter, with little proselytising. Many Latin monasteries were built, but the Orthodox ones also prospered, becoming important centres for the preservation and fostering of Byzantine culture. Now that Byzantium was no more, Crete became an important staging post for Greeks fleeing to the West. They brought with them manuscripts and works of art, creating a revival of Byzantine learning. The larger monasteries built up huge libraries and became centres of Greek learning. In Herakleion Aghia Aikaterini, a daughter foundation of the Orthodox monastery on Mount Sinai, became a renowned centre for Greek scholarship and religious art. Fresco painting petered out in the first quarter of the 16th century (the last church fresco is in Siteia and is dated to 1525). Not so icon painting, which flourished with Mikhail Damaskinos towards the end of the 16th century. Like him a number of Cretans were also looking west and came into contact with the Italian Renaissance via Venice. Among these was Domenico Theotokopoulos, who became famous as El Greco (*see p. 52*).

The pursuit of knowledge also bloomed with the establishment of Neoplatonic academies in the major towns. A number of their members had been educated in Italy at the universities of Padua and Bologna rather than in the local monasteries, or on the mainland at Athens or Ioannina. The scholars' interests ranged from poetry and plays to mathematics and science and general self-improvement. At the same time Venice was taking the lead in the publication of Greek texts.

Over time a large Greek colony had become established in Venice. They had their own church (San Giorgio dei Greci), their own quarter, they dressed in their own way, spoke a mixture of Venetian and Greek and had an interest in maintaining and disseminating their cultural heritage. A Cretan émigré, Zacharias Kallergis, had earlier on set up a printing press for this purpose. He later went to Rome where he became a pioneer printer of Greek texts in the papal capital. Aldus Manutius was no Greek but could see that there was a market in Venice. The Greek colony itself had amassed a wealth of manuscripts and could be called upon for copyists, typesetters and editors in the difficult work of preparing textual editions. By the time of the death of its founder in 1515, the Aldine Press, with the collaboration of the Cretan humanist Markos Mousouros, had given the world access to all major Greek Classical authors. Back in Crete, libraries were no longer the preserve of the monasteries: they also flourished in private houses.

Soon however it became evident that the very existence of Venetian Crete was under threat from the Turks, who were steadily moving west while Venice was weakened by conflicts in Italy. There was also the question of the shifting pattern of trade routes in Europe and the impact of Vasco da Gama's rounding of the Cape of Good Hope in 1488. On this commentators are divided: some maintain that if Venice had been able to defend her position in the eastern Mediterranean, Alexandria would have remained the main outlet for caravans transporting luxury goods for the European market. Unfortunately, in spite of repeated requests from dukes and rectors, Venice was not in a position to increase her involvement in the defence of the Kingdom of Candia. Moreover, as incursions and raids multiplied, the spirit of Lepanto dwindled and Venice was left almost alone to deal with the Turks in Crete. Things came to a head in 1645, when the Turks landed in the west of the island with 450 vessels and an army of 50,000. The pretext had been the capture by the Knights of Malta of a ship carrying pilgrims to Mecca. They made their way first to Chania and then, after a long siege (the longest in history), conquered Candia in 1669. Venice was left with only three strongholds (Souda, Gramvousa and Spinalonga), which it held until 1715.

THE TURKISH OCCUPATION
(1669–1898)

The period of Turkish occupation is generally described as a time of decline, with Crete left struggling to cope with a heavy burden of taxation. On the other hand, Ottoman rule meant that the risk of pirate attacks abated, as Crete was now a Muslim country (see p. 270). The island was divided in four *pashaliks* and Candia became Megalo Kastro, the 'Great Fortress'. The new occupants settled in the cities, where many churches became mosques. Penetration into the countryside remained negligible: there are no rural mosques. Discriminatory practices in taxation and in the job market meant that it became expedient for a proportion of the indigenous population to convert to Islam. The 1881 census found that 60 percent of the population in the large towns on the north coast had gone that way; the figure for the island as a whole was significantly lower.

Remote mountain areas remained beyond the control of the pashas, and it is there that rebellion brewed. Sporadic revolts in the remote districts became a way of life. The docile people of the lowlands often had to endure reprisals while the rebels retreated to their mountain strongholds. The preservation of the Orthodox Church became an issue now, far more so than under the Venetians: they at least were Christian, though of a different rite. The transmission of Hellenic culture and tradition through education also became important. Occasionally monasteries also became involved in the struggle.

In 1770 a major revolt was led by Giannis Vlachos (better known as Daskalogiannis, or 'John the Teacher'), a Sphakiot from Anopolis who had lived most of his life abroad. He had become a pawn in the hands of the Russians who wanted to expand south at the expense of the Ottoman Empire. As things soured when the Cretans were left alone to bear the brunt of the Turkish onslaught without the promised Russian assistance, Daskalogiannis surrendered. He was executed and the whole of the Sphakia district suffered reprisals. He is honoured as a hero today. Chania airport is named after him.

After the Napoleonic interlude revolt flared again in the early 1820s, when the Greek mainland began fighting successfully for its independence. The rebellion was crushed, however, with the assistance of the Egyptians, so while Greece achieved independence in 1832, Crete had to endure ten years of Egyptian rule. The Great Uprising of 1866, in which fighters from Greece and elsewhere in Europe participated, brought the plight of the Cretan people to the attention of the wider world. The Ottomans regained control after three years and defused the situation by passing a law granting equal rights to Muslims and Christians. But by now Crete had *enosis*, the union with Greece, fixed in its mind, and unrest continued.

In 1897 the Great Powers (Britain, France, Russia and Italy) intervened militarily by occupying the main towns to restore order and, a year later, they took the opportunity of peace negotiations that were being conducted between Greece and the Ottoman Empire over mainland territory, to impose a settlement on the island. *Enosis* was not considered at this stage. The Ottoman forces were expelled and Crete was granted a limited form of independence. Prince George, the second son of the King of Greece, was appointed *Armostis* (High Commissioner) and governed from Chania. His rule brought *enosis* no closer and he was faced with a rebellious Cretan Assembly, one of whose leaders was Eleftherios Venizelos. Born in Mournies near Chania in 1864, but technically a Greek subject, Venizelos had been prominent as a young man in the struggle for the island's independence and had first raised the Greek flag on Cretan soil in 1897. In a further crisis in 1906, Prince George resigned. The crisis was temporarily resolved with the appointment of the veteran politician Alexandros Zaimis to the post of *Armostis*, but in 1908, taking advantage of internal turmoil in Turkey and the absence of Zaimis, temporarily away from the island on holiday, the deputies declared union with Greece. With the Treaty of Bucharest in 1913, which ended the Balkan Wars, *enosis* was formally sanctioned by the international community and Crete became part of the Kingdom of Greece.

MODERN HISTORY

In spite of its geographical isolation, Crete became involved from 1913 in events unfolding in Athens, the more so because the Cretan-born Venizelos was playing a prominent role in national and international politics. During the First World War his personal convictions led him to favour the cause of the Allies and brought him into conflict with King Constantine I, whose wife was the sister of the German Kaiser. Things came to a head in 1916, when Venizelos issued a proclamation establishing a rival government in Salonica (now Thessaloniki). The king eventually abdicated in favour of his second son, Prince Alexander, and Greece entered the Great War on the Allied side.

In 1920–22 Greece played a part in a disastrous campaign of expansionism over the Turkish mainland, rooted in an old irredentist concept (the *Megali Idea*) aimed at the restoration of the Byzantine Empire with its capital in Constantinople. The timing was opportunistic: the Ottoman Empire was being dissolved and Turkey was in turmoil. Nonetheless the Turkish forces, under the leadership of Mustapha Kemal (later Atatürk), were able to repel the invasion. The trauma of defeat and the sack of Smyrna (modern Izmir) are still painful memories in the Greek collective memory. The ensuing population exchange between Greece and Turkey, sanctioned by the Treaty of Lausanne in 1923, brought more than a million refugees to Greece. In Crete those Turks who had stayed behind after the departure of the Ottoman government now left, and their land was distributed among the newcomers. The population movement also included a number of Armenian families fleeing Turkey for a different reason. Venizelos continued to play a prominent role in national politics until he fled into exile in France in 1935 after plotting to install a republic, dying a year later. He is buried on the Akrotiri near Chania. The new figure in Greek politics was now General Metaxas. He ruled as a dictator, having persuaded the king to dissolve parliament. Metaxas could see that war was inevitable in Europe and it is thanks to him that Greece was better prepared than the neighbouring states to resist aggression when it came.

Mussolini occupied Albania in April 1939 and the threat posed by a fascist power on Greece's border led to a British and French guarantee of Greek territorial sovereignty. In spite of reaffirming Greece's neutrality, Metaxas was still confronted with an Italian ultimatum on 28th October 1940. He rejected it with a single word: 'No'. His gesture is now commemorated in a national holiday (Ochi Day). At the time of the ultimatum Mussolini's troops were already on Greek soil but the defending army, with the assistance of the harsh Greek winter for which the Italian troops were ill equipped, was able to drive them back to a position of stalemate on the mountains of Albania.

The balance was altered by Hitler's decision to intervene in Greece to protect the southern flank of his planned Russian front. In March 1941 a small expeditionary force composed of British, Australian and New Zealand troops was dispatched to assist the Greek army in halting Hitler's advance but proved unsuccessful. By the end of April evacuation was on the cards, and Crete was the only possible choice.

The Battle of Crete (1941–45)

The withdrawal took place in the last week of April and the beginning of May 1941. King George was evacuated with his government, headed by the Cretan-born Emmanouil Tsouderos. He stayed briefly at the Villa Ariadne at Knossos and then moved to Chania. As the campaign on the mainland ran into difficulties in 1940, Churchill insisted on the importance of holding onto Crete as a secure base in the Mediterranean. Unfortunately, resources were overstretched and the defence proved inadequate. Moreover, for all its remoteness, Crete was badly exposed to enemy airborne incursions. All airfields were situated along the narrow strip of the north coast at Herakleion, at Maleme near Chania, and at Rethymnon, and all the main harbours and anchorages were on the north coast as well. The more protected fishing ports on the south coast were useless for supply purposes as the road network cutting across the island north–south was underdeveloped. The road from Souda to Sphakia had yet to be completed.

There had been several changes of command on the island in the six months leading to the events of spring 1941. The Cretan garrison (Creforce) was under the command of General Freyberg, a New Zealander. He had a garrison of 43,000 British, Australian, New Zealand and Greek troops, including the 21,000 that had been evacuated from the mainland. To its lasting chagrin, the Cretan division could not be repatriated and had remained on the Albanian front. The Creforce headquarters were in the Souda area, east of Chania, while to the west the New Zealanders, with the assistance of a Greek contingent, were responsible for the defence of the vital airfield of Maleme. British, Australian and Greek battalions were in charge of the areas around Rethymnon and its airstrip, and Herakleion and its airport.

Hitler's principal objective in the planned invasion of Crete was to use the island as a base against British forces in the eastern Mediterranean. He knew he could only rely on air power, as the strength of the British Navy made a seaborne assault too dangerous. The German operation was masterminded by General Student of the XI Air Corps, and aimed to take advantage of the Luftwaffe's undisputed command of the air. The plan included the use of gliders and parachute troops.

The airborne invasion began on 20th May. As expected, landings concentrated on the airfields and on the main towns of the north coast. In the west, the Germans established a toehold not far from the airfield of Maleme. A detachment of parachutists attempted to land in the broad valley (nicknamed Prison Valley) running northeast–southwest from Chania into the White Mountains. The aim was to converge with the forces on the coast road and advance on Chania, but in the end the German troops in this sector proved disorganised and unable to respond to central control. The glider assault on Akrotiri failed entirely. The Rethymnon airstrip was successfully defended by the Australians, while around the airfield at Herakleion the Germans were in considerable disarray. In the town itself their initial success had developed into heavy fighting with the civilian population which led to a stalemate. The first wave of landings met with much more resistance than German intelligence had expected and it became clear that the mood of the local population had been severely misjudged.

It is generally agreed that at the end of the first day the final outcome hung in the balance, with the narrowest of margins in favour of the invading force. However, what turned out to be the crucial battle had developed to the south and west of Maleme airfield, centred on Hill 107. With hindsight it can be seen that the position of the German forces was extremely precarious, but in the confusion of the battle, which was compounded by an almost total breakdown of communications due to a shortage of wireless sets, essential defence reinforcements did not become available on time. The commanding heights had to be evacuated, leaving the airfield undefended. The balance was tilted at this point in favour of the Germans, who were quick to take advantage of the situation. They used the airfield to land reinforcements and supplies and were able to defend it successfully. By the fourth day of the battle German fighter planes were operating from it. Although the German invading fleet had been successfully routed by the Royal Navy (though with appalling losses), the Allied position in Crete was becoming untenable as Chania and Souda were now indefensible: a retreat to the south was the only option left. King George and the government had already been escorted down the Samaria Gorge to embark at Aghia Roumeli. The troops were to take the Sphakia direction 40km south along the eastern flank of the White Mountains. The operation was only made possible because of the determined action of a Greek regiment cut off at the south end of Prison Valley in the area of the Alikianos river-crossing. For two days (24th–25th May) these troops, with the help of the gendarmerie and of the local population, held up the Germans and prevented them from cutting off the road south.

The shambles of the march over the mountains by Stylos, over the Askiphou plateau and down the Imbros Gorge, have been described in many records, including General Freyberg's official report. However, the column was successfully protected against enemy action by relays of rearguard troops. Some 12,000 men were involved, and during the nights of the 28th–31st May, three quarters of them were evacuated by the navy from the beach at Chora Sphakion. At Rethymnon the Australians fought hard for the control of the airstrip but were overwhelmed on May 31st. The garrison was evacuated from Herakleion by the Royal Navy through the Kasos Strait with appalling human losses. In total 18,000 men were evacuated, 12,000 taken prisoner and 2,000 killed. A considerable number, though, had gone into hiding, with the help of the local population. They formed the nucleus of the resistance movement and guerrilla warfare that developed on the island, assisted also by supplies coming in from North Africa. This made the task of the Germans increasingly difficult, sapping morale and tying down resources in the pursuit of an invisible enemy. The civilian population, caught between the two, suffered cruel losses in the inevitable reprisals. One extraordinary account of the period is *The Cretan Runner* (*see p. 320*). Its author, the Cretan George Psychoundakis, was involved in the resistance. His description throws light not only on the progress of the guerrilla war but also on the quirky characters of some of the foreigners as seen through native eyes, and also on many essential traits of the Cretan character. A comprehensive and authoritative account of the whole episode, drawing from published and unpublished material from both sides and also on personal recollections, was published by Antony Beevor in 1991, on the 50th anniversary of the Battle of Crete.

Crete since the war

The end of the war and of the German occupation left Crete impoverished and locked in a cycle of revenge and retribution against the defeated Germans and the collaborators. Events on the mainland, where civil war raged until 1949, meant that many young men found themselves conscripted to fight over there. In the late 1960s Crete turned to industrial agriculture, with the establishment of large cultivations under plastic. The 'Costa Plastica' along the south coast may not be very sightly, but it has brought prosperity to that part of the island. It is also responsible for an unwelcome overuse of fertilisers. Mass tourism has done the rest. It first took off along the north coast, there again with mixed results—at least according to environmentalists. With an improved road network and a taste for walking holidays, it is now percolating slowly into the darkest recesses of the island.

Environmental questions are now hotly debated and words like 'traditional', 'biological', organic' and 'hand-made' are the hallmark of a new Cretan hospitality that is welcoming and the same time mindful of the fragility of the island.

The last 50 years have brought great social changes to Crete. Whole villages have been depopulated as people follow jobs. Herakleion has grown and grown to become a substantial city, the fifth most populous in Greece. The European Union (of which Greece has been a member since 1981) has stepped in to lay down the foundations for a sustainable pattern of development. This includes sheep rearing and the preservation of a mountain environment of *madares* (summer pastures) and *mitata* (the stone huts where cheese is made), a way of life that has existed for millennia but which is now under threat. According to the latest figures for the Sphakia region, the programme has had some success: the number of shepherds may have diminished, but sheep are up as flocks are larger.

MINOAN RELIGION

Evans's very first publication of his finds at Knossos in 1901 was concerned with the religion of the new civilisation he was uncovering. One hundred years on, things are only marginally clearer in this respect, probably because, in spite of their high level of literacy, the Minoans did not use writing to record ritual texts. The answers must therefore be found in the interpretation of objects, architecture, iconography and the way all these things appear to fit together. The dual role that the ruling class seems to have played, wielding both administrative and religious power, makes it hard to unravel the different strands of evidence in the palaces and in the mansions.

The Minoan religion had a multiplicity of sacred sites where the presence of the divinity could be experienced in a variety of ways. These places are defined by the presence of categories of objects for which a ritual purpose is assumed. These include horns of consecration, double axes, libation vessels (in particular rhyta; *see p. 390*), offering-tables and figurines. Large numbers of finds come from palaces and mansions where they are associated with architectural features that are clearly not residential or utilitarian. Various areas have been recognised, from the balustrade shrines with a clear focal point and the 'pillar crypts' (named thus by Evans, under the influence of contemporary Victorian church architecture) to the 'lustral basins'. The purpose of these sunken chambers has been, and still is, hotly debated. They were first interpreted as baths, ritual or utilitarian, but being lined with gypsum, a material that loses its finish when in contact with water, and lacking drains, they make poor candidates for the job. Moreover, proper baths, with drains, are known from residential apartments in Minoan palaces. These chambers, which are rather small with L-shaped steps and a balustrade, are often found together with evidence of a pier-and-door partition system, suggesting that the arrangement of the surrounding rooms could be altered, access controlled and light regulated. There is no evidence that 'lustral basins' were roofed, and the possibility that whatever took place in them was intended to be watched from above cannot be ruled out.

The idea that Minoan ritual involved actors and spectators is reinforced by the layout of the western courts of the palaces, with seating areas and raised processional ways. This suggested to Nannos Marinatos that the Throne Room at Knossos did not have a secular purpose but was used for staging the epiphany of a member of the ruling class impersonating the goddess. He saw the repetition of the griffin motif on either side of the throne and of the door to the inner sanctuary as an indication of the route followed by the goddess as she emerged from the inner sanctuary, used as a robing room. We can only speculate about the nature of this divinity. Although the image of the snake goddess, with her exposed full breasts and arms stretched out clutching two snakes has captured the popular imagination, it is important to remember that such a representation is comparatively rare. Snakes are traditionally associated with chthonic underworld cults, but this is a later development and one should be careful in extrapo-

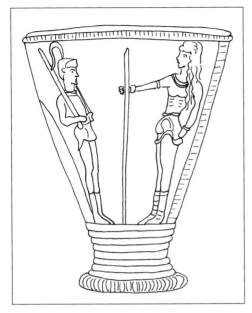

Drawing of the Chieftain Cup (c. 1650–1500 BC), a stone vessel found in 1903 in Aghia Triada. On the right is a figure which has been interpreted by scholars as the image of the Young God. According to some commentators the scene represents two children impersonating dignitaries.

lating backwards from classical Greek traditions. Iconography, in particular the well-preserved Minoan frescoes on Santorini at Akrotiri, suggest a goddess of fertility, a mistress of the animals in tune with nature, and a concern with the cycle of death and renewal.

The male role in religion is twofold. Priests carrying a curved axe or a mace can be recognised by a long fringed robe with diagonal bands. The young god, e.g. the tall slim young man with a short kilt and codpiece holding a staff and exuding authority on the Chieftain Cup from Aghia Triada cup (*illustrated left*), is associated with the wilderness, hunting, and rites of passage. Male deities also appear as protectors of towns and institutions (Chania's Master Impression, for example; *illustrated on p. 331*). A motley collection of animals, either exotic or fantastic, also interact with the gods and attend to them, as shown on the Malia Triton (*see p. 181*). The bull sits neatly between the two. It is not as dangerous as the demons but it is real and is the largest and fiercest animal in Crete. It is shown either in complete submission, tied up and ready for sacrifice, as on the Aghia Triada larnax (*illustrated on p. 45*), or manipulated and subjugated by human cunning. This may be the meaning of the bull-vaulting scenes on frescoes and seals.

There are no urban shrines at the time of the palaces. The preferred setting for public observance was outdoors. Peak sanctuaries, located high up on the mountains but still visible from the settlements they served, flourished from the Prepalatial Period (*see illustration on p. 256*). They show palace influence later in the form of prestige offerings. With no cult images, activity in the peak sanctuaries is difficult to understand. The presence of animal bones and storage facilities suggests communal feasting. Votive objects may have been ritually 'killed' in periodic bonfires. The type of material (figurines of worshippers and limbs) shows a preoccupation with the ordinary human condition.

The same thing could be experienced in the other preferred location of popular cult, namely the caves, frequent in Crete because of its plentiful limestone. The combination of darkness, strangely shaped stalactites and mysterious pools of water clearly acted on the collective psyche and led to the belief that the divinity could be approached and experienced in that setting. On the other hand, venues like Kamares Cave on the slopes of Mt Ida, where no votive objects have been found, point to periodic gatherings to celebrate agricultural festivals in which different classes of society mingled. The site, not accessible in the winter because of snow, is well known for its deposits of high-status vessels (Kamares ware; *see p. 30*).

Both in the palace and in the great outdoors, ancient Cretan religion projects an altogether benign image, which goes hand in hand with Evans's idea of his beloved Minoans. Later finds, however, suggest that there were flaws in the 'Pax Minoica'. Just as the demise of the palaces is now no longer attributed entirely to external forces, so religion had its darker side. The evidence is slim but compelling. It centres mainly on Anemospilia (*see p. 89*) where Giannis and Efi Sakellarakis excavated a temple destroyed in a violent event. Here they found four skeletons. Three belonged to people trying to flee to safety. The fourth person (a male youth on an altar) was apparently already dead by the time the earthquake struck. Forensic examination has concluded that he had been bound and that the main blood vessels in his neck had been severed. The murder weapon (a 40-cm long bronze lance) was still laying across his body. It is enough to make a case for human sacrifice.

The demise of the palaces did not mark the end of Minoan religion; it shifted the focus from a ruling class that had lost its credibility to the urban setting, where shrines become more accessible. A number of architectural features (e.g. pillar crypts, subterranean chambers, pier-and-door systems) go out of use. Figurative art is no longer expressed in frescoes but on pottery and on larnakes, with a stress on symbolism. The ritual furniture in the town shrines tends to be basic; it includes wheel-made pottery figures of a goddess with a headdress, large eyes, raised arms and snakes. Snakes appear also on the so-called 'snake tubes', which are actually pot stands. Meanwhile, in the refuge settlement of Karphi, overlooking the Lasithi plateau (*map p. 430, D2*), abandoned at the very end of the Bronze Age in the 11th century BC, the inhabitants still worshipped a goddess of nature, just as their ancestors had.

MINOAN POTTERY

Pottery has always played an important part in the understanding of Minoan civilisation. An early breakthrough came when J.L. Myres recognised among the material that Evans was unearthing in the early days of excavation at Knossos the same kind of pottery that Flinders Petrie had found at Kahun in Egypt and which was securely dated to the Middle Kingdom (this pottery on Crete was later called Kamares ware, because it was abundantly found in that cave; *see p. 171*). The stratigraphical sequence could be tied to a definite date and Evans's 'oldest European civilisation' was born.

Pottery is not a Cretan invention. It arrived here from Anatolia in the Neolithic period—not with the first settlers, though, as there is an acknowledged aceramic phase when containers must have been in wood or leather or other organic materials that leave little trace in the archaeological record.

Early Neolithic pottery is coarse and utilitarian with the usual addition of grit to ease the firing process. Construction techniques are standard, using coils or slabs pinched together, or shapes formed over inverted bowls. Decoration is scanty, with burnishing and incisions. Vessels are fired at low temperatures in closed conditions, producing a dark surface. Only towards the end of the Neolithic, i.e. almost 2,500 years later, do things start moving and at Knossos, from where most of the evidence for the Cretan Neolithic comes, we see an improvement in quality and in the variety of shapes. This goes hand in hand with evidence of foreign contacts and a beginning of stratification in society, creating a market for finer material. It is the dawn of the Minoan Age, a development that can now be traced across the island: art is produced on demand and clay is an accepted medium. Technically pottery is still hand-made, but by EM II there are specialised craftsmen working with small turntables that probably looked like the clay and stone discs found at Myrtos and Phaistos; these, though, are still devices on which the pot is worked, not thrown. It is a time of exuberant experimentation generating a variety of new shapes with exaggerated spouts, handles and high stems, and figurative vessels as well. Decoration follows the trend, with the addition of paint to incisions. Burnishing gives way to new techniques such as the mottled ware from Vasiliki. Here the surface was covered with a slip high in potassium that vitrified upon firing to a hard glossy surface. Further evidence

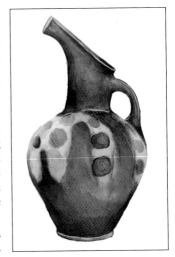

Example of a Vasiliki ware vessel with long, teapot-like spout.

of increased technical mastery is forthcoming at the end of the Early Minoan period with the appearance of the 'white on dark' ware. In this case the vessel was fired to a pale brown colour and covered with a dark slip; then a linear decoration of spirals and zig-zags was painted on top.

The pivoted wheel, the proper potter's wheel, harnessing centrifugal force to produce thin-walled ware in large quantities, is again an import: evidence shows that it was already present in Greece, in Anatolia and in Cilicia some 500 years earlier. In Crete the last hand-made pots date from MM IA towards the end of the Prepalatial period and include some intriguing shapes.

The Proto- and Neopalatial periods

Kamares ware jug found at Phaistos (1800 BC).

The Kamares ware that follows is wheel-made in the palaces by specialised painters and potters to satisfy a specific demand from the upper strata of society, those that either lived in the palaces or gravitated around them. It is characterised by a polychrome decoration on a dark background with the addition of barbotine (a ceramic slip) and relief, freely associating abstract figures and forms arranged in such a way as to produce a sophisticated effect of movement and torsion. Technically it is a challenge as it is very thin and it required firing for several hours at an even temperature ranging between 950 and 1100°C. Kamares kilns have not been identified in Crete, but contemporary suitable structures with perforated floors and clay pillars have been identified on the Greek mainland. The style, mainly found in Knossos and Phaistos, has several unique forms and is well known for its inventiveness. It peaks in the Protopalatial period, prompting speculation that high-status pottery was later replaced by metalware. Probably the pottery industry suffered in the turmoil that followed the destruction of the first palaces c. 1700. The recession in MM III is apparent in

Giant pithos at Malia, 164cm tall.

style and technology, with material poorly fired. Certainly the pottery that immediately follows is of lesser quality: fine carinated drinking cups give way to coarse, conical, utilitarian vessels.

As things pick up with the rebuilding of the palaces, new shapes include stirrup jars and libation vessels open at both ends (rhyta; *see p. 390*). The simplified pictorial decoration with flowers and animals borrows heavily from contemporary forms of decorative art, i.e. frescoes, seals and faïence. Among the large shapes, the pithoi (*see p. 101*) are particularly well represented. They are huge (one from Malia is 164cm tall; *see picture opposite*) and lavishly decorated with rope motifs, medallions and incisions. It does appear, though, that the large number of pithoi recovered from this period does not mean an increase in storage capacity. The evidence from the Protopalatial period is incomplete and additional evidence points to a reduced storage function in the palaces. These are times of great expansion for Minoan pottery, which is found throughout the Aegean and also, but in lesser quantity, in the Middle East.

The flagship fine ware of LM times is known as tortoiseshell ripple ware, characterised by reddish brown decoration on smooth, dense, light clay, with waves, flowers and spirals. Technically it is more demanding, as it requires higher temperatures, a finer slip of a specific composition, as well as control of the oxygen supply in a proper updraft kiln. The ripple effect is achieved by alternating areas that are burnished or painted, onto which some vitrification occurs, with plain surfaces that remain porous and therefore fire differently. Shapes are extremely varied, from tableware to large storage vessels. Tortoiseshell ripple ware is found in Mycenaean Greece, from where, according to some, it may have contributed to the development of Greek and eventually Roman pottery.

The Postpalatial period

This period represents the beginning of Mycenaean influence on the island, with Knossos the only palace left, dominating the production of pottery as well as everything else. The previous trends continue with the explosion of the Marine Style, in which argonauts, tritons, seashells, octopuses and seaweed provide an endless source of inspiration for sinuous designs. Alongside it flowers, reeds and papyrus as well as abstract motifs, possibly inspired by metalwork, offer ideas for alternative decorative schemes. Larnakes, the clay burial chests first appearing in EM III, become very prominent as a vehicle for art, with a new emphasis on the representation of people and animals at the expense of the natural world. Gradually the overwhelming mainland influence, with an emphasis on abstraction, on stylisation and on stretching the material to fill the space, takes over, and while the population retreats to refuge sites, shapes become stereotyped, the repertoire is limited and the artistic syntax uninspired. The Geometric style that follows, with its precise ruler-and compass-design, has nothing to do with Minoan art; it is an entirely new idea.

THE BOTANY OF CRETE

Crete is not only famous for its medicinal plants (*see p. 203*) but for its flora as a whole. It may be a comparatively small place (250km from end to end) but its complex topography has resulted in a great diversity of environments, biotopes and habitats. Moreover its geological history first connected it to the mainland and then isolated it, thereby promoting speciation. Crete is home to some 170 endemic plant species, the result of evolution and selection to meet the challenges posed by climate and animal and human activity. No wonder that since the 15th century it has attracted botanists from all over Europe and that several plant species are protected by the 1982 Berne Convention.

Climatically the island is very diverse: in the winter, from November to March, the west winds brings in the rain; in the summer the meltemi (the north wind) sweeps the moisture from the Aegean and as it hits the heights it creates storms in the mountains. Rainfall decreases from west to east and from north to south in inverse correlation with temperatures. As one can see from pollen cores, documents and travellers' accounts, apart from a few fluctuations, this situation has remained stable since the Bronze Age, when the climate became drier.

The wettest parts of Crete are the northwest flank of the White Mountains and the Fasas valley, west of Chania between Skines and Nea Roumata in the district of Selinos. The Fasas valley is a wetland and in the past there was a bog where the nearby artificial lake of Aghia is today. This is a good place for hygrophiles, with rare species of mosses and liverworts. The extreme southeast is the driest part of the island and has developed into a refuge for North African desert-like flora such as *Viola scorpiuroides*, a perennial with yellow flowers, and a number of tropical grasses and ferns.

Cretan flora has learned to adapt, with a number of species high up in the mountains postponing the flowering season until the summer. Others have adopted defensive tactics against browsing, developing spines and pungent smells. The relic endemic species have made the most of the island's varied topography, seeking refuge in specific habitats unsuitable for other plants like calcareous cliffs and naturally treeless mountains where there is little or no competition.

The island's present tree cover is the result of human and animal activity. The original vegetation was very different. It is probably wrong to imagine that Crete was ever fully forested; the island lacks specialised tree species for very high altitudes. Tree cover has waxed and waned with agriculture. The treeline is 1450m on the north-facing slopes and 1700m on the other side. Beyond, there is some grassland but water is scarce. Only specialised prickly dwarf shrubs and geophytes manage to survive. The high desert (*see p. 362*) is no different now from what it was in Minoan times. In the lowlands, woodland degradation due to deforestation and browsing has given rise to different habitats. Where there is enough rainfall, Mediterranean scrub has developed, an impenetrable thicket 1–3m high: it is a good place for orchids. At the far end of the spectrum, in cases of extreme woodland degradation, the garrigue or *phrygana* (to give it its Greek name, meaning 'twigs' or 'firewood') has taken over, especially on limestone soils. This is the land of spiny, aromatic, colourful dwarf shrubs punctuated by empty spaces where geophytes and orchids will bloom in the spring.

EDWARD LEAR IN CRETE

The well-known nonsense poet and artist Edward Lear paid a short visit to Crete in 1864. He was coming from Corfu, where he had lived for nine years; when the British government returned the Ionian islands to the Greek state, the British community dispersed. At that point in his life he needed to find a warm place for his indifferent health and to produce another book like his *Views in the Seven Ionian Islands*, which had sold steadily. Lear chose Crete, and arrived in Chania on 11th April, with his faithful valet George Kokali and armed with Pashley's *Travels in Crete*. Although he was aware of the presence of Venetian monuments and of some earlier ruins, what he was searching for were beautiful, exotic landscapes that he could sell in England, possibly in a book reworked from notes in his diary. Crete proved a disappointment in many respects. The landscape, vast, rugged and raw, did not lend itself to artistic composition according to the classical canons. The weather did not help and living conditions, from the food to the ever-present fleas and the state of the pavements, proved a perennial source of complaint. The only things that seemed to cheer him were the wine, the birds and the flowers. Lear took more notice of the latter than of the people. Unlike Pashley he makes very few ethnographical observations, even though he spoke Greek and took lodgings with local people.

Lear first travelled west in the Kissamos direction, venturing as far south as Topolia. He then went back to Chania for the Akrotiri and continued east to Souda and Aptera, cutting across to Vamos and Lake Kournas, finally sailing from Rethymnon to Megalokastro (i.e. Herakleion), which failed to impress him. He continued south, ascending Mt Juktas on the way. This he pronounced 'Cumberlandish', a term that he had already applied to Lake Kournas and of which he was obviously fond. The Mesara reminded him of the Beka'a Valley in Lebanon, but wanting in colours, lines and shape, and Mt Ida, around which he skirted from Tymbaki on his way north through the Amari Valley, was forever lost in the clouds. Lear was probably relieved to arrive back in England on 11th June. He had with him some 200 sketches and a diary: nothing of either was ever published in his lifetime. A few drawings were reworked and completed on commission and are now in the Ashmolean Museum in Oxford. The bulk of the sketches found their way onto the London art market in the late 1920s. The Gennadius Library in Athens has 92; the remainder are in private collections and museums. The diary was published in 1984.

THE REDISCOVERY OF CRETE

There has been a long continuum of civilisation on Crete, but until comparatively recently not much was known about it, despite the fact that legends about its glorious past had been embodied in tradition from the time of Homer onwards. Antiquity honours Minos as the original, mythical lawgiver (he is featured laying down the law in Dante's *Inferno*) and it was well known that Crete, the land of 90 cities, had performed brilliantly at Troy under Idomenaeus. In Roman times the Labyrinth, the central element of the Minotaur legend, was well established as part of popular culture, as a graffito in Pompeii implies. Attempts at pinpointing its location by Pliny the Elder, however (*Natural History 35.19.85*), testify to a certain degree of confusion.

From the 14th century the island had been a regular stopover for pilgrims to the Holy Land. In 1322 Simeon Simeonis, a monk from Clonmel in Ireland, paid a visit and commented favourably on Chania (not so on Herakleion), left a few words about the local produce—the wine, the cheese and the fruits—and took an interest in the gypsies, who were living in caves and in oblong, black tents.

It is only in the 16th century, when the antiquarian movement in Europe became interested in the past and its material remains, and by which time relations between Venice and Crete had improved, creating an environment in which the Cretan Renaissance could flourish, that western travellers to Crete started looking around and recording what they saw in their letters home. The bulk of these travellers were merchants connected with the Venetian trade in the East. Some were pilgrims like Sir Richard Guyforde, who came here with his chaplain on his way to the Holy Land in 1511 and left a description of Aghios Titos in Gortyn, or inquisitive spirits like the Frenchman Pierre Belon, an apothecary by training, who collected observations on the natural history and archaeology of the island.

In 1583 Onorio Belli from Vicenza, a contemporary of Andrea Palladio, came to Crete as the personal physician to Alvise Grimani, a Venetian official. Belli remained for 16 years (his wife Bianca Saracena is buried in Chania, in the church that is now the archaeological museum). He toured the island surveying, recording buildings and inscriptions and occasionally also excavating. He collated his finds in a manuscript, *Rerum Creticarum Observationes*, never published and now lost. Fortunately, he left a number of letters and drawings. What most interested him were the Roman remains. They were prominent and he could relate to them. The same was true of his contemporary, the astronomer and mathematician Francesco Barozzi, who collected Roman inscriptions later edited by his nephew Iacopo. The manuscript is now at Oxford University.

Roman monumental remains were indeed also attracting Venice's attention but for different reasons. The Serenissima quarried Crete for Roman statuary, which she shipped back home, while in the island itself, Roman architectural elements were moved to the main towns to beautify them. Roman Ierapetra suffered greatly in this regard. About the same time Venice was busy mapping its colony. The work of Francesco

Basilicata and Marco Boschini, among others, is an important reference for students of the Venetian period, together with the Venetian archives that the defeated Republic was able to ship back to Venice when ousted by the Ottomans.

The superb Cretan flora was also attracting interest. In 1615 the poet and traveller George Sandys, the youngest son of the bishop of York, paid a visit on his grand tour of the East and commented on ethnographical, archaeological and botanical features. Richard Pockoke did likewise in his *Description of the East* over 100 years later. Joseph Pitton de Tournefort, one of the founders of modern botany, was in Crete in 1701 collecting rare endemic species on Mt Ida. He was followed by John Sibthorp, professor of botany at Oxford, at the end of the 18th century. His *Flora Graeca* lists numerous endemic Cretan species. In 1837 Robert Pashley, a Cambridge-trained economist, published his *Travels in Crete*, with important social, economic and ethnographical observations. He also recorded a number of archaeological sites and proposed identifications with lost ancient Hellenistic cities known from written sources. Another Englishman, Captain T.A.B. Spratt, pursued a brilliant career in the navy where he was mostly associated with surveying the Mediterranean. Spratt was also versed in the Classics and made important observations on the geology, archaeology and natural history of Crete in his *Travels and Researches in Crete*, published in 1865.

The crucial period for the exploration of Crete's past is the second half of the 19th century, when archaeology as an established research method was finding its feet, and when Schliemann's discoveries in mainland Greece and at Troy were the talk of every town. Crete acted like a magnet for a crowd of willing archaeologists, not for its visible remains, which were Roman or later, but for an elusive civilisation that had produced the seals that were cropping up here and there, suggesting the presence of a writing system and inviting comparisons with Mycenae. Moreover a merchant and antiquarian by the name of Minos Kalokairinos, in his excavations of 1878–79 at Knossos, had hit upon huge structures and intriguing finds. In the last decade of the 19th century, Sir Arthur Evans and John Myres were not the only ones looking for a site. The Italians had already established a presence with Federico Halbherr, who had been working as an epigraphist at Gortyn since 1884 where, as early as 1577, Barozzi had spotted Greek lettering. The French and the Americans also had an interest.

Though archaeological opportunities were manifold, the early 20th century was a politically troubled time for the island. The Cretan question loomed large and the great powers (France, Britain, Italy and Russia) hoped to engineer a solution that would spell the end of Ottoman occupation while also avoiding union with Greece. Meanwhile there were fears that finds from excavations would find their way into the newly-built Imperial Archaeological Museum in Istanbul: it is for this reason that the Cretan Assembly had halted Kalokairinos's excavations.

The advent of independence signalled a different outlook from the local authorities, led by the Cretan archaeologist Joseph Hatzidakis. Excavations began all across the island involving American, British, Italian and Greek teams. The French, temporarily sidetracked at other Greek sites, came back to Crete for Malia in 1921. The history of archaeology in Crete is also notable for the careers of two remarkable women. Harriet

Boyd and Edith Hall were pioneers in a society that barely allowed women to study Classics at a higher level and certainly barred them from fieldwork, for which they were considered and too great a distraction for the men. Boyd's exploration of Crete began in 1900. Unable, apparently, to secure a position with any ongoing excavation because she was a woman, she decided to run her own site, becoming the first woman to do so. With her at Kavousi, northeast of Gournia, was a fellow American, Edith Hall, who went on to run her own excavation at Vrokastro in 1910–12. In spite of their success, both women gave up fieldwork in order to raise a family, after which they pursued distinguished careers in academia. Nevertheless, the way was now open: Mediterranean archaeology ceased to be a male preserve.

Fragment of Venetian masonry with billeted edging and traces of foliation. Photographed by Giuseppe Gerola in the Ottoman cemetery of Herakleion, where it was functioning as a grave marker.

Excavations at this early stage covered pre-Roman sites. Roman Crete had to wait a while longer. Ian Sanders was the first to make an exhaustive survey of the Roman sites in the wake of John Pendlebury's comprehensive fieldwork, published in 1939.

The end of Ottoman occupation also signalled a renewed Italian interest in the remains of the Venetian period, and the Istituto Veneto in Venice spearheaded a mission to document them. On Halbherr's suggestion, the task was entrusted to a young medievalist, Giuseppe Gerola (*see p. 54*). Gerola documented Venetian architectural remains *in situ* and in secondary locations such as Herakleion Ottoman cemetery, where several architectural fragments had been used as tomb stelae. Gerola also extended his enquiries to any evidence of the past, be it Byzantine, Roman or indeed Ottoman. He photographed people and places, a precious testimony of contemporary life on the island, a world now vanished. He may have been inspired in his holistic approach by a local photographer, Beha Eddin. Of Turkish extraction and with a keen eye, Eddin operated on the island on a freelance basis. He had a studio on Odos Daidalou in Herakleion and took an interest in everything, including Cretan revolutionaries (of whom he made fine portraits). He also edited the first picture postcards of the island, some of which are still on sale. Unfortunately his original negatives, numbering approximately 1,500–2,000 are now lost, thrown away in 1982 according to a newspaper report. With them went a precious testimony of Crete's Ottoman heritage, a heritage to which, on the whole, the island has been none too kind. After independence and then union with Greece, the Turkish interlude was considered best forgotten. Mosques were returned to their original function as churches; other evidence has suffered from neglect and indifference, if not downright hostility. Only now is the Ottoman past beginning to be rehabilitated: the restoration of a minaret in Rethymnon is a sign of changing times.

HERAKLEION PROVINCE

The *nome* or province of Herakleion is set in the middle of Crete stretching from north to south, from coast to coast. It is well served by a road system radiating from the capital city of Herakleion itself. This means that it is possible to drive along the coast east to Aghios Nikolaos and west to Rethymnon in a short hour and also to venture inland using an improved network, to explore the Mesara plain and the stunning south coast.

There is much in the province for visitors keen on the cultural and historical aspects of Crete. The new archaeological museum in Herakleion, when completed, will be a necessary stop for anyone interested in the island's archaeology. It has a huge collection and artefacts are hardly ever allowed to leave the island. In addition to this, three of Crete's best-known Minoan palaces—Knossos, Malia and Phaistos—are in the province, together with the largest Roman site on the island, Gortyn. The Byzantine period is well represented with a number of monasteries in quiet rural locations, such as Angarathos and Epanosiphis. Vrondisi is well known for its frescoes. These can all be visited in a day trip from Herakleion; indeed, in the low season, it may be convenient to be based in the city itself. It is different when the heat sets in; at that point, a location by the sea, or inland for the breeze (the sea is not very far anyway), will probably be preferable.

Walkers will be able to follow the E4 long-distance route coming in from the west on the south slopes of Mt Ida towards Zaros. It can then be followed to Venerato, Temenos and Archanes, and east through Kastelli Pediadas onto the Lasithi plateau.

There are beaches at either end of the province, but readers would be well advised to go south for a swim. The development on the north coast, especially to the east of Herakleion, caters to the needs of mass tourism, which at least means that there is plenty of it. It does fill up quickly though and, more importantly, it may not be exactly what one wants. Having said that, it is possible to find something between Amnisos and Chersonisos, and west (Fodele and Bali). On the south coast, tourism is still on a comparatively small scale. Visitors with their own transport will be able to reach delightful coastal villages such as Kali Limenes or Tsoutsouros, but here the problem is the other way round. Facilities may not be numerous, and soon fill up at the height of the season. Further east, the region of Viannos is even more remote from the tourist track and development is more rudimentary still. It does, however, have good road communications to the coast and the east, and can be an excellent base for exploring the Lasithi plateau.

HERAKLEION

The city of Herakleion (Ηράκλειο; pron. Iráklio; *map p. 430, B1–C1*), centrally placed on the north coast facing the Aegean, became the capital of the island only comparatively recently, supplanting Chania. When Prince George was installed as High Commissioner of Crete in 1898, after the expulsion of the Turks, he operated from there;

Herakleion's hopes of supremacy were blighted by its problem harbour, prone to silting. Only in 1971 did its central location emerge triumphant. Since then Herakleion has not looked back. It has expanded to become fifth largest city in Greece, with a population more than double Chania's. It is now the main hub for the island, with ferries to mainland Greece, Thera (Santorini), Rhodes, Haifa and Egypt, and a busy international airport, second in traffic volume in Greece only to Athens. It is a thoroughly modern city. A quick look at a town plan, showing the outline of the Venetian fortifications, gives an instant and vivid idea of the vast size of its sprawling suburbs. That said, once crossed, these are quickly forgotten, as the historic centre is fairly self-contained.

In itself, Herakleion is not a particularly beautiful city. It suffered greatly in the Second World War when it was heavily bombed by the Germans, and that came at the end of a history of earthquake damage, foreign occupation, pirate raids and internal conflicts. It can be very busy, very congested, and very noisy (it does not help that the airport is so close and is also used by the army). Attempts have been made to ease the traffic with a one-way system, which is fine once you understand how it works. Pedestrian areas have also been increased, with a view to extending the scheme to the whole of the old town.

Visitors will want to be in Herakleion principally for the Venetian remains (the impressive star-shaped fortifications, the Arsenali, the castle guarding the port and the occasional surviving building), for the maze-like street plan of the old city, and for a clutch of fine museums that will be finer still when the new archaeological museum eventually reopens.

Fortunately Herakleion is blessed with a good road network. The E75 coastal highway bypasses it to the south and a web of minor roads gets you quickly to a beach on either side of the town. A couple of stops by bus to the east will take you to Amnisos in 15mins. The west coast with the bay of Lygaria (15km) and Fodele (another 10), is more peaceful but requires private transport.

HISTORY OF HERAKLEION

Evidence of Neolithic occupation has been found in the high ground above the Kairatos stream bed to the east of the present town. The modern suburb of Poros, where the Greek Archaeological Service has been excavating, was the site of one of the two Minoan harbours of Knossos. It was known as Katsambas. In Roman times, according to the geographer Strabo, it was still functioning as the harbour of the Roman colony of Julia Nobilis Cnossus, though the precise location of the installations is not known. At that time it acquired the name of Heracleum. The Arabs recognised the potential of the location and, after their conquest in the 820s, built a large defensive ditch which gave the town a new name: Rabdh el-Khandak, literally 'the castle of the ditch'. According to Christian tradition, the town developed into a centre of piracy and became the chief slave market of the Mediterranean.

The emperor Nicephorus Phocas reclaimed Crete for the Byzantines in 961 but the island was eventually sold to the Venetians in 1204. They settled in for a spell that lasted until the 17th century. Herakleion became known first as Candica, then as Candia (a

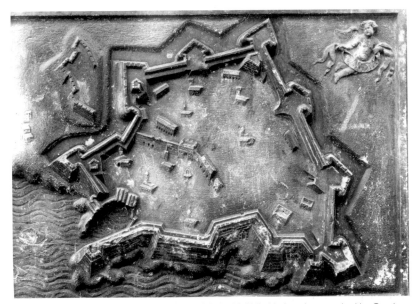

Relief map of Candia from the church of Santa Maria del Giglio, Venice, photographed by Gerola. The shape described by the Venetian city walls is very clear, with the harbour, the arsenals and the castle. The Piazza delle Biade with its fountain and church of St Mark is also shown.

corruption of its former Arab name), and families from Venice began arriving in 1212. The town was developed as the leading seaport of the east Mediterranean and the capital of the Kingdom of Crete, known then as the Regno di Candia. It became the seat of government for the Duke of Crete and his councillors, with a Ducal Palace in the main square opposite the church dedicated to Venice's patron saint, St Mark. There were no walls, as Phocas had forced the inhabitants to pull them down and fill in the ditch. The city prospered with an expanding population that included Armenians from the Black Sea area (they had their own church by 1363) and Jews moving in from the countryside or possibly, judging by the name of one of their three synagogues (Siviliatico), from Seville. The ghetto was in the northwest of the city, where Jews were involved in the tanning business, traditionally a smelly activity kept out of the town centre.

Eventually, in 1364, a circuit of walls was built. Inland it ran roughly along Odos Daidalou and Odos Khandakos and along the sea from the Porta del Molo by the castle westwards to the Jewish quarter, and to the east by the convent of the Franciscans (now the Archaeological Museum). The circumference became too small as surrounding villages expanded and coalesced with the town. New city walls were planned and the old ones became incorporated into stores, shops, depots and a jail.

These new Venetian defensive walls, originally 5km long with seven bastions and four gates, still surround parts of Herakleion. The circuit was built over a long period between the 15th and the 17th centuries. The final plan belongs to Michele Sanmicheli, a 16th-century military architect from Verona, whose work can also be seen in Chania and Cyprus, though he was hardly ever on hand to supervise the execution, which he mainly left to his nephew Gian Girolamo. Work was dogged by chronic lack of money and by the population's understandable reluctance to live in a town that was either expensive, because of the extra tax imposed by the government to finance the wall-building, or else unsafe, because its fortifications were inadequate. Two out of the original four city gates survive today: the Chanioporta (the Chania Gate) to the west and the Porta tou Eissou (Jesus Gate), also known as Kainourgia Porta ('New Gate'), to the south at the end of Odos Evans. Of the other two, one was pulled down by the British in 1898 to improve traffic flow. The other met its fate in 1917 at the hands of the locals. They would have removed the whole wall circuit, a symbol of foreign occupation, but Sir Arthur Evans was able to persuade them otherwise. All seven bastions are preserved. The tomb of the famous author Nikos Kazantzakis (1883–1957), with its epitaph: 'I wish for nothing, I fear nothing; I am free', can be seen at the Martinengo Bastion.

When it became clear in the 1640s that the Turks had set their sights on Crete and that Venice's dominion in the eastern Mediterranean had become severely impaired by piracy, the Serenissima put together a coalition to defend its position, receiving assistance from Naples, Tuscany, the Papal States and Malta. The Christian fleet totalled well over 100 ships. In 1648 the Turks began the siege of the city. Their camp was on the south side on the hill of Fortetsa, 4km away, from which cannons operated against the town. In spite of military assistance from the French king Louis XIV, the Venetian commander Francesco Morosini the Younger eventually negotiated a surrender on September 6th 1669. It is not clear why Morosini gave up at that point; he took the decision without even consulting the Venetian senate. He may have been prompted by the decision of the French to leave Candia in August. On the whole, during the war, Venice had been on the offensive and had won stunning victories over the Turks, narrowly missing the chance to set up a permanent base in the Dardanelles. In the 21-year siege the losses had been considerable. Over 100,000 Turks and some 30,000 Christians lost their lives, a tally that included 280 Venetian noblemen, the equivalent of one quarter of the Gran Consiglio, the main hereditary body governing Venice. No one counted the local civilians.

The Venetians were allowed to sail away unharmed—and with them sailed the state archives, an invaluable source of information for later historians (unfortunately, of the five ships, only three made it home). Some Cretans also left to start new lives in the Ionian islands. Morosini's reputation was blighted by the experience, but not for long. Re-elected Captain General in 1683, he led the anti-Turkish coalition to oust the Ottomans from Europe, regaining Venetian control of the Morea (now the Peloponnese). He was eventually elected Doge and died in 1693.

After the surrender, Candia was no more. Officially Kandiye to the Ottomans, it became known as Megalo Kastro ('Big Castle') because of its impressive fortifications, and was the seat of the Turkish government until 1850, before it was transferred to Chania. The name Herakleion dates from 1898, after the end of Turkish rule. The suburb of Nea Alikarnassos is a reminder of the population exchanges which followed the collapse of the Ottoman Empire, when Greeks in Turkey were 'repatriated' to Greece and vice versa. The Greeks from the western coast of Turkey brought back with them an expertise in the sultana and currant industry, which flourished until quite recently. In 1971, because of Herakleion's economic development and central location, it was chosen as the capital of the island.

ARCHAEOLOGICAL MUSEUM

Open in low season Mon 12–5, Tues–Sun 8.30–3; high season daily 8.30–7. Entrance on Doukos Bofor; ticket office (T: 2810 279000) on Odos Hatzidakis, around the corner to the right. NB: At the time of writing the museum was closed for renovation and refurbishment and no firm reopening date had been set. A temporary exhibition shows a small selection of the 15,000 exhibits the museum owns. A visit provides a good introduction to the archaeological wealth of the island. There are serious drawbacks though. The display is too limited and condensed: the experience induces a slight feeling of indigestion as every single object is a top find and there is no time to take them in. Physical space is a problem. The two rooms are really small and as soon as a guided tour gets in with loud commentary, visitors are seriously cramped.

The museum stands on the site of the monastery of St Francis, where Pope Alexander V (*see p. 190*) studied. The monastery was demolished in 1937, but fortunately (or unfortunately) not completely. Surviving remains have come to light in the course of the present renovation works and they cannot be ignored. Everything seems to have come to a halt and the temporary exhibition has taken on an unsettling air of permanence.

The display is set out in two small rooms and shows a limited selection of artefacts, arranged chronologically, with emphasis on the showpieces of the Minoan period.

Entrance: At the entrance, the controversial *Prince of the Lilies*, the relief fresco now forever associated with Knossos, where its fragments were found in a heap, welcomes visitors. This is Evans's version—by no means unchallenged. The original appearance of the artwork may never be known.

Neolithic: Case 1 displays Neolithic finds from Knossos and Katsambas (7000–3400 BC).

Prepalatial: Case 2 shows material from further afield with examples of the Prepalatial period (3400–2000 BC), with mottled Vasiliki ware and an excellent example of a **teapot vase** with a long, delicate spout. Note the **bull from a Mesara tomb** with tiny acrobats clinging to its horns: clearly the bull fascination has deep roots in Crete.

Case 3 features an excellent display of early metal and jewellery of the same period. The **gold lion** with delicate granulation is an early example of the technique.

Cycladic figurines from the Prepalatial Mesara in Case 4 testify to foreign contacts with the Aegean, while **seals and sealings** show the early rise of administration and power.

Old Palace Period: Cases 5 and 6 display dazzling examples of **Kamares**

ware from the Old Palace period (2000–1700 BC) from Knossos and Phaistos. These are unique pieces showing craftsmanship at its best, with a variety of shapes and an uncanny ability to bring movement to the decoration that seems to coil and twist itself around the vessel.

Old Palace finds from Malia in Case 7 show the quality of the goldsmith's work of the period. The well-known **Bee Pendant** in granulation and filigree is but one instance of the gold work buried at the cemetery of Chrysolakkos (*see p. 127*).

Domestic housing of the 18th–17th centuries BC is illustrated in Case 8 with the **Archanes Model**. The small terracotta piece shows a two-storey Minoan house with small windows, a light-well opening onto a Minoan hall, a stairway, pier-and-door partitions, a balcony and columns supporting a reconstructed roof. Together with the faïence inlays of the façades of houses in the **Town Mosaic**, and the as-yet-unpublished house model from Monastiraki (now in Rethymnon Museum), the Archanes Model gives a good idea of the appearance of an ordinary town house such as the House of the Fallen Blocks at Knossos.

New Palace Period: Case 9 shows examples of New Palace (1700–1370 BC) ceramics. The famous **octopus vase from Palaikastro**, an outstanding instance of the Marine Style, is next to a kalathos (a clay vessel in the shape of woven reed basket) from Pseira with a ritual motif of double axes.

Crafts and tools are shown in Case 10, with finds mainly from Zakros. Note the copper ingots in the shape of an ox hide, and the elephant tusk, one of a number retrieved during excavations.

From the palace of Knossos comes the wooden **game board** (alternatively a calendar, according to some scholars) inlaid with rock crystal, glass paste and lapis lazuli, and decorated with gold and silver leaf (Case 11), while in the next case the **rock crystal rhyton** is both a testimony to the virtuosity of the ancient craftsmen who made it and the skill of the modern conservators who reconstructed it by piecing together its 300 fragments.

Case 13 shows another virtuoso piece, the **Bull's Head Rhyton** from the Little Palace in Knossos (*illustrated left; see also p. 76*).

There are monumental double axes in incongruous modern stands in the corners of the room.

Artefacts from Knossos with faïence inlays in the Marine Style (flying fish,

The magnificent rhyton (ritual libation vessel) in the shape of a bull's head, made of steatite with eyes of jasper and rock crystal.

Detail of the scene on the Harvester Vase (1500–1450 BC), found at Aghia Triada. Reapers are shown in procession, with a group of singers in the centre. One of their number rattles a sistrum.

shells and nautilus) take pride of place in Case 14 with the world-famous **snake goddesses** that have become emblematic of the Minoan civilisation (*see box overleaf*). Case 15 displays a limestone lioness rhyton.

From Aghia Triada (Case 16), comes the much-restored **Boxer Rhyton**, with scenes of boxing and wrestling matches and bull sports, side by side with the **Harvester Vase**, of which only the upper shoulder is preserved (*illustrated above*). The scene shows a procession of youths with the leader carrying a long rod while the rest have pitchforks and scythes. They are accompanied by four singers, one playing a sistrum like the one found in Archanes. Both artefacts are in serpentine and are believed to have been manufactured in Knossos. Equally outstanding and unique is the third vessel of the display, namely the slender **rhyton from Zakros** showing a peak sanctuary (*see illustration on p. 256*). It was originally covered in gold leaf, as the scanty remains indicate.

The back wall of the room is the culmination of the show, with a selection of the original fragments of the **Knossos frescoes** (*Bull-Leaper, Parisienne, Saffron Gatherer, Monkey in a Rocky Landscape, Blue Bird* and *Cup Bearer*). They are so well known that they hardly come as a surprise; one has to imagine what impact they made on Evans as he first cast his eyes on them. Since then, of course, extensive and more complete examples of Minoan frescoes have come to light on Santorini (*see Blue Guide Greece the Aegean Islands*).

In Case 18 the **Phaistos Disk** (*see p. 152*) is in a class of its own.

THE TROUBLE WITH SNAKE GODDESSES

Over 100 years on it is hard for the modern reader to appreciate the excitement engendered by Evans's finds in Crete. Here was a whole new civilisation with artistic achievements rivalling Egypt's. Evans himself fostered expectation by dwelling on the modernity of the style and by embarking on a (now) controversial restoration programme which owed much to his own romanticised image of the 'Minoan' (his own word) past. As Minoan artefacts became prestige objects for museums, unscrupulous dealers, smugglers and restorers were quick to react. Top of the wish list was the snake goddess. With her full exposed bosom, pinched waist, flounced skirt and modern expression, she looked exactly what was expected: an art even superior to that of Classical Greece and comparable to the Italian Renaissance. The Getty curator Kenneth Lapatin has suggested that the famous snake goddess might not be a genuine antiquity.

It is certainly true that from modest beginnings in Crete in 1903, the production of modern Minoica moved onto a world-wide market. In 1914 the Boston Museum of Fine Arts paid a staggering $950 for a very damaged chryselephantine snake goddess with no detailed provenance. It has affinities with the faïences from the Temple Repositories but also a number of crucial unexplained differences, not least that it is the only example in Minoan art in which ivory is used for a female figure. Questions about its authenticity remain unanswered. In the 1920s the curator at the Fitzwilliam Museum, Cambridge, wishing to enhance the status of her department, fell for a marble snake goddess, once again with no provenance except for a vague 'east of Knossos'. £2750 were duly paid to a local intermediary who said he had it through a Paris dealer. Doubts raised by the ephor in Crete were set aside and ascribed to jealousy and embarrassment at having allowed such a unique artefact to leave the island. Yet questions soon began to be asked. No archaeologist had actually seen the artefact come out of the ground. Authentication was based purely on style, subjective judgement and expectations. Evans was still defending it in 1935 but the Fitzwilliam Museum after demoting its status to 'dubious' in 1964, last showed it in 1991. Who dunnit? Evidence points in two directions: first the Gilliérons, père et fils, who worked as restorers for Evans from the very beginning and eventually set up shop in Athens producing fine detailed replicas of Knossos finds for academic collections; alternatively it was one of the Cretan workers trained by them. Sir Leonard Woolley in his memoirs tells how a forger who apparently confessed on his deathbed, had wept bitter tears on discovering how much money his work could ultimately command.

Case 19 displays the celebrated **larnax from Aghia Triada**, carved from a single block of limestone and found in a LM IIIA context. The stone was covered with plaster and painted with the fresco technique (*see illustration below*).

Cases 20 to 24 have a selection of finds from cemeteries, dated 1500–1400. These include gold jewellery with the famous and controversial **Minos Ring**— or at least one of them, since apparently copies were made by Evans when it came to his notice in the 1930s. This one received the seal of approval from the Greek Archaeological Service in 2002.

Case 21 testifies to overseas contacts with Egypt with finds from the old harbour of Katsambas dated to the 18th dynasty (16th–13th centuries). Case 22 shows the **ivory inlays belonging to a footstool** found in Phourni Tholos Tomb A (*see p. 86*). The 87 ivory fragments had not been disturbed and it was thus possible to reconstruct the whole object and its decorative scheme (even though the wood, possibly ebony, had long perished) as a 35cm-long footstool with the helmeted Mycenaean heads acting as

Both long sides of the Aghia Triada larnax portray funeral ceremonies. Above: Two scenes are shown here, distinguished by background colour and by the direction the participants are facing. On the left the figure pouring the contents of a vase into a krater is conducting a purification ceremony for the deceased. The sacred surroundings are symbolised by the double axes with birds perching on them. On the right, a procession conveys gifts, including a model boat, towards an individual in front of a richly decorated building. The figure is thought to represent a priest. Below: Female figures are officiating at the sacrifice of a bull to the accompaniment of a flute. On the short sides (not shown) are representations of a procession and chariots drawn by horses and griffins.

handles. The stool was not piled in the corner like the other offerings; its location in front of the tomb chest suggests that it was used in the interment ritual.

Case 24 has another object showing Mycenaean connections. The **boar-tusk helmet** would originally have been sewn on a leather base. Homer (*Iliad X, 260–70*) gives a vivid description of Meriones, brother-in-arms and charioteer of Idomenaeus, and the boar-tusk helmet he gave to Odysseus.

Post Palatial and Graeco-Roman:
The rest of Crete's history is dealt with at breakneck speed, with metal finds from the Idaian Cave, from Dreros (the bronze statues made with the sphyrelaton technique by hammering the bronze plates onto a wooden core) and Kato Symi.

For Hellenistic and Roman Crete, one has to be content with a handful of statues. On the other hand, there is a chance to have a good look at the **Eleftherna Kore** (*see p. 289*). The front is quite damaged but the headdress is better preserved at the back and the eight braids could be clearly made out if it were not pushed so far against the wall.

A WALK THROUGH OLD HERAKLEION

The walk starts from Plateia Eleftherias (*see map overleaf*). A pedestrian shopping area leads through Odos Daidalou to **Plateia Venizelou**, the Venetian Piazza delle Biade, where the grain market was held. It is known to the locals as Lion Square because of the four lions of the **Morosini Fountain**, built in 1626–28 by the Venetian governor Francesco Morosini the Elder. The lions, recycled from an earlier monument, are the original elements of the fountain together with a statue of Neptune, now lost. The sinuous basin, made of hollowed-out Byzantine capitals, is a later addition and not of the same quality artistically, although some of the marine scenes with sirens and tritons engaging in various activities are quite fetching. During the Turkish occupation the monument underwent drastic modifications. The Neptune was destroyed and an incongruous superstructure of iron gates and marble pillars with Sultan Abdul Megid inscriptions was added. The monument has recently been restored and includes the interesting addition of two glass panes set into the lower basin to show the underground workings.

Opposite the fountain, the **church of St Mark**, the protector of Venice, is a three-aisled basilica with a wooden roof. Built in 1239, the first Venetian church on the island, it underwent a series of repairs and re-buildings, attaining its present dimensions in a final overhaul at the time of the Ottoman domination, when it became a mosque. Its original appearance is not known in detail. According to Gerola (*see p. 54*), its plan can be compared to Santa Maria dell'Orto in Venice. It is now used as an exhibition hall.

From the square a short walk east leads to the reconstructed **Venetian Loggia**, once the meeting place for business and other transactions. The Turks closed the arches and turned it into a government building. The present construction is a careful copy of the

Photograph by Gerola of local children against a blocked-up doorway of Palazzo Ittar, in old the centre of the Venetian city.

1628 loggia destroyed in a direct hit in the Battle of Crete in 1941. The first mention of such a building in Herakleion dates to 1269. There were at least five loggias during the course of the Venetian era, not all in the same place or to the same plan.

On the north side of the loggia is the **Sagredo Fountain**, built in 1602 and named after one of the dukes of Crete. The fountain has a defaced female figure assumed to represent the nymph Crete, mother of Pasiphaë, Minos' wife according to Greek mythology. She holds a shield in her left hand and a club in the right.

Further on is **Aghios Titos**, probably the only mosque in Crete that later became a church. Originally there was a Byzantine church on the site, dedicated to Titus, the first bishop of the island, appointed by St Paul. The church was destroyed in an earthquake followed by fire in 1544 and rebuilt as a mosque in 1872. It became an Orthodox church in 1926. After a fire in 1544 the Venetians removed St Titus' head, St Saba's tibia and St Ephraim's arm to St Mark's in Venice, while the icon of the Mesopanditissa went to Santa Maria della Salute, also in Venice. To this day only the head of St Titus has been returned, amidst general jubilation in 1966.

The Bembo Fountain, Aghia Aikaterini and Aghios Matthaios

From Plateia Venizelou a wide avenue leads to the Chanioporta (Chania Gate). In early Venetian documents, Odos Kalokairinou appears as Via Imperiale. Continuing south along Odos 1866, where the outdoor market is, the road leads to Plateia Kornarou, with another fountain: the **Bembo Fountain**, by the Venetian architect Zuanne (Gianmatteo) Bembo. It was built in 1588 using antique fragments from Ierapetra, including the headless statue. The statue was painted black and was apparently venerated by the Turks and was known as ἀραπης ('Moor', and also 'bogeyman'). This was the first fountain to supply fresh running water to the city, from Mt Juktas. The aqueduct, built by Morosini, started nine miles to the south and supplied the town with 1,000 barrels a day. Before that the town had to rely on cisterns and wells and on water-sellers plying their trade from the nearby stream, six miles away to the east. The fountain has now lost its upper structure, which Pashley saw. Close to it, the Turkish pump-house, Koubes, is now a café. At the back a *Romeo and Juliet* with extra heads and limbs is an attempt at representing movement in sculpture.

Heading west, Odos Karterou leads to Plateia Aikaterini with the neo-Byzantine Cathedral of Aghios Minas, built in 1895. In its shadow lies the **old Aghios Minas**, in which is a beautiful icon of Minas, the patron saint of Herakleion, on his white horse. According to tradition, Minas was a 3rd-century Egyptian soldier.

The former monastic church of **Aghia Aikaterini Sinaïtes** is on the edge of the same square. The monastery, a *metochi* (dependency) of the monastery of the same name on Mt Sinai, was an important cultural and artistic centre from the 15th–17th centuries, the period between the fall of Byzantium and the capture of Herakleion by the Turks (1669). It became a famous centre for the arts and learning, playing an important role in the preservation and dissemination of Byzantine culture. This church dates from 1555 with 17th-century alterations. The only church in Herakleion still owned by the monastery is Aghios Matthaios Sinaïtes close by (*see below*), with a collection of icons.

Airport & OLD ROAD TO EAST CRETE

KNOSSOS & NEW NATIONAL ROAD

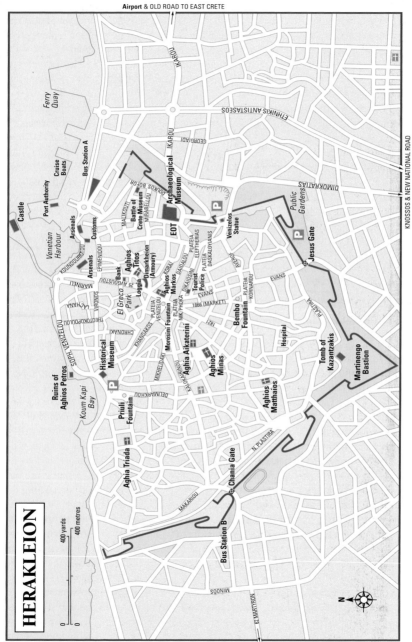

HERAKLEION

400 yards
400 metres

PHAISTOS, RETHYMNON & NEW NATIONAL ROAD

The church of Aghia Aikaterini Sinaïtes used to be the theological museum, but at the time of writing it was closed due to restoration work. It has an important collection of works by leading Cretan icon-painter Mikhail Damaskinos (*see box below*).

Mikhail Damaskinos (active 1555–91)

The *Divine Liturgy*, by Damaskinos, in the church of Aghia Aikaterini.

Damaskinos first studied at Aghia Aikaterini and then, like many of his contemporaries, looked for employment abroad. He was in Venice from 1577 to 1582 and worked on the decoration of San Giorgio dei Greci. He painted the fresco in the apse and the individual panels on the tier of the iconostasis, with icons representing the 12 great festivals of the church. His production is now widely dispersed, but six major works belonging to his mature period, after his return from Venice, are to be seen here. They were originally in the Vrondisi monastery on the south slopes of Mt Ida but were housed for safety at Aghios Minas in 1800 and from there they were moved to Aghia Aikaterini. The works include the *First Ecumenical Council at Nicaea*, the *Divine Liturgy*, the *Virgin and the Burning Bush*, *Noli me Tangere*, the *Last Supper* and the *Adoration of the Magi* with camels, horses and Turkish-looking soldiers, said to show more clearly the influence of Western art.

In the church of **Aghios Matthaios Sinaïtes** are two more icons now attributed to Damaskinos. The church is situated in Taxiarchou Markopoulou, a few minutes' walk from Aghia Aikaterini (*it looked firmly closed at the time of writing and had no timetable for visitors; this may change when the museum in Aghia Aikaterini Sinaïtes reopens*). The two panels by Damaskinos are *Aghios Symeos Theodochos* (Receiver of God) illustrating the message of the Presentation in the Temple, and *Aghios Ioannis Prodromos* (St John the Baptist). The scene shows adherence to the iconographical tradition of the Palaeologan style with the saint wearing a sheepskin garment with one hand raised in blessing and the other holding an open scroll. The traditional severed head at his feet has been omitted, however, while the addition of wings is certainly a departure from the standard representation.

Retrace your steps to the Morosini Fountain, from where **Odos 25 Avgoustou** heads north and leads to the harbour. This is a pedestrian area with banks and tourist agencies.

THE MARTYRS OF 25TH AUGUST

Many streets in Greece are named after dates commemorating important events in history. The street connecting the harbour to the old city centre of Herakleion, anciently the Venetian Ruga Magistra, is no exception: it is named after a day in 1898, when the struggle for independence from Turkey was nearly over. *Enosis*, the union with Greece, had been temporarily ruled out, but autonomy had been granted. On that day a detachment of British soldiers was escorting officials of the new Executive Council along the street to harbour. They were attacked by a mob of Turkish Cretan rioters. In the subsequent disturbances many civilians were killed as well as 17 British soldiers and the British honorary consul. The British navy moved in, and the Turkish Cretan ringleaders were apprehended and hanged. Eventually the city was cleared of Turkish forces and on 2nd November of the same year the last Turkish soldier left Crete.

The waterfront

The harbour is guarded by the 16th-century **Venetian castle** (Rocca al Mare; *open low season Mon–Sun 8–3, high season 8–7*). Sited at the end of a long pier, it still has the symbol of the Serenissima, the Winged Lion of St Mark, stamped upon it. The original castle on

this site was a *castellum comunis*, intended to shelter the inhabitants in case of attack. It was destroyed in an earthquake in 1303. The building that replaced it was ambitious but ill-fated. It developed immediate problems because of exposure to the waves and to the north winds. Alterations to the configuration of the harbour to improve the castle's situation only exacerbated the harbour's tendency to silt up and, according to documents, the sea was still getting into the fortress in 1638.

The entrance is on the ground floor, where 26 vaulted rooms were used as stores and to house the garrison. The upper platform is accessible via an inclined ramp designed to move guns while pack animals would have been able to negotiate the shallow steps. There is a fine view from the top.

Winged Lion of St Mark on the wall of the Venetian Rocca al Mare, Herakleion's castle.

Opposite the castle, the **Arsenali** of the same date are well preserved. They are the remains of the great dockyards Venice built as soon as it took control of the island, to shelter and repair its vessels; they were never intended for ship-building.

On the seafront not far from the Historical Museum (*see below*) is **Moni Aghios Petros**. This is an old Dominican foundation; in its original setting it stood much closer to the sea. Travellers in the 15th century wondered how the monks could hear their own voices during services with the noise of the waves breaking against the walls. The building, with its fine slender windows, survives to the second storey. Restoration was in progress at the time of writing.

Herakleion is a fast-changing town; visitors wishing to get an idea of how the modern city has developed, literally on top of its past, might like to have a look immediately east of the Hotel Megaron (by the bus station) on the landward higher entrance. In an empty plot between two high-rise constructions you can see the roof of a Venetian building that was at some point completely filled in and presumably built over.

Historical Museum of Crete

Odos Sophokli Venizelou 27; open Mon–Sat 9–5. With the ticket you get a plan which is no longer accurate. However, the display has exhaustive information panels, also in English, and makes good use of interactive technology.

The museum houses an important collection of material touching upon the history of Herakleion and Crete from Early Christian times to the present. The building itself, the Neoclassical **Kalokairinos House**, is of interest as an example of the island's architecture. It belonged to Andreas Kalokairinos, an important local benefactor, and dates from 1870. After it went up in flames in the events of 25th August 1898 (*see p. 51*), it was rebuilt according to the old plans, with a colonnaded entrance and windows framed by caryatids. The interior is decorated with friezes of scenes from the *Iliad* and the *Odyssey*. It is now a listed building. Over time, to increase exhibition space, a wing in the same style was added to the west, and eventually a glass and aluminium bridge linking the two was built, to a design by the Cretan architect J. Pertselakis. The nucleus of the collection is the Kalokairinos Bequest, to which the Society of Cretan Historical Studies (of which Andreas Kalokairinos was a founding member) has been adding over the years.

The **Sculpture Collection** (Rooms 5, 6 and 7), covering the Byzantine–Venetian periods, includes a number of beautiful marble well-heads, a multi-spouted tall fountain from Palazzo Ittar in working order, a marble medallion from the now demolished St George's Gate in the city walls, a comparative analysis of three representations of the Lion of St Mark and tombstones laid to good effect in the floor. Notable among the paintings (Room 11) are **the only two El Grecos on the island**: the *View of Mount Sinai and the Monastery of St Catherine* (1570) and the *Baptism of Christ* (1567). These are both early works, painted before the artist moved west, first to Venice and then to Spain. The (unsigned) *View of Mount Sinai*, in tempera on wood, is an imaginary rendering of the location at the foot of the holy mountain where Moses, according to the Old Testament, received the Tablets of the Law. A computer display nearby gives a potted history of the life of the artist (the one with a working display in English is to the right). Note by the door leading to Room 12 (ecclesiastical vestments, a chance to learn the difference between 'epimanikia' and epigonation'), a collection of **Byzantine religious artefacts** together with the moulds to mass-produce them.

On the second floor (Room 16) is a **display on Nikos Kazantzakis** (1883–1957), Crete's most influential modern writer, with a reconstruction of his study with desk, library and other personal belongings from his home on the island of Aegina, as well as paintings and engravings inspired by his writings. Kazantzakis died in Germany but is buried in Herakleion at the Martinengo Bastion, at his request. At the far end on the same floor is Room 15, furnished as the **study of Emmanouil Tsouderos**, a native of Rethymnon

Two versions exist of El Greco's *View of Mount Sinai*, one in Herakleion and another in Modena, Italy.

who became Prime Minister of Greece in 1941, after the German invasion of northern Greece and days before the evacuation of the Allied forces from the Greek mainland to Crete, by then the only remaining free territory. The space in between has an exhaustive **display on the Battle of Crete** (*see p. 22*), with memorabilia and film footage.

The top floor (Room 17) has a fine collection of **Cretan folk art**, with beautiful textiles, needlework, traditional costumes, jewellery, musical instruments and dowry chests (*sandik*, the Turkish word, or *kassella*, the Venetian one). The walk-in reconstructed house interior of c. 1900 is well worth a visit. Note the hand quern for the preparation of the daily bread, the wooden stand for the oil lamp, and the tiny door with the huge bolt. But there is colour as well: see the hangings, the bedspread and the magnificent loom.

OTHER MUSEUMS

Museum of the Battle of Crete and the National Resistance

Behind the archaeological museum at the corner of Doukos Bofor and Hatzidakis. Open Mon–Fri 9–5, Sat 9–2.
The museum commemorates the German parachute landings and the Battle of Crete in May 1941 and the history of the Cretan Resistance during the Second World War. The collection includes photographs, uniforms, drawings, paintings, books and newspaper cuttings illustrat-

ing those difficult and traumatic times in Cretan history.

Natural History Museum of Crete

On Sophokli Venizelou, west of the harbour. Open Mon–Fri 8.30–2.30, Sun 10–3.
The museum operates a joint programme with the Peabody Museum at Yale to investigate ecological biodiversity on the island. The Stavros Niarchos Discovery Centre is an excellent way to introduce a young person to the various aspects of the Cretan environment and biotopes.

CretAquarium

Open 1 May–15 Oct 9–9, 16 Oct–30 April 10–5.30; T: 2810 337788 or 337888; parking; www.cretaquarium.gr.
Situated 15km east of Herakleion within the old American base of Gournes, and signposted from everywhere on the island, the aquarium is part of Thalassocosmos, a complex devoted to marine research. The display includes 32 tanks of various sizes representing Cretan seascapes. Touch-screens provide information in five languages

---

Giuseppe Gerola (1877–1938)

Kitted out with a camera, Giuseppe Gerola criss-crossed Crete on horseback

between 1900 and 1902 taking pictures (over 1,000) of buildings, fragments of inscriptions and of architectural elements, intended for a museum of the Venetian occupation of the Levant, to be set up in Venice but which never materialised. This archive and Gerola's five-volume *Monumenti Veneti nell'Isola di Creta* (1905–32) remain a fundamental testimony to the state of the island at the turn of the last century. A number of the monuments that Gerola photographed have since disappeared, victims of neglect or indifference. As late as 1974 the church of the Holy Saviour in Herakleion, photographed by Gerola as a mosque and later turned into flats and then into a school, was pulled down.

Herakleion: interior of the monastery complex of the Capuchins, who offered lodging to medieval pilgrims on their way to the Holy Land. Photographed by Gerola: his shadow and that of his camera can be seen in the bottom left. The monastery church of St Mary of the Crusaders still stands, on Mousourou, the continuation of Odos 1821, between the Bembo Fountain and Aghios Minas.

PRACTICAL INFORMATION

GETTING AROUND

• **By air:** Nikos Kazantzakis International Airport (*T: 2810 397129; www.hcaa-eleng.gr/irak.htm*) is 4km east of the city on Odos Ikarou, which connects directly into the eastern part of the old town. The airport also handles internal flights to Chania and Siteia. Though small, it processes five million passengers a year; it can therefore be very busy and occasionally passengers have to wait outside for their flight. Note that the airport is also used by the Greek army and photography is strictly prohibited.

Airport bus: On exiting Arrivals, cross the car park behind the row of kiosks. The stop for the bus into town (no. 1) is on the near side of the road by the taxi rank. The bus to get to the airport leaves from Plateia Eleftherias on the north side by the kiosk, starting at 6.15am. Both locations have computerised displays that bear no relation to reality; both have coin-only ticket machines (you will need an orange ticket). Tickets cannot be purchased on the bus. Buses run until late at night; during the day they are relatively frequent, from 10pm onwards you are easily in for a 30-min wait. The trip takes about 20mins. Getting to the airport by public transport from other parts of the island involves getting into Herakleion first, and taking the airport bus from there.

Transport by previous arrangement: Private companies (e.g. www.resorthoppa.com and www.keytransfers.com) offer shuttle transfers to Herakleion (quoted prices per person based on an occupancy of four minimum) and a private taxi/minibus/coach service by previous arrangement to a list of resorts in Crete. A local company (*T: 2810 228220 www.taxireservations.gr*) is more pricey but is not based on sharing and allows for late reservation up to 8hrs before arrival; no surcharge for late flights.

• **By car:** The New National Road (E75) is Herakleion's bypass. At the Knossos junction, turn north towards the sea. After about 2km you are in the old town in Odos Evans and arrive at the Morosini Fountain near Plateia Venizelou.

Parking: There is no point using a car to get around the old town. Streets are narrow and many have been pedestrianised; more will be in the future, with the idea of eventually barring cars from the old centre completely. There are a number of pay parking spaces, either in designated car parks or payable with a parking card, which can be bought from kiosks. When visiting Herakleion it makes sense to arrive by taxi and postpone renting a car until you leave to visit the island.

• **By bus:** Herakleion Bus Service (www.crete-buses.gr) has two bus stations for long-distance buses (which are green):

Bus Station A: This station (*T: 2810 245020*) is between the Venetian Harbour and the modern port on the south side of the road. It has four departure platforms. Destinations to the east depart on the seaside road outside the ticket office. For Chania and Rethymnon the departure is opposite the taxi rank, near the Knossos stop (for Knossos buy the ticket at the kiosk). Other destinations (south and west) are served by the buses parked below the Megaron Hotel. Some announcements are in English.

Bus station B: This station (*T: 2810 255965*) is outside the Chanioporta, at the beginning of 62 Martyron in the west side of town. It covers Anogeia, Rogdia, Aghia Galini, Mires, the Mesara and places in between.

Local buses: Buses for Herakleion town,

for Knossos and for the beaches are blue in front; the rest is covered with adverts (*T: 2810 220755*).

• **By taxi:** T: 2810 210102 or 210146 or 210168 or 210124. At the airport the taxi rank is in front of the terminal building. In Herakleion there are a number of taxi stands in the centre and at the bus stations (where the tariffs are displayed).

• **By sea:** Ferry services operate to and from Herakleion (*T: 2810 244912; www.ferries.gr*). Three operators serve Crete: ANEK, Minoan Lines and Blue Star. The ferry quay is east of the old Venetian harbour. Connections with Thessaloniki (two or three times a week depending on the season, 23hrs with stops on various islands en route. The mainland stretch is by connecting bus from Piraeus), Piraeus (6–9hrs, arriving in the morning), the Cyclades, the Dodecanese and Dia.

TOURIST INFORMATION

National Tourist Organisation (EOT): Odos Xanthoudidou, opposite (north of) the Archaeological Museum (*Mon–Sat 8.30–5.30; T: 2810 228203*).

Post Office: Odos Giannari, the street parallel to (south of) Dikaiosini, where the police station is (*Mon–Fri 8–8, Sat 8–3*).

Travel agencies and banks: Most travel agencies (normally with long opening hours up to 10pm) and banks are in Odos 25 Avgoustou, the broad pedestrian street connecting the centre to the Venetian port.

Tourist Police: Dikaiosini 10, opposite Marks & Spencer (*T: 2810 283190*).

Venizelos Hospital: (*T: 2810 237502*) on the Knossos road.

Apolloneion Medical Centre: Two blocks west of Plateia Kornarou, at the top of Odos 1866 (*T: 2810 229713*).

Emergency services: T: 100

Herakleion Ambulance: T: 166
Tourist Police Emergency: T: 171
Laundrette: corner of Khandakos and Kydonias (wash and dry in 90mins).

WHERE TO STAY

€€€ **Capsis Astoria Hotel**. A modern, functional building with rooftop swimming pool and facilities for disabled guests, centrally located in Plateia Eleftherias. *T: 2810 343080; www.capsishotel.gr.*

€€€ **Galaxy Herakleion Hotel**. The largest outdoor freshwater pool in Herakleion. Also sauna, parking, facilities for disabled guests. Renovated in 2008. *Dimokratias 75, just outside the city centre on the way to Knossos; T: 2810 238812; www.galaxy-hotel.com.gr.*

€€€ **GDM Megaron**. A luxury hotel overlooking the harbour in a restored listed building known as Megaron Fytaki from the name of the firm that built it (in 1925) on the foundations of a stretch of the Venetian seaward walls. It started life as a processing centre for citrus fruits. Here lemons were prepared for shipping in barrels full of seawater to the UK, where they were turned into citrus peel for Christmas pudding. The industry went into terminal decline in the 1930s, as a result of competition from Corsica. The building suffered heavily during the war and was recently restored. *Doukos Bofor 9; www.gdmmegaron.gr.*

€€ **Arolithos**. A theme hotel in a completely made up 'traditional Cretan' village on the west side of Herakleion on the Old Road after Gazi, close to the New Road and connections to the south. It is ideal as a base to explore the region from. The theme-park style has attracted the purists' criticism, but as a hospitality model it works well. The spacious and attractive rooms are set in mature grounds with plenty of flowers and greenery and the recently-built swimming pool, though not exactly traditional, is a welcome addition. *T: 2810 821050; www.arolithosvillage.gr. Map p. 430, B1*

€€ **Atrion Hotel**. In the old city close to the Historical Museum and to the Venetian fortress. *Chronaki 9, T: 2810 246000; www. atrion.gr.*

€€ **Athinaikon Hotel**. At the south end of town, just inside the Venetian bastions. A good choice for a family holiday. It even has a garden. *Ethnikis Antistaseos 89, T: 2810 229312.*

€€ **Castello City Hotel**. On the west side of the city next to the Chania Gate, within easy reach of the airport. Free parking. *Leoforos 62 Martyron, T: 2810 251212; www.castellohotels. com.*

€€ **Kastro Hotel**. A comparatively small hotel (39 rooms) right in the heart of the old city on with private parking. *Theotokopoulou 22, T: 2810 284185 or 285020; www.kastro-hotel.gr.*

€€ **Lato Boutique Hotel**. Perfectly located on Epimenidou with a fine view over the Venetian harbour. Very modern and sleek, the latest word in boutique hotels, in Crete at least. *T: 2810 334955; www.lato.gr.*

€€ **Lena Hotel**. Small hotel in the maze of narrow streets at the north end of the old town, in a quiet location near the old harbour. Renovated in 2004. *Lachana 10, T: 2810 223280; www.lena-hotel.gr.*

€ **Hellas Rent Rooms**. Probably the cheapest rooms in town after the Youth Hostel, in a very central, pedestrianised street. Thirteen rooms on four floors (no lift) with shared showers. *Khandakos 20, T: 2810 288851.*

€ **Mirabello Hotel**. Small, quiet hotel in the centre of town near the El Greco Park. *Theotokopoulou 20, T: 2810 285052; www. mirabello-hotel.gr.*

WHERE TO EAT

For fish the best tavernas are at the end of 25 Avgoustou (**Ta Psaria** and **Ippokambos**, just off the seaside road into Marineli). For a more upmarket experience try:

€€€ **Istioploïkos**. A fish restaurant belonging to the Herakleion Yacht Club and right on the edge of the harbour. *T: 2810 228118.*

€€€ **Loukoulos**. Situated at the heart of the old city in an old, renovated house with plenty of space for eating al fresco. It serves a selection of Mediterranean cuisine, not strictly Cretan. *Odos Korai 5, T: 2810 224435.*

€€€ **Thalassina**. With a more exotic menu including cuttlefish and sea urchins. Some way out of the centre, south of 62 Martyron. *Kalon Limenon 27, T: 2810 251378.*

€€ **Erganos**. Just outside the city walls to the east. Rated one of the best places for traditional Cretan food. *Georgiadi 5, T: 2810 285629.*

€€ **Merastri**. On Chrysostomou, the continuation of Evans beyond the Jesus Gate. Situated in a Neoclassical building, the restaurant has a reputation for traditional Cretan food (try the stuffed zucchini flowers) and Cretan wines. *T: 2810 221910; evenings only.*

€€ **Pagopoieion**. The 'Ice Factory', one of Herakleion's hotspots. The building is an old ice factory tastefully and imaginatively renovated. Food varies and is not strictly traditional, but the crêpes with Roquefort sauce are certainly worth a try. Near Aghios Titos church. *Plateia Aghiou Titou; T: 2810 346028.*

€€ **Parasties**. Next to the Historical Museum, particularly good for grilled meats and desserts. *T: 2810 225009, closed Mon lunch.*

€€ **Pardalos Peteinos**. At the north end of town, serving a Cretan equivalent of tapas with an interesting Greek wine list. *Marineli 11, T: 2810 245528.*

€ **Outopia**. A chocolate rendezvous for the

local youth attractively set out in comfortable sofas in a pedestrian area. Try the chocolate fondue if you dare. *Khandakos 51.*

SHOPPING & MARKETS

Herakleion has **street markets** in different parts of town according to the day of the week: Mon: Kaminia; Tues: Alikarnassos; Wed: Mastabas (Panaghitsa); Thur and Sat: Patelles; Fri: Therissos. There is also the very central **open market** in the pedestrianised Odos 1866 (Mon–Sat) for souvenirs, gold, furs, clothes and traditional Cretan products (olive oil, wine, cheese, raki, honey, herbs and dried fruit and nuts).

Other good places include the **Simandiraki cheese shop** (*Kalokairinou 257; near Chanioporta; south side of the street*), a small outfit with an excellent choice of cheeses and yoghurt. The **Road Travel Bookstore** (*Khandakos 29, T: 2810 344610*) has an extensive selection of travel guides, maps and books about Cretan history and folklore. **Lexis** (*Evans 56–58, T: 2810 244457; www.lexisbooks.gr*) has reading matter in English and some maps and guidebooks.

FESTIVALS & EVENTS

Herakleion hosts a variety of cultural events in the summer ranging from ancient Greek and Renaissance dramas to ballet and Greek music, both modern and traditional. Most events take place either on the roof of the Rocca al Mare, the Venetian fortress, or at the Kazantzakis Garden Theatre and the Manos Hadzidakis Theatre. Information is normally available only at short notice. Try the Tourist Information Office on Alexandrou Papa (the short street immediately opposite the Archaeological Museum).

WALKING

The Mountaineering Association of Herakleion (*T: 2810 227609*) can give information about refuges, paths and organised excursions. For trekking maps and information on excursions and outdoor activities, go to the Mountain Club shop at Evans 15 (*T: 2810 280610; www.geocities.com/mountain_club*).

BOOKS & FURTHER READING

Candia Veneziana, Venetian Itineraries through Crete, by Michele Buonsanti and Alberta Galla, describes itself as 'a guide to the historical remains of the Venetian dominion'. Nicely produced little book on Venice's heritage, both in Herakleion and the island as a whole.

KNOSSOS

Inland from Herakleion along the road leading south to Peza, in the beautiful countryside dominated by Mt Juktas, there are a number of important Minoan sites. Foremost among them is Knossos, the large 'palace' complex where the Minoan civilisation was first discovered.

KNOSSOS

Map p. 430, C1. Open April–mid-Oct Mon–Sun 8–8; mid-Oct–March Mon–Fri 8–5, Sat, Sun 8.30–3. The entrance ticket is for admission to the main palace site only. At the moment plans to open an archaeological park, admitting the public to some of the dependencies that make up the Knossos archaeological landscape such as the Royal Tomb, the Little Palace and the Caravanserai (see map on p. 77), have not yet come to fruition. The locations are signposted from the road but they are closed.

Because of its proximity to Herakleion, its association with the legend of the Labyrinth and Sir Arthur Evans's evocative—though at the same time disputed—reconstructions, the Palace of Knossos (Κνωσός) is the most visited site in Crete. Indeed, it ranks third in the whole of Greece after the Athens Acropolis and Olympia. It is therefore advisable to come early in the day (or later in the afternoon, when there may be fewer tour groups) and at any rate to be prepared for some company. The management of the site is geared to handling crowds: guardians blowing whistles to warn visitors when they step out of line are just one aspect of it. As it is, although the site is large and there would theoretically be room for almost everyone, tour groups moving as a block have a momentum of their own and can make it difficult for individual visitors to go against the flow. Disabled visitors are catered for by a system of wooden walkways, though the network is far from complete. The site is provided with explanatory panels, in Greek and English.

Knossos lies 6km south of Herakleion, an easy drive if you have your own transport. There are also buses, which stop right outside the site entrance (*see p. 79*). By car the best way to approach from Herakleion is to drive east of the castle on the coast road and take the first right immediately after the bus station into a boulevard with palm trees in the middle. Eventually the built-up area gives way to the archaeological zone; you know you are approaching Knossos when you enter a green landscape about 6km on. First the drive crosses the **North Knossos Cemetery**, an important funeral area in use from the later phases of the Minoan period to Early Christian times. The stream bed marks the edge of the settlement that spread around the palace in the Bronze Age. Later the Roman city extended this far, though not much can be seen above ground. **Villa Dionysos**, on the right (*see map on p. 77*), is undergoing a major restoration programme to prepare it for public display. It was first investigated in the 1930s and excavated in 1971. The building is named after the motif of its fine mosaic showing the god Dionysos at the centre of a medallion surrounded by his companions, including Pan and Silenus. Other finds, such as amphorae and lamps with erotic decoration and fragments of plaster with women and satyrs, have confirmed the attribution. The villa, built in the 1st century AD and redecorated a century later, was destroyed by an earthquake around 200. The statue of Hadrian found here by Sir Arthur Evans is now the centrepiece at the **Villa Ariadne**, up a private driveway further on. Evans had the villa built as his dig house in 1906 by Christian Doll, one of the architects working on Knossos. He used it as his residence when he was working on the palace excavations. Between 1926 and 1955, Villa Ariadne belonged to the British School at Athens. After that it became the property of the Greek state together with the site. It was used to house King George of the Hellenes at the time of the evacuation from mainland Greece in 1941. It then became the residence of the occupying German commander. The German surrender was signed here in 1945.

Parking at Knossos is not a problem provided you do not arrive at peak times: it can get tight close to the entrance. The best area is the one signed among the olive trees on the left coming from Herakleion, about 100m before the entrance. It is free provided you patronise the nearby taverna at the end of your visit. And you will certainly need a cool drink by then.

History of the excavations

The archaeological potential of the Knossos area had been known for some time because of its surface finds. The locals gathered stone seals called *galopetres* ('milk stones'); nursing mothers strung them around their necks as amulets: on their breasts to increase lactation, slung backwards to stop it. The site was first investigated by Minos Kalokairinos, a local collector. He had useful contacts in his capacity as dragoman (interpreter) to the British vice consul. The only visible ruins at the time were the Roman theatre and basilica, but Kalokairinos pitched his trench further south at Kephala Hill. After three weeks' work in April 1879, he hit the walls of a 30m by 60m building containing many pithoi and the first Linear B tablet, though he missed a number of fragmentary tablets and seal impressions that ended on the spoil heap. At that point Kalokairinos thought he had found the Royal Palace, Minos' Courts of Law and the Labyrinth. News of the discoveries spread fast—and alarmed the newly established Cretan Assembly who thought, probably correctly, that the best place for Cretan antiquities was 'mother earth' until the Turks had left the island. They were well aware that Osman Hamdi Bey, a statesman and art expert, was keen to raise the profile of the planned Imperial Museum in Istanbul with Cretan artefacts. Even so Kalokairinos's finds were not safe: it is true that they remained on the island, but they were destroyed in disturbances at the end of the century together with his notes. His excavation report appeared 22 years later but, by then, things had moved on considerably.

The late 19th century was a period when Schliemann's excavations at Mycenae were putting archaeology, and particularly Greek archaeology, on the map. Schliemann in fact took an interest in Knossos as soon as he heard about Kalokairinos's success. He tried to negotiate the purchase of the site from the owner, but the asking price (£4,000) was too steep. Shortly afterwards he was dead. Enter Arthur Evans. A widower with no children, he was at a watershed: his career as a journalist had probably spent itself and he had had enough of the Ashmolean Museum at Oxford, where he was curator, and probably of Oxford itself, its establishment and its closed academic circles. He was well acquainted with Mycenaean material, which he had seen in Athens. In Crete he was in touch with some of the prime movers in the archaeology of the island: Federico Halbherr (*see p. 143*), Ioannis Mitsotakis, who had been involved in the discovery and the retrieval of the bronzes from the Idaian Cave, J.L. Myres, who had identified and dated the crucial Kamares ware. Evans had also had a chance to see Kalokairinos's finds and visit the small archaeological museum in the courtyard of Aghios Minas cathedral in Chania. From his activity as Balkan correspondent for the *Manchester Guardian* he had acquired a reputation for being sympathetic to the plight of Christian populations oppressed by Ottoman rule and this stood him in good stead with the Cretan Assembly.

Evans arrived in Crete in 1894 and over the next few years toured the island extensively, buying up objects for his collection and indulging every now and again in some illicit digging. The political situation was volatile, coming to a head late in 1898, when the Ottomans left. Evans had already been able to buy one quarter of Kephala Hill for £235 and had no difficulty in persuading Prince George, the newly appointed regent, to help him negotiate a reasonable price for the rest (an additional £200) and grant him permission to excavate.

Evans lacked training in digging. Aware of this, he enlisted the assistance of Duncan Mackenzie, a Scotsman who had excavated four seasons on Milos. Mackenzie stayed with Evans for 31 years, though the partnership was sometimes difficult. The Cretan Exploration Fund that Evans set up to finance the operation never really took off as the British were apparently reluctant to support a 'rich man's son chasing his dreams in the sun'. Financially, Evans was indeed well off: he had private means and eventually inherited from his family. His father was not only a scholar and antiquarian of repute, but also run a successful paper business.

When he began digging on 23rd March 1900, with 31 workers and a foreman, Evans was in a strong position since he owned the whole site. But though the British flag was flying on Kephala Hill, Evans could not consider the area as British soil. Crete's Antiquity Law was extremely strict: all finds belonged to the state, a circumstance which was to prove a constant source of friction between Evans and the Cretan authorities. Several digging seasons ensued during which the palace and the surrounding areas were explored. Restoration started as early as 1901. In 1924, Evans handed over everything, the site, his own residence (the Villa Ariadne) and the vineyards, to the British School in Athens. Though he was no longer digging, the interpretation and understanding of the 'Minoans', as he called them, remained his province until his death. He resisted attempts to question his conclusion that the Minoans had ruled Mycenaean Greece and was able to make life difficult for those who opposed him. Evans controlled access to the finds and crucially to the Linear B tablets. It was only after his death in 1941 that scholars were able to look at the stratigraphical sequence and get back to the dig's records (the daybooks that Mackenzie had kept up to 1903; after that the general feeling had been that the palace had been excavated and it was just a case of clearing up).

After a short spell with Mackenzie as curator, John Pendlebury (*see p. 340*) took over in 1930 and started studying the pottery that had accumulated over the years. Eventually he came to concentrate on his survey work, which resulted is his pioneering book *The Archaeology of Crete*. The site now belongs the Greek state.

HISTORY OF KNOSSOS

The Neolithic, Prepalatial and Old Palace periods

The Knossos area shows evidence of Neolithic occupation with simple, rectangular mud-brick houses on stone foundations. The deposits, in places as much as 7m thick, provide the best record for the period in Crete. They show a population practising mixed farming and using pottery after an initial aceramic period in which containers in organic material (leather, bark or wood) must have been the norm. A copper axe was apparently found in the very late Neolithic levels. Unfortunately it can no longer be traced and the context is dubious, but given its shape from the extant drawing it must have been imported, as such a type was never produced in Crete. The earliest metallurgy in Crete was not at Knossos but in the east of the island, where it appears to have developed through a Balkan connection at the very end of the Neolithic period.

Occupation continued through the Bronze Age until the first palace was built, roughly contemporary with that in Phaistos, at the end of MM IA. Extensive deposits of pottery from the period immediately before the foundation were found in a number of locations below the building and the Central Court (laid out on top of two MM IA houses). The construction of this first palace required some remodelling of Kephala Hill. Deposits of Prepalatial material removed for this purpose and dumped in the northwest part of the site have yielded objects showing overseas links with Egypt, the Levant, mainland Greece and the Cyclades at this crucial period in Minoan history. The building itself was originally constructed as a series of discrete units but over time additions and modifications brought greater architectural unity to the whole complex.

The New Palace period

The building was destroyed in a fire at the close of MM II and rebuilt almost immediately: it is this 'Second Palace', extending over 20,000 square metres and with innumerable rooms, that survives today. Whether visitors are helped or hindered by Evans's reconstruction and naming of the rooms and quarters, in a way much influenced by the imperial environment in which he lived, is now a moot point. Knossos as it stands is part of the history of archaeology; a visit to it in its present state can help us to understand and visualise other comparable sites that escaped Evans's attentions.

Towards the close of MM III, a severe earthquake necessitated some rebuilding and restoration of the West Façade, and both the Central Court and the West Court were covered with paving. In that period the Knossos area underwent the same development as can be traced in other centres throughout Crete. A number of important buildings were erected in the vicinity, not rivals to the palace but associated with it: the Treasury, the House of the Frescoes, the South House, the House of the Chancel Screen, the Little Palace, the Royal Villa and the Temple Tomb, to name but a few.

The Final Palace period

At the end of the LM IB period, some 150 years later, there was a major break in the history of Knossos but, while a certain amount of physical damage can be seen in the palace and town, it is nowhere near the wholesale fire destruction of other excavated sites of this date throughout the island. Both the palace and the dependencies continued in use, though changes in culture are apparent. The event marks the end of 'palaces' in the rest of Crete, but not in Knossos, where the palace continued to function. It may, however, have been in different hands. The archaeological record shows new burial customs (individual or family graves with weapons instead of communal tombs) and an evolution in the style of pottery which points to links with the mainland. This was confirmed by the discovery of a large number of clay tablets, accidentally fired in the conflagration, inscribed with Linear B, which Michael Ventris and John Chadwick deciphered as an early form of Greek. The same script is also known from Mycenaean centres in the Peloponnese such as Pylos, Mycenae and Tiryns. The latest thinking among archaeologists, though by no means unanimously accepted, is that in the period LM II to LM IIIA, Knossos was inhabited by mainland Greeks and operated as a Mycenaean administrative centre for the whole of Crete.

Later periods

After the final destruction, occupation of the site was subdued, bar some LM IIIB activity in the Shrine of the Double Axes, in the Little Palace and in various locations in town. At some point a Classical Greek temple stood in the southwest corner of the Central Court. Otherwise, while life continued in the Knossos area, the palace site was left undisturbed. Popular mythology had it that the area was cursed: the myth of the Labyrinth and of the labrys, a powerful, enigmatic symbol that appears on Knossos' later coins (*see p. 70*), grew and grew. By the time Evans was excavating, his guards reported seeing ghosts and hearing voices at night.

There are few remains from the subsequent development of the site. The contents of the cemetery to the north show that there was an important community in the Geometric period. Later on, Knossos, with Gortyn and Chania, became one of the leading towns of the island, losing its pre-eminence to Gortyn after the war with Lyttos in 220 BC. With the Roman conquest in 67 BC, Knossos lost out again to Gortyn, which was chosen by the incoming administration as the capital of the new province of Cyrenaica. In the civil war that followed Julius Caesar's assassination, Crete was caught up in the tussles between various Roman generals. Eventually, it proved expedient for Octavian, the future emperor, to use Knossos and its land to pacify his veterans. Thus it was that Knossos became connected to the town of Capua in southern Italy and was renamed Colonia Julia Nobilis Cnossus around 27 BC. The civic centre was north of the Minoan palace while the town expanded to the east. The plan of the Roman town is not fully known but the imported marbles, the mosaics and the abundant statuary, removed over time to Venice, speak of a degree of opulence. As it is, most knowledge of the Roman town comes from areas overlying the Bronze Age remains. In the Early Christian period churches were built at Knossos. Two basilicas have been excavated north of the Roman city: a large mortuary church dated to the 5th century and a 6th-century martyrion built over Christian graves. The bishop of Knossos was present at the early Church councils of 431 (Ephesus), 451 (Chalcedon) and 787 (Nicaea).

With increased Arab raids, Knossos's position became difficult since it could not be defended. When Rabdh el-Khandak, modern Herakleion, was fortified, it supplanted Knossos as the principal settlement of the area.

WHY IS KNOSSOS WHERE IT IS?

Much has been written about Knossos, the cradle of the first European civilisation, with a continuous occupation of some 8,000 years from the Neolithic through to early Byzantine times. The site, though, is fairly nondescript: there is not much in the location that would seem to justify such success. It does face the Aegean, but Cycladic imports appear in Knossos later than in other parts of Crete (though the levelling of Kephala Hill to build the first palace may be partly responsible for this lack of evidence). The key, according to Jennifer Moody and Oliver Rackham (*The Making of the Cretan Landscape*), lies in the harbour facilities—but not those that are normally quoted, that is Amnisos and what became known later as Herakleion, but another harbour altogether.

Crete is short of good harbours. The Aegean coast is exposed to the prevailing north winds which means that ships risk being dashed against the high cliffs or thrown onto the rock ledge close to the shoreline. This ledge consists of a razor sharp, shallow, sand conglomerate cemented by calcium carbonate. In addition to this, the western peninsulas run north–south, which does not help, because the prevailing wind comes from the north. Souda Bay is very deep and is an excellent harbour once you are in it. The problem for sailing ships would have been to negotiate the comparatively narrow entrance in fierce northerly winds without the help of the tide. Souda Bay only took off as a harbour with the development of steamships. The south coast suffers from sudden storms and squalls from the high mountains. The truth is that the best Cretan harbours are not on Crete itself but opposite Knossos on the small island of Dia. Here ships could safely anchor in four excellent harbours and wait for favourable weather conditions to cross to Herakleion or Amnisos. The island has not yet been fully investigated but it does show occupation from the Neolithic.

Facing page: The famous *Bull-leaper* fresco.

KNOSSOS IN MYTHOLOGY

According to Greek mythology, when Minos claimed the Cretan throne, he dedicated an altar to Poseidon and asked the god for a suitable animal to sacrifice. Poseidon promptly obliged and a beautiful bull emerged from the waves. Minos, reluctant to part with such a fine specimen, kept it and slaughtered another bull from his herd instead. Cheated, the god took his revenge by causing Pasiphaë, Minos' wife, to become infatuated with a bull. She sought the assistance of the palace's chief architect, Daedalus, who constructed a hollow wooden cow for her to hide inside. It was wheeled to the field where the bull was. The result was the Minotaur, half human half animal, for which Minos had the labyrinth built by the same architect. At regular intervals a tribute consisting of seven Athenian youths and maidens was offered to it. Eventually Theseus, son of Aegeus the king of Athens, volunteered to join the next consignment in order to kill the Minotaur and free Athens of the servitude. He enlisted the assistance of Minos' daughter Ariadne, who gave him a sword and a ball of string to unwind so that he could find his way out of the maze. Having successfully concluded his mission, Theseus sailed from Knossos harbour with Ariadne, but abandoned her halfway on the island of Naxos. As a punishment the gods made him forget to hoist white sails to signal to his father that all was well. In despair Aegeus threw himself to his death from the cliffs, which is how the Aegean Sea acquired its name.

The myth has been variously interpreted. It is assumed that the youths represent a time of subservience to the mainland, though their fate was probably not as grisly as the myth suggests. They may have been engaged as attendants to the Moon Priestess with whom Pasiphaë ('The Shining One' or 'Little Moon') is identified and may have performed risky bull acrobatics during the ceremonies. Pasiphaë's reputation did not suffer despite her unorthodox tastes: in the 1st century AD the emperor Galba was claming descent from her in a family tree, prominently displayed in the entrance of his residence in Rome.

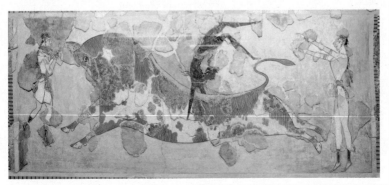

THE PALACE

After the ticket kiosk, the visit starts through a tunnel of bougainvillea, the very last shade for a while, which leads past a bust of Evans into the **West Court**, paved with limestone flags. To the left are three large pits, the circular **kouloures**, which may originally have been grain stores; Evans believed that they were associated with the disposal of sacred objects. Excavation has shown that they were eventually used as rubbish dumps; these days they attract the odd coin from tourists who obviously wish to return to Crete. Note at the bottom of one of them the remains of a MM IA house: when it was excavated the red plaster rendering on the walls and on the floor could still be seen.

The court itself may have had multiple uses: as a gathering place, as a market, or even as Ariadne's dancing floor, mentioned by Homer (*Iliad XVIII, 591–92*). It is crossed by raised walkways, a standard feature in Minoan palaces, and extends to the **West Façade (1)**, in front of which is an altar base. The massive West Wall is a prime example of high-quality Minoan ashlar masonry. It is faced with gypsum blocks, now severely weathered as this material is unsuitable for outdoor use. It was quarried from the hill of Gypsades, close by to the south.

Entrance to the palace

The palace was entered via the **West Porch (2)**, built after the earthquake of MM III when the West Façade underwent restoration. Evans found here fragments of a relief fresco with painted bull's hooves which made him think that visitors entered the building amidst a representation of stampeding animals. It led via a wooden door (no longer extant; you now go along a modern walkway), into the **Corridor of the Procession (3)**, paved with gypsum flagstones flanked by blue schist set in red plaster and named after the fresco showing people bearing offerings (*see below*). The end of the corridor affords a fine view of the south dependencies of the palace, the **South House** immediately below. You are directed to turn left now, through the **South Propylaion (4)**, where you get a taste of the restoration techniques used at Knossos over time. Note the faux wood and the red inverted-tree-trunk columns: it is all concrete. On the other side of the Propylaion, behind perspex, are some examples from the Procession Fresco (visitors should be aware that all the frescoes at Knossos are modern copies: a selection of the original fragments can be viewed in the Temporary Exhibition at Herakleion Archaeological Museum; *see p. 43*). The **Cup Bearer** is the best known and best preserved of these figures, reminiscent of 18th-dynasty Egyptian funerary scenes. On the parapet wall here, the original south front of the palace, the large **horns of consecration** in stone have been restored and erected. The small Classical Greek temple that once stood in this area, on top of the ruined palace, has been removed.

With the Cup Bearer on your left and some giant pithoi on your right, a wide **staircase (5)** leads to the upper floor, heavily restored by Evans on the evidence both of architectural elements found at ground level and of the surviving walls. With Renaissance Italy in mind, he called it the 'Piano Nobile'. The corridor runs along the **West**

Magazines (6) at ground level below, where many pithoi were excavated together with stone stands for double axes on poles. Beyond this, the passage leads to a series of rooms above the Throne Room area. One of them has been reconstructed to look down into the lustral basin in the Throne Room below. One of the theories put forward to explain this sunken structure holds that the room was meant to be viewed from above and had nothing to do with ablutions (the basin has no drain) but was more probably used in ritual initiations. Here also are copies of well-known **Knossos frescoes**. These include the *Ladies in Blue*, two panels of the Miniature Frescoes, the *Bull-leaper* and the *Captain of the Blacks*, all from the palace, and a couple from the House of the Frescoes (*see pp. 75–76*), namely the *Blue Bird* and the *Blue Monkey*. This marks the end of one element of the First Palace complex, as shown by the rounded finish of the northeast corner (clearly visible at ground level from the Central Court).

THE MYSTERY OF THE LABYRINTH

If the purpose of the Labyrinth was to disorientate, it can be safely said that it has been successful. According to Plutarch, writing in the 1st century AD, a 'labyrinth' was the palace of the double axe (*labrys*). According to Herodotus (*Book II*), writing in the 5th century BC, 'labyrinth' was an Egyptian word designating a huge structure with 12 courts and 3,000 rooms; excavations by Flinders Petrie at Hawara in the Fayum unearthed the mortuary temple of Amenemhet III (19th century BC) which is unusually large and complex and might be what Herodotus referred to. Before him, Homer (*Iliad XVIII, 590–93*) used the word to describe a complex dancing ground for Minos' daughter Ariadne. What is referred to here is not a building but a pattern. As such it was inscribed on Achilles' shield and has been found incised on a clay tablet from Pylos. The layout, square or round, is a development of the meander theme and represents a game or a dance in which one goes from the edge to the centre via the longest route. The same pattern appears on the reverse of Knossos coins from Hellenistic times; indeed, there is no firm evidence of any connection of Knossos with the Labyrinth before then, at which period the palace was no longer visible.

The Minotaur, which is another reason for building a labyrinth, is first associated with a labyrinth on a graffito from Pompeii. By then, Minos had completed his transformation from Homeric good king and lawgiver to despicable tyrant who fed young Athenians to a monster, and ancient Knossos had been partly overlaid by a new Roman town. Pliny the Elder quoted three different locations for the Labyrinth, including the ancient quarries at Gortyn which were still an official 'labyrinth' in the 18th century of our era. However when Richard Pockoke visited in 1739 he was not taken in. He recognised the place for what it was, 'the ancient quarries from which the city of Gortyna was built', and firmly placed the Labyrinth in Knossos, though at the time there was not much to be seen there.

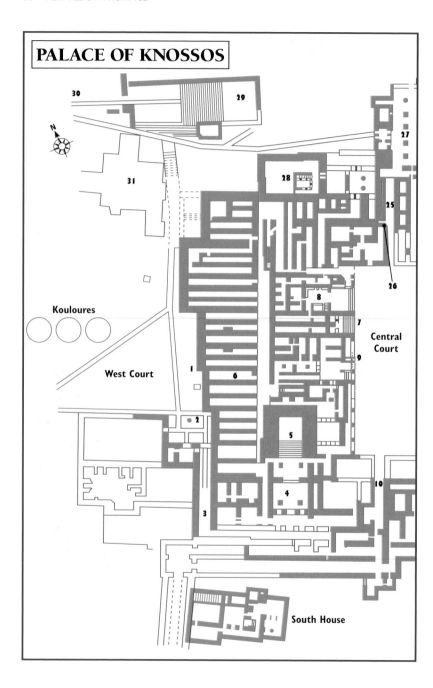

PALACE OF KNOSSOS

30

29

27

N

31

28

25

26

8

7

Kouloures

Central
Court

9

West Court

1

6

2

5

10

3

4

South House

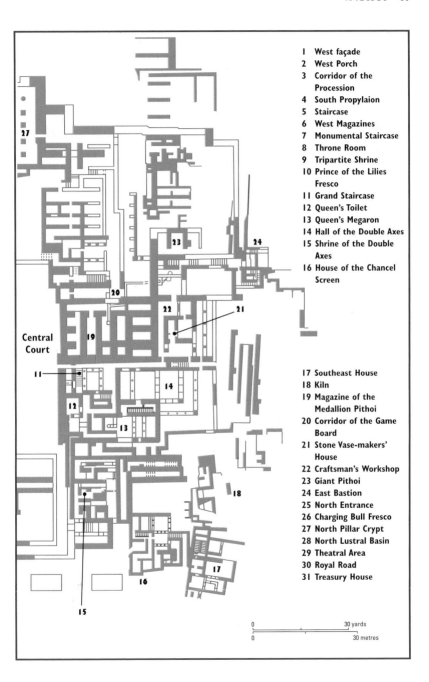

1 West façade
2 West Porch
3 Corridor of the Procession
4 South Propylaion
5 Staircase
6 West Magazines
7 Monumental Staircase
8 Throne Room
9 Tripartite Shrine
10 Prince of the Lilies Fresco
11 Grand Staircase
12 Queen's Toilet
13 Queen's Megaron
14 Hall of the Double Axes
15 Shrine of the Double Axes
16 House of the Chancel Screen

17 Southeast House
18 Kiln
19 Magazine of the Medallion Pithoi
20 Corridor of the Game Board
21 Stone Vase-makers' House
22 Craftsman's Workshop
23 Giant Pithoi
24 East Bastion
25 North Entrance
26 Charging Bull Fresco
27 North Pillar Crypt
28 North Lustral Basin
29 Theatral Area
30 Royal Road
31 Treasury House

Central Court

0   30 yards
0   30 metres

THE LABRYS

Symbol of the double axe, inscribed on a stone block at Knossos.

The iconic artefact of the Minoan period, the labrys, was not a local design. The earliest hafted double-blade axe, from Susa (modern Iran), dates from the 4th millennium BC and is in the Louvre. The object, some 22cm long and about 2kg in weight, was made in pure copper with traces of arsenic and lead. It was cast and then hammered; one of the blades was left blunt. It is possible that this was a tool, not a standard or a symbol. Two-in-one tools like hammer axes and double axes are known from Europe and from the Middle East.

The labrys design features in early forms of script in Mesopotamia where it is associated with war; by the mid-3rd millennium it was obsolete and the single-blade axe had taken over. It is at this point that the earliest double axe appears in Crete, in a ritual context in Mochlos, where three small examples, one in lead and two in copper, were found. Given Crete's connection with the Middle East, where the idea of seals and writing might have originated, and in particular with Syria, as exemplified by imported metal artefacts in Early Minoan graves, it is possible to think of a straight migration, bringing in craftsmen with new metalworking technology and old ideas.

In Crete the labrys took on a life of its own and was strictly associated with ritual activity. It may have symbolised the waxing and waning of the moon and represented the creative and destructive power of the Moon Goddess. Double axes are found in cultic deposits, in graves, and in the stores where they were housed between ceremonies. Huge stone stands found *in situ* show where they would have been displayed (as illustrated on the Aghia Triada larnax; *see p. 45*). The symbol was depicted in a variety of media: painted on pottery, incised on pillars and in a variety of materials in miniatures. At the ruins of Knossos and Malia, incised labryses can be seen in some of the masonry.

The Central Court

From the Piano Nobile you descend to the Central Court down the **Monumental Staircase (7)**, which continued to a second storey as the marks for the ascending steps indicate. As is often the case in Minoan palaces, the west side of the **Central Court** was not residential but has been interpreted as a cult area. These days one can but take one's turn to peer at the **Throne Room (8)** through a plexiglass screen under the eyes of an ever-watchful guardian, who sits on an imitation wavy-backed throne (the benches on either side are genuine). Behind, and not accessible, is the Throne Room itself, with the alabaster throne, gypsum benches and restored frescoes of guardian griffins. This is also the location of the lustral basin. Immediately to the south of the Throne Rome, also on the Central Court, is more evidence of ritual in the form of a structure known as the **Tripartite Shrine (9)** (*no access*). A number of rooms here produced finds, including the faïence snake goddesses which still baffle archaeologists. Double axe signs on the pillars and a fresco of a tripartite shrine all seem to suggest that this was a cult area, though it is difficult to speculate beyond that, especially since the finds associated with these rooms are commingled with objects that fell from above. Moreover, the area shows signs of having been damaged and repaired several times. Evans thought he had found dramatic evidence of the last moment of life in the palace, with overturned jars and ritual vessels lying on the floor. It seems now that the profusion of cult-related objects was due to the fact that they were stored here while building repairs were being carried out.

EVANS'S RESTORATIONS

Mindful of the criticism Schliemann had to endure for having no architects on his team, Evans hired one from the start. David Theodore Fyfe, a 25-year-old Scot, had been engaged to draw plans and produce watercolours of fresco fragments, but from the second season he was busy shoring up the crumbling structures and underpinning walls. Minoan building techniques had not been developed for the long term. Structures were mainly built with a framework of squared timber beams packed with rubble and occasionally faced by well-finished sandstone, purely for aesthetic reasons. Moreover, the extensive use of gypsum for outer walls was problematic. Gypsum, a crystalline form of alabaster, is a very soft material, 2 on the scale of hardness. Though probably easy to saw with a bronze tool and abrasive powder, it is not very resistant to the elements. It can be very attractive, especially in its translucent variant: the Egyptians ground it and used it as plaster. Otherwise it was used for vases and indoor ornament.

In archaeology, as long as structures remain underground in a stable environment, they survive. Evans immediately faced problems and used the expertise of some of his workers, who had been miners, to prop up walls. In the Knossos restoration timetable, Fyfe belongs to the age of wood. He inserted wooden beams where they had rotted away, put a roof on the Throne Room and even built a watchtower in the Central Court to allow Evans to enjoy an overall view of the excavations. Christian Doll followed in 1904. He introduced the use of stone, replacing columns originally in wood with stone ones coated in red plaster. He became aware that Fyfe's beams had already rotted and inaugurated the age of iron girders. The rebuilding of the Grand Staircase is his work. It was competed in 1906 ready for an impromptu dance performance by Isadora Duncan. The third age of restoration is linked to the name of Piet de Jong, who was with Evans for nine years from 1922. De Jong introduced the use of concrete. Even so today, almost 100 years on, the Cretan climate and geology emerge the winners in this game as Evans's reconstructions are in continuous need of restoration.

In the middle of the south side of the Central Court, the fresco of the Priest or **Prince of the Lilies (10)** still draws the crowds. This is probably one of Evans's most notorious reconstructions, made from fragments that may belong to more than one figure. A copy can be viewed on the wall under which the original remains were found, in a heap at the end of the Corridor of the Procession.

Domestic Quarters: lower south side

The so-called Domestic Quarters are situated on the east side of the central court and were accessed in antiquity via the **Grand Staircase (11)**, of which five flights of gypsum steps are preserved. The area is not open to the public, though it is possible to catch a glimpse of the **Queen's Toilet and Bath (12)** fitted with a drainage system testifying to a truly royal lifestyle. The **Queen's Megaron (13)** with the famous Dolphin and Rosette fresco is firmly behind plexiglass and to all intents and purposes invisible. The **Hall of the Double Axes (14)** or King's Megaron has a reconstructed wooden throne and a reconstructed portico providing some welcome shade.

Detail of the mural of dolphins and fish from the so-called Queen's Megaron.

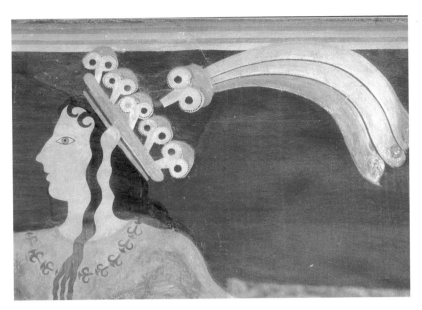

Detail of the *Prince of the Lilies* fresco.

The visit continues towards the **Shrine of the Double Axes (15)**, roofed and gated for protection, a tiny room with small idols with drum-shaped bases and miniature horns of consecration. The shrine dates from the period of limited reoccupation following the great fire that destroyed the palace (LM IIIB, c. 1300 BC). The remains of the **House of the Chancel Screen (16)** occupy the space to the south next to the **Southeast House (17)** with a good example of pier-and-door partitions and, under a roof, a LM I–II **kiln (18)**.

The northern area

The northeast side of the palace (industrial and storage) can be entered down narrow steps past the terrace covering the **Magazine of the Medallion Pithoi (19)**, with some relevant specimens in residence. Under your feet just outside, at the beginning of the **Corridor of the Gameboard (20)** (*for the game board, see p. 42*), under a metal grate, is evidence of the palace **sewer system**. The water supply of the palace has not yet been fully elucidated; there is a spring some 500m southwest of the building from which water was fed to the palace by gravity; moreover, elements of an aqueduct were apparently identified by Evans. Additional evidence of water management can be found continuing downwards past a room **(21)** with a supply of stone imported from the Peloponnese ready to be made into vessels, another room, a **craftsman's workshop (22)** and storerooms with **giant pithoi (23)** dating from the Old Palace, at the **East Bastion (24)**. Here the reconstructed stone channel built beside the staircase has a design intended to break the flow of the water: an impressive testimony to Minoan hydraulic engineering skills and to the torrential downpours that must have afflicted the area.

The **North Entrance (25)** is a ramp with 'bastions' on either side. It underwent a number of alterations over time resulting in restricted, controlled access to the central court, a drive towards tighter security which can be traced throughout the evolution of this and other palaces in Crete. A large deposit of Linear B tablets and the stucco relief of the **Charging Bull (26)**, which now adorns the reconstructed west 'bastion', come from this area.

From the rooms immediately to the west of the ramp comes an alabaster lid with the cartouche of the Egyptian Hyksos king Khyan. Connections between Knossos

Two giant pithoi in the storeroom below the Central Court to the east.

and the Hyksos are attested by finds from recent excavations at Tell el-Dab'a, thought to be the Hyksos capital Avaris and located in the eastern Nile Delta. During the 1990s, work by the Austrian Institute of Egyptology concentrated upon an area on the western edge of the site, known as Ezbet Helmi with a large palace-like structure dating to the Hyksos period (c. mid-2nd millennium BC). In the location of the ancient garden there was a heap of refuse containing many fragments of Minoan wall-paintings with bull-leapers, much in the style of the well-known fresco at Knossos. Apparently the fresco came off the wall in antiquity, which is why it was thrown away. But by then, presumably, the Cretan artists had left.

The palace is exited down the ramp, through the **North Pillar Crypt (27)** with two rows of monumental gypsum rock pillars, and past the **North Lustral Basin (28)** into the **Theatral Area (29)**, where up to 500 people could watch religious processions. The paved **Royal Road (30)** with its raised walkway fades into the distance and eventually leads to the Little Palace, now out of bounds (*see map overleaf*). The exit is to the left, past the location of the now backfilled **Treasury House (31)** (*not visible*), from where a large hoard of bronze vessels was retrieved. You may wish to stray amidst the bougainvilleas to catch a last look at the West Façade and the kouloures. There are peacocks too, their cries as shrill as the custodians' whistles.

AROUND THE PALACE

Several buildings have been excavated around the palace, but they cannot normally be visited. Nevertheless, a walk through the surrounding area will give a better idea of the environment and the setting of the palace complex.

Minoan Viaduct: The viaduct is on the southern side of the Vlychia stream. It is a structure that is unique in Crete, which does not help with interpretation. It is assumed that it was built when the South House was erected, as part of a new, impressive approach to the town and palace from the south.

Caravanserai: Evans thought travellers would stop here to rest and wash in the stone trough, hence the name. Its fine paintings, in the same style as the House of the Frescoes, and the Spring Chamber prompted suggestion that it was used to wash ritual vessels. It may also have been connected to the water management of the area.

Hogarth Houses: These are two elegant, high-status houses built in MM III, repaired about 100 years later before a major destruction in LM IB. Occupation apparently continued but possibly on a reduced scale; the nearby well was abandoned. They are named after David Hogarth, who put in a season at the beginning of Evans's excavation but then moved east to work at Psychro.

House of the High Priest: Of uncertain construction date, it my have been connected to the Temple Tomb a short distance to the southwest via a paved road. It contained a shrine with a pillared hall, an antechamber and a room with an altar and two double-axe stands, an ar-

rangement reminiscent of the shrine in the House of the Chancel Screen, with which it is possibly contemporary.

Temple Tomb: Evans was much taken with the grand scale of the building and suggested a tentative connection with King Minos, though according to Diodorus Siculus (*IV, 79*), writing in the 1st century BC, there is already a tomb of Minos in Sicily where, according to legend, he died. There is no primary evidence that this building was originally a tomb. Its features, the elaborate plan and the quality of the construction, suggest a temple. The façade is reminiscent of a tripartite shrine while the internal layout, with a pillar crypt and descent into darkness, has parallels at Phourni cemetery at Archanes. The Temple Tomb may have been a cult building, with evidence of disruption and repairs around LM IA when some 20 victims of the disaster were placed here. It remained in use for a while longer until the palace was destroyed.

Royal Villa: Located to the northeast and close to the original route to the sea, this had a central hall and an upper floor. The abundant use of gypsum, dados and balustrades marks it out as a special building. Probably built in LM IA and destroyed some 200 years later.

House of the Frescoes: This building, located to the west of the palace, was in a heavily disturbed area with much Graeco-Roman intrusion. The house is the findspot of frescoes such as the *Blue Bird* (now in Herakleion Museum; copy in the palace). These were no longer on the walls when the house met its fate. The building was already in ruin and the frescoes had been stacked on the ground prior to removal or while the house was being repaired.

Unexplored Mansion: Situated on the line of the Royal Road leading west from the palace, this is roughly contemporary with the Little Palace beside it (*see below*), c. 1600 BC. There were originally two buildings on this spot separated by a road a hundred or so years earlier. After destruction the area was designated for the construction of two buildings which although distinct were linked by a bridge. The Unexplored Mansion can be treated as an annexe of the Little Palace. Stylistically it presents similarities with the construction style of the Palace and of the Royal Villa, but it was unfinished and may not have been occupied at the time of its demise, though an upper-floor room had already been decorated with a plant mural.

Little Palace: This is the largest building after the main palace itself and shares the high-status features of the latter, with an abundance of pillar crypts at the south end used for storage or for perhaps for cult, and a series of stately halls to the east. It also yielded exceptional finds like the Bull's Head rhyton (*see p. 42*). Excavated in 1908, this stone vase is made in an astonishing combination of materials: steatite for the head, shell (*Tridacna squamosa* from the Persian

Gulf) for the nostrils, rock crystal and red jasper for the blood-shot eyes; the wooden horns were covered in gold leaf. Evans assumed that this was a bull's head, though normally bulls were represented in full to show their sex. The Egyptian goddess Hathor was represented with a cow's head, but Evans was not interested in a connection along those lines. The double-axe stand from a drainage shaft was built very much like those in the palace domestic quarter.

Evans was convinced that the building's history followed that of the main palace but the evidence is not conclusive. It appears certain, though, that the Little Palace went through a change of use: the lustral basin was filled before any form of destruction and the space between the fluted wooden columns around it was blocked. In the area thus created a number of rough stones were found prompting the suggestion that it was a 'fetish shrine'. Doorways were narrowed; tighter security set in.

North House: West of the Stratigraphic Museum (*not open to the public*), the North House has been dramatically renamed the House of the Sacrificed Children, after finds which have shed a sinister light on Bronze-Age Crete. The semi-articulated remains of at least four healthy children whose corpses had been expertly butchered were found in 1979. As the context has a LM IB date, a time of great upheaval throughout the island, the find was linked to possible deviant practices in time of stress and famine. Times were certainly difficult by then, but it must be borne in mind that excarnation i.e. the processing of body parts prior to reburial, was an estab-

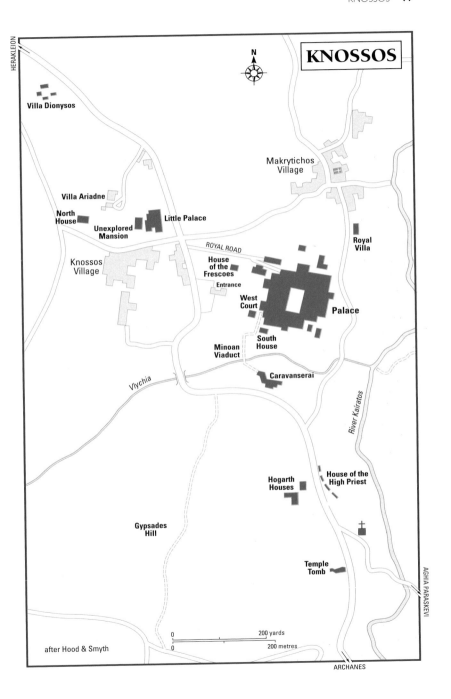

HERAKLEION

N

KNOSSOS

Villa Dionysos

Makrytichos
Village

Villa Ariadne

North
House

Little Palace

Unexplored
Mansion

Royal
Villa

ROYAL ROAD

House
of the
Frescoes

Knossos
Village

Entrance

West
Court

Palace

Minoan
Viaduct

South
House

Caravanserai

Vlychia

River Kairatos

House of the
High Priest

Hogarth
Houses

Gypsades
Hill

Temple
Tomb

AGHIA PARASKEVI

0   200 yards

0   200 metres

after Hood & Smyth

ARCHANES

lished practice in parts of Greece until comparatively recently. The finds at the Anemospilia Cave (*see p. 89*), though, suggest more sinister goings-on.

THE BEAST OF MINOS

Palaces are special places, and Knossos, where the Minotaur lived, was even more so, as the animal bone remains suggest. Crete's Neolithic levels show that the first farmers' cattle, sheep, goats and pigs arrived from the Middle East or from Anatolia in a pre-domesticated state, that is, small enough to be controlled on the perilous sea voyage and in general handling. In Bronze Age Knossos the picture is different. As zoöarchaeologist Günter Nobis has shown, a number of animal remains belong to wild species ancestral to the farmyard animals. The study is particularly relevant for cattle. Minoans had clearly a thing about bulls and cows. Remains at Knossos include domesticates but also aurochs, that is the primitive wild variety, which is considerably larger, as well as hybrids of the two. It has been suggested that large cattle were a status symbol and that the elite would go out hunting for aurochs to retrieve juveniles to domesticate and use for breeding. This practice of tapping into a fresh gene pool in order to improve the domestic strain is attested in ancient Asia in the case of camels.

Going out to hunt for juvenile aurochs was not without danger and may have been an activity linked to rites of passage (it was clearly not part of a subsistence economy, as contemporary Minoan farmers went on rearing small cattle). One's prize bull could be displayed somewhere in the palace grounds, with leapers performing daring jumps. The sport represented on vases, frescoes and sealings was

by no means exclusive to Crete. Other ancient societies that had cattle also engaged in some form of ritual activity with them, as shown by evidence found around the Mediterranean and as far away as China. Quite where at Knossos this happened is disputed. None of the proposed venues appears suitable for containing a fiery bull. The Central Court is too small and lacks evidence of any fencing. Moreover, the paving could have caused skidding. The West Court is too open. Evans and Pendlebury opted for a huge palisade outside the palace, but so far a credible post hole alignment has proved elusive.

Charging Bull fresco, from the reconstructed west bastion of Knossos palace.

PRACTICAL INFORMATION

GETTING AROUND

• **By car:** By car it is 20mins to Knossos from Herakleion (6km). Follow the coast road from the Venetian fortress to the bus station, continuing east and taking the first turn right into an avenue of palm trees. Signs to minor sites (Royal Tomb, Caravanserai) can be safely ignored as these are not open to the public.
• **By bus:** The bus stops to and from Herakleion are right on the road past the site. For information about catching the bus in Herakleion, see p. 55.

WHERE TO EAT

Interspersed with the souvenir shops, on the other side of the road from the palace enclosure, are a couple of simple places to have a bite to eat. None of them is anything special. They are all geared, quite reasonably, to tourists, and serve adequate, simple food.

BOOKS & FURTHER READING

Dilys Powell's *The Villa Ariadne* provides an eloquent and amusing portrait of life at Knossos during the latter days of Evans's tenure. Her return to Crete after the war to revisit scenes from the past is poignantly described. Cathy Gere's *Knossos and the Prophets of Modernism* postulates how Evans and his discoveries inspired a host of idealistic intellectuals who, disillusioned with a Europe torn by war and ugly demagoguery, embraced the idea of a gentle, matriarchal Minoan society where bare-breasted priestesses and wasp-waisted youths presided over palaces frescoed in bright, sunlit colours.

ARCHANES & ENVIRONS

South of Knossos the countryside is dominated by the impressive Mt Juktas and by extensive vineyards and olive groves. The whole area, the mountain and its surroundings, are part of the 'Natura 2000' programme, set up by the European Union to monitor and protect threatened flora and fauna. A tour can easily be made as a day trip from Herakleion, a welcome relief from the congested city.

Between Knossos and Archanes

Driving from Knossos note, before Spilia (Σπήλια; *map p. 430, C1*), the remains of an aqueduct supported by two tiers of arches spanning a ravine. It was built in the mid-1800s to improve the water supply to Herakleion. Beyond that, at Patsides (Πατσίδες), a sharp right turn at a T-junction marks the spot where the German general Heinrich Kreipe was kidnapped in his own car in 1944. The spot is marked by a sculpture of a broken column and a tangle of wire. A little further on, towards Archanes, is a tiny museum of old wartime vehicles, including a black Mercedes, apparently the very same (*see box below*).

THE KIDNAPPING OF GENERAL KREIPE

The kidnap plot organised by the Cretan resistance movement was intended to demoralise the German occupying force and boost the morale of the local population. General Kreipe, the divisional commander of the German forces, was being driven from his headquarters in Archanes to the Villa Ariadne at Knossos, his private residence. The kidnap was masterminded by Patrick Leigh Fermor, the travel writer, then a major in the army, and Captain W. Stanley ('Billy') Moss, with the assistance of local *andartes* guerrillas. They ambushed the general's Mercedes, handcuffed him and bundled him onto the floor in the back. Then, with Moss at the wheel and Leigh Fermor sporting the general's cap, they bluffed their way through the checkpoints and the heavily guarded gates in and out of Herakleion. The car was left on the shore with evidence incriminating the British in order to minimise reprisals against the Cretans. The general was taken on an 18-day march on foot and muleback to the south across Mt Ida. German search patrols were eluded and eventually the party made it to the cove of Rodakino, west of Plakias, from where a submarine took them to Cairo. German reprisals did follow, but the effect on the locals' morale was undeniable: 'We all felt two centimetres taller the next day', as one of them put it. The story is told in Moss's *Ill Met by Moonlight*, which was later made into a film with Dirk Bogarde in the role of Leigh Fermor.

ARCHANES

Archanes (Αρχάνες; *map p. 430, C2*) is divided into two, the hamlet of Kato Archanes ('Lower Archanes') and the main village, Ano (or Epano, 'Upper') Archanes. The area is known for its table grapes (Rozaki) and its wines (Archanes and Armandi). It should be even more famed for its water. The Venetian aqueduct for Herakleion, the one that Morosini built and which terminates in the Morosini Fountain (*see p. 46*), started here. The toponyn of Archanes itself is associated with water. Etymologically, the Indo-European root 'ach' or 'arch' tends to denote it (see many names of rivers and lakes such as Acheloös, Inachos and Acherousia). Water brought fertility to the region. It was settled early, though not much is known of the very first Neolithic inhabitants apart from sporadic finds of stone tools, ornaments and idols.

The name of Archanes appears for the first time in a 5th-century BC inscription from Argos in the Peloponnese, though the discovery of ancient roads leading from Archanes to Juktas, Anemospilia and Vathypetro confirms that the location was already an important regional hub in Minoan times. The presence of a palace here also bears this out.

The village

The main street of Archanes is the narrow Georgios Kapetanakis. At the beginning of it on the right-hand side is the large Open University building, the war memorial, and the beautiful three-aisled church of the **Panaghia Vatiotissa**, with a free-standing white clock-tower and a fine collection of icons dating from the 16th century (*church open Tues–Thur 9–2; otherwise the key is with the local papas, enquire at the museum*). Parking is not easy in Archanes; here at the top end of Kapetanakis there are sometimes some free spaces.

If you are driving into the village from the Knossos direction, you will be diverted anticlockwise off the main street shortly after the church of the Panaghia by the one-way system, which brings you round to the bottom of the pleasant, triangular **main plateia** (Kapetanakis is the return street of the one-way system). The plateia is surrounded by tavernas and cafés, those at the Kapetanakis end still redolent of old Greece, with high ceilings, bare walls, and small tables occupied by elderly men playing backgammon or cards, smoking and drinking tiny Greek coffees. At the bottom end of the square the new Greece makes itself felt, with the Pizzeria Sofia and design-conscious bars with plump teenagers drinking frappé, a frothy iced coffee concoction.

A short way up Kapetanakis on the left, look for a sign to the **Archaeological Museum** (*open Wed–Mon 8.30–2.30*). It offers a picture of Archanes in the Bronze Age, with particular focus on tomb architecture, rituals and foreign relations. Funerary ritual is illustrated with different types of burial (pithoi, larnakes and children's coffins). Some of the finds from Phourni (*see p. 84*), the Archanes palace (*see overleaf*) and Anemospilia (*see p. 89*) are here, but the best material is in Herakleion. A visit is recommended before setting out to see the sites. The sistrum from Phourni (replica) is presented alongside an illustration of the Harvester Vase from Aghia Triada showing how such an instrument was used. A wine press from Vathypetro is also here. Of particular interest is the reconstruction of the painted offering-table from the Tourkogeitonia and the huge steatite lamp from the same site. At the end of the display, towards the exit, finds from Roman Archanes are a reminder that life did not end with the demise of the palaces.

The palace

The excavations, in Tourkogeitonia (the old Turkish quarter of Archanes), are not open to the public, and can only be viewed from the street, behind a fence. Little can really be seen (to get there, walk uphill from Kapetanakis and its parallel street; 5mins from the church of the Panaghia). Nevertheless, the history of the site is interesting and it has yielded some good finds. As early as 1912, Stefanos Xanthoudides had noted the archaeological potential of the site, but it was Arthur Evans, who in 1921 excavated a Minoan circular structure successively known as the Spring Chamber, Well House or Reservoir, who first characterised the site as palatial. He believed that Archanes was probably a summer palace for the Knossos kings and on his frequent visits was able to enlarge his collection of Minoan artefacts, now in the Ashmolean Museum in Oxford. These include a number of fine seal stones and the well-known gold signet ring with the bull-leaping scene. Spyridon Marinatos and Nikolaos Platon excavated minor areas in the region, but nothing supporting Evans's theory came to light until 1964 when Giannis (John) Sakellarakis dug trial trenches at Turkogeitonia and uncovered the first evidence of a palace site. It became clear then that, unfortunately for the archaeologists, old Archanes lay right beneath the modern town. Since 1966, Archanes has been excavated by the Greek Archaeological Society under the supervision of Giannis and Efi Sakellarakis. The excellent, well-illustrated guide written by the husband-and-wife team is on sale in the bookshop on Kapetanakis. It covers the whole Archanes area.

The excavators established that the settlement had been continuously inhabited from the Pre-Minoan times until the New Palace period. The well-preserved palace, built between 1700 and 1400 BC, was constructed on a scale comparable to Knossos and Phaistos, with the use of luxury material like marble, schist and gypsum. It was surrounded by high walls and had a sophisticated drainage system. It may have risen to three storeys, judging by the thickness of the walls. There was evidence for fresco decoration and painted reliefs.

Finds confirming the high status of the building include marine style pottery, faïence, stone vases, a section of a tusk and a block of red jasper which may have been imported from as far away as modern Iran. Parts of at least six acrolithic figurines (with the main body made of perishable material like wood and the extremities in ivory) were also recovered. They showed traces of paint and it is believed that gold scraps found with them were part of their accoutrements. Smaller than the Palaikastro Kouros (*see p. 237*), in the region of 12cm in height, they share the chryselephantine technique. The archive, a crucial indication of the importance of the site, was located in a separate excavation to the southwest. Here a number of Linear A tablets (including a double-sided one) were recovered. Because of the nature of the excavation, it was not possible to investigate fully the architecture of the area. Finds of obsidian, rock crystal and steatite indicate that there may have been a workshop here as well. The best find remains, however, the clay model of a house showing a two-storey building with windows, columns and pilasters now on display in Herakleion (*see p. 42*). It has added greatly to our understanding of Minoan architecture.

Other elements of the place complex have come to light a short distance away to the southeast near the church of Aghios Nikolaos. The Theatral Area, paved with flagstones, was crossed by raised walkways. A stepped altar was identified and it is assumed that the horns of consecration with an incised branch found nearby belonged to it. The whole arrangement is comparable to representations on seal stones and on the Zakros rhyton (*see p. 256*) and is believed to be linked to a form of cult.

The first palace of Archanes, built around 1900 BC, shared the fate of the other palace centres in Crete with a series of destruction phases each followed by a repairs and reconstruction. A first event, contemporary with the destruction of Anemospilia, occurred at the end of MM II about 200 years later. But while Anemospilia never recovered from the earthquake damage, Archanes was rebuilt only to be struck again around 1600 BC. Whatever the cause of the catastrophe, the comeback was swift, not just here but in the whole of Crete. More damage occurred around 1450 but Archanes bounced back 'under new management', so to speak. It is believed that it became the seat of a powerful magnate of foreign origin. Mycenaeans have been mentioned together with a possible identification with the city of Lykastos (*Iliad II, 647*). The grave enclosure at Phourni (*see overleaf*) does support this, as do the rich quality of the funerary offerings and their more martial character. Everything came to a final end around 1100 BC, possibly due to a combination of invasion and a natural catastrophe.

What such a large palace was doing so near to the palace of Knossos (just 10km away) has not been explained. Evans's idea that it was the summer palace of the king of Knossos is now discounted. All the archaeological finds reinforce the view that the palace of Archanes was an autonomous and powerful administrative centre around which an extended settlement had developed and that many other settlements and isolated farms, scattered all over the surrounding area, were dependent on it.

ENVIRONS OF ARCHANES

Archanes lies below the summit of Mt Juktas, the contours of which have been compared to those of a sleeping bearded man, which may be an origin of the persistent legend that this is the resting place of Zeus—if gods ever die. The area is noteworthy for the funerary remains at Phourni, while at Anemospilia the Minoans come under a cloud with evidence of human sacrifice. Further south at Vathypetro, you can see a Minoan country house with industrial installations. The circuit is completed by a visit to Temenos, a wild place where the Byzantines had planned to move their capital, away from the sea and its dangers. Moni Epanosiphi further south is certainly worth a visit if you are here on April 23rd, the feast of St George, otherwise it is a quiet place, 'a retreat from the busy hum of men' in the words of Robert Pashley, who visited in the 1830s.

PHOURNI NECROPOLIS

Phourni is located northwest of Epano Archanes on a hill slope. The site, fenced, should be open daily 8–2 but it is better to check with the Archanes museum first. It is accessible from the south following signs beyond (or before, if you approach from Knossos) the church of the Panaghia Vatiotissa. You can easily accomplish the distance on foot (about 30mins). After crossing the Archanes bypass, keep on past houses and waste ground (there are intermittent signs, some very faded). Past a ramshackle sheep farm you turn right uphill to follow the road used in antiquity, with a surface not dissimilar to the paving uncovered in the cemetery itself. After about 10mins' gentle climb you see the site fence. Keep right; the entrance gate is this way. From Kato Archanes a badly signed secondary road leads to the north end of the cemetery with space to park at the top after 2km. From here it is a particularly pretty walk of c. 15mins along a track with a fine panoramic view amid olive groves and wild flowers, an ideal place for a picnic.

History of the cemetery

In use from 2400 to c. 1000 BC, the necropolis of Phourni (Φουρνί) offers a unique concentration of different types of funerary structures; excavations have provided archaeologists with an impressive amount of information about funerary practices and customs. Moreover, the understanding of the functioning of a cemetery as a going concern has been heightened by the study of ancillary building, paved roads and drainage systems. Finds have shown contacts far and wide, with the Cyclades, Egypt and the East.

The earliest use of the cemetery is Prepalatial in date and is attested in the southern area at the bottom of the hill. However, individual tombs were sometimes in use for many decades and occasionally later burials were cut into these Prepalatial levels. The very last burials, dated to c. 1000 in the Sub-Minoan period, were cut into the collapsed roof of Tholos Tomb D, which had been built c. 300 years before.

The name Phourni originates from the oven-like appearance (*phournos* = oven) of the stone buildings, which farmers used later for storage while tending the surrounding vineyards. The majority of the necropolis has now been excavated. Twenty-six structures have come to light. The numbers by which the features are known refer to the order in which they were excavated, not to a chronological sequence.

Tholos Tomb D

At the very south of the cemetery, this is a pristine grave dated LM IIIA, in which a young woman was buried with all her gold and jewellery while still holding her mirror in her left hand. The grave had been hewn out of the rock and had a stone superstructure which later collapsed. The deceased has been laid out on a wooden support and decked in her finery. This included a gold diadem of 37 rectangular beads with a marine motif encircling her head and necklaces in gold, glass paste, faïence, chalcedony and electrum (a very rare occurrence in Minoan Crete). Gold spirals found nearby were presumably woven in her hair. According to the excavators the 67 gold rosettes did not form part of another necklace. They were part of a cloth covering the head and shoul-

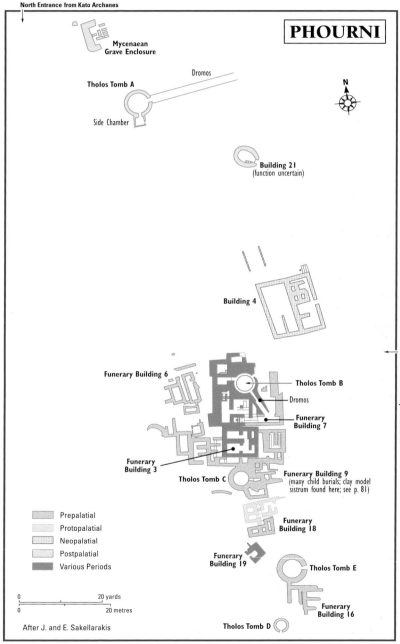

North Entrance from Kato Archanes

PHOURNI

Mycenaean
Grave Enclosure

Dromos

Tholos Tomb A

Side Chamber

N

Building 21
(function uncertain)

Building 4

Funerary Building 6

Tholos Tomb B

Dromos

Funerary
Building 7

Funerary
Building 3

Tholos Tomb C

Funerary Building 9
(many child burials; clay model
sistrum found here; see p. 81)

Funerary
Building 18

Funerary
Building 19

Tholos Tomb E

Funerary
Building 16

Tholos Tomb D

Site Entrance from Epano Archanes

Prepalatial
Protopalatial
Neopalatial
Postpalatial
Various Periods

| 0 | 20 yards |
| 0 | 20 metres |

After J. and E. Sakellarakis

ders, onto which they had been sewn. Additional offerings underline the high status of the deceased. An ornamented clay pyxis contained a necklace of gold beads, unique because of the variety of designs and techniques shown.

Tholos Tomb A

The most spectacular find in the necropolis came from a grave (Tholos Tomb A, dated to the same period, uphill towards the north end) that had already been disturbed by robbers. Back in 1964 when Sakellarakis first explored the hill, he realised that one of the huts used by the locals as a store and during the Second World War as a hiding place, had been originally a vaulted Mycenaean grave. With the passing of time, the original entrance, the dromos, one of the longest in Crete, dug into the soft *kouskoura* rock, had filled up to the lintel and was obscured. The modern entrance was via a hole made by grave robbers near to the actual roof of the structure. Earth fallen through the opening had created a new floor over the years, some metres higher than the original floor of the grave. When the earth was removed, Sakellarakis saw that the grave had been looted in antiquity but was able to conclude that the deceased was a prominent person, indicated by evidence of a horse sacrifice as part of the funeral ritual. The remains of the six-year-old animal show that it had been dismembered and disembowelled with the greatest care. The cut-marks on the bones were still apparent. At the end of the procedure the skeletal remains, with some flesh still attached, were reassembled in a neat pile. Sakellarakis also noted a peculiarity in the structure of the wall on the south side of the construction which made him suspect that there was a side room behind it, a feature known in similar vaulted graves in Mycenae and Orchomenos. After removing the stones, he discovered the head of a bull. This was identified as an aurochs (*Bos taurus primigenius*) and lay hidden between the stones at an angle. It had been dispatched in honour of the dead, as shown in the bull sacrifice scene in the famous stone larnax from Aghia Triada. Bull sacrifices in ancient Crete were performed not only in honour of the gods but also for dead kings and priests. At that point, for safety reasons, Sakellarakis decided to excavate from the outside. Eventually almost 5m below the surface, the first undisturbed royal grave in Crete came to light. The chamber was very small, only 3.5 square metres. It contained a huge larnax originally sealed with yellow plaster. The deceased had been placed in the foetal position, facing west, sometime in the first half of the 14th century BC. A careful study of the finds and of their position over the bones enabled excavators to conclude that he or she was wearing a long gown trimmed with gold, comparable to the garments trimmed with decorative bands that feature in some wall paintings. There were also seal stones and necklace beads. More offerings had been placed beside the larnax. These included stone lamps, tripods and a mirror with an ivory handle with a representation of a cow suckling her calf. A large number of worked ivory fragments, 87 in all, belonged to a wooden footstool placed in front of the larnax, possibly as part of a funerary ritual. It would have been c. 35cm long and has been compared to the representation of a similar object on a gold ring from Tiryns, providing an unequivocal Mycenaean connection. Its boar's tusk handles were carved with relief heads of helmeted Mycenaean warriors. While the skeletal remains were in poor shape and offered no clue as to the age and sex of the occupant of the side chamber, the finds unequivocally suggest a woman. For a start there are no weapons; moreover, the domestic utensils and jewellery all point in that direction. But this was no ordinary woman. The quality of the offerings and the fact that they include iron beads (rusty, but still the only known for the period) plus the evidence for elaborate ritual, suggest someone of elevated rank, possibly royal, but who also fulfilled some religious function, as shown by careful study of the scenes engraved on the rings.

Mycenaean Grave Enclosure

North of Tholos Tomb A is the Mycenaean Grave Enclosure, a unique structure in Crete containing seven LM III graves from the 14th century. The rectangular graves were cut in the soft rock at a regular distance in three rows. They all have the same orientation except the one in the middle, which lies at right angles to the others. The enclosure wall is incomplete but it is assumed that the entrance would have been from the east. Excavation showed that each shaft had contained a larnax. These were found broken and almost empty. Many offerings were found in the burials but outside the larnakes, prompting the conclusion that the bodies had been exhumed after a time and reburied.

Finds included a group of bronze vessels of comparable quality to those found in the side chamber of Tholos Tomb A, and stone vases, one in Egyptian diorite. Among the ivory objects, a large pyxis with a lid had a relief decoration of a lion. A mirror handle shared the motif of the cow and calf from Tholos Tomb A. An ivory comb was decorated with facing pairs of lizards in relief. Amethyst and chalcedony seal stones were also recovered.

It is not only the finds that make the enclosure interesting. Some of the graves had stelae marking them, which is a new departure. Three were found in all, not particularly beautifully worked stone slabs but important in view of

The Mycenaean grave enclosure at Phourni (14th century BC) with the excavated grave shafts and the three upright stelae, still *in situ*. The sacred pit for funerary offerings is outside the enclosure wall to the right (not shown in the photograph).

the later development of grave markers in Mycenaean Greece (either painted or plain or with carved relief). These are quite early. The enclosure must be viewed as a whole, which is what makes it unique in Crete. There are Mycenaean shaft burials elsewhere, mainly in Knossos, but they do not have the same unity. A possible comparandum can be found outside Crete, in the Grave Circles at Mycenae, which also had stelae and an enclosure. Moreover, they might also have had a bothros, a sacred pit for offerings. Here at Phourni, at a small distance from the enclosure, a circular pit over 2m in diameter had been excavated in the rock; it had a stone lining all around and a slab floor. It contained pottery fragments from libation vessels and not much else while its mouth was littered with more sherds. The absence of animal bones suggests that only liquid offerings were made here, not animal sacrifices. Liquids accumulated and decayed over time which may account for the unbearable stench the excavators had to endure while they were digging. Apparently the lower levels were the worst. According to Homer (*Odyssey XI, 24–28*), offerings consisted of milk and honey, followed by sweet wine and water. Unfortunately for the excavators, they were well past their sell-by date.

Building 4

Not all the buildings at Phourni are graves. A large rectangular structure in the centre of the necropolis, known as Building 4, was used by the living to care for the dead. Here were workshops for the manufacture of the artefacts necessary for funeral ceremonies. Finds include loom weights, a 'tortoise', i.e. a bronze ingot, storage vessels, stone colanders and whetstones. One of the rooms housed a press for the production of wine used in funeral libations. The building was in use in the LM IA period and is unique not only to Minoan Crete but in the whole Aegean area.

Tholos Tomb B

Just south of Building 4, Tholos Tomb B remains the most complex structure of the cemetery. It was built on top of a MM IA funerary building, therefore no earlier than 2100, but according to the pottery, before the end of the Early Bronze Age. It was used for 600 years up to the 14th century, undergoing modifications over time. Fundamentally it is a tholos accessed via a dromos and set within a rectangular complex which at one time had two storeys. During the early years of its use, a pillar crypt was added to the south carefully constructed against the then outer wall of the tholos. The crypt and the room above it became an integral part of the funerary rituals enacted in Tholos B and remained so for the entire period of use. High-quality finds including a gold ring with a goddess and a griffin, and a silver pin inscribed in Linear A, point to high, even royal status. A larnax used as an ossuary was found in a concealed space. It was full to the brim with the remains of no fewer than 19 people. It had remained sealed over the centuries and the excavators remarked on the bright red colour of the bones upon discovery, suggesting they might have been washed in wine prior to deposition. It was also remarkable that the bones had been grouped by type. Those that did not fit had been placed in neat piles in the surrounding space.

ANEMOSPILIA

The sanctuary of Anemospilia (Ανεμόσπηλια; the 'Cave of the Wind') is c. 3km west of Epano Archanes on the eastern flank of Mt Juktas on the secondary road leading to Vasiles. The site is fenced but usually accessible, at the end of a track starting on the left-hand side coming from Archanes. The cave, situated where ancient roads met, can reward the lucky visitor with sweeping views: east to Mt Dikte, west to the Mt Ida while Knossos (where the cypresses and pines are) and Herakleion stretch out to the north.

The site was identified by Giannis and Efi Sakellarakis during a survey of the area and excavated in 1979. The building, which has been interpreted as a shrine, has a simple plan with three rooms to the south fronted by a corridor to the north. An enclosure wall runs around it. Analysis of the pottery has allowed excavators to pin down the period of operations to a comparatively narrow bracket between MM II and MM IIIA, between the 19th and 17th centuries. The finds include a large number of ritual vessels, pithoi and the clay feet of wooden statue, a xoanon. More interesting, though, were the human remains of four people buried under the fallen blocks, showing that the building was destroyed in a violent event, assumed to be an earthquake, followed by a fire. One of the victims was about to leave the building carrying a highly distinctive Kamares ware relief vase similar to the one on the Aghia Triada stone larnax, where it can be seen under the altar ready to collect the blood of the sacrificed bull (*see p. 45*). The remains of three more people were found in the west room; obviously they had not been able even to attempt an escape to safety at the first tremors. A woman in her late 20s and a man of about 38 were on the floor. The last skeleton, a male youth, was found lying diagonally on a structure in stone and clay probably covered with a wooden plank, reminiscent of the altar found in the west court at Knossos. Forensic evidence suggests that his ankles had been bound and the discoloration of the skeleton showed that he had lost his blood while still alive. A bronze weapon, a lance or a knife, had been placed across his stomach. Perhaps here is conclusive evidence of human sacrificers 'caught red-handed'. Up to now archaeologists had to be satisfied with literary and historical references.

ASOMATOS

Outside Archanes there are a few small chapels, prominent among which is the one dedicated to Aghios Mikhail Archangelos. Ask for the keys at museum in Archanes before going, and be prepared to leave your passport as security. To get there, drive south on the Archanes bypass in the Vathypetro direction and immediately after the junction from the south end of the village take the narrow road to the left, signed Asomatos (Ασώματος; though it is easy to miss the sign). Bear right at the first fork, and at the next turning keep straight on (left). The tiny chapel, signed after a sharp bend across a stream bed, is all that remains of a Venetian settlement. It is particularly known for its well-preserved frescoes, showing scenes from the life of the Archangel Michael, a stern Pantocrator in the apse, a remarkable Crucifixion and scenes from the Old Tes-

Crucifixion scene in the chapel of the Archangel Michael at Asomatos. Note the armour of the soldiers at the foot of the Cross. Above the crucified Christ is a scene of Christ in Majesty. Orthodox iconography frequently places the two together, to emphasise the glory of Christ the Lord after the humiliation of Christ the man.

tament including a *Fall of Jericho* (west corner of the right wall) with soldiers portrayed in 14th-century armour, contemporary with the chapel. The St Michael cycle is one of the largest in Crete. The style is archaic, indeed these frescoes are the oldest example of Byzantine Palaeologan style on the island (dated to 1315), with some concessions, however, to the tastes of the donor Mikhail Patsidiotis, who can be seen with his wife on the west wall (bottom left) reverently offering a model of the church to his patron saint.

MOUNT JUKTAS

The cave of Anemospilia (*see above*) is not the only holy place on Mt Juktas (Γιούχτας). The mountain, which dominates the surrounding countryside, had a number of Minoan shrines. The one at the top has been shown to be one of the most important peak sanctuaries in Crete, which is not so surprising since it overlooked Knossos, from where it could be seen. In Classical times this was believed to be the last resting place of Zeus and as such was a pilgrimage destination. Travellers were still visiting on the same quest in the Venetian period and later. The locals were only too ready to oblige with a show of caves, piles of stones and to embellish everything with an appropriate legend.

Approaches

You can reach Mt Juktas by a narrow asphalt road that winds its way up 3km south of Archanes (turn right off the Vathypetro road; signed 'Giouchtas 5km'). The E4 hiking trail leads off from the road immediately after the turn (signed 'Minoan Peak Sanctuary'). You can also climb on foot along a direct path from the village, signed 'Afendis Christos' from the road that bypasses Archanes to the west. Look out for the telecommunication masts that mark the site. Griffon vultures are often to be seen circling round the peak.

The tiny chapel of St Michael Archangel at Asomatos, south of Archanes.

The peak sanctuary

Mt Juktas was first investigated by Evans, who found substantial structures and a temenos wall of cyclopean masonry built with irregular but close-fitting stones. He also established a communication link from Knossos and identified traces of a paved road both at Anemospilia and on top of the mountain. Later, in 1977, the sanctuary was investigated by the Greek Archaeological Service. Its time of activity was dated from the Prepalatial period through to LM IIIB, well into Mycenaean times. The excavation is fenced but can be viewed from a vantage point on the hillside above it. At the south end of the temenos is the key feature of any peak sanctuary i.e. the crevice into which offerings were made. This one is 10m deep and is surrounded by a building intended for cult practices. The visible features date from the New Palace period. On the west side of the cleft was a stepped altar. Cult objects including a kernos with 100 or so depressions, presumably for offerings, a hoard of bronze double axes, libation vessels and remains of sacrifices were excavated in the vicinity. A large number of offerings were retrieved from the cleft itself. They were mainly linked to the day-to-day troubles of life: terracottas of women in labour, heads, hands, torsos and phalli. Objects in precious material (faïence, rock crystal, gold leaf and bronze) and fragmentary stone offering-tables with Linear A inscriptions, show that not only the poor walked all the way up to seek solace and divine assistance. Artefacts are mainly dated to the Old Palace period, but not exclusively: a headless sphinx establishes the continuity of the shrine into Mycenaean times. To the north of the temenos, by its northern entrance, remains of a potter's kiln testify to industrial activity in the New Palace period. From the summit on a clear day you can see Mt Dikte in the east, the White Mountains in the west and look south across the island to the Asterousia range and the Libyan Sea beyond.

View from the ruins of Vathypetro.

VATHYPETRO

The road south of Archanes continues to Vathypetro (Βαθύπετρο; *map p. 430, C2*). The Minoan Farm is signposted to the right, just before the village. The site (*open Tues–Sun 8.30–2.30*) is beautifully positioned on a bluff overlooking a wide vista of mountain, fields and olive groves. The ruins were excavated in the 1950s by Spyridon Marinatos. Further investigations were carried out by Driessen and Sakellarakis.

The settlement

The complex, not just a single house but a small settlement, was built in LM IA and was badly damaged about 30 years later. This first structure had some high-status palatial features such as light-wells, ashlar masonry, halls, a west façade and a north–south orientation; it may indeed originally have been planned as a palace. The tripartite shrine may belong to this phase, but not everyone agrees that there was such a feature at all. The reconstruction work, which took place in LM IB, may have included a smaller building to the east mainly devoted to food processing and industrial activities. This new phase changed the character of the complex from its original administrative, ritual and residential purpose to an agricultural and industrial one. Olive and wine presses were installed and storage areas developed. The site also had a pottery kiln and weaving facilities, judging by the numerous loom weights. The final destruction is dated around 1470 BC. It is quite likely that this was the most important building of a settlement extending over three hills, since ashlar masonry has only been found here.

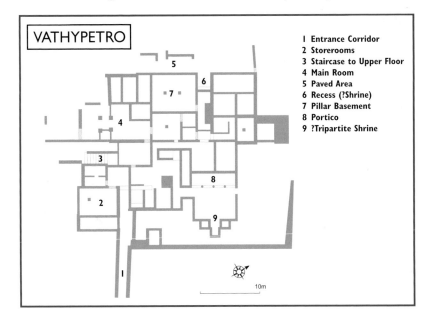

VATHYPETRO

1 Entrance Corridor
2 Storerooms
3 Staircase to Upper Floor
4 Main Room
5 Paved Area
6 Recess (?Shrine)
7 Pillar Basement
8 Portico
9 ?Tripartite Shrine

10m

It may now be too late to investigate fully the true character of the site, however. Much has been lost to vineyard cultivation, though this is wholly appropriate—judging from the wine press found here (now in the museum in Archanes), vineyard cultivation has been practiced at Vathypetro for several millennia.

THE MEDITERRANEAN TRIAD

Cretan cuisine is excellent and makes abundant use of the basic ingredients of the Mediterranean diet (the triad: corn, oil and wine). The health benefits of the combination are part of an image that the islanders would like to anchor to a distant past. But is that really so? Did the Minoans thrive on such a diet? Archaeologists have identified grape pips and olive remnants as far back as the Neolithic. Certainly in the early Bronze Age both these crops were cultivated. But it is a question of scale. Minoan Crete had a subsistence economy in which the food supply in most cases stretched no further than the productive season. Neither wine nor olive oil fit that pattern. Both require a huge investment in labour and time before any harvest.

Traditionally in Crete the wild olive stock would be taken from the Mesara plain, immersed in water and planted somewhere else in a cleared field. It would then be grafted and require constant attention: annual pruning, fertilising, regular irrigation and three ploughings a year. Twenty-five years later serious production would start, with the yield still dependent on a number of climatic imponderables. It is therefore doubtful, although per unit volume olive oil contains more calories and fat than butter or lard, that it was used in ancient Crete as part of the daily diet.

Evidence shows that olive oil and wine were consumed as prestige items: oil in balms, unguents, perfumes and lighting (its use in food preparation is a recent development), wine in feasting and social display. Not surprisingly, most processing installations are found in palaces and villas and cease to function when these do.

Eventually both commodities became a major earner for the island. The long period of the *Pax Romana* and the opening up of the Italian market (Italy became a wine importer during the time of Augustus in the 1st century BC) created a demand for Cretan wine, especially of the sweeter variety, the type that the poet Martial called the 'poor man's mulsum' (a mixture of wine and honey). The establishment at Knossos of a colony of veterans from Capua might have helped. The same success story was repeated in Venetian times with Malmsey (*see p. 133*). The boom days of olive oil production had to wait even longer. Venice unwittingly helped by trying to enforce cereal production while being unwilling to pay the market price for it. Then the Marseilles soap industry burst onto the scene: by the 1730s Crete was exporting 1600 tonnes of olive oil a year, and that was only the beginning.

Of the Mediterranean Triad, the average Minoan probably only consumed the wheat grain, which he supplemented with pulses, milk and whatever else he could lay his hands on.

Visiting the ruins

A visit to the Vathypetro farm starts from the southeast along the corridor **(1)**. On the left are the storerooms **(2)** where the wine-making equipment was found; at the end a staircase **(3)** led to the upper storey above the storerooms. The main room **(4)** has four central pillars and a paved floor. Along the west façade, a paved area **(5)** is reminiscent of the west courts in the palaces, though much smaller. An olive press was found here. The deep recess **(6)** could have housed a shrine. The roofed area is a pillar basement **(7)** with 16 huge pithoi to store the wine and oil. The residential quarters are thought to have been in the northern area, which is poorly preserved. The entrance to this part of the house was through a portico with three columns **(8)**. East of it, across a small court, the excavator identified what he saw as a tripartite shrine **(9)**, with a central recess flanked by two square niches, a typical Minoan architectural style which can be seen in the Knossos miniature frescos and on the Zakros Rhyton (*see p. 256*).

MONI EPANOSIPHI

From Vathypetro the road joins the main north–south link at Choudetsi from where a 5km drive leads to the junction for the Epanosiphis monastery (Μονή Επανωσήφη), just after Partheni. The monastery's foundation is thought to date towards the end of Venetian rule. Indeed it was then a small affair but came to prominence in 1655, on the occasion of a plague epidemic, when the faithful flocked here to seek the protection of the patron saint. On that occasion the monastery expanded and acquired its current shape, and an imposing new church was built. That church is no more, having been destroyed in an earthquake in 1856. However, the offerings that the faithful left in the church sometimes accompanied by a prayer, show that they were as terrified of the plague as of the Turks besieging Candia. The foundation was prosperous, with valuable land and property, and a community still flourishes today under the jurisdiction of the cathedral in Herakleion. During the Ottoman occupation is was a centre of learning like other religious foundations. The main reasons to come here would be to join Cretan families on a Sunday outing (*ekdromi*), to look at the view stretching to the Asterousia range to the south beyond the village of Ligortynos, where the road enters the Mesara plain, or just to enjoy a quiet spot. Alternatively you may want to participate in the celebrations marking the feast of Aghios Georgios on April 23rd (if the date falls in Holy Week, the festivities will take place on Easter Monday).

TEMENOS

A reasonable road (13km) leads northwest to Kyparisos past **Roukani** (Ρουκάνι; *map p. 430, B2*). Note, on the edge of the village, the picturesque domed cruciform church of Aghios Ioannis, dated to the 11th–12th century. A left turn at Kyparisos takes you to Venerato and Moni Palianis (*see p. 138*), but if you keep straight on you will arrive, 6km later, at **Profitis Ilias** (Προφήτης Ηλίας; *map p. 430, B2*). Above the village to the southeast a twin-peaked hill was once the site of the fortress of Temenos, a name

The ruins of the fortifications at Temenos, north side.

meaning 'enclosure'. Nothing much apart from the circuit wall remains, but the views are stunning.

Here the Byzantine emperor Nicephorus Phocas had intended to build Crete's new capital after regaining control of the island from the Saracens in 961. He wanted it well inland in a fully defensible position, but the population would not follow. When he was recalled to Byzantium in 968 only the fortress had been completed. On the occasion of the first revolt against Venetian rule in 1211, it provided sanctuary for the Duke of Candia, Giacomo Tiepolo, who after fleeing Candia disguised as a woman, took refuge here, waiting for reinforcements. The fort was restored in 1303 after an earthquake and again in the 16th century, with the Ottoman peril looming. The old name of the village (Kanli Kastelli, meaning 'Bloody Castle') refers to an event that took place in 1647, when the Venetians and the locals inflicted a heavy defeat on the invading Turks.

The path marked from the village 'to the Byzantine fortress' is nothing short of suicidal but it does lead to an almost life-size statue of Phocas in his imperial finery. To get to the top it is advisable to take the low road from the modern church and look for a track and stone steps to the right. Temenos may have been the site of the ancient city-state of Lykastos, which was destroyed Knossos, who then took over its territory. The saddle between the two hills was defended and was meant to be a refuge in times of trouble. Some of the walls now being restored may include reused Hellenistic material. The church of Aghia Paraskevi, just inside the entrance, is also receiving some attention, but the frescoes that the Italian scholar Giuseppe Gerola admired 100 years ago remain open to the elements. The saddle between the two peaks is fenced—understandably so—for safety reasons. It is therefore not possible to get to the church of Aghios Nikolaos, rebuilt on old foundations, and the substantial remains of a Venetian building nearby to the east, nor to the remains of fortifications (the Rocca) and the double cistern to the west. The site is spectacular not so much for the structures but for the spread of irises, the birds, the view and the ferocious, gusty wind. The Megali Pigi ('Great Spring') is at the foot of the hill to the south of the village.

From Profitis Ilias, the valley road due north via Malades and Phoinikia follows the path the Byzantines and Venetians would have taken to come out here. It leads to Herakleion, to the Chania Gate.

PRACTICAL INFORMATION

GETTING AROUND

• **By car:** Archanes is on the same route as Knossos. The right turn is signed 4km south of Knossos. The village is 5km further.
• **By bus:** From Bus Station A in Herakleion (*see p. 55*) buses leave for Archanes hourly from the area below the Megaron Hotel. Other destinations require private transport.

WHERE TO STAY

Epano Archanes (*map p. 430, C2*)
€€ Archontiko Archanes. Four self-contained apartments in a beautifully restored and furnished 19th-century building, just above the main street. *T: 2810 752985, www.arhontikoarhanes.gr.*
€€ Kalimera Archanes. ▪ Four self-catering cottages in a little walled garden (one is just outside). Old stone houses very attractively restored and thoughtfully furnished with a mixture of antique pieces and modern fittings. A comfortable place to base yourself. Right in the heart of the village, but in a traffic-free little kernel, beautifully silent at night. *T: 2810 287760 or 2810 752999.*
€ Villa Orestis-Archanes. Simple traditional

rent rooms. *T: 2810 751619; mobile 6942 445784.*

WHERE TO EAT

Epano Archanes (*map p. 430, C2*)
In the main plateia there are two good tavernas, the Spitiko and Mesostrato, situated side by side. Lykastos, on the same side of the square, is another popular place, with a good choice of wines. Diagonally opposite the church of the Panaghia is the Ampelos, popular with locals at weekends.

FESTIVALS & EVENTS

Archanes hosts a Wine Festival between August 10–15, as well as a variety of cultural events in summer. St George's Day celebrations at **Moni Epanosiphi** (April 23).

BOOKS & FURTHER READING

J. and E. Sakellarakis: *Archanes.* A full account of the excavations in Archanes, Anemospilia and Phourni.
W. Stanley Moss: *Ill Met by Moonlight.* The story of the abduction of General Kreipe.

THE PEDIADA DISTRICT

A visit to the Pediada district (meaning 'flat country') takes you southeast of Herakleion towards the Lasithi plateau across an unspoilt landscape with the possibility of visiting the Kazantzakis Museum, a couple of potting villages, Moni Angarathou, some frescoed churches, and the ancient remains of Lyttos and Smari. It can be combined with a visit to Malia and an exploration of the beaches on the north coast.

The E4 long distance walking route crosses this landscape west to east and enters the Lasithi plateau south of Lyttos. The district is well known for its agricultural production, especially olive oil and wine; 70 percent of Crete's output originates from the Peza area. Free tastings are available at a number of wineries on the way.

Myrtia and the Nikos Kazantzakis Museum

Leave Herakleion on the road leading south to Knossos and take the left turn to Skalani after Spilia. A country road leads to Myrtia (Μυρτιά; 6km; *map p. 430, C2*), which was the home of Kazantzakis's father. The museum (*open March–Oct Mon, Wed, Sat, Sun 9–1 & 4–8; Tues and Fri mornings only; signposted to the far end of the village*) was founded in 1984 by set- and costume-designer Georgios Anemogiannis with the assistance of Eleni Kazantzakis, the author's second wife, and her adopted son Patroklos Stavrou. The premises belonged to the Anemogiannis family, who was related to Kazantzakis's father.

Kazantzakis (1883–1957) is best known for *Zorba the Greek*, which made it to the big screen to great acclaim with Anthony Quinn in the title role. The film was shot in Crete, mainly on the Akrotiri peninsula near Chania. The theme music, by Mikis Theodorakis, brought *syrtaki* into every home. Kazantzakis's output was much more varied though, and not constantly informed by his nostalgia for his native Crete. He was a philosopher influenced by Nietzsche and Bergson as well as by Christianity, Marxism and Buddhism. His views led the Orthodox Church to excommunicate him.

The display is arranged chronologically in five rooms covering the author's childhood and early works, followed by the periods 1921–38, when he travelled extensively, and 1939–45, which he spent on the island of Aegina. Room 3 offers an audiovisual presentation of his life in six languages, while the two remaining rooms on the upper floor display material relating to *Zorba the Greek* and his other works.

The museum is also a resource centre for researchers with over 50,000 archival items relating to Kazantzakis's life and works.

Moni Angarathou

Continue to the main road to Kastelli and take the turning north to Episkopi, keeping right after c. 3km for Moni Angarathou (Μονή Αγκαράθου; *map p. 430, C2*). This is an old foundation, apparently dating as far back as 960. It flourished as seat of learning after the Fall of Byzantium, second only to the Sinai College in Herakleion. The monastery was still sufficiently close to the coast to suffer from Turkish incursions, which explains why it was fortified. In the 17th century valuables and documents were removed for safety to the island of Kythera, where the abbot had connections. Among the items was the icon of the Panaghia which, according to tradition, had miraculously marked the spot where the monastery was later built. When the Turks invaded the island the abbot led a lively group of fighters and according to a contemporary account, he was responsible for exhibiting the severed heads of the Turkish warriors on the Herakleion city walls in order to impress the Venetian commander inspecting the defences.

The present church was built in 1941 but the structures around it, in the triangular courtyard, go back to Venetian times, as the inscriptions show. Look out for the gateways at the north and south entrances (1583 and 1565 respectively), a sarcophagus built into the north side of the court (1554), and the barrel-vaulted storeroom opposite the west end of the church (1628).

LITERARY MEDIEVAL CRETE

What was life like for a well-to-do Venetian in 15th-century Crete? The story of Marinos Falieros is quite enlightening. He numbered among his ancestors the very early settlers who had come to colonise the island in 1211. By the early 15th century the family had obviously prospered. Marinos owned eight villages in the Pediada and Malevisi districts; he was a member of the Cretan senate and dabbled in the wine trade. That was clearly not enough to fill his days: he was a poet as well. A true Cretan, though still a Catholic, he wrote in the Greek of his day with traces of Venetian dialect but otherwise very few Italianisms. However, he sought his poetic inspiration firmly in the West. His *Threnos*, a dramatic lament on the sufferings of Christ, was inspired by the Umbrian *Laudae*, lyrical or dramatic pieces sung and acted by confraternities of laymen at religious festivals. This text and his other productions, two dreams of love and two moralising poems, have foundered into obscurity. There is only one copy of his works, dated to 1585, buried in a library in Tübingen. Nevertheless, Marinos Falieros can be credited as one of the first to experiment with the dramatic form in modern Greek.

Galatas

Returning to the main road from Moni Angarathou, take the right turn to Voni for the Minoan excavations at Galatas (Γαλατάς; 4km; *map p. 430, C2*). Here on the hilltop above the village, the Greek Archaeological Service has been excavating a Minoan palace since the 1990s. The area is a protected zone because of its archaeological potential. In the spring you might come across interesting flowers on way up (the Cretan iris, orchids and asphodels): this is not the place to pick them. The area is fenced but you can get a fair idea by walking around the perimeter. The building is centred on a 16m by 37m paved central court. The east wing is the best preserved; there seems to be little room on the plateau for much development to the west to include a west court. Many features typical of Minoan 'palaces' have been identified: the monumental north façade on the central court with ashlar blocks with several mason's marks; the pier-and-door partitions, a pillar hall with a monumental hearth, and the store facilities with pithoi in the east wing. There is also evidence for frescoes in miniature, recalling those from Knossos. Evidence for fresco decoration has also been found in the remains of the surrounding houses.

The main interest of Galatas, though, is its close dating (meaning that the dating bracket for the finds is narrower than for the other sites). From Early Minoan times through to the Old Palace period the area appears to have been occupied by a substantial house with grain-processing facilities. The present building with its high-status features was built at the very beginning of the New Palace period and had a very short life. It was already in a state of decay, with frescoes removed from the walls, when an earthquake tentatively dated to LM IA destroyed it. The reasons for its decline are not clear unless the seat of power moved to a more convenient location such as nearby Kastelli.

Thrapsano

If you are desperate to go home with a pithos, and can fit it in your hand luggage, Thrapsano (Θραψανό; *map p. 430, C2*) is the place to go, from Galatas via Voni. According to the Cretan monk Agapios Landos, all men in Thrapsano were potters, and he was writing in 1642. The tradition is probably much older than that.

Ten years ago Thrapsano was still a potters' village filled with small workshops. The success of the industry was due to the availability of water and the quality of the local clay. Pottery in those days was a strictly seasonal occupation, beginning in the early summer so that freshly-thrown pots could air-dry before firing. Pots of all sizes were manufactured, from table jugs to the occasional pithos, individually fired. Things have now changed somewhat. Pottery is still very much a male preserve, and to a large extent the pots are still made by hand, but the potteries have turned industrial. There are no more cottage potters to be seen in the village itself; they have all moved to hangars on the outskirts, where they can be watched at work. These days only pithoi destined to be garden features or umbrella stands are manufactured. In antiquity itinerant potters moved around to build and fire pithoi where they were needed. Only smaller items like tableware would be centrally produced and shipped to market.

In modern Thrapsano the procedure for making a pithos starts with the preparing of the clay, which comes in huge bags full of grey powder which is hydrated and churned in giant electric mixers. The paste is then put through a mangle to make it completely homogeneous. The turning is still done by hand. For smaller pithoi (up to 1m) a single operator can swing the turntable with his feet and build up the vessel at the same time. For larger specimens a team of two is required. In this case, an assistant sits on the floor and turns the table while the master potter adds a new coil to the pithos, smoothing the surface with a wooden spatula. At each stage of the process the fabric is strengthened by applying heat with a blowtorch. A team of two people can prepare up to eight large pithoi a day. The finished vessels are left to dry until they reach the right consistency (known as 'leatherhard'). They are then stacked with clay spacers and fired in electric kilns for about 12 hours. Each kiln load is well over 100 items.

PITHOI

By sheer virtue of their size, pithoi and their smaller siblings *pitharakia*, loom large in Cretan prehistory and history. Not all are as large as the one from Knossos pictured on p. 74 (185cm tall with an estimated capacity of 2500–3000 litres) or the one from Malia pictured on p. 30 (164cm high). Most are 50 to 80cm in height with a capacity of 50 to 400 litres. Because of their size and thick walls, pithoi are not easy to make even today. The procedure involves building up coils to the intended height and circumference on a turntable rotated by an assistant. In antiquity potters would have used the same approach, though there is evidence that the base and lower section were shaped with slabs of clay. The problems have not changed either. The sheer weight can cause the pot to sag as the higher coils are added. Handling the unfired vessel remains problematic. The situation is neatly summed up by the Greek proverb 'trying to learn the potter's art by making pithoi' which is the equivalent of 'wanting to run before you've learned to walk'.

The function of a pithos depends on its shape and size. Beyond 80cm in height pithoi become difficult to move, even when empty. Moreover, some have an awkward shape that makes it difficult to get a purchase on them. Traditionally pithoi have been connected with domestic storage, and indeed they are often found in that capacity in palaces and lesser dwellings. That accounts for about 60 percent of pithoi in Bronze Age contexts. Another 30 percent were used in burials, interpreted by some as a return of the deceased all trussed up into the womb. The earliest evidence for the practice is contemporary with the introduction of the clay chests, the larnakes, towards the end of the 3rd millennium. Otherwise pithoi were used in workshops or in agricultural installations with wine and olive presses, where they would also be used to store water. There is little evidence for their use in bulk transport; they are too heavy, too fragile and difficult to seal. According to petrographic analysis, Cretan-made pithoi have been identified only in Sardinia and on Thera (Santorini). Other Minoan-looking pithoi found outside Crete are locally made according to Cretan models. Even in more recent times pithoi were not much used for Cretan exports. In antiquity bags, sacks and baskets were employed in conjunction with containers made of animal skins for liquids. The British traveller John Bowring witnessed the practice in Crete as late as 1840. The use of wooden barrels, introduced to the Aegean area by the Franks and the Venetians in the Middle Ages, only gained currency in Crete much later, around the 18th century.

Evangelismos and Sklaverochori

From Thrapsano the road to Kastelli crosses the village of **Evangelismos** (Ευαγγελισμός; *map p. 430, C2*), where in 1981 14th-century frescoes were uncovered in the west arm of the domed cruciform church of Aghios Evangelismos in the middle of the village (note how the transept is higher than the nave). The paintings include, unusually for Crete, Old Testament scenes such as the *Creation of Adam and Eve*, the *Garden of Eden* and the *Expulsion from Paradise*. The key to the church may be found in the café across the street. At **Sklaverochori** (Σκλαβεροχώρι), 4km further on, is another Byzantine church with well-preserved frescoes dated by a graffito to 1481. The church of the Eisodia Theotokon (the Presentation of the Virgin) is at the north end of the village. In the customary position in the apse is the *Panaghia Platytera*, the Virgin 'Wider than the Heavens', framed by angels, hierarchs and deacons. In the nave are the *Birth of the Virgin*, the *Presentation in the Temple* (on the vault) and scenes from the life of Christ including a *Baptism* with male and female river gods. The south wall has a scene with St George slaying the dragon and rescuing the princess, whose parents watch from the city walls, with the hand of God stretched out from above. The figures opposite include St Francis, a saint of the Western church and an unusual appearance in Crete (one of only three). The name of the village is apparently derived from the little bells shepherds hang around the necks of their sheep; it bears no connection with slaves or Slavs.

Smari and the Moni Kallergis

The road joins the main connection to Kastelli. For more antiquities, drive less than 1km west and take the turn right at Galeniano to Smari (Σμάρι; *map p. 430, C2*), a picturesque village from where a track leads to the **Smari acropolis**. Here Greek excavations next to the church of the Profitis Ilias have established continuous occupation from the Middle Minoan period well into the Iron Age on top of the hill, and to Roman times in the wider area. On the top of the hill inside a fortification wall, in a location known as Troulli, the sanctuary of Athena Ergani was identified together with a number of buildings dated to the Geometric and Orientalising periods in the Iron Age. Poorly preserved earlier Minoan remains were also present. The excavators have proposed that this was the seat of a ruler and have put forward an identification with Homeric Lyttos, though there is already a place by that name in the area (*see below*).

Before entering Kastelli west from Galeniano, a left turn leads to a scenic drive (5km) to **Moni Kallergis**, in a shaded and cool position and connected to the Byzantine family of that name, who eventually moved to Venice. The monastery no longer functions, having been abandoned in 1931 after a fierce fire. The church of Aghios Ioannis has been restored but still reveals Venetian elements in its architecture.

Kastelli Pediadas and its nearby churches

Kastelli Pediadas (Καστέλλι Πεδιάδας; *map p. 430, C2*) sits oblivious to tourism at the centre of a prosperous agricultural community. Excavations have shown that there was a sizeable Minoan settlement here. The town takes its name from a Venetian castle, the imposing ruins of which could still be seen in the early 20th century on the hill where the modern school is. Kastelli is a good place to take time off from sightseeing. The weekly market is held on Wednesdays; in August the festivities of Xenitemenou are held (*see p. 106*). Walkers will find Kastelli a good place to plan their route to the Lasithi plateau. The E4 walking route comes past here on its way east.

For devotees of Byzantine churches there are a couple of excursions from Kastelli. To the south is **Liliano** (Λιλιανό), where the church of Aghios Ioannis presents a puzzling mixture of Venetian influence with features normally associated with much earlier churches. The church is on the way to Liliano from Kastelli, though the key must be obtained in Liliano. After the sign (right) for the military airfield, take the turning to the village; the church is immediately to the right on a concrete road, well hidden among the trees. The ground-plan is that of a basilica, with three aisles ending in apses, but the short square nave is not typical and may have been designed to support a dome. The church now has a wooden saddle roof and, across the west end, a barrel-vaulted narthex supports a bellcote. Inside, the columns of the aisles have Ionic capitals with plain abaci. Other reused material, possibly from Lyttos (*see below*), can be seen outside: the stone bench against the west wall has an inscription in ancient Greek, while a fragment of an Early Christian altar forms part of the threshold at the church entrance. The basilica plan, with the floor well below the level of the narthex and altogether c. 1m lower than the modern cemetery, has suggested to some the reworking of an earlier Byzantine structure but the Italian scholar Gerola saw it as one of the last of the Cretan basilicas, with a 12th–13th-century date. The roof structure and other architectural details (the corbels for instance), show Venetian influence. On the south wall the remains of a pulpit (five stone steps and part of a column) indicate the practice of the Latin rite: any adaptation of a Byzantine church did not happen before the 13th century.

The other church, **Aghios Pandeleimon**, is north of Kastelli near Pigi (named after the spring that fed the Roman aqueduct to ancient Chersonisos). To get there, take the main road to Chersonisos and watch for the sign to the right after 1km marked 'Byzantine church and Paradise tavern'. Two kilometres on you cannot miss the church. It stands in a well-watered spot by the spring itself. The key should be with the taverna when it is open, otherwise ask in Kastelli. The church, of the Second Byzantine period with 13th–14th-century frescoes, stands on the foundations of an earlier Christian basilica: Hellenistic inscriptions as well as architectural fragments suggest an earlier sanctuary. As Aghios Pandeleimon is traditionally a saint connected with healing, continuity from the site of an earlier Asclepieion is a strong possibility. When Gerola saw it in the early years of the last century the church was almost in ruins; it was restored in 1962. The plan is that of a three-aisled building, though it is quite an unconventional structure incorporating many reused architectural blocks as well as inscriptions of Roman and Hellenistic date. One of the columns is made of four superimposed Corinthian capitals resting on a square abacus plate. The frescoes in the apse and in nave are well preserved. They are dated stylistically to the late 13th or early 14th century. On the north wall at the east end is a rare scene of St Anne nursing the infant Mary.

LYTTOS

Lyttos (Λύττος; *map p. 430, C2–D2*) is signed from the centre of Kastelli, 5km on a good road to the east, leading to the modern village of Lyttos or Xydas. On the way, the small chapel of Aghios Georgios, which has been recently restored, can be seen from the village across the valley. The path leading to it starts by the modern church near the war memorial. The chapel has frescoes in the apse and on the south wall dated to 1321 by inscription; the key can be obtained in the village.

The ancient site of Lyttos is signposted and there is parking space at the end of the track. It is high on a ridge with a view of the sea to the north, where in antiquity Lyttos had its harbour, at Chersonisos. Down in the valley to the south, the E4 route follows a traditional mule path into Lasithi past Kastamonitsa. The ancient Graeco-Roman city of Lyttos therefore occupied a nodal point in communications between the coast and the interior. There is not a lot of the ancient city to see above ground but it is a beautiful location with a dramatic view of the Lasithi escarpment and the possibility of some interesting wildlife.

HISTORY OF LYTTOS

According to one version of the legend, Rhea gave birth to Zeus here, at a safe distance from his father Kronos (*see p. 208*). She then concealed the infant in a cave on Mt Dikte. Traditionally the town was founded by Dorians from Sparta and was, according to Polybius, the most ancient city in Crete. Homer spoke of 'Broad Lyttos' and enthused over the exploits of the Lyttian force under Idomenaeus, the leader of the Cretan contingent of '80 black ships' to Troy. Coeranus, the leader of the Lyttians, gave his own life to save Idomenaeus. In Hellenistic times Lyttos was a powerful city-state and a rival of Knossos, with a territory stretching to the north and south coasts. In the war of 221–219 BC Lyttos came to grief when it attacked Hierapytna (now Ierapetra) leaving its own city unguarded. Knossos swiftly moved in and destroyed it. After c. 150 years the city had recovered sufficiently to put up a fierce resistance to Metellus, the future Creticus, who conquered Crete in 67 BC. Lyttus prospered in Roman times and in the First Byzantine period. Statues and inscriptions dedicated to Trajan and Hadrian (early 2nd century AD) are particularly abundant. Defensive walls were built at the time of the Arab invasion, but clearly they were not enough.

When the first travellers started coming to Crete, a visit to Lyttos was a must as apparently there was plenty to see. Onorio Belli, who came to Crete in 1583 (*see p. 34*), spent quite some time touring, botanising and collecting antiquities. He had a natural interest in fostering the study of Classical antiquity. He conducted 'excavations' at Lyttos in the theatre, the largest in Crete, and in the town; he found statues and inscriptions which he duly sent to Venice, and identified the location of a temple dedicated to the imperial cult. Belli also recorded Christian basilicas with mosaics.

The Italians returned to explore in 1893–99. At that time the theatre that Belli had described could still be seen. Lyttos is now being investigated by the Greek Archaeological Service.

View of the countryside at Lyttos, with the Pediada in the distance.

The site

A **Hellenistic house** has been excavated. Four column bases and a built altar were preserved in a main hall, as well as storage and workshop areas. The house had been destroyed in a fire in 221–220 BC, probably while the Lyttians were away at Hierapytna (*see History, above*). The chapel of the **Timios Stavros** (Holy Cross) is built over the foundations of a large 5th-century basilica in the centre of the city. A second church, **Aghios Georgios**, lies over a 2nd-century building with painted wall plaster. Note the architectural fragments from ornate piers with crosses set in acanthus foliage built into the church's southwest corner. The **bouleuterion** or city council chamber, with platforms and benches, has been excavated nearby. It was destroyed in AD 200 in an earthquake. Traces of the **city wall** can be made out on the hilltop between the two churches. The style of masonry, with a rubble core faced with squared stones, is reminiscent of the fortifications of the acropolis at Gortyn built by the emperor Heraclius. That would date it to the 7th century AD. Of much later date are the **grain mills**, strategically placed on a very windy ridge and probably operating until quite recently. Crossing the narrow valley to the southeast, traces of the Roman aqueduct bringing Lasithi water from springs near the Kera convent can be seen. North of Lyttos, a long descent (12km) leads to Avdou and more frescoed churches (*see p. 204*).

PRACTICAL INFORMATION

GETTING AROUND

• **By car:** Kastelli Pediadas is easy to reach from the E75. You can take the Knossos road and turn 4km after Peza. For Myrtia either take the left turn from Skalani after Spilia, or go via Astraki on the Kastelli Pediadas road. Galatas and Thrapsano are on side roads east of Aghia Paraskies on the way to Kastelli. Kastelli has good connections to the beaches (16km to the north coast at Chersonisos) past the Aquasplash water park.

• **By bus:** From Herakleion, local buses (blue) depart hourly to Kastelli Pediadas from Bus Station A near the harbour (*T: 2810 245020; www.crete-buses.gr*). The departure bay is in the area below the Megaron Hotel. Tickets are sold at the kiosk outside the ticket office. Ask the driver to tell you when to get off. Other destinations require private transport.

WHERE TO STAY

Kastelli Pediadas (*map p. 430, C2*)
€ **Hotel Kalliopi**. A small hotel in the centre of Kastelli in a quiet location. *T: 28910 32685, www.kalliopi-hotel.gr.*
€ **Elena Rooms**. Both rooms and small apartments in Kastelli, on the Lyttos road. *T: 28910 31093.*

WHERE TO EAT

There is no shortage of tavernas in this area. For something unusual try the Steiakakis at **Skalani** (*T: 2180 731217; map p. 430, C1*). Here you may get snails in season and sample the stew with branches of wild fennel. Elia and Diosmos (*T: 2810 731283*), also in Ska-

lani, offer a taste of nouvelle Cretan cuisine. In **Thrapsano** (*map p. 430, C2*) there is the very simple Taverna Anemomylos ('windmill').

FESTIVALS & EVENTS

At **Kastelli Pediadas**, the Xenitemenou Festival (The Celebration of the Expatriate; 4–6 Aug) hosts concerts, exhibitions and plays. Also at Kastelli, Carnival is held on the last Sun of the carnival season according to the Orthodox calendar.

LOCAL SPECIALITIES

The area is a huge wine and olive oil producer. The **Boutari Exhibition Hall** (*open 10–8; T: 2810 731617, www.boutari.gr*) is situated on the estate of the Fantaxometocho vineyard on the outskirts of Skalani near Myrtia. The visit offers a tour of the underground wine cellars, an introduction to the art of wine-tasting, an opportunity to enjoy wines in combination with local, traditional dishes, a chance to purchase current and older vintages of Boutari wines as well as wines of limited production and wine-related books and accessories. **Minos Wines** (*T: 2810 741213; open Mon–Fri 9–4, Sat 11–4 in summer; by appointment in winter; www.minoswines.gr*) is situated on the right side of the road close to the exit from Peza village. Visitors are offered tastings and there is also a shop for wine and other traditional Cretan products. **Peza Union** (*T: 2810 741948; open 9–3 every day otherwise by arrangement, www.pezaunion.gr*) is the local cooperative, with over 3,000 members. The exhibition centre is located 2km out of Peza (*map p. 430, C2*) on the way to Aghia Paraskies on the left.

ANO VIANNOS &
THE SOUTH COAST

The southeast part of the province of Herakleion is relatively little known, but with the Lasithi mountains to the east and the inviting beaches of the south coast, it is well worth exploring. It offers stunning landscapes and, at the right time of the year, quiet coastal villages.

Arkalochori

The main road from Herakleion strikes south past Knossos and Peza. At Aghia Paraskies take the right turn to Arkalochori: otherwise you end up in Kastelli Pediadas, heading back to the north coast. The road runs through vineyards for the Rozaki table grapes trained on tall wire trellises. After 9km note the left turn to Galatas for the Minoan palace excavations (*described on p. 99*).

Around 30km from Herakleion, **Arkalochori** (Αρκαλοχώρι; *map p. 430, C2*) is the busy centre of an agricultural region with no time for tourists. Nearby is the cave of Profitis Ilias (*not accessible*), an important cult centre from the Early Minoan period to Neopalatial times. A huge assemblage of metal finds (altogether one of the largest in the Aegean area) has been retrieved from it over time. Locals first found metal objects in the Ottoman period: these were melted down for agricultural tools. Spyridon Marinatos went back to the site in the 1930s and excavated more metal including several LM I rapier blades suggesting the cult of a warlike deity. One particular specimen, an axe, bore characters considered by some to be comparable to those of the Phaistos Disk (*see p. 152*). There were also miniature double axes in silver and gold, some decorated with an intricate pattern and one with a vertical inscription in Linear A.

Arkades and Embaros

From Arkalochori you can drive due south to the coast down to Skinias, Kato Kastelliana and Tsoutsouros (*see p. 109*); otherwise follow the road east towards Viannos and the western slopes of Mt Dikte. After Panaghia (13km), a right turn to Afrati (Αφρατί; *map p. 430, C2*) leads to **Arkades**. Not much remains above ground of this powerful city founded by immigrants from the Peloponnese. The Italians excavated here early in the 20th century, finding evidence of settlement from Minoan times. The town flourished in the Iron Age with contacts with Egypt, Rhodes and Corinth, as indicated by the material from the cemetery, which is reminiscent of the Orientalising objects found in the Idaian Cave. Arkades was destroyed in 221 BC but its fortunes must have picked up later as it appears in the *Tabula Peutingeriana*, a document showing the layout of the late Roman Empire.

The site is high up, west of Afrati on the hill overlooking the village. It is unsigned, and when making enquiries in the village it is advisable to ask for 'Archazía', the name by which it is locally known. North of Afrati by a concrete water cistern, a rough, unmade road unsuitable for hire cars leads to the top of the hill keeping left at the first fork. The site is very overgrown and there is not much to admire nowadays apart from the strategic position—which, admittedly, is very fine.

Back on the main road 3km later, a 1km detour to **Embaros** (Έμπαρος) is recommended because of the frescoes in the church of Aghios Georgios. They are dated 1436–37 and are by Manuel Phokas, who also worked at Avdou in the Pediada district and at Epano Symi southeast of Viannos. Walkers will enjoy exploring the path after Xeniakos, one of the traditional entry points to the Lasithi plateau.

Kefali

Further south, skirting the Dikte massif, the road comes to a right turn marked Chondros and Keratokambos. Three kilometres from the main road, on a right turn above the village of Chondros (Χόνδρος; *map p. 430, D3*) is the site of Kefali. There is not very much to see and in the spring, flowers may prove a distraction. This, however, is an important site because it is one of the few settlements founded in LM IIIA after the Minoan civilisation had suffered a crippling blow. Other sites such as Stylos, Samonas Apokoronou and Kastelli in Chania, also have features belonging to the Postpalatial period but these were commingled with older structures. The excavation is on the saddle above the village. After the first houses, watch for signs right: after less than 1km, the site is 3mins on foot uphill to the left. There are two groups of buildings separated by a double wall. Each complex has several houses. The architecture is typical of LM III, with thick walls, stone-flagged floors, low benches and sunken pithoi. The western complex is grander in scale and may have been the house of the local ruler. Fragments of ritual objects, including a stone offering-table decorated with lions in relief, have been interpreted as evidence for a shrine possibly located on an upper floor. The settlement had a short life. It was destroyed by a fire, either by hostile action or after an earthquake, and was certainly not reoccupied.

Ano Viannos

Ano Viannos (Άνο Βιάννος; *map p. 430, D3*) is a large village laid out on a steep hillside, built on the spot of the ancient city of Viannos, which minted its own coins with a flower on one side and a woman on the reverse. It reputedly produces the best olive oil in Crete. Ano Viannos also boasts a couple of interesting Byzantine churches. **Aghia Pelagia** is signposted from the main square and has well-preserved frescoes dated by inscription to 1360. The representation of Hell to the left of the entrance, showing sinners entangled both in a serpent and a symbol of their sin, is very direct. Follow the brown Ministry of Culture signs up the stepped side streets to a terrace with a splendid view. The church of **Aghios Georgios** has fine doorways and a bellcote.

The **Folklore Museum** at the western end of the village is well worth a visit (*opening hours are unfortunately erratic*). Exhibits cover everyday life in the area in the last 200 years, and exhibits include fine local dresses, Cretan bagpipes and a raki still. The material from the Second World War is a reminder that this was the land of Manoli Bandouvas, one of the more colourful chiefs of the Cretan resistance. In September 1943 the area suffered greatly because of its proximity to the Italian-occupied zone in eastern Crete. When the Italian armistice with the Allied forces intervened, the Germans decided to flush out the resistance to prevent any colluding with the Italians. Six villages in the area were burnt and about 500 men shot. According to Antony Beevor's account, males called Bandouvas were particularly targeted. They were not relatives of the guerrilla chief; they simply shared a surname dating from the time of Venetian occupation and meaning 'from Padua'.

From the main square a rough road (2km, signed) leads to **Aghia Moni**, an ancient foundation with a fine church with a Gothic doorway and an interesting collection of icons, two of which are attributed to the 15th-century master Angelos.

Keratokambos, Tsoutsouros and ancient Priansos

For a day out at the seaside in a still unspoilt part of Crete you might want to investigate **Keratokambos** (Κερατόκαμπος; 12km from Ano Viannos; *map p. 430, D3*). From there the coastal road leads east, and eventually picks up the main road at Myrtos.

Tsoutsouros (Τσούτσουρος; *map p. 430, C3*) lies further west, at the end of a good coastal road (11km). The village is now beginning to be known, which may be its downfall, but the water is still deep and blue. The road to Tsoutsouros is cluttered with the debris of horticultural activity, but the birds do not seem to mind; they still flock to the area of the Anapodiaris river. Development has now taken over, but the swimming is still one of the best in the island. Tsoutsouros is the ancient Inatos or Binatos, the harbour of Priansos (*see below*). It was known in antiquity because of the cult of the Binatian Eileithyia, the goddess of fertility. Her temple may have been at the top of the hill where the chapel of Aghia Eleni now stands. The goddess was also venerated in a cave like the one near Amnisos on the north coast (*see p. 114*). The cave at the back of the beach, just before the road ends, is not accessible. It was excavated in the 1970s by Nikolaos Platon and Kostis Davaras, who found evidence of activity from the Minoan to the Roman periods. Finds include a Neopalatial stone altar, several bull figurines and double axes, as well as a large number of terracottas on the theme of fertility and the safe delivery of children. Finds from as far afield as Egypt suggest pilgrimages. The model boat is possibly a reminder that the harbour was a safe one, a fact not lost on the Allies in the Second World War, who used the deep waters of Kerkelos, the cape to the west, for their submarine landings, keeping contact between the Cretan resistance and Cairo.

From Tsoutsouros the road leaves the coast to climb inland into the Asterousia Mountains. It is also possible to drive due north to Kato Kastelliana and from there to continue towards Garipa for Priansos. The Archaic city-state of **Priansos** (*map p. 430, C3*), known through written sources and from its coins, flourished around the 5th century BC. Its precise location, however, is not clear. Coins with Poseidon and other marine motifs suggest a strong connection with the sea. A stele mentioning Priansos was found in Venice built into a house with a text of an oath between Priansos, Hierapytna and Gortyn. In the early 13th century Enrico Pescatore, the Genoese freebooter who controlled the island for a short while before the Venetians, built a castle on the flat hilltop with a commanding view of the sea and may have used spolia from the ancient city.

Pyrgos and Charakas

From Tsoutsouros a scenic route to Achendrias leads 20km west to **Pyrgos** (Πύργος; *map p. 430, C3*). Travellers may find it a convenient, cool and breezy spot from which to explore either the Mesara plain or the wild reaches of the Asterousia Mountains, on whose northern slopes it sits. It is worth a stop here for a visit to the old heart of the village, with an interesting church. The church has a double dedication to Aghios Georgios and Aghios Konstantinos; it is located at the eastern end of the main street, not far from the stream. The key should be with the laundry next door. Originally there were three naves, but the one dedicated to Aghia Eleni (Constantine's mother) was pulled down to widen the street. The earliest painting, featuring Aghios Georgios, is in the north aisle. The south aisle has the Constantine cycle (Constantine is a saint in the Orthodox Church), which is dated by a donor inscription in the apse to 1314–15. In the eastern half of the vault are: the *Birth of Constantine*; his parents with the young Constantine on horseback with his father, the emperor Constantius Chlorus; the *Battle of the Milvian Bridge* with the Vision of the Cross that inspired Constantine to victory against his rival Maxentius and which afterwards led him to declare Christianity the religion of the Roman Empire. The style of the frescoes is conservative and shows no influence of the Palaeologan art recognised in Byzantium at the time. For stylistic features typical of the period, with more generously moulded figures, see the 14th-century panels in the west bay of the same aisle.

From Pyrgos it is 50km north to Herakleion in the direction of Tefeli. The left turn for Moni Epanosiphi and Temenos (*see p. 95*) is just after the village. If you want to explore the Mesara, you can pick up the road west through Asimi. It is barely 20km to Gortyn. On the way take time off at **Charakas** (Χάρακας; 4km; *map p. 430, B3*) to visit the Venetian fortification on an isolated outcrop with a commanding view of the Mesara and of Lasithi in the far distance. The short ascent among wild flowers and to the sound of sheep bells is well worth the effort, though it is not possible to visit the chapel (with frescoes) nor the building itself. According to the archives, the village of Charakas in the mid-14th century belonged first to the Malipiero family and then to the De Mezzos. The local population had different rights: some were serfs, others enjoyed more freedom.

East of Viannos: the sanctuary of Symi

The main road east of Viannos eventually enters the province of Lasithi and then hugs the coast to Ierapetra. Before that, there are some side roads to the right leading to good beaches; and to the left, just after Kato Pevkos (9km from Viannos), is a left fork signed to a **war memorial** (commemorating the destruction of six villages in the area on 14th September 1943; *see pp. 108–09 above*) and leading to Kato Symi. Here you may want to make enquiries about the key to the church of Aghios Georgios in Ano Symi.

The ascent starts at the Aphrodite taverna. After 2km a right fork, marked, leads to **Ano Symi** (Άνω Σύμη; *map p. 430, D3; also known as Epano Symi; Επάνω Σύμη*). This short stretch of road is narrow, unmade and unsuitable for hire cars. The frescoes in Aghios Georgios, dated by inscription to 1453, are by Manuel Phokas, who also worked at Embaros and Avdou. The village itself is now almost deserted and extremely picturesque; it is a good place to explore.

It is not possible from the village to reach the **Sanctuary of Hermes and Aphrodite** higher up, as the path is unmarked and is blocked by fencing. Back on the tarmac road, a wooden sign promises the sanctuary 9km on. And there indeed it is, provided you turn left at the next junction and stop just before the end of the tarmac when you see to your right a sign warning of forest fires and below it another wooden sign, barely legible, saying 'Αρχαιότητες' and pointing right. The site is entirely fenced and sits right at the bottom of the cliff. There is not much point in looking for a hole in the fence (there is one on the west side, but all it affords is a close look at the huge tree in the southeast corner. It may not be part of the archaeological record but is probably just as old). A bird's-eye view of the site can be enjoyed legally by walking a few hundred metres further along the road in the Omalos direction and taking the first turn right up an unmade track.

Situated at 1200m on the slopes of Mt Dikte, in a spectacular natural setting, the Sanctuary of Hermes and Aphrodite affords superb views down to the south coast and the sea. The nearby spring immediately to the east explains why it is also known as Krya Vrysi ('cold spring'). The sanctuary associated with this water source occupies several terraces across the natural amphitheatre on the mountainside. It was excavated by Angelika Lebessi in the 1970s and it is now being investigated by the Greek Archaeological Service. It is extremely significant that such an isolated spot should continue as a cult centre from the Old Palace period to Roman times, for well over 2,000 years. The first sign of activity goes back to MM II and was followed by developments dated MM III. The paved, open-air sacred enclosure of this latter phase was extended in the Geometric period to include a monumental altar and in Roman times a temple was built.

Huge quantities of finds accumulated over the centuries. The Minoans left stone offering-tables, many inscribed with Linear A, stone vases and clay and bronze figurines. Three bronze swords with incised decoration have a Postpalatial date. From the Iron Age come a number of bronze cut-out plaques (a selection of these is displayed in the Temporary Exhibition at Herakleion Archaeological Museum). These are similar to the gold ones found on Mt Ida and were hammered on a leather or wood support to create a votive tablet with a pseudo low relief. The worship of Hermes and of Aphrodite is attested by ex-votos, by a stone inscription and by graffiti on the tiles of the house shrine of the Hellenistic and Roman periods. Hermes was worshipped as Hermes Dendrites, 'Hermes of the Trees', and indeed a 7th-century BC bronze votive plaque shows him in the branches of a tree. This remarkable continuity has led some to believe that, over time, elements of the Minoan religion with the duo of the 'Goddess' and 'Young God' became incorporated in the cult of Hermes and Aphrodite.

PRACTICAL INFORMATION

GETTING AROUND

• **By car:** From Herakleion it is 65km to Ano Viannos on the Knossos road going straight on at Aghia Paraskies to Arkalochori. From further east at Chersonisos or Malia, take the Kastelli direction and continue south to Liliano until you find the road 3km east of Roussochoria (25km from Chersonisos). If you are already south in the Mesara, the road that crosses the plain continues east to Ano Viannos via Asimi and Pyrgos (53km from Aghii Deka to Ano Viannos).

• **By bus:** from Herakleion Bus Station A (*T: 2810 245020; www.crete-buses.gr*) there are daily buses to Arkalochori and Ano Viannos; in the Pyrgos direction to Asimi and to Mesochorio (either side of Pyrgos), and to Arvi on the coast east of Keratokambos.

WHERE TO STAY & EAT

Ano Viannos (*map p. 430, D3*)
€ **Lefkes** (*T: 6978 327812*) offers two rooms and taverna on the west side of the village. € **Plantzounakis** (*T: 28950 22448; markelllla@hotmail.com*) consists of eight large rooms in a block of flats at the east end of the village above the shop. The bakery in the middle of town has an excellent *galatopita*, a sort of baked semolina pie.

Arkalochori (*map p. 430, C2*)
€ **Domatia Sakavelis**. Three double rooms. The owner only speaks Greek, but there is little else around in the way of accommodation. The rooms are signed (in Greek) on the outskirts of the village on the way to Viannos. *T: 28910 22877; open March–Dec.*

Arvi (*map p. 430, D3*)
€€ **Ariadni**. A modern hotel at the western end of the village overlooking the beach. *T:*

28950 71300, mobile 6972 307681; www.ariadnihotel.com.

Other options include € **Gorgona Rooms** (*T: 28950 71353*) in a modern block of flats and € **Taverna Kima** (*T: 28950 71344*), which has also rooms.

Keratokambos (*map p. 430, D3*)
€€ **Komis Studios**. Close to the beach. Restaurant open July and Aug. *T: 28950 51390; www.komisstudios.gr.*

€ **Doriakis Apartment**. Behind Komis, with a reduced view and less greenery. *T: 28950 51359.*

Pyrgos (*map p. 430, C3*)
Pyrgos, inland at the east end of the Mesara, on a hill off the heat of the plain, is a good location as a base. € **Saridakis Rooms** offers seven double rooms in a modern block of flats at the top end of the village. *T: 28930 22238 or 22861; www.travel.diadiktyo.net/saridakis-nikolaos.* € **Hotel Arhontiko** is a small modern hotel on the main road crossing the village. *T: 28930 23118.*

Tsoutsouros (*map p. 430, C3*)
€€ **Mouratis Apartments**. Small and large independent apartments by the beach with views of the Asterousia Mountains (*open April–end Oct and by arrangement for groups off season. T: 28910 92244 or 28910 24550; www.mouratis.gr*). € **Lytos Rent Rooms** (*T: 28910 92321*).

FESTIVALS & EVENTS

Every July, the village of **Archontiko**, north of Arkalochori, organises a feast in honour of snails ('*chochli*' in the local Cretan dialect). Thin or fat snails are cooked according to various time-honoured recipes.

At **Charakas** near Pyrgos, an effigy of Judas Iscariot is burned on Easter Sunday.

EAST OF HERAKLEION
TO MALIA

The north coast highway, known both as the 'New National Road' and as the E75, connects Herakleion to Malia and then continues inland to Aghios Nikolaos, 70km away. As you drive east, apart form the palace at Malia, the places to visit include the villas at Amnisos and Nirou Chani. Chersonisos may be worth a stop, if only for the innovative open-air museum. Detours are possible to beaches around Kato Gouves and Analipsi and to sacred caves (Eileithyia and Skoteino).

AMNISOS

To get to Amnisos (Αμνισός) from Herakleion (7km; *map p. 430, C1*) it is probably better to use the old road, which runs closer to the coast. Starting from Plateia Eleftherias, drive east past the suburbs of Poros and Katsambas, where one of the harbours of Knossos used to be (Amnisos was the other one), past Nea Alikarnassos and the airport. Beyond that the road descends into the bay of Amnisos the very place from which, according to one tradition, Idomenaeus, the grandson of Minos, set sail for Troy. You may want to try out the beach, though bear in mind that it is very popular with tourists and locals alike in the summer. The site is signposted from the east end of the bay.

The site

Starting the visit from the east, the first building is the so-called **Villa of the Lilies**, named after the frescoes depicting papyrus, irises and lilies built in the New Palace period. The site is fenced but there is a vantage point on the seaward side close to the villa's paved terrace. The building is noteworthy because of its ashlar architecture, a colonnaded court and a system of halls facing the sea. To the northeast is a lustral basin, to the south a number of small rooms with a staircase that once led to the first floor. The building was designed on a grand scale with six sets of pier-and-door partitions (polythyra), but it does lack storage and service areas. The frescoes were found in the southwest area of the house in a room with two column bases. To the north stands a well, built with reused ashlar blocks; the same technique is employed in the megaron 30m to the west.

The site was first excavated by Spyridon Marinatos in the 1930s and re-examined in the 1980s by German archaeologists. Marinatos found quantities of pumice stone which he attributed to the eruption on Thera only 100km away. This led him to believe that he had found a destruction layer and that this explained the demise of the building. Later analysis has concluded that this was not the case. The dating evidence provided by pottery styles shows that the wholesale destruction in Crete in LM IB happened possibly 100 years after the Thera event. The pumice stone may indeed have been washed to the shore but it could hardly have created any serious damage. On the other hand, something did change in this villa and not for the better: the nature of the finds and the very scarcity of them suggest that it ended its life as a workshop.

How else to account for the 13 boar's tusks and the ivory? Eventually it may have been damaged in an earthquake (some ashlar blocks of the west façade had been displaced) and finished off by a fire in the LM I period, but it was already in decline by then. The abundant pumice stone, used as an abrasive, fits the workshop explanation well.

West of the excavation, on the other side of the hill, are the remains (fenced) of an **Archaic temple** (6th century BC) dedicated to Zeus Thenatas and also excavated by Marinatos. Apart from the two limestone eagles associated with a round, open-air stone altar with traces of burnt sacrifices, the most important survival is the 40m long façade with mason's marks in the shape of a trident. It has a return pointing west at the north end and incorporates reused blocks from an earlier building. A large staircase leads to the terrace with two podia at either end. The original construction is dated to late MM IIIB and was not in use beyond LM IB. It might have been associated with the cult in the Eileithyia Cave. The site suffered extensive destruction in LM I and shows signs of reoccupation in LM III and beyond. While the dating provided by the layer rich in ashes by the LM I wall has not been conclusive, the pottery and the figurines suggest that a form of cult activity was being carried on here in the 10th century, at the very beginning of the Geometric period, as at Kommos. The cult of Zeus Thenatas continued well into Roman times, to the 2nd century AD. According to Marinatos, the epithet by which Zeus was worshipped here was related to the town of Thenon in the Omphalion plain (Pediada district); he saw that as a reference to the worship of the Crete-born god, which would account for the endurance of the cult.

The remains of the **Minoan harbour works** are now underwater, a little further west by the Aghii Theodori chapel.

THE EILEITHYIA CAVE

To reach the cave take the road south from Amnisos to Episkopi; after 1km watch for a sign on the left. The cave (*not open to the public*) is one of the 15 or so Cretan caves used in antiquity as sanctuaries. It measures 60m in length, 12m across and is 2–3m high. Near the centre is a stalagmite some 150cm tall with a roughly shaped stone in front interpreted as an altar. Figurines and votive objects have been found in the cave, investigated first by Hatzidakis and then by Marinatos between 1929 and 1938. The location is believed to be associated with the cult of Eileithyia, the goddess who assisted women in childbirth. It is she who was in attendance when Leto gave birth to Apollo at Delos and when Athena sprang fully armed from Zeus' head.

The cult of Eileithyia, mentioned by Homer and Hesiod (c. 8th century BC), is a very ancient one, probably dating from the Neolithic. It can be traced also in mainland Greece during Hellenistic and Roman times. Pausanias mentions sanctuaries in Athens, Sparta and Argos but the most important one was at Aigion, where there was a xoanon, a wooden statue of Eileithyia with face, hands and feet in Pentelic marble, by the 2nd-century BC sculptor Damophon. The goddess was represented holding torches in both hands, because she brought children into light out of darkness. The cult in the Eileithyia Cave is believed to have continued from the Late Neolithic up to the 5th century AD.

NIROU CHANI

The site (*map p. 430, C1; open Tues–Sun 8.30–3*) is 5km east of Amnisos on the Old Road past Chani Kokkini beach, signed to the right just before a bridge. The remains are of a large country house excavated in 1918–19 by Stefanos Xanthoudides. Built by the sea in MM III, it is remarkable because of its state of preservation. Only part of the excavated building is on view. The entrance is from the east, where a paved court **(1)** with raised paths and a stepped platform with remains of horns of consecration **(2)** led to a colonnaded porch **(3)** separated by a polythyron system from a hall with a gypsum dado and decorative paving **(4)**. A corridor **(5)** continued into the house. Note the light-well **(6)** next to a room with benches **(7)**. In a room **(8)** only accessible from this direction, four stone lamps were found. Further west two rooms **(9 and 10)** contained 40 tripod tables for offerings, stacked in piles. Across the corridor a room had a bench decorated with triglyphs **(11)**; the one next to it **(12)** had three more tables for offerings. The north area was used for storage. It had a mud-brick structure creating five storage bins **(13)** with steps up to them and pithoi. At the south end there is a room **(14)** where an unusual concentration of ritual finds was excavated. It included four large bronze double axes, remarkably thin meaning that they were use for ceremonial purposes. The second floor was accessed via a staircase **(15)**.

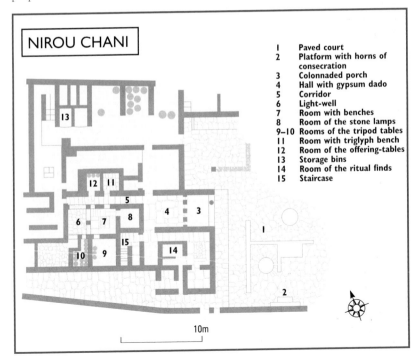

NIROU CHANI

1	Paved court
2	Platform with horns of consecration
3	Colonnaded porch
4	Hall with gypsum dado
5	Corridor
6	Light-well
7	Room with benches
8	Room of the stone lamps
9–10	Rooms of the tripod tables
11	Room with triglyph bench
12	Room of the offering-tables
13	Storage bins
14	Room of the ritual finds
15	Staircase

10m

HORNS OF CONSECRATION

Reconstructed horns of consecration at Knossos.

Horns of consecration, a term invented by Sir Arthur Evans, are widely—though not universally—accepted as the stylised representation of a bull's horns. As such they are not a Minoan idea. The use of bucrania for apotropaic purposes dates from the Neolithic; instances dating to the 6th millennium BC are known from the Middle East and from northern Greece. Here an ox skull covered with a thin layer of plaster was found in a Neolithic house; it had been suspended in the middle of a room on a tall pole, from where it crashed when everything went up in a blaze.

In Crete horns of consecration first appear towards the end of the Prepalatial period, as small appliqués on models of altars and on vases, but achieve much higher visibility some 400 years later in the Second Palace period. Now they become truly monumental, like the stone ones at Knossos crowning the southwest and northwest entrances of the palace (though there is no evidence for a countless number of them side by side as Evans imagined), and on Mt Juktas on the terraces around the sanctuary. These were up to 2m in height. Examples on a smaller scale, made of a stone or clay core covered in stucco, appear in other palaces and villas in central and eastern Crete, either in ritual contexts or in storerooms, where they were deposited when not in use. Still smaller versions are represented in frescoes and on seal rings. It is possible that at this point horns of consecration were bound up with Knossos's hegemony in the religious life of the island. After the devastation of LM IB, the symbol was apparently appropriated by the new rulers, the Mycenaeans, though later it begins to feature in funerary contexts, across the whole island from Chania to Palaikastro, as a symbol of the individual power or status of the deceased. The Aghia Triada painted larnax is just one example.

At the beginning of the Postpalatial period at Knossos, when the palace authority, both secular and religious, was no more, the symbol became incorporated into the new cult that flourished in bench sanctuaries such as the 'fetish shrine' in the Little Palace. Outside Knossos, horns of consecration are found as mass-produced painted clay artefacts in caves and in open-air cult places in central and east Crete: these are now votive objects, not tokens of power.

Horns of consecration disappear in the Sub-Minoan period, but the garlanded bucranium lives on. It is found carved on public buildings among metopes and triglyphs as an element of Classical and later Roman architecture, and to this day Greek farmers still hang an ox skull at the edge of their fields for protection.

Alternative interpretations of the 'horns' include the raised arms of the goddess and the sun rising between two peaks.

While the Nirou Chani house had pretensions to luxury and was nicknamed by the archaeologists 'The House of the High Priest', it appears that before being destroyed by fire in LM IB it underwent substantial structural modifications. These included the blocking of entrances and the addition of supporting walls on the east façade and in the storerooms. It is therefore possible that the building underwent a change of function. The large number of stacked clay altars found in the store area and the double axes might mean that the place was given over to the industrial production of ritual objects, possibly connected with the nearby harbour facilities, and was being remodelled for commercial purposes when it met its end.

THE SKOTEINO CAVE & CHERSONISOS

To get to the Skoteino Cave, take the south road from Kato Gouves. The site is signposted from Gouves to the right. A 6km detour will take you to Skoteino (Σκοτεινό; *map p. 430, C1*) and then to the church of Aghia Paraskevi; the opening of the cave is next to it. There are gates but the entrance to the cave is normally unlocked. The cave is a complex of four levels connected by sloping and slippery corridors for a total length of 160m. The name means dark—and dark indeed it is when you reach the third level. Modern visitors have compared the experience to descending into the womb of mother earth; ancient Cretans obviously felt the same way. They worshipped here, at least according to the finds, from MM I well into Roman times. Analysis of the pottery suggests ritual eating and drinking but a limited catchment area: worshippers were mainly local. The Venetian church nearby suggests that the appeal of the cave endured into the Middle Ages. First investigated by Evans, Skoteino Cave was excavated by Kostis Davaras in 1962. He recovered three Neopalatial bronze votive figurines in the characteristic pose of salutation to the goddess, with the right hand raised to the forehead. These are now in Herakleion. The shapely stalactites that have inspired visitors over the centuries are still there.

The mouth of the Aposelemis
The Aposelemis river, actually more of a torrent, was believed in antiquity to be the exit of the Chonos on Lasithi (*see p. 202*). Bird-watchers will be amply rewarded by a stop here. The site is not a beauty spot. It may be part of Natura 2000, an EU programme to create a network of protected sites for migrant birds, but the scheme unfortunately does not exclude human activity from the area, which is, indeed, a rubbish dump in places; but birds on the move do not care. The wetland is also used for alternative pursuits, as the seizure of a large haul of cannabis by the Greek police in 2007 testifies.

Chersonisos
The present Limenas Chersonisou (Λιμένας Χερσονήσου; *map p. 430, D1*), the official name of Chersonisos, owes its fortune to its sheltered harbour away from the treacherous north wind which made it, in antiquity, the only safe place for ships between Herakleion and Elounda. It was the port of Lyttos (inscriptions refer to it as 'Lyttos on the sea'), 15km inland, and it flourished in Graeco-Roman times, issuing its own coins

from the 4th century BC. A temple to Britomartis on the Kastri headland on the harbour is quoted in Strabo in his *Geography* (*10.4.14*), and indeed an inscription to the goddess, whose image frequently also appears on Chersonisos' coins, has been found in the vicinity. Remains of the Hellenistic and Roman harbours are now underwater. Standing by the much-restored **Roman fountain** along the waterfront and looking at Kastri, remains of the **Roman quay** follow roughly the present harbour defences. The Roman harbour works consisted of massive breakwaters made with large boulders edged on the inside with concrete moles that served as quays. Immediately to the south, large dressed blocks are the remains of the **Hellenistic harbour works**.

The fountain, with remains of a 2nd–3rd-century mosaic of a fishing scene, was fed by aqueduct from **Xerokamares** near Potamies (*map p. 430, C1*), where remains are still visible. The Kastri headland, probably the acropolis in Classical period, was walled in late antiquity; the 5th-century **triple-aisled basilica**, one of the largest in Crete, with a fine floor mosaic, was the seat of the bishop (the presence of a bishop is attested at Chersonisos in the 5th–8th centuries). With a landmark like that, seafarers probably did not need a lighthouse. On its seaward side, the headland meets the sea with a flat rock-shelf into which **fish tanks** (now submerged) were cut in Roman times. Three of them (the largest 4m by 3m) can be seen at the east end. They were originally walled. Here fish were kept fresh for export by a system of channels ensuring a continuous water supply. The rest of the Roman town has all but disappeared under the relentless tourist development, though ancient public buildings were still visible in the 16th century and remains of the theatre could be seen as recently as 1897. As a port, Chersonisos was too exposed to Saracen raids and was eventually abandoned. The inhabitants resettled inland, to another Chersonisos, now called Old Chersonisos to distinguish it from the present town, which has been booming since the 1950s. Visitors will find an 18-hole golf course, water parks, a large aquarium and Fun Beach and the usual array of clubs and discos.

Lychnostasis Museum

For those with different inclinations and an interest in the traditional life and rural economy of Crete, a visit to the **Lychnostasis Open Air Museum** (*open April–Oct Tues–Sun 9.30–2; entrance charge covers a return visit on another day*) is a good alternative. The museum is on the coast road, well signed a short distance towards the town centre from the eastern end of the bypass. The display is centred on the collection of a local professor of ophthalmology and is laid out around his family's former summer home. It aims at preserving Crete's fast-disappearing heritage and traditional way of life. Chersonisos is certainly an appropriate site considering the huge impact of the tourist industry in the area. The museum houses exhibits on traditional architecture, furnishings, domestic equipment, customs and occupations. The museum also displays work by Cretan folk artists and offers live dance performances as well as educational programmes for adults and children. There are regular guided tours, also in English.

South of Chersonisos the land climbs steeply to an almost empty plateau edged on the west by the road into Lasithi via Potamies. It is well worth exploring for a quiet day in the cool. A steep, winding minor road leads inland from Stalida, east of Chersonisos, to **Mo-**

chos (Μοχός; *map p. 430, D1*), an isolated village with a large, shady plateia. Olaf Palme used to holiday here (Villa Palme is now a pilgrimage destination for Swedish visitors).

MALIA

From Chersonisos the coast road continues east to Malia (Μάλια; *map p. 430, D1*), now a resort of beaches, pool bars and 'famous night life'. The archaeological site, the Minoan palace, is 3km east of the town, signed from the main road towards the sea. The area is particularly attractive because of the rich red colour of the soil contrasting with the severe greyness of Mt Selena (1560m), which rises to the south.

HISTORY OF MALIA

The ancient name of the settlement is not known and the association with Minos' brother Sarpedon is the stuff of legend. A long archaeological investigation, begun in 1915 by Joseph Hatzidakis and continued since the early 1920s by the French School in Athens, has revealed a settlement going back to the Neolithic and peaking in the MM period, when the Old Palace as well as a number of semi-public buildings were erected. Only limited remains of the Old Palace have been identified, though levels belonging to that date are known. A sword of this period, with a pommel covered with a stippled sheet of gold with a repoussé figure making the full circle with its body in a backwards leap (the Sword of the Acrobat), was found under the floor in the northwest sector of the later palace. A town, possibly walled, extended around the Old Palace according to a system of radiating paved roads.

The Old Palace was damaged in an earthquake at the end of MM II. The New Palace that replaced it went through at least two phases before being destroyed at the end of LM IB. After violent destruction some 200 years later, the rebuilt Neopalatial settlement was smaller. Controversy about the final days of Malia still rages among French archaeologists: was the palace destroyed at the same time as the town? Opinions are divided, with a slight preference for some occupation lingering on in the palace by the time the town was deserted, not later than LM IB. Reoccupation has been identified in *quartiers* E and Nu, where Linear B tablets were found.

Like the other contemporary sites caught up in the great catastrophe of the LM I period, Malia town as well as the palace were undergoing repairs when disaster struck; entrances were being blocked, remodelling was going on and changes of use were taking place. Security was a problem. On the other hand, Malia stands out in Minoan architecture for the type of building material used: local stone (*sideropetra*, a type of grey limestone, and *ammouda*, or sandstone), abundant rubble and mud-brick. This explains why part of the site is sheltered under lofty covers, which unfortunately have not proved a solution to all the conservation problems.

THE PALACE

At the time of writing visitors may only visit the Palace and view the Crypt and Agora. Quartier Mu (*see map on p. 125*), with its daring, futuristic covers, is closed to the public. The site (*open Tues–Sun 8.30–3*) is equipped with an excellent preliminary display showing maquettes of the ruins, of the reconstructed Palace and of Quartier Mu, and complemented by plans, aerial photos, illustrations of finds and exhaustive explanations. The display greatly adds to an understanding of the site.

The ground-plan of the New Palace is very similar to the other Minoan palaces, with a Central Court and the West Court. It belongs to the second phase. The visit starts from the North Wing, through the main entrance situated in that area, as at Zakros and Knossos. Note the double system of massive **thresholds (1)**: they mark a narrowing of the entrance. Immediately to the east is a row of small **rooms for storage (2)**. Beyond is the **Northwest Court (3)**, opening off which a room **(4)** yielded metalwork (bronze tools and daggers). Across the hall is the **Oblique Room (5)** with a completely different alignment, a later construction dated to the latter part of the 14th century BC, after the destruction. Some form of lunar observation has been proposed for this structure, though it was roofed, which makes this unlikely. At the south end of it, up three steps, are traces of the **Keep (6)**. To the east is the residential area, with typical Minoan features: light-wells and pier-and-door partitions. To the west are a small **Paved Hall (7)** and a **Lustral Basin (8)**. The Sword of the Acrobat (*see History, above*) was found under the floor in a room west of this area, while the **Palace Archives (9)**, with tablets in Linear A and Cretan hieroglyphs, were south of it.

The **Central Court**, measuring 48m by 22m, compares well with those of the other palaces, and is oriented north-northeast–south-southwest, as in Knossos and Phaistos. It may originally have been completely or partially paved. The feature in the middle has been interpreted as a bothros or sacred pit. It was found lined with mud brick and with four stands of the same material in it. It is aligned with the Pillar Crypt in the West Wing (*see below*) and may have been associated with the cult activities taking place there. Some 600kg of charred lentils and the remains of ten pithoi were found in the north portico area. Perhaps parts of the Central Court had been turned over to storage at the time of abandonment.

The West Wing was divided by a **corridor (10)**: to the east of it, facing the Central Court, was a ceremonial cult area, and to the west were stores. In the former, note the **Hall of the Leopard (11)**, where a fine mace with a leopard's head was found hidden in a vase together with a bronze bracelet, a dagger and a sword with a rock crystal pommel (now in Herakleion Archaeological Museum) and the **Pillar Crypt (12)**, with cult symbols carved on the pillars. It originally looked east through a porch into the Central Court. Later the opening was closed and the width of the court reduced.

A large doorway with a bronze pivot suggesting an impressive construction led to the first floor via the **Northwest Staircase (13)**. Immediately to the north of it, a small

Malia in springtime, overgrown with tall grasses and blue alkanet.

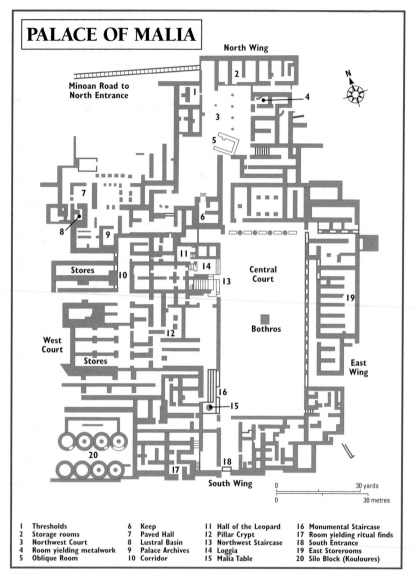

PALACE OF MALIA

North Wing

Minoan Road to
North Entrance

Central
Court

Bothros

West
Court

Stores

East
Wing

Stores

South Wing

0   30 yards
0   30 metres

1	Thresholds	6	Keep	11	Hall of the Leopard	16 Monumental Staircase
2	Storage rooms	7	Paved Hall	12	Pillar Crypt	17 Room yielding ritual finds
3	Northwest Court	8	Lustral Basin	13	Northwest Staircase	18 South Entrance
4	Room yielding metalwork	9	Palace Archives	14	Loggia	19 East Storerooms
5	Oblique Room	10	Corridor	15	Malia Table	20 Silo Block (Kouloures)

room is known as the **Loggia (14)**. It stands on a platform and has steps descending into the court. Researchers have suggested some form of ceremonial purpose for it, or even that it might have been the setting for the epiphany of the goddess, with the little room behind as a 'robing room'.

At the south end of the Central Court is the **Malia Table (15)**, a round limestone object with 34 hollows set around a large central one. It is displayed where it was found, on the floor of a paved terrace. It has been interpreted as a cult object (*kernos*) connected with the offering of the first fruits and alternatively, by more imaginative commentators, as a solilunar calendar or a clock. The whole area was devoted to some cult activity. To the north of it are the lower steps of a **Monumental Staircase (16)**. **Room 17** is one of the few places where objects were found *in situ*. These included a small altar with incised signs, tripod tables, tubular vases, shells, lamps and two terracotta feet. The unfinished stone vases found in an adjoining room also indicate some activity cut short by a sudden event.

Above: Stairway in the East Wing, leading to an upper floor formerly above the storage area.

Below: The kernos known as the Malia Table.

The South Wing lies to either side of the **South Entrance (18)**: judging by the finds, the area was devoted to cult activity. It has several mud-brick walls suggesting very late alterations. The **East Wing (19)** was used for storage. It was fronted to the west by a portico of alternating columns and pilasters. At some point (the date is not certain) the use of the area was switched from liquid storage (oil and wine) to the storage of solid foodstuffs. An earth floor was laid above an earlier one that had collecting vessels and gutters; grain was stored here, to be found charred 3,500 years later.

Considering its overall size (8000 square metres, smaller than the other main palaces), Malia had a lot of storage space. The **Silo Block (20)** in the southwestern corner (access by the West Court), with its eight kouloures and which was probably originally roofed, added an estimated

4000 hectolitres to the storage capacity of the palace. The venue was short on frescoes though, and generally speaking on high-status finds. It is possible that repairs and refurbishment were not complete at the time of the final destruction. What fresco fragments have been found—and they are not numerous—may have belonged to the previous construction. Only on one occasion is a fragment with a human figure mentioned, found somewhere in the West Wing. It appears that at the time of destruction part of the building had been blocked off and abandoned, a circumstance paralleled by evidence from the town.

Northwest of the palace, the complex known as the **Agora** was excavated in the 1960s. It is aligned to the cemetery of Chrysolakkos (*see below*) and was in use in the First Palace period. It is basically a walled building (the remains of houses on the east side have a later, Neopalatial date) arranged around a large courtyard (29m by 40m). Note the three entrances. The northeast gate faces the direction of the cemetery. The access to the upper floor of the complex, known as the **Hypostyle Crypt**, is via the southwest gate; the roofing is intended to protect the plastered walls. The building consisted of two interconnected halls with benches on three sides. Finds have been scarce; not so hypotheses and interpretations: these range from a 'council chamber' in operation at the time of the Old Palace, to a storage place for olive oil.

THE TOWN

In contrast with Phaistos and Knossos, where only the areas in immediate proximity to the palaces have been investigated, the town at Malia has been extensively explored, uncovering houses and street systems. **Quartier Mu** (they all have Greek letters and French denominations) west of the Palace is by far the most interesting; unfortunately at the time of writing it was not accessible. It can only be viewed from behind the outer fence.

Early building activity at Malia (from EM III to MM II) is generally represented by simple structures. Not so at Quartier Mu. Here the style is clearly palatial and a sign of the things to come in Minoan Crete. The Central House, the largest of three, a 450 square-metre building has some 30 rooms, and that is just the ground floor. Stairs led to the upper storeys. There are provisions for liquid storage with elaborate drainage systems, buried jars and channels, and evidence of writing. The very earliest lustral basin in Crete, a regular feature of the later palaces, is here. Industrial, storage, ritual and residential areas are segregated. The architecture includes ashlar masonry and cut stone column bases.

The finds (some of which can be seen at Aghios Nikolaos museum), including numerous stone vessels, bronze bowls and cauldrons and a hieroglyphic archive, are equally revealing. Ceremonial weapons have also been found and they include a dagger with a gold pommel worked in what appears to be a precursor of the cloisonné technique. The pommel had regular round perforations on its entire surface and it is assumed that it was studded with multicoloured beads and stones. The emerging Middle Minoan elite lived here. Opposite, on the other side of a narrow road, smiths, potters, stonemasons and seal engravers toiled away for their masters producing the

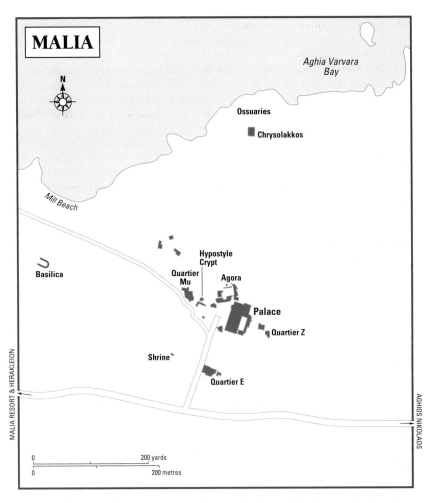

goods emblematic of their new, elevated status. In the workshops, an unfinished kernos was found at the stonemason's while at the potter's, figurines, miniature vases and offering-tables, as well as shell and *agrimi* horns, showed a production centre for goods related to cult activities.

Neopalatial developments in the town can be seen in **Quartier E**, immediately south of the palace along the road to the car park to the east. Here stood a large house with a north entrance, a portico, a hall with pier-and-door partitions, a lustral basin with niches and evidence of painted plaster. The house, remodelled in LM II with the addition of a pillar room and a hearth on the east side, was re-occupied in LM III after the destruction of the palace.

GLYPTIC ART

The art of making seals is named after the Greek work for engraving precious stones, but it is not a Greek idea. It comes from Mesopotamia and it is strictly linked to the requirements of a stratified society with a complex administration. Seals are found in structures connected with authority: in palaces and villas and also in high-status graves. The first seals were pyramidal in shape with a perforation at the top and an incised drawing at the base. They would have been strung and worn around the neck or the wrist. Many shapes developed from this, sometimes dictated by the material used (ring seals, for instance, were made of segments of long bones) or by personal requirements, which may explain why there are polyhedral seals with as many as six surfaces. Cylinder seals, that is the Mesopotamian type, are known in Crete, but they are a minority.

Materials are extremely varied. Ivory (hippopotamus or elephant) had to be imported. Recent analysis of the 'ivory' category has reclassified a number of seals to animal bone and boar's tusk, which would have been available locally. Hard and semi-precious stones like amethyst, jasper and cornelian were used, as well as steatite, which is softer. The choice of tools included bronze chisels that blunt quickly, obsidian blades that fared better and, later, drills. Over time, alternative solutions were worked out. The 'whitepieces' common in the Mesara were made of a paste of pulverised steatite and adhesive fired at 850 degrees, then incised and glazed; at the other end of the market there was gold.

For a craftsman, seal-making could be a full-time occupation. In Quartier Mu in Malia, alongside a potter who specialised in making moulded votive objects, the workshop of a seal-maker was found. It contained 150 seals and a supply of raw material (rock crystal and steatite); from the offcuts it seems that he specialised in prismatic seals with three incised surfaces.

THE CEMETERY AT CHRYSOLAKKOS

The meaning of the site ('pit of gold') is a great giveaway: its contents were clearly known before the archaeologists got here. The site is immediately north of the Palace, not far from the sea. It would originally have been further inland. This part of the north coast has been sinking over time and the islet of Aghia Varvara, on which a Minoan farmhouse has been excavated, would have been part of the mainland. To the east further remains are known, including a workshop of the Old Palace period. Present-day swimmers have encountered underwater hazards in the bay, suggesting old port installations.

Chrysolakkos cemetery was in use mainly in the MM period. It had a large rectangular enclosure built in dressed limestone blocks and divided into several compartments surrounded by a paved area. The east façade had a portico. The purpose of the structure is debated. In Prepalatial times this was already a burial ground and, judging

The so-called Bee Pendant, showing two golden wasps, dated c. 2000–1600 BC. Found at Chrysolakkos, it is now in Herakleion Museum.

by the high-status finds, may have been used for royalty. The later structures though, belonging to the Old Palace phase (which is the one that can be seen), have no parallel among funerary structures on the island. The list of finds, with clay figurines and a stuccoed altar, suggests a cult area or a sanctuary. The famous gold pendant with the bees (or wasps) holding a berry (on display at Herakleion Archaeological Museum Temporary Exhibition) comes from this area. It shows the use of metal granulation, a technique imported from Mesopotamia or Syria-Palestine.

East of Chrysolakkos the path follows the line of defensive walls built at the beginning of the New Palace period. At Mill Beach to the west (*see map on p. 125*), by a small peninsula with the ruins of a mill, are the remains of a large Minoan harbour. The whole coastal area is under pressure for development and it is hoped that the archaeologists will be able to carry out investigations before developers move in. South of the beach the remains of an early Christian basilica, dated to the 6th–7th centuries and built on top of a tomb with an imported Attic sarcophagus of the 2nd century AD but reused in a later context, cover the last period of activity in the area.

After Malia, the E75 cuts through to Neapolis and Aghios Nikolaos (26km). To the south an alternative scenic road into Lasithi starts at the bypass in Neapolis.

NB: For the far east of Herakleion province and the approach to the Lasithi Plateau, see p. 204.

PRACTICAL INFORMATION

GETTING AROUND

• **By car:** The New National Road runs along the whole of the coast. For Limenas Chersonisou (28km) keep left on the old road at Gournes. For Malia (34km) go straight on, the site is 3km east of the modern town. For Amnisos take the old road in the direction of the airport from the archaeological museum in Herakleion. It runs through the suburbs of Poros, Katsambas and Nea Alikarnassos, skirts the airport and then descends to the beach.

• **By bus:** From bus stop on the north side of Plateia Eleftherias in Herakleion, bus 7 goes to Amnisos and to a choice of beaches in the summer (blue ticket). In other seasons long-distance buses on the E75 make request stops. For Chersonisos and Malia there are services from Herakleion Bus Station A. There are also services to Malia archaeological site (the Aghios Nikolaos bus will stop there on request).

WHERE TO STAY & EAT

For those who want to be near the sea the coast offers plenty of choice, ranging from luxury hotels to rooms to rent. From Chersonisos to Malia the coast is a non-stop tourist development with plenty of accommodation to choose from (see www.travelinfo.gr/her.htm for a list; note that some may not be open year-round; most may not be precisely what you had in mind).

Accommodation inland is more sparse but preferable; the land is higher and it is cooler and altogether more pleasant in the summer.

Amnisos (*map p. 430, C1*)
€€€ **AKS Minoa Palace**. Completely modern with swimming pool. *T: 2810 300330 or 220088, www.ellada.net/minoapal.*
€€€ **Karteros Hotel**. Near the beach, with swimming pool and a bus stop for city and long-distance buses nearby. *T: 2810 380402 or 380522, www.karteros.gr.*
Chani Kokkini (*map p. 430, C1*)
€€ **Kamari Hotel**. A holiday resort in a quiet place near the famous sandy beach. *T: 2810 761340 or 761002, www.kamari-hotel.kokkini-hani.com.*
(Old) Chersonisos (*map p. 430, C1*)
€€ **Village Apartment Villa Medusa**. Self-catering up on the hills in the old village. *T: 28970 22624.*
Mochos (*map p. 430, D1*)
€ **Mary Hotel**. A family-run modern hotel with pool on the outskirts of Mochos, well up on top of the escarpment but within easy reach of the excellent tavernas in the village. *T: 28970 61534 or 61526; www.hotelmary.gr.*
Piskopiano (*map p. 430, D1*)
€€ **Palatia Village**. The address is Chersonisos but the complex is 1km away from the beach in a quiet inland location. *T: 28970 22017, www.palatia.gr.*

On the coast the best food is at the tavernas closest to the Malia archaeological site to the west of it. Inland, try the two tavernas at **Krasi** (*map p. 430, D2*), driving due south from Malia towards Lasithi. One is by the Venetian fountain and the immense plane tree (Platanos); the other one immediately below to the right (Kares). Both offer traditional Cretan food of very good quality.

WEST OF HERAKLEION

From Herakleion there is the choice of two roads leading west. On the coast, the New Road, the E75, will take you to beaches and to the Almyros Gorge (though not the finest the island has to offer, it is good walking country and the body of water is a good place for bird-watchers). Palaiokastro and Rogdia along on the way are of interest because of their Venetian heritage. Inland the old road west is more scenic and highly recommended. It is a slow drive and rightly so: it should be savoured and enjoyed. Minoan remains are on the way at Tylissos. The drive to Rethymnon, barely 80km, runs through beautiful countryside with vineyards, becoming more rugged later as it skirts the north slopes of Mt Ida. From Herakleion the exploration of the slopes of Ida can be a long operation. It is better to be based closer by.

THE COAST ROAD

Leave Herakleion at the Chania Gate. At Gazi continue north and some 5km later, after the Pantanassa bridge, watch out on the right for the ruins (*signed*) of the Venetian castle, built just before the beach in 1573 to fend off pirates. The **Palaiokastro** (*map p. 430, B1*) can be visited following a narrow path along a precipitous and spectacular cliff edge, but the parking on the busy road is not ideal. The archway of the main entrance, partly carved in the rock, is still extant. The rest is in a sorry state. For a full view of the well-preserved foundation work, drive down to the beach at the end of the bridge (*parking and taverna*) and take a swim out about 50m. The small cove has been blighted by the road bridge above it, but the sea is good.

Rogdia looks down on you from on high. To get there, retrace your steps a couple of kilometres and wind your way up. You will be rewarded with a splendid view of the bay of Herakleion and the island of Dia, marred only by the ugly motorway bridge.

Rogdia

Rogdia (Ρογδιά; *map p. 430, B1*) was the centre of a Venetian feudal estate belonging to the Kallergis family, originally from Byzantium but later much linked to Venice (*see pp. 17 and 18*). In the village, the Kallergis mansion and church have now been restored. The complex is organised around a courtyard, which had a monumental entrance to the east which Gerola photographed; today it is no more. It consisted of a rusticated archway set in a circuit wall incorporating the tympanum in its profile. The house, built in local slate with two storeys, is grand by Cretan standards; the church is set at right angles to it and can only be entered via the courtyard. It has a very fine marble door frame and decorative arches. House and church are presumed to be contemporary, although the church has Byzantine features and could be earlier. The chapel next to it and completely separate from it is much later (1809 according to the inscription on the doorway).

Moni Savathianon

From the entrance to the village a signed 5km drive to the northwest leads to Moni Savathianon (*map p. 430, B1; open daily 8–1 & 4–7, daylight permitting*), a Venetian foundation at the end of a valley among tall trees. After the entrance gates, the red-roofed Aghios Antonios protects the grotto, the original nucleus of the monastery. The main church is the Panaghia nearby, dated to 1635. An old bridge has a 1535 inscription. The monastery suffered greatly at the time of the Turkish invasion. During the siege of Candia the monks fought so fiercely that they were sold into slavery in Africa by the victorious Ottomans. Only the intervention of the patriarch secured their return to their ravaged monastery.

Apart from the beauty of the place, the shady trees and the hospitality of the 20 or so nuns, the main attraction of the location is an icon that resurfaced here in 1991. It was known through old records and had last been seen in 1854 but was believed lost. When it was found it was in a very poor state but after careful restoration it has been attributed to Ioannis Kornaros (1745–96). The theme is the same one that the painter developed in his well-known masterpiece at Moni Toplou, dated 1770 (*see p. 265*). It is generally believed that this icon is a forerunner of it. Kornaros belonged to a family originally of Venetian extraction but assimilated to Crete over the years. He started his life as a painter at this monastery and later worked also at Moni Toplou, in Cyprus, in Sinai and perhaps also in Egypt. The icon is known by the first words of the Orthodox prayer for the sanctification of water: 'Thou art Great, O Lord', traditionally attributed to Sophronius, 7th-century patriarch of Jerusalem. It depicts many figures, unusually for an icon, and covers as many as 61 themes from the Old and New Testaments. The style blends Byzantine and Western influences.

Lygaria and Aghia Pelagia

Back on the main road, the drive continues to some interesting beaches. **Lygaria** (*map p. 430, B1; Λυγαριά*) can be a good choice. Further west is **Aghia Pelagia** (*map p. 430, B1; Αγία Πελαγία*), now a fully developed tourist resort, which is the reason why Achlada up on the hills is semi-deserted. People have moved where the jobs are.

Classical and Hellenistic ruins have come to light in the area of Aghia Pelagia, and a tentative identification with the city-state of Apollonia has been proposed, though Gazi, to the south, is another contender. Ancient Apollonia came to grief in 171 BC when the Kydonians (from modern Chania), who were their friends and allies, paid a surprise visit. They came off the boats and slaughtered the Apollonians as they rushed to the beach to welcome them with open arms (Polybius, *28, 14*). After the event the site was fought over by Gortyn and Knossos, which eventually led to Roman diplomatic intervention. A hundred years later the whole island fell to Rome.

Fodele

The road continues inland and meets the sea again at Fodele beach. The village of that

The church of the Panaghia Loubinies at Fodele.

name (Φόδελε; *map p. 430, B1*) is some 2km uphill. Traditionally this is the birthplace of Domenikos Theotokopoulos (better known as El Greco), but opinions vary and scholars now believe he was born in Herakleion. The University of Valladolid in Spain, the city where the painter lived and worked for the last 38 years of his life, seems to believe, though, that some of El Greco's magic lingers here: they have erected a bilingual inscription in his honour at the end of the main street by the stream. For the **Panaghia Loubinies**, cross the stream by the larger village bridge. It leads southwest to the church, a few hundred metres on. It is dedicated to the Birth of the Virgin, celebrated on 8th September. The plan is cross-in-square with a dome supported by a drum lit by 11 narrow windows and built into the central nave of an earlier 8th-century basilica. It is possible to see traces of the apses and of the medieval village that was built around the church. Several layers of frescoes have been uncovered in the latest restoration. They show a variety of styles. The oldest, in the sanctuary, is 13th-century Venetian; frescoes in the south cross-arm include a donor inscription dated 1323.

Further inland from Fodele, the road leads through unspoilt countryside to the former monastery of **Aghios Pandeleimonos**, a Venetian foundation. The church is still operating but the best icons have been moved to the Historical Museum in Herakleion for safety. The surrounding buildings are farmsteads. From here visitors can drive on to Rethymnon along the coast and visit Moni Atalis (*see p. 285*), a flourishing monastery overlooking Bali and signposted from the highway (*closed Fri*) or rejoin the old road down a partly unpaved track from the monastery itself.

ON THE OLD ROAD

Taking the old road from Gazi, Tylissos is the next main stop, but on the way keep an eye out for two interesting features. The first, west of Gazi, 3km on, is the **Voulismeno Aloni** (*map p. 430, B1*), meaning 'sunken threshing floor'. In fact this is not a threshing floor at all, but an area of subsidence some 90m in diameter, in fact a cave whose roof collapsed some time in the Pleistocene era. Smaller examples of the phenomenon, which is caused by rainwater dissolving limestone, can be seen elsewhere in Crete, on Mt Ida for instance. This one is 60m deep (there is a path leading to the bottom from the southwest). A very large instance of the same phenomenon is the Lasithi plateau itself.

The other curiosity is the **Koumbedes Café**, by the roadside to the right shortly after the new and the old road part company. The structure, now fully restored, has two domes (its name means 'cupola' in Turkish), which has spawned the legend that it was formerly a hamam, a steam bath. In reality it was a wayside inn, where in Venetian and later in Turkish times, travellers halted if they could not reach Herakleion before the town gates were locked. The domes were probably a device to dissipate heat. It is now a café offering musical entertainment most evenings. Tylissos is signed to the left and the drive takes you across the district of Malevisi, famous in Venetian times for its wine, Malvesey or Malmsey (*see box opposite*).

MALMSEY

This sweet dessert wine of Shakespearean memory (the Duke of Clarence was famously drowned in a butt of Malmsey in the Tower of London) may originally have come from the Monemvasia region in the southeast Peloponnese, but by the 15th century it was regarded in Europe as a Cretan product. It was widely exported to Venice, England and the Netherlands. When Henry VIII appointed the first English consul to Candia, Crete was the second wine exporter to England. The first was France, whose wine was half the price. What made the fortune of Malmsey, apart from a European sweet tooth, was that this wine was stable because of its high sugar content and travelled comparatively well. It was made sweet not by the old-fashioned technique of allowing the grapes to dry in the sun as in Roman times, but by being stewed in cauldrons, as the French naturalist Bellon testified. An alternative technique, producing something akin to Madeira and sherry and involving blending different vintages, was used only for wine exported to Venice.

By the 16th century one third of cultivable land in Crete was vineyard and Venice had to intervene to foster wheat production. Soon enough, however, the Malmsey trade diminished. With the introduction of corked glass bottles, it became easier for any wine, sweet or not, to travel, and the peace with Spain made the fortunes of the sherry and sack producers at the expense of Crete. Though wine continued to be produced on the island, output went into grave decline under the Ottomans.

TYLISSOS

Tylissos (Τύλισος; *map p. 430, B1; site open Tues–Sun 9–3; signposted from the village; parking is tight*) is the site of one of the major Minoan settlements in north central Crete. It is overlooked by a peak sanctuary that remained in use into the Neopalatial period. Known since the 19th century because of the chance find of four huge bronze cauldrons, the site was first excavated in 1909–13 by Joseph Hatzidakis; Nikolaos Platon took over between 1953 and 1955 and finally Anastasia Kanta worked here in 1971. The main features are three high-status Neopalatial buildings, destroyed by fire in LM 1B. As at Knossos and at Aghia Triada, the site was later reoccupied early in LM IIIA, when it flourished. Further activity is noted in Classical times, with the reuse of earlier material. In the Classical era Tylissos was a city-state with its own coins.

Soundings have revealed that the town is quite extensive and that occupation goes back to the EM period. Unfortunately there have not been further systematic excavations, which hampers a full understanding of the remains. The site is now practically in the middle of the village, with the built-up area reaching to its edges.

Houses A and B

House A, perhaps the best understood, was entered from the east into a peristyle court

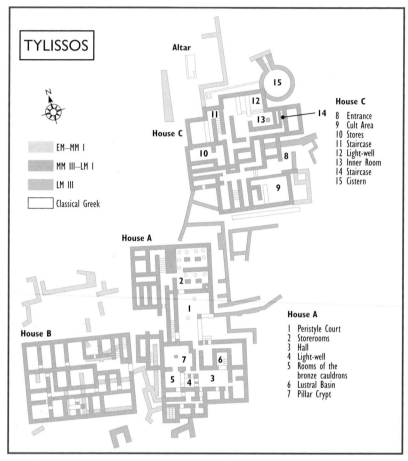

TYLISSOS

Altar

House C

N

EM–MM I
MM III–LM I
LM III
Classical Greek

House C

8 Entrance
9 Cult Area
10 Stores
11 Staircase
12 Light-well
13 Inner Room
14 Staircase
15 Cistern

House A

House B

House A

1 Peristyle Court
2 Storerooms
3 Hall
4 Light-well
5 Rooms of the
    bronze cauldrons
6 Lustral Basin
7 Pillar Crypt

(**1**) which linked the two wings. Immediately to the north, two large rooms (**2**) were used as stores with pithoi set into the floor. The rectangular pillars supported an upper floor reached by a staircase off the main hall. The upper floor may have been residential. The jars, vases, loom weights, and a very fine bronze figurine found in the northwestern rooms probably fell from above.

The southern wing of the house is reached through a paved corridor. The rooms are set around a hall (**3**) with a light-well (**4**) surrounded by three columns. The four huge bronze cauldrons mentioned above (now in Herakleion) came from the two little rooms (**5**) immediately west of the light well. Clay sealings and Linear A tablets suggest that this was a store or a treasury. The Minoan Hall itself did not yield anything significant but its architecture confirms the high status of the building, with pier-and-door (polythyron) partitions and a lustral basin (**6**) in the area to the north. A staircase led to the upper floor. The portico to the north of the light-well leads to a pillar crypt **(7)** where the excavators found pyramidal stands for double axes similar to those recovered in the corridor of the West Magazines in Knossos.

House B has a much simpler design. It may have been an annexe and probably predates House A. It has storage rooms but little was found apart from a large collection of LM I vases.

House C

House C is the best of the three, with store-rooms, a possible shrine and residential area. The complex is difficult to interpret because of later Doric activity, when much of the material was reused to build a structure similar to Aghia Triada's megaron on top of it. The building, with pier-and-door partitions and other high-status features, had over 20 rooms on the ground floor with three flights of stairs leading

Pithoi at Tylissos.

up. The entrance **(8)** is on the east side with a cult area immediately to the left around a room with a central pillar **(9)**. The stores **(10)** are on the west (the column base belongs to later occupation). The staircase **(11)** is in two styles: the lower part belongs to the original Neopalatial house, the upper part was remodelled in the Classical period. The north end is residential with a light-well **(12)**. The inner room **(13)** received light through an internal window, now restored. The transverse corridor south of it leads east to a staircase **(14)** and a toilet with a drain through the outer wall.

To the northeast of the building is a stone cistern **(15)** of slightly later date. It has walk-in steps like the one at Zakros. It was connected to the aqueduct carrying the water from the spring at Aghios Mamas. Clay pipes have been found some 38m to the northwest of the house. The present village is still using the same water source. The altar to the north is a later development. It originally stood in a courtyard paved with flagstones and stands on top of an earlier building.

There has been much speculation about the quasi-palatial character of these buildings. The site is too close to Knossos to have been in competition with it; Evans's original explanation for buildings like this, namely that they were summer residences for the Knossos ruling elite, resulted in a glut of summer palaces and is now discredited. More likely the houses, or at least two of them, were the residences of minor officials.

SKLAVOKAMBOS & KAMARIOTES

From Tylissos a country road leads west in the Gonies direction to a **Minoan country house** (7km) overlooking the open plain of Sklavokambos (*signed by the road*). The architectural style of this Neopalatial building, excavated by Marinatos, is quite different from that of Tylissos. Floors are unpaved, masonry is cruder, and there is abundant provision for storage. In the north façade a pillared veranda opened onto the valley; in the south a small open court with three pillars supported a peristyle roof. It has been suggested that the building was connected with Knossos' trade to the west. Indeed, the discovery of several clay sealings with bull-leaping scenes similar to those from Aghia Triada, Gournia and Zakros supports the hypothesis. The area is fertile and also has outcrops of serpentine, much used in antiquity for the manufacture of stone vases.

From Sklavokambos an 8km drive into the mountains to the north among the pines and the chestnut trees, leads to **Kamariotis** (Καμαριώτης; *map p. 430, B1*), a remote village with a couple of pretty fountains in its main square. The church of Aghios Georgios is up on the hill overlooking the village. The tone is set by the Kallergis eagle on the outside of the apse window. Inside, beyond the narthex, is the *pièce de résistance*: a Gothic archway with three twisted polychrome columns at either side. On the architrave two blue and white Kallergis crests flank a lion of St Mark. Here a Latin bishopric replaced an Orthodox one. All this is completely irrelevant to Kamariotis's other claim to fame. As tradition recalls, in 1645 a local child, Evmenia Vergitzi, was kidnapped and taken to Istanbul where she entered the sultan's harem; she went on to become the first and favourite wife of Mehmed IV and the mother of two sultans. By then she had changed her name and probably also her religion.

PRACTICAL INFORMATION

GETTING AROUND

• **By bus:** From Bus Station A in Herakleion (*T: 2810 245020; www.crete-buses.gr*), by the harbour, there are several departures for Rethymnon with stops at the coastal sites. From the bus station by the Chanioporta a limited number of routes go to Rogdia.

WHERE TO STAY & EAT

Most accommodation is on the coast. Huge compounds with all mod cons exist in Lygaria and in Aghia Pelagia. For something simpler try € **Amoudi Apartments** (*T: 2810 811339*

or *811478*) at Made, a small village before Lygaria. € **Vivi's** (*T: 2810 811747 or 811748*) offers rooms to rent above the supermarket in Made. € **Zorba's Rooms** (*T: 2810 256072*) is a simple place in Aghia Pelagia. The best **tavernas** are in Lygaria along the beach.

For the Arolithos 'traditional' village (*map p. 430, B1*), see p. 56.

FESTIVALS & EVENTS

The **Koumbedes Café and Restaurant** (*T: 2810 821509*), 2km west of Gazi just before Arolithos on the right, offers live Cretan music (*normally Mon, Tues, Fri, Sun*).

SOUTH OF HERAKLEION
& THE MESARA PLAIN

This chapter covers the countryside southwest of Herakleion, starting with the Archaic site of Rizenia and moving onwards along minor roads to the eastern slopes of Mt Ida. It then enters the Mesara plain, where there is a string of important sites along the east–west road to Mesara Bay. Two final sections deal with the area south of this (by the sea) and north of it (on the southern slopes of Mt Ida). This is, of course, also walking country. The E4 comes in at Venerato, from where it continues east to Archanes. The eastern slopes of Mt Ida have several stretches of this particular route. It leads south to the Nida plateau and the Kamares Cave (*see p. 171*) and north to Zominthos and Anogeia (*see pp. 294–95*). Walkers should bear in mind that the slopes of Mt Ida can be a steep climb in an environment at times harsh and unforgiving.

KROUSONAS & VENERATO

Krousonas (Κρουσώνας; *map p. 430, B2*) is 14km south of Tylissos; from there it is another 2km to Moni Aghia Eirini. The drive is picturesque across vineyards first, then the climb into the mountains begins. The village sits at the top of the valley at an altitude of 460m. The monastery is signed to the south of the village.

The religious foundation of **Aghia Eirini** dates back to at least 1589. It prospered under Venetian patronage and Turkish rule and was an important centre for Hellenic education. The original buildings were destroyed by the Turks in 1822 when Crete joined the mainland in the war of independence, as revenge for the slaughter of 370 Albanian soldiers in the service of the occupying power. The Albanians had been trapped in a church in Krousonas and were shown no mercy by the locals in spite of the fact that they held a Cretan child hostage. The present buildings date from the end of the Second World War, when four nuns took up residence here and a small, self-supporting community developed. You may like to visit for coffee and cake like Cretan families do. Needlework and other craft products are for sale. To the west, an unmade road, which might eventually be surfaced, joins the south road from Anogeia to the Nida plateau. In antiquity this would have been the eastern approach to the Idaian Cave from Knossos. It might be worth making time for a hike to look for birds and flowers right now, before it is too late.

From Krousonas there is a choice of roads. An unmade road continues due south in the Aghia Varvara direction. At Kato Asites (5km) a sign marks the steep climb to **Moni Gorgolaïni** (*map p. 430, B2*), a Venetian foundation (*normally open only in the morning*). The first buildings are too recent to be of any interest but the view is superb. At Ano Asites the road crosses the E4 path. If you follow it east it takes you to Temenos and Archanes. To the west it reaches into the Ida range via the Prinos shelter, run by the Greek mountaineering Club EOS, at 1100m. As the road climbs it becomes more interesting, not least for flowers and wilderness.

Alternatively you can drive to **Pendamodi** (6km; Πενταμόδι; *map p. 430, B2*), for what was once a fine Venetian fountain, rated by Gerola as one of the best in the island. That entails taking the sharp left in the centre of Krousonas. The fountain is in the lower part of the village after the church of the Panaghia by the road. The level of the road has been raised and as a result the bottom half of the fountain has disappeared, but there are still the elegant volutes framing the coat of arms of the powerful Querini family. When Gerola visited at the beginning of the last century, he was able to photograph it in its full glory and in working order. Below the opening now closed with a metal door, it had an elaborate mascheron spouting water into a basin.

Moni Palianis and Aghios Thomas

The main north–south road passes through Venerato (Βενεράτο; *map p. 430, B2*). **Moni Palianis** (Μονή Παλιανής) is southeast of the village on the E4 hiking route. It is a very old foundation; indeed it apparently goes back to 668. The church itself is 13th-century with many later additions but it has retained the old 6th-century basilica plan. It suffered great damage both from earthquakes and from Turks, who stormed it in the 19th century and massacred the nuns. Ancient architectural fragments can be seen inside (marble columns, two 6th-century Byzantine capitals *in situ* and four supporting the altar) and outside in the courtyard. The time to visit is September 24th, when the convent holds a celebration for the Panaghia Myrtidiotissa ('Virgin of the Myrtle') in honour of an icon miraculously found under a very old myrtle tree near the southeast wall of the church after the Turks left. Now a lamp burns perennially in its branches, an echo perhaps of the Minoan tree cult. The convent is home to about 50 nuns, who make a living by selling their needlework.

Five kilometres south of Venerato on the main road, a left turn leads to **Aghios Thomas** (Άγιος Θωμάς; *map p. 430, B2*), a village that boasts an improbable number of churches, as many as 40. The church of Aghios Thomas itself is a fine three-aisled, domed construction of the Second Byzantine period. More interesting though, is the geology of the place. The spot is 530m above sea level, at the watershed, on a saddle between curious rock formations. Opposite the church (*signed to Roman tombs*) you can walk up to a good vantage point. The rocks belong to the original spine of the island connecting Ida and Dikte. Edward Lear was attracted to the place and on 16th May 1864 he sat down to sketch just after dawn among the 'great rox'. He was looking down on the village with the church of Aghios Thomas in the middle. More geology awaits on the main north–south road just below the Rizenia acropolis. The circular erosion features are locally known as 'old lady's cheeses'.

RIZENIA

The Patela of Prinias (*patela* meaning 'naked expanse') is a naturally defended position 5km south of Ano Asites. Here stood the acropolis of the Archaic city of Rizenia (Ριζηνία; *map p. 430, B2*). From this strategic position it could control the road linking the north and south coasts.

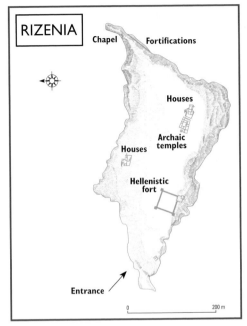

The site

There is room to park and the site is always accessible. The entrance is along the path on the north edge of the flat expanse. It leads to the small white chapel of Aghios Pandeleimon on the edge of a precipice overlooking the north–south road.

The site was first surveyed by Federico Halbherr in 1894 and then excavated by Luigi Pernier in 1906–08. Later work was carried out in 1969. The Patela is a roughly triangular expanse accessible only from the west, with occupation dating from the Postpalatial period. It is therefore a refuge site like Karphi and Vrokastro, but unlike them, it continued into the Late Hellenistic period. Older settlements have been identified at nearby Siderospilia (late 3rd millennium; *see overleaf*) and Flega (New Palace period).

On the Patela itself remains of houses, defences and lookouts dated to the Geometric period and a square **Hellenistic fort** with bastions have been identified. Excavations have concentrated on **two Archaic temples**. These are remarkable for integrating features that look back in time with others that herald the future development of Classical Greek architecture. For instance, the single central pillar between the side posts of the porch, instead of the customary arrangement of the later Greek temple with two columns, is Minoan, though some commentators have also seen an Egyptian influence, drawing parallels with mastabas. The cella, moreover, had an axis in line with the above pillar with two wooden columns on low stone bases and a hearth in between them. In the hearth a large quantity of burnt animal bones and ashes were found; the arrangement is reminiscent of the temple at Dreros (*see p. 191*). On the other hand, the sculptural ornaments speak a different language and show a sophisticated decorative scheme. Intriguingly, the combination of low reliefs from friezes with parading horsemen and the two goddesses seated in Daidalic style, originally from above the doorway into the cella (now in Herakleion), appears fully formed here, well before it is found on the Greek mainland and ultimately on the Parthenon, and with no previous inkling of any development in this direction in Crete itself. Other finds from the temples include votive terracottas with snake tubes, goddess figurines with stiff cylindrical skirts and raised arms, typically Postpalatial in style.

Taking the small white chapel as the starting point of the visit, it is possible to find, in the midst of the abundant vegetation and of the confusing clearing cairns, the remains of the temples (*fenced*) and of the Hellenistic fort, recognisable by the superior quality of its wall construction technique. A visit to the area is of interest, apart from the birds and the flowers, to appreciate fully the sheer scale of its natural defences. The Patela had no water sources and so far no cisterns have been identified.

Siderospilia

The necropolis of Siderospilia is 500m northwest of the Patela on a slope facing the acropolis. It was excavated by Italian archaeologists between 1972 and 1976. The 680 burials have revealed a cemetery in continuous use from the 13th–mid-6th centuries BC. Phases are distinguished by different burial rites. A number of crouch burials with no grave goods are thought to be much earlier and associated with the Prepalatial settlement nearby. Later burials included pit graves, inhumations in tholos tombs and cremations. Sporadic Roman activity was also observed. Two particularly well-preserved **Roman rock-cut tombs**, complete with niches and benches and cists in the floor, can be seen from the road. In the cemetery animal graves associated with tholos tombs (13th–6th centuries BC) contained carefully interred horses and the occasional dog, confirming the practice of animal sacrifice mentioned in ancient literature.

THE MESARA PLAIN

From Prinias you regain the north–south road, which winds its way south towards the Mesara plain (pron. Mesará). On the approach to the village of **Aghia Varvara** (Αγία Βαρβάρα; *map p. 430, B2*), the little church of Profitis Ilias is perched on a rock known as Omphalos ('navel'), said to be the centre of the island.

HISTORY OF THE MESARA PLAIN

The Mesara plain is an alluvial deposit stretching from the Dikte massif to Mesara Bay. It enjoys a favourable climate and a rich soil, and has been an area of agricultural prosperity since Neolithic times. It boomed in the Early Bronze Age with settlement spreading along the slopes of the Asterousia range. The monumental collective tholos tombs of the Mesara type belong to this period. By the 2nd millennium, Phaistos had developed as the palatial centre of the region and its economic focus. Later Gortyn took over as the capital of the whole of the Roman province of Crete and Cyrenaica. The area retained a position of importance to the 7th century.

In the village of **Aghii Deka** (Άγιοι Δέκα; *map p. 430, B3*) the church of the same name is signed to the left in the older part of the village, south of the road. The 'Holy Ten' alluded to in the dedication are the martyrs executed by order of the emperor Decius on 23rd December 250. According to tradition, five were from Gortyn, while the others came from far and wide, from Knossos, Lebena, Panormos, Herakleion and Chania. They all ended up in Gortyn because Paul, the local bishop, went out to collect the bodies when Christianity was legalised under Constantine. The building itself has been much restored using stone from ancient Gortyn, and more of the same can be observed in the houses around the main square. Inside the church is a glass case with the stone the martyrs knelt on when they were executed; above it an icon depicts the gruesome scene. The stone has shallow impressions believed to be from the knees of the martyrs. A path (*signed*) to the southwest outskirts of the village leads to a modern chapel. Beside its portico in a crypt are six tile graves believed to be the martyrs' tombs.

You are here at the edge of a huge archaeological area that stretches all the way west to the sea. The site of Gortyn is nearby. Indeed, a back road from the Aghii Deka graves leads to its Roman praetorium. Normally, though, one would start the visit 1km west, where the car park is. Phaistos and Aghia Triada are not far, barely 15km away.

GORTYN

Also Gortys, Gortyna. Map p. 430, B3. Open daily 8.30–7; Nov–March free Sun; parking.

Federico Halbherr at Gortyn, in front of the Law Code.

HISTORY OF GORTYN

In the Roman period Gortyn rose to become the main city in Crete and the capital of the province of Crete and Cyrenaica (in Roman north Africa); the site on the acropolis, though, shows evidence of much earlier occupation going back to the Neolithic and the Bronze Age. Homer (*Iliad II, 646*) refers to the city's defences, though no walls of that date (8th century BC) have come to light so far. The town that developed below the acropolis was certainly flourishing around 500 BC, the date of the Law Code (*see opposite*). It was organised around wells, sanctuaries such as that of Apollo Pythion, and public buildings such as the Ekklesiasterion. Here the Law Code was displayed for everyone to see and abide by.

Hellenistic Gortyn was one of the cities of the Cretan *koinon* and extended as far as Mitropolis. Unfortunately its remains are buried under the later buildings. It had two harbours: Matala to the west and Lebena on the south coast. According to Cornelius Nepos, the 1st-century BC historian, Hannibal fled to Gortyn in 189 BC after being defeated by the Romans at Magnesia; eventually the Romans caught up with him and he committed suicide. With that in mind, perhaps Gortyn did really help Rome with the capture of Crete in 67 BC. The city was certainly handsomely rewarded but the choice of Gortyn as provincial capital may have more to do with the town's geographical location, looking south towards the other half of the province, namely Cyrenaica.

With Rome, peace and prosperity came for Gortyn. This translated into something of a building boom, with the town expanding towards the southeast. It is estimated that the Roman town covered 200 hectares. Unfortunately, not even Roman patronage could stop earthquakes and the town suffered accordingly.

The town made a seamless transition to Christianity. The first bishop of Crete, St Titus, lived here. He was a follower of St Paul, recipient of the Epistle to Titus. Byzantine Gortyn, which occupied the same area as Hellenistic Gortyn, had at least six basilicas and smaller churches. It was dealt the final blow by the Saracens around 823–28, at least according to tradition. There is no unequivocal evidence of destruction linked to the Arab occupation, and probably the town was already in advanced state of neglect and disrepair by then.

Remains litter the whole area and attracted the attention of spolia hunters very early on. Indeed, in the 16th century the ruling power put in a request for Gortyn's antiquities to be shipped to Venice for the embellishment of Doge's Palace. Archaeological investigations began in the late 19th century, when the first fragments of the Law Code were found by two French travellers in a watermill near the church of Aghii Deka, though the earliest record of the inscription goes back to 1577, when Barozzi had spotted some Greek lettering.

The discovery of the inscription attracted interest in Italy, where Classical archaeologists were keen to extend their research to Mediterranean areas formerly under Italian or Roman influence. The leading linguist and epigraphist of the time was Domenico Comparetti. In 1884 he sent his star pupil, Federico Halbherr, also an epigraphist, thereby starting Halbherr's lifetime involvement with Crete, and resulting in the establishment of the first Italian archaeological mission to the island in 1899. Halbherr almost drowned while studying the inscription in the 1880s. The stones had become incorporated in the leat and the owner of the mill had opened the sluice without due notice. Since then the area has been investigated but because it is so vast and amorphous, it has suffered from lack of systematic excavations as well as from security problems. Recently, in 2007, a full-size statue of Apollo that Halbherr had excavated and which was exhibited at the site, was returned to the Greek authorities via a Swiss antique dealer, having been stolen in 1991. On the whole, the high visibility of the Roman remains has caused the earlier phases of Gortyn's development to be neglected.

Visiting the site

A short walk north past the church of Aghios Titos and the odeion leads to the **plane tree** by the Lethaios river, now called Mitropolianos. According to myth, Zeus in the guise of a bull brought Europa to lie with him here after abducting her from Phoenicia. Triplets were born to Europa: Minos, Rhadamanthys and Sarpedon. It is said that the plane tree, which had to witness all this, has refused, mindful of its modesty, to shed its leaves ever since. The 4th-century BC Greek philosopher and botanist Theophrastus believed the story, but the true explanation is more prosaic. Normally plane trees are deciduous: this one is a rare evergreen subspecies of which about 50 specimens have been recorded in Crete.

The odeion and Law Code

South of the area is the **odeion**, built in the 1st century BC and restored by Trajan after earthquake damage at the beginning of the 2nd century AD. The blocks of the **Law Code** came to light during excavations. They had become incorporated into a public building of Hellenistic date, within which the odeion was built. They are thought to have belonged to an earlier circular building, the Ekklesiasterion or meeting place. They set out the laws informing the work of the council and of the day-to-day life of the citizens.

The text was laid out in 12 columns to a total of some 640 lines written in boustrophedon (that is, one line from left to right and the following one from right to left, just as an ox ploughs a field). The technique was developed to avoid interpolations. The code, dated c. 500 BC and written in a Dorian dialect, dealt with civil and criminal offences including property rights, assault, adultery, divorce and inheritance. It shows a stratified society in which citizens, serfs and slaves had different rights and obligations. The testimony, for instance, of five witnesses was required to convict a free man, while for a slave, one was enough. At Gortyn one can view the majority of the inscription. The remainder, two more blocks, has been in the Louvre since 1868.

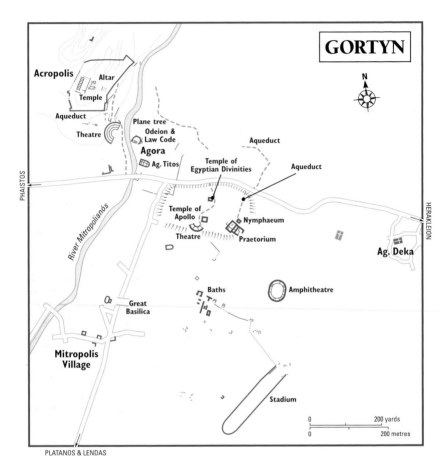

PHAISTOS

HERAKLEION

PLATANOS & LENDAS

Aghios Titos

South of the Odeion, across what was the **agora**, is the church of **Aghios Titos**, a 6th–7th-century Byzantine construction of which the imposing apse survives because it was used until recently as a separate church. According to tradition the bishop-saint Titus was buried in it. Investigations were started by Gerola in 1900 and continued by Xanthoudides in 1902 and Orlandos in the 1920s. The original plan, which might also have included an atrium, reflects the influence of Eastern architecture. The name of the original dedicatee is not known (*see below*). The earlier metropolitan see of Gortyn was in another building, the **Great Basilica**, also dedicated to St Titus, further south. It was discovered in 1978 during roadworks, which is why its mosaic floor with colourful birds and flowers is cut by the provincial road at Mitropolis. The huge three-apsed building, the largest of its kind in Crete with impressive granite columns, suffered extensively in an earthquake in AD 670 and was abandoned; it must have been demolished and pillaged since the remains are so shallow: there was no accumulation of debris. It is possible that the smaller church to the north took over and was rededicated to Gortyn's first bishop.

The praetorium, theatre and temples

The rest of the Roman area is best explored at leisure by going back to the main road from Aghii Deka and looking for the remains of the aqueduct along its south edge. Water for Roman Gortyn was piped from Zaros, 15km away. A marked path in the midst of beautiful mature olive trees follows the arches past a cistern and leads to a **nymphaeum**, and next to it the **praetorium**. The complex, first built in the 1st century BC to house the Roman governor and accommodate the administrative buildings of the newly-formed province of Crete and Cyrenaica, is very typically Roman in its construction technique, with a concrete conglomerate core with brick facing and monolithic columns. It included a basilican hall used as law courts, a shrine dedicated to Augustus, and a bath house. Parts of it lived on after the fall of Rome as a monastery, which survived until Venetian times. The Nymphaeum, originally built for the Praetorium, became a public fountain in Byzantine times, one of the 40 or so that the town boasted.

Like any Roman town of some standing (and the abundance of marble sculptures by the cafeteria testify to that), Gortyn had its entertainment buildings for the populace. Following the uncertain path along the fence, the **theatre**, with over half its cavea surviving, comes into view. Next to it are the remains of the **Temple of Pythian Apollo**, the holiest sanctuary in Gortyn and known throughout the ancient world. This was the religious centre of the town well before the Archaic period, when the temple was built, and remained as such until the advent of Christianity. The temple was erected above an earlier Minoan temple and was remodelled in the Hellenistic period. The original building had a rectangular cella with a treasury in the northwest corner. Later a pronaos was added with six half-engaged Doric columns. Between them were stelae used to record Gortyn's treaties with other cities and with King Eumenes II of Pergamon. In front of the temple stands a stepped monumental altar of the 2nd century BC.

A little to the north are the remains of a Roman **Temple to the Egyptian Divinities**, specifically Isis, Serapis and (probably) Anubis. Statues of the triad would have stood on the tripartite podium at the east end of the cella: those of Isis and Serapis were recovered. The west façade was fronted by six Ionic columns. The architrave records the construction of the building by Flavia Phylira and her two sons (1st–2nd centuries AD).

Further south, by the Megali Porta, the 'Great Gate', are the remains of **baths**. The remains have not yet been fully investigated, but it is believed that the tall wall that was mistaken for a city wall (hence the denomination 'Great Gate') is in reality a part of a large hall of a public bath house. To the east are the remains of the 2nd-century **amphitheatre**, and further south, traces of a **stadium**.

The acropolis

The acropolis, on the hill of Aghios Ioannis, is to the northwest of the archaeological site. It is better to drive to it: Gortyn is a large site and it gets hot. The hill reveals oc-

Monumental stepped altar in front of the Temple to Pythian Apollo at Gortyn.

cupation from the Neolithic through the Bronze Age and again in the Byzantine period up to the 10th century. A fortified settlement was established during the Geometric period (10th–7th centuries BC). It remained fortified in Hellenistic times and parts of the circuit can still be traced. The defence was damaged in an earthquake but the acropolis was not fortified until Byzantine times. On the southern brow of the hill are the remains of the small, 7th-century BC **Temple of Athena Poliouchos** ('Guardian of the City'), with a central bothros, a sacred pit. The temple remained in use, with alterations, into Roman times. It contained a cult statue of a naked female triad, now in Herakleion. Excavation of the dump on the east slope of the acropolis, near the remains of an **altar** over 10m long, have brought to light a mixed assemblage of terracotta figurines, painted clay plaques with relief figures and bronze artefacts of all periods from LM III to Roman. The site of the temple was built over in the mid-5th century, and again sometime later between the 6th and the 10th centuries with the construction of a Byzantine basilica which incorporated some of the worked stone. The rest was disposed of in the dump.

A second **theatre**, on the southeast slope of the acropolis, has not yet been investigated, but it is known from notes by the Italian antiquary Onorio Belli, who came to Crete in 1583 and toured the island extensively, recording ancient monuments (*see p. 34*). In the 7th century the emperor Heraclius fortified the acropolis to allow the population to take refuge in it. The urban fabric of the city had by then become disjointed and Gortyn was no more.

MESARA TOMBS

For a sample of the Mesara tholos tomb, take a short detour 5km along the south road from Mitropolis. At **Platanos** (Πλάτανος; *map p. 430, B3*), signposted to the far side of the village to the west, you will find two of them, the largest yet known, linked by an area paved with alluvial stones from the nearby river. This type of communal tomb, dated to the 3rd millennium but sometimes with a long period of use, is comparatively common in the region though rare elsewhere in Crete, and shows little variation. It consists of a free-standing circular structure with an east entrance and a set of smaller rooms in front. These may have been used for ritual purposes or as ossuaries when the main chamber became too full. The tholos itself was probably corbelled with stone slabs, though for the larger structures like these at Platanos, the possibility of an organic superstructure of mud brick or thatch or a combination of the two should not be discounted. A number of these tombs have yielded rich finds, with stone vases, three Egyptian scarabs and a Babylonian haematite cylinder seal from the period of Hammurabi (1792–1750 BC).

PHAISTOS

Map p. 430, A3. Open daily 8–7; note that if you are planning to visit Aghia Triada in the same day, the latter will close at 3 (4.30 in summer).

Approaching from Mires, the palace of Phaistos (Φαιστός) comes into view to the left of the road, on a ridge jutting into the plain. Note the Venetian water mill on the way up to the palace.

Phaistos: view from the Upper Court with the West Court stretching below and the Great Staircase rising on the left.

HISTORY OF PHAISTOS

The settlement of Phaistos, mythological seat of King Rhadamanthys, brother of Minos, looks out over the Mesara and lies in the shadow of Mt Ida, the highest mountain in Crete (2456m). To the south the Asterousia range runs parallel to the coast. Occupied since the Neolithic (the only round Neolithic hut in the whole of Crete is here; otherwise houses of this period are rectangular), the site became the seat of a palace excavated since the beginning of the last century by the Italian School in Athens. This accounts for the Italian-sounding names ascribed to some of the features. Two main phases have been identified: a First Palace built in the early MM period and destroyed by fire in MM III, and a Second Palace mainly built in LM IA, almost exactly on top of the ruins of the previous one. This building incorporates some of the features of the First Palace, such as foundations and paving. The phases are separated by a thick layer of debris made of lime, stones and sherds, used as a levelling platform. The fill, which the Italian called *calcestruzzo*, was known locally as *astraki*. It was as hard as concrete and broke many an excavator's pick. The visible remains belong to the Second Palace, which has escaped the somewhat excessive restoration of Knossos. This building was destroyed by fire in LM IB and subsequently abandoned.

Excavators have been intrigued by the contrast between the monumental character of the building and the comparative shortage of prestige finds. It is true that portable objects could have been removed or looted, but it is the absence of frescoes, tablets and sealings that is intriguing. The comparison with Zakros and Knossos poses difficult questions that have not yet been fully answered. Moreover, nearby Aghia Triada, which is a villa and not a palace, *does* have these kind of finds from the Neopalatial period. It could be that the two sites were complementary, with Aghia Triada in the ascendant when they both met their end.

After the wholesale destruction of LM IB, there was subdued occupation at Phaistos towards the end of the Bronze Age and in the Geometric periods. On the whole though, upon excavation, very few signs of this immediate later activity were found or, more precisely, recorded. The Hellenistic town that followed was apparently was quite large, with wide streets and city walls. It was built on top of the Minoan settlement to the west of the palace and also extended to the south. The actual site of the palace before excavation was covered with houses of that period; unfortunately they were removed and not recorded in the early excavations.

Hellenistic Phaistos lived on and prospered until it was crushed by nearby Gortyn in the 3rd century BC. The area subsequently saw only sporadic occupation.

In Roman times Phaistos was an agricultural estate. Later the Byzantines built a chapel and in the 14th century the Venetians established a monastery here (Aghios Georgios at Phalandra, just west of the excavations). Over time the Phaistos toponym, which appears in Linear B tablets and in Homer, in his words 'fair to dwell in' (*Iliad II*, 648), fell into disuse. When Captain Spratt visited in the 19th century, and later in 1900, when Federico Halbherr and Luigi Pernier began excavating, the hill on which the palace was later found was known as Kastri because of the huge blocks that were strewn across the area.

On the whole the location of Phaistos, like that of Aghia Triada, is geologically not a very good choice for a large settlement. It may have abundant building stone (limestone, marl and gypsum) and plentiful water, but it lies on a scarp fault. There is no way of knowing in detail what earthquakes occurred in Minoan times—though the recorded destruction by fire may well have been started by such an event—but in more recent times, between 1902 and 1976, as many as five tremors, measuring 6 to 7 on the Richter scale, have been recorded within a 50km radius.

Visiting the site

The entrance to the site is across the Upper Court and down the stairs into the West Court. The site has information panels, also in English, but no set route: it is difficult at times to get around without stepping on walls. The plan you get with your ticket is useful up to a point as it shows more than is visible or accessible.

The visit starts from the West Court with the **Theatral Area (1)** and remains of the First Palace just in front of the later monumental facade belonging to the Second Palace, 7m to the east. Immediately below the wide staircase is a small **shrine complex (2)**. A large clay offering-table, stone vases and cult objects were found here. To the south are a few rooms also belonging to the First Palace and preserving elements of its original **West Façade (3)**; further to the south, traces of the **monumental entrance** of the First Palace can just be made out **(4)**. The whole area beyond both the railings and the huge pits (the kouloures) is out of bounds. What you can see from this vantage point belongs to the First Palace (immediately to the left) and to the Second Palace (further left).

The **Great Staircase (5)**, carved partly into the living rock, leads to the **West Propylaia** (6), possibly the most impressive entrance to any Minoan palace. It consists of a landing, followed by a porch, a portico and a light-well. Beneath this area are stores belonging to the First Palace: they can be viewed by descending a level via the staircase to the right. Dark, cramped and creepy, with pithoi in place, they do look the part.

The same staircase leads to the north, to a **Peristyle Hall** (7) with remains of the original stone paving and wall revetment. A fine collection of faïence inlays was found nearby. From here there is a good view of the **Royal Apartments** (8), under cover and complete with **Lustral Basin (9)**. This, the quality of the finds and the presence of frescoes, testify to the high status of the North Wing.

Another celebrated findspot is nearby in the **Northeast Quarter (10)**. According to the excavators, it was built and destroyed in MM III, though the **Central Hall (11)** was still in use at the time of the demise of the Second Palace and burnt down with it. The highly controversial **Phaistos Disk** (now in Herakleion museum; *see box on p. 152 below*) was discovered this area, in one of a series of **storage chests (12)**.

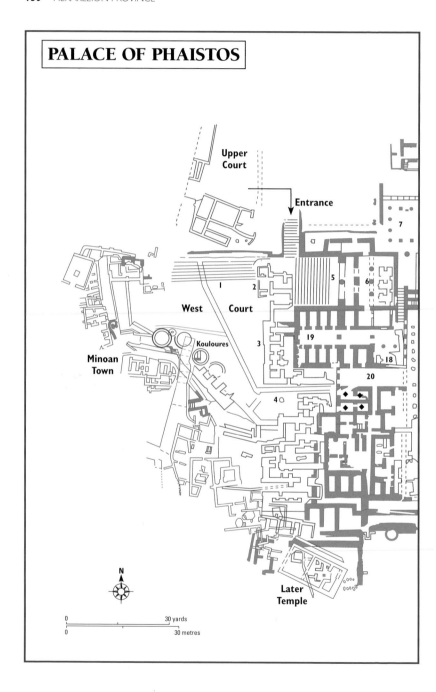

PALACE OF PHAISTOS

Upper Court

Entrance

West Court

Kouloures

Minoan Town

Later Temple

N

0   30 yards

0   30 metres

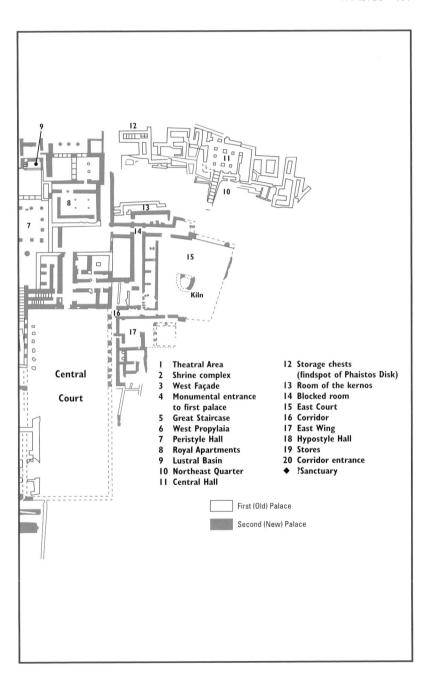

Central

Court

1 Theatral Area
2 Shrine complex
3 West Façade
4 Monumental entrance
   to first palace
5 Great Staircase
6 West Propylaia
7 Peristyle Hall
8 Royal Apartments
9 Lustral Basin
10 Northeast Quarter
11 Central Hall

12 Storage chests
   (findspot of Phaistos Disk)
13 Room of the kernos
14 Blocked room
15 East Court
16 Corridor
17 East Wing
18 Hypostyle Hall
19 Stores
20 Corridor entrance
◆ ?Sanctuary

Kiln

First (Old) Palace

Second (New) Palace

THE PHAISTOS DISK

On 3rd July 1908 Luigi Pernier, working in House 101, northeast of the palace, found an object with symbols on both sides, next to a Linear A tablet. This was the Phaistos Disk, as intriguing and mysterious now, a hundred years later, as it was then. Physically it is round, hand-made, about 1.5cm thick and approx. 16.2cm in diameter, with an incised spiral. The signs, 241 or so of them stamped on fresh clay, represent the earliest evidence of the use of movable type. The clay is free from impurities and the object, unlike the tablets, was fired deliberately.

The excavator assumed it had fallen from the upper storey and that it was of Cretan manufacture. Not much progress has been made since then, though not for want of trying. Nothing else remotely similar has ever been found, and that is the main problem. Accusations of foul play were made as early as 1913. The villain of the piece was said to be Pernier who, jealous of the Halbherr's success at Gortyn with the Law Code and of Evans's discoveries at Knossos, deliberately planted a forged object with an invented script in order to raise the profile of his site. However, while it is true that Phaistos could not rival Knossos as to finds, at Aghia Triada nearby, also excavated by the Italians, the quality and quantity of material was truly amazing. Pernier and the Italian School had their hands full. Besides, Pernier's track record and distinguished career marks him out as an unlikely accomplice in a forgery of this magnitude.

The case should not be allowed to linger, since it is possible to put it to rest one way or another with appropriate testing. Modern techniques such as thermoluminescence are not invasive and can ascertain the date of the firing, thereby deciding once and for all the question of authenticity, while the analysis of a minimal quantity of the clay could assist in determining provenance.

Though a second disc has not been forthcoming, similar characters have been found on a few objects, namely a Kamares ware vase now in Herakleion, on the Arkalochori Axe, excavated by Spyridon Marinatos in the 1930s, and on a stone block from Malia, though the parallels are not unanimously accepted.

Interpretations of the object's function and meaning are extremely diverse, ranging from an astronomical or astrological calendar to a hymn to victory, a nursery rhyme or, according to Evans, a sacred text. Current thought assumes it is a piece of writing though the direction of it, from the centre to the periphery or the other way round, has yet to be established. The small number of characters, 45 in total, suggests it is a syllabic scripts and close to Linear A, which has not yet been deciphered. There has been no shortage of proposed translations, based on languages as diverse as Chinese, Dravidian, Georgian, Hittite, Luwian, Semitic, Slavic and Sumerian. Indeed it was this abundance that prompted the late John Chadwick, who decoded Linear B with Michael Ventris, to appeal to those producing their own solutions 'not to send them to him'.

Turning south, visitors walk past a room **(13)** where a stone kernos with 14 hollows around a central one, probably belonging to the earlier phase, was found. It is similar to the Malia Table (*see p. 123*), which had 34 hollows in all but is equally enigmatic in interpretation. Further south, beyond a room **(14)** that is blocked, suggesting that the two rooms immediately to the north were abandoned before the LM IB fire, the **East Court (15)** can be recognised by the kiln built in the middle of it; this became an industrial area in the LM period. Beyond a corridor **(16)** is all that remains of the **East Wing (17)**, built behind a portico. It contains a lustral basin with mud-brick walls and has produced an assorted collection of finds, including double axes, a rhyton with a human head, stone horns of consecration, a number of bronze blades and shell plaques decorated with monstrous creatures. The interpretation as a shrine is not unanimously accepted.

The **Central Court**, which belongs to the First Palace, is aligned with the Kamares Cave (*see p. 171*). Note the blocks on the upper west side: according to some commentators, they may have been used by bull-leapers in their performances, though there is no ready explanation of how bulls could have been kept under control in such a space. In the West Wing, a **Hypostyle Hall (18)** with marble revetment and a triple doorway may have been used for cult purposes. It shows signs of a change of use in the time immediately preceding the destruction, with the blocking of doors. To the west is a double line of **Stores (19)** where a number of pithoi were found.

The wide **Corridor (20)**, representing the main entrance of the second palace, has a block of rooms on the south side, four of which (♦) were only accessible from the West Court. The finds and the benches suggest that this may have been a small **Sanctuary**. The rooms to the south contained two lustral basins. This area, devoted to cult activity, was heavily remodelled in antiquity when a large wall (the Antemurale) was constructed in front of the southwest façade. This has been variously interpreted as part of an intended monumental entrance, or a terrace wall, or even an anti-seismic device. Further south still, a number of walls close off the area providing support, just as the south terrace basement does at Knossos.

The two faces of the mysterious Phaistos Disk.

On the whole, excavators have been puzzled by the lack of finds of value in the LM IB destruction layer of the palace; indeed only in a dozen rooms were vases found *in situ* and pithoi are quite scarce. All in all it would seem that while the Second Palace was planned on a grand scale, it was ultimately smaller than its predecessor, as large areas to the west were given up. Much of the paved area to the west went out of use and was found under a levelling layer of *calcestruzzo*, as if waiting for a redevelopment that never materialised.

AGHIA TRIADA

Situated less than an hour's walk west of Phaistos or a short drive on the same fault scarp with the same geological problems (*see p. 149 above*), the settlement of Aghia Triada (Αγία Τριάδα; *map p. 430, A3*) was excavated by the Italian School in Athens in the very early days of Cretan archaeological research, at the beginning of the last century, when record-keeping both of the excavation and of the many finds still left something to be desired. At the time Halbherr was busy with Phaistos; he was probably happy to leave this 'minor site' to somebody else. Finds, however, proved that Aghia Triada was no such thing. Test pits and soundings replaced systematic excavation in an attempt to reach an evaluation of what land should be bought. After the Second World War publication plans by Luisa Banti were frustrated by the loss of important documents in the 1966 Florence flood. As a result the interpretation of the site, especially of the village area, is still controversial. The location is named after the small Venetian chapel dedicated to the Holy Trinity. The site includes a large, lavish, high-status building (dubbed the Villa Reale by the excavators) and a village.

The site shows continuous occupation from the Neolithic to the end of the 13th century AD. Two Prepalatial tholos tombs have been excavated in the area to the north. Contrary to other Minoan sites, Aghia Triada had its first floruit in LM I, at the same time as the Second Palace at Phaistos. It went up in flames in the general destruction that blighted so many sites in Crete, but it was rebuilt and regained importance in the Postpalatial period, possibly becoming the focus of economic and political power in the fertile western Mesara plain after the demise of Phaistos. Although smaller in size, Aghia Triada is characterised by true palatial architecture, with frescoes, paved roads and the extensive use of gypsum. The plan, on the other hand, is not palatial at all. It represents a clear departure from the standard arrangement around a central court so characteristic of Minoan palatial buildings. The site has also yielded important finds. For reasons that are still little understood, the site was not ransacked, though occupation and building activity went on. Finds rank among the most stupendous of Minoan art and also the most extravagant, such as a hoard of copper ingots weighing over 500kg. The largest Linear A archive was also found here. The rebuilding in the Postpalatial period dates to the 14th century, slightly after the final destruction of Knossos. The style is monumental, suggesting influence from Mycenaean Greece. Buildings include a rectangular hall, a possible megaron (if so, it is the earliest on the island), a shrine and an arrangement looking like a prototype stoa, with shops or storerooms along the side of a court. The well-known painted limestone larnax dates from this period and is linked to the reuse of the Prepalatial tholoi. There is evidence of reoccupation in the Geometric period c. 900–700 BC, with finds of figurines and ritual objects suggesting cult activity. In Hellenistic times there was a shrine of Zeus Velchanos (a manifestation as god of fire and volcanic eruptions). The small Byzantine church of Aghios Georgios Galatas has a fine portal and the remains of much-worn frescoes dated 1302.

It was once thought that the whole area was closer to the sea in antiquity, which would have made Aghia Triada Phaistos's harbour. Unfortunately there is no evidence for embayment in the Ieropotamos alluvial plain. Ground level at the foot of the ridge is still 15–20m above sea level. Moreover, surface sediment analysis seems to suggest that the sea did not reach this far. The structure north of the villa, which the excavators dubbed Rampa al Mare, probably did not lead to a port. Kommos makes a much more likely harbour for the area.

Visiting the site

The present sorry state of the site (*open daily 10–3; 4.30 in summer*) reflects the chequered history of the excavations. The location, amidst tall trees and twittering birds with fine views of the mountains, is enchanting. Unfortunately, visitors who have ventured this far are not rewarded for their efforts; they are left to make sense of a jumble of walls with no labels, no panels, no directions, no set route, not even a plan to go with the ticket. Halbherr does have a commemorative bust here, but he is unlikely to approve of the way his site is being presented.

Past the ticket booth follow the fence to the site entrance down a flight of steps to the left at the end of it (*see plan overleaf*). This is the top north end of the village. In order to get your bearings the best strategy is to home in on the chapel of Aghios Georgios, crossing the village and going up the steps to the left of the covered area.

Looking north from the chapel, the area immediately in front is the Paved Court. The first villa, the Minoan one of Neopalatial date, is opposite and to the left, in the form of an L-shaped building. Evidence shows it had an upper storey. The Lower Court is beyond to the north, roughly in front of the covered area. The excavated remains beyond belonged to the village. The cemetery area is to the northeast. The eastern end of the villa was used as a reception area while the '*quartiere signorile*', that is the grand apartments, were at the northwest corner. A service block with kitchen and storerooms is immediately to the left of the church. The megaron belonging to the second phase of occupation was built directly on top of the villa, in the middle of it and above its main storage area. It had a paved loggia facing onto the court.

The Minoan Villa

The southwest area, consisting of several small rooms with earthen floors, suggests storage; this interpretation is confirmed by the finds, which included several pithoi, sealings and bronze objects besides the ubiquitous pottery, as well as stone basins for

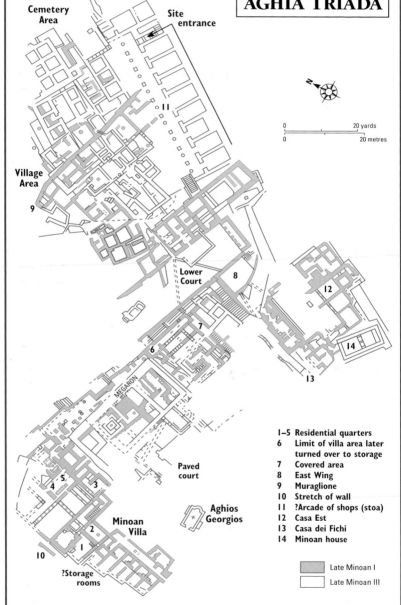

AGHIA TRIADA

Cemetery Area

Site entrance

Village Area

11

9

Lower Court

8

12

7

6

14

13

MEGARON

Paved court

Aghios Georgios

5
4
3

Minoan Villa

2

1

10

?Storage rooms

1–5 Residential quarters
6 Limit of villa area later turned over to storage
7 Covered area
8 East Wing
9 Muraglione
10 Stretch of wall
11 ?Arcade of shops (stoa)
12 Casa Est
13 Casa dei Fichi
14 Minoan house

Late Minoan I
Late Minoan III

0   20 yards
0   20 metres

collecting water. It may be a later addition to the villa as there is LM pottery below the floors. Rooms 1 and 2 have thick ashlar walls suggesting that the villa originally ended there. **Room 1** marks the transition to the residential quarters, which may have had an upper storey. In antiquity there was no entrance to the villa from this direction. It probably served as a food preparation area because of the stone troughs and the clay basins found in it. **Room 2**, to the right, was probably originally a pillar hall but was given over to storage as the finds suggest. It was packed with mint-condition LM I pottery, stone and clay lamps and two bronze cauldrons one inside the other. A short corridor leads on to the hall and **Room 3** (*under cover*), which has fitted benches decorated with triglyphs similar to those found at Myrtos Pyrgos; the gypsum facing has been restored, with red stucco between the slabs. Here and in the small room to the north, lamps and stone vases, including the steatite Harvester Vase, probably fallen from above (*see p. 43*) were found. One of the steatite lamps with relief decoration probably came from the same workshop as one found near Knossos in the Isopata Royal Tomb. In the small room to the north (*not visible*) a huge raised gypsum slab on the paved floor has been interpreted as a divan base. It could have held a wooden bed similar to the one found in the excavation of the Minoan settlement of Akrotiri on Thera. Back in the hall, one is looking down into another hall to the west with pier-and-door partitions on two sides and beyond to the area from where 179 sealings, Linear A tablets and the Boxer Rhyton, an elongated steatite ritual vessel, were retrieved. More sealings (450) come from a gypsum chest in **Room 4**, as well as fresco fragments. The pier-and-door parti-

Room 3 at Aghia Triada, with its fitted benches and restored gypsum revetment.

tion along south wall of this room had been modified in antiquity into some sort of cupboard. One section had a hollowed stone slab in it suggesting a toilet. It is indeed reminiscent of the comparable arrangements in the 'Queen's Toilet' in Knossos. The presence of a sealing inscribed with Linear A remains unexplained. In **Room 5** the *Cat and Sitting Lady* fresco, with a cat stalking a partridge (now in Herakleion) was found partly *in situ* on the north mud-brick partition, no longer extant. The room has been interpreted as the shrine of the area and may have been a relatively new development after some earlier fire damage.

According to the excavators, the north area communicated with the southwest area and not with the northeast part of the villa; it remains difficult to interpret because of the Mycenaean megaron built on top of it. The complex produced a cache with 19 inscribed copper ingots weighing some 28kg each, gold foil and bronze statuettes, an abundance of pithoi with tablets and sealings. The whole area up to **Room 6** was indeed eventually devoted to storage, though judging by the quality of the construction this may not have been its original function. Several rooms were built in ashlar with gypsum paving and dadoes. It should be pointed out, though, that the difference in paving can be imputed to intended storage functions: stone paving for liquids and trodden earth for everything else.

The eastern area (*under cover*) produced a very limited number of finds, but the quality of the construction does contrast with the nearby stores. It appears to have undergone a number of alterations just prior to the fire, with doorways blocked and mud-brick partitions. Some of the finds, such as incense burners, suggest a ritual use. It can be viewed by entering the **covered area (7)** to the east.

The East Wing or **Avancorpo Orientale (8)** is to the east beyond the stairs connection the lower and upper courts. It was probably a later feature since its installation involved the cutting away of the east façade. It may have been used for storage. Finds of heaps of discarded fresco fragments hint at ongoing repair work.

North of the villa
From this area a road led to the village to the northeast. Originally the village extended as far as the wall known as the **Muraglione (9)**, which can be recognised by its thickness (c. 1m) rather than by a different construction style. It runs east–west and may be related to a similar **stretch of wall (10)** immediately to the west of the villa. The Muraglione has a LM I date. North of it, MM IIIB/LM IA destruction deposits were found with very slight traces of immediate reoccupation. The large Complesso della Mazza di Breccia apparently had a storage function. In the village proper, south of the Muraglione, the situation is more complex because the houses were more densely packed with several phases of destruction and rebuilding. Here and to the east there is extensive evidence of LM III reoccupation after the destruction of the palaces and of other main sites in Crete. Notable among these is a building that looks like a **stoa (11)**, a row of shops under a porch dating from a long time before such arrangements became a regular feature of ancient towns.

East of the villa

The area east of the villa is very messy and the remains are difficult to make out. Excavators' plans show a fine mansion, the **Casa Est (12)**, with a LM IA construction date. It burned with the villa but may already have been uninhabited by that time since, apart from a few pithoi, very little was found in it. The west part of the building had a row of stores with several pithoi. Two dagger blades and a bronze double axe were found underneath two of the vessels. To the south, beneath a later shrine, was the **Casa dei Fichi (13)**. It was named after the charred organic remains, which included figs (*fichi*) as well as lentils barley, peas and *cyperus* (a kind of sedge). **House no. 14** was a Minoan house cut into by the cella and vestibule of a shrine of the Postpalatial period. The floor had remains of a fresco with a marine seascape with dolphins and octopuses.

The cemetery

The cemetery area (*not accessible*) is to the northeast. Of the two Prepalatial tholos tombs, the best preserved is Tholos A, used as a communal burial from EM II to MM I, a period of 1,000 years beginning in the early 3rd millennium. The outer annexes were used as ossuaries to make space for more interments, as well as for offerings. At least 150 individuals had been laid to rest there. Grave goods included bronze daggers, jewellery, stone vases and humble clay pots as well as a deposit of over 100 sealstones, some carved in ivory some in faïence. The famous **Aghia Triada larnax**, decorated with a funerary scene (now in Herakleion Archaeological Museum Temporary Exhibition; *see p. 45*) was found in Tholos B, which had been cleared out and reused in Postpalatial times. It has been noted that while the decoration of the sarcophagus is typically Minoan, the figures are Egyptian in style, a connection which is supported by other finds from a neighbouring tomb, namely a seal of the Egyptian queen Tiye (1411–1375 BC), wife of Amenhotep III, and a Hittite sphinx. Nearby excavations have uncovered a settlement which may be connected with the earlier phases of this cemetery.

FROM PHAISTOS TO THE COAST

From Aghia Triada it is only possible to return to Phaistos anyway and visitors may welcome the opportunity to sample something different—not Minoan, not Classical, but a curious building with a long history, possibly a rare instance of the use of a pagan structure for a Christian building.

The church of **Aghios Pavlos** is situated just beyond Aghios Ioannis, 1km south of Phaistos, in a cemetery to the left of the road (*map p. 430, A3*). Recent investigations have shown that the oldest part of the building was originally a cupola supported by four massive piers with open arches. That is hardly a church: indeed the structure is reminiscent of Late Roman spring chambers and there is a well behind the present church. The nave with a dome resting on a drum is a later addition. The open arches of the first structure were blocked and later still, in Venetian times, a narthex was added. The frieze around the dome bears a painted inscription dated 1003–04, though it is not clear what event is commemorated, the construction or the restructuring of the building. The text mentions the dedication of the church to the apostle Paul in the village of Baptistiras (meaning Aghios Ioannis, that is, the village of St John the Baptist). Also mentioned are the church's restoration and the building of a wall around it by order of the Byzantine emperor Andronicus II Palaeologus (1283–1328), his wife Empress Irene and their son Michael. The choice of St Paul may have something to do with the Apostle's visit to nearby Kali Limenes, when he was being taken from Caesarea to Rome to be tried. It was late autumn, not a good season to be sailing on the Mediterranean. The Cretan harbour offered safety for a while, but not for long. Soon passengers and crew were out again, with a view to finding safe wintering at Phoinix (modern Loutro), but driven by a strong northerly wind they strayed south of Gavdos and were eventually shipwrecked on Malta. Paul only reached Rome in March (*Acts 27, 12*).

Vori

On the right of the main road in the Tymbaki direction, after the Phaistos turning, is Vori (Βῶροι; *map p. 430, A3*), where a visit to the **Museum of Cretan Ethnology** (*open daily April–end Oct 10–6; cretanethnologymuseum.gr*) is strongly recommended. The museum focuses on Crete's more recent history and way of life (beginning roughly in the 11th century) with systematic ethnological research through rural Crete in order to document its recent, fast-fading past.

The collection is very large and only a fraction of it is displayed (though plans for expansion are afoot). The display is organised by theme.

Case 1 deals with food production, nutrition and agriculture, starting with the traditional tools to work the earth and break the sod (the sledges with flints or with metal attachments). Food-processing tools include a variety of sieves for different purposes (one even made of goatskin), as well as a *cheiromylos*, a hand quern.

House furnishings take up much of Cases 2–4, while Case 5 has models of different types of Cretan house (the *pyrgos*, or tower-house, fortified with access by ladder, and the *kamara*, with an arch dividing different areas in one big room; *see illustration opposite*). Furniture and clothing follow, with a collection of knapsacks, saddle covers, shepherds' cloaks woven and felted for waterproofing, and the tools and the looms used for the purpose.

Cases 10–15 deal with various trades (blacksmiths, basket-makers and potters). In Case 16 we are reminded that until quite recently the most common means of transport in Crete was one's own two feet, a stout pair of boots and a *bastouni*, or walking stick. The next two cases deal with the lighter side of life, such as the pranks played on the afternoon of Easter Sunday, when the local youths set fire to the *sklapatzikia*, sort of large crackers full of gunpowder. The display closes with a section on religion, music, more recent history and the Battle of Crete.

Besides the bewildering variety and quantity of the objects displayed, the museum is of particular interest because it explains (also in English) how tools were used and matches exhibits with pictures of the objects 'in action'.

VERNACULAR ARCHITECTURE

After the Minoan palaces there is not much architecture in Crete that is distinctive and unique: successive occupiers imported and imposed their styles on public and high-status buildings. This, however, did not reach beyond the cities, and it is in the small villages that Cretan vernacular architecture can be found, albeit mostly in ruins.

While mud-brick construction was used in the Neolithic, showing the first farmers' Anatolian connection, over time it became customary for peasants' dwellings to be built of stone mortared with mud levelling courses. Timber framing remained rare. A typical house consisted of a single rectangular room some 5m by 8m. The roof was flat, of timber joists covered with vegetable matter (vine, oleander prunings or reeds) topped by a layer of clay and finally levelled and compacted with a roller. This type of roofing can still be seen in Anatolian villages today, though it is been rapidly replaced or covered over by tiling. In Crete roof tiles were not used even when they became standard on mainland Greece in antiquity. The advantage of this system is that it produces a structure that breathes and is cool in the summer. It may be a drawback colder seasons, but it has been shown, over the centuries, to be able to survive Anatolian winters, certainly harsher than Crete's.

The inner arrangement of the room varied according to how the problem posed by the size of the roof joists, at least 5m in length, was solved. One approach (*kentis* house) was to have a central beam running along the length of the room supported by a forked post. Roof joists ccould then be half as long as they rested on the beam. A variation on the theme reduced the required length of the central beam by resting it on a short wall projecting from the narrow side of the rectangle. One of the recesses created on either side of the wall was traditionally used as kitchen. This construction has been seen as step towards the *kamara*-type house.

In a *kamara* the central beam is entirely dispensed with: the roof joists are supported by an arch spanning a portion of the central length. An arch with a full length-span would have created an unstable structure. The four recesses in each corner can be used as kitchen/storage and bedrooms, with the advantage of some privacy.

A further refinement on the *kamara*, more commonly found in the western part of the island, is a two-storey construction with the arch outside housing the kitchen fronting a narrower building (thereby solving the problem of the length of the roof joists) with storage space below and living quarters, occasionally with carved ceilings, upstairs.

Very little work has been done on investigating and recording of this type of architecture: it is thought to be Byzantine or post-medieval and to have remained in use until the 1900s.

Kamilari tholos tomb

From Vori, the west end of the Mesara now stretches west and terminates in a glorious beach running north south from Kokkinos Pyrgos almost to Matala. On the way from Phaistos, take the right turn at Aghios Ioannis to visit Kamilari tholos tomb, excavated by Italian archaeologist Doro Levi. After 2km at the crossroads, the village of Kamilari (Καμηλάρι; *map p. 430, A3*) is on the left. Keep right and follow the signs. After leaving your car by the side of the road, it is less than 20mins on foot to the tomb (keep left at both forks). The large communal tomb is over a hump in direct view of the sea and of Mt Ida: the view in itself makes the visit worthwhile. It was built in the Protopalatial period and remained in use for many centuries. Its walls stand to almost 2m and evidence for the roofing points to a wooden structure with masonry. It is a standard Mesara type with annexes for ritual purposes later used as ossuaries. Although it was robbed in antiquity, it still yielded interesting finds, namely three clay models (on display at Herakleion Archaeological Museum's Temporary Exhibition) related to the cult of the dead: the offering, the banquet and the circle dance, still performed to this day in Crete. The horns of consecration and doves add to the ritual character of the activity.

Kommos

It is barely 3km from Kamilari to the sea, but before going to the beach it is worth taking a look at Kommos (Κομμός; *map p. 430, A3*), even through the fence. Plans are afoot for a glass, steel and plastic cover to be erected over the whole area, and for the public to be admitted. Unfortunately at the time of writing this has not yet come to fruition. If you are lucky (and persuasive) you may be able to enlist the help of the excavators. Their dig house is in Pitsidia (Πιτσίδια; *map p. 430, A3*) and they are there in the summer, working on post-excavation. You may be able to borrow the keys, a guide book and perhaps even an excavator. Kommos can be reached from Pitsidia by turning right in the village. Alternatively, there is a second turning just over 1km west at the crest of the hill. The excavation is below by the shore.

At first sight this may not look like the best bet for a harbour, with the prevailing west winds battering the coastline. That said, the choice is either here or the precipitous cliffs to the south. Indeed, in Roman times that is where the harbour was, at Matala. Both the archaeology and the written references support the hypothesis that Roman Phaistos and Gortyn used Matala. The possibility of a submerged Roman platform has been mooted and there may have been a shipshed at the south end of the harbour. But Matala has a drawback: there is no room for anchorage. In any case, there are no Minoan remains there. The Minoans must have gone somewhere else, and Kommos is the place. What makes this possible is the difference in sea level. Archaeologists think that in Minoan times the sea was 2m lower; as a result the shoreline extended for a further 50–100m; moreover, the protection afforded to the coastline by a reef was more effective. That reef is now submerged and in poor shape, after being eroded by the sea over the centuries and damaged by the Germans, who used it for bomb practice in the last war.

Kommos was first recognised by Evans, who mused about a 'customs house' for the Minoan navy. Excavations were carried out by the American School of Classical

Studies at Athens from 1976–94. These revealed a very long occupation, from the late Neolithic to MM I, when the town was founded, to the end of the Minoan period and beyond into Roman times, when the site was abandoned.

The earliest houses were on the hill. Below, by a paved road, a series of buildings of monumental proportions with ashlar masonry were erected. The largest building block used in Bronze Age Crete is here: 94 by 344 by 35cm. **Building T** was truly planned on a grand scale, almost as big as Phaistos. It had pier-and-door partitions, a staircase and a central court paved with cemented sea pebbles. At least part of it seems to have fallen out of use by the end of the Neopalatial period when a pottery kiln was constructed in the south area. Then, in LM IIIA, a building with six galleries, each over 5m wide and almost 40m long, was erected on top of it. It has been suggested that these were **shipsheds** as described in the *Odyssey* (*VI, 262–69*) for boats to be pulled up for shelter in the winter months. Unlike most of the rest of Crete bar a handful of sites such as Knossos, for instance, the settlement shows no sign of decline in the Postpalatial period: that is when the shipsheds were erected and the finds show an increased range of foreign contacts with Cyprus, Syria, Egypt, and Italy.

On the whole, the economy of the town shows a marked shift from small-scale subsistence agriculture to industrial production, with large olive-oil presses and abundant evidence for metalwork in LM IIIA. Kommos had developed into the harbour for Phaistos, Aghia Triada and the Mesara and survived their demise.

Between 1200 and 1020 the town went through a phase of abandonment only to resurface in the Protogeometric period when a small temple was erected almost 3m above the level of the Minoan paved road. A later shrine, with an 8th-century foundation date, has been widely discussed because of the pillared structure found inside, which is Phoenician. That Phoenicians should be present in Crete is no surprise. Their pots are in Knossos in a roughly contemporary burial context and there is a fair amount of iron in the west of the island; Phoenician merchants could easily have been involved in trading it to the Assyrians. Kommos appears to have been a Phoenician trading and watering point, peaking in the 9th century; this temple remained in use beyond that period while, in the 7th century, settlement on the hill expanded. A third temple was superimposed in the 4th century. It had two central columns, a hearth in between, benches around the walls and a cult statue, of which only the eye remained for the excavators to find. It is therefore not known which deity was worshipped. The style is unique to Crete and has been found with an earlier date in Dreros and Rizenia. Here the double doors opened onto a courtyard where eventually four altars were erected. On the basis of evidence for feasting, a room to the northwest has been interpreted as a dining hall, while buildings to the north of the court were used for storage and residence. Towards the end of the life of the site, well into Roman times, the only recorded activity came from this building: it may have functioned by then as a residence rather than as a temple.

Matala

From Kommos it is a short drive to Matala (Μάταλα; *map p. 430, A3*), with its beautiful cove and spectacular cliffs with Roman rock-cut tombs. You might want to enjoy the place in the quiet season, that is when the influx of tourist coaches abates and the place dies down—to the delight of the Loggerhead turtle.

THE LOGGERHEAD SEA TURTLE

The Loggerhead Sea Turtle (*Caretta caretta*) is the most common sea turtle in the Mediterranean and in Greece. When Guy Crouchback (the central character in Evelyn Waugh's *Officers and Gentlemen*) was hallucinating in his hospital bed in Cairo after a harrowing crossing from Crete, he could hear whales singing and see 'myriad cat's eyes…and the whole surface of the water encrusted with carapaces gently bobbing one against the other and numberless and ageless lizard faces gaping at him'. You may not wish such a close encounter—and indeed you should not. These turtles live in the sea, but mature females return every 2–3 years to bury their eggs in the beaches where they hatched. It is then that they are at their most vulnerable, being very bulky (up to 100kg) and with an awkward locomotion system as their feet have evolved into paddles. In Crete the areas of the Mesara Bay north of Matala and specific beaches on the north coast are used as nesting sites. More are located further north, on the island of Zakynthos and in the Peloponnese. Unfortunately, the nesting and hatching season is from June to September, at the height of the tourist influx which brings humans and their clutter onto beaches. This could spell disaster for the turtles and the hatchlings as they race for the sea and become disoriented by lights and noise.

The Sea Turtle Protection Society (STPS) has played a major role in assisting the implementation of legislation intended to protect the sea turtle and its habitat while at the same time accommodating the need for local development and encouraging sustainable tourism. There are now restrictions on the use of beaches at night and arrangements regarding the cleaning and floodlighting of sensitive areas in the breeding season. Volunteers monitor the beaches and rescue nests. The society also runs a programme of sea turtle rehabilitation, with a centre in Athens to assist animals that have been injured or trapped in nets. For more information, see www.archelon.gr or ask at the STPS information hut in Matala (*summer only*).

ON THE SLOPES OF THE ASTEROUSIA MOUNTAINS

The south coast of Herakleion province is still comparatively unspoilt, probably because it lacks a serious coastal route along the whole of its length; and long may it remain thus, one hopes. The access routes from the Mesara are long, winding and at times a hair-raising drive, but they are certainly well worth the trouble. The landscape is rugged and barren, wild and unspoilt, a beauty to behold, though you should keep your eyes firmly on the road. Moreover, though the state of the roads is generally good, the pace of driving can be slow; extra time must be allowed and notices such as 'Last petrol station before Lendas' should be taken very seriously. This section proposes a number of separate excursions, most of them culminating in a fine swim in the Libyan Sea. They should be planned from a local base and undertaken in no hurry.

FROM THE ODIGHITRIA MONASTERY TO THE SEA

From Phaistos an 8km detour on a secondary road leads south to Sivas and the Moni Odighitrias. Beyond the monastery you can either walk to the sea down the Aghiopharango Gorge or drive on to Kali Limenes, though it is an unmade road from the monastery onwards. (Kali Limenes has a slightly better road from Pombia to the east.)

The drive starts in a landscape of olive groves and cypresses but as the road starts climbing the hillside, it winds its way through a typical *phrygana*, the Greek word for firewood. This is the last stage of woodland degradation after the Mediterranean scrub has failed and the impenetrable woodland has given way to maquis and garrigue and finally evolved into its present state with a ground cover of highly scented spiny dwarf shrubs, no taller than 50cm and resistant to drought and grazing. Here and there, in among the bare patches of land, geophytes (bulb plants) prosper and you might find the occasional orchid. The bees have a feast and the view is wide and unimpeded towards the White Mountains, Mt Kedros and the Mesara Bay to the northwest.

The Odighitria Monastery

The Odighitria Monastery (Μονή Οδηγήτριας; *map p. 430, A3*) is named after a type of icon (the 'Hodighitria'), in which the Virgin is represented pointing to the Child Christ as the way to salvation. According to the Venetian archives there was a convent here as early as 1393, when a monk asked permission to leave Crete to be ordained by an Orthodox bishop. It was flourishing in the 16th century, when it belonged to the Kallergis family and its income was 1500 ducats. At present the complement of monks is small. The monastery commands a high ridge over a tributary of the Aghia Kyriaki, which flows through the Aghiopharango Gorge. Its position inland afforded some protection against pirate raids and a tall stone-built tower was an additional security. Gerola visited at the beginning of the 20th century. He noted three gates in a quadrangular enclosure, the courtyard around a church, and a gravestone with a 1564 inscription.

The **Xopateras tower** is named after the legendary defrocked monk (*xopateras* means 'ex-priest'; his real name was Ioannis Markakis) who achieved fame in the 1828 revolt as the chief of a local band. The Turks pursued him into the tower where he had taken refuge with all his family. Popular legend maintains that he defended himself by hurling beehives at them, but to no avail. This may be fictional, but the fortress style of the buildings and the round opening above one of the doors of the tower (meant for the pouring of hot oil) shows that defence was a consideration.

The two-aisled **church** has some frescoes in the vault with scenes from the life of the Virgin and a fine deësis. The *Embrace of Peter and Paul* and the Christ with the Twelve Apostles in the branches of a vine have been attributed to the 15th-century painter

Angelos. An icon of Aghios Phanourios by the same artist is now in Herakleion at Aghia Aikaterini.

Just north of the monastery are two excavated **tombs of the Mesara type** (*see pp. 146–47*) in use in the Prepalatial period, an early date confirmed by the obsidian blades and the stone axes. Both tholoi had been looted but still contained superb finds, including stone vases, pottery, seals and jewellery, three gold diadems and a bracelet that had accompanied some of the 150 burials. In an ossuary between the tombs an undisturbed deposit yielded 22 seals.

The Aghiophrarango Gorge

For a walk down the Aghiopharango Gorge (the 'Holy Gorge') to the beautiful beach by the Libyan Sea, drive on towards Kali Limenes. About 1km after the road crosses the river bed there is room to park (*NB: Walkers should not plan this expedition in the early spring or after heavy rains. Also bear in mind that it takes a good hour to get to the sea. Moreover, since there is no coastal path, the only way out is the way back*). The gorge was a sacred place populated by hermits until comparatively recently. They lived in the caves and came together once a year in the Iegoumenospilios ('Abbot's Cave') for a head count. The track (about 3km) starts there. At first it is a clear path but soon there is only the stream bed to follow, while the gorge narrows and its sides become more precipitous. Towards the end, with the sea in sight, note to the left the substantial domed church of Aghios Antonios, built into the rock wall. It encloses the chapel of Aghios Ioannis Xenos, the evangelist St John the Stranger, born in the area at Sivas in 970.

St John Xenos (active 970–1027, canonised 1632)

After a century of Arab occupation had adversely affected Crete's religious landscape, the island was in need of evangelists to reproclaim the faith and of builders to pick up the pieces of the damaged infrastructure. St John Xenos, a true Cretan from Sivas in the Mesara, was both, though he was by no means the only Byzantine saint engaged in this type of missionary work.

He was led by visions and spent his life criss-crossing the mountains of Crete following imperatives from saintly apparitions and from God himself. He is credited, among other things, with the building of a church on the site of the tombs of Sts Eftychios and Eftychianos and the monastery at Myriokephala, southwest of Rethymnon; he also took care of existing foundations, making sure they were on a good economic footing and that the monks had sufficient land and the wherewithal to support themselves. He went to Byzantium to acquire books, icons, ecclesiastical furnishings and vessels for monastic life. Eventually he retired to Kissamos, though he is also associated with the Katholiko on Akrotiri (*see p. 335*), suggesting that the caves on the hillside had an anchorite community. According to one tradition he was buried in Corfu but his skull remained in Crete and is presently in Tsourouniana, a village south of Kissamos.

Kali Limenes

Kali Limenes ('Fair Harbours'; Καλοί Λιμένες; *map p. 430, A3*) is only 7km from Moni Odighitrias. The beach is lovely, not so the view, marred by an oil installation on one of the islands. The site was one of the ports of Gortyn when it was called Lasaia (and also, according to the coinage, Thalassa or Alasa). The place enjoyed a reputation as a safe anchorage, 'secure for ten galleys', according to a Venetian document. It certainly did not work for St Paul on his disastrous trip from the East to Rome (*see p. 160*). So far there have been no official excavations of the Graeco-Roman city-state, though unofficial digging has taken place. The centre of the city has been located on the island of Taphos or Palaios Molos, 100m offshore at the eastern end of the beach. A narrow channel was left at the southern end before the island to allow boats to move to a shel-tered position on either side, according to the direction of the winds. A survey of the headland and the coast has identified the site of a temple, a possible basilica church, house walls, cisterns, an aqueduct and harbour works at the island, as well as evidence of Minoan presence (settlement and tombs).

The place was visited by Onorio Belli in 1586. He was able to name the city after seeing some stray finds, but by then it was in a ruined state with no recognisable struc-tures. In 1854 the English surveyor Captain T.A.B. Spratt did a better job at working out the area of the ancient city on the seashore, on the island and on the hill with the cemetery area to the west, but he took more interest in the goings on at Taphos. Con-vinced that the inhabitants were pirates (the island was in fact a base for Greek freedom fighters against the Turks) he dispatched a ship to kill them and a bloody battle ensued.

Apesokari, Moni Apezanon and Miamou

Some way inland, at **Apesokari** (Απεσωκάρι; *map p. 430, B3*), a Mesara tomb is con-veniently located and signposted by the road with a clear path leading to it (a short walk among olive trees). The remains are not spectacular, as is true of many of these ancient structures, but the location on an eminence at the foot of the Asterousia range, overlooking the Mesara plain, Mt Ida and the sea in the distance, is truly engaging.

For **Moni Apezanon** (*map p. 430, B3*), continue to Plora, a couple of kilometres on, and then continue southwest. A right turn before Andiskari leads to the monastery (c. 2km), whose buildings are marked from a distance by a line of cypresses. The original north entrance is just beyond the modern gate into the courtyard. The monastery, a Venetian foundation, was dedicated to Aghios Antonios of Aghiopharango (*see above*) and, according to tradition, the monks had to retreat inland for safety. Gerola, who vis-ited at the beginning of the last century, described a pentagonal wall circuit enclosing the monastic buildings, with towers, a defended gateway and crenellations. Enough remains nowadays, in spite of modern alterations, to convey some of the original effect.

Lendas with its fine beaches is certainly worth a visit, but rather than cutting across the Asterousia mountains, visitors are advised to take the south road from Apesokari, just east of Plora. From there a good road climbs into the mountains via **Miamou** (Μιαμού; *map p. 430, B3*), a very picturesque village on the mountainside. Here a cave excavated at the end of the 19th century produced evidence of occupation dating to the Final Neolithic. The site is at present under the modern village. The road now winds its way towards the sea with fine views of **Mt Kofinas**, the highest point in the range (1231m), to the east. At Kofinas critical finds such as a bull rhyton, statues and a Linear A inscribed bronze vessel have confirmed the presence of a Minoan peak sanctuary of the early 2nd millennium, for which the British School is now carrying out a survey.

Lendas

On the way down to Lendas (Λέντας; *map p. 430, B3*) visitors will be able to judge for themselves whether the name of the village is justified. Apparently it is derived from the Greek word for lion, inspired by the profile of the promontory to the west of the village, which resembles a crouching lion. Here was the site of ancient Lebena, a place that prospered as a harbour (Minoan remains show early occupation, and in Roman times it was used by Gortyn) and even more so as a spa. Water and health went hand in hand in antiquity, and here the therapeutic springs (the spring water is alkaline and has traces of arsenate minerals, good for blood conditions) ensured a long-lasting veneration of Asclepios, the healing god, dating from Hellenistic times. It had developed from an earlier cult of the water nymphs and of the river god Acheloös. The place was first identified by Onorio Belli. He was very taken with it and drew a plan. Taramelli and Halbherr visited in 1894 for the inscriptions and conducted excavations.

The **Sanctuary of Asclepios** (*signposted 'Archaeological Site'; always accessible*) is at the foot of the hills just above the beach. It was damaged in the Second World War by the Germans, who blew up the pillars. Recent work has reorganised the remains but they are still pretty difficult to make out. The temple, on an artificial terrace, was made of local limestone and consisted of a 12m by 13m cella with a podium for the statue of the god against the inner west wall. In Hellenistic times the walls were in stone but they were given a brick veneer by the Romans. Near the statue, dedicated by Xenion (inscription on a loose fragment), are remains of a Roman mosaic. In the northeast corner of the temple was the treasury with a 3rd-century BC sea-pebble mosaic showing a seahorse set in a scroll of waves with two delicate palmettes. The floor was damaged in antiquity by the sinking of a shaft for offerings, which were subsequently looted. Two free-standing colonnaded porticoes stood north and west of the treasury but are no longer visible. Archaeologists have found other evidence of the complex, namely c. 15m to the east, where traces of a brick and tile structure near the spring may be linked to a nymphaeum, as well as down the hillside below the temple, where two great basins were perhaps for the total immersion of the sick in the warm water. None of that can be viewed these days. Hard evidence of a long building interpreted as pilgrims' lodgings has also vanished. Inscriptions from it include votive tablets in the Doric dialect. One gives a vivid description of a miraculous cure of sciatica performed by the god on the sleeping patient. The complex suffered an earthquake in AD 46 and was rebuilt. In Byzantine times the small basilica church of Aghios Ioannis Theologos, erected using spolia just below the Asclepieion, testifies to a decline of the cult. It was later partly built over by a Venetian church, which sits neatly inside the two rows of columns.

The Minoan settlement on Cape Lendas has not yet been excavated. However, finds from tholos tombs of the Mesara type (*see pp. 146–47*), which include Egyptian scarabs, Cycladic figurines and seals, testify to the far-reaching connections of the area.

Modern Lendas is a small village awaiting salvation by way of tourism. In the '60s the hippies descended here because of the beautiful beaches and the 'away from it all, end of the world' atmosphere. Indeed from Lendas the next stop is Libya. Now they are gone. The place has acquired some regular accommodation: wild camping is frowned upon. The area is not short of beautiful beaches. To the east past Loutro, a visit to Trachoulas beach can be the starting point for a walk up to the gorge of the same name to Krotos. Ditykos beach to the west may be overtaken by campers in the summer; it is also popular with nudists.

THE SOUTH SLOPES OF MOUNT IDA

Leaving the main road south of Herakleion just out of Aghia Varvara, a wonderful scenic drive opens up to the west along the south slopes of Mt Ida. In this section the proposed excursions go as far as the Kamares Cave, with some fine churches on the way. Alternatively, continuing west in the Phourphouras direction, it is possible to make the complete loop to the north coast to Rethymnon via the Amari valley. This itinerary is much recommended to nature lovers, bird-watchers and flower aficionados. Serious walkers and hikers will not be disappointed either. It is possible to pick up the E4 route 10km north of Gergeri and go east to Venerato and Temenos via the Prinos refuge, and west to the Nida plateau and the Idaian Cave; for more leisurely activities there are walks around Lake Votomos, an artificial lake with an interesting bird population, and the Rouvas Forest.

Rouvas Forest and Moni Vrondisi

The road starts a few hundred metres south of Aghia Varvara in the Gergeri direction, with fine views of the Libyan Sea and of the Paximadia islands in Mesara Bay. At Gergeri the path to the **Rouvas Forest** (*map p. 430, B2*), a large grove of prickly oak (*Quercus coccifera*), is marked to the right. **Zaros** (Ζαρός) is the next village (15km), known for its abundance of water and fine trout. Gortyn's water supply started here. Remains of the Roman aqueduct can be seen on the road to the artificial Lake Votomos.

A track up in the mountains 500m out of Zaros leads to **Moni Aghios Nikolaos**, 2km up the valley. In the church of the monastery the older frescoes are in the original chapel. The 14th-century paintings include, in the sanctuary, a particularly moving scene representing the Birth of the Virgin. For walkers there is an alternative route along the stream bed (20mins) or from Lake Votomos on a longer marked footpath. The monastery is at the foot of the Rouvas Gorge. Up the hillside is the cave church of **Aghios Efthymios**, also with frescoes, and along the gorge itself a marked path leads to the chapel of Aghios Ioannis (2hrs), where it connects with the E4 route.

Panorama of Mt Ida.

From Zaros, **Moni Vrondisi** is not signed. Do not enter the village and keep west. The monastery (*map p. 430, B2; open all day*) is 4km on, signposted to the right. It sits on a panoramic, shaded terrace with a fine Venetian fountain, the Monofatsi, near the entrance by the huge chestnut trees. It has a relief framed by pilasters with Corinthian capitals. It shows Adam and Eve before the Fall and the four rivers of the Garden of Eden in the lower register. The gateway to the monastery was destroyed in 1913. An inscription from it dated to 1630–36 has been incorporated into the door frame of one of the cells. By the end of the Venetian period, this monastery was a very influential community, a centre for scholars and artists. It had six icons by Mikhail Damaskinos, eventually moved for safety to Aghia Aikaterini in Herakleion (*see p. 50*). In the court-yard (try to ignore the concrete construction to the north) the two-aisled church pre-serves important frescoes in the older south aisle dedicated to Aghios Antonios. These date to the first half of the 14th century and are early examples of the Cretan School, a specific trend in Palaeologan painting. The *Last Supper* appears here on the vaulting of the apse, a position unique in Crete. Below is the *Communion of the Apostles*. On the right of the Hierarchs, Simeon holds the Christ Child.

Moni Valsamoneros

Back on the road a shortcut leads walkers straight to Moni Valsamoneros (*map p. 430, A2*); otherwise the road to the monastery starts from Vorizia (3km) at the bottom of the village past a bridge with plane trees. Of the monastery, once an influential centre, only its beautifully frescoed church, dedicated to Aghios Phanourios, remains (*not open to the public*). It appears that after an early period of prosperity, the monastery was overshadowed by nearby Vrondisi. The original church was built in 1328 and shows a strong Venetian influence over the current Byzantine style. This can be seen on the south façade in the elaborate doorways with rosette decoration and in the Venetian coat of arms above the entrance to the narthex. The ground plan is complex and unusual because of numerous alterations and additions. The original nave runs along the north wall and is dedicated to the Panaghia, the Virgin Mary: on its barrel vaulting is the most complete set of scenes from the life of the Virgin (the Hymns to the Mother of God) known in Cretan fresco painting (*at the time of writing, sadly, it was not possible to view them*). The transept is dedicated to Aghios Phanourios, a saint originally from Rhodes but particularly venerated at Valsamoneros, known for his power over lost causes and lost articles. Apparently he still assists the faithful in finding anything from a lost piece of jewellery to lost health and happiness.

The Kamares Cave

From the village of Kamares (Καμάρες; *map p. 430, A2*), 4km west of Vorizia, a steep climb of 4–5hrs leads to the cave that gave its name to a style of fine polychrome Protopalatial pottery that was instrumental in building the first Minoan chronology (*see illustration on p. 30*). The cave is quite high up (1524m), overlooked by the summit of Mavri, and is accessible only in the extended summer months. The start of the hike is marked at the eastern end of Kamares; from then on watch for yellow paint splashes and E4 signs. The first part is along the watercourse following the pipeline; after about one hour you will reach a group of water troughs. There you go east along the edge of the trees up to a second group of troughs and a spring. From that point there is another hour to go. From the cave the E4 path continues north to summit of Mt Ida (2456m) and east to the Idaian Cave, the Nida plateau and beyond. Walkers should not embark lightly on such expeditions.

The location was first investigated by the Italians in 1904 after a shepherd discovered it in 1890; the British then conducted excavations in 1913, assisted by a particularly mild winter. In 2002 speleologists and pottery experts from the Canadian Institute in Greece joined forces to undertake a re-examination of the cave and its finds. They explored the interior of the cave, made of two chambers, and identified walls possibly of Minoan date. The material excavated in 1913 consists mainly of large quantities of pottery, a few animal figurines, some stone and bone tools, animal bones and six iron spearheads, a later deposition. According to the style of pottery, the cave was visited in the period 3000–1100 BC, with activity peaking at the time of the First Palace at Phaistos. The sheer quantity suggests sustained use, but there is an intriguing shortage of utilitarian items. Moreover, the pottery is in pristine condition, probably hardly used.

Caves have a special place in the Minoan religion. Kamares is no exception, but while other locations have produced finds clearly linked to cult and ritual activities such as ex-votos, offering-tables and double axes, at Kamares these are absent. Yet some ritual activity did take place here. Looking at the typology of the pottery, one finds a preponderance of storage jars and of libation vessels, hinting at a cult in which the setting aside of foodstuffs and the pouring of liquids were important activities. Petrographic analysis has shown that most of the pottery originated from the Mesara plain, though a very small amount came from further afield, including the island of Gavdos. As for the actual ceremonies performed in the cave, the charred remains of seeds and animal bones have prompted speculation that the site was used for a religious festival connected with the harvest when the fruits of the earth were offered in a blaze to the gods.

From Kamares the drive to Phourphouras is strongly recommended (though possibly not in the evening sun).

PRACTICAL INFORMATION

GETTING AROUND

• **By car:** From Herakleion take the straight through road south to Aghii Deka from the E75 bypass as it leaves the town (38km) then turn right. It is less than 20km to the sea.
• **By bus:** From the bus station by the Chanioporta in Herakleion (*T: 2810 255965; www. crete-buses.gr*) buses go all the way south to Aghii Deka (the stop for Gortyn) then continue to Mires and Tymbaki. Phaistos is in between and eight buses a day go specifically there. A stop in Pitsidia might get you to Kommos. Kamilari has a bus service to and from Herakleion and Tymbaki. For the eastern foothills of Mt Ida there are services from Herakleion at the bus station by the Chanioporta going to Krousonas, Prinias and Asites. Buses to Lendas from Herakleion are infrequent and involve a change.

WHERE TO STAY & EAT

The area around Venerato and Krousonas is well stocked with accommodation. In the Mesara it is best to avoid the villages by the main road on the plain, where it can be very dusty and hot, and either go to the seaside (where there is plenty to choose from) or take to the hills, either here or further east. Matala and the coast to Tymbaki and Kokkinos Pyrgos are not short of accommodation (including a well-known camp site) and places to eat. For Gortyn the nearest tavernas are at Aghii Deka. Phaistos and Aghia Triada are badly served as far as food is concerned. Phaistos has something in the Tourist Pavilion at the entrance to the site; Aghia Triada nothing at all. The nearest taverna is along the main road that crosses the Mesara.

Krousonas/Venerato (*map p. 430, B2*)
€€ **Agioklima**. Three apartments on the outskirts of the village of Petrokefalo, 8km northeast of Krousonas, in old renovated houses. *T: 2810 223861; www.agioklima.gr.*
€€ **Earino**. Studios and maisonettes in a superb commanding position above Kato Asites. *T: 2810 301977; www.earino.gr.*
€€ **Viglatoras**. Traditional apartments in a forested area on the eastern slopes of Ida in Sarchos, east of Krousonas. *T: 2810 711332 or 252581; mobile 6979 349286; www.viglatoras.gr.*
€€ **Villa Kerasia**. Attractive small country hotel in a quiet location west of Venerato. Breakfast is served; dinner optional. *T: 2810*

791021; www.villa-kerasia.gr.

€ **Babis Tselentakis**. Rooms at Oulaxiana Palianis in a small hamlet between Kerasa and Ano Asites. The turning is marked in Venerato opposite the Kostis Varouchas taverna (*T: 6971 896310*), which serves good Cretan food. *T: 2810 791021.*

Pitsidia (*map p. 430, A3*)

€€ **Filia**. Studios, apartments and rooms in a modern building. *T: 28920 45206, www.interkriti.net/hotel/pitsidia/filia/index.html. See also www.pitsidia-villa.com.*

€€ **Vrisi**. Studio and apartments with swimming pool in a green setting. *T: 28920 45114, www.pitsidia-studios.com.*

€ **Pension Sofos**. Five renovated rooms with air conditioning. *www.pitsidia-apartments.com.*

Vori (*map p. 430, A3*)

€€ **Portokali** (*T: 28920 91188, mobile 6932208534; portokali@messara.de*) offers studios and rooms to rent. Near the top of the village is the € **Pension Margit** (*T: 2892 091129, www.pensionmargit.messara.com*). For somewhere to eat, try the **Tavena Alekos** or **Oi Velgoi** ('The Belgians', run by Greeks who have lived in Belgium) at the south end of the village, for good wholesome Cretan cuisine.

Zaros (*map p. 430, B2*)

€€ **Keramos Studios**. Basic but comfortable family guesthouse. *T: 28940 31352, www.studios-keramos.com.*

€€ **Hotel Idi**. Situated at the foot of Ida, a modern hotel in attractive grounds, outside the village of Zaros. *T: 2894 031301 or 031302; www.idi-hotel.com.* The **Taverna Votomos** next to the hotel has a well-deserved reputation for fresh trout straight from the lake.

FESTIVALS & EVENTS

Dafnes, just north of Venerato, has been hosting a wine festival since 1976. It normally takes place in first two weeks of July, though the programme may not appear on the website (*www.winefest-dafnes.gr/main_english.htm*) in time for you to take a decision. Probably the best tactic is just to turn up: with luck you will be able to join in the music, the dancing and the wine tasting. This is the land of the famous Liatiko, an early-ripening red grape.

LASITHI PROVINCE

East of Herakleion province, Crete stretches another 90km or so as the crow flies to the shores facing the island of Karpathos. Lasithi, the easternmost province, takes its name from a mispronunciation of the Venetian name of one its main towns, La Sitia, now Siteia. Lasithi is ecologically very diverse. To the west are the tall mountains of the Dikte range (2080m), the Lasithi plateau (850m), too cold for olives trees, and the sheltered bay of Mirabello, true to its name meaning 'beautiful view'. In the far east, before the stormy Cape Sideros, there is a touch of the exotic with Vai beach and its palm trees: the hippies and their colourful lifestyle have moved out and on; now developers and their golf courses would like to move in (*see box on p. 263*). In the centre of the province the isthmus of Ierapetra, barely 15km wide, is crossed by a good road leading to an area that is warmer and drier than the rest of the island. That has had its effects on the landscape as, rather than tourists, locals have been cultivating fruit and vegetables. The stretch east of Ierapetra with its polytunnels well deserves its nickname of 'Costa Plastica'.

The province offers a good choice of sites to visit, whether you want to see the ancient and Classical side of Crete or the more recent Byzantine developments. Archaeologists have been busy here too. There are several excavated Minoan sites: on the south coast, at Myrtos, two side by side. Another type of settlement, the refuge site, which developed in the troubled times following the unravelling of Minoan society, is well represented at Kavousi on the north coast and at Karphi in the Lasithi area. The Lasithi plateau is in a class of its own because of its bizarre geology and complex historical development. A visit to the plateau can be done as a day trip, even by bus from Aghios Nikolaos.

Further east, the coast is still remote and comparatively unspoilt. The main centre of attraction is obviously Zakros, with a Minoan palace and town, but visitors should not overlook Palaikastro, possibly less spectacular but no less thought provoking, nor ignore what the coast itself has to offer for a day on the beach, now that the pirates and their ravages (*see p. 270*) belong to history.

Hikers can walk the whole length of eastern Crete on the E4 long-distance route. You can pick it up as it enters the province east of Kastelli Pediadas, skirt around the Lasithi plateau, cross Mt Dikte and strike east, keeping to the high ground where the view, the birdlife and the wild flowers are superb. After dipping at Vasiliki in the Ierapetra isthmus, the E4 climbs up into the Thrypti mountains and continues on a gentle slope all the way to Zakros and the sea.

AGHIOS NIKOLAOS

Situated on the western side of the Gulf of Mirabello, a stone's throw from the island of Aghii Pandes (a designated sanctuary for Kri-kri goats; *see p. 365*), is the small resort town of Aghios Nikolaos (Άγιος Νικόλαος; *map p. 431, B2*). 'Ay Nick', as it is familiarly known to the British, has managed to turn itself into a pleasant, well-behaved tourist resort—and that in spite (or perhaps because of) the scarcity of good beaches in the immediate vicinity. There is a strip of sand along the road north from the centre (Ammoudi), a pebble beach in the Kitroplateia cove (quickly crowded in summer), a municipal beach southeast of the marina and another, further south, the reed-fringed Almyros beach. The success of Aghios Nikolaos is due to a combination of good-quality service and facilities, the friendly feel of the place, and 'location'. The town is also greatly helped by its varied topography, full of ups and downs and unexpected vistas, breaking the townscape into different focal points.

Aghios Nikolaos is a good choice as a base for day trips to Spinalonga and the rugged Aghios Ioannis peninsula, to the Lasithi plateau and along the coast to Siteia.

HISTORY OF AGHIOS NIKOLAOS

The location was originally the harbour of the ancient inland town of Lato near Kritsa (*see p. 198*). It was then known as Lato pros Kamara meaning 'towards the arch', a toponym perhaps referring to the cliff overhanging Lake Voulismeni. The coastal settlement flourished in Roman times on the low hill jutting into the bay between the modern port and the south-facing shore of Kitroplateia. The Venetian anchorage was slightly to the north, by the chapel of Aghios Nikolaos (*see p. 183*), and it was called Porto San Nicolò. The position was strengthened with the Mirabello fortress that stood where the prefecture (Nomarcheion) is today. The original fort, built by the Genoese in 1212, was taken over by Venice but later the Serenissima concentrated its efforts on the more strategically placed Spinalonga, where a defensive position was built in 1579. The Turks sacked the Mirabello fort in 1537, and when the Venetians got it back, realising that they needed all the defences they could muster, they reinforced it, only to lose it to the Ottomans again through treason. When they re-conquered it they razed it to the ground, or nearly so. Giuseppe Gerola visited in 1900 and found just one wall left of a structure that had originally been square in plan with four bastions and a tower. Nowadays only the name lives on: both the prefecture and the gulf are called Mirabello.

The present town of Aghios Nikolaos is a comparatively recent development. When it was chosen as capital of the province in 1905, it numbered 95 inhabitants and had no harbour. Its main attraction must have been Lake Voulismeni (*see below*). A name for the new capital had to be found, and the Byzantine chapel above the old Venetian port provided inspiration.

The centre of town

The **main harbour** at Aghios Nikolaos is lined with cafés on Akti Koundourou. The two **shopping streets**, 28 Oktovriou and R. Koundourou, feed into it. On the other side of the harbour, across the modern road bridge, is the old **port authority building**, part of which houses the inconspicuous folklore museum (*see opposite*). The bridge spans a short channel built in 1867 to link Ay Nick's most famous feature, **Lake Voulismeni**, then a brackish body of water, to the sea. Since then the quality of the water has improved and it is now easier to believe that Artemis and Athena once washed their hair in it. The other legend about the lake, namely that it was bottomless, was exploded by The surveyor Captain Spratt, who measured its depth to 64m round about the same time. Today the lakeshore is lined on the south and east by cafés, and small fishing boats tie up. The north side is the sheer cliff that may have given the place its name in antiquity (*see History, above*). Now pigeons roost in it. Past an old Turkish fountain, steps lead up to the streets of the higher town and eventually to the archaeological museum (*see p. 179*).

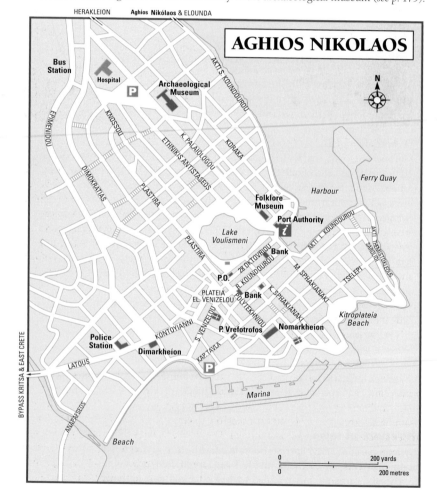

View across the Gulf of Mirabello from Aghios Nikolaos, looking towards Kavousi.

To the south of the old harbour, past the ferry dock where the Nostos boats leave for Spinalonga, the coast road and promenade lead around to the pebbly **cove of Kitroplateia**, a name reflecting a historical association with citrus shipping. From this point there is a magnificent view across the gulf to the great wall of the mountains on the other side (*illustrated above*). In the evening the lights of Kavousi can be seen twinkling. A short walk to the south from Kitroplateia leads to the **marina**, with its fine display of yachts. Just above it, in an old part of town on Kapetan Tavla, is the church of the **Panaghia Vrefotrofos** ('Our Lady Feeding the Infant'). The building dates to the 12th century and has remains of 14th-century wall paintings and the 17th-century Venetian tomb niche of a Lorenzo Maripietro, who died at a young age and is here commemorated in a Latin inscription set up by his father, the governor of the region. The church is normally locked but a verger comes to light candles in the evening.

The Folklore Museum

The museum (*by the tourist office at the north end of the bridge over the lake where it connects to the sea. Open Sun–Fri 10–2; T: 28410 25093*) provides an excellent introduction to the traditional Cretan way of life, with a large collection of embroideries, linens and clothing together with icons and household implements. It also offers the rare chance to see a reconstruction of a house interior. The elevated conjugal bedstead was a standard feature of a Cretan house and was intended to ensure a degree of privacy. The area was surrounded by a balustrade and enclosed with richly-embroidered hangings. On a table by the entrance lingers a book of old postcards, a true treasure trove of views of

Chania and Herakleion c. 1900. There are images of dervishes from Chania, the original Bedouins from Koum Kapi (*see p. 330*), Chania market standing in empty fields and an array of Cretan beauties.

EMBROIDERY

Traditionally in Greece and in the Greek islands it was expected that a young girl's dowry would include a number of embroidered articles to wear and to adorn the house. These she would make herself and store in a chest, known in Crete as a *kassella* (a Venetian name) or *sandik* (its Turkish counterpart). Travellers and archaeologists alike have taken an interest in these items over the centuries. One of the best collections is in Britain, acquired by the Victoria and Albert Museum in 1876 from Thomas Sandwith, British Consul in Crete from 1870–85.

The two focal points for embroidery were women's clothing and bed hangings. The latter were designed to create a private space in shared accommodation. The bed would be on a raised platform decorated by a valance and surrounded by a curtain (called *mostra* in Greek, an Italian word meaning 'display').

The best Cretan work, however, is found in the clothing. Early travellers report that Cretan women wore very full skirts (five loom widths, making the skirt sometimes over 3m wide at the hem), much fuller than in the other islands. These were suspended high up from the shoulders with short straps and may have been worn over an underdress with wide sleeves. Alternatively, women wore a loose drapery with long sleeves, gathered at the neck, and which a pilgrim in 1322 compared to a choir boy's surplice.

Embroidery went on the hem (sometimes a very wide band) and on the edge of the sleeves. With the Turkish occupation women started wearing *shalvar* (baggy trousers) under the skirt: these were decorated at the lower end, where they showed beneath the skirt. The neckline also received attention and was covered with a tippet of fine linen with silk and metal thread embroidery and lace insertions. This garment had a Venetian name (*koleto*), which suggest that the Cretan *décolletage* had been a source of worry even before the arrival of the Ottomans. Indeed, as early as Venetian times women were confined to the house, and according to Belon and Sandys, who visited the island in the early 17th century, women would welcome the chance at funerals to 'let their hair down' and wear a low-cut dress leaving their hair uncovered.

Embroiderers in the Greek islands tended to be quite conservative in their choice of patterns. Once a design was established, it was repeated through the generations. Crete is no exception. A Venetian colony until 1669, longer than anywhere else in the Aegean, it retained its designs with stylised flowers and figures that can be traced to contemporary motifs on Italian silks, which it was possibly trying to imitate.

The Archaeological Museum

Almost at the top of Konstantinou Palaiologou and close to a colourful fruit and veg-etable market (held on Weds), the Archaeological Museum (*open Tues–Sun 8.30–3; T: 28410 24943*) houses artefacts from eastern Crete, though nowadays material from the extreme east of the island is more likely to be exhibited in Siteia. There is an illustrated publication by the museum's first director, Kostis Davaras, describing the major ex-hibits and setting them in context. Sites and categories of artefacts are presented with excellent introductory panels in Greek and English and on the whole the collection is well curated, though the labelling is not yet complete. The museum, founded in 1970 and recently renovated, is set around a central court with eight rooms. The display begins in Room III (you get a plan with your ticket) and is arranged clockwise.

Room III (Neolithic to Prepalatial):

The **limestone idol** facing the entrance is from the cave of Pelekita, north of Kato Zakros on the seaward side of Mt Traostalos; here Neolithic activity, possi-bly prompted by the awesome stalactites, has been identified. The other cases are mainly taken up by pottery from the large EM cemetery of Aghia Photia on the coast east of Siteia. Note the burnished surfaces, possibly imitating wood, and the incised decorations, often with clay filling. Shapes include biconical goblets or chalices and cult vessels known as fry-ing pans. Multiple vases (double, triple and quadruple) are also well represented. A bird-shaped vase with incised decora-tion (to suggest plumage) represents an early example of a form that became a favourite with Cretan potters. Among the **bronze weapons** note the one that was bent to make it deliberately harm-less, a practice that may be linked to the funerary ritual of a warrior, symbolising the end of his battle days. On the whole the finds show strong connections with the Cyclades to the north but also with Phaistos to the west.

Room IV (Prepalatial to Old Palace):

Straight ahead as you enter are finds from the Prepalatial cemetery at Moch-los, now a small island close to the north coast on the way to Siteia, excavated first by Seager and, in the 1970s, by Kostis Davaras. Here, from one of the tombs built like a house, came the delicate **gold jewellery** folded in a silver box. The treasure included bracelets, chains and a diadem decorated with schematic representations of the Cretan wild goat

The EM II 'Goddess of Myrtos', a libation vessel in the form of a stylised woman holding a jug.

in repoussé dots. Three symbolic representations of *agrimi* horns are attached to the upper part of the diadem.

The most famous exhibit is the well-known **Goddess of Myrtos**. This anthropomorphic libation vessel with painted geometric decoration was found at Phournou Koryphi, one of the two sites at Myrtos west of Ierapetra. The only opening is the small jug with a beak spout cradled by the goddess. Other finds from the site (potters' wheels, seals and figurines) are also exhibited in the same room. To the left of the entrance is a good display of **Vasiliki pottery**, so called after the first site where it was identified. Since then it has become clear that it was by no means exclusive to that locality. The vessels have a characteristic mottled, slightly lustrous surface, the result of an uneven firing combined with the use of different coloured slips. Note also the astonishing examples of **Minoan stone vases**, some with closely fitting lids. The manufacture of plain stone containers probably predates the production of fired clay vases. Soft stones like gypsum would have been used in the aceramic phase of the Neolithic period, together with organic containers in wood and leather. The technique was first developed in Egypt and the earliest stone vases in Crete are imports from there. Local production started in the early 3rd millennium BC and is geared to the manufacturing of prestige goods (since by then pottery was used for day-to-day needs) in a variety of stones including alabaster, rock crystal, steatite, marble and serpentine. Finds of unfinished vases show that the vessel was first hollowed with a bronze tubular drill. After the core had been removed with a chisel, the surface was smoothed to shape with an abrasive substance, desert sand rich in quartz in Egypt or emery, more prevalent in the Cyclades.

The five **clay sistra** (*for their use see Herakleion museum, p. 43*) come from Aghios Charalambos, a cave on Lasithi excavated in 2002 by the American Philip Betancourt and Kostis Davaras. Apart from a large hoard of finds in good condition (pottery, jewellery and stone vases), the site is of particular interest because of the large sample of human skeletal remains dating to the Early and Middle Bronze Age (3rd–2nd millennia BC). It is expected that the bone analysis will provide information on diet, lifestyle and lifespan. The deposit, the reburial of hundreds of individuals, and the number of domestic animal bones unearthed, suggests that already in antiquity Lasithi supported a flourishing society practising a stock-raising economy.

Room V: At either side of the entrance are **votive offerings from peak sanctuaries** in eastern Crete. These include figurines and ex-votos deposited by pilgrims, all of which give some insight into their physical appearance, their clothing, as well as their trials, tribulations and aspirations; just as in Greek or Italian churches today, the body parts offered for ailments are mainly legs, hands, feet; here we also find genitalia. The animal figurines are believed to represent substitutes for sacrifices. From Petsophas, the peak sanctuary overlooking Palaikastro, come the unusual **composite horns of consecration** in lime plaster. The rest of the room is taken up by a display on the palace and the town of Malia, courtesy of the French School

Above: Lidded pyxis of the 8th century BC, with Geometric decoration of young men engaged in battle. Found at Itanos, in the far east of the province.
Below: Example of the many clay larnakes (tomb chests) in the Aghios Nikolaos museum collection.

(thus the explanations are in French). Note the green steatite **triton shell** with the relief carving of two facing genii, one pouring libations from a double-spouted jug into the outstretched hand of his companion (dated to LM IA) and in the same case a beautiful **gold pin** decorated with a bramble motif on one side and an inscription of 18 Linear A characters on the other. It has an interesting history. It was illegally exported from Crete and was bought in Brussels by archaeologist J.P. Olivier, who donated it to the museum in 1981.

Room VI: A good collection of **clay larnakes** is displayed here, with particular emphasis on the Marine Style. Note

the one with a large fish in the interior. The superb **vase with octopus decoration** (*illustrated overleaf*) was found at Makrygialos on the south coast and shows the quality of life and range of contacts in large villa estates of the New Palace Period (1700–1370). It is thought to originate from a Knossos workshop. From Milatos cemetery comes a selection of grave goods including jewellery and combs. On a more utilitarian level, note the collection of loom weights from the Siteia district. They would vary in size and weight according to the cloth being woven.

Room VII: Shown here are finds from the Postpalatial cemeteries at Myrsini and Kritsa and from Gournia. They show contacts with mainland Greece as well as with the west of the island. In the middle the **child burial in a pithos** from the cemetery of Krya, inland from Siteia (LM III–Protogeometric), is shown exactly as it was found and complements the collection of Minoan larnakes of the previous room. The incense burner with multiple holes and the stand with painted horns of consecration are from Gra Lygia, a cemetery near Ierapetra dated to the 14th century BC.

Above: Marine Style jar from Makrygialos. Octopuses were popular motifs because their ability to renew lost tentacles was taken as a symbol of the renewal of life.

Room VIII (Archaic period): The large collection of finds comes from a shrine deposit near the centre of modern Siteia. Note the hollow clay **head of a youth** with the typical Archaic smile. Originally the face was painted, but the paint has faded; only the blue of the eyebrows can be made out. Of particular interest is the very fine **late Geometric pyxis** (8th century BC) from the cemetery of Itanos, painted with a scene of warriors engaged in a fight (*illustrated on previous page*).

Room IX: There is a collection of coins in the centre as well as four display cases covering **ancient Olous**, the town now underwater between Elounda and Spinalonga. While the town itself (7th–5th centuries) is mainly known from inscriptions and coins, information has been forthcoming from its cemetery on the mainland and the votive deposits excavated in the 1960s on the rocky eastern tip of Spinalonga.

Room X (Roman period): Particular emphasis is placed on Roman on Aghios Nikolaos, then known as Kamara. Prominently displayed is the **skull of a young man**, dated to the 1st century AD, probably an athlete since he was buried wearing a gold wreath of stylised olive leaves and with a gold ring with a representation of Victory hanging up a trophy. A silver tetredrachm of the city of Polyrrhenia, dated to the time of emperor Tiberius (early 1st century AD), had been placed in his mouth to pay the ferryman's fare to the underworld. Also found with him were his aryballos (oil jar) and strigil, the implement used for scraping off dust and sweat mixed with the oil.

The rest of the material displayed in the room testifies to a wide web of contacts. The ostrich shell must have come from Africa. The opening would have been fitted with a spout in faïence or wood.

Votive head of a young man in the Archaic style. Found near Siteia.

The Byzantine chapel of Aghios Nikolaos

NB: The chapel contains painting of importance for the student of art history. That said, a visit is for the truly committed. There is not much left to see and access is not particularly easy.

The chapel is approached by the coast road (Akti Koundourou) in the direction of Elounda from the harbour, aiming for the headland with the Minos Palace Hotel (c. 3km from the city centre). It is possible to get there on foot, though it is a dusty and not particularly pretty 40-min walk. You arrive at the long horseshoe-shaped cove

The chapel of Aghios Nikolaos, site of the only examples of Iconoclastic-era art on Crete (*see example illustrated below*).

that was once the Venetian Porto San Nicolò. Nothing is left of it: today the inlet is filled with hotels in various stages of construction, occupation and abandonment. From the parapet as you arrive you can look across the bay and see the tiny chapel nestled among the trees. It stands within the precinct of the Minos Palace Hotel (*closed off-season until Easter*) and they keep the key. You will have to leave your passport as security (*NB: insert the key upside down and turn anticlockwise*).

The chapel has one nave with three bays; the central one supports a dome. The architecture is not specific enough to allow a dating. Restoration work in the 1960s and

more recently has uncovered two layers of frescoes. There is some 14th-century work, including a ruined Pantocrator with a fragmentary inscription, in the conch of the apse. Below are remains of the earlier wall paintings, which can be dated to the Second Byzantine period (10th century), after the Saracen interlude. These provide the only examples in Crete of the style of painting inspired by the Iconoclastic movement of the 8th–9th centuries, which banned any anthropomorphic representation in religious art. Motifs include crosses, lozenges, interlocking circles and quatrefoils, and, in the drum of the dome, floral motifs in a free-flowing and imaginative style.

PRACTICAL INFORMATION

GETTING AROUND

• **By car:** Aghios Nikolaos (www.agios-nikolaos.gr) is on the New National Road from Herakleion (69km). Taxi rides to Aghios Nikolaos are available from Herakleion airport. Arriving from other parts of the country, take either bypass on either side of the town. Aghios Nikolaos operates a one-way system. Drivers need to keep an eye out for that. Both routes arrive at the harbour front.

There are designated parking areas (by the Marina, by the hospital and in front of the Nomarcheion). Free parking is very limited in the centre but it is possible to leave a car towards the edge of town out of season.

• **By bus:** The bus station is on Epimenidou (*T: 28410 22234; www.crete-buses.gr*) to the north of town. Several buses go to Herakleion Bus Station A and fewer to Chania and Rethymnon. There are also a number of services to Ierapetra via Pachia Ammos, to Siteia, to the north coast (Sisi and Milatos), inland to Kritsa and Kroustas, and to Elounda and Plaka.

• **By sea:** Aghios Nikolaos is on a car ferry route from Piraeus to Siteia and Rhodes stopping at various islands (*www.ferries.gr/lane; T: 28410 89150*). Be alert to unexpected changes.

Trips to Spinalonga depart from the main harbour.

VISITOR INFORMATION

Tourist office at the bridge by the lake (*Koundourou 21/a, open 8.30am–9.30pm; T: 28410 22357; gr_tour_ag_nik@can.gr*) for information, maps, brochures, currency exchange and accommodation.

Taxi ranks are in Plateia Venizelou and near the tourist office (*T: 22810 24000 or 24100*

or 22786).

Post office at the top of 28 Oktovriou, south end of the lake.

The foreign community of Aghios Nikolaos has its own website (www.inconews.com) with useful links. The association organises events and runs clubs.

Port Authority T: 28410 22312.
Tourist Police T: 28410 26900.
Emergency Police T: 100.
Ambulance T: 166.

WHERE TO STAY

Aghios Nikolaos's reputation has been built on the quality of its tourist accommodation, and indeed there is plenty of it to choose from along the coast both north and south, including the luxury hotel 'villages' St Nicolas Bay (*www.stnicolasbay.gr*) and Candia Park Village (*www.greekhotel.com/crete/agiosnikolaos/candia/home.htm*). Consult the Tourist Office for cheap rooms to rent. A more limited choice is available inland, where it is quieter.

€€ **Du Lac**. In a fabulous position overlooking the lake with the entrance on 28 Oktovriou, right in the centre of town. *T: 28410 22711, www.dulachotel.gr.*

€€ **Lato Hotel**. A small establishment on the way to the chapel of Aghios Nikolaos, with 37 rooms overlooking Ammoudi beach. *T: 28410 24581/2, www.lato-hotel.com.gr.*

€€ **Palazzo Apartments**. ■ Family-run rooms (10 small apartments) with self-catering facilities on Kitroplateia beach. In a modern building, nicely done with mosaic floors. Home-baked cakes for breakfast. Warm and welcoming. *Open April–Oct. Tselepi 18, T:*

28410 25080, www.palazzo-apartments.gr.
€ **Pension Mylos**. With balconies and views of the sea. *Sarolidi 24, T: 28410 23783.*

WHERE TO EAT

In Aghios Nikolaos the seafront, harbour front and the lakeside offer a wide choice of tourist-oriented tavernas, with touts posted outside to lure you in. The Du Lac Hotel mentioned above has a fair reputation, probably deserved, but you pay for it. Other choices include:

€€€ **Migomis**. An expensive place overlooking the lake and the harbour with an international menu and an amazing wine list, which comes with the accompaniment of subdued piano music. *Restaurant open Easter–late Oct; café open all year. Nik. Plastira 22, T: 28410 24353, www.migomis.com.*

€€ **Pelagos**. Between the lake and the waterfront in an old house; recommended for seafood lovers. *Open March–Oct. Katechaki 10 (corner of Koraka), T: 28410 25737.*

€€ **Portes**. Near the sports stadium, if you fancy stewed rabbit with plums and figs served in an imaginative décor. *Anapafseos 3, T: 28410 28489.*

€ **Faros**. On Kitroplateia beach, for fish and meat cooked on an open brazier. *T: 28410 83168.*

€ **Roumelli**. Family taverna specialising in spit-roast and grilled meat. On Akti Koundourou, past the port, towards the Aghios Nikolaos headland. Open lunch and evenings.

€ **Sarri's** family taverna, inland on Kapetan Tavla, with tables on an outdoor terrace overlooking the church of the Vrefotrofos. The menu is long; ask what she has freshly cooked. *T: 28410 28059.*

For *mezedes*, try (on Kitroplateia beach) Maistrali, Chrysofillis and Mouragio (the last of the line along the promenade towards the port, just before the road divides). They cater for local custom and are not open till the evening, but will serve you until the small hours.

SHOPPING

The main shopping area, for anything from souvenirs to jewellery, is between the harbour and the main square on R. Koundourou and 28 Oktovriou (pedestrian). **Anna Karteri** (*T: 28410 22272; http://karteri.gr/site*) on R. Koundourou has an excellent choice of reading matter on things Cretan. **Bio Aroma Essential Oils Distilleries** (*open 9–2 & 5–8, T: 28410 82293; entrance free, parking*) near the Aghios Nikolaos/Herakleion crossroads and garden centre, is a museum, distillery and outlet for Cretan herbs and essential oils: the place to learn about the distillation of the herbs of Crete and their therapeutic properties.

FESTIVALS & EVENTS

There are a number of events in Aghios Nikolaos, mainly in the summer (see the Aghios Nikolaos website or enquire at the tourist office: the programme is normally available only at very short notice). Other regular festivals include **Nautical Week** (biennial in summer): water sports events and fireworks. The night of the **Anastasi** (Resurrection, Easter Saturday) is celebrated with a candlelit vigil around the lake followed by the burning of the effigy of Judas and fireworks. **Dec 6th**: feast of the patron saint. **Jan 1st**: New Year's Day celebrations with two fishing boats, one leaving the port (symbolisng the year ending) and the other coming in, (the year beginning). St Nicholas disembarks, welcomed by the city officials, the municipal band and the cheering crowds and proceeds to the main square to give out presents to the children.

AROUND ELOUNDA

The itinerary covers a roughly triangular area between Aghios Nikolaos, Sisi, on the north coast and Cape Aghios Ioannis. It forms a peninsula edged to the southwest by the E75, the New National Road, via Neapolis. A number of minor roads to the east branch off it, bisecting a plateau with an altitude not exceeding 750m. Things are very different south of the E75, where the landscape is dominated by the Lasithi range.

North of Aghios Nikolaos, the Spinalonga peninsula (12km) bears a name traditionally derived from a Venetian mispronunciation of 'Stin Elounda' (meaning 'in Elounda') until it became Spinalonga. It is worth pointing out, though, that there is a Spinalonga (a long, narrow island in the shape of a thorn, *'spina'*) in Venice and that the name predates the Venetian occupation of the Crete. That island is now known as the Giudecca.

Between Aghios Nikolaos and Elounda

The road follows the coastline climbing to the tiny village of **Ellinika** (Ελληνικά; *map p. 431, B1*). Here a small 2nd-century BC temple in local limestone was excavated in the 1930s. It had a portico and two cellae, each with a bench altar, but no door between them. The temple was dedicated to Ares and Aphrodite. According to ancient sources it was a cause of much friction between the city-states of Lato and Olous. Remains are signposted inland. The descent from the headland is a good spot to enjoy the view of Spinalonga and of the Gulf of Mirabello. There is parking (unfortunately the view is marred by an incredible amount of tangled electric wire). From this vantage point it is also possible to make out the site of ancient Olous, an important harbour in Classical times (now submerged). Focus on the Poros isthmus, cut in the recent past by a canal. A causeway has now been built over it and Spinalonga is a peninsula again. Ancient Olous straddles the isthmus. Beyond is the modern resort of **Elounda**, (Ελούντα), which has developed to meet the challenge of a booming tourist industry in this particularly appealing landscape.

SPINALONGA

For ancient Olous (Όλους), Spinalonga (Σπιναλόγκα; *map p. 431, B1*) and the Venetian fort, follow the sign to the Akti Olous Hotel on the seaward side of the road in the middle of the village. It is a tight hairpin bend coming from Aghios Nikolaos. It is possible to drive all the way over the isthmus.

Ancient Olous

The area around the isthmus of Poros, which connects Spinalonga to the mainland, was an important natural harbour for sailors escaping the battering winds of the north coast and finding shelter in Mirabello bay in the lee of Cape Aghios Ioannis. The port developed on both sides but is now submerged because of rising sea levels. In 1898 the

French navy, then part of an international occupying force, dug a canal across Olous itself to create a direct link with the open sea. In the process, and later in excavations in the 1930s and again after the Second World War, many inscriptions were recovered. They are the main source of information about Olous in the absence of underwater archaeological excavations. It is from these that we know its name; that somewhere there was a great temple to Zeus Talaios (a title connected with Talos, the giant to whom Minos entrusted the protection of Crete) and Britomartis, with a xoanon of the goddess; that Olous cooperated with Rhodes in Hellenistic times to stamp out piracy; and that Knossos intervened in the dispute with Lato over the temple at Ellinika (*see above*). Inscriptions also occasionally mention individuals: one Asclepiodotos, whom we know was involved in the restoration of an official building in Gortyn in the 4th century, has a dedication here.

Some structures are visible underwater from the isthmus. Others were reused as salt pans by the Venetians (and are now good spots for bird-watchers). A Minoan presence from c. 1700 BC is also attested. There was a settlement on the west side of the north harbour while the burial grounds were south of the isthmus. Hellenistic and Roman remains have also been identified on the immediate mainland.

There is no attested development after Roman times apart from the **two Early Christian basilicas**. The same French sailors mentioned above obligingly cleared the mosaic floor of one of them. To get there, take the rough path at the isthmus to the right of the restored mills and follow the signs to the fenced area nearby. The site is padlocked but the mosaic can easily be seen from the outside. It is black and white with an asymmetrical layout and a combination of geometric and naturalistic motifs, with some fine dolphins. This suggests that there may have been two building phases, with the mosaic belonging to an earlier, possibly smaller church. The writing style of the two inscriptions naming the donors suggests a 4th-century date.

A visit to the second basilica can be combined with a swim in what is reputedly one of the best spots in the area. Spinalonga is not a place for average hire cars, but a 40-min walk due east to **Kolokythia beach**, opposite the island of the same name, will be handsomely rewarded. The remains of the small basilica can be seen on the water's edge together with traces of a Roman or Hellenistic road leading to it.

Spinalonga fortress

The fortress stands on Kalydon, a rock off the top northern end of Spinalonga peninsula. It can be reached by regular boat services from Aghios Nikolaos, Plaka and Elounda. The trip from Aghios Nikolaos, which is the longest (about 1hr) may, if you are lucky, include a sighting of the *agrimia* goats on the island of Aghii Pandes, one of their reserves. Moreover, as the boat takes the route on the east side of Spinalonga, past the island of Kolokythia, bird-watchers might see some interesting birds at the time of the spring migration.

The fortress was built by the Venetians in 1579 on top of and incorporating a pre-existing structure, in a bid for increased security. They used limestone quarried on the northeastern shores of Spinalonga and manpower from Akrotiri (which they paid for)

The fortress of Spinalonga, on the rocky islet of Kalydon.

as well as forced local labour (which they did not). The fort was intended to control access to Mirabello Bay and the port of Elounda and had been planned to cover an ambitiously wide circuit. This created problems which remained unsolved in spite of repeated inspections from Venice. Another difficulty was the sheer altitude of the peninsula itself, overlooking Kalydon. Water was also scarce, and with a population fluctuating between 150 and 300, it proved impractical to rely on supplies shipped in from the mainland. Eventually a cistern was built.

The fortress remained in Venetian hands until 1714, well after Crete had fallen to the Ottomans, and was used as a stopping point for trade with the East. The Turks then took over and held it until 1903, using it as a refuge in the last troubled years of their occupation. From 1903–55 it functioned as a leper colony, one of the last in Europe. Not surprisingly, it acquired a reputation as a place of sadness and hopelessness. The setting up of the colony was one of the first measures of the newly-established Cretan Assembly to tackle a real problem in the island, where leprosy was endemic. At Spinalonga, Crete's lepers were assured food, water, medical attention and social security payments; over time the problem was brought under control. The last person to leave the island was a priest in 1962. He had stayed on to ensure compliance with the Orthodox requirement that the dead be commemorated at regular intervals up to five years after their demise.

A guided visit to the island, which provided the setting for Victoria Hislop's novel *The Island* and for Werner Herzog's experimental short film *Last Words*, includes a tour of the battlements and fortifications. Within the enceinte the lepers' village is in an advanced state of decay.

WEST OF CAPE AGHIOS IOANNIS

Plaka (Πλάκα; *map p. 431, B1*), on the mainland opposite the fortress, is a good place to plan an exploration of the peninsula west of Cape Aghios Ioannis. The E75 cuts across to the southwest from Malia to Aghios Nikolaos and the area is mainly served by minor roads. Walkers and bird-watchers will find it rewarding to reach Cape Aghios Ioannis and explore the sandy beaches of Boufos and Avlaki on the north coast, 4km east of the palace of Malia. The area is being developed and has facilities including camping.

Alternatively, visitors can join the locals in a pilgrimage to **Milatos Cave** (*map p. 431, A1*). Signposted at a junction from Milatos village on the road to Tsambi on the north coast east of Sisi, it is the site of a Turkish atrocity. As the story goes, in 1823, when Crete wanted to join Greece in its successful bid for independence, a large number of Christian women and children, as many as 2,700, and a few armed men, found refuge in the cave. They were betrayed and eventually found themselves besieged by a large Turkish force. They negotiated a surrender only to be slaughtered or sold into captivity.

The village of **Milatos** (Μίλατος) has a long history. Minoan occupation has been identified, and important LM III tholos tombs have been excavated (finds in Aghios Nikolaos museum). The settlement developed into a city-state, eventually destroyed by Lyttos. It is said that the great city of Miletus on the Ionian coast of Asia Minor was founded by people from Milatos. While Minoan influence has been detected in Miletus, it is still not possible to make a direct connection with this particular settlement. According to the geographer Strabo, the founding fathers of Miletus came from Crete, but for Homer they came from Caria, further south on the Ionian coast of Turkey.

Well inland, on the north side of Mt Kadisto, **Moni Aretiou** (*map p. 431, B1*) is set between Karydi and Valtos. Established in the 16th century, it prospered during the time of the Turkish occupation and bought up seven other institutions in the Mirabello area. It suffered damage in the 1821 disturbances and has only recently undergone a programme of extensive restoration. In nearby **Dories** (Δωριές; 2km) the former monastic church of Aghios Konstantinos has a 14th-century icon of the Panaghia Odighitria, with later alterations and restorations. One of the oldest remaining on Cretan soil, it had been incorporated into a slightly later *Crucifixion* as part of a double-sided icon.

This whole area, which is isolated on the far side of the main road, is very scenic and thick with villages, some of them in a state of picturesque abandonment. For some fine windmills go to **Pines** (Πινές; *map p. 431, B1*), on the ridge overlooking Elounda.

NEAPOLIS & DREROS

Northwest of Aghios Nikolaos the main road leads to Malia and Chersonisos. On the way visitors might like to shun the bypass and take time off in sleepy Neapolis.

Neapolis

During the Venetian occupation Neapolis (Νεάπολη; *map p. 431, A1*) consisted of two settlements. In 1868 the Turkish governor of Lasithi province transferred the seat of government here from Kastelli Pediadas and renamed the two settlements Neapolis ('New Town'). He liked the place so much that he built a Large Palace (now the Courts) and a Small Palace. Neapolis remained the capital of Lasithi until 1905, when Aghios Nikolaos, better placed and perhaps more dynamic, took over.

Neapolis today is a pleasant, relaxed town. It boasts churches dating from Venetian times, as indicated by relief inscriptions on their entrances. The Archaeological Museum (*open Tues–Sun 8.30–3*) houses important exhibits from nearby sites, including Dreros, Elounda, Ellinika and Kalo Chorio.

Neapolis' most celebrated citizen is Petros Philargos (1340–1410), who studied at the universities of Padua, Paris and Oxford, became bishop of Piacenza, was made a cardinal and eventually contested the pontificate, as Pope Alexander V, for ten months in 1409–10. This was the period of the Great Schism, when popes and 'antipopes' claimed power simultaneously. Philargos died and is buried in Bologna. In his short spell as antipope, he made a gift to the Franciscan friary in Herakleion, where he had originally trained, of a fine marble portal with his emblem. This can now be seen in Herakleion at the entrance of the law courts in Odos Dikaiosini. Though his name does not appear on the official pontifical list, at least one man publicly acknowledged his legitimacy: Rodrigo Borgia, when he took the regnal title of Alexander VI in 1492.

DREROS

From Neapolis a winding route west offers a scenic drive into the Lasithi plateau. Close by, a much shorter excursion will take you to Dreros (Δρήρος; pron. Dríros; *map p. 431, A1*). The site is signposted from the bridge crossing the National Road (E75). Go right at the next two forks and after c. 3km there is parking. The site is fenced but open.

Ancient Dreros was a typical small city-state of the Archaic period, with a long history of settlement. Most finds belong to the Geometric and Archaic periods, but the cemetery goes back to the late Bronze Age, a couple of hundred years before, and the cistern is Hellenistic. The city went into decline towards the end of the 2nd century BC. Traces of occupation dating to the second Byzantine period have been identified on the east acropolis hill, named after the chapel of Aghios Antonios. Dreros is best known, however, for the discovery of one of the earliest temples in the whole of Greece.

The site

The plan of the city can be compared to that of Lato (*see p. 196*): a square **agora** with a retaining wall and a large **cistern** (13m by 5.5m by 6m) edged with dressed stone, essential in this rather dry environment. Other public buildings are less evident. Unfortunately the site has been neglected over the years and the path that should lead to the stone-built shed protecting the famed temple excavation soon disappears into a jungle.

The **temple**, dedicated to Apollos Delphinios (a reference to his cult in Delphi) and dated to the Geometric period, was excavated in 1932 by Spyridon Marinatos; it overlooked the agora and could be reached from that direction via a flight of steps which is still preserved. It consists of a small cella oriented northeast–southwest. The entrance may have been at the north end through a porch; unfortunately the area was disturbed by a later lime kiln. In the long axis of the cella, excavators found a sunken hearth full of ashes and the base for a wooden column. If the assumption that there were originally two columns is correct, the arrangement is very similar to that in Kommos and Rizenia. On the ledge in the southwest corner were a 6th-century bronze gorgoneion (a gorgon's mask), vases and figurines; in front on the floor stood a stone offering-table. Three bronze statues of 650 BC were also found and it is thought that they originally stood on the ledge. They represent Apollo, Artemis and their mother Leto (the 'Dreros Triad') and were made in an Orientalising style by hammering the metal onto a wooden core (sphyrelaton technique). They are now displayed in Herakleion museum's temporary exhibition. Beside the ledge was a *keraton*, a stone box filled with the horns of young goats. There are echoes here of the Crane Dance, the dance imitating the twists and turns of the Labyrinth, which, according to Plutarch, Theseus and his companions performed around the horn-built altar known as the Keraton at Delos upon their victorious return from Crete (*Life of Theseus, 21*). According to another version, Theseus actually danced on Dia, after abandoning Ariadne on Naxos.

A good crop of inscriptions was found at Dreros, beginning with the *kyrbis*, a four-sided inscribed pillar, dated to the end of the 3rd century BC and found in 1855. It contains the text of the 'Oath of the Ephebes' in which local youths were required to proclaim their love of Knossos and hatred for Lyttos. Blocks of Archaic date cleared from the cistern turned out to be the text of the earliest known constitutional law in Greece. Another text written in the Greek alphabet could be a bilingual inscription combining Greek and a local Eteocretan language. Unfortunately it is short and there is no certainty that the two texts have the same meaning. Dreros was essentially a defensive site and it is possible that the last of the Minoans lingered on here, hanging on to their language and traditions as they did in Praisos (*see p. 243*).

KRITSA, THE KATHAROS PLATEAU & LATO

From Aghios Nikolaos a road branching off from the bypass leads to Kritsa (8km). Along the road, take the right turn for the church of the Panaghia Kera, which houses one of the finest and most complete set of frescoes in the island. Further on, Kritsa itself is a beautiful sight on the slope of the Lasithi mountains and the starting point for an excursion to the ruins of Lato.

Rear view of the Panaghia Kera church, clearly showing its three-aisled, pitched-roofed structure, with apses at the end of each aisle and a tall central dome.

THE CHURCH OF THE PANAGHIA KERA

The church (*map p. 431, B2; open daily 8.30–3*) is clearly signed to the right of the road from Aghios Nikolaos, immediately opposite the Paradise restaurant. Leave your car by the ticket office. The church is a two-minute walk up the track. In low season the ticket offices are shut and you pay the custodian at the church itself. Good books on the church paintings are available for sale in the adjacent shop.

The church, a three-aisled structure with a dome, is dedicated to the Assumption of the Virgin and dates from the early years of the Venetian occupation.

The nave

The central aisle or nave is believed to be the most ancient part of the church (mid-13th century). Two phases of painting, both falling within the 13th century, have been identified. Remnants of the earlier decoration are preserved only in the apse (*Ascension*; Hierarchs dressed in chasubles decorated with crosses and holding scrolls; the deacons Stephanos and Romanos on the jambs) and on the flat surfaces of the arches supporting the dome (a female saint on the south arch). Both dome and nave are decorated in the later style (late 13th century). In the dome itself the usual Christ Pantocrator has been replaced by four Gospel scenes (anti-clockwise from the west: *Presentation, Baptism, Raising of Lazarus* and *Entry into Jerusalem*). Some traditional elements have been retained, though: the four angels in the apex triangles, the twelve prophets around the cylinder of the vault and the four Evangelists in the pendentives. This replacement of the Pantocrator may have something to do with the architecture of the dome itself and its heavy ribs. Other scenes from the Gospels occupy their usual places in the nave vault. Note the Venetian glass and pottery in the scene of the *Last Supper* (*illustrated below*) and in *Herod's Feast*. On the side walls are the worshipping saints: on the north-west pillar is St Francis, rarely depicted in Greece and thus reflecting the influence of the Latin Church during the Venetian occupation. On the west wall are the remains of a *Crucifixion* with soldiers dressed in 13th-century armour; below are gruesome scenes of the punishment of the Damned.

North aisle

In the north aisle, dedicated to St Anthony, the decoration, dated to the 14th century, is centred on the theme of the Second Coming. Below the Pantocrator in the apse are the Hierarchs, each pointing to the appropriate text. Towards the east end of the vault, the enthroned Apostles and the massed ranks of angels, with saints below them, wait for the salvation of the world. On the reinforcing arch an angel holds a scroll of stars, the Book of Revelation. Next, in the vault to the south side, Paradise is depicted as a walled garden with fruit trees and birds; the four rivers of Paradise (Tigris, Euphrates, Geon and Phison) can be identified by their (very faded) initial letters. Beside the enthroned Virgin, the patriarchs Abraham, Isaac and Jacob protect the souls of the just. The gate of Paradise is guarded by St Peter, who admits the righteous thief. Across the vault is the *Dance of the Female Martyrs* and *Saints Entering Paradise*. On the south side two

The Last Supper (late 13th century), depicted in the nave vault of the Panaghia Kera. Only one of the disciples—Judas—shows any interest in the food.

panels show the *Wise and Foolish Virgins* symbolised by candles lit and extinguished. In the scenes at the west end of the vault the Earth (with a snake) and the Sea (with a boat) deliver up their dead for the Day of Judgement. High up on the west wall, above the angel supervising the judgement scales, the Archangel Michael sounds the last trumpet proclaiming the Second Coming. In the very northwest corner you can see a contemporary portrait of the donor, Georgios Mazizanis, with his wife and child.

South aisle

The south aisle, which is slightly later (early 14th century), is dedicated to the Virgin's mother, St Anne, who is depicted in the apse. On the west wall is an inscription with the name of the donor, Antonios Lameras and the village, 'Kritzea'. The date cannot be read but is recorded to translate as 'the century beginning 1292'. The vault is decorated with scenes of the life of the Virgin from the Apocrypha, arranged on either side. The chronological order of the scenes is the following (*see plan*):

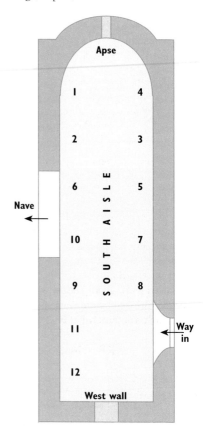

1: The Tent of Joachim. Joachim, husband of Anne, has retreated to the wilderness, in despair at his wife's failure to bear a child. He is visited by an angel announcing that is wife will give birth to a daughter.

2: The Annunciation to St Anne. Anne, likewise dismayed at her barrenness, is greeted by an angel with the news that she is with child.

3: The Meeting at the Golden Gate. Joachim and Anne, overjoyed at the news, meet and embrace at the Golden Gate in Jerusalem.

4: The House of Joachim. Joachim and Anne return home to a feast.

5: Nativity of the Virgin. Anne lies on a bed. Her baby is shown swaddled, in front of a decked table.

6: Blessing by the Priests. The one-year-old Virgin is presented to the High Priests to receive their blessing.

7: Admiration of the Virgin. Mary, now a little girl, is shown being dandled on her father's knee.

8: Presentation of the Virgin: Mary is led to the Temple by a procession of virgins, to receive the blessing of Zacharias.

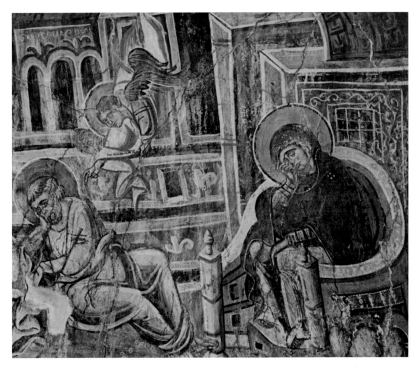

Joseph's Sorrow: The grieving Virgin weeps because her husband believes her unchaste. Joseph is visited by an angel, who tells him that the child his wife is bearing is conceived by the Holy Ghost.

9: Joseph's Sorrow. Joseph, husband of the now adult Mary, learns that she is with child and is grieved at the news. An angel appears to inform him that the child is God's and his wife is undefiled.

10: The Water of Trial: The Virgin's innocence is tested by the Water of the Lord, which will putrefy her body if she is not innocent.

11: Journey to Bethlehem: Mary and Joseph travel to Bethlehem for the census ordered by Caesar Augustus.

12: The Sealed Gate. In accordance with a prophecy of Ezekiel, Mary is revealed as the 'Sealed Gate', in other words *virgo intacta*.

KRITSA & THE KATHAROS PLATEAU

Kritsa (Κριτσά; *map p. 431, B2*) is an attractive terraced village on a steep hillside. The local industry is weaving and needlework, and has been so for a long time. The work is displayed everywhere and there is no getting away from it. The traditional designs are based on geometric patterns and natural variations of the wool. The village repays some time spent exploring; the best way to enjoy it is to press on, on foot, past the centre, higher up towards the main church, **Aghios Georgios**, which can be seen from the car park at the lower village entrance. The streets become narrower and the embroidery disappears. The real village is here. The church has fresco remains by two painters dated from the late 13th to the mid-14th centuries.

Less than 2km south of Kritsa is the church of **Aghios Ioannis Theologos** (Second Byzantine period), beside the road (right) on the way to Kroustas. It sits in a fine position at the head of the valley. Further south from Kroustas, on the way to Prina, another **Aghios Ioannis** (4km) is signed on the left. The Byzantine chapel has frescoes dated 1347–48. You may wish to enquire about both these from the guardian at the Panaghia Kera.

Walkers can explore the area south of Kroustas on the way east to Pyrgos across country paths, old *kalderimia* and paved donkey tracks. Alternatively they can venture further inland to the Katharos plateau, or, north of Kritsa, the **Kritsa Gorge**, signed on the road to Lato: in the dry season walkers can get to Tapes in the north in c. 2 hours.

The Katharos plateau

The asphalted road to the plateau (*map p. 431, A2*) is 16km from Kritsa in the Avdeliakos direction; walkers can shorten the climb a bit by taking shortcuts. The plateau is quite high up and only seasonally inhabited by shepherds. They do not own the land, which belongs to Kritsa, but pay four percent of their produce to that community. Because of the altitude (1200m), crops are mainly confined to a few potatoes, grapes, almonds and apples, but in the spring the area is very green and provides excellent grazing for sheep and goats. Shepherds come up on May 15th, which is when the three tavernas also open. It is a good chance for visitors to sample *myzithra*, a fresh white sheep's cheese which can be eaten with honey as a dessert, or with olives and tomatoes as a *meze*. The climb is recommended for the fine views of the mountains and the variety of wild flowers. From Avdeliakos a dirt track winds its way north across the mountains to Mesa Lasithi, one of the traditional points of entry to the Lasithi plateau.

LATO

Open Tues–Sun 8.30–3. Outside these hours the site is not seriously locked; there is a ticket booth, so payment may be required when it is manned, possibly in high season.

Approaching Lato from Aghios Nikolaos, follow the road signed to the right before you get to Kritsa. At the beginning of the road, note the signs to the Kritsa Gorge (*see above*).

The site of Lato (Λατό; *map p. 431, B2*), locally known as Goulas, is 3km on, situated at 400m with two acropolis peaks. The city sits in the saddle between them. The site is well presented and tidy; the vegetation is kept under control and there is a map. It is a site well worth a visit for the fantastic views over Mirabello, Pseira and Aghios Nikolaos below. It also brings home the cramped living conditions of a Hellenistic city-state at a time when defence was an overwhelming consideration.

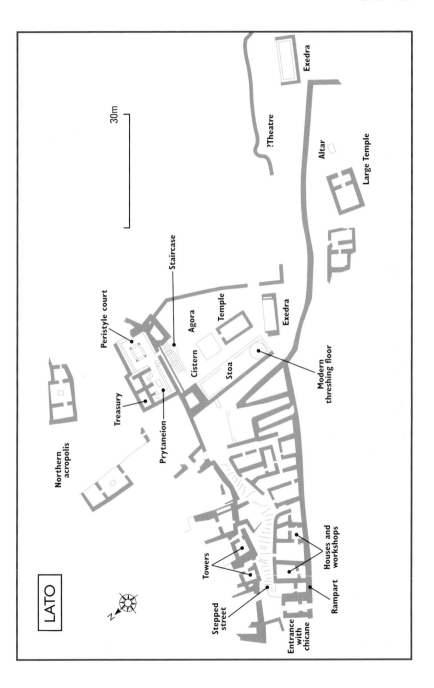

LATO

Northern
acropolis

Treasury

Prytaneion

Peristyle court

Staircase

Cistern

Agora

Temple

Stoa

Exedra

Modern
threshing floor

?Theatre

Exedra

Altar

Large Temple

Towers

Stepped
street

Entrance
with
chicane

Rampart

Houses and
workshops

30m

HISTORY OF LATO

The settlement is a foundation of the Geometric period, though there are traces of LM III occupation. As a city-state Lato was still flourishing in Hellenistic times when it was known as Etero Lato, the 'other Lato'. Evidence of Roman occupation is very slight and abandonment is presumed around the end of 2nd century BC in favour of its harbour, Lato pros Kamara, today's Aghios Nikolaos. The position is defensive, high up, controlling a pass with extensive views of the surrounding countryside, of the route connecting east and west Crete, and of the sea. Visitors may wish to climb the path leading to the top of the northern acropolis. Such a strategic choice came at a price. The location has no water: the nearest spring is in Kritsa, 3km away. So the city was planned around a natural depression, a sinkhole turned into a huge cistern with sheer sides and a capacity of c. 125 cubic metres. The building stone is local limestone.

The city had been identified by French archaeologists in 1899–1900, but at that time Cretan archaeology was focused on Minoan sites. Sustained investigation only started in earnest in 1967. Lato is now one of the most thoroughly excavated towns of its period in Crete. Cyclopean walls still standing several metres high in places, have provided refuge for interesting flora.

Visiting the site

Just beyond the ticket booths and old guardian's hut, you come to the **entrance** to the stepped street leading to the agora. This was fortified by a chicane. To the right, a free-standing **rampart** was added for security in the 3rd century BC; the space in between was filled with a row of **houses and workshops**, some with interesting features still *in situ*. On the left a stout wall follows the steep slope; it is interrupted by several entrances leading into the north sector of the town. The wall was strengthened by two **towers**, also used as dwellings.

At the top of the long stepped street is the **agora**. In its present form it is Hellenistic, but finds of figurines indicate an earlier 6th-century temple. The shape is a rough trapezoid with the **cistern** in the middle. To its south are the remains of a small **temple**

and to the west, a **stoa** that had stone benches behind a Doric colonnade (the circular threshing floor is a modern instrusion). Behind the small temple is an **exedra** with benches. The northern side was monumental with an elaborate **staircase** (note the triple flight of

Part of a stone press in one of the houses or workshops of Lato.

The site of Lato, viewed from the prytaneion. The cistern is clearly visible, surrounded by a modern fence, with the remains of the small temple behind it. To the right of this, the circular threshing floor cuts across the agora. Beyond, where the people are sitting, is the benched exedra.

broad steps separated by two flights of narrower, shallower ones for easier ascent) set between two bastions. The grand arrangement is reminiscent of the Minoan theatral areas in the western courts of Knossos and Phaistos, but at the same time prefigures the seating arrangements of the Classical Greek theatre.

The **prytaneion**, the administrative centre of the Hellenistic city-state, stands between the bastions. The building consisted of a dining hall to the west with couches for eight people set around a hearth; it opened to the east onto a **peristyle court**. The two small rooms to the north have been interpreted as a **treasury**, where the city archives would have been kept. One of the inscriptions that made it possible to identify the function of the building recorded a treaty between Gortyn and Lato.

On the other side of the agora is a terrace supported by a retaining wall of polygonal masonry. On the terrace the so-called **Large Temple** still stands four courses high. In the square cella the inscribed base for a cult statue was found. In front of the pronaos stood a stepped altar. Further east still, below the temple terrace, is a wide open space supported by a wall with two semicircular bastions. Here a rectangular **exedra** stands next to the remains of 10–11 steps cut in the rock and overlooking a semicircular area to the north. The arrangement has been interpreted as a form of theatre.

PRACTICAL INFORMATION

GETTING AROUND

• **By bus:** The bus station in Aghios Nikolaos is on Epimenidou (*T: 28410 22234; www. crete-buses.gr*) to the north of town. There are buses to the north coast (Sisi and Milatos), to Elounda and Plaka, as well as inland to Kritsa and Kroustas.

• **By sea:** Boats operate tours to Spinalonga from Aghios Nikolaos. Elounda and Plaka have regular services in the summer.

TOURIST INFORMATION

Elounda Tourist Office: T: 28410 42464; dhmosan@agn.forthnet.gr.

WHERE TO STAY

The Elounda area is well equipped for tourists and caters for both ends of the market. For luxury hotels visit www.elounda.com, where they are listed. Plaka has rooms to rent (enquire at Aghios Nikolaos Tourist Office).

Elounda (*map p. 431, B1*)
€€ **Hotel Aristea**. On the main street out of the main square by the waterfront. An acceptable alternative to the 'luxury' tourist complexes. *T: 28410 41300.*

Kritsa (*map p. 431, B2*)
€€ **The Olive Press**. Apartments and guestrooms in a historic building in the quieter part of Kritsa, near the main church. *Mobile: 6973 091201; www.olivepress.centerall. com.*

€€ **Argyro**. Rooms and apartments at the lower entrance to the village, to the left opposite the car park. *T: 28410 51174, www. argyrorentrooms.gr.*

Neapolis (*map p. 431, A1*)

€€ **Hotel Neapolis**. Not far from the main square on Plateia Evangelistrias, this is the only hotel in town. It is a sensible choice for a base: Neapolis has a nice atmosphere and road connections are good. *T: 28410 33967; www.neapolis-hotel.gr.*

WHERE TO EAT

Elounda (*map p. 431, B1*)
Elounda has a number of tavernas by the waterfront patronised by the clientèle of the luxury resorts. For a cheaper alternative and traditional fare, keep away from the sea and try a couple of places at the far end of the main square. There is also **Kanali** (across the isthmus near the remains of the Christian basilica).

Exo Lakkonia (*map p. 431, B2*)
Taverna Stavrakakis. At Panaghia, 10mins from the coast near the hamlet of Exo Lakkonia, famed for its huge bougainvillea and honest food. Patronised by locals as well as visitors. *T: 28410 22478.*

Kritsa (*map p. 431, B2*)
Kritsa has a number of tavernas: try **Lato** in the main street (for *mezedes*) next to Kastelli, with a roof garden. The best Cretan food though is on the way out of Kritsa at the **Konaki** taverna.

Neapolis (*map p. 431, A1*)
€ **To Steki tou Lagou**. The 'hare's hideout' in Plateia Aghiou Vasileiou, a little square off the main one. *T: 28410 33184.*

WALKING

To see and experience local sights and life off the beaten track, contact Hilary and Phil Dawson on 6945 246983 or by email: hilary72051@hotmail.com. They arrange informative and enjoyable walks around local villages and the countryside.

LOCAL SPECIALITIES

Cretan Olive Oil Farm (*T: 28410 24741*) 1km from the Aghios Nikolaos/Kritsa crossroad on the way to Kritsa. Local and organic products. **Kritsa** for lace and embroideries, probably more than you really want.

FESTIVALS & EVENTS

The **Analipsi of Almyros**, an open-air market with traditional Cretan festivities, is held on Ascension Day, the 40th day after Easter. In early June the Feast of the Klidona, an ancient fortune-telling custom largely connected with girls' future husbands, is held at **Kroustas**. At **Elounda** they hold a *Psarovradia* ('Fish Night'), with fish, drink and live music in the summer. In August **Kritsa** hosts a Cheese Pie Festival, with music and dancing.

BOOKS & FURTHER READING

Victoria Hislop: *The Island*. A novel set on Spinalonga. Two books on the frescoes of the Panaghia Kritsa are available, both from the shop next to the church. One is a commentary by M. Borboudakis; the other, very well illustrated, is by the Byzantinist Katerina Mylopotamitaki.

THE LASITHI PLATEAU

The Oropedio Lasithiou (Οροπέδιο Λασιθίου; *map p. 431, A2*), the high plateau of Lasithi, is one of the 25 or so areas of fertile upland in Crete, the only one at this altitude (850m) inhabited all year round. It was formed when the subsidence of a portion of the earth's crust between faults allowed water and then decaying vegetation to collect. This caused the limestone to dissolve further: as a result, the sunken plain is surrounded by lofty mountains. The basin has gradually filled with scree, gravel, blown dust, snow-melt and organic matter, a process that over the centuries has ensured its fertility.

There are two main approaches to Lasithi. From the east there is a road from Neapolis (30km): officially it has been upgraded but it is still narrow and winding. It is a slow drive: allow plenty of time to take in the beautiful wooded landscape up a scenic mountain valley. Alternatively there is the north road via Potamies and Kera, less engaging and normally more crowded.

There is evidence for Neolithic occupation at Trapeza Cave. An important sanctuary, the Diktaian Cave at Psychro, was a place of pilgrimage for almost ten centuries from Middle Minoan times; Lyttos, over the mountains to the west, controlled the area in the Hellenistic period, and Roman farmers settled to exploit the rich soil.

Agriculture and mills on the Lasithi plateau

The area has been farmed since time immemorial because of its fertility and the protection afforded by the surrounding high peaks (Selena to the north, Afendis to the west, Katharo and Varsami to the east, and the Spathi, the highest, at 2148m, to the south).

Water management has always been a problem in Lasithi as the Chonos, which drains the plain in its west corner through a large sinkhole, has been known to become blocked. When that happened in the past, the plain was more of a lake. The numerous windmills dotting the landscape (apparently there were once as many as 10,000) are part of the Venetian solution to the problem of irrigation and power supply.

In the 13th century the inhabitants put up a fierce resistance to Venetian occupation and, as a result, Venice cleared the plateau, demolishing villages, laying waste the land and relocating the inhabitants. Later, at the beginning of the 16th century, Venice redeveloped the area in a bid to boost wheat production, an important export. The authorities rented part of the land to citizens from Candia (Herakleion) in exchange for an exemption from galley service and corvées. The balance was used to compensate the noble Venetian families of the Peloponnese, who had lost everything in the war against the Turks. Engineers from Padua set up a system of ditches (known as *linies*) defining plots called *voudea*, a noun related to the Venetian name for an ox, which implied a measure of what an ox could plough in a day. This (and not, as some have suggested, Roman centuriation) is what gives the west end of the plain the appearance of a chessboard.

The windmills are of two types. The smaller ones dotted around the plateau, with sails fixed onto a stand, are for water. Some are a comparatively recent development, taking over from dipping wells. The D-shaped stone mills, of which there is an impressive battery on the ridge at the north entrance into Lasithi from Herakleion, are for grinding corn, and those go back to Venetian times. Nowadays most mills are in ruins and have been replaced by less picturesque but more efficient petrol pumps. Plans for restoration are afoot; meanwhile, visitors wishing to see a complete corn-grinding mill with all its machinery (millstones, wheels and trough) will find one at Moni Toplou (*see p. 264*).

MEDICINAL & AROMATIC PLANTS

Geologically linked to the Peloponnese and the Balkans on one side and to the Taurus Mountains in Asia Minor on the other, Crete is home to a stunning number of plant species which have survived and evolved thanks to its varied morphology and relative isolation. The island was well known in antiquity for its medicinal plants. Nero's doctor, Andromachos the Cretan, made remedies using 33 Cretan plants, two of which could not be found anywhere else. Later, in the 2nd century AD, Galen and the pharmacists of his time were still advocating the use of herbs from Crete for their preparations.

Cistus creticus, source of the resin called labdanum.

Though some of the plants could be found in the Roman *campagna*, the quality of the Cretan plants was deemed to be superior because of the drier climate. Plants were harvested at different times depending on whether the flower, the fruits, the seeds, or the essential oils in the leaves were wanted, by trained slaves under the supervision of procurators. Three at least were cultivated in Roman times (seseli, oregano and anis); others such as thlaspi, a form of cress, could only be found in the wild, high up at over 1300m.

Plants were packed in woven, breathable containers made of vitex and shipped to Rome when the Mediterranean was 'open' i.e. in the late spring or summer. More delicate specimens were laid flat on lower-grade papyrus sheets (known as *emporitica*, the equivalent of shop wrapping paper) and rolled up with name and place of origin written on it.

Essential oils, which plants produce as a form of defence against browsing animals, were also important Cretan exports. Oils and gums may have been distilled in the so called 'fireboxes' that can be seen at Siteia archaeological museum. These pots, with their rounded perforated capsule topped by a flaring rim, fit the description by Theophrastus (*De Odoribus 5, 22*) of a process of slow heating and dry distillation. They are exclusive to Crete. Labdanum was also an important export. This resin, used in perfumery and medicine, is exuded by the leaves of the rockrose (*Cistus creticus*) and was traditionally collected with a *ladanastirio*, leather straps aimed at the leaves and then periodically scraped. The process was witnessed by the French botanist Belon in the mid-16th century.

THE NORTH ROAD TO LASITHI

From Chersonisos (*see p. 117*) take the Kastelli road past the Aquasplash Park. Keep left at the junction and head towards **Potamies** (Ποταμιές; *map p. 430, D3*). As you approach the village, a sign to the left before it indicates a side road to the frescoed Byzantine church of the Panaghia. Dedicated to the Assumption of the Virgin, the church is all that remains of the **Gouverniotissa Monastery**, built, according to tradition, at the very beginning of the Second Byzantine period and abandoned in 1942 (*it should be open in the morning; otherwise enquire in Potamies at the first kafeneion on the right on the main street*). The climb to the church is about 1km past the chapel of the Sotiros Christos (Christ the Saviour, also with frescoes) overlooking the Langada valley. Cruciform in plan, with three arms of almost equal length, its dome rests on a drum lit by eight blind, arcaded windows. Venetian influence is only apparent in the quatrefoil window and pointed arch above the entrance, and in the window in the apse. The frescoes, dating from the second half of the 14th century, are best preserved in the west arm, with a double tier of Gospel scenes above the worshipping saints. The church is dominated by the Pantocrator in the dome above the four Evangelists in the pendentives. The 16th-century icons, the beautiful carved wood iconostasis and the sanctuary doors have been removed for safety to Herakleion Historical Museum. Outside, one of the monks' cells has a small folklore museum.

Further on is **Avdou** (Αβδού; *map p. 431, A1*) with more frescoed churches. Aghios Konstantinos, with work by the brothers Manuel and Ioannis Phokas and a donor inscription dated 1445, is signposted to the right before the village. Manuel is also known for his work in the churches at Embaros and at Epano Symi near Viannos. The other church, Aghios Antonios, with 14th-century paintings, is in the middle of the village. For access to either inquire in the village.

At **Krasi** (Κράσι; *map p. 431, A1*), Spyridon Marinatos excavated in 1929 a Mycenaean tholos tomb discovered by Evans. The pretty village has additional attractions. In the centre stands a huge plane tree that once even had a café inside it and is reputedly 2,000 years old. Next to it an abundant spring, probably closely related to the plane tree's longevity, gushes out of the mountainside. Under one arch is a pool of water and above it a quote by Nikos Kazantzakis; under the other arch, local women must have exchanged many words of wisdom while doing their laundry in the stone basins.

At Kera the nunnery of the **Panaghia Kardiotissa** is to the right just before the village below the road. The name, Panaghia Kardiotissa, is a Cretan variation of the Virgin of Tenderness. There must have been a foundation here as early as 1415, because Cristoforo Buondelmonti, a Florentine monk and author of the *Descriptio insulae Cretae*, published in 1417, mentions the miraculous powers of the Kardiotissa icon, then venerated here. According to legend the icon was removed to Istanbul twice and twice flew back here. Its present whereabouts are now not very clear. According to some, it was stolen in the 15th century and taken to Italy by a merchant. It performed its first miracle on its way to Rome when it saved the ship it was travelling on; eventually, after many adventures, it took up residence in the church of Sant'Alfonso on the Esquiline

Hill in Rome, where it adorns the high altar and is worshipped under the name of *Madonna del Perpetuo Soccorso.*

The monastery expanded during the Turkish period but also suffered destruction at the time of disturbances in 1866. The church has an unusual ground plan, the result of successive building phases, four at least. The exterior, on the other hand, has attained a degree of homogeneity. Originally there was a three-apsed chapel, now the sanctuary of the convent church. An extended narthex was added forming a triple transept, with steps to negotiate the change in level of the terrain. The church is accessed via a conventional narthex parallel to this transept; the north chapel is a later addition. Frescoes were uncovered in the 1960s. Those in the sanctuary have an early 14th-century date, the others are slightly later and show the influence of the Macedonian School.

Beyond Kera, with the limestone knob of Karphi in sight to the left, the road climbs towards the Seli Ambelou Pass at 900m, with stunning views and the first sight of the famous windmills of Lasithi. Official monuments since 1986, 24 windmills have been partially restored, but they do not look the part without their white sails; and sadly they are all disused. The Lasithi plain, ringed by a road connecting the villages, stretches to the south. Eighteen villages are dotted around the plateau leaving the land in the centre free for farming (Lasithi vegetables, apples and almonds are famous throughout Crete and as far away as Athens). The largest village is **Tzermiado** (Τζερμιάδο; *map p. 431, A2*) to the east, from where visitors can make their way to Karphi.

KARPHI

The site of Karphi (Καρφί; *map p. 431, A1*) is signed from the western approach of Tzermiado, left along a 2km track to the Nisimos plateau (*20mins on foot and less by car; the alternative route from the Seli Ambelou Pass is for walkers only. Leave your car at the chapel and follow the track which is signposted to the site. It is a steep half-hour walk*).

Karphi (meaning 'nail' or 'spike') lies in a saddle between two peaks. On the way note the **Astivideros spring**, one of the two that supplied water to the settlement, and a group of four small **tholos tombs**. Seventeen more tombs were uncovered by the other spring, the Vitzelovrysis. Flower enthusiasts should look out for local species such as the *Paeonia clusii*, a species endemic to Crete and Karpathos, with its distinctive white flowers flushed with pink. On the last stretch the direct path to the site leads between two outcrops of rock. The **survey post** on the peak of Mikri Koprana to the right marks the eastern limit of the first excavations. A scramble to that point and the whole of north and central Crete is in view. This explains why this remote area, 1100m above sea level with a commanding view of the entrance to the plain, was chosen as a refuge site by the last true Cretans (the Eteocretans), still following Minoan religious traditions 300 to 400 years after the collapse of Minoan power. They settled here around the end of the Bronze Age and held out for 150 years or perhaps a while longer into the Protogeometric period, and then left. They lived by hunting, herding and cultivating the lower slopes, as the palaeobotanical remains imply. Finds show that in spite of the remoteness of the location, they maintained contacts across the Aegean

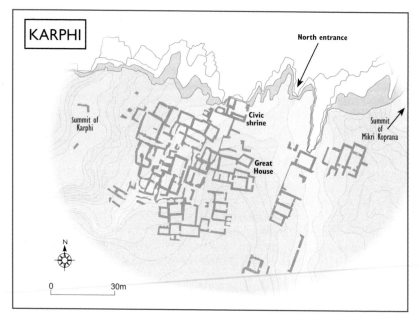

and as far afield as Cyprus. An alternative, less benign theory, suggests that in troubled times this sizeable settlement (estimated to 3,500 people) had become a hiding place for brigands, a tradition upheld by later developments in Lasithi history.

Visiting the site

The site, partially excavated between 1937 and 1939 by John Pendlebury, spreads across the saddle between two peaks. Encroaching vegetation, erosion and intensive grazing have all taken their toll: as a consequence the original plan can be difficult to make out and these days hikers tend to visit Karphi for its dramatic setting rather than for the archaeology. The location is sheltered from the north wind, which makes it inhabitable all year round—but even so winters must have been hard and difficult. Houses were roughly built in stone with no plaster; thresholds and door jambs alone had carefully cut blocks. Only the **Great House** stood out, for its superior construction and finds of pottery and bronze ornaments. Paved streets separate clusters of rooms but individual house plans remain difficult to understand fully. Of particular interest are the numerous shrines identified by the excavators. At the top of a steep northern ascent a stepped entrance led to a temple or **civic shrine** built at the edge of the precipice. Part of it has been eroded away. The largest room, with remains of an altar, was entered from the east and had two small adjoining rooms opposite this doorway. Finds, now in Herakleion, include clay goddesses with stiff cylindrical skirts and hands raised in blessing (one, almost a metre tall, has birds perching in her crown) and a unique rhyton in the form of a chariot driven by three oxen represented only by their heads. If there was indeed a Middle Minoan peak sanctuary on the knob at Karphi, it is possible that the particular religious significance of the location influenced the choice of this remote, inhospitable site later in time.

A new programme of excavations was begun in the summer of 2008 by the British School at Athens.

THE TRAPEZA CAVE & AGHIOS GEORGIOS

The **Trapeza Cave** is signed from the middle of Tzermiado (*map p. 431, A2; open daily 10–6, but it would be wise to seek confirmation about opening hours in the village first. The cave mouth is reached after a steep 10-min climb after leaving your car; access is cramped and awkward*). The cave was cleared in 1936 by John Pendlebury; since then the interpretation of the finds has been dogged by controversy. There are traces of Late Neolithic activity continuing into the Bronze Age. By EM II (mid-3rd millennium) it was used for communal burials. The quality of the finds, including sealstones, jewellery, figurines, metalwork, stone vases and a glazed steatite scarab, indicates high status, summed up by Pendlebury who described it as 'a fashionable burial place'. The cave appears to have been abandoned at the beginning of the Neopalatial period. It may have been related to a nearby site to the east on the hill of Kastellos.

The road continues south past Moni Kroustallenias, where the access road from Neapolis joins the Lasithi circuit. From Mesa Lasithi a track leads to the Katharo plateau and joins the road coming up from Kritsa. You are now on the slopes of Mt Dikte, and walkers can join (after careful preparation) the E4 walking route at Avrakondes beyond Aghios Georgios. The way to the summit (1884m) can be long but the first approaches to the Limnakaro Plateau (90mins) should be within the reach of any enthusiastic, albeit unfit, walker.

At **Aghios Georgios** (Άγιος Γεώργιος; *map p. 431, A2*) there is an exhibition dedicated to the life and times of the Greek statesman Eleftherios Venizelos, a native of Crete, with many documents and memorabilia, located in a restored old building signposted from the road. Traditional Cretan life can be sampled at the **Lasinthos Eco Park** (*open April–Nov 10–6.30; disabled access; www.lasinthos.gr*) that opened in the vicinity of the village in 2005. The park runs an exhibition centre and also aims to offer agrotourism. That might have to wait until the trees planted around the brand new studios and apartments, on a very barren slope, grow a bit taller and produce some reasonable shade. The exhibition side of things is up and running and offers an excellent opportunity to watch potters, spinners, weavers, woodworkers, and candlemakers at work. Beyond the modern church, a small zoo-cum-botanic garden is home to some native Eteocretan species. Goats are of course the chief exhibit, with *agrimia* and a larger variety with impressive horns, called *kateika*. Cretan pigs are special too, looking more like wild boar with a light brown furry coat. The botanic garden is small but labelled: there is no prize for spotting a clump of dittany (*Origanum dictamnus*) with its furry, fat rounded leaves and pungent scent. In the wild it normally grows up steep cliffs, out of reach of tourists but not of goats, who reputedly eat it when they are injured.

THE DIKTAIAN CAVE

Psychro (Ψυχρό; *map p. 431, A2*) is the starting point for a visit to the Diktaian Cave (*open daily Oct–March 8.30–3, April–Sept 8.30–7*). *The turning is signed at the end of the village. A steep, rocky path some 800m long leads from the car park to the entrance. Donkey rides are available, and lanterns can be hired if you have no torch. Good footwear and a warm sweater could be useful. The place is slippery and chilly.*

THE BIRTH & INFANCY OF ZEUS

According to legend, the Diktaian Cave is the site of the infancy (and in some traditions also the birth) of Zeus, chief of the Olympian gods. His father Kronos, mindful of an oracle predicting that he would loose his throne to a son, decided to play safe and devoured his own children. When Zeus was born, his mother Rhea duped Kronos with a stone wrapped up in swaddling clothes and spirited Zeus away to the safety of this cave, where he was suckled by the she-goat Amaltheia. Zeus spent his infancy here, nurtured by the Curetes (Kourites), a male confraternity of demigods. They covered the noise of Zeus' childhood tantrums with their drumming and dancing, clashing their swords against their shields, so that Kronos would hear nothing. In due course the boy was raised to manhood by shepherds on Mt Ida (*see the Idaian Cave, p. 296*). Zeus went on to dethrone his father.

Halbherr and Hatzidakis made preliminary investigations in the outer areas of the cave in 1886. Evans and Myres paid a visit some ten years later and bought some of the objects found by the locals; this explains why some of the finds are in Oxford. In 1899 the cave was excavated by Hogarth, whose somewhat unorthodox methods included the use of dynamite to remove fallen boulders. Unsystematic excavations followed. As a result the stratigraphy is blurred and sequencing is based on style: it shows that the site was in use from MM IIB to the 6th century BC. Finds of Roman lamps and even a Byzantine cross suggest a dwindling continuity.

The cave is entered via a narrow passage leading to a hall with a rectangular stone shrine. Neolithic potsherds, EM burials and MM votive items, including limestone and serpentine offering-tables, were found here. At the very northern edge an area with a paved floor has been interpreted as a temenos, a sacred enclosure. Further on are other halls with natural formations: visitors in the right frame of mind will recognise the cradle of the chief of the gods, his mantle, his very image and even the spot where the goat Amaltheia used to nurse him. A good number of votive offerings, mainly bronze statuettes, knives, spearheads and double axes, were found around the lake in the lower cave. The body of water would have been deeper in antiquity. Finds were found around it and

Limestone formations inside the Diktaian Cave.

at times embedded in stalactites. They mainly have a LM I date (16th–15th centuries BC), corresponding to the main period of use of this part of the cave, though there was a revival in the 8th–7th centuries with characteristic votive open-work bronze plaques.

PRACTICAL INFORMATION

GETTING AROUND

• **By car:** From Herakleion leave the E75 6km after Gouves on the Kastelli Pediadas road, taking the left turn 1500m after Aquasplash in the direction of Potamies. From Aghios Nikolaos take the E75 west to Neapolis, then go left to Vryses and Exo Potami. The road is winding and extremely scenic.

• **By bus:** There are daily services to Psychro from Herakleion Bus Station A (*www.crete-buses.gr*). Tzermiado has a bus connection with Aghios Nikolaos on Mon, Wed and Fri.

WHERE TO STAY & EAT

Lasithi is comparatively new to tourist development, which is probably part of its appeal. Accommodation is still rather scarce and as the plateau gets a fair amount of snow in the winter, the tourist season tends to be curtailed.

Aghios Georgios (*map p. 431, A2*)
€ **Hotel Dias**, on the main street, also has a good taverna (*open May–Oct, T: 28440 31207*) as does € **Maria**, a modern hotel in a quiet location (*open April–Oct, T: 28440 31774*).
Avdou (*map p. 431, A1*)
€€€ **Avdou Villas**. Purpose-built accommodation in an organic farming estate (citrus, apricot, kiwi). *T: 2810 300540, www.avdou.com.*
Krasi (*map p. 431, A1*)
There are two tavernas here: one (Platanos) is by the Venetian fountain and the immense

plane tree; the other immediately below to the right (Kares). Both are good.
Magoulas (*map p. 431, A2*)
The **Dionysos Taverna** has a few rooms to rent. *T: 28440 31672.*
Mesa Potami (*map p. 431, A2*)
€ **Marianna**. Rooms to rent in a fine rural location on the eastern approach to Lasithi. An excellent place to stay and to eat; the owner rears his own rabbits and goats and Marianna makes excellent Easter *kaltzounia* (sweet cheese tartlets). *Open April–Oct. T: 28440 22497.*
Tzermiado (*map p. 431, A2*)
€€ **Argoulias Apartments**. In the older part of the village, where it traditionally first developed, higher up, close to the springs, leaving as much of the plain as possible free for cultivation. Eleven stone-built apartments with cooking facilities and heating. Traditional local produce is supplied for breakfast. *T: 28440 22754 or 0810 918368, www.argoulias.gr.*
€ **Kourites Hotel**. A modern hotel on the edge of the road by the taverna of the same name (a winner of the Greek tourist prize for catering, with excellent oven-roasted meat). *T: 28440 22194, www.kourites.eu.*

FESTIVALS & EVENTS

Aug 30th: *Panigyri* in honour of Aghios Alexandros in **Plati** near Psychro; also Feast of the Holy Girdle (Aghia Zoni) at **Psychro**. 1st July and 1st Nov: Feasts of Sts Cosmas and Damian (Aghii Anargyri) in **Mesa Lasithi**.

THE ISTHMUS & IERAPETRA

From Aghios Nikolaos the road hugs the rocky shores around Mirabello to Pachia Ammos and the Minoan town of Gournia just short of it, then moves inland for a scenic drive to Siteia, 70km away. The southernmost point of Mirabello Bay marks the Ierapetra isthmus, only 14km wide. Driving south past Vasiliki, the warm Libyan Sea beckons and it is just one hour to the island of Chrysi from Ierapetra. To the west, the Bramiana Dam lures bird-watchers; those who understand the pleasure of ruins will want to visit the Minoan site of Myrtos Pyrgos. Up the valley of the Sarakina Gorge it is about 15km to the southeast slopes of Mt Dikte to Males and beyond, with some fine views and walks along the E4 route.

Vrokastro

Leaving Aghios Nikolaos on the E75 heading east, it is less than 10km to **Istro** (Ἴστρο; *map p. 431, B2*), with a number of beaches in sheltered coves on the way. As you drop downhill at the beginning of Istro, the site of the Early Iron Age settlement of **Vrokastro** is on the seaward summit of the hills ahead, with a terraced gully pointing up to it. (*The site is accessible on foot if you fancy 20mins of stiff climb. Leave the main road after the Golden Bay Hotel in Istro and follow the road to pick up a track in the direction of the gully. Aim for the saddle connecting the highest peak on the left with the hills behind. By car, or for a gentler climb, follow the coast road another 4km and watch for a right turning past the Istron Bay Hotel.*)

The settlement, clearly a refuge site on a limestone outcrop 313m above sea level, with difficult access and sweeping vistas over the sea and the east–west route, was excavated by Edith Hall in 1910–12. Seventy years on, a reassessment of the whole region, roughly from Istro to Gournia and stretching inland some 5km, has been undertaken by an American-led international team. It covers both the settlement pattern and the environmental evidence. At the close of the Vrokastro survey a specific area on the coast was selected for further investigation.

At Vrokastro occupation is attested between the 12th and 7th centuries BC. The plan of the site is complex: houses, both on the upper and lower settlement around the peak and down the terraced north slope, follow the morphology of the terrain. They are now tangles of walls with units difficult to make out. Unpaved floors of beaten earth seem to rule out grand buildings, but column bases have been found suggesting the possibility of more complex architecture. Shrines have been identified. The remains to the north belong to a defensive town wall. There is no ground water at Vrokastro and no trace of cisterns; the nearest spring is 20mins away. Finds of iron slag (*see box overleaf*) provide evidence for early metalworking. Pottery and artefacts indicate more sustained contacts with the Cyclades, Dodecanese and mainland Greece than with inland Crete.

The cemetery has yielded evidence of a variety of burial practices over time (both cremation and inhumation), with the use of pithoi, rock-cut chamber tombs and walled bone enclosures.

THE ISTRON & PRINIATIKOS PYRGOS
GEOARCHAEOLOGICAL PROJECT

After excavating Vrokastro, Edith Hall began investigations on the coast at Prini-atikos Pyrgos, where she believed the Minoan harbour to be located. She identi-fied occupation from the Minoan to the Roman periods.

The Priniatikos Pyrgos Survey (2002–06), part of a larger project involving three decades of fieldwork in the area, concentrated on the coastal region using remote sensing techniques and more conventional fieldwork undertaken by ge-ologists, soil experts and topographers.

The survey explored the site of Priniatikos Pyrgos in the bay of Kalo Chorio at the mouth of the Istron river, where it crosses a rich, fertile alluvial plain. The remote sensing showed well-preserved, shallow architectural remains, probably port installations belonging to the Graeco-Roman period. According to finds from the test pits, this occupation was preceded by an earlier phase with a large settle-ment dating from the end of the Neolithic and the Bronze Age. Magnetic sensing identified a large concentration of iron slag on the west slopes of the promontory and also to the east on the larger headland of Nisi Pandeleimon, thought to be the centre of the Greek harbour town of Istron. Researchers believe that kilns in that location could have made good use of sea breezes to achieve a sufficient temperature, and indeed remains of a kiln have been identified. The raw mate-rial (clay and iron) was available in the surrounding area. Geological prospecting has shown that the igneous diorite and granodiorite found in the Mirabello area are accompanied by iron ore in the form of magnetite. It appears therefore that the area was an important centre on the Mirabello coast, from early days up to the Venetian and Ottoman periods. It made good use of the location (a protected anchorage on an important route, with a fertile and well-watered hinterland) and exploited the local resources for the production of ceramics and metal.

GOURNIA

The coast road continues towards Gournia (Γουρνιά; *map p. 431, B2; open Tues–Sun 8.30–3*). Opposite the Gournia Moon campsite, a steep climb leads to an austere mo-nastic building on a rock ledge with fine sea views. There is not much left of the origi-nal Moni Phaneromeni, a foundation of the second Byzantine period. Presently the focus of veneration in the church is a grotto with a miraculous icon of the Virgin. But it may be worth coming up here in the spring for the wild orchids and the *Ranunculus asiaticus*, a perennial that has extended its habitat to Kythera and Karpathos via Crete.

Gournia is a Minoan town, one of the few to have been extensively excavated, though the total size of the settlement is known to have been up to four times greater than the

The ruins of Gournia spread out on their low hill, with views of the Gulf of Mirabello and Aghios Nikolaos in the distance.

excavated acropolis. Settlement probably extended to the sea in antiquity: submerged remains of Minoan houses associated with the port have been identified by the shore.

The site lies on a small hill, a few hundred metres from the sea on the Ierapetra isthmus, meaning that it controlled not only the east–west route, but also the access to the south shores of the island, at this point a mere 14km away. This road would certainly have been more attractive to ancient travellers and traders than embarking on a difficult sea voyage around the east coast.

The ruins of the settlement were visible before the excavation and the name Gournia was given to the area by the villagers because of the many stone basins (*gourni*) littering the area. Its ancient name is not known. The site was excavated between 1901 and 1904 by American archaeologist Harriet Boyd-Hawes. There is a superb view of it from the road, with the tiny whitewashed chapel of Aghia Pelagia next to it in a clump of trees.

The site

Although the area had been occupied since the 3rd millennium, serious building first began at Gournia in MM III or LM I, c. 1600 BC, when a small palace was erected on the top of the hill. This was destroyed, along with the town, at the same time as the other palaces on the island, around 1450 BC. The structure was built to the north of a

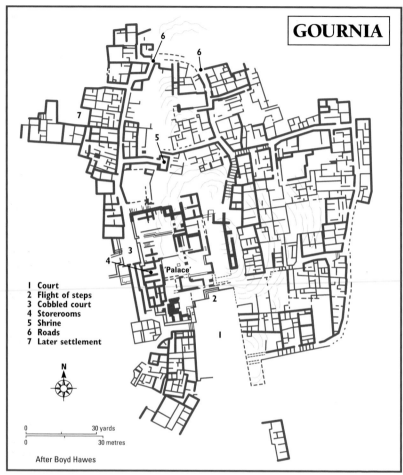

GOURNIA

1 Court
2 Flight of steps
3 Cobbled court
4 Storerooms
5 Shrine
6 Roads
7 Later settlement

N

0   30 yards
0   30 metres

After Boyd Hawes

rectangular court (**1**) onto which opened many private houses. A low **flight of steps** (**2**) attached to the south side of the palace and facing the court suggests a primitive theatral area, perhaps for watching ceremonies in the courtyard. Behind the steps to the west, a small room with a perforated stone in the paving is thought have been used for bull sacrifices, assuming the hole was for slotting in a table or draining the blood. Beside it was a *kernos*, a small stone with 32 hollows used for ritual offerings, a larger version of which was found at Malia (*see p. 123*). In the portico fragments of stylised bull's horns, fallen from the pillars, point to some cult use.

The west side of the palace opened on a narrow **cobbled court (3)**: it had a monumental façade with recesses and projections, and a central door. **Storerooms (4)** with benches and channels for collecting liquids were located behind the west façade, as is traditional in the layout of Minoan palaces. The palace also contained a lustral basin and light-well. There were three entrances: from the south, west and northeast. Although comparatively small (50m by 37m), the palace at Gournia, with its many features common to the larger palaces of Minoan Crete, adapted for storage, administration (but no Linear A archive so far) and religious activities, may have been the centre of its own independent polity in the centre of Mirabello Bay in the LM I period. According to estimates, the area covered some 200km square; Knossos' territory is thought to have been five times larger at least. The palace did not survive long and was destroyed by an earthquake. Early in the LM I period it was turned into workers' accommodation and an industrial settlement developed around it; the whole settlement covered an area of 25,000 square metres, divisible into seven separate quarters.

To the north of the palace, and separate from it, stood a small **shrine (5)**, 3m by 4m, dating to the LM I period; it had a ledge on the south side for cult objects. Finds from the shrine, with a date later than the construction itself, include a goddess with raised arms, clay tubes with snakes modelled in relief, and horns of consecration.

Two **roads (6)** joined by steps encircled the lower and upper parts of the town. The numerous houses were small and tightly packed. Many of the surviving rooms were, most likely, basements used for storage; entry to the houses would have been in many cases via steps leading up from the street. Some of these steps can still be seen. Access to the basements would have been from inside the houses, down wooden stairs through a trap door. Other dwellings were entered directly at street level, as the large threshold stones, still in place, indicate.

Finds from the **later settlement (7)**, thought to have been abandoned towards the end of the 2nd millennium BC, have increased our understanding of the economy of a Minoan town. There was evidence for stone vessel manufacturing, pottery making, oil or wine production, carpentry and metalworking.

Sphoungaras and Pachia Ammos

In 1910, a while after Harriet Boyd's work at Gournia, Richard Seager, also an American archaeologist, excavated a cemetery at **Sphoungaras**, on a hill slope at the end of the cove directly below the site and which had first been explored by Boyd in 1904. Seager uncovered 150 pithos burials, the majority contemporary with the last phase of Gournia; grave goods included an important series of seals. As the road continues east, it is possible to get a fine view of the site.

At **Pachia Ammos** (Παχειά Άμμος; 'Deep Sand'), now a coastal resort, a Minoan cemetery was exposed on the beach in 1914 after a severe storm (this part of the Mirabello gulf is not as idyllic as it looks: swimmers should be aware of strong currents). Upon excavation, Seager found six larnakes and over 200 pithoi, the majority of Neopalatial date. Among the earlier ones, belonging to the Prepalatial period, one had been buried with the base uppermost so that the body, which had been folded and introduced head first, could enjoy a sitting position in the afterlife. Seager also found some of the jars below the waterline, a confirmation that this part of the coastline has been sinking since the Bronze Age, as at nearby Mochlos.

ACROSS THE ISTHMUS TO IERAPETRA

From Pachia Ammos it is barely 14km to Ierapetra. If you are not in a hurry and wish to enjoy some fine countryside, the route from Istro via Kalamavka to the south-west and the Bramiana Dam (*see p. 222*) will be rewarding, though longer (25km) and slower. The road to Ierapetra is dominated by the Thrypti massif to the east, cut by the narrow cleft of the spectacular **Cha Gorge** (*map p. 431, B2*), a 700m deep V-shaped crack. Geologists have noted a remarkable match in the two sides, showing that Cretan gorges are the result of cracks in the earth's crust through tectonic upheaval, only subsequently deepened by river erosion. The Cha Gorge is truly spectacular with pools and waterfalls, but it is not easy to climb.

Vasiliki

Shortly after the gorge, on the other side of the main road, is Vasiliki (Βασιλική; *map p. 431, B2*). Look out for the sign to the site, which is reached up a path through carob and olive groves. The ruins are fenced, but there is no custodian now, and the fence has been pulled up high so it is easy to get in. The site occupies a commanding position overlooking the north end of the isthmus route down to the south coast, controlling traffic from Mochlos and Pseira along the Mirabello gulf through to Myrtos and Makrygialos on the south coast. Excavations by Richard Seager in 1903–06 were followed by further work and re-evaluation by Antonios Zois in the 1970s. Vasiliki shows signs of early occupation from the middle of the 3rd millennium. The first phase has houses with a crammed, egalitarian architecture reminiscent of Çatal Höyük in Anatolia, but this gives way to more high-status buildings showing the emergence of a stratified society. The characteristically mottled Vasiliki ware (*see p. 29*) dates from this period. Aghios Nikolaos museum has good examples of 'teapots' with extravagantly long spouts. Talk of a palace, however, is certainly premature. Zois's re-evaluation of Seager's stratigraphy of the House on the Hill showed that the 'palace' was in reality the result of a confusion in the phasing of two distinct buildings (the West House and the Red House). The settlement peaked in the early MM I period and was still important in LM I, c. 500 years later. Destruction through fire and earthquakes did occur but was promptly followed by levelling and rebuilding. Vasiliki was re-occupied in Roman times, when it acquired an aqueduct bringing water from Episkopi, 4km away. It is a surprising move given that modern Vasiliki, which is not far, has good springs. This may not have been the case in the past; moreover, evidence of industrial activity (ceramics, weaving and glass-making) suggests that the community did not rely only on agriculture and may have been in need of an additional water supply.

Because of its complexity, continuous rebuilding and troubled excavation history, the site is not easy to present to the general public, and in fact there has been no attempt to do so. In spring the ruins are overgrown with tall grass and wild flowers. For archaeologists it has provided interesting insights into Minoan building techniques,

View across the ruins of Vasiliki to the great cleft of the Cha Gorge.

Episkopi church. Detail of the decorated blind arches around the drum of the dome.

including the imprints in the plaster of long gone structural timbers. In the Red House (with deep basement rooms) it has been possible to establish an early use of plaster for rendering rough surfaces. In Late Minoan times these plastered surfaces would have been frescoed; here, in the basement rooms of the Red House, builders used a sort of stucco made of hard red lime plaster. Small patches are still preserved, as are the channels for structural timbers. For ceramicists the discovery of five sherds predating Vasiliki ware, decorated with dolphins, a motif that resurfaces at the height of the Neopalatial period in the Marine Style, gives an insight into the evolution of Minoan pottery.

Episkopi

On the way south, visitors interested in church architecture should consider stopping at Episkopi (Επισκοπή; *map p. 431, B2*) for an intriguing medieval church dedicated to Aghios Georgios and Aghios Charalambos, in the centre of the village close to the modern cathedral (below the road in a dry river bed filled with mature eucalyptus trees). Access can be difficult (the keys are with the *papas*) but even a look at the exterior is worth the detour. The unusual ground plan of the church, the bishop's church in medieval Episkopi (*episkopos* = bishop), is the result of the addition of a south nave (Aghios Charalambos) to an earlier domed church (Aghios Georgios) with conch-shaped cross-arms and a north aisle which was only accessible originally from the inside (the doorway in the west conch is Venetian in date). On the outside, the 19 blind arches around the drum below the dome are outlined with a pattern of tiles set upright in mortar and fringed with an upper band of small rosettes, a style only rarely found in Byzantine churches in Greece. The closest parallels are with churches in Bulgaria at the end of the 12th century. This, in conjunction with the absence of evidence of Venetian influence, helps date the building to the end of the Second Byzantine period. The plan suggests a martyrion and according to the Service for Byzantine Antiquities, it may have been associated with a system of early Christian catacombs with access from inside the church. Giuseppe Gerola saw it slightly differently. The area had a Latin-rite cathedral, the Panaghia Eptatroullis, 'of the seven domes', which is no more. It was demolished and the material used to build another church, though according to the locals, some marble friezes were moved to Aghios Nikolaos by the German occupying force in 1942. This curious church might have been the cathedral baptistery.

In 1946 during road building, chamber tombs of the Postpalatial period were uncovered under the village street in Episkopi. A fine painted larnax is now in Ierapetra museum (*see p. 221*).

IERAPETRA

Ierapetra (Ιεράπετρα; *map p. 431, B3*) is proud of its status as the southernmost town in Europe. You know it is true when you get there. It is dry and hot. This has helped in Ierapetra's chosen destiny, which is not catering for tourists, but developing as a centre for the cultivation of fruit and vegetables. Tourism here is almost an afterthought, but the beaches are excellent.

HISTORY OF IERAPETRA

The small archaeological museum next to the town hall in the Plateia Kanoupaki (*see opposite*) is living proof that Ierapetra is quite ancient. The name of Hierapytna, by which the city was known in antiquity, first appears when the Dorian city-state destroyed neighbouring Praisos c. 145 BC and became the main rival of Itanos, situated at this extreme end of the island. Hierapytna put up fierce resistance to Roman occupation but later bent to the inevitable and made the most of its position opposite the African coast, where the rest of the newly-created province of Crete and Cyrenaica was located. Contacts with the west were strengthened and a local girl, Flavia Titiana, daughter of a local worthy, made a spectacular ascent in 193 when her soldier husband Pertinax became Roman emperor. Unfortunately his reign lasted only lasted 86 days. In the late 4th century, Hierapytna was as important as Knossos. The *Tabula Peutingeriana* shows that it had road links with Knossos, Lyttos and Gortyn.

The ancient city covered an area larger than the present one. In 824 it was destroyed by the Saracens but resurfaced as a centre for piracy. It prospered in Venetian times and not much is heard about it until June 1798 when, according to tradition, Napoleon, then a young general, stayed with a local family on his way to Egypt. The house where he spent the night can still be seen opposite the clock tower near the fortress.

Investigations have started in recent years in the harbour areas and west of it, but little has yet been excavated of ancient Ierapetra and nothing remains of the amphitheatre, two theatres, naumachia, temples, baths and aqueducts mentioned by earlier travellers. Unfortunately systematic looting and destruction by locals and by well-meaning travellers (Spratt sent two sarcophagi to the British Museum in 1861) reduced the Jewel of the Mediterranean to a 'miserable townlet in the last stage of dilapidation and dead rot'— to quote Evans, who visited in 1894.

Much has been done now to improve the image of the city. On the promenade cafés like Pink Semiramis or ice cream parlours like Chocolicious are decidedly modern, and further north, Koundouriotou has been pedestrianised and is a smart shopping area.

The old town

Old Ierapetra is small—and not much of what remains is particularly old. The present **Kale (fort)** dates from the 17th century (rebuilt in 1626 by Francesco Morosini after earthquake damage and later by the Turks) but is on the site of an earlier structure; according to tradition the earliest fortification was Genoese, predating the arrival of the Venetians. The building is now being restored and is worth having a look at on your way to choose a restaurant on the waterfront. The beautiful Roman drainage slab abandoned in the entrance is an extra attraction.

The old **Turkish quarter**, with the inevitable fountain next to a former mosque, now a concert hall, is just inland from the harbour.

The Archaeological Museum

The museum (*open Tues–Sun 8.30–3; T: 28410 22462*) is housed in one of the few remaining old buildings in the town, an Ottoman school set up in 1899 for Turkish children. The first room is taken up by **finds from nearby sites**. Of particular interest are the goddesses and snake tubes from Kavousi and Vronda, the collection of LM pottery from Episkopi, and the assemblage of Minoan pottery from Ierapetra itself, attesting the ancient occupation of the location.

The **burial reconstruction from Vronda** in the next room testifies to the use of the site as a cemetery after the Late Minoan town had been abandoned in the second half of the 8th century BC. It is thought that settlement had by then moved to Azorias or to Kastro. Cremation no. 26, in a stone-lined cist, holds three bodies. First an adult and a child were cremated on two separate occasions and grave goods were deposited after the burning. Later a body was burnt elsewhere, packed in an amphora and buried in the same cist.

The star exhibit is the **Postpalatial larnax from Episkopi** (*see p. 219*). The clay coffin is in the shape of a rectangular chest decorated with 12 painted panels with scenes of hunting, a chariot procession and a stylised octopus; the gable of the lid has a bull's head modelled at one end and a human figure at the other. The last room concentrates on **Ierapetra in the Graeco-Roman era**; of particular interest is the 2nd-century AD statue of Demeter, a sheaf of corn in her left hand and in her headdress two snakes beside an altar. Displayed on either side of the door are fragments of treaties showing dealings with King Antigonus Doson of Macedonia (229 BC) and much later with Roman Gortyn.

Chrysi Island

Chrysi (Χρυσή; *map p. 431, B3*), formerly known as Gaidouronisi or 'Donkey Island', is only an hour's boat ride from Ierapetra. The main attraction for visitors are the beaches, which is what has prompted the local tourist office to return to the ancient name, associated with the Greek word for gold and much more evocative than wild donkeys of inviting sandy expanses. The island is now uninhabited; it has been suggested that rising sea levels may have affected the coastline and interfered with harbour facilities and the water supply. Minoan occupation has been identified and, in Roman times, a village with a field system and tombs developed. Medieval remains suggest a chapel and a possible monastery. Up until the early 1950s locals living on the mainland would row across to till their fields. Now Chrysi belongs to rabbits. Botanists braving the fierce sun to explore the island will spot lentisk and juniper, both the land and sea varieties. You may be told that sea juniper is cedar (sea cedar, as the Cretans call it) but experts disagree. To them this plant, with its distinctive berries and often gnarled and distorted trunk, is *Juniperus oxycedrus macrocarpa*, rare on Crete itself and now threatened by encroaching tourism.

WEST OF IERAPETRA

The main road runs close to the shore and the hothouses all the way to Myrtos and the two interesting Minoan sites nearby. This is the 'Costa Plastica', where fruit and vegetables are grown in polytunnels and polythene-sided greenhouses. A short drive inland will transport you to a much more pleasant hilly landscape with good views. Here ornithologists will find an excellent spot both for migrant birds and year-round residents.

West to Myrtos

The road signed to Bramiana and Kalamavka branches off north upon leaving Ierapetra. As you approach the **Bramiana Dam** (*map p. 431, B3*), the road climbs to the east end of it. The dam, the largest in Crete, was built in the 1970s to provide water for the budding horticultural industry on the coast. The area is now the most extensive wetland in Crete, with interesting flora and fauna. It is possible to make a tour of the reservoir; the best points for bird-watching will depend on the water level and the time of day.

Further inland to **Kalamavka** (8km; Καλαμαύκα; *map p. 431, B2*), the road climbs towards the watershed. The village is situated in a cleft on the spine of the island which accounts for the bizarre hard limestone rock formations, where the core of the massif is exposed. The E4 is 4km north in the Prina direction, in a landscape good for orchids. From Kalamavka the road sweeps south to Anatoli and then west in the Males direction to **Moni Panaghia Exakoustis** (the 'Virgin Renowned'), a nunnery of no great antiquity (a 19th-century foundation twice dissolved and brought back to life in the 1960s) but enjoying a fine view of the Myrtos valley. At **Males** (Μάλες; 580m; *map p. 431, A2*) you are at the foothills of Mt Dikte. Here shepherds' tracks lead to the Katharo plateau west of Kritsa and join the E4 at Mathokotsana to cross the mountains in the Lasithi direction to Avrakondes and northwest to Lyttos. To return to the coast and to Myrtos (13km), a walking detour via **Metaxochori** (Μεταξοχώρι) is recommended. Alternatively you can follow the Sarakina Gorge in the Mythi direction for a pleasant drive down a fine valley.

At Myrtos, two important Minoan sites occupy the hill overlooking the Libyan Sea: Myrtos Pyrgos and Myrtos Phournou Koryphi.

MYRTOS PYRGOS

Taking the road from Myrtos to Ierapetra, Myrtos Pyrgos (Μύρτος Πύργος; *map p. 431, A3*) is the first site, high up to the left along a well-marked path off the main road (*parking*). Excavated by Gerald Cadogan in the 1970s, it is named after the 17th-century Ottoman beacon tower (*pyrgos*) overlooking the coast. This was a good defensible position in antiquity also, with water available from the stream in the valley. The first signs of occupation date to EM II, as at the other site nearby. But unlike Myrtos Phournou Koryphi, Myrtos Pyrgos was reoccupied and rebuilt following destruction by fire. In the Neopalatial period, the settlement was dominated by a high-status house with ashlar masonry and gypsum, overlooking the sea across a court. The building may have had two, possibly three storeys. Only the lower one cut into the rock now remains.

MYRTOS PYRGOS

1	Street
2	Paved court
3	Cistern
4	Veranda
5	Raised walk
6	Column base
7	Entrance passage to house
8	Gypsum staircase
9	Light-well
10	Bench
11	Pantry
12	East access passage
13–14	Storerooms

Ottoman tower

5m

Visiting the site

The visit starts along the **stepped street (1)** leading along the ashlar façade to the **paved court (2)**. The plaster-lined **cistern (3)** with a capacity of 23 cubic metres dates from the Protopalatial period; when the court was laid out, it was filled with river pebbles and used as a soakaway for storm water. The front of the house had a gypsum-floored **veranda (4)** with two wooden columns on purple limestone bases on either side of a pillar. A **raised walk (5)** runs in front of it. To the south, a **column base (6)** indicates a building, a small pavilion or a shrine, closing the east end of the courtyard. The main entrance to the house was along a **passage (7)** leading to a **gypsum staircase (8)** in an area that is now disturbed by pits made in modern times to quarry ashlar masonry for reuse.

The upper floor would have been at the same level as the hillside at the back. In the passage and in the three rock-cut basements beside it, excavators found gypsum slabs fallen from the first floor, sealings, a red faïence triton shell, tubular stands and a Linear A tablet, an assemblage highlighting the close connection between religion and administration in Minoan society. North of the staircase is a **light-well (9)** and across from it, a **bench (10)**. At the bottom of the stairs was a stone basin. The staircase was separated from the light well by a stepped parapet with an arrangement for wooden columns, a set-up reminiscent, in a more modest form, of the Grand Staircase at Knossos. The bench had gypsum back panels and, below the seat, triglyph decoration imitating carved wood. The rock-cut **pantry (11)** held a large tub and a quantity of plain cups. More gypsum was used in the construction of the light well, in the walls and floors. The rainwater would have been directed by the eaves into the central basin, thereby protecting the delicate gypsum lining. The fragment of an obsidian vessel from this area points to connections with the Dodecanese islands.

The east wing of the house was accessed from a **passage (12)** and contained, behind the ashlar façade, a couple of **storerooms (13, 14)** with large pithoi. Clay and stone vessels found in the **street (1)** indicate a grander room above these stores. The whole area went up in flames in the second half of the LM I period in a localised violent blaze that vitrified the pottery, baked the mud brick and the Linear A tablet, and splintered the ashlar masonry; yet it left the houses of the surrounding settlement untouched. At the back of the house up the hill are remains of a large Protopalatial cistern that went out of use in antiquity and of terrace walls with the lower courses of the Ottoman tower.

On the way back to the main road, visitors pass the well-preserved stretch of a paved road leading to a two storey **communal tomb**. The area fell out of use in LM I, roughly at the same time as the destruction of the main house, but the tomb had been built around the very end of the 3rd millennium using debris from a much earlier, Prepalatial phase. Finds include high-status objects with metalwork, a triton shell and stone vases. Examination of the skeletal remains showed a healthy population with a diet that included plenty of pork.

MYRTOS PHOURNOU KORYPHI

This Early Bronze Age site lies 1.5km to the east of Myrtos Pyrgos. (*NB: Although it is signposted from the main road, the track does not look viable. The site is not open and can only be viewed from the fence—if you can get there.*) The settlement was built in EM II and was abandoned after a fire a few centuries later. Traces of a defensive circuit, with a main entrance to the south with a bastion and a door on a pivot, have been identified. All water had to be fetched: there are neither wells nor cisterns.

The settlement consists of 90 densely packed small rooms and passages, thought to correspond to six family units. Buildings were in mud brick on undressed stone directly on the bedrock and had a single storey. Material recovered from the site includes seals and sealings, important because they could be securely dated, and agricultural equipment. In the southwest part of the site, a domestic shrine held a figurine of a goddess clutching a miniature jug of a shape similar to those vessels found in the village;

this is one of the earliest pieces of evidence of early Minoan religion (*illustrated on p. 179*). According to the finds, villagers made a living by farming cereals, potting and weaving, making wine and oil, and herding sheep, goats, cattle and pigs.

Myrtos village nearby (Μύρτος; *map p. 431, A3*) is a pleasant place known for its mild winters (apparently even swallows find it congenial). Tourism has developed but in the small way, and the village has not lost its charm. Road connections are good, and it makes a good base to explore the region from; alternatively it offers peace and quiet for a relaxing stay.

PRACTICAL INFORMATION

GETTING AROUND

• **By car:** The E75 runs from Aghios Nikolaos to Siteia. The turning to Ierapetra is 19km after Aghios Nikolaos. From Ierapetra it is 14km to Myrtos. Parking in Ierapetra is not a big problem outside the old town.
• **By bus:** Ierapetra bus station (*T: 28420 28237; www.crete-buses.gr*) is on the continuation of Lasthenous at the north end of town after Plateia Plastira. There are regular services to Ierapetra from Herakleion's Bus Station A near the harbour and from Aghios Nikolaos. From Ierapetra a service runs to Myrtos and a more limited one continues west to Viannos. Services also to Siteia and the south coast to Makrygialos.
• **By sea:** Chrysi island is 8 nautical miles away. Frequent day trips are advertised from Ierapetra.

VISITOR INFORMATION

Ierapetra
Police on Plateia Eleftherias (*T: 28420 90160*); **Tourist Police** in the same building, but entrance on Markopoulou (*T: 171*).
Taxi ranks are in the main squares (*T: 28420 26600*).

Hospital on Mamounaki, north of the bus station (*T: 28420 22488*).
Post office in Plateia Kanoupaki on the edge of the old town, not far from the archaeological museum.

WHERE TO STAY

There are a number of options in the area, from rent rooms and apartments to luxurious resorts along the north coast, which is well developed for tourism. The south coast is less developed. Ierapetra and Myrtos remain the main centres.

Ierapetra (*map p. 431, B3*)
€€ **Arion Palace Hotel**. A modern building just outside the old town on Kothri. *T: 28420 25930 or 22240, www.greekhotel.com/crete/ierapetra/arionpalace.*
€€ **Cretan Villa Hotel**. A small hotel three blocks north of Daidalou, in a restored 18th-century house with plenty of character. *T: 28420 28522, www.cretan-villa.gr.*
Two other good-value hotels in the old town are € **Hotel Koral** (*T: 28420 22743*), a small place at Ioannidou 106 and € **Greco** (*T: 28420 28471 or 28472*) on Kothri. **Rooms to rent** are advertised in the old part of town be-

hind Stratigou Samouil and near the harbour.
Istro (*map p. 431, B2*)
€€€ **Istron Bay Hotel**. A self-contained
luxurious hotel overlooking the bay, with its
own cove and much else. *T: 28410 61303,
www.istronbay.gr.*
€€€ **Mistral Hotel**. High up in a position
commanding a fine view of the bay, with
private beach. *T: 28410 61112, www.mistral-
hotel.gr.*
Kalo Chorio (*map p. 431, B2*)
€ **Elpida**. The village of Kalo Chorio is
slightly inland from Istro. The loss of the bay
view is more than compensated by the fine
garden. *T: 28410 61403, www.elpidahotel.com.*
Myrtos (*map p. 431, A3*)
€€ **Villa Mertiza**. A family-friendly apartment hotel set back from the beach in a lovely garden. Recently the owners have acquired
holiday flats in the village of Tertsa, 6km to
the west, completely off the main road and in
a village smaller than Myrtos. *T: 28420 51208,
www.mertiza.com.*
€ **Myrtos Hotel**. Small, family-run hotel
with a good taverna attached. *T: 28420 51227
or 51209, www.myrtoshotel.com.*
€ **Nikos House**. Rooms and apartments to
rent in the village. *Open Easter–Nov. T: 28420
51116.*

WHERE TO EAT

Ierapetra (*map p. 431, B3*)
The restaurants are mainly along the harbour.
Napoleon, which has now been in business
for almost 40 years, is still a strong favourite.
Near the fort is **To Archontiko**. In among
them has recently sprung a new breed of
eateries and cafés characterised by modern
design and international-sounding names.
Istro (*map p. 431, B2*)
Zygos Taverna has whole lamb and suckling
pig on the spit.
Myrtos (*map p. 431, A3*)
There are a number of tavernas in Myrtos.
Katerina, next to Nikos House, a couple of
blocks from the beach, is a firm favourite
(try the lamb). There is another good taverna
attached to the **Myrtos Hotel**.

FESTIVALS & EVENTS

Ierapetra
The Kyrvia Festival (July and Aug) features
singing, dancing, open-air theatricals in the
Kale, art exhibitions and lectures. During
Nautical Week (Aug) swimming competi-
tions, water sports events and a fireworks
display are held.

THE EAST COAST TO SITEIA

From Pachia Ammos it is 45km to Siteia on the E75 across high ground, with Thrypti and the Ornon mountains to the south and fine sweeping views of the sea to the north. From Kavousi walkers can explore the slopes of Thrypti with the sites of Vronda and Kastro. By the sea, there is scope for a boat trip to Pseira and Mochlos. Past Khamaizi and its intriguing oval building, Siteia, the main town of eastern Crete, offers a good base for exploration of the area beyond.

KAVOUSI, AZORIAS & VRONDA

The village of Kavousi (Καβούσι; *map p. 431, B2*) is known because of its association with the sites of Vronda and Kastro, though it has a couple of interesting Byzantine churches too. The area in the mountains behind Kavousi was first explored by American archaeologist Harriet Boyd at the beginning of the last century. She investigated three main sites: Azorias, Vronda and, higher up, Kastro, on a pinnacle that can be seen from the main road. All are in strategic positions overlooking the coast, the mountain plain and the mountain passes. As Boyd became involved with Gournia from 1901, the area received no further attention until recently in the 1990s when the American School of Classical Studies in Athens set up a programme of systematic re-evaluation in collaboration with the 24th Ephorate of Prehistoric and Classical Antiquities. Vronda and Kastro are important for understanding the dynamics of change from the Bronze Age to the Iron Age at a time when Minoan coastal settlements were being abandoned and the population was moving inland. Azorias may be the key site to chart the process of urbanisation in the area in the Archaic period.

Churches in Kavousi

Two churches in Kavousi are of interest: Aghios Georgios, with well-preserved 14th-century frescoes, and Aghii Apostoli, with works charting the transition to the style known as the Cretan School. These take some determination to find. Old Kavousi is up the slope to the south. Walk up beyond the large modern church to the village's old main road running east–west. At the west end, before a No Entry sign and a mini market, take the alley uphill to the left. **Aghios Georgios** is up at the top, signed to the right. It is locked but the fine portal can still be admired. Back down to the mini market, take the alley alongside it to its left and follow it for **Aghii Apostoli**. The frescoes were being restored at the time of writing and are certainly worth the trouble.

The sites

The way to the sites is indicated just outside Kavousi by a large explanatory panel by the road on its south side. It is a one-hour walk to Azorias and two to Vronda. The road goes straight up the valley along the sideroad next to the panel. The first landmark is an extravagant modern construction halfway up the mountainside. It is possible to drive that far on a bad road. Beyond that the path follows the contour of the mountain and is very convoluted, though well marked. The oldest olive tree in Crete is somewhere on the way.

Azorias

In her limited excavation on the rounded hilltop of Azorias, Boyd identified four phases and concluded that the site had been in continuous use from c. 1200–700 BC. Later excavations from 2002 onwards have ascertained that by the early 6th century the site has been substantially rebuilt, using the debris of earlier structures as a foundation but also significantly transforming the ground plan and its spatial and architectural organisation. This is exemplified by the repetition of formal house types and the construction of a 'spine wall', a single architectural element regularising the uneven terrain and organising the urban fabric across the settlement. The wall, built in large blocks of local dolomite and limestone, created an impressive façade which has survived to almost 2m in height. It probably acted as a retaining wall in places but it may also have had a segregating function, controlling access to various parts of the town. Central and administrative cult buildings such as andreia and prytaneia, known so far in Crete only from written sources, with attendant store rooms and used for communal banquets and public ceremonies, have been identified. They confirm the existence of a ruling group and the restructuring of the town's political space in the 6th century BC. A destruction layer shows that the town was badly damaged by fire, but only after it had already been abandoned.

Vronda

At Vronda (meaning 'thunder') the earliest evidence is Late Neolithic and after that Early to Middle Minoan. The remains on view are Postpalatial, c. 12th century. Part of the site has been lost through erosion; moreover, its reuse as a cemetery in the 8th century BC has hampered interpretation. The exposed part measures c. 60m by 40m. By the ridge, Boyd's 'House on the Summit', now known as **Building A**, was apparently peacefully abandoned in the Sub-Minoan period. In the north part of the court is an oval shaped stone *kernos* with 24 circular depressions, similar to those at Malia and Gournia. A cobbled street ran west from the court; structures on its southeast side may be **basement storerooms**. The massive wall is probably a **retaining wall** and not for defence. The building on the southwest slope of the ridge was a **shrine**. Evidence for at least 17 goddess figurines, with raised hands in the typical late Minoan attitude, has been discovered together with snake tubes and *kalathoi* (vessels in the shape of baskets), one of which was decorated with horns of consecration.

The study of the **Late Geometric cemetery** has added new information about funeral ceremonies and burial practices. In some cases Bronze Age tholos tombs were reused but there are also cist tombs, in two of which a cremation burial was followed by an inhumation. Remains of pyres showed that cremations also took place in abandoned Bronze Age houses. This may be relevant to Burial 26 exhibited in Ierapetra archaeological museum (*see p. 221*). The contrast between the sparse offerings in the earlier burials in the tholos tombs on the north slope, and the abundant goods in the

8th-century graves is striking. The latter included a rich selection of iron tools and weapons. It is not clear where these people lived. Kastro was still occupied in the 8th century but it is quite a way away, probably too far to use this site as its burial ground.

Kastro

The refuge site of Kastro, on the peak towering above Vronda, is another 45mins from Vronda and it is a steep climb. It can be reached by taking the paved road from the chapel of Aghia Paraskevi. When this reaches the head of a cultivated valley, it turns right, away from the site and towards Thrypti. At that point you leave the *kalderimi* and cross the valley aiming for the saddle behind the pinnacle. The site stands at 710m; the view and the flora are worth the climb.

The refuge settlement clings to the sides of a tall outcrop in a precipitous position overlooking one of the passes to the hills behind. The cemetery is on the nearby slopes. There is no water and the nearest water source is 45mins away. Kastro, now thought to be larger than Boyd had originally believed, was first occupied in the 12th century BC. It expanded in the 8th century and went into decline from the early 7th century. Houses were built on terraces, with floors, benches and lower walls cut into the bedrock. Structures were made of undressed limestone. On the terraces on the eastern slope, a room with two centrally aligned columns and a hearth in between is reminiscent of the temple at Dreros. The precipitous profile of the area suggests that the terraces were accessed with wooden ladders. Finds included a number of crude unpainted figurines, a stone kernos, weaving equipment and tools. The analysis of the animal bones suggested that the settlement exploited a very wide area.

A regional survey has shown that the stable and constant system of clustered agricultural villages, characteristic of much of the Early Iron Age, evolved into a pattern of fewer and smaller settlements. A hierarchy emerged at the end of the Early Iron Age, with a long-term population shift in favour of Azorias. The size of Azorias, which is roughly 10–15 times greater (as much as 15 hectares) than adjacent Early Iron Age sites, leads to the hypothesis that a nucleation of population and attendant processes of urbanisation were under way here during the Archaic period, leading to the dispersal and gradual abandonment of the smaller villages.

PSEIRA

Beyond Kavousi the E75 climbs inland. By taking the left turn at Platanos (6km), it is possible to reach the coast at Mochlos (*see below*). All the way the island of Pseira (Ψειρα; *map p. 431, B2*), c. 3km from the coast, remains in view. Richard Seager excavated here in the early 1900s. Further investigations were carried out in the 1980s.

The settlement is on a peninsula overlooking a natural harbour with deep anchorage on the southeast side of the island, which was well protected from the fierce north winds. It had to rely on rainwater and wells, as there are no springs on the island. The first signs of activity date from the Final Neolithic; occupation was continuous, with phases of rebuilding to the end of the LM I period when there is evidence of destruc-

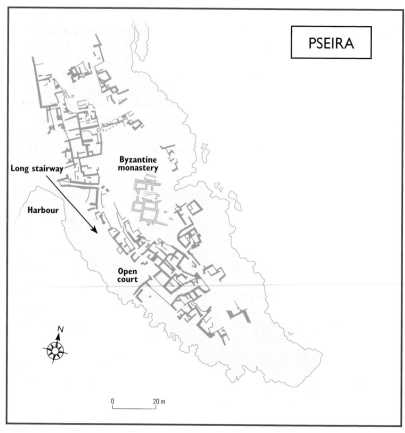

tion and abandonment. By then the town numbered some 60 houses strung out along the peninsula, set on terraces overlooking the harbour and connected by streets and flights of stairs, including a long one from the harbour to an open court at the top. Architecture had some pretension, with floors flagged with the abundant local stone and fresco decoration in the town shrine. Finds of fine ware, imported pottery and some metal also show a degree of opulence. After a limited LM III reoccupation c. 100 years later, Pseira saw some Roman activity and later became the seat of a Byzantine monastery. The cemetery, with 19 tombs, remained in use to MM II.

MOCHLOS

The site of Mochlos (Μόχλος; *map p. 431, C2*) is on an island facing the modern village of the same name. To get across you will have to rely on a local boatman and wait for propitious weather conditions. The narrow channel is subject to strong currents and rough seas. Alternatively, the site can be viewed in comfort from the **restaurant To Bogazi**, the furthest one on the small harbour, while sampling local specialities such as fish or lamb with artichokes. In antiquity there was an 180m isthmus connecting the island to the mainland. The sea level here has changed dramatically. Along the shoreline to the east of the modern village are some **Roman fish tanks**, now fully submerged. This suggests a considerable upheaval sometime after the 3rd century AD, possibly the 'Byzantine Paroxysm', a violent earthquake in late antiquity. Geology to this day plays an important part in Mochlos life. To the west of the village huge, noisy quarrying operations have been going on for the past 30 years carving out vast chunks of gypsum from the mountainside. Otherwise the place could be described as idyllic.

HISTORY OF MOCHLOS

The area was first investigated by Richard Seager in 1908 and later, in the 1970s and 1980s, by Kostis Davaras and Jeffrey Soles. In Minoan times there would have been an excellent harbour with good shelter from the prevailing north winds. The remains of the town are Neopalatial, but evidence for earlier occupation comes from the cemetery on the western side of the island. Here 26 tombs shaped like houses and built against the cliff have been excavated. Burial gifts from the richest tombs included spectacular jewellery and sealstones, silver cups and the earliest faïence as well as the finest collection of stone vases in Minoan Crete (now in Aghios Nikolaos and Siteia museums). Raw materials include rock crystal, marble, steatite and breccia. In recent years further excavations have opened more graves in the cemetery, some of which had been reused in Neopalatial times. The Prepalatial settlement below, the one that Seager had exposed, has also been investigated, revealing a paved street. The street system of the Neopalatial town was also uncovered, and three houses were found with their contents intact.

Research on the mainland around the modern village has led to the identification of a LM settlement of around the mid-15th century. It had a bench shrine and produced evidence of bronze-working, pottery and the manufacture of stone vases. The kilns were found with stoking chambers full of olive pits, a by-product of oil production used around the Mediterranean up to very recently as fuel. The evidence gathered from the pottery sequence and from the presence of volcanic ash in the stratigraphy supports the view that the Minoan civilisation continued to flourish in this period, a long while after the major volcanic eruption on Thera. This settlement was destroyed, like many others sites in Crete, at the end of LM I. Unusually, human skeletons were found in the debris. Some reoccupation took place in the Postpalatial period. A house has been identified on the island and there was also a cemetery on the mainland. Later the island was strengthened to the north with a curtain wall with towers and a fort, probably Byzantine in date, a move intended to control either pirates or the Saracens or both.

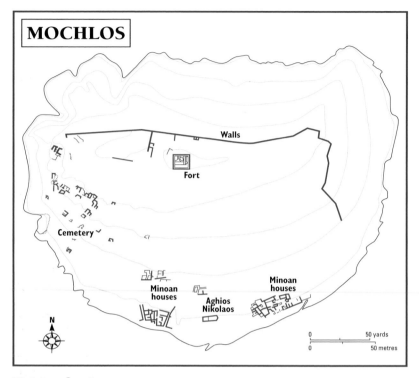

Visiting the site

When visiting the island, it is best to take the white chapel of Aghios Nikolaos by the shore to the south as a starting point. The excavations of the **Neopalatial settlement** extend on either side. On the east is the larger house exposed by Seager: the main entrance to the south led to a light-well with a bench, a main room and stairs to an upper floor. West of the chapel, a building was interpreted as the main administrative centre of the settlement. It had an ashlar façade and was terraced in three storeys against the hillside: the lowest floor had a pillar crypt. The building material was sandstone from the mainland, the same used in the palace at Gournia. To the north are remains of the **Byzantine village**; the fort and the defensive wall are beyond. The **Early Minoan cemetery** is signposted to the west. Here about 20 tombs in the shape of houses have been excavated. They would have been closed with huge stone slabs and covered with a flat roof of reeds and clay. The most important group of tombs opened to a paved court with an altar.

FROM MOCHLOS TO SITEIA

Beyond Sfaka the road continues past **Myrsini** (Μυρσίνη; *map p. 431, C2*), with tracks to the south up the slope of Mt Ornon. North of Myrsini on a hill by the sea, 12 rock-cut chamber tombs of the Postpalatial period were excavated in the 1960s. The grave goods included a rich variety of vases, weapons and utensils, now in Aghios Nikolaos museum. Also on the slopes below Myrsini, a much earlier tholos tomb of the Mesara type, one of the few found in eastern Crete, contained 60 burials dated by finds to the end of the Prepalatial period. Further on the E75 goes through **Mesa Mouliana** (Μέσα Μουλιανά; *map p. 431, C2*) Here two tholos tombs with a LM III date but reused some 400 years later, yielded rich offerings: a gold mask, bronze vessels and a sword reflecting Mycenaean influence. Of particular interest was a 10th-century BC bell krater with a huntsman pursuing two wild goats (probably *agrimia*) on one side and a man on horseback on the other, the first such representation known in Crete.

Khamaizi

On the last crest before the bay of Siteia at Khamaizi (Χαμαίζι; *map p. 431, C2*), a 10-min walk along a track to the right leads to the remains of an **early MM I house** (*site fenced but open*). It is visible from a distance on top of a conical hill, from which it enjoys extensive views over the eastern part of the Mirabello gulf, with the islands to the north and the valley and the land beyond to the south (including the highly visible motorway). The house, excavated in 1901 and reinvestigated in 1971, is unique because of its oval plan. The **entrance (1)** is to the southeast and the rooms are arranged around a small **paved courtyard (2)**. It sits within a thick perimeter wall probably meant to protect the building from the north winds, particularly strong in such an exposed position. In a northeast corner of the court is a deep, massive **cistern or well (3)** lined with masonry. Three figurines found in one of the rooms **(4)**, with remains of a hearth and of a portable clay altar, led first to its identification as a house shrine. The building had an upper storey as the **steps (5)** in the room near the **north entrance (6)** indicate. It is now believed to have been a look-out post. The idea that it was a sanctuary (the cistern was originally believed to be a votive pit) is now discredited because the cistern turned out to have a conduit. The building is superimposed on

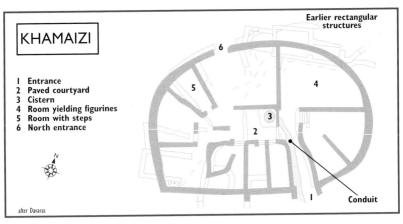

KHAMAIZI

1 Entrance
2 Paved courtyard
3 Cistern
4 Room yielding figurines
5 Room with steps
6 North entrance

Earlier rectangular structures

Conduit

after Davaras

earlier rectangular structures, suggesting that the oval shape was not the result of the lie of the land but was intended.

In the middle of the village of Khamaizi, the small **Folklore Museum** (I Kamara; *opening hours erratic; normally 9–1, also 5–7 in high season*) offers the chance to see a typical Cretan interior in a *kamara* house with its old furniture, the chest for the bride's dowry (the *kassella*), the low table (*sofra*), the grinding stone for the daily bread, and to imagine life with no running water or electricity, as was the case for most of rural Crete up until the late 1940s. The loom was for the womenfolk to produce decorative weaving for the house and the clothing. A bride's most precious piece of weaving would have been slung for display from a *kontada* (a wooden pole suspended from the beams). The new extension of the museum has old olive and wine presses and a smith's workshop. If you visit at the end of September, you will be able to join in the *Kazanemata*, a feast celebrating the production of *tsikoudia* (*see box below*).

HOW OLD IS RAKI?

Rakí, or *tsikoudiá*, as it is called in Crete, is the result of a process of distillation of grape marc, i.e. what is left over after wine-pressing, including skins, stems and seeds. It is flavoured with terebinth, a deciduous shrub of the pistachio family which Chadwick identified on a number of Linear B tablets, and has a strong, distinctive taste. The alcohol content should be 38 percent but it is much more variable in the home-produced variety where it can escalate to 65 percent. Raki is traditionally believed to have been introduced by the Turks and is celebrated at the feast of St George the Drunken on 2nd November. Recent finds of carbonised grapes and grape pips in the palace of Monastiraki, however, have prompted Rethymnon University to conduct an experiment to see if raki, which modern Crete shares with mainland Greece and Turkey, could be claimed as a Minoan invention. The researchers fermented the trodden grapes in a pithos for two weeks and then transferred them to a bronze cooking pot inside which a small empty bowl was placed. The pot was closed with a lid and sealed with dough. It was placed over a slow fire and the lid was cooled with a wet cloth. The vapour condensed into the bowl, apparently producing a very acceptable raki.

Liopetra and the Moni Phaneromeni

North of Khamaizi, a track (7km) leads to **Liopetra** (Λιόπετρα; *map p. 431, C1*), a corruption of Leon di Pietra, the 'Stone Lion', with the remains of a Venetian fortress. The building was started in 1579 and never completed—though never quite abandoned either. The stronghold, planned by Giacomo Foscarini to house 6,000 inhabitants fleeing Siteia, threatened by Turks and pirates alike, was built in a strategic position on top of an earlier fortress, of which the cisterns remained.

Following the coastal route, the road leads to **Moni Phaneromeni** (10km). The area is not as peaceful and quiet as it used to be. Works on the enlarged Siteia airport are to blame. However, the Panaghia Phaneromeni (the Virgin 'Revealed' or 'Made Manifest'), a church of the Venetian period perched on a ravine overlooking the sea, is still a pretty sight. Built on a north–south axis, it rises above a grotto traditionally associated with the miraculous appearance of an icon of Mary; the grotto is still revered. Frescoes have a graffito dated 1465.

SITEIA

Siteia (Σητεία; *map p. 431, C1*) is the harbour town and commercial centre of eastern Crete. A quieter place than Aghios Nikolaos, it will appeal to visitors looking for a base from which to explore the remote countryside. The town is clustered around two harbours with a tree-shaded waterfront at the Plateia Iroön Polytechniou. The main museum is a few minutes away. From the sea the land rises steeply up the hillside along wide, decorative stairways in a maze of narrows streets between colour-washed houses.

HISTORY OF SITEIA

Archaeologists have identified occupation dating back to the 4th millennium BC at various points in the area; major excavations at nearby Petras have focused on the Minoan occupation. It is thought that the town was built on top of the ruins of ancient Eteia, the port of the city of Praisos. When the Dorians invaded the island, the inhabitants fled to the interior. Later, in 146 BC, Praisos was destroyed by Hierapytna, and its inhabitants moved to Eteia. The town continued to flourish in the subsequent centuries. While it is known that Myson, one of the seven sages of ancient Greece, was born here, the Graeco-Roman period remains inadequately documented, though Eteia is mentioned in the 6th century AD by Stephanos of Byzantium, but with no precise location. The first mention of a settlement where the town now is dates from the First Byzantine period. During the crusades, Siteia was taken by the Genoese who rebuilt the ruined Byzantine castle. The city continued to prosper until 1508, when it was destroyed by a great earthquake. Thirty years later, Siteia was destroyed again, this time by the pirate Barbarossa. In 1648, when the Turks were at the gates, the Venetians had already moved the inhabitants to a castle on the steep hill of Liopetra, about 10km to the west. After a spirited defence lasting three years, the Turks captured Siteia and reduced it to a pile of ruins. They were preceded in this work of destruction by the Venetians themselves who, wishing to deny a strategic stronghold to the enemy, had destroyed the castle, the Kazarma (a name derived from the Italian for 'military building'). Its ruins are still there today for all to visit. After this Siteia was deserted for two centuries until 1869, when it was rebuilt by the Turks, who needed an administrative centre in the easternmost part of the island.

EROTOKRITOS

Vitsentzos Kornaros (1533–1613/1614) was one of the leading figures of the Cretan Renaissance. He is the author of the epic *Erotokritos*, considered to be one of the masterpieces of Cretan literature, a five-part poem in rhymed lines of 15 syllables. The plot revolves around Erotokritos, son of Pezostratos, adviser of the king of Athens, and Arethousa, the daughter of that same king, and the many twists and turns in their love story. The storyline owes much to a medieval French romance, popular throughout Europe as an archetypal example of idealised courtly love, as well as to 16th-century Italian poetry, of which Ariosto's *Orlando Furioso* is a prime example. Within the stylised conventions of epic-romantic verse, Kornaros finds space for philosophical digressions, descriptions, analysis of emotions and reflections on underlying meanings often only thinly disguised.

The poem may be understood on many levels. Kornaros wrote in the Cretan dialect, which made the poem accessible to his compatriots. The theme of national pride was also a unifying force wherever Cretans gathered, and *Erotokritos* often helped to keep hope alive during the centuries of foreign rule. Many Cretans are said to have memorised the whole poem (10,000 lines). The first printing of *Erotokritos* was in Venice (there were no local facilities, the Cretan market was too small) in 1713. One copy from that print run is preserved in the Gennadios Library in Athens while the British Museum in London has a slightly earlier handwritten edition. Over time *Erotokritos* became regular popular reading; quotations from it have found their way into everyday language, into folk songs and recitations.

Nothing much is known of Kornaros himself. Born in Siteia in 1533 into a distinguished Hellenised Venetian family, he worked as an administrator in Herakleion. His brother Andrea was also a literary figure, a poet and historian and the founder of one of the three Neoplatonic academies of Crete.

The Archaeological Museum

Siteia's Archaeological Museum (*open Tues–Sun 8.30–3*) opened in 1984, exactly 100 years after the first excavations at Praisos (*see p. 243*). It has good maps of sites and explanations in English and is arranged in roughly chronological order around a central court. Prominent at the very entrance is one of its showpieces, the skilfully restored Palaikastro Kouros, showing different degrees of discoloration as a result of burning.

The display starts immediately to the left with remains of extinct fauna (Cretan hippo and pigmy elephant) followed by Neolithic finds from Siteia and the cave of Pelekita on the coast north of Zakros. The Bronze Age display includes finds from the cemetery of Aghia Photia, where over 250 tombs of the Prepalatial period were excavated. Note the beautiful obsidian pressure blades. The pottery shapes (frying pans) show links with the Cyclades. Votive terracottas from peak sanctuaries of the region, including

Petsophas overlooking Palaikastro, are on display in Case 4. The next cases contain material from the islands of Mochlos and Pseira, with some fine stone vases and a particularly interesting stirrup jar, an excellent example of the Neopalatial Marine Style. The recent excavations at Petras have attracted much interest in the archaeological world on account of their discoveries. Some can be viewed in the next free-standing case. The Minoan town of Palaikastro is represented in the next display with rhyta, stone horns of consecration and stone vessels.

THE PALAIKASTRO KOUROS

One of the most spectacular finds from the recent excavations at Palaikastro, on the east coast north of Zakros, has been a chryselephantine statuette about one quarter life size, found in a fragmentary state in an open space and in the adjacent building in the northern area of the town. It represents a young male in the characteristic pose of a kouros, with the left leg slightly forward. It was manufactured in hippopotamus ivory and the head was of serpentine with inlaid eyes of rock crystal worked at the back to take an iris, perhaps a small stone. Scraps of gold indicate that the kouros originally had footwear, a belt and bracelets. The figurine was made of at least eight ivory pieces, separately carved and fitted together with dowels (the ninth piece was the pommel of the missing dagger). A rectangular ivory peg behind the face fits a cavity in the back of the head. The first ivory and gold leaf fragments, belonging to the torso and arms, were recovered in 1987. A year later systematic sieving brought rewards: scraps of neck, eyebrow, ear and eventually the serpentine head which fitted neatly into the rectangular dowel at the back of the ivory face. Success was complete when the rock crystal eyes were retrieved. In 1990 the ivory legs and feet were found. The figure may represent the Boy God, the companion to the Minoan Goddess, and has prompted speculation that its findspot must have been a cult place. The later development of the cult of Cretan-born Zeus in the nearby Diktaian temple at Palaikastro may also be significant. The Kouros appears to have been deliberately vandalised when Palaikastro was destroyed at the end of the LM I period.

The back of the room is entirely devoted to finds from the palace of Zakros save for an exhibit from a Minoan country house just outside modern Ano Zakros. The wine press with a LM I date was found with a pithos inscribed in Linear A (unfortunately the assemblage is not complete as the pithos has been sent to Herakleion museum). The rest of the display covers various aspects of the life of the palace, from the huge bronze saw (a reminder that the palace was a production centre) to the display of Linear A tablets (underlining the palace's function as an administrative hub for storage and distribution). The strangely shaped vessels in Case 11 have been interpreted as fireboxes for the dry distillation of aromatics (*see p. 203*). The importance of the palace as a storage and distribution centre is again underlined by the display of massive pithoi, some showing the marks of the fire that heralded the end of the palace. There is also a selection of Minoan cooking pots and basins alongside cases showing fine ware with a good display of spouted jars. Cult activities are also represented, with lamps and stone offering-tables, horns of consecration, double-axe stands and kernoi.

The Geometric and Archaic periods are illustrated with a map of the local sites. Material mainly comes from cemeteries in the area. The Daidalic terracotta heads and figurines were a chance find during road works in modern Siteia. The Archaic sanctuary of Roussa Ekklisia is represented with a display of Daidalic sculpture.

The last section is devoted to the Hellenistic and Roman periods, with material from Trypitos (a lead slingshot, coins, weights and amphorae with seals advertising the local wine) and from Xerokambos. A useful drawing illustrates the functioning of a hopper mill. Finally, a display covers the island of Kouphonisi (*see p. 246*) with some useful pictures. In Roman times the place developed a thriving production of purple dye extracted from the shellfish *Murex trunculus*.

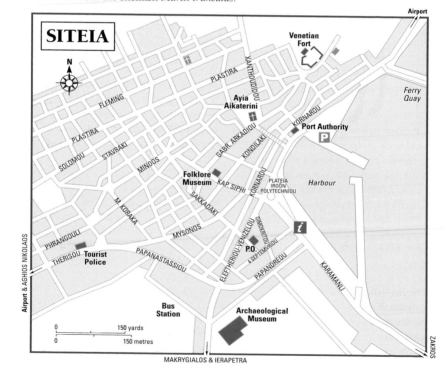

The Folklore Museum and castle

The **Folklore Museum** (*closed at the time of writing*) is on Kapetan Siphi. It houses an ethnographic collection in a beautifully restored period building. The interiors are particularly well arranged, with traditional Cretan furniture and equipment. The display covers domestic crafts such as weaving, lacemaking, woodcarving and embroidery, showing both the products and the tools to make them. The Museum Society encourages a revival of traditional skills in the area by keeping for sale a small stock of contemporary embroidery, normally made to old, traditional designs.

Northeast of the old centre stand the ruins of the **Kazarma**, the Venetian castle. The huge tower (a Turkish building on Venetian foundations) stands at the apex of a triangular-shaped fortified enceinte that ran down to the sea, though it had no proper harbour. Apart from the military installation, the compound also had a church and a rector's residence but lacked an independent water supply.

PRACTICAL INFORMATION

GETTING AROUND

• **By air:** Siteia airport operates internal flights to Herakleion and Chania.
• **By car:** Siteia is 46km from Pachia Ammos; 19km from Aghios Nikolaos; 147km from Herakleion; 30km from the south coast (all on good roads).
• **By bus:** Siteia bus station (*T: 28430 22272; www.crete-buses.gr*) is at the south end of town on Papanastassiou (off Venizelou) close to the Archaeological Museum. Regular services run to and from Ierapetra, Herakleion (Bus Station A by the harbour) and Aghios Nikolaos. Limited services run inland to Paraspori, Chrysopigi (crossing the E4) and Stavrochori (east of Mts Ornon and Thrypti); to the south coast at Makrygialos; to Palaikastro and Vai; to Zakros; to Armeni and Ziros past Etia and Chandras (close to Voila).
• **By sea:** From Siteia there are ferries to Aghios Nikolaos. Also to Piraeus and the islands of Kasos, Karpathos, Rhodes and Milos. LANE Lines (*Siteia office T: 28430 25080*).

TOURIST INFORMATION

Siteia
Post office: On Eleftheriou Venizelou.
Taxis: Grey, T: 28430 61380 or 22317.
Tourist information: On Karamanli by the harbour (T: 28430 61546).
Ambulance T: 166.
Police T: 28430 22266 or 22259.
Tourist police: On Therisou (west side of town).
Hospital T: 28430 24311.

WHERE TO STAY

There is plenty to choose from along the Mirabello coast. As the road dives inland, accommodation becomes more scarce.

Mochlos (*map p. 431, C2*)
If you ignore the gypsum quarry this can be a good choice as it is off the main road and is comparatively well set up.
€ **Meltemi Studios**. Above the village with

views of the island (not all the rooms) in a modern purpose-built building. Minimum stay required. *T: 28430 94200*.

€ **Pension Mirabello/Mirabello Rooms**. A very small place (2 rooms) above the village in a sleek, modern, functional style (German-owned), the exterior in 'Greek' colours (bright white and ocean blue) with a perfect view of the island. *T: 28430 94681, mirabello@ pension-mirabello.de, pension-mirabello.de (website in German)*.

€ **Sofia Hotel**. Down in the village by the sea. *Open April–mid-Oct. T: 28430 94554 or 94738*.

Siteia (*map p. 431, C1*)
Siteia has a number of modern hotels open all year round by the harbour, and some quieter, more interesting accommodation (normally closed in the winter) in the old part of town, up the steps from the harbour.

€€ **Elysee Hotel**. On Karamanli, the main road running along the port. Private parking. *T: 28430 22312; www.elysee-hotel.gr*.

€ **Hotel Archontiko**. A small hotel in the old town, on Kondilaki up the steps close to Aghia Aikaterini. *Open April–end Oct. T: 28430 28172*.

€ **El Greco**. Uphill on the way to the fort. Plain, unpretentious and comfortable in an old-style building. *Open April–Oct. Gabr. Arkadiou 13, T: 28430 23133*.

€ **Mariana Hotel**. A modern hotel close to the beach on Odos Misonos. *T: 28430 22088; mobile 0977 564595*.

WHERE TO EAT

Mochlos (*map p. 431, C2*)
There are a number of tavernas by the sea. **To Bogazi**, the last one (closest to the island), offers an interesting menu. The **Sofia Hotel** also has a taverna attached.

Siteia (*map p. 431, C1*)
The Balcony on the corner of Fountalidou and Kazantzaki in the old town (*T: 28430 25084*) is a bistro-style place with a good atmosphere and Cretan traditional fare with a Mexican touch (evenings only).
For fish try the **Siteia Taverna** (*T: 28430 28758*) at Venizelou 161 on the other side of the harbour.

FESTIVALS & EVENTS

Siteia celebrates the Kornaria Festival from mid July-end Aug in and around the Kazarma, a tribute to the author of *Erotokritos*. Events include plays, concerts, art exhibitions, readings and lectures. A wine festival is held on the quays in Aug. In **Kavousi** there is a raki festival in May

LOCAL SPECIALITIES

Siteia has a long wine-making tradition: it is the home of a number of well-known vintages, namely Vilana, Moschato, Thrapsathiri and Liatiko. The stable humidity, the constant sunlight and the minimal changes in yearly temperature provide a very favourable environment for wine production. Siteia's wine is celebrated in a lively festival in August. The Siteia cooperative (www.sitiacoop.gr), set up in 1993, represents 43 local cooperatives and almost 9,000 farmers. The headquarters are on the way to Aghios Nikolaos, just out of town. The cooperative runs a small museum and offers a chance to sample and to buy the local wine, raki and oil.

At **Myrsini**, halfway between Pachia Ammos and Siteia, Nikos Makrinakis creates ceramic artefacts in his workshop (*T: 28430 94590*) in a traditional and not-so-traditional style.

SOUTH OF SITEIA

From Siteia the main road south crosses the island and it is only 30km to the south coast at Analipsi. It would be a pity, however, to drive straight through without taking time to explore the unspoilt countryside. This chapter explores the country on either side of this main road.

Manares, Kato Episkopi and Zou

The main road south from Siteia is signposted Lithines. After c. 3km at **Manares** (Μανάρες; *map p. 431, C2*) it cuts through a Neopalatial Minoan villa, terraced into the hillside and overlooking the fertile valley (*signed*). The lower part of the building, which included storerooms, was protected by massive stone blocks. These have been interpreted by some as an anti-seismic device, by others as an embankment in view of the river below. At the northern end of the building stairs gave access to the upper floor.

For the Byzantine church of **Kato Episkopi** (Κάτω Επισκοπή; *map p. 431, C2*), take the east turn in Piskokephalo (1km). Though Aghii Apostoli, now the cemetery chapel, is signed (to the right) from the village, it is probably best to leave your car and find your way on foot. This tiny cruciform building, with a dome on an octagonal drum, was originally an episcopal church dating from the beginning of the Second Byzantine period.

Just short of **Zou** (Ζού; *map p. 431, C2*), up the road bank to the right (*fenced but open; parking problematic*), is another Minoan villa. The commanding position overlooking the valley is comparable to that of Manares. The entrance, with a small room with a bench at the south end of the façade with megalithic masonry, is well preserved; walls stand over 1m high in places. Two deep pits nearby may have been involved in the storage of grain. The farmhouse had its kiln. The land to the east, past modern Zou, a village noted for its abundant springs, now part of the Siteia water supply, is quite empty. Walkers and flower lovers would be well advised to explore it north to **Roussa Ekklisia**, the site of an Archaic sanctuary, and east to Karydi and Sitanos overlooking Zakros, especially in the spring when Crete's endemic tulip is in bloom.

THE ACHLADIA VALLEY

The road to Achladia branches out from Piskokephalo to the west. After a couple of kilometres, signs to the left direct to **Riza** (Ρίζα; *map p. 431, C2*) and the massive foundation of a Neopalatial building known as Achladia House A, constructed in MM III and destroyed in LM I. It was investigated by Platon. The Minoan farmstead or house was part of a small settlement stretching south and west along a low hill. The house had some 12 rooms and an entrance in the centre of the southwest façade. The main hall was through double doors on the left of the entrance passage, with storerooms on the right. The hall had three columns along the central axis and opened onto an area with a stone bench in one corner. Finds in the area behind the north façade suggest a kitchen. The owners of the villa may have been living in a remote location but they were certainly up to date with the architectural trends of the time, including pier-and-door partitions.

South of the villa, along a dirt track, is the **Platyskinos tholos tomb** (c. 1km), dated c.1340–1190, to the period of Mycenaean control of the island. It is one of the best preserved of its time. It was excavated during and immediately after the Second World War and again in 1991–93 by a joint Italian and Greek team. These latest investigations have ascertained that the area had been previously settled in the Prepalatial and in the Neopalatial periods. In Postpalatial times there was a radical change of use: the area became a necropolis and a Mycenaean tholos with a long dromos was built on top of it. At the end of the dromos two uprights support a massive lintel in the low doorway. The circular chamber was built in large stones with a corbelled roof closed by a keystone. Opposite the entrance, a small doorway against the natural rock was found blocked by two walls; it has been compared with the false doors provided for the spirit of the deceased in Egyptian tombs. The tomb had been robbed and some of the finds from the first excavations were lost in the war. However, three larnakes remained, one decorated with a double axe, horns of consecration and a griffin. The lid of another was shaped like the back of a bull, including the head and tail at the gable end.

Monte Forte and Epano Episkopi

From the crossroads before Achladia a slow and winding road connects to the main coastal road. On the way, by the banks of the Lapsanari, the deserted village of **Kimouriotis** (Κιμουριώτης; *map p. 431, C2*) has some interesting examples of traditional stone-built houses with cobbled yards close to a church and a spring.

Visitors wishing to explore the deserted area to the south can venture on the road south past Skordilo, to **Kato and Epano Krya** (bearing in mind that the name may really reflect the intense cold of the winter; *kryo* = cold). Two kilometres east of the village (*signposted*), on a hill at the end of a very narrow concrete road, are the ruins of the Venetian castle of **Monte Forte** (*map p. 431, C2*), probably a Genoese construction and certainly in use in the 14th century, when it was damaged in the 1303 earthquake. Set in a strategic position on a rocky outcrop, it controlled the region. As many as 3,000 locals took refuge here in 1579; later it fell into disrepair. There was not much left of it when Gerola took pictures at the turn of the last century except the ruined circuit of walls following the contour of the rock, the tower, the huge cistern (10m by 7m) and Aghios Nikolaos church, restored at the end of the 19th century. There is even less to see now, but the place is wild and beautiful. Moreover, on the lower slopes of the hill, a cemetery with a Sub-Minoan–Protogeometric date was excavated in the 1970s. A stone-lined complete tomb with a pithos and human remains are now in Aghios Nikolaos Museum.

From Monte Forte it is a bit of a twist and a turn to get back to the main road, but if you go via Vouvali and Sotira (which could involve some slow roads), you end up in **Epano Episkopi** (Επάνω Επισκοπή; *map p. 431, C2*) and will be able to compare Orthodox and Latin church architecture. In Venetian times the two rites co-existed: Latin for the occupying force, Orthodox for the locals. The Orthodox bishop had his seat in Kato Episkopi (*see above*). The residence of his Latin counterpart was here, at least by the early 16th century, when pirate raids made Siteia too insecure. In Epano Episkopi the basilica of the Panaghia, with its pointed arches, detailed stonework in the doorway and Italianate bellcote, is a far cry from the cruciform domed church at Kato Episkopi. To dispel any doubts, the coat of arms of Gaspare Viviani, who moved from here to take up the position of Bishop of Siteia in 1566, is emblazoned in full view on the portal.

PRAISOS & THE COAST

After Epano Episkopi, on the main south road from Siteia, there is abundant scope for exploration along quiet roads in open countryside. Praisos, regarded by ancient authors as the city of the Eteocretans, and more recent remains at Etia and Voila, are on the way to the Ziros plateau. Back on the main road south, the coast beckons with some good beaches (the bay of Makrygialos boasts the longest sandy beach in eastern Crete) and good walking country north of Analipsi in the beautiful Pefki Gorge, or by the But-terfly Gorge from Koutsouras or, to the east, up the Perivolakia Gorge in a spectacular dry and barren environment, up from Moni Kapsa. Alternatively, a short boat ride will take you to the island of Kouphonisi, the ancient production centre of purple dye.

PRAISOS

From Epano Episkopi, the minor road east descends along the fertile Pantelis valley, below the hilltop where the ancient city was, and climbs (7km) to **Nea Praisos** (Νέα Πραισός; *map p. 431, C2*). The ancient site is signposted from the main square. After c. 2 km and past some tholos tombs and the so-called Third Acropolis to the left, the First Acropolis, distinguished by a network of terrace walling, is straight ahead. The entrance to the First Acropolis and the remains of the temple on top are not difficult to find (*the site, though fenced, is always accessible*). Unfortunately, of late, Praisos has been somewhat neglected and has become quite overgrown. The other archaeological remains are very

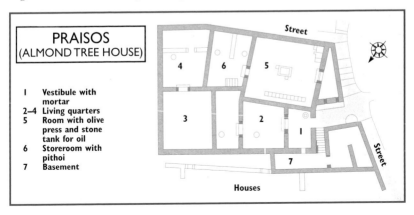

PRAISOS
(ALMOND TREE HOUSE)

I   Vestibule with
     mortar
2–4 Living quarters
5   Room with olive
     press and stone
     tank for oil
6   Storeroom with
     pithoi
7   Basement

Street

4   6   5

3   2   I

7

Street

Houses

difficult to see. The location, on the other hand, is stunning, and the walk among the fruit trees (almonds, figs, pomegranates and lemons) is well worth the trouble. It will also help you to work out the relationship between the different parts of the ancient city.

HISTORY OF PRAISOS

The town flourished from the Archaic to the Hellenistic periods. Herodotus mentions it, but it was the 1st-century AD geographer Strabo (*10.4.6–12*) who made the connection with the Eteocretans, the true or original Cretans, suggesting that the inhabitants were descendants of the Minoans. Indeed, inscriptions using the Greek alphabet but for a non-Greek language are one of the most intriguing finds from the site. It has been suggested that the language was related to that of Linear A. The area was first investigated by Federico Halbherr in 1894; as an epigraphist he was naturally interested in the inscriptions. Bosanquet excavated it in 1901 and the Greek Archaeological Service has been carrying out survey work since 1995.

The site shows evidence of Neolithic occupation in a nearby cave and of Minoan activity. The Megalithic House to the southeast of the hills has a Neopalatial date, and cemeteries have produced finds dating from LM III through to Hellenistic. There is, however, no continuity with a Bronze Age settlement. The city spread across three knolls (First, Second and Third Acropolis) and was mainly built on the bare rock with no underlying settlement. Hellenistic Praisos had contacts with the neighbouring cities of Hierapytna (modern Ierapetra) and Itanos. Its territory spread east and south, possibly including Kouphonisi. A major cause of dispute with Itanos was the control of the Temple of Diktaian Zeus at Palaikastro. At some stage in the Hellenistic period, the Praisians even shared citizenship with Hierapytna, but that did not stop the latter from obliterating Praisos sometime between 145 and 140 BC. The site was never reoccupied.

The city lay in the saddle between the First and the Second acropoleis where the **Almond Tree House** is. This is a Hellenistic andreion of some standing, named after a fruit tree that overhung it at the time of excavation. The structure was quite substantial, with ashlar masonry and joints finished with lime mortar. It was built into the slope, with the upper part making use of the native rock and a strong retaining wall below. Floors would have been of native rock or hard clay, though there are traces of a cobbled pavement. The house fitted into a street plan, its roof was tiled and there were steps to a second storey. The architecture is characterised by wide doorways and substantial stone jambs. The doors turned on pivots and the windows had wooden shutters. Living quarters were entered via a vestibule to the north, away from the sun, while the rest of the basement area was devoted to storage and industrial activities centred on olive oil production, as suggested by a press and a stone tank with a lid. On the summit of the **First Acropolis** the scant remains of the limestone foundations of a temple can be made out and on the south side of the **Second Acropolis** (at the further end of the saddle), rectangular cuttings show where houses were built into the slope in the Hellenistic period. These had rock-cut shelves and alcoves. The two hills were enclosed by a wall which can still be traced in places. The **Third Acropolis**, also known as Altar Hill, lies across the gully to the southwest. The five Eteocretan inscriptions were found here. On the summit, a primitive altar with rock-cut steps and ashlar masonry marked a sanctuary used, according to the finds, from the 8th–5th centuries BC. Interesting terracottas among the offerings included three painted figurines of lions.

THE SOUTH COAST & KOUPHONISI

The sea is not far from Praisos, and the main road will take you there past **Lithines** (Λιθίνες; *map p. 431, C2*), a very pretty village that remembers proudly its heroic feats against Ottoman occupation. One involves a three-storey fortress in which some 400 beleaguered Turks barricaded themselves at the time of the disturbances. The locals could not get them out, but at some point the wooden floors of the building caught fire. The Turks reached for a barrel thinking it was water, but it turned out to be raki— and that is why there is nothing left of the fortress. There are also miraculous icons in the church of the Panaghia, if you can get the key from the *papas*. Alternatively, aim for the church of Aghios Athanasios, a 15th-century building downhill from the main square, and see the ceramics embedded in its south façade. Tradition has it that these were the builders' dinner plates, though this is a form of decoration widely spread across the Mediterranean.

Upon reaching the coast, a 10km detour east leads to **Moni Kapsa** (Μονή Καψά; *map p. 431, C3*), dramatically situated on the cliff edge just beyond the mouth of the Perivolakia Gorge. The present building is mid-19th-century, but the grotto church, now the north aisle, dedicated to Aghios Ioannis Prodromos, is much earlier. According to tradition much of the work in it, including the carved wood iconostasis, is by the hand of an eccentric monk named Gerontogiannis, whose remains are still revered in the church.

The **Perivolakia Gorge**, some 4km long, is signed and has a convenient beach opposite the entrance across the road. It takes about 2–3hrs to walk up, and one hour less to come back. It is a very barren dry landscape, so a swim is recommended before and after. There are some facilities at Perivolakia including a bar, and a visit to the tiny deserted village of **Pezoulas** (Πεζούλας; *map p. 431, C2*), less than 1km away to the west, is recommended.

Makrygialos

The coastal village of Makrygialos (or, as the locals say, correctly, 'Makrys Gialos'; Μακρύγιαλος; *map p. 431, C3*) has merged more or less with the village of Analipsi to form a string of holiday rent rooms and tavernas along the long, sandy shore: the beach stretches away to the east, backed by the cliffs of the extreme southeastern corner of Crete. Kouphonisi is in view from here and is a summer boat ride away (*see below*). If you are approaching Makrygialos from Ierapetra, you will first see a sign pointing left to a Minoan villa, and then another pointing right to a Roman villa. Both sites are disappointing to visit. The very scanty remains of the **Roman villa** stand on the headland just west of the harbour, locked away behind a rusting fence. The remains of the **Minoan country house**, on a site that has been identified by the French archaeologist Paul Faure as ancient Syrinthos, are situated on an elevation with commanding views of the sea and of Kouphonisi. The ruins are aggressively fenced, however, and overgrown with grass. Only a vague idea of the villa outline can be had from behind the chicken wire. The site was excavated between 1973 and 1977 by Kostis Davaras and has produced finds of very high quality, some of which are displayed in Aghios Nikolaos museum. The building, in local sandstone and mud brick, much damaged by later development and farming activity, is dated to LM I. It exhibits palatial features and the excavator has suggested that it was no isolated building but may have been a manorial villa with a religious role, as well as exercising control over the local economy. Features would have included a central court with colonnaded porticoes, an altar and benches; a monumental west façade with recesses; a complex entrance system to the north; and possibly a walled east court. All of these are established palace features, but in Makrygialos everything is on a miniature scale. The central court, for instance, measures a mere 6m by 12.5m (Knossos is over four times that). Among the finds from the central court were a stone chalice and a sealstone carved with a scene of a ship carrying an altar flanked by a palm tree and an adoring female worshipper, suggesting a marine association for the Minoan goddess.

Marine associations are certainly what Makrygialos offers to visitors today. Out of season the **beach** is very lovely, a narrow strip of beautiful sand which extends for some way under the water as a shallow ledge, with a few tufts of eel grass growing near the shoreline. The beach is fringed by low-rise concrete buildings, yellow- and white-washed rent rooms and bars and tavernas offering cocktails, 'drought' beer, karaoke nights and other temptations for a clientèle that wants the familiarity of home under bluer, warmer skies.

Kouphonisi

This small island (*map p. 431, D3*), measuring 2km by 4km, lies to the southeast of the coast with daily trips in the summer from Makrygialos. Vegetation is scarce apart from a few tamarisks by the shore; the winds have eroded the soil and created sand dunes. No one lives there now and there is no record of any settlement for the past 1,000 years. But in antiquity it was different. There is evidence of activity from the Bronze Age; in the Hellenistic period the island, then known as Lefki (or 'White Island'), was the cause of a dispute between Itanos and Hierapytna. The arbitration, recorded in a stele now set into the façade of Moni Toplou (*see p. 264*), took place in 132 BC, when the court of Magnesia awarded the island to Itanos. Later a considerable Roman town developed, a possible port of call en route to Egypt and the East, but more importantly a production centre for the purple dye (*see box*). The settlement petered out c. 400 AD.

In the middle of the 19th century Captain Spratt, the British cartographer, visited and reported seeing ruins; later, in 1903, Bosanquet made an inspection; proper archaeological investigations only started in 1971. They have identified a theatre with an estimated capacity of 1,000 people, a temple, cisterns, mosaics and a settlement with workshops for the preparation of purple dye. The workshops are of particular interest as some commentators believe that the idea of extracting the dye from the murex mollusc should be credited to the Minoans and not, as is traditionally the case, to the Phoenicians. The dye is obtained from mucus secreted by the mollusc's hypobranchial gland. Twelve thousand murex were needed to make enough dye for a single toga.

On the whole, preservation is pretty poor; the remains have suffered since Spratt visited. The temple, for instance, was dismantled in the 1920 to build the lighthouse (bombed in 1944), which also incorporated the broken remains of a colossal statue.

THE COLOUR PURPLE

Kouphonisi was an important centre for sponge fishing and for the preparation of purple dye much valued in the Mediterranean textile industry and associated with Roman emperors, though their shade of purple was more a deep crimson. It was extracted from two species of the murex family (*Murex trunculus* and *Murex brandaris*). The gastropod, according to Aristotle and Pliny the Elder, was gathered at the beginning of autumn or winter and kept alive in baskets until a sufficient quantity had been collected, as each shell only produced a single drop of dye. The smaller shells were crushed with stones to extract the dye while the larger ones were pierced and a tiny gland (known as the *anthos* or flower) was removed from the neck of the mollusc. This had to be done quickly while the animal was still alive. The milky fluid from this was put into brine, a little vinegar was added, and it was left in the sun where the colour gradually ripened and changed from yellowish to a deep purplish red. It was then either diluted or concentrated further by boiling it down. In those days this purple dye was sold for its own weight in silver. Traditionally the Phoenicians from Tyre have been credited with the discovery of the process, though legend has it that Heracles' dog accidentally chewed a *Murex trunculus*, unwittingly staining its mouth deep blue. Recently the discovery of murex shells in Minoan contexts in Palaikastro, Malia and Kouphonisi suggests that the process may be much older.

The use of purple as a colour designating high status has endured through the centuries. It is well exemplified by the restricted use of porphyry for imperial buildings and statuary and of the purple dye for exclusive garments. Only comparatively recently was a suitable alternative to the processing of the murex found: in 1856 the first aniline dye was invented by the 18-year-old William Henry Perkin. It was called 'mauve'. Queen Victoria endorsed it in 1862, shortly after the death of Prince Albert, by appearing in a gown dyed in the new shade at the Royal Exhibition. However, it was the fashion-conscious Empress Eugénie of France who started the 'mauve madness' that swept Europe and then America in the 1860s, bringing the imperial colour to the masses.

Pefki and its gorge

Seven kilometres from Makrygialos on a good road is the little of Pefki (Πεύκοι; *map p. 431, C2*), its name reflecting the wealth of pine trees in the area. It is built in tiers on the hillside, surrounded by well-tended olive groves, with the bare crag behind it crowned with the bright white Stavromenos church (a steep walk from the village). For walkers, the route up the beautiful Pefki Gorge from Aspros Potamos (follow signs to the Art Studio, from where the route is signed by red dots, red and yellow arrows, and intermittent signboards) is recommended. Sunflower's *Eastern Crete* has a described walk. In early spring and autumn, the gorge has abundant water and picturesque waterfalls. The white *Cyclamen creticum* grows here as well as dwarf iris, and stick insects are also to be found.

PRACTICAL INFORMATION

GETTING AROUND

• **By car:** East of the main north–south road from Siteia to Anlipsi, transport is along a sparse network of secondary roads in good condition and perfectly adequate as long as the traffic is not too heavy. Petrol stations are few and far between.
• **By sea:** Boats to Kouphonisi leave from Makrygialos.

WHERE TO STAY & EAT

Aspros Potamos (*map p. 431, C2*)
€€ **Aspros Potamos Traditional Houses**. A rare chance to experience true Cretan rural life in renovated cottages hewn out of the rock with stone sleeping platforms and limited electricity. The place is tucked away in the mountains up an unmade road (walkable) from Analipsi. *T: 28430 51694, www.asprospotamos.com.*
Makrygialos (*map p. 431, C3*)
€ **Rooms Fedra**. For those who prefer 24/7 electricity, a standard bed and a view of the sea. *T: 28430 51482, mobile: 6973 901955.*

There are several tavernas in Analipsi/ Makrygialos. The better bets are **To Chani** (in Analipsi on the main road on the eastern side of the village) for Athenoula's simple and tasty Cretan food; **Tramuntana** in Analipsi on the sideroad to the beach opposite the sign to White River Cottages; *T: 28430 51904*) for *mezedes*, tomatoes from the owner's greenhouse, and freshly cooked meat and fish; the **Cave of the Dragon** (signed from the main road on the way to Kalo Nero) for traditional Cretan fare; and **Kalliotzina** (in Koutsouras to the west; *www.kalliotzina.gr*) for Greek cuisine. **Piperia** (in Pefki, 7km inland on a good road) is the place to go to in winter. There is also a very simple bar-cum-grocery shop in Pefki which will serve a simple lunch.

LOCAL SPECIALITIES

Jewellery-maker Myrto Botsaris runs a shop (Anemi, on the through road in Makrygialos) with modern **jewellery and pottery** of her own production and also from craftsmen from Crete and mainland Greece.

The village of Pefki.

THE FAR EAST

Crete's east end is a world apart, rugged and wild with a varied coast seldom reached by the road. The interior, dominated by the Ziros plateau, is good walking country for flowers and, in the right season, for the endemic *Tulipa cretica*. Up the Itanos peninsula the road reaches almost the extreme east end of the island at Cape Sideros, in the teeth of the prevailing north wind, the meltemi. The top end, a military area, is off limits. The rest of the peninsula, though, has already attracted the interest of developers, to the dismay of conservationists (*see p. 263*). Down south Xerokambos is advertised on the net as somewhere 'away from it all'—meaning that such a state of bliss may not last long. The archaeology of the area is varied, with Zakros Palace as the main magnet; but visitors will also be rewarded by more recent remains like the Venetian villa at Etia, the medieval village of Voila, and Moni Toplou.

The Venetian villa at Etia

The turning for Etia (Ετιά; *map p. 431, C2*) off the main road is about 15km south of Siteia, signed Ziros. The Venetian villa dates from the 15th century and is said to have belonged to the De Mezzo family, powerful landowners from Siteia. When Captain Spratt visited in 1856, he described a castellated villa combining strength, luxury and taste. Villas like Etia were built as residences or holiday homes for Venetian landlords with a desire to emulate, albeit on a reduced scale, the fine mansions in the hinterland of Venice (the *Ville Venete*), hence the elaborate portals and windows. Crete, though, was not as safe as home, which explains the need for fortifications. The three-storey villa certainly impressed the locals with its grandeur. They nicknamed it *ekatoportes*, meaning 100 doors. When the Turks occupied Crete, the building was used to house one of their high officials and suffered accordingly, being targeted by rebels in the 1828 revolt and again in 1897, when it was quarried for building material for the village church. In Spratt's time the paved courtyard, the flight of steps to the entrance, as well as the top storey could still be seen. When Gerola visited less than 50 years later, he was able to establish that both the first and the second floor had vaulted ceilings and were planned around a central corridor. He was much taken with the elaborate atrium with staircase and column-cum-caryatid; he admired the relief sculptures on the arched doorways and the De Mezzo emblem with chimeras on either side above the front door on the façade. Unfortunately the choice of building material was not well advised, as tufa does not weather very well. The building has now been cleared and restoration work is in progress. It should eventually become a venue for public performances.

The villa dominates the village of Etia, with two Byzantine churches. It is now deserted but was still inhabited in 1971. Some of the stone houses are of the *kamara* type (*see p. 161*) with huge fireplaces. Remains of the old flat roofing are still in place, showing a construction of beams with a layer of reeds topped by clay and beaten earth.

Armeni, Chandras and Voila

Past **Armeni** (Αρμένοι; *map p. 431, C2*) and the imposing three-aisled church of Aghia Sophia, which is all that remains of the Venetian monastery now abandoned because of earthquake damage, the road reaches Voila (5km) after **Chandras** (where the church of Aghia Paraskevi has the latest dated fresco of the island, 1565, in the arch above the door).

The medieval deserted village of **Voila** (Βόιλα; the name apparently derives from the Byzantine word *voilas* or *volias*, meaning nobleman) is now a protected site; its evocative ruins are spread along the hillside to the right of the road. A side road leads to an Ottoman fountain at the start of what was the main street. The site is dominated by remains of the 15th-century double-naved church of Aghios Georgios, with a tomb of the Salomon family, a powerful family from Siteia. It is decorated with a fresco of the Virgin flanked by various members of the family. The tower house of the Turkish period next to it is very similar in style

The Ottoman fountain at Voila.

to the one in Petras. It has two vaulted rooms on the ground floor. One has a huge fireplace while the other houses a massive staircase supported by an arch. The inscription on the doorway with the date 1153 (equivalent to 1742 in our calendar) is now very worn. Remains of a Venetian fortress are on the top of the hill. A tour of some of the other abandoned stone houses allows you to catch a glimpse of a typical Cretan interior. Note the bread oven constructed with discarded bricks and tiles; the wine press; the wooden mezzanine with ladder access and the trapezes swinging from the roof to keep food away from vermin. The small apsidal structure at the back is a toilet.

The Ziros plateau and Xerokambos

From Voila there is plenty of scope to explore the **Ziros plateau** (*map p. 431, D2*), its vineyards and beautiful flora, heading north to Sitanos and Karydi, or east to Ziros and beyond. This is wine country, and not surprisingly the southernmost vineyard in Europe is here. Whether that adds to the quality is another matter. The E4 walking path can be followed all the way from Chandras to the sea at Zakros, via Ziros.

From Ziros it is less than 20km to **Xerokambos** (Ξερόκαμπος; *map p. 431, D2*) and its promise of eternal peace: no pubs, no discos, not even a cashpoint. The area is certainly attractive with its sandy beaches and Mediterranean vegetation with a touch of the subtropical. It can be very dry, which accounts for the abundance of heavily scented species (thyme, lavender and oregano), though palms, hibiscus and bougainvillea flourish as well, thanks to newly-tapped water sources. Captain Spratt, the British naval surveyor who visited in the mid-19th century, described the remains of a small walled city located at the south end of the beach before the main road strikes inland. There is very little to see there these days except the remains of houses built directly on a rocky outcrop facing the sea. Nevertheless, it is a good place for a swim. The site has now been investigated and it has proven to be a Hellenistic settlement, possibly ancient Ambelos.

ZAKROS

No matter where you approach from, the way to Kato Zakros (Κάτω Ζάκρος; *map p. 431, D2*), the site of the Minoan palace, involves getting to Ano Zakros, the village inland at the head of the Gorge of the Dead. From Xerokambos it is about 10km along a panoramic road north; from Siteia (34km) the best approach is via Sitanos and Karydi, leaving the main road south at Kato Episkopi; from Palaikastro it is about 20km along sparsely inhabited windswept hills with the opportunity for serious walkers to explore the Chochlakies Gorge from the village of that name down to the sea at Karoumbes beach.

The traditional way on foot from **Ano Zakros** (Ἄνω Ζάκρος; *map p. 431, D2*) is down a spectacular gorge on the last stretch of the E4 walking route. Caves in the gorge were used as burials in the Early and Middle Minoan period which resulted in the present name of the valley, the *Pharangi ton Nekron*, the Gorge of the Dead; the path is c. 7km and will take a couple of hours. It may not be passable after storms; walkers should enquire at the village. For motorists the road to Kato Zakros is signposted from the village. On its way out it cuts through a Neopalatial farmstead, where in 1965 a wine press and a Linear A inscribed pithos were found.

HISTORY OF ZAKROS

The settlement lies in a sheltered position affording some protection from the dangerous north winds from Cape Sideros to the northeast. Zakros bay provides the best sheltered harbour on the coast and was well placed for trade with the east. Finds from the palace such as elephant tusks and an Egyptian jug show that the Minoans exploited this trading advantage. It was overlooked by the peak sanctuary at Traostalos (above Azokeramos) and was protected by a defensive system. Recent surveys have shown that all approaches except to the main gorge were blocked by walls and guarded by a series of watchtowers linked by a purpose-built road. The discovery of these defensive structures is not an isolated instance and has prompted a reappraisal of the traditional assumption of Minoan Crete as a land free from strife.

The settlement consists of a harbour town on the slopes of three hills surrounding a palace occupying the flat land in the middle. The valley is fertile but subject to flash floods down the Gorge of the Dead. Water might have come from an aqueduct from Ano Zakros and from wells in Minoan times when the land was higher. Now part of the site is under water in the early part of the year and the old coastline can no longer be traced. Zakros was inhabited in Prepalatial times; it has been noted that the town comes up to the palace, suggesting that this was a harbour town in existence before the palace, not one that grew or was planned around it. The visible palace remains are chiefly from the Neopalatial period, but traces of the old palace have been encountered, including evidence for a central court and features by the main entrance gate and beneath the west wing. The main axis of the town, the harbour road, dates from this Protopalatial period.

In modern times the site was first mentioned by Captain Spratt in 1852 in his *Travel and Researches in Crete*; he identified it with Itanos. It was later explored by D.G. Hogarth of the British School at Athens, who excavated 12 houses in the town, which extended to the northeast of the palace, occasionally incorporating elements of the first palace, and had narrow cobbled lanes and terraces very much like Gournia. Houses could be grand though, up to 30 rooms, with storage areas arranged around large areas fitted with benches. Dwellings were divided in blocks and also had industrial installations as attested by the olive oil and wine presses. The spectacular nature of the finds continuing to be unearthed locally, including gold objects, prompted a resumption of excavations. When Nikolaos Platon reopened the excavations in 1961, he immediately found the palace itself, which had not been looted at the time of destruction in LM I. This 'second palace' covers some 8000 square metres with 150 rooms and a Central Court measuring 30m by 12m, smaller than that of Knossos. It probably served as the Minoan gateway to the East, a view supported by finds from the site originating from the Middle East. It is also believed that the palace was producing faïence, an Egyptian procedure for the manufacture of blue-glazed pottery, in one of its workshops.

The relationship between the palace and the town, which dominates it from the hill, is poorly understood. They seem to complement each other, with a marked distinction between palace and town in terms of wealth and elite status. On the whole there are no high-status finds from the town and no evidence for the manufacture of luxury items. Industrial activities with large storage facilities were centred on oil and wine production and cereal processing, which were absent from the palace. If the palace was imposed on a pre-existing town, as the current thinking goes, suggesting that it may have been some sort of 'outpost from Knossos', it took over the town's destiny, since eventually they met their ends together.

The palace

The site (*open Tues–Sun April–Sept 8–7, Oct–March 8–3; limited parking in the shade*) is signed 300m inland along the road from the beach towards the foot of the Gorge of the Dead. With the ticket you get a plan, which is presently out of date. The site has no explanatory panels; the board in the car park is about ancient olive oil production.

Entrance and Central Court: The palace is entered from the southwest end **(1)** past the location, to the right, of **workshops** for faïence, rock crystal, ivory and scent, which have now been backfilled. Like other Minoan palaces, Zakros is built around a **Central Court**, which visitors enter at the south end. The alignment of the court is different from that in other palaces, the result of topographical constraints.

East Wing: Generally speaking, although Zakros is set back from the sea, water encroachment is now a problem. The site is often marshy and waterlogged. This is due to eastern Crete's slow subsidence and also to the **cistern (2)**, whose outflow has now silted up. The feature, which may once have supplied fresh water to the nearby Royal Apartments, has a balustrade and seven steps leading to a paved floor. The purpose of such a grand construction is still poorly understood and hypotheses ranging from swimming pool to aquarium have been mooted. Nearby are **wells (3–4)** connected to the operation of the workshops mentioned above and to the general supply of water to the palace. The abundance of water may have negative effects on the archaeology, but on the bright side it supports a sizeable population of small tortoises.

On the basis of Evans's appraisal of Knossos, Platon placed the **Royal Apartments** here in the East Wing of the palace. A portico ran the length of the east side of the court and behind it Platon identified the King's **(5)** and the Queen's **(6)** apartments, connected by multiple doors (note the remains of the luxurious flooring). In his view, the bedrooms would have been on the upper floor.

West Wing: On the opposite side of the court is the West Wing, the cult centre, as shown by the double axes inscribed on the walls, entered via a massive threshold next to an equally massive altar in the northwest corner of the Central Court. Note the **façade (7)** in ashlar masonry incorporating vertical and horizontal beams, as in the other palaces. The stone originated from the nearby quarry at Pelekita, some 5km to the north. **Storerooms (8)** are to the north. A number of outstanding finds have been recovered from this area, possibly fallen from the floor above. They include six copper alloy ingots from Cyprus, three elephant tusks from Syria and two rhyta, elongated libation vessels. The first was a bull's-head rhyton, the second showed a tripartite peak sanctuary similar to a standard one with three doors, but with the graceful addition of leaping animals, vegetation and mountains in the background (*see illustration overleaf*).

To the south is an area not entirely accessible. It includes a **lustral basin (9)**, a sunken feature with steps down into it next to a small shrine with two benches. Controversy on the use and purpose of these sunken features still rages among Minoan archaeologists. According to some they were bathrooms for domestic use, especially when located close to high-status living quarters; on the other hand, many claim that they had a purely religious function and were used for ritual cleansing. However, lustral basins do not have drainage and the abundant use of gypsum in their construction seems to rule out the use of large quantities of water. One school of thought considers them to be sunken chambers with a ritual purpose for ceremonies that

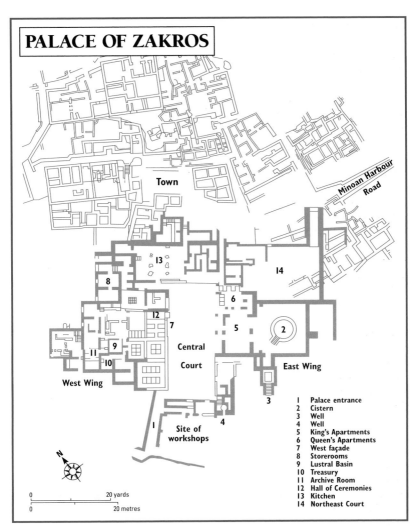

PALACE OF ZAKROS

Town

Minoan Harbour Road

13

8

14

6

12

7

5

2

Central Court

9

11

10

East Wing

West Wing

3

I

Site of workshops

4

N

I	Palace entrance
2	Cistern
3	Well
4	Well
5	King's Apartments
6	Queen's Apartments
7	West façade
8	Storerooms
9	Lustral Basin
10	Treasury
11	Archive Room
12	Hall of Ceremonies
13	Kitchen
14	Northeast Court

0   20 yards
0   20 metres

may have been meant to be viewed from above; the Piano Nobile reconstruction at Knossos may enable visitors to visualise proceedings.

In the **Shrine Treasury (10)** eight tightly-packed clay chests yielded a remarkable collection of porphyry, alabaster and basalt vessels and an exquisite rock crystal rhyton, all 300 fragments of it (now skilfully restored and exhibited in Herakleion Archaeological Museum's temporary exhibition). Valuable raw material, including three large elephant tusks and six copper ingots, was also found in the area, but it is assumed that it fell from the upper floor. The **Archive**

The Late Minoan 'Sanctuary Rhyton' from Zakros palace, now in Herakleion museum's temporary exhibition. Made of soft stone, much darkened by fire damage, it is decorated with an elaborate scene in relief which seems to depict a Minoan peak sanctuary in a mountainous landscape. At the bottom is what appears to be the approach to a tripartite shrine decorated with horns of consecration. Above is the elaborate shrine door on top of which are seated four *agrimia* with splendid horns. Further round the rhyton (not shown here) are *agrimia* leaping, and more horns of consecration, this time with birds perched on their tips.

Room (11) held Linear A tablets. Unfortunately only 13 of these have survived. Many were crushed when the boxes they were in fell off the shelves; as they had not been fired, they were reduced later to a clay mass by the encroaching water. Under the covered area to the west are remains of internal stairs.

Returning to the Central Court the visitor will pass the **Hall of Ceremonies (12)**, lit by a colonnaded light-well and supplied with polythyra (pier-and-door partitions) characteristic of high-status Minoan architecture. It had relief frescoes and decorative panelling on the floor framed by narrow strips of stucco painted red (some still in place). It was probably used for banquets judging by the large number of drinking vessels found in it. Immediately to the north is the **kitchen (13)**, the only one ever identified in a palace, conveniently located close to the storerooms **(8)**. The six rugged column bases are taken to indicate structural support for a dining room above. The staircase is on the eastern side.

Northeast Court and Harbour Road: In the **Northeast Court (14)** are remains of the ancient Minoan Harbour Road, which was paved with a contrasting pattern of blue and white stone slabs. It can be traced from the north end of the central court to the northeast court, up the heavily reconstructed stepped entrance (but the huge threshold at the top is probably original) and on into the town. In the Northeast Court under a protective roof are the remains of an industrial installation belonging to the first palace.

The town

The town, as yet partly unexplored, extended to the northeast of the palace well beyond the fenced area. A walk through the maze of narrow alleys and steps, minding the odd snake, is a perfect way to end the visit. From the restored clay bench (cordoned off) there is an excellent view of the palace layout.

PALAIKASTRO & PETSOPHAS

The coastal plain of Roussolakkos (the 'Red Pit') is north of Zakros on the way to Itanos past Chochlakies. In Palaikastro (Παλαίκαστρο; *map p. 431, D2*), aim for the bay of Kouremenos for excellent swimming and the best windsurfing in Crete. This is a place where the meltemi, the north wind, is positively welcomed.

To find the site, follow the signs for the Hotel Marina Village near Angathia. The road leads in 2km to the excavations, just in from the beach. The flat-topped promontory of Kastri is to the north. From the top on a clear day it is possible to make out the islands of Kasos and Karpathos in the distance, past Grandes in the middle of the harbour. This was the notorious Kasos Strait, a gateway to the Aegean Sea used by the Allied forces from their bases in North Africa in the Second World War. The Germans had an air base on Karpathos and used stukas to harass the British Mediterranean fleet. In the process, the site of Roussolakkos received a hit.

Palaikastro is fully accessible in a very pleasant setting and with good explanatory panels that make up for the discontinuous presentation due to the complex excavation history of the site and the frequent backfills.

The excavations at Palaikastro

Excavations on the headland of Kastri have revealed occupation at the beginning and at the very end of the Bronze Age. These were times of troubles, and the hill offered a defensive position. Later, in the Middle Ages, the Venetians established a fortress here, which is how the location acquired its name (Palaikastro = 'Old Castle'). The new castle (Kastri) was on the hill, and the old one, Palaikastro, a reference to the prominent building remains of the Bronze Age town, was below. The Minoan settlement was first investigated in the early 20th century by British archaeologists and again in the 1960s. The current programme began in 1983. It was during this phase of the excavations that a most spectacular find came to light. The Palaikastro Kouros, a chryselephantine statuette of a young man, recovered in innumerable fragments over three seasons of digging, is now in Siteia museum (*see p. 237*).

There was evidence of occupation in the fertile plain from the Neolithic to the end of the Minoan period while the cult of Diktaian Zeus is attested from Geometric up to Roman times. By 1900 BC (the time of the first palaces at Knossos and Phaistos), a large, well-planned town had been established. It had overseas contacts, including with Egypt and Asia Minor. It was destroyed twice but lived on to become the largest town in eastern Crete in the Postpalatial period with a sheltered harbour and a fertile hinterland on the alluvial plain. The settlement was eventually abandoned around the 12th century BC when the population gave up the coast and fled to the mountains for safety.

The site

The town of Palaikastro was laid out to a grid with evenly spaced blocks comprising two to four units. It exhibits a high degree of axiality in contrast to Gournia and Zakros town. On the other hand, while roads would facilitate movement across the town, and suggest a form of central planning, there is a surprising lack of public places where social interaction could occur outside the house. Additional anomalies include the shortage of storage space, which sits uneasily with the evidence for public works such as the street system with large paving blocks and the exploitation of the sandstone quarries at Ta Skaria to the southeast, among the largest yet known for a Minoan site. The analysis of the buildings shows social stratification, though evidence for the very

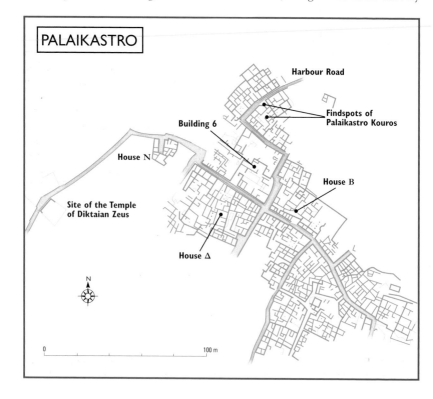

top strata is lacking. Elite architectural elements such as ashlar masonry (House Δ), pier-and-door partitions (Building 6), lustral basins (House B), mason's marks, upper storeys (Houses B and N), halls and frescoes are present but no building stands out as central; moreover, there is a shortage of public administrative buildings. All this may yet be excavated; estimates put the total size of the town at 50,000 square metres, so there is hope.

Many of the earliest excavations at Palaikastro have since been backfilled and the site has suffered damage, during the war and also from bulldozer activity. Not much remains of the Temple of Diktaian Zeus, whose location was identified during the early excavations. The existence of the temple is known from a 2nd-century BC fragment of an inscription from Magnesia in Asia Minor, now at Moni Toplou, regarding the arbitration in a dispute over the control of the temple between the city-states of eastern Crete. The temple building had been completely demolished, but surviving architectural fragments date back to the 6th century BC and include a section of a clay sima, a water spout with a chariot scene in relief. Scattered pieces of an inscribed limestone slab of the 3rd century AD recorded part of the *Hymn to Diktaian Zeus*, an invocation used in re-enacting the dance of the Curetes who, according to legend, protected the infant Zeus after his birth (*see p. 208*).

Petsophas Peak Sanctuary

Palaikastro is overlooked to the south by the steep hill of Petsophas (Πετσοφάς; *map p. 431, D2*), on which a peak sanctuary was established in Minoan times. It was first explored by British archaeologists in 1903 and fully excavated in the 1970s by Kostis Davaras. He found a walled precinct, a small shrine with plaster benches, evidence of animal sacrifice and feasting. Votive offerings found in the crevices and in the summit area included unique animal figurines of tortoises, hedgehogs and weasels, suggesting a cult of the Minoan goddess as Mistress of the Animals. According to archaeoastronomers, the alignment and orientation of the sanctuary may have been connected to the summer solstice. A good selection of the finds, which also include stone offering-tables inscribed with Linear A and horns of consecration, are in Siteia and Aghios Nikolaos museums. The climb to Petsophas is signed from Angathia, but it is possible to take a short cut from the Palaikastro excavations along a *kalderimi* to the summit (215m), aiming for the tin roof covering a well on the red earth to the south up the hillside.

THE ITANOS PENINSULA

From Palaikastro the road strikes inland to the north and 7km on, just after Vai village, you can take a right turn to the sea for a touch of the exotic.

Vai

Vai beach (Βάϊ; *map p. 431, D1*) became famous in the end of the 1970s when hippies moved here fleeing Matala and Preveli, which had become too well known. It did not do the place any good to be turned into a chaotic camping ground-cum-garbage dump. Now things are back to normal, the area is protected and the palm forest is in fine fettle. Access to the beach is regulated and you have to pay to get in. The palm grove was already known in Classical times and Theophrastus had described the species as early as the 4th century BC, which accounts for its scientific name (*see box below*).

THE PALM TREES AT VAI

Although tradition has it that palm trees were introduced by the Arabs, there is little doubt that the Minoans knew about them. They figure often in their iconography and remains have been found in the Pleistocene levels on Thera (Santorini), where the tree still grows wild.

The grove at Vai, the largest natural palm forest in Europe, was known in Classical times. The Cretan date palm, *Phoenix theophrasti Greuter*, to give it its scientific name, is a distinct native species. The fruit, though, is dry, smaller than a date, and has an unpleasant acrid taste; even so, some locals do eat it. The tree can grow to 15m tall with several slender stems. It can be found elsewhere in Crete, not perhaps in such fine shape as at Vai, in the Aegean and on the west coast of Turkey.

There must be a special microclimate here. Not only do palms prosper, but there is also a banana plantation up the road producing delicious small bananas. This is the only place in Crete where they grow and ripen out of doors; down south by the coast they are under plastic. The plantation can be visited, affording a rare chance to see the deep crimson-coloured banana flower with its multitude of tiny fruits (the future bananas) emerging to form a bunch.

ANCIENT ITANOS

The Vai area was the territory of ancient harbour town of Itanos ('Ιτανος; *map p. 431, D1*), thought to have been around Erimoupolis, a village immediately to the north, whose name means 'deserted place'. Beaches here today afford excellent swimming and snorkelling. In antiquity they offered more: this was the first sheltered place after braving the winds around Cape Sideros, on the coast or on the island of Elasa, which also has ancient remains.

In Graeco-Roman times Itanos grew to become one of the most influential cities in eastern Crete, with a territory possibly stretching as far as Kouphonisi, the dye-producing island off the south coast. Buondelmonti in the 15th century and later Captain Spratt reported visible ruins in the area, but the site was first explored by Halbherr at the very end of the 19th century, and later on after the Second World War. An extensive survey, which ended in 2005, has looked at the area as a whole (town and surrounding territory) in order to get a complete picture of the landscape; one of its discoveries were the pink marble quarries near Vai.

HISTORY OF ITANOS

There is evidence of Minoan occupation in the area in the form of a Neopalatial country house to the south of the Graeco-Roman site, but it appears that the town was not founded before the 9th century BC, prompting speculation that Phoenician traders may have been involved. According to Herodotus (*IV, 151*), Itanos was a flourishing centre in the 7th century and a local fisherman led people from Thera to establish a colony on the shores of Libya. It minted its own coins in the 5th century, one of the first Cretan cities to do so, and had at least four temples in Classical times. Around 260 BC Itanos asked for support from Egypt against neighbouring Praisos. An Egyptian garrison was established on a fortified acropolis overlooking the harbour. Until the end of the 3rd century BC and again some 50 years later, Ptolemaic Egypt played a role in Aegean politics and probably found Itanos a convenient stopping-place for its fleet, based in Alexandria. On top of that, eastern Crete was good recruiting ground for mercenaries.

With the defeat of Praisos by Hierapytna c. 155 BC, the latter became the chief rival of Itanos, especially over the control of the prestigious Temple of Diktaian Zeus at Palaikastro. It took 20 years to settle the dispute. The Treaty of Magnesia of 132 BC (*see p. 264*) marks the first clear show of interest by Rome in Cretan affairs. The history of the Roman city is not very well documented apart from a few dedications by emperors. Itanos was important in Byzantine times with at least two basilicas. Occupation came to an end in the 7th century AD when the location became unsafe and the population moved inland.

The site

Itanos had a double acropolis with two low hills linked by terracing; not much remains of the fortifications except a **Hellenistic watchtower** and the foundations of the limestone walls. The exact extent of the town is not known and one must bear in mind that because of intense seismic activity, part of it may be under the sea. In the saddle between the acropoleis excavations have uncovered an Early Byzantine residential district built on top of earlier Classical and Roman occupation with a short break in the 3rd century when the site was apparently deserted. The two Byzantine basilicas, also incorporating spolia, with massive thresholds and monolithic columns, belong to this last phase of occupation; one of them, **Basilica A**, was part of an extensive religious complex.

Up to coast to the north of the town, the **necropolis** shows that the funerary use of the area lasted until the 7th century BC. At the end of that period a building of a public nature was erected on top of the graves. It has been interpreted as a gymnasium because of the finds (a disc and a weight for jumping), possibly the oldest known gymnasium in the Greek world. The building was abandoned c. 450 BC. The rest of the area went on being used for burial, but the ruined Archaic building was respected and only in the 1st century BC was it partially reoccupied, with a single tomb.

Finds from the town and the necropolis show contacts with central Crete, the Aegean islands and the Greek mainland from the Archaic period onwards and intermittently with the Levant.

CAPE SIDEROS

Cape Sideros (*map p. 431, D1*) runs north in a desolate wind-beaten landscape to the extreme northeast point of Crete. A temple to Athena stood here in antiquity, consecrated by the Argonauts. Now part of it is off limits because of military installations. But the skies are free, and ornithologists may get a chance to spot **Eleonora's falcon** from the reserve at Paximada, the northernmost island of the Dionysades group to the northwest. Eleonora's falcon (*Falco eleonorae*) is named after Eleonora d'Arborea (1350–1404), a Catalan who became queen of Sardinia. Her *Carta de Logu*, hailed as a very early form of constitution, which she promulgated in 1392, contains provisions to protect the adult birds against hunters and their nests against raiders. The bird, known in Greek as *varvaki* or *mavropetritis*, is a medium-sized falcon with long wings and tail. It spends the winter in Madagascar, returning in April or May and nesting in islets all over the Mediterranean, with an isolated population in the Canary Islands. Egg-laying occurs in late July and when the young hatch they feed on migrating moths and butterflies, as well as on smaller birds, before making their way back south in early October. Three quarters of the world population (some 12,300 pairs) of Eleonora's falcon is concentrated on the Greek islands; with the expansion of tourism to the desolate spots they prefer, they are under threat though loss of habitat and poaching. The chicks are apparently delicious.

As for the name of the cape itself, it was Cape Samonion in antiquity, and its present denomination owes more to Aghios Isidoros, who has a chapel right at the tip, than to any connection with iron (*sideros*).

ITANOS, AN ENVIRONMENT UNDER THREAT

The arid and windswept Itanos peninsula may not survive long in its wild, desolate beauty. This protected ecotope, recognised as a natural monument by Europa 2000, the EU initiative to halt biodiversity loss, is firmly in the sights of property developers. A recent plan by a British firm included a string of 5-star luxury hotels, a marina, three golf courses, an athletics stadium, 474 villas, 595 apartments and town houses for a total of 7,000 beds in an area of 2600 hectares. The project had strong backing from the Greek government and the owner of the lease of the land, Moni Toplou. It was also endorsed by a leading environmental organisation which described the Environmental Impact Assessment as 'best practice'.

In 2008 the properties were already advertised on the net (though with a 'price to follow' tag). Environmentalists, headed by archaeologists Oliver Rackham and Jennifer Moody, authors of the seminal book *The Making of the Cretan Landscape*, did not lie idle. An appeal was lodged and at the time of writing it is still not settled.

The main objections are as follows: the development is completely out of character with the present landscape and is not sustainable as there is not enough water to keep all those golf greens. Plans to set up a desalination plant are unrealistic because they are too energy-greedy. The normal ratio for sustainable tourism is in the region of 40 percent of the local population, which, in this case, is 2,500 people. The area is biologically unique: its fragile equilibrium may not survive such a gross intrusion. Finally, there has been no archaeological assessment. Because of its remoteness, semi-arid climate and exposure to pirate attacks, the Itanos peninsula has seen reduced human activity in the more recent past. But it was not always so. Surveys have shown a landscape of terraces, check dams and fields which may go back to Minoan times, the last vestige of ancient Mediterranean farmed landscape.

The economic downturn of 2009 may signal the downfall of the project. On inspection in early summer of that year, there was no sign of any building activity. With a bit of luck this lovely location will be spared the abandoned shells of failed developments that litter so many of Crete's other beauty spots.

MONI TOPLOU

The fortified monastery of Moni Toplou (Μονή Τοπλού; *map p. 431, D1; open 9–1 & 2–6*), once a lonely outpost in a barren landscape, has now become a regular stop for visitors in eastern Crete thanks to its history, its museum and its hospitality; it is best avoided in the height of the season. The name is Turkish and refers to the gun installed by the monks in Venetian times against pirates. Its original dedication was to the Panaghia Akrotiriani (the 'Virgin of the Headland'). The earliest records for a church here go back to the 14th century and this may have been the nucleus of the later Venetian buildings. The foundation acquired great wealth and power over the island. The **forti-**

fications date to the end of the 16th century, after the Knights of Malta attacked it in 1530, overlooking the fact that the monks were fellow Christians. The Turks targeted it over and over again and in 1612 an earthquake also caused extensive damage. The fortress-like appearance of the monastery with its tall, closed wall, dates from that time (the Venetian Senate contributed 200 ducats; see the plaque on the church wall). The monastery maintained close links with the cause of Cretan independence and operated an underground radio transmitter in the Second World War. The Germans got wind of it and the abbot, Gennadios Silignakis, and two monks were jailed in Chania and executed. Before the main entrance, there is a **restored stone windmill** for grinding corn. It shows a good reconstruction of the original workings, with the machinery in place, the iron-bound millstones and the trough to feed the grain into.

Visiting the monastery

The main entrance is by the loggia gate through a reception and workshop area and into the monastery proper. Note the **double doorway** with a massive door operated by a wheel mechanism. The heart of the monastery is a small cobbled court surrounded by the **church**, the **monks' cells**, the **refectory** and the **abbot's quarter**. On the court façade of the double-nave church, four embedded stone slabs are of interest. The two central ones deal with reconstruction work after the 1612 earthquake. One is a *Virgin and Child*. The last is a fragment of an inscription dated 132 BC, known as the **Treaty of Magnesia**. It records an arbitration whereby the Roman city of Magnesia in Asia Minor settled territorial disputes between Itanos, Praisos and Hierapytna. One of the

Detail of the stone tablet known as the Treaty of Magnesia (2nd century BC).

bones of contention was the control of the Temple of Diktaian Zeus at Palaikastro. The inscription, originally in Itanos, was being used as an altar table in the cemetery chapel across the road from the monastery when it was spotted by Pashley in his visit in 1834. He suggested the present setting.

The **museum** in the cloister houses maps, icons (15th–18th centuries), manuscripts and other ecclesiastical treasures, including a 15th-century icon, an example of the type known as the Hodighitria, the Virgin showing the Way. In the monastery church, dedicated to the Panaghia Akrotiriani and Aghios Ioannis Theologos (the Evangelist), restoration work has uncovered frescoes with Gospel scenes dated stylistically to the 14th century. On the north side a small room was used by women attending the services. On a stand between the two altars is a portable icon entitled 'Lord, Thou Art Great', with over 60 densely painted scenes inspired by the Great Benediction used by the Orthodox Church on the feast of the Epiphany. The 7th-century patriarch Sophronius is shown kneeling to the right of Eve. The prayer is often attributed to him, but it is more likely to have been composed by Basil the Great, one of the three Cappadocian Fathers of the Church. The four central themes from the lowest level show the Descent to Hell, the Mother of God enthroned between Adam and Eve, the Baptism of Christ and the Holy Trinity. The intricate arrangement and the use of narrative both from the Old and the New Testaments follow a tradition dating back to the time of the Palaeologan emperors before the Fall of Byzantium. Two inscriptions in the lower part of the icon establish the artist, Ioannis Kornaros, the date, 1770, and the donor, Demetrios, with his wife and children. An earlier version of this icon had been painted by the same artist at Moni Savathianon (*see p. 130*).

AGHIA PHOTIA & TRYPITOS

From Moni Toplou the road reaches the coast at Analoukas; the site of Aghia Photia is 5km on, signed to the right on the headland of Kouphota.

Aghia Photia

Aghia Photia (Αγία Φωτιά; *map p. 431, D2*) consists of a large stone rectangular building with earth floors for a total of 37 rooms communicating only with an elongated central court or corridor and arranged symmetrically. The construction, with an early MM I date, was surrounded by a stout wall with buttresses, an arrangement reminiscent of Lerna in the Argolid. It was abandoned after a short period of use; a couple of tholos tombs were built on top some 200 years later. The unusual layout poses questions. It is possible that the building belonged to several families, maybe a clan. On the other hand, Rodney Castelden has drawn parallels with Khamaizi, which is not far away (*see p. 233*) and suggested that they may have been part of a ring of military bases protecting Crete. The Early Minoan cemetery, excavated in the 1970s and dating to the first part of the 3rd millennium, is nearby. Over 250 tombs have been found, with rich offerings including pottery and bronze and stone artefacts, showing contact with the Cyclades. These are now in Aghios Nikolaos and Siteia museums. Some of the graves were simple shallow pits, but most were primitive forms of chamber tomb closed with slabs. A number of tall cups with pedestals were found in paved antechambers associated with the cult of the dead.

Trypitos

The site of Trypitos (Τρυπητός; *map p. 431, C2–D2*) is signed from the road to a headland a short distance from Aghia Photia. It has been known since the 1960s but excavations only started in 1987. The Hellenistic city minted its own coins and covered the whole headland; it had a massive defensive wall to the south with military installations and housing built against it on its seaward side. An unroofed shipshed cut in the rock (30m long, 5.5m wide and 5m high), tilting downwards towards the sea, would have been used to shelter a craft in the winter. The town is accessible via a bad road, but not the shipshed below.

PETRAS

The site of Petras (Πετράς; *map p. 431, C2*) is only 1km from Aghia Photia, signed to the left on a hill overlooking a sheltered stretch of bay where the Minoans established two safe harbours on either side of a little point. The settlement covers the hill behind. The remains were first investigated by Evans (1896) and Bosanquet (1900). Since 1985 Petras has been the object of extensive excavations by Metaxia Tsipopoulos of the Greek Archaeological Service.

View of the ruins of Trypitos.

HISTORY OF PETRAS

There has been occupation in the bay from the Neolithic. The earliest evidence at Petras is Prepalatial (towards the end of the EM II period) but the occupation flourished in the Neopalatial period when a high-status building on top of the hill was at the centre of an urban settlement clustered around it. The visible remains belong to the second palace, rebuilt c. 1600 BC on top of the original one dated early MM II. Little is known of the Prepalatial occupation. As a palace, the structure is small, but a number of tell-tale features do set it apart from ordinary dwellings. It has a central court in the canonical north–south direction, with a grand staircase at its north end, a monumental west façade, large storage areas, exceeding the need of the complex, one upper storey, possibly two, ashlar architecture, a small number of Linear A tablets and a hieroglyphic archive. The area covered by the building (2800 square metres) is certainly small when compared to the other palaces; moreover other standard features such as light-wells, lustral basins, pillar crypts and lavish use of gypsum are absent. However, this could be a local variation (schist dados instead of gypsum, for instance) for a high-status building on a smaller scale. Metaxia Tsipopoulos, who has extensively surveyed the surrounding landscape, suggests that this was the central focus of an agricultural community with little contact with the sea—unlike Zakros, which had been built as a gateway to the East in an area not particularly renowned for its fertility.

The site was abandoned at the beginning of the LM period following violent destruction; only a small part of the hill was reoccupied in the Postpalatial period with two houses erected on the ruins of the palace. Petras was completely deserted by the time a small Byzantine cemetery was established in the palace area around the 12th century, partly carved in the rock and also using Minoan remains.

The site

The site is always accessible and is 400m along a marked road (*well signed; parking is tight*). Note, before entering, the cyclopean Protopalatial **fortification wall** with towers just below the road. At the entrance the **Venetian tower** (in a line of sight with the Kazarma at Siteia and with Liopetra) shows that Petras has always been of strategic importance. The site is well supplied with explanatory boards, clearly illustrated, allowing visitors to link visible remains with the key finds as well as placing the site itself in its geographical setting by explaining relationships with other excavated sites in the hinterland. Of particular interest is the Hieroglyphic Archive, where two four-sided bar inscriptions, nine medallions, and several sealings from 42 different seals used on parchment and papyrus were recovered from a context securely dated by the associated pottery, proving beyond doubt that the palace had an administrative function. The items fell from the upper floor of the palace in the MM II destruction in the gate area. The location was not cleared but was levelled for rebuilding, preserving for posterity this unique assemblage.

HIEROGLYPHS, LINEAR A & LINEAR B

Crete in the period of the palaces had a complex society with a degree of literacy; it was indeed the first European country to have a form of writing. Three scripts have been identified, mainly linked to administrative and religious functions.

Before coming to Crete, Evans was already acquainted with Cretan hieroglyphs, indeed this is what first attracted him to the island after he saw his very first sealstone in Oxford at the Ashmolean. This is the oldest form of Minoan script, locally developed but inspired by the Egyptian hieroglyphs, which predate it by well over 1,000 years. The script is found on clay bars, sealings and labels, where it was used in the cursive for labelling, counting, certifying and recording (archival function) and in the monumental form on stone offering-tables, in a ritual context. The largest hieroglyph archives are from Knossos, Phaistos, Malia and Petras, and were found in Old Palace contexts. The system then died out, but not entirely, and was largely superseded by Linear A, which may have evolved from it. This is a syllabic script, though still using ideograms as shorthand, and has a decimal numerical system. Linear A began to be used in the older palaces and flourished after these were destroyed and rebuilt. It was also found in non-palatial contexts such as Aghia Triada (the largest archive), Tylissos, Palaikastro and Myrtos Pyrgos, and outside Crete on Samothrace and Thera. Both hieroglyphs and Linear A have so far resisted any attempt at decipherment. Linear A appears to have affinities with Linear B but crucially experts have concluded that they represent two different languages.

Evans found his first Linear B tablet at the very beginning of his excavations, on 31st March 1900, followed six days later by the discovery of an important archive: all had been fired in the final conflagration that spelled the end of the palace at Knossos. The final count of Linear B tablets for Knossos stands at 4,360. Over time Linear B tablets were also found at Chania and, more importantly, on the Greek mainland at Pylos, Tyrins, Thebes in Boeotia and Midea in the Argolid. When Linear B (a syllabic script but still using ideograms) was deciphered in 1953, the result proved that Evans had been mistaken in his interpretation of the final days of the palace of Knossos. The people running the place and the economy were Greeks, not Minoans. They used a pre-Doric Greek dialect of the Arcado-Cypriot family to keep track of their livestock and to monitor textile production. The Mycenaeans had arrived. The honour of deciphering Linear B belongs to Michael Ventris and John Chadwick. Ventris built on the work already done by the American archaeologist Alice Kober, who in the 1940s had identified patterns in the language and had applied techniques derived from wartime code-breaking. Ventris was as surprised as anyone to discover that Linear B was an ancient form of Greek.

With the end of the palaces all form of script disappeared from Crete for several centuries.

PRACTICAL INFORMATION

GETTING AROUND

• **By bus:** See www.crete-buses.gr. From Siteia there are limited services to Palaikastro, Vai beach and Kato Zakros; Ziros is on a different bus route. From Ierapetra use the bus to Siteia and get off at Papagianes for the connection to Ziros for Voila and Etia. A daily service runs from Herakleion to Vai. Unfortunately it leaves Vai at 4 which means one will spend almost as much time travelling as enjoying the palm trees.

TOURIST INFORMATION

Taxi Palaikastro T: 28430 61380; mobile 6944 534848
Taxi Zakros T: 28430 93383
Police Palaikastro T: 28430 61222
Police Zakros T: 28430 93323
Doctor in Palaikastro T: 28430 61143
The mayor of Itanos has set up tourist offices in the OTE (telephone centre) at Palaikastro (*T: 28430 61546; open daily May–Oct 9am–10pm*) and in the guest area at the Vai forest.

WHERE TO STAY & EAT

www.palaikastro.com/hotels and www.eastern.cretefamilyhotels.com have good listings.

Ano Zakros (*map p. 431, D2*)
€ **Zakros Hotel**. Long-established, good-value base from which to explore this corner of the island. *T: 28430 93379.*
Kato Zakros (*map p. 431, D2*)
€€ **Kato Zakros Palace**. Rooms, studios and one apartment with views of the beach, the palace and the plain. *T: 28430 29550, mobile 6974 888269; www.palaikastro.com/katozakrospalace.*

€ **Bay View** offers rooms and apartments next to the Gorge of the Dead (*T: 28430 26887; www.palaikastro.com/bayview*); € **Rooms Poseidon** (*T: 28439 26893*) is on the sea's edge.
Palaikastro (*map p. 431, D2*)
There is an advantage in staying in modern Palaikastro rather then on the plain below: it will be cooler. There is a good choice of tavernas. **Myrtos** (*T: 28430 61243*) opposite the Hellas Hotel has an appetising selection of vegetarian *mezedes*, traditional *magirefta* dishes (meaning 'cooked': meat braised with vegetables) and fish and grills. Down by the sea the **Taverna Chiona** has a reputation for fish.
€ **Hotel Hellas**. Completely renovated in 1999, with good facilities including an internet café. *T: 28430 61240 or 61276, www.palekastro-hotel.gr.*
€ **Hotel Palekastro**. Very small, just six rooms, but very welcoming and with a good taverna serving traditional Cretan food. *T: 28430 61235.*
€ **Chiona Hotel**. Newly-built modern hotel on the beach. *T: 28430 29623, www.palaikastro.com/hionaholiday.*
Rooms to rent include € **Senie Rooms** near the main square (*T: 28430 61414*) and € **Thalia Rooms** (*T: 28430 61448*) just behind it. If you run out of reading matter, they have a small library. The €€ **Hotel Marina Village** offers accommodation in bungalows in the middle of the olive groves surrounding Palaikastro. *T: 28430 61284/61407; www.palaikastro.com/marinavillage.*
Xerokambos (*map p. 431, D2*)
€€ **Villa Petrino**. A modern building among the olive trees, exactly like the rest of the accommodation available at Xerokambos, a place that only exists because of tourism. *T: 28430 26702, www.xerokampos-villas.gr/villapetrino.*

€ **Taverna Kostas** has a reputation for fish.

Ziros (*map p. 431, D2*)

There is not much choice in Ziros, a village at the centre of a wine and oil producing region; € **Hazkliolakis Rooms** (*T: 28430 91266*) is a good place to eat and sleep.

PIRACY ON CRETE

According to Thucydides (5th century BC), King Minos freed Crete from Carian and Phoenician pirates. He does not mention the Cretans themselves, and yet from antiquity the island's history is tied up with piracy, with the locals cast in the role of both victims and villains. Indeed the ancient Cretans enjoyed a reputation as untrustworthy, grasping savages. Odysseus had no qualms about passing himself off as a successful Cretan pirate when he landed icognito on Ithaca (*Odyssey XIV*).

The waxing and waning of piracy in Crete can be charted against the extent of coastal settlement. It increases in the Bronze Age, when the Minoan 'thalassocracy' ruled the waves, and shrinks considerably in the troubled times at the end of it. During the Hellenistic period, pirates used the island as a base for operations and refuelling, and the occasional kidnapping: no wonder the Gortyn Law Code had a long section on slaves and ransom. One of the main reasons for the Roman conquest was to clear the east Mediterranean of pirates—and they were indeed successful. Under the Byzantines, after the Fourth Crusade that broke Byzantium's sea power at the beginning of the 13th century, the situation took a turn for the worse. Pirates appeared from everywhere: Muslims from the coast of Turkey and North Africa and Christian Knights from Malta. The Venetians occupied the island as a way of controlling their trade routes. Local manpower was pressed to man the patrol ships and the northern harbours were fortified. Despite this, Rethymnon was sacked repeatedly by Kheir ed-Din Barbarossa. A network of coastal lookouts (*vigle*) was set up for early warning of imminent raids, but it was not Venice's policy to build too many harbours that had to be fortified and which might also encourage smuggling. The eastern coast was more or less given up as it was too exposed to attacks. The consequences in the Siteia region were dramatic: the town and a string of villages up to 15km inland were deserted. Those who stayed on, like the monks in the monastery of Toplou, built fortifications, but they were still attacked, this time by fellow Christians, the Knights of Malta, in 1530. On the whole the Venetian occupation was characterised by the abandonment of the coastal plains with attendant consequences on agricultural production. Things improved under the Ottomans: Muslims at least did not attack fellow Muslims; by the 1820s the eastern Mediterranean was free of pirates. Siteia was re-founded and prospered, and people trickled back to the abandoned settlements. Coastal reoccupation moved more slowly in the south, where it was only firmly re-established by the 1930s. Today the process is operating in reverse. Instead of pirates depopulating the coasts, it is tourism that keeps them filled, while the villages of the hinterland lie abandoned.

RETHYMNON PROVINCE

The province of Rethymnon, between Herakleion province and the Ida massif to the east, and Chania and the White Mountains (the Lefka Ori) to the west, stretches for 30km from coast to coast. It offers visitors a wide range of landscapes from the old Venetian city, at the heart of the town, to the beautiful countryside in the Amari Valley with fine Byzantine churches and their interesting wall paintings. The road to Anogeia, eventually leading to the Idaian Cave after a scenic drive, is on the old road to Herakleion, while the well-known Postpalatial cemetery at Armeni is a short drive south of Rethymnon on the way to the south coast past Spili, an excellent central location to explore the countryside from. The Libyan Sea is a better bet for beaches than the north coast, especially at the beginning and end of the season, when the water is noticeably warmer than the Aegean. Plakias can be a good choice for a relaxing holiday. Preveli, with its spectacular monastery and gorge, is not far.

Walkers will not be disappointed either. The E4 long-distance walking route crosses the province's sparsely populated expanse with two trails. To the north, it links Lappa (modern Argyroupolis) on the border of Chania province with the Armeni cemetery and, past the peak sanctuary of Vrysinas, crosses the Amari Valley continuing east to Eleftherna, Axos, Anogeia, Zominthos and eventually the Idaian Cave. The second branch runs to the south connecting Spili and the Kamares Cave. Much of the hinterland, served by reasonable (albeit at times quite narrow) metalled roads, offers plenty of scope for motorists looking for flowers and birds off the beaten track.

RETHYMNON

'Built on the border between tameness and wilderness' in the words of the local-born novelist and art historian Pandelis Prevelakis, Rethymnon (Ρέθυμνο; *map p. 429, B2*), known to the Venetians as Retimo and to the Ottomans as Resmo, is famed for its sandy beaches which give way, to the west towards Chania, to barren cliffs the colour of lead. The town is the third largest in Crete and the seat of the university arts faculties. It prides itself on a long intellectual tradition dating back to the late 15th century when two locals were involved in the printing industry in Venice: Markos Mousouros with Aldus Manutius for the Aldine Printing Press and Zacharias Kallergis, who started the first wholly Greek publishing house. The promontory is dominated by a great fortress, a failed Venetian plan to make the locals safe from pirates. The harbour next to it was another Venetian headache. It had—and still has—a tendency to silting. Even with constant dredging it is unsuitable for large vessels. Nowadays it is mainly used for fishing boats and provides a fine backdrop to the Turkish lighthouse. Modern Rethymnon has considerably expanded; tourist development has spread along the sandy beaches of the east coast—to the despair of the loggerhead turtle (*see p. 164*).

HISTORY OF RETHYMNON

The area shows continuous occupation since Minoan times (Late Minoan remains including a LM III tomb with offerings have been found in the area of Mastabas to the southeast), when it probably acquired its name, Rithymna, which is pre-Greek in origin. Rethymnon followed the fate of other Cretan cities after the Classical period. After the Byzantines, the Arabs settled in. Finally the Venetians arrived in 1204, after a short interlude under the Genoese buccaneer Enrico Pescatore. The Venetians first occupied the area of Palaiokastro (which they called Castelvecchio) in the centre of town. This was already surrounded by a fortified wall and housed some 3,000 people. As the settlement grew, however, it became necessary to build new city walls. The task was undertaken between 1540 and 1570 by Michele Sanmicheli, also known for his work in Chania and Herakleion. The new wall probably ran along an older loop of fortifications at the base of the small peninsula. The magnificent city gate (Porta Guora, named after the rector Giacomo Guoro) is all that remains of it. The Sabbionara Gate was pulled down at the end of the 19th century by the Russian occupying forces. The defences proved no match for pirate attacks, first by Kheir ed-Din Barbarossa and, on July 7th 1571, by Ulutz Ali. In this second attack Rethymnon lost most of its buildings. The present city dates from after this time.

Rethymnon's defences also needed a complete overhaul, a task which was completed by 1590. The new castle, the Fortezza, had originally been intended to house all the inhabitants, as Liopetra had done for Siteia, but this never happened. The interior of the polygonal structure, designed by the architect Sforza Pallavicini, was only ever home to public buildings: the storeroom of the artillery, where cannons and weapons were kept; the residences of the councillors and of the rector; and the cathedral. The bishop refused to move his residence inside the enceinte. The populace also preferred to remain outside. Space within was cramped and the proximity of the women to the soldiers was deemed to be a problem. In the end the Venetian authorities relented and the new rector, Francesco da Molin, agreed to the reconstruction of the old town. The main street (Ruga Grande) ran along the present Odos Arkadiou. The bishop went on clamouring—in vain, as it turned out—for a plot in town that was large enough for an adequate church.

The Rethymniots did take refuge inside the Fortezza, in 1645, but the Turkish siege only lasted 23 days. When the white flag was finally hoisted the inhabitants had the choice between becoming Ottoman subjects or emigrating to Khandak (Herakleion)—which in any case fell to the Turks in 1669. The Ottomans renamed the town Resmo, and settled in for a long occupation that was to last until 1897. Considerable changes took place in the architectural landscape of the old town below the Fortezza. The dressed stone of the Venetians was replaced by a construction technique using a wooden framework filled with rubble and mud brick and heavily plastered for protection against the elements. Some fine examples of the period can still be found in the maze of narrow streets; moreover these symbols of a once-hated domination are now cherished and restored. Upper storeys faced with wood can still be seen projecting over the street. Occasionally the characteristic lattice work (*kafasoto*) is still in place. In 1897, as a result of the intervention of the Great Powers, the Russians took over as an occupying force, remaining to 1909. Eventually the Greek flag was hoisted from the fortress walls, after Crete's achievement of its much-coveted union with Greece.

A SHORT WALK THROUGH RETHYMNON

Starting from the Porta Guora, a short walk through Rethymnon will reveal much of its Venetian and Turkish heritage. Down Odos Ethnikis Antistaseos, the church of **Aghios Frangiskos** has a very fine door frame. Note the inverted acanthus motif carved on the keystone of the arch. The original church, all that remains of the Franciscan friary, was a very simple single-aisled basilica with a wooden roof. The door frame may be a later embellishment. Further on, at the crossroads of Palaiologou and Arkadiou, is the **Loggia** (built by Sanmicheli); recently restored, it is probably the best Venetian building in Crete. Here the ruling class would congregate to discuss the running of the city, to do business deals, to gossip and to gamble. Under Turkish rule it became a mosque. The minaret was demolished in 1930. The Loggia is square in plan with round-arched window openings originally closed only on the south side. The cornice rests on 22 corbels along each side above a defining moulding. Internally four pillars supported the wooden roof beams and wooden corbels were carved with a decoration of acanthus leaves. The flat roof is a 17th-century alteration. Now the Loggia has reverted to its commercial function. It is the seat of the Archaeological Receipts Fund, where illustrated guides

The Rimondi Fountain, built by the Venetian rector of Rethymnon in 1629.

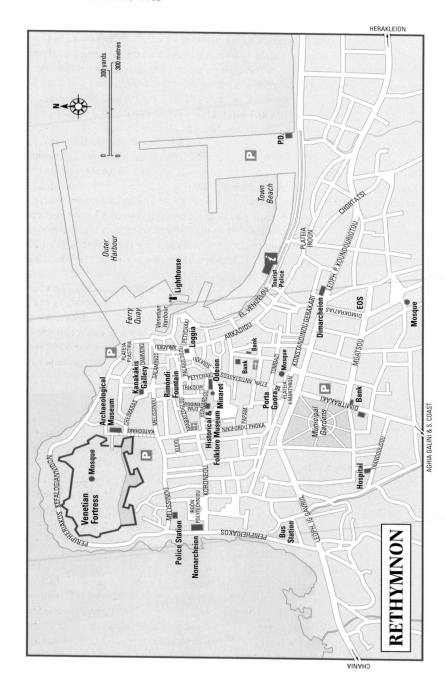

and high-quality replicas can be purchased (*open Mon–Fri 8–5, Sat 9–2*). Next to it are the foundations of the Venetian clock tower which bore the effigy of St Mark and had a clock with the signs of the Zodiac; it was destroyed in an earthquake in 1596.

Continuing west, the **Rimondi Fountain**, built in 1629 by the rector Alvise Rimondi, with its waterspouts in the shape of lion's heads and its Corinthian columns, stands at the junction of several streets. This is the heart of the city, with cafés, bars and shops. Turning into Vernardou is the **Neratze Mosque**, formerly a church belonging to the Augustinian monastery; note the Venetian monumental portal after a design by Sebastiano Serlio, the 16th-century Mannerist architect from Bologna who set down the canons for the use of the Classical orders in his influential treatise. The three domes are a later addition dating from 1657, when the church was turned into a mosque. They replace the original timber roof. At that point the bell-tower became a minaret, the highest in town. At no. 25, **Palazzo Clodio** still retains its family crest and motto. According to local lore, at the time of the Turkish occupation a descendant of the family was granted permission to remove a memento of his ancestors. He left with a wooden beam full of gold coins. The Historical and Folklore Museum (*see p. 278*) is at no. 28 in a restored Venetian mansion.

To the right (north), in Odos Nikiphorou Phoka, is a church popularly known as the **Mikri Panaghia** ('Little Virgin'), formerly a Dominican church dedicated to Mary Magdalen. It too became a mosque in due course; its minaret collapsed in 1680. One of the best examples of Venetian architecture is in the narrow **Odos Kleidi**, off this street. Here is a fine door frame with putti, columns and a family motto. At the other end of Nikiphorou Phoka, at the junction with Odos Papamichelaki, a **stone iconostasis** built into the wall is well worth searching for.

THE FORTEZZA & ARCHAEOLOGICAL MUSEUM

The Fortezza of Rethymnon (*open Tues–Sun 10–5*) is one of the largest Venetian castles in Crete. At the top of the steep street which leads to its entrance, the building on the right, the old Turkish prison, is now the Archaeological Museum (*see below*).

Begun in September 1573, probably on top of the acropolis of the ancient Rithymna, and built on a rocky outcrop where the geology changes from sand to rock, the Fortezza was a response both to damaging pirate raids and increased Turkish pressure in the sea around Crete. It took ten years to complete, at enormous cost and with a large input of forced local labour. The immense ramparts still stand with their intriguing loophole battlements, circular guard turrets and four great bastions on the exposed landward side.

The **East Gate**, a long barrel-vaulted passage through the ramparts, through which visitors enter, was designed to accommodate large-scale movements of wheeled traffic or cavalry and the recess above the gateway at its outer end would have held Venice's symbol: the Lion of St Mark. There were also two minor gates in the defences. The **Sea Gate** allowed access for small boats by a stairway in the rocks, but when the Venetians were besieged by the Turks, it proved ineffectual as severe storms prevented the landing of much-needed help. The other gate was to the west. The church by the east gate, near

The Fortezza. View from the north, over the storeroom complex to the Mosque of Ibrahim Han and what is thought to have been the prison building of the rector's palace.

the Aghios Nikolaos bastion, **Aghios Theodoros Trichinas**, a denomination that refers to the wearing of animal-hair garments as an act of penance, is comparatively recent. It dates from 1899 and was erected to mark the departure of the Turks from the island. In the lower ward a deep **well** is reached by a sloping subterranean passage which may have been part of a defensive scheme for counter-mining. The fortress also had cisterns.

The chief landmark in the centre of the enclave is the recently restored **Mosque of Ibrahim Han**, occupying the site of the Venetian cathedral church of Aghios Nikolaos. The building dates from the time of the fall of Rethymnon to the Turks in 1645. Inside, the huge dome rests on eight supporting arches and the mihrab on the southeast side faces Mecca. At the time of writing the mosque was not open to the public. A large **storeroom complex** is situated by the Sea Gate. It had barrel-vaulted rooms both above and below ground, the latter for more perishable products such as cheese, wine and oil. To the west are the **councillors' residences**; the Turks added a hamam on the upper floor.

At the time of the final siege the fortress showed its shortcomings: the south ramparts should have had a moat and the harbour was unable to accommodate Venetian galleys. As a result the Fortezza held out for only 23 days. During the Turkish occupation the fortress gradually filled up and by the middle of the 19th century a sizeable settlement had developed. Its intrusive structures were levelled in the 1960s and a programme of restoration has been in place ever since.

The Archaeological Museum

The museum (*open Tues–Sun 8.30–3; T: 28310 54668*) occupies the free-standing pentagonal bastion opposite the main gate of the Fortezza, built by the Turks as an additional defence and a prison. The display is housed in a single space with an atrium at the centre. Labelling is rather erratic and in most cases minimal. The exhibits are mainly from the Rethymnon area and are arranged chronologically.

The prehistoric section starts at the left of the entrance, with **material from cave sites** (Gerani, Elenes and Melidoni). The important **Protopalatial settlement of Monastiraki** in the Amari Valley is well represented with a selection of finds, including the clay model of a sanctuary and an incised stone kernos. From **Mt Vrysinas**, the peak sanctuary overlooking Rethymnon from the south, comes an assemblage of offerings excavated from the high rock clefts. These include figurines of worshippers and cattle and a rare stone altar with an incised Linear A inscription, mercifully displayed with a transcription.

The **Postpalatial material from Mastabas** confirms the occupation from early times of the immediate neighbourhood of modern Rethymnon. Another Postpalatial cemetery, **Armeni**, figures prominently, with a lavish display of the grave offerings. Of particular interest is the reconstructed boar's-tusk helmet. The larnakes nearby are from the same cemetery; their painted decoration ranks among the finest achievements of Postpalatial Crete. Note the abundant fauna: octopuses, bulls, birds and *agrimia* in a ritual hunting scene; a double axe; horns of consecration and a tree of life motif. The end of the Bronze Age is represented by finds from the **chamber tomb of Pangalochori**, east of Rethymnon. The display includes jewellery, a mirror with an ivory handle and anthropomorphic figurines of the 'phi' type, so called after their shape, reminiscent of that letter of the Greek alphabet (Φ). They are found in this period widely scattered around the Mediterranean and are an indicator of Mycenaean presence. In the same case is a tall figurine of a goddess with a stiff skirt, in the characteristic pose with raised arms.

The display dealing with the historical period starts with **material from the Geometric and Archaic cemetery of Orthi Petra** on the western slopes at Eleftherna. Finds include miniatures as well as human and animal figurines and a tripod table for offerings. The display of **Roman and Hellenistic glass** from various sites is of particular interest, with a mould-blown flask and core-formed amphoriskoi. The latter technique involved forming a core

Statue from Roman Lappa (Argyroupolis) of the Empress Faustina, wife of Antoninus Pius (2nd century AD).

of sand or clay of the intended shape, cemented with an organic binder, on a rod. A trail of molten glass was then wound around the rod; alternatively it could be dipped into the molten glass itself. On the wall are a couple of **inscriptions**. One, written in boustrophedon, is from Eleftherna and deals with the dangers of excessive drinking. The other is an alliance treaty between Eleftherna and the Macedonian king Dosos (227 BC).

OTHER MUSEUMS

Folklore Museum

Vernardou 28–30. Open Mon–Sat 9.30–2; T: 28310 23398. Labelling also in English.
Housed in a restored Venetian mansion next to a shop where you can learn how to make phyllo pastry. On the ground floor is historical material, with documents and mementoes of a broad spectrum of public and professional life in Rethymnon. The display on the upper floor, amassed over the years through donations and purchases, bears witness to a fast-disappearing world. The exhibits cover all aspects of Cretan crafts and deal in detail with traditional agricultural methods. One room is devoted to the traditional method of preparing bread in Rethymnon province.

Kanakakis Gallery

Odos Cheimaras 5 (near the Archaeological Museum). Open April–Oct Tues–Fri 9–1 &
7–10, Sat–Sun 11–3; Nov–March Tues–Fri 9–2, Wed and Fri also 6–9, Sat–Sun 10–3; T: 28310 52530.
Dedicated to the memory of the Rethymniot painter Lefteris Kanakakis, it covers a wide spectrum of modern Greek figurative art from the mid-20th century to the present. It includes a permanent collection by Kanakakis as well as works by other contemporary Greek artists.

Fratzeskakis Collection

Closed at the time of writing; normally housed near the Kanakakis Gallery.
The collection is based on the late Eleni Fratzeskakis's bequest to the city. The work of this self-taught Cretan artist was inspired by the traditional motifs she collected all over the island. It covers a number of traditional handicrafts including weaving, lacemaking and embroidery.

PRACTICAL INFORMATION

GETTING AROUND

• **By air:** Rethymnon is about halfway between Herakleion and Chania airports. Taxi rides are available from both. By bus you will need to get into town first and then catch a long-distance bus to Rethymnon.

• **By car:** From Herakleion (60km) and Chania (50km), Rethymnon is on the E75. The inland road from Aghia Galini (50km) is winding and at times narrow, but otherwise good.

Parking: There are several designated parking spaces (next to the tourist office, north of the bus station, on Dimitrakaki and next to Plateia Iroōn) but outside the main tourist season spaces are available on the marina along Venizelou and in other streets as long as you avoid the old town. Scratch cards are sold at kiosks and in the street.

• **By bus:** The bus station is on the Peripheriakos at the west end of town (*T: 28310 22212 or 22659 for both long-distance and local lines*). Regular services run from Herakleion Bus Station A and from Chania. A more limited service connects to several destinations in the province including Preveli, Aghia Galini, Argyroupolis, Eleftherna and Anogeia. www.bus-service-crete-ktel.com/maps4reth.html has a very clear map with all the routes.

The string of hotels on the coast to the east is served by the bus to Panormos.

• **By sea:** ANEK Lines (*www.anek.gr*) runs a ferry connection between Rethymnon and Athens (10hrs). The office at Rethymnon is at Arkadiou 250 (*T: 28310 29221 or 55518 or 26876*). Minoan Lines also runs ferries to Athens (*T: 28310 22941*).

TOURIST INFORMATION

Tourist Information Office: The only building on the seaward side of Venizelou (*T: 28310 29148*).

Taxis: (white; *T: 28310 25000*) can be hired from ranks on Plateia Iroōn and on east side of the municipal gardens on Dimitrakaki, south of Porta Guora.

Port authority: T: 22820 22276.

Road assistance: T: 104 and 28310 54554.

Rethymnon Hospital: On Trandoulidou near the municipal gardens (*T: 28310 27491*).

Rethymnon Police: On Iroōn Polytechniou in the west part of town, south of the fortress (*T: 28310 22289*).

Rethymnon Tourist Police: On the marina near the tourist information office (*T: 28310 28156*).

WHERE TO STAY

The whole of the cost east of Rethymnon is a huge development with back-to-back hotels and apartments. Below are some recommendations in the old town and just outside. The tourist office will have information about alternative accommodation and rooms to rent.

€€€ **Palazzino di Corina.** A very luxurious set of suites in a renovated building. *Corner of Damvergi and Diakou, www.corina.gr.*

€€ **Eliza Studios.** Recently renovated, offer a choice of 2–3 person accommodation. *Plastira 12, T: 28310 51594 mobile 6944 645117; lefteris.rethymnon.com.*

€€ **Hotel Fortezza.** In a modern building with private pool south of the fortress. *Melissinou, T: 28310 55551 or 55552; www.fortezza.gr.*

€€ **Hotel Ideon.** A brand new hotel with facilities for guests with disabilities overlooking the ferry port east of the Fortezza. *Plateia Plastira, T: 28310 28667/9; www.hotelideon.gr.*

€€ **Palazzo Vecchio.** One of the oldest Venetian mansions at the southwest end of the Fortezza, recently restored and turned into studios and apartments. *Corner of Iroōn Polytechniou and Melissinou, T: 28310 35351, www.ellada.net/vecchio.*

€€ **Valari.** In a modern building just on the east edge of the old city. *Open April–Oct. Koundouriotou, T: 28310 22236 or 25140, valari-hotel.com.*

€ **Hotel Leo.** Near the Loggia. *Corner of Arkadiou and Vafe, T: 28310 26197; liberty@reth.gr.*

€ **Zania.** A small place on Vlastou a side street off Arkadiou inland from harbour. *T: 28310 281693.*

WHERE TO EAT

Venizelou by the marina has a string of un-
interesting eating places. It is best to favour
those close to the Venetian harbour on the
way to the Archaeological Museum and the
Fortezza. These are good for fish and *mezedes*.
The more upmarket restaurants are to be
found in the maze of the old town.

€€€ **Gefsiplous**. By the sea, in Koumbes in
the western outskirts. Try the fish, the lobster
and ravioli. *Akrotiriou 3, T: 28310 58897.*

€€ **Avli**. Expensive but a good place for
Cretan cuisine. Good wine list. Just west of
the Raimondi Fountain, between Trikoupi
and Epimenidou. *Xanthoudidou 22, T: 28310
58250.*

€ **Fanari**. Taverna with good homely cuisine
on the waterfront between the harbour and
the fortress. Try *loukaniko* sausages and fish.
Kefalogiannidon 16, T: 28310 54849.

€ **To Pigadi**. Family-run restaurant serving
Greek and Mediterranean cuisine. *Xanthoudidou 27 (between Trikoupi and Epimenidou), T:
28310 27522.*

LOCAL SPECIALITIES

For leather goods, jewellery, textiles and
Cretan food, the best area is along Ethnikis
Antistaseos and Arkadiou on the eastern edge
of the old town north of Porta Guora. Qual-
ity antique reproductions are available at the
Loggia.

FESTIVALS & EVENTS

Rethymnon has a varied cultural life, details
and updates of which can be found on www.
rethymnon.biz/Reth/event. The **Renaissance
Festival** (details on above website), now in
its 22nd year and normally held in July, offers
concerts, films, theatre street performances
and dance exhibitions in various locations
throughout the town. **Carnival** (*carnival-in-
rethymnon-crete-greece.com*) with traditional
parades through the streets, fancy dress
parties and other events in the Lent period.
Fishermen's Festival (end of June) in the
Venetian Harbour with a free supper of bread
and grilled fish. **Feast of the Klidonas** (June)
is a celebration in which the traditional First
of May wreaths are burnt. The **Rethymnon
Cretan Wine Festival** has now been going
for almost 40 years. It is held in the municipal gardens at the end of July. It offers dance
and folklore music and the chance to sample
the local vintages.

WALKING

The Happy Walker (*Odos Tombazi 56, near
the Mitropolis church; office open April–end
Oct 5–8.30; in the summer closed Sat; T: 28310
52920; www.happywalker.com*) organises walking tours and hiking activities in the province
from March–Nov with experienced guides.
The EOS, the Greek Mountaineering Society
(*T: 28310 29148 or 56350 or 24143; www.eos.
rethymnon.com*) at Dimokratias 12 organises
more demanding hikes.

BOOKS & FURTHER READING

Pandelis Prevelakis: *Tale of a Town*. This delightful, evocative story of Rethymnon, the
author's native home, was written in 1938.
Available now only in second-hand editions,
it is nevertheless well worth tracking down
and reading while you are here.

EAST OF RETHYMNON

Visitors motoring along the coast east of Rethymnon, now given over to tourism, should cast their minds back to a very recent past when the area witnessed one of the crucial events in the Battle of Crete, namely the German parachute landing on 20th–30th May 1941. The defence of the area was in the hands of two Australian battalions together with some 2,000 or so ill-equipped Greek soldiers. The German objective was the airfield 7km east of Rethymnon just before **Stavromenos** (Σταυρωμένος; *map p. 429, B2*). On 20th May as many as 160 German planes flew in from the Herakleion direction dropping paratroopers, most of whom were lost at sea or shot down. The defenders were successful in mopping up the rest and capturing the German commander. The event is commemorated near Stavromenos, the scene of a fierce battle with the German parachutists holed up in the local oil factory. The memorial is signed from the old road to Herakleion at the Stavromenos junction.

From there onwards, the old Herakleion road takes to the hills and continues inland. To reach Panormos, keep to the E75 past the location of the airfield mentioned above.

THE ARKADI GORGE & MONASTERY

Aghios Dimitrios, Pikris and Amnatos

The church of **Aghios Dimitrios** is in the village of that name (Άγιος Δημήτριος; *map p. 429, B2*) south of Pigi off the New National Road. Past the whitewashed village, the church is some 200m downhill. The plan is a cross-in-square and the date is about the end of the Second Byzantine period. Note the decorative arches echoing the barrel vaulting of the cross-arms, the pattern of ornamental tiling and the eight arched windows separated by slender columns in the dome, recently restored. Inside, four columns with Corinthian capitals from an earlier church support the dome. There is evidence for 12th-century frescoes; the full-length figure of a saint is dated to the 14th century.

From Pigi the road leads to **Loutra** (Λούτρα; *map p. 429, B2*), with a fine Turkish fountain (all that remains of the Ottoman population that left in 1922) and the house of Ilias Spantidakis, who went on to become the leader of the Union of Coalminers in Colorado under the name of Louis Tikas. The village of **Pikris** or Pikri (Πίκρης; *map p. 429, B2*) in the Arkadi Gorge used to live on its mills, but the river now has almost run dry. The Clodio family had a villa here. The monumental entrance still bears a date, 1610, and a couple of inscriptions. We learn here (in Latin) that the owner, Georgius Clodius, had a doctorate in both civil and canon law. Another fine Venetian portal can be seen at **Amnatos** (Αμνάτος; *map p. 429, B2*). It belonged to the local lords, the Sanguinazzo, and has Doric columns and the inevitable Latin motto. In Turkish times the village, with a fine view towards Rethymnon, had a mosque, which Pashley mentions. Remains of a Turkish tower of the same period have been located outside the village.

This is the site of the Arkadi School, where future monks for the monastery (*described below*) trained. The place is very much bound up with the history of Arkadi, as indicated by the memorial at the centre of the village and explained in the two local museums.

MONI ARKADI

The famous monastery of Moni Arkadi (Μονή Αρκαδίου; *map p. 429, B2*) is 15km southeast of Rethymnon. There are various ways of getting there. It is only 8km west of Eleftherna; otherwise take the turning at Platanias or at Adelianos Kambos on the coast east of Rethymnon to Adele. Alternatively, if you turn at Pigianos Kambos, a bit further on towards Pigi, you will be rewarded with a Byzantine church (*see above*). From either approach follow the Loutra and Amnatos direction.

Moni Arkadi is one of the best-known spots in Crete. Everyone has been here: Lear painted it in 1864, Pashley made a fine drawing of the façade as it stood in 1834, just as Franz Sieber, the Czech botanist and collector, had done earlier in 1823. Cretans come here in droves on 9th November to commemorate a tragic episode during the uprising against the Ottomans in 1866–69.

THE MASSACRE AT ARKADI

The official version of events is as follows: the fortified monastery, the headquarters of the revolutionary committee of Rethymnon, was besieged by an overwhelming Turkish force. The rebel defenders under the leadership of the abbot, Gabriel, together with some 600 women and children who had taken refuge here, chose death rather than capture or surrender. When the enemy broke down the west gate, the defenders blew up the gunpowder magazine, with the abbot featuring prominently in the heroic act, killing themselves and at the same time hundreds of Turks. All this is proudly related in the monastery museum.

The alternative version, published in 1874 by William Stillman, then American consul in Chania, confirms that the monastery acted as the headquarters of a group of volunteer rebels who made sorties to harass the Turks under the leadership of a Greek commander. It also states that there were many women and children refugees. The rebel commander had wanted to send them away, but some belonged to Abbot Gabriel's extended family, so everyone stayed. Upon hearing that some 23,000 Turks were coming from Rethymnon to flush them out, the rebels sortied to meet them. They were defeated and promptly melted into the mountains. The defence of the monastery was left to the monks and the refugees. The powder magazine was blown up by one of the monks (not by the abbot himself), killing fewer than 100 Turks. The siege ended in a bloodbath, and the lives of the Christians were not spared. All were executed except 33 men who could claim connections with the Turkish governor, and 61 women and children.

News of the tragic event spread across Europe, mobilising public opinion. Victor Hugo wrote an emotional letter to a Trieste newspaper; Garibaldi expressed his sympathy with the Cretans as 'brave children of Ida'. It was a turning point in Crete's quest for independence and the principle of the 'moral intervention' of the Western powers was established.

The origins of the monastery date to the early days of the Venetian occupation when the powerful Kallergis family owned it and its surrounding land. A 14th-century document mentions the name of the founder, Archiatos, but the foundation really flourished in the 16th century when it was refurbished and enlarged. The monastery became an important cultural centre with an impressive library housing Greek and Latin philosophical texts.

The monastery today looks more or less as it did in the 17th century; the gateway destroyed in 1866 has been rebuilt to the same design. The ornate 16th-century façade of the church, dedicated to the Transfiguration of Christ and to Aghios Konstantinos (the Roman emperor) and his mother Aghia Eleni (St Helen), shows a mixture of different styles Gothic, Renaissance, Neoclassical and Baroque. The twin pediments have been unified by a tall bellcote with an inscription of 1587. Below are four pairs of Corinthian columns, equally spaced to form three bays, each with a door. The two lateral doors serving as entrances and the central doorway has been converted into a niche. The refectory, on the north side of the courtyard, still bears the scars of the bullets, and the powder magazine is still short of a roof. Below the monastery, where the modern road up from Rethymnon crosses the stream bed, a narrow bridge bears the date 1685.

PANORMOS, BALI & MONI ATALIS

Panormos and Bali, at either end of a rocky promontory, are two resort harbour villages that can be used as a base from which to explore the hinterland.

Panormos

Panormos (Πάνορμος; *map p. 429, C1*), c. 22km east of Rethymnon, has a long history. Coins from the ancient site, of which little is known, cover the period from the 1st century BC to the 9th century AD. Its main monument is the early Christian basilica of Aghia Sophia (*see below*). The port was important as a trading centre in Venetian times and beyond, before a land link—what is now known as the Old Road—was built between Rethymnon and Herakleion in the late 19th century.

To find the **basilica of Aghia Sophia**, follow the main road entering the village until you reach the post office. Aghia Sophia is signed from the opposite end of the square. The road goes under the highway and climbs uphill. The building, excavated in 1948, was one of the largest basilicas in early 6th-century Crete. The church had a nave and two aisles, transepts and a single apse. The nave was divided by stylobates of four columns topped with Ionic capitals. Under the chancel floor, a small container filled with bones was interpreted as a foundation deposit. Pebble and slab floors, with a notable absence of mosaics, contrast with the high quality of the capitals and the details from the narthex. West of the narthex is an atrium which originally had a Corinthian colonnade around a central cistern. The baptismal font is in the south transept, but the original baptistery may have been located in the room nearest to the narthex. The tile grave in the north transept is known from inscription to be the tomb of Theodoros, a minor cleric.

At the eastern end of town, on the rocky coast by the mouth of the river Milopotamos, is the **site of a castle** built by the Genoese pirate Enrico Pescatore, who briefly held Crete before the Venetians.

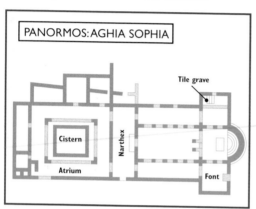

PANORMOS: AGHIA SOPHIA

Tile grave

Cistern

Narthex

Atrium

Font

Upturned Corinthian capital amid the ruins of Aghia Sophia.

The castle already figures in an early Venetian document dated 1212 which records the carving up of the old Byzantine provinces. In 1455 it was undergoing repairs and the bill for the work on two towers was sent to the Duke of Candia. The other six towers were privately owned. But come 1560 it was in a poor state, in ruins and deserted because of corsair attacks. Later, in 1620, the castle passed to one Giorgio Gritti on the understanding that he would restore it using forced local labour. This he did, but eyebrows were raised in Rethymnon about his treatment of the indigenous population and the rector put in a request with Venice to have the concession revoked. These days there is nothing left of the castle at all.

Bali

Bali (Μπαλί; *map p. 429, C1*), with fine views of the coast, is another 10km east, well placed almost midway between Herakleion and Rethymnon. The name comes from the Turkish word for honey, but in Classical times the city state of Axos (*see p. 293*) had its seaport here, and then Bali was called Astale. This name was still in use on Venetian maps and survives in Moni Atalis (*see below*). Bali is an attractive village set around several small coves, with the original fishing harbour at its centre. For good swimming, take the cliff path to the west (signed Evita Beach), aiming for the Karavostasis cove.

Moni Atalis

The Monastery of Aghios Ioannis of Atali, or Moni Atalis (*map p. 429, C1; open Sat–Thur 9–2; summer also 4–7*), signed inland on the E75 south of Bali (5km), has been in the middle of nowhere for most of its existence, since at least the 17th century if not earlier. The coastal road only dates from the 1960s, and the so-called 'Old Road' inland is of no great antiquity. So it comes as no surprise to discover that its foundation is connected with a local hermit, who settled here on the slopes of Mt Kouloukonas (also known as the Talaia Mountains). As the Ottomans settled in, the monastery played an important role in the Greek fight for freedom. It made good use of its pivotal position, commanding the access to the interior across the mountains to the Milopotamos valley and the resistance strongholds on Ida. After mainland Greece achieved independence in 1821, it acted as a lifeline to keep communications open with the outside world, a fact which resulted in the bombardment of the bay by Turkish ships. In 1866 the monastery came under attack, narrowly escaping complete destruction. Gerola, who visited at the beginning of the 20th century, noted Venetian architectural details on the arched buildings and also the roofed main entrance with an inscription of 1635. Later the monastery fell into decline and was deserted after the German invasion in 1941. It stood empty until 1983. The double-naved church, with wall paintings dated to the early 17th century, is associated with St John the Baptist, whose feasts are held on the day of his birth (24th June) and of his martyrdom (29th August). The monastery is now being restored and is well worth a visit, certainly for the grand view of the coastline from the terrace and along a narrow path from the old Venetian fountain.

THE FOOTHILLS OF IDA

While it is possible to reach almost all the interesting spots in Crete by car, this is really walkers' country: the E4 route crosses the territory, linking Moni Arkadi to Eleftherna and east to Axos and Anogeia, from where it strikes south on the way to Zominthos and the Idaian Cave. This itinerary goes all the way round the tall, imposing Psiloritis (as Mt Ida is also called), Crete's highest and most significant mountain range, covering landscapes and sights of interest clinging to its northern and eastern sections. It ends at the Idaian Cave, where according to one tradition Zeus spent his early years (*see p. 296*).

ELEFTHERNA

Before heading for Eleftherna from the coast road east of Rethymnon, church enthusiasts might wish to make a detour via **Ano Viran Episkopi** (Άνω Βιράν Επισκοπή; *map p. 429, B2*), signed south near the Australian War Memorial near Stavromenos. At the village take the right turn from the centre and go right again. The church of Aghios Dimitrios, now in a serious state of disrepair, is by the road. The site has a long history. Originally there was a temple to the goddess Diktynna (*see p. 386*) here, as the milestone recording road repairs on her behalf suggests. In the 10th–11th century a four-aisled basilica was erected over the temple ruins. Columns and pillars and the dome on a drum are still standing. The basilica may have succeeded Sybrita (Syvritos; modern Thronos) as the seat of the bishop after the latter had been destroyed by the Arabs.

ANCIENT ELEFTHERNA

Ancient Eleftherna (also transliterated as Eleutherna; Ελεύθερνα; *map p. 429, B2–C2*), on the northern foothills of Ida, is on the edge of the village of Archaia Eleftherna. Walkers can follow the E4 route to it; drivers can approach from Perama, past Margarites to the south (c. 12km) or from Moni Arkadi (8km). The site, fortified by nature and by man, stands on a narrow ridge overlooking the plain to the north. The spur is made of marly limestone with alternating horizontal layers of soft and hard material suitable for the construction of platforms, building foundations and connecting staircases on the slopes. Sea access is 10km away down the valley to the north, with Panormos or Stavromenos as possible harbours. Two seasonal streams run 40m below the summit on either side: the Chalopota to the west and the Kyriaki to the east.

The site

The ruins spread along both the east and the west slopes of the acropolis, extensively terraced to keep erosion in check. Water came from a spring up the valley to the west, and was collected in huge cisterns dug into the limestone on the slopes. Traces of a vaulted aqueduct have been found, which would have brought the water below the acropolis

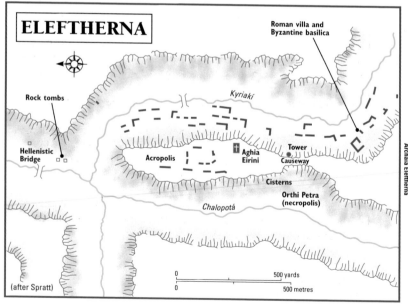

ELEFTHERNA

Roman villa and Byzantine basilica

Rock tombs

Kyriakí

Hellenistic Bridge

Acropolis

Aghia Eirini

Tower

Causeway

Cisterns

Orthi Petra (necropolis)

Chalopotá

Archaia Eleftherna

0   500 yards
0   500 metres

(after Spratt)

from the cistern to the city terraces on the east side. You can choose which part to visit first. On the way in from Margarites, the remains on the east slope are signed right ('To Ancientry'). For the acropolis, carry straight on to the T-junction and turn right.

HISTORY OF ELEFTHERNA

Eleftherna was one of the most important Dorian city-states, with continuous occupation from the Dark Ages to the Byzantine period. Its remains are spread far and wide and the site is in places quite overgrown. Even without aiming to see everything, one should allow time to take in the feel of the rugged landscape.

There are signs of Early Minoan activity, with some figurines showing contacts with the Cyclades, but Eleftherna really takes off with the arrival of the Dorians. While Iron Age Eleftherna is better known through the cemetery of Orthi Petra (*see overleaf*), there is little doubt that it was a flourishing settlement at the time, with contacts with mainland Greece, Cyprus and the Levant. The city prospered, kept on the fringes of Crete's internal political conflicts, and became known for its sculptors and its musicians (Ametor on the lyre and Antipatros on the hydraulic organ). It put up a fierce resistance to Roman occupation—according to Cassius Dio (*36.18.2*), the Roman commander Quintus Caecilius Metellus Creticus used vinegar to soften the upper courses of the mud-brick walls—but eventually bowed to the inevitable; it thrived in the Roman period and enjoyed a building boom.

Eleftherna was important in early Byzantine times, with at least four basilicas (one on the acropolis and the others on the east slope) and a bishop until the 8th century. The last of these was Epiphaneios the Unworthy. The city's demise was due to a combination of earthquakes (three major ones in the 4th, 7th and 8th centuries) interspersed with Arab raids and barbarian incursions from the Peloponnese. Eventually the inhabitants took to the mountains, only returning when Nicephorus Phocas re-established Byzantine rule in 961. They resettled on the acropolis, protected by the massive late Roman–early Medieval tower, which still stands to a height of 8m and controls access to the site via the narrow causeway (only 3m wide). Eventually the modern village developed. It was called Prines after the local holm oaks, and changed its name to Archaia Eleftherna in 1997.

Captain Spratt visited in the mid-19th century, leaving a description, some fine drawings and a sketch plan. The site was investigated by the English archaeologist Humfry Payne in 1928. He noted the massive walls of the Classical period and the Roman repairs but did not think that the site warranted another season. Eleftherna had to wait a while longer for sustained attention. The University of Crete has been studying the site and the surrounding area since 1985.

The acropolis and Orthi Petra

The entrance to the **acropolis** is beside the taverna. The remains of a tower stand beside a narrow causeway, a bridge of stone with its slabs carved to resemble paving. Once across it, an overgrown path leads onto the acropolis proper. Here is a fenced area where a large structure of the early Christian period has been uncovered. It was built on top of a sanctuary that flourished in Archaic and Hellenistic times and was of central importance to the town, at least judging by the number of inscriptions recovered. Next to it was a three-aisled basilica. Down the hillside to the east, archaeologists have identified traces of ancient fortifications with square towers. The chapel of Aghia Eirini probably stands on top of an earlier cult building.

The cemetery of Orthi Petra (*not open to the public; recognisable by its metal roofing*) is down the valley to the west, along a *kalderimi* still paved in places past two huge and impressive **rock-cut cisterns**. These come in groups of three separated by rock-cut pillars and measure 40m by 25m, with an average depth of 5m.

The locality known as **Orthi Petra**, meaning 'standing stone', was used as a cemetery between the 9th and 6th centuries BC. Later the Romans quarried it for building stone and also laid a paved road across it. Burial practices vary according to areas. Pithoi and amphorae were used for babies, children and adolescents. More conspicuous were the stone enclosures representing families or clans. They included both inhumations and cremations. Studies of the pyre remains showed that the wood used was olive, cypress and pine. Parallels with representations on 5th–4th-century red-figure vases

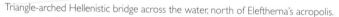

Triangle-arched Hellenistic bridge across the water, north of Eleftherna's acropolis.

have been put forward. The varying degree of combustion of the offerings suggests that they were placed at different times of the procedure, including after the burning had ceased (which is why some pots showed no traces of scorching). It is estimated that pyres burnt to c. 900° for a long time, after which they were quenched with water. The remains of the deceased were washed in wine and placed in an amphora. The pyre was then sealed with stones, altogether a process reminiscent of Patroclus' funeral as described in the *Iliad* (Book XXIII). In 1990, excavators uncovered evidence pointing to human sacrifice; it included a 30-cm iron knife found near the neck of the victim (whose head was missing), a whetstone (presumably to sharpen the knife) and a jar that might have held the water to use with the whetstone. Analysis of the grave goods and evidence for ritual feasting show connections with communities on the island and also overseas, on the Greek mainland, Cyprus, the Phoenician coast and Egypt. Rethymnon Archaeological Museum has an extensive display of the finds including gold, crystal and bronze artefacts and the diminutive ivory heads thought to have originally belonged to xoana. A Phoenician cippus suggests that people from the Levant were living and dying in Eleftherna, prompting speculation that they may have been involved with the manufacturing of the shields from the Idaian Cave (*see p. 296*). A similar artefact, though smaller, was found in Eleftherna where it was used as a lid of a pithos. This throws an altogether new light on the Ida finds, suggesting that perhaps they were not ceremonial shields at all.

Sculptural fragments, some of which became incorporated into modern terracing, have shown Crete's contribution to the development of Greek sculpture. In particular the discovery of fragmentary remains with traces of paint of an early Archaic *kore* have been instrumental in dating and provenancing the so-called *Lady of Auxerre*, which combines Minoan and Egyptian influences. This female figure was found in the stores of the museum of the French town at the beginning of the 20th century with no clear provenance. The Eleftherna Kore (now displayed in Herakleion archaeological museum; *see p. 46*) is the closest in style to it.

The Hellenistic bridge

Beyond the point where the two streams meet, to the north, is a fine **Hellenistic bridge**, which can be reached following red waymarks from the hairpin bend beyond the cisterns on the west flank of the acropolis (ignore the wire gates; those are for sheep). This can be a long walk involving a stiff climb back up, but it is highly recommended. The cliffs around the bridge have Roman rock-cut tombs.

The remains on the eastern slope

On the eastern slope are Hellenistic and Roman remains of private and public buildings some with mosaics (*site fenced, but visible*). On this side of the ridge the terraces are wider and the gradient smoother; this and the many springs prompted the ruling classes to favour this location for their houses and baths. The site is reached down a concrete road. The vandalised guardian's hut marks the location of the current excavations. The impressive site can only be viewed by walking around the fencing, but quite

Christ Pantocrator (12th century) in the dome of the Sotiros church.

a bit can be seen. Note the huge Hellenistic retaining walls, standing in places up to 4m, in pseudo-isodomic style; they mark the beginning of the urban development. The paved street running north–south had a sewer which was in use up to the 3rd century AD. The buildings on either side of it are later, although archaeologists have identified earlier underlying structures. To the west the early Byzantine basilica stands on top of a Roman temple. According to the finds it was dedicated to Hermes and Aphrodite. It has been speculated that Hermes Psychopompos (the 'Leader of Souls') was venerated here, which may have a connection with the dedicatee of the Christian basilica, namely the Archangel Michael, also a leader of souls. The three-aisled basilica, built around 430–50, had mosaic floors and opus sectile floral decoration on walls and pillars. In the narthex an inscription set into the mosaic floor gives the name of the bishop, the date and the dedication to St Michael. The church suffered in the 7th-century earthquake and was abandoned. In the nearby earlier building archaeologists uncovered the skeletons of a man, a woman and a child, gruesome evidence of the ravages of the earlier earthquake of AD 365.

A megaron stood to the east of the road in the Geometric period. The visible structures, however, are Roman. They include two high-status houses, a public building, the possible residence of a city official with an altar in honour of the emperor Trajan, and a couple of baths. These produced a great hoard of statuary, including an almost complete Aphrodite '*Sandalizousa*', in which the goddess is represented fastening or unfastening her sandal. The theme was popular in Hellenistic and Roman times and is known in at least 200 instances in terracotta, bronze and marble. The settlement is believed to have extended to the wide terraces to the south of the basilica, but this area has not yet been investigated. Lower down, the path leads to a cistern near the stream. The pillar foundations mark the emplacement of an ancient bridge.

The church of the Sotiros
On the way down to the Roman remains (or on the way back up, depending on how you choose to visit it) is a curious double church. The domed cross-in-square church of the Sotiros Christos (Christ the Saviour) dates to the 10th century and has a 12th-century Pantocrator in the dome. The church was built on the foundations of a 6th-century basilica and reused material from it. In the 16th century the church underwent modifications with the addition of the pitched-roofed structure with an elegant Gothic entrance. This was dedicated to Aghios Ioannis. Venice still controlled the island at this date, and may have wanted to accommodate the Latin rite.

AROUND ELEFTHERNA

From Eleftherna, one way forward is to get back onto the provincial road, in this case the Old Road at Perama, via Prinies and **Margarites** (Μαργαρίτες; *map p. 429, C2*), taking time off in the latter to have a look at the pottery. In 1333 the village was at the centre of a rebellion against Venetian requests for taxes and forced labour. The leader was one Vardas Kallergis, who did not toe the family line (*see the Pax Kallergi, pp. 18–19*): he was defeated by another Kallergis and spent the rest of his life in prison with his sons as an example to all. Potters no longer work in Margarites but the village is pretty, with interesting old houses with ornate doorways and the colourful ceramics displayed everywhere. The fine houses that Gerola saw and photographed are unfortunately no more but the church of Aghios Ioannis Prodromos (St John the Baptist), dated 1383, has fine frescoes. Note at the entrance to the left the depiction of the founder. The village also offers a fine view over the wooded gorge and the deserted settlement of **Kato Tripodos** across the valley.

An alternative is to take a winding road east from Eleftherna via Pigouniana, stopping at **Kalamas** (Καλαμάς; *map p. 429, C2*) for the cross-in-square church of Aghios Georgios, once the seat of a bishop and dating from the 11th century. It has two narthexes in the front, set at right angles to the main axis and added at different times. Early frescoes (13th century or earlier) with six scenes of the life of the saint have survived in the vault and in the inner narthex. On the outside, the building has blind arches and brick decorations.

The Melidoni Cave
To continue the exploration of the Ida foothills, at Perama take the old road and go east. Alternatively, for the Melidoni Cave, another high point of Crete's struggle for independence, follow the sign from Melidoni village (Μελιδόνι; *map p. 429, C2*). The cave is a further 2km to the left. A path leads to the cave, marked by a small church. The main cave measures 40m by 50m and is about 25m high. It is quite impressive with

huge stalactites, lit to theatrical effect which means you can dispense with a torch—but you will still need stout shoes for the slippery steps and a warm sweater to cope with the drop in temperature.

According to tradition, the cave was the site of a Classical sanctuary to Hermes Talaios, an epithet possibly connected with Talos, the giant to whom Minos entrusted the protection of Crete and its laws. Investigations have confirmed that it was visited from the Final Neolithic up to Roman times. Levels with abundant Minoan pottery, with traces of ashes and charcoal, may indicate Neopalatial cult activity. In 1823, when the Turks were wintering in the area, about 400 men, women and children hid in the cave. When the Turks found them and were unable to get them out, they blocked the entrance with stones and earth and lit a big fire to suffocate them. Pashley, who visited in 1834, met one of the men who had been keeping watch outside and had been able to escape. Ten years on the cave was still strewn with human bones. Now a cenotaph has been placed here in remembrance.

FROM PERAMA TO AXOS & ANOGEIA

The old road from Perama to the east follows the Milopotamos valley, a slow drive strongly recommended. At Aghios Syllas, dive a couple of km inland to **Damavolos** (Δαμαβόλος; *map p. 429, C2*) for Aghios Pnevma, a chapel belonging to the Kallergis family. The best plan is to get a guide in the village. The chapel is in the valley along an unmarked and uncertain path with some old watermills. It is at the centre of a Kallergis estate, as the two family crests (black bands on a silver background) on the façade show. These were the old Kallergis arms (with a variant of blue or red on a gold background); later they favoured a double-headed eagle with or without a crown and the old crest on its breast.

From Damavolos, **Episkopi** (Επισκοπή; *map p. 429, C2*) can be reached cross-country via Mourtzana. In the village are the remains of the church of Aghios Ioannis Prodromos (St John the Baptist), also known as Frangoklissa, belonging to the bishop of Milopotamos. It was built in the Byzantine style, possibly as early as the 13th century, but for the Latin rite, on top of an earlier construction of the Second Byzantine period. Only the apse has been fully restored; the rest is open to the elements but it is still a fine and sizeable ruin. In the apse the frescoes include a *Virgin with Angels*, a *Virgin and Child* and *Twelve Apostles*. In 1568 the then bishop, Jacopo Sorreto, had it refurbished: his small crest can be seen on the entrance.

The next south turn just after the village (signed Garazo) leads straight into the mountains following the E4 walking route. For **Moni Diskouri** (*open daily 9–12 & 4–9; closed 12–4; map p. 429, C2*) take the Livadia turn after Garazo. The foundation is Venetian, though the name, meaning 'youths of Zeus', and its association with Castor and Pollux, Zeus' twin sons, the Dioscuri, points to an earlier cult. The monastery, a flourishing foundation in Venetian times, is now much reduced. Its present sphere of influence does extend to the summit of Ida, however: the chapel of Timios Stavros (the Holy Cross) at an altitude of 2456m, as far as the E4 walking route will go, belongs to it. A visit to the whitewashed building set around a serene courtyard full of flowers does bring home the peace and tranquillity of past religious communities.

Further east (7km) on a signed right turning from the main road, **Moni Chalepa** (*map p. 429, C2*) offers an interesting contrast. The stone building of the main monastery has now been restored and is not open to the public. Just below it, however, on the slopes, it is possible to wander around the ruined buildings connected with the agricultural estate associated with the community. There is a fine *kamara* house (*see p. 161*; note the slot in the arch to take the cross beam to support a cooking pot on a central fire), a wine press, a mill installation, animal troughs and a fantastic view of snow-capped Ida. Presently only one monk (and his dog) live there. Following either the chanting of the former (broadcast though loudspeakers) or the barking of the latter, you can find the double-apsed chapel built inside the shell of the previous church, now under restoration.

Beyond Zoniana, the **Sedoni Cave**, also known as Sfentoni or Zoniana cave (*open daily April–Oct 9–6; guided tours only; map p. 429, C2*) is signed left. In a land of caves this is the most spectacular, and the word has got about. You will not be alone. On the bright side, the cave is well equipped with lighting and 270m of wooden walkways. Plans to extend it further have not yet come to fruition, which is just as well given the unique fauna that has colonised such a specialised environment. Archaeologists have investigated the cave and have found evidence of activity dating from the Neolithic up to Roman times. The guide is sure to supplement that with legends and fairy tales.

Axos

Axos (Αξός; *map p. 429, C2*) is a short way downhill from Zoniana. The modern village clings to a high ridge in a beautiful position on the lower slopes of Ida. The church of **Aghia Eirini** stands in the centre. Originally a single-naved chapel, it acquired a narthex and a dome with blind arcades in the 14th century. The track next to the church leads to the ancient site of Axos. On the way is the **church of Aghios Ioannis** by the cemetery, built into the central nave of a basilica, possibly of the First Byzantine period as indicated by the mosaic remains. It has fine 14th–15th-century frescoes. Do not miss the representation of sinners in Hell in twelve scenes to the left of the entrance. Among the highlights are the usurer, the couple lingering in bed on Sunday morning and the dishonest innkeeper. The scenes represent the sin and the punishment with an abundance of little devils.

Nothing much remains above ground of **ancient Axos**. The site was first occupied in Late Minoan times and flourished as a city-state the Archaic and Hellenistic periods; the climb, though, is short and pleasant and the view is stunning. The *polis* occupied a saddle between two hills with a steep acropolis to the south. At the very top stood the temple of Aphrodite, excavated by Halbherr at the beginning of the 20th century. He found many ex-votos and important metalwork, namely a bronze pectoral and helmet with cheek-pieces in the form of winged horses, representative of the Oriental influence in the 7th century BC. The rest of the city continued down the northeast slope.

Anogeia

On the way to Anogeia the road passes **Aghia Paraskevi**, a derelict Byzantine church incorporating spolia probably from Axos. **Anogeia** (Ανώγεια; *map p. 429, C2*) sits in a commanding, scenic position on the edge of the province of Rethymnon, at the start of the road to the Nida plateau and to the Idaian Cave beyond. Anogeia is famed for its weaving (every house is said to have a loom) and embroidery as well as for its singers and lyre players. The village is laid out in two centres: one along an upper road on the way to Herakleion, with a *plateia* set back from it, and the other around a little square downhill where the road from Axos joins. Steps and passages link the two levels.

Anogeia has a tradition of resistance and revolt going back well beyond the Second World War, when the village suffered great losses (*see below*). In the words of the poet Ioannis Kostantinides, the men of Anogeia have 'feet of hares, hearts of lions…slim waists …trunks of cypress trees; when they had no knives, they fought the Turks with the staff in their hands. Now they have swords and rifled muskets', and he was writing in 1867.

During the Second World War the village had a reputation as a centre of pro-British resistance and espionage. As Anthony Beevor relates, even the local priest was involved. Father Ioannis Skoulas trained as a parachutist with the Allies and received permission from the Orthodox Church to cut his hair and shave his beard for the duration of the war. Things came to a head in August 1944, when resistance fighters shot the German commander of a small local garrison. After a German punitive expedition was intercepted with considerable loss of life, revenge knew no bounds. The village was burnt to the ground and a number of its inhabitants were shot. The event is commemorated in the *Partisan of Peace*, a sculpture created by the German artist Karen Raeck, near the entrance to the Idaian Cave.

MOUNT IDA & THE IDAIAN CAVE

Dominating the view south from Anogeia, is Mt Ida, in Greek Psiloritis (from *psilos*, meaning high or lofty) reaching to 2456m, the highest peak in Crete. To the east Herakleion is not far (c. 40km) past the Minoan sites of Sklavokambos and Tylissos. The Idaian Cave is open only in the summer; the road south to the Nida plateau (20km) has been asphalted in its entirety to offer access to the Schinakas observatory and the ski resort just north of the cave. The road itself is old: it has belonged to shepherds since time immemorial. They still come to these high summer pastures with large flocks of sheep and goats and live in *mitata*, where they make cheese—you might be able to sample some on the way. Archaeologists have drawn parallels between these simple stone structures with their corbelled roofs, and the Bronze Age Mesara graves, though none of these was found intact, so the roofing architecture is not known. Walkers may wish to follow shepherds in their footsteps. The E4 walking route follows the contour of the mountain and from the Nida plain climbs to the summit where the Timios Stavros chapel is. It is a recommended climb, especially in the early summer when the snow recedes and the wild flowers are at their best, though it is not to be undertaken lightly. Pilgrims also came this way, as the evidence for cult activities in the Idaian Cave, covering the period from Late Neolithic to Roman, shows. They probably needed some facilities on the way, as suggested by the remains at Zominthos, 10km south of Anogeia.

Zominthos

The large Neopalatial structure at Zominthos (Ζόμινθος; *map p. 429, C2*), dated c. 1600 BC, has been interpreted as a Minoan caravanserai, a stopping place for visitors on the road leading into the massif from Knossos via Tylissos or Krousonas. The site, which has retained its pre-Greek name, was discovered in 1982 and excavated from 1983 to 1990 by a team lead by Giannis Sakellarakis. The dry stone building, set at an altitude well above the modern Cretan settlement, had at least 16 rooms and a second storey; it was destroyed by earthquake and a subsequent fire that burnt ceiling, floors and roof. It now stands at places over 2m high and has, on the north façade, some of the best surviving Minoan windows. A room has been identified from finds, including a potter's wheel and bronze tools, as a potter's workshop. The current Zominthos research project, begun 15 years after the end of the excavations, aims at applying an interdisciplinary approach to the understanding of this unusual structure in its Minoan landscape. The site (*not marked*) is immediately after the right turning for Aghios Yakinthos on the road from Anogeia to the Idaian Cave. It is securely fenced and not accessible to the public. Apart from the location, there is not much to see.

The left turning for the observatory is 6km on. On a clear day, a walk to the top at 1750m is recommended for the view over the Nida plain and beyond to Psiloritis. It is possible to drive, but it is 4km of a steep and narrow road. Continuing to the right, the road leads to the Nida plateau at an altitude of 1400m, ending roughly at the signs for the ski slope. The path to the cave (10mins) is further on by the taverna.

The Idaian Cave

The exploration of the cave (*open summer only; Tues–Sun 9.30–4; map p. 429, C3*) is quite hazardous because at the entrance, which is downhill, there is snow even in the summer. There are a total of four chambers, past the altar carved out of a fallen rock at the entrance. The first chamber, on a slope, opens onto a couple of side chambers at a lower level, while steps in the rock higher up at the back lead to the inner sanctum. Here, among the stalagmites, the archaeologists made amazing discoveries.

Shepherds probably knew about the cave before Ioannis Mitsotakis, the Russian consul, visited in 1885. News of his finds of metalwork prompted the Cretan authorities to dispatch Halbherr for an investigation in 1888. After work by Spyridon Marinatos in the 1950s, Sakellarakis set up a wide-ranging programme of excavation and study from 1982–86. This involved a thorough and meticulous examination of the cave and its structures. It has confirmed that this was one of the most frequented cult centres in Crete, with activity beginning at the end of the Neolithic, developing in the Middle Minoan period and continuing to Roman times. The site is remote, there is no nearby settlement; moreover, it is snowbound for half the year. The sheer volume and quality of the votive finds and the cave's association with the cult of Zeus, including a plaque naming Idaian Zeus, point to a sanctuary of national, not local importance. It has been suggested that it could be the precursor of the Panhellenic sanctuaries.

The most spectacular finds, now in Herakleion museum, are dated to the Geometric period and include a large number of bronze tripod cauldrons (only Olympia and Delphi have more). Ceremonial 'shields' of a slightly later date, with sphinxes and griffins, point to a connection with the Near East, though material from Eleftherna may indicate local manufacturing according to the fashion of the day (*see p. 289*); the same consideration applies to the metal bowl with the lotus handle, a possible Cypriot import, though something similar has also been found also at Amnisos, Eleftherna and Kavousi. Carved ivories dated to the 8th–7th centuries indicate contacts with Syria. Particularly notable among them are the pin with two female heads back to back, a fragmentary plaque in Daidalic style, and the seals. Gold jewellery and evidence for large statues both in bronze and terracotta contrast with more humble finds, the terracotta figurines and the thousand or so Roman lamps, the indispensable tool of the pilgrim.

THE IDAIAN CAVE & THE CULT OF ZEUS

There are several versions of Zeus' troubled early life, when he had to be spirited away by his mother Rhea to escape being devoured by his father Kronos. He found safety in Crete, but was it in the Diktaian Cave or here? If it is accepted that he was born on the Lasithi plateau, then he may have been sent to Ida as a small boy, to grow to manhood among the shepherds. The Idaian Cave is associated with cult activities from the early 2nd millennium. Offerings and abundant burnt animal bones and ash, associated with sacrifices and ritual meals, increased over the centuries with no interruptions, peaking in the 8th–6th centuries BC. Ex-votos from both men and women indicate that warfare and fertility were the main concerns.

The cult did not abate in Classical times. The philosopher Pythagoras visited in the 6th century BC to be initiated, according to some, into the local mysteries; alternatively he had a day out with a friend, the seer Epimenides, a native of Phaistos. Theophrastus, the 4th-century BC Greek botanist, knew about the place and its tradition of hanging votives on trees at the entrance (though he fell short of explaining how they moved to their present findspots). Evidence points to continued use to the 5th century AD. The Cretan version of Zeus, it would seem, was bound up with the annual cycle of vegetation involving death (Zeus' grave is traditionally on Juktas) and rebirth, and an emphasis on to the god's younger years. It probably originated with the Minoan Young God tradition and fed into mainstream Greek religion.

PRACTICAL INFORMATION

GETTING AROUND

• **By car:** There is a choice of two good roads, one on the coast, the E75 (the New National Road) and the old road inland. The latter, running through a shady, beautiful landscape, is far preferable, and is not to be driven in a hurry. The roads inland on the foothills of Mt Ida can be very scenic, but you will have to share them with sheep and other animals.

• **By Bus:** Regular bus services connect Rethymnon to Panormos and Bali on the coast. Anogeia, Zoniana, Margarites, Eleftherna and Arkadi all have limited bus services from Rethymnon. The Anogeia service from Herakleion runs from Bus Station B (at the Chania Gate). A map of services is on www.bus-service-crete-ktel.com/maps4reth.html.

TOURIST INFORMATION

Perama Health Centre: T: 28340 23075.
Anogeia Health Centre: T: 28340 31208.
Perama Police: T: 28340 22349.
Anogeia Police: T: 28340 31208.

WHERE TO STAY

Tourism in the area is developing inland along the beautiful stretch of the old road between Ida and the Talaia (Kouloukonas) mountains and to the south of it, serving a clientèle that appreciates mountains and other 'green' pursuits. The local municipality (Kouloukona) is trying to tap the agrotourism market and has set up a website that contains some useful information (www.kouloukonas.gr). Anogeia is well equipped for tourists, with rooms for rent and a number of tavernas.

Anogeia (*map p. 429, C2*)
€€€ **Delina Mountain Resort**. A brand new luxury hotel, also suitable for guests with disabilities. *T: 28340 31701, www.delina.gr.*
€€ **Hotel Aristea**. On the outskirts on the way in from Zoniana, with a fine view from the balcony. *T: 28340 31459.*
€ **Kitros**. Inexpensive, simple accommodation in the centre of town, with taverna. *T: 28340 31429; mobile 6976 808036.*
Apladiana (*map p. 429, C2*)
€ **Oasis Rooms and Taverna**. Along the Old Road in a particularly scenic stretch just over 1km west after the turning to Moni Chalepa. *T: 28340 41471 (better to ring in the evening if you need an English speaker).*
Astiraki (*map p. 429, D2*)
€ **Traditional Rooms Elena**. Accommodation and half-board. Technically in Herakleion province, Elena's rooms serve a clientèle of walkers and hikers who will naturally gravitate west towards Anogeia and Mt Ida. The village is really in the middle of nowhere, but is it well signposted and the welcome is great. *T: 2810 510141, www.psiloritis.net.gr/Elena.*
Axos (*map p. 429, C2*)
€€ **Enagron**. Rooms, studios and apartments situated in the valley below Axos in the grounds of a farm, part of which is still operating to supply the restaurant. Enagron offers relaxation, with a swimming pool as well as a chance to explore the Cretan way of life and the surrounding countryside, on donkey rides and walks. *T: 28340 61611 or 61818; 2810 285752, www.enagron.gr.*
€€ **Yakinthos**. Traditional apartments and studios on the highest point in Axos. *T: 28340 61760; www.yakinthos.gr.*
Drosia (*map p. 429, C2*)
€€ **Aposperitis Traditional Guest Houses**. Self-contained accommodation in a quiet

rural location on the old road. An added attraction is the ostrich farm at Apladiana, 4km away, which means you can try ostrich *stifado* the Cretan way. *T: 6976 618968; www.aposperitis-villas.gr.*

Nisi (near Garazo; *map p. 429, C2*)
€€ **Nisi Nature Club**. Apartments in a green setting with pool and a fine view of the mountains. *Open in winter by arrangement only. T: 28340 41336; mobile 6932 906411.*

Panormos (*map p. 429, C1*)
€€ **Villa Kynthia**. ■ Five beautifully furnished rooms in a restored 19th-century merchant's house in the centre of the village, on a very quiet street. Small enclosed courtyard with pool. *T: 28340 51102; call the Herakleion number (T: 2810 228723) in winter), www.villakynthia.gr.*

Tzanakiana (*map p. 429, C2*)
€€ **Kouriton House**. Traditional Cretan house in renovated 18th-century stone buildings in a small village near Margarites. Ideal as a base to explore the countryside. *T: 28310 55828; mobile 6945 722052 or 6942 968714; www.kouritonhouse.gr.*

WHERE TO EAT

Anogeia has a clutch of tavernas. There are also tavernas in **Margarites** and at **Apladiana** (*see above*). The taverna at **Arkadi** does not have a particularly good reputation; the traditional Cretan solution is to take a picnic. The **Idaian Cave** has a taverna at the start of the ascent; there is nothing at the top. **Bali** has several tavernas clustered around the coves. Psaropoula in the main cove, the one that has the fishing harbour, is a good choice.

Aghios Syllas (*map p. 429, C2*)
€ **Psiloritis' Tastes**. The restaurant on the Old Road specialises in Cretan food with a particular stress on local gastronomic traditions, with wine and raki of course. Teetotallers are also catered for with Byral (a drink made from carobs), Soumada (from almonds) and Kanalada, a refreshing potion. Also rents rooms. *T: 28340 20716; mobile 6972 875684; info@agios-silas.gr.*

Eleftherna (*map p. 429, B2–C2*)
There is a taverna near the entrance to acropolis, open in high season. Out of season, the well-situated **Panorama**, on the main road east of Eleftherna, will do a good lunch.

Panormos (*map p. 429, C1*)
Geronimos is best taverna in Panormos, in the heart of the old village at the corner of two streets. Konstantina cooks delicious traditional meals, served in convivial surroundings with locals watching the TV. There is the usual handful of places on the waterfront, too.

LOCAL SPECIALITIES

Perasma next to Psiloritis' Tastes in **Aghios Syllas**, has a selection of colourful local ceramics as well traditional Cretan food such as jams, olive oil, raki, honey and herbs. **Anogeia** is the land of weavers and embroiderers. For a particularly large selection look out for Archandoula, up a tiny alleyway from Plateia Livadi in the middle of town. Those who do not 'do' needlework may take an interest in the local knives. Here knives are so beloved that they are even framed.

THE AMARI VALLEY

The Amari Valley (*map p. 429, B2–C3*) stretches deep into the countryside between Mt Kedros (1776m) to the west and the Ida massif to the east, on a diagonal line southeast of Rethymnon. It is first mentioned by that name in Venetian documents. Before that, the area was known as Syvritos or Panakron. The valley is broad, much unlike the gorges, sometimes wide enough for one side not to be visible from the other, though north of Phourphouras this is because Mt Samitos is in the way. The valley is not normally on the commercial tours: the shortage of beaches is to blame. The drive along it is beautiful and scenic, on a reasonable road with interesting wild flowers and a good crop of Byzantine churches, especially in the area between Thronos and Apodoulou, and also along the alternative way back by the eastern slopes of Kedros. Other aspects of Crete's history are represented at Chromonastiri (a Venetian villa) and further into the valley at Monastiraki, Syvrita and Apodoulou.

The E4 walking route crosses the valley from east to west with a loop to the top of Mt Kedros, keeping north of Mt Samitos. At Phourphouras experienced walkers will be able to plan a climb of Mt Ida past the Stoumbotos mountain refuge. Most tourists explore the valley as a day trip from Rethymnon. It is 25km from the turnoff inland to Aghia Photini and roughly as many again to Apodoulou, which is only 12km from the south coast, signposted to Aghia Galini. If you have no compulsion to be near a beach and your interest is in flowers and a drive across a fine stretch of countryside, the approach from the west, from Spili to Aghia Photini (17km) can be very rewarding.

The Myli Gorge

The road is signed from the eastern end of the Rethymnon bypass. On its way south it runs along the west side of the Myli Gorge (*map p. 429, B2*), where once stood the water mills that ground the flour for Rethymnon's daily bread. Some 30 mills have been identified, all a very poor state of repair. Access to the gorge is via a stairway with wooden rails, signed to the left c. 4km after the turnoff (*parking*). The gorge is now covered with lush vegetation, a sign that the water that powered so many mills all year round is still there. Remains of the recent past are difficult to make out: by the stream bed, Kato and Pano Myli are now deserted and near the chapel of Aghios Ioannis, the overseer's 16th-century villa now stands in ruin. He controlled the millers' production and taxed them accordingly, and also baked batches of bread for the town. Keeping right after the chapel there is a bridge to Pano Myli. The path follows the stream to Kato Myli and leads back up near the Chalevi church, all that remains of the monastery of that name.

Chromonastiri

Chromonastiri (3km; Χρομοναστήρι; *map p. 429, B2*) offers not one, but two churches with 11th-century frescoes, among the earliest surviving in Crete, and a Venetian villa. In the middle of the village a track to the left leads to the abandoned church of Aghios

Eftychios at **Perdiki Metochi**, about 2km away; it can also be reached from the north via Xiro Chorio. The building, dating to the Second Byzantine period, is of interest on account of the architecture and of the paintings. The nave, unique in the island, consists of five bays with the central one raised to form a cross-arm and surmounted by a dome. Note the magnificent Pantocrator. The 11th-century frescoes have survived only in the sanctuary and show a flat, linear style influenced by the conservative tradition of the Macedonian dynasty in Byzantium. There is a deēsis (Christ between the Virgin and St John the Baptist) and a St Peter among the apostles.

The second church, dedicated to the Panaghia, is at **Kera**, c. 1km from Chromonastiri. The building is the result of several phases. To start with there was a domed construction (11th century) with a single nave and apses in the north and south walls. In the 14th century a taller narthex was added, with an opening between columns giving the effect of an extended nave. Later a bellcote and a side chapel were built. In the sanctuary the incomplete deēsis is dated to the 11th century. The other scenes are later. In the apse on the south wall, the Virgin is portrayed in the arms of her mother. She is not represented as a child; she is an adult looking out at the world, arms raised in blessing.

In Chromonastiri itself the **Villa Clodio** has been restored to a doubtful pink but otherwise does look the part: an elegant country house for a wealthy Venetian family escaping the summer heat of Rethymnon. It was not their only one. The Clodio family had at least two more, in Argyroupolis and Pikris. The villa is set to become a war museum, though at the time of writing there was not much sign of activity. It is a shame, because what can see peeping through the gates—the well among the orange trees, the loggia and *piano nobile*—looks much more welcoming than the forbidding exterior.

THE AMARI VALLEY

The road to the Amari Valley has to be picked up from the bypass in Rethymnon (marked 'Amari'; Αμάρι). Trying to go cross-country is not a good plan as minor roads are unmarked and not very good. At **Prasses** (Πρασσὲς; *map p. 429, B2*), a village with interesting Venetian remains, you are right on the eastern slopes of Mt Vrysinas and its peak sanctuary, reputedly one of the westernmost in the island. The site yielded rich finds, including a Linear A tablet, stone tables, miniature vases and boar tusks. A number are displayed in Rethymnon archaeological museum.

After the village, the Amari Valley proper starts past the ridge and it opens up like a lush oasis. Here the road narrows and it is slow driving all the way. This is a good place for birds, possibly attracted by the reservoir further south. After the Amari dam (9km) a turning right leads to Pantanassa (5km) and **Patsos** (9km; Πατσός) through beautiful countryside. From Patsos it is 30mins on foot to a sanctuary down in the gorge which has been in use on and off for a long time. At the chapel of Aghios Antonios, the spring marks the spot of a pilgrimage destination since Minoan times as attested by the ex-votos, which include figurines of worshippers and of animals, horns of consecration, offering-tables and a double axe. The theme of the figurines suggests a fertility cult.

The location remained in use through the Iron Age and beyond: an imperial inscription shows that in Roman times Hermes Kranaios was worshipped here. The place is now sacred to St Anthony, the protector of children. Hermes had a plethora of epithets, ranging from 'splendid', to 'bringer of luck', but Kranaios does not appear to have a recognised meaning or association.

Back on the main valley road, the **war memorial** with the figure of a heroic freedom fighter commemorates another episode in the resistance. It took place in September 1944, towards the end of the German occupation, against the express wishes of the Allies and in the general atmosphere of confusion created by different local factions vying for position, with the end of the war and victory in sight. The operation, which started as an ambush of German lorries, escalated and left many dead on both sides.

At the watershed beyond the war memorial, **Apostoli** (Απόστολοι; *map p. 429, B2*) has a fine Venetian church. From its terrace there is a stunning view of Mt Ida in the distance and of the site of the city-state of Syvritos to the northeast. In the cemetery just outside the village, the chapel of Aghios Nikolaos is worth a visit for the frescoes—if you can get the key. These include portraits of the donors, Mikhail Bafa and his wife, and a representation of Hell with the damned sprouting worms from their heads.

ASOMATHIANOS KAMBOS

From Apostoli the valley divides in two. The eastern part takes its name from Moni Asomatos while the western valley, which is smaller, is known as Smilianos Kambos. They are reunited at Apodoulou. The visit proceeds clockwise.

Thronos and Syvritos

Thronos (Θρόνος; *map p. 429, B2*) is signed uphill: the frescoed church of the Panaghia (*keys with Taverna Aravanes*) in the middle of the village was built on the foundations, still apparent with mosaic flooring, of an early Christian basilica. The frescoes belong to two periods at either end of the 14th century. A depiction of the Presentation of the Virgin has survived from both cycles, on the north wall of the sanctuary (early 14th century) and on north side of the vault of the nave (western bay, lower register; late 14th century). It is interesting to compare the two styles.

The site of the **acropolis of ancient Syvritos** is on Kephala Hill just above Thronos. It has recently been investigated by a Greek-Italian team, and is signposted from the village. The path peters out but as long as you keep going up you will get to the top in c. 15mins. Traces of occupation go back to the 12th century BC, making the site roughly contemporary with Karphi and with Kastro above Kavousi, which both acted as refuges in the eastern part of the island. But while these show no further occupation, Syvritos flourished in Hellenistic times and beyond because of its position on an important north–south trade route, until it suffered under the Arabs. The city that once minted coins with Hermes and Dionysos spread over the hill where the village of Thronos is and down the slope to Aghia Photini. A cemetery has been identified at Genna in the valley below. The basilica preceding the church of the Panaghia was probably a focal point in Byzantine times. Its harbour was on the south coast where Aghia Galini is now; it was then called Soulia or Soulina. On the way to the acropolis, a stretch of the fortification wall is visible. The excavations on the acropolis, now temporarily interrupted, have uncovered remains of a monumental building, a section of a paved road and remains of houses. According to Lorenzo de Monacis, a Venetian chronicler writing a long time after the events, the first Duke of Candia moved from Temenos to Syvritos at the time of the rebellion (*see p. 96*) and built a castle here, turning the ancient town into the capital of the *castellania*. However, this did not last long: by 1367 everything was in ruins and the capital of the *castellania* of Amari was moved to the village of the same name.

Monastiraki

At Kalogeros (Καλόγερος; *map p. 429, B2*) leave the main road and turn right at the junction for the small church of **Aghios Ioannis Theologos** (2km). If the missing lock has not been replaced, you will be able to see the frescoes of 1347, with Christ flanked by the Virgin and St John the Evangelist. The scene is repeated on the south wall of the nave.

The cruciform domed **church of Aghia Paraskevi**, originally a chapel of the Chortatzis, a distinguished Byzantine family, is on the main road to the right, 1km on. The chapel later passed to Moni Asomaton. At its north end is a tomb with a 13th-century fresco above it showing the donors Georgios Chortatzis and his wife. Another scene, now much damaged, represents a farewell, with a knight in armour taking leave of his wife and (?)son. According to popular legend this refers to the two Chortatzis brothers (Georgios and Theodoros), who left in 1272–73 to lead a rebellion against the Venetians which ended in 1278 with their flight to Asia Minor.

The former **Monastery of the Asomaton**, 1km south, was dissolved in 1930 (the buildings now belong to an agricultural centre specialising in cattle-breeding research). It was founded, according to tradition, by a Byzantine noblewoman who took a liking to the place, its quiet atmosphere with birds singing and tall, leafy trees. The monastery grew steadily in power and influence and, throughout Ottoman rule, Moni Asomaton played an important part in fostering Hellenic education. A number of its liturgical furnishings are now in the Historical Museum in Herakleion.

From Asomatos it is 2km to **Monastiraki** (Μοναστηράκι; *map p. 429, B2–C2*), where the University of Crete and an Italian team have been investigating a Minoan building since the 1980s. The site occupies a low hill at the foot of the modern village. It was first excavated by the Germans in 1942. Work has uncovered a MM II building of the First Palace period, with some 60 interconnecting rooms, storerooms, workshops and evidence of a second storey. The monumental character of the architecture, in local limestone blocks, has suggested a palace, one of the few in western Crete. Two archives of clay sealings show connections with Phaistos, as does the pottery. The destruction of the building in an earthquake and fire c. 1700 BC was followed by a Hellenistic reoccupation of the site. The site is erratically signposted from modern Monastiraki on a bad road below the village. It is very effectively fenced and shows no signs of being accessible to the public. That said, it is well worth taking the time to find it. The site is absolutely idyllic: anyone would want a palace in those lovely surroundings.

GERMAN WARTIME EXCAVATIONS

The German army was in Crete from May 1941 to early 1945 and reading Antony Beevor's account of the Battle of Crete and the ensuing occupation, one would hardly think there was any time for archaeology. But this was not the case: excavations and surveys were carried out from 1942, by order of the military authority with the assistance of professionals drafted in from the German Archaeological Institute in Berlin. The list of sites investigated is quite impressive, though it is only fair to say that most excavations were rather short, more a matter of days than weeks. Attention focused on two main sites: the Temple of Diktynna at the top end of the Rodopos peninsula (*see p. 385*) and Monastiraki in the Amari Valley. The former had been extensively looted in antiquity; work concentrated on recovering the plan of the building. At Monastiraki the Germans thought they had found what they had set out for: the westernmost Minoan palace in Crete. In 1942 there was nothing palatial west of Phaistos; Chania's impressive Minoan past had not yet been discovered. Whether the Germans were fully aware of the significance of their find is another matter. There was no time for further investigations after the autumn of 1942.

Apart from these excavations, in May–August 1942 the German army also carried out a multi-period survey covering western Crete, looking at settlement pattern and development and later, in 1944, a campaign of aerial photography to record field and road systems in the Mesara. By early 1945 everything (write-ups, plans and pictures) was ready for printing but unfortunately it suffered in air raids in Berlin. What was able to be rescued was published in 1951. All the finds were entrusted to the Cretan authorities.

In the modern village of Monastiraki two churches may be of interest, both with frescoes. The church of Archangel Michael (Archistratigos), with an elaborately carved doorway and a fresco of the *Assumption*, is downhill from the main square. Higher up on top of the village the apse of the partly ruined Aghios Georgios has a well-preserved *Platytera* (Virgin with Child symbolising the Incarnation).

Amari to Phourphouras

In nearby **Amari** (officially Nefs Amari; Αμάρι; *map p. 429, B2*) note the domed basilica of the Panaghia Kera with its Greek-cross plan and the impressive 15th-century coat of arms of the Kallergis family above the doorway. On the outskirts, the church of Aghia Anna has frescoes dated to 1225 in the apse, which is very early for Crete. The date is given as 6733, the year according to the Orthodox calendar, in use at the time. Its starting point was the creation of the world, taken to be the year 5508 BC.

For more churches stop at **Lambiotes** (Λαμπιώτες; *map p. 429, C2*), where the church of the Panaghia is signposted (it has remains of 14th-century frescoes) and Platania—

but it is probably time to go out into the fields for a change. According to Turland (*Flora of the Cretan Area*), in the plain of **Gious Kambos** northwest of the Kedros massif (*map p. 429, B2–B3*), the *Tulipa doerfleri* is endemic. This sterile variety of edible red-flowered tulip propagates by offsets and stolons (runners). It obviously prospers with the assistance of agriculture and ploughing; Turland has speculated whether it was introduced by Neolithic farmers as an undercrop, in case the main one failed.

On the approaches to Phourphouras, in the hamlet of **Ellinika**, just outside Vizari (*map p. 429, C3*), taking a side road towards the bottom of the valley, is the site of a Roman town; the best remains, though, belong to an early Christian basilica excavated in the 1950s and tentatively dated to the period just before the Arab conquest. Two Saracen coins were found in the destruction debris suggesting a 9th-century destruction date. The three-aisled construction with raised stylobates and small apses for the side aisles has an unusual plan, known from Bulgaria and Syria but not from Crete itself at such an early date. Evidence for a screen across the central aisle providing a spacious chancel (look for the slots to take the upright slabs), a font in the south aisle, floor tiling and the sheer size of the building suggests that at the end of the First Byzantine period, life was relatively prosperous in this remote valley, away from the troubled coastline. The basilica, built with rough boulders interspaced with fragmentary tiles, is a few minutes away from the main road and is always accessible.

In **Vizari** itself (Βιζάρι; *map p. 429, C3*) look out, as you come up from Ellinika to meet the main road, for the remains of a Venetian villa with fine windows and a small balcony. It belonged to the Saonazzi family. The arch in the front marks where the staircase to the first floor was. Somewhere hidden under the abundant vegetation is a sundial. The villa ended its life some 150 years ago as an oil factory and has been abandoned since.

Phourphouras (Φουρφουράς; *map p. 429, C3*) is one of the starting points for the ascent of Mt Ida, an 8-hr walk along the E4 past the Stoumbotos Prinos refuge to the very top at 2456m. Immediately south of the village, the church of Aghios Georgios has 14th-century frescoes with a fine Pantocrator. There the road enters the very end of the valley with grand views of the Libyan Sea, of the Mesara plain and the Asterousia range beyond.

Apodoulou

After a drive of some 10km on the slopes of Ida, the road reaches Apodoulou (Αποδούλου; *map p. 429, C3*) in an empty landscape. For a touch of romance stop at the very entrance to the village, where you will see the **ruins of a 19th-century mansion**. As the story goes, in the 1821 disturbances, a local girl, Kalitsa Psaraki, was abducted by Muslims who put her up for sale at Alexandria slave market. She was rescued by a Scotsman, Robert Hay, who was in Egypt drawing and recording antiquities. They were married in 1828 in Malta. When the couple returned to Crete, to the delight of her family, they built this house in her native village.

A sign leads higher up to **Aghios Georgios**, a single-nave church with 14th-century frescoes by Iereas Anastasios including a well-preserved figure on horseback. Above this fresco note a depiction of the Lion of St Mark in a different, hybrid style with pointed ears and powerful wings.

The main attraction of driving so far, however, are the **Minoan remains** investigated in the 1930s by Spyridon Marinatos, then by the Germans during the war and currently by a joint Greek and Italian team. The presence of Minoan activity here shows the importance of the location in controlling access to the south. There are two main sites: a necropolis and a settlement. The necropolis at Tournes, signed left from the village and dated to the early Postpalatial period has three impressive chamber tombs with long dromoi. The graves had been looted but excavators found larnakes, bronze weapons, jewels, a necklace with a Linear A inscription and even the remains of a wooden litter. The settlement, west of the village on the same road leading to the church above, 2km on, on the left and fenced, shows a long occupation from the Late Neolithic to the end of the Minoan period. The first investigations revealed a Neopalatial complex with cult area, as shown by the finds (gold and bronze double axes and a bull's-head rhyton). More recent excavations have uncovered older Protopalatial remains to the south, destroyed by earthquake. These include three buildings with evidence of upper storeys and extensive storage facilities. The presence of painted plaster and the quality of the masonry suggests that this was more than just an agricultural settlement.

SMILIANOS KAMBOS

Just after Apodoulou the road divides east to Kamares and Zaros and west to complete the valley circuit. Due south, Aghia Galini and the sea are only 10km away. In the village of **Aghia Paraskevi** (Αγία Παρασκευή; *map p. 429, C3*), the church of the Panaghia, on a rise in the centre of the village, will retain the interest of specialists. The incomplete fresco decoration, dated to 1516, is a fine example of the later developments of the Cretan School, both in its technique and composition. In the apse the figure of the *Platytera* (the symbol of the incarnation) is well preserved; the donor (a priest) and his wife are on the west wall. Further on, on the other side of the valley towards Mt Kedros (note the medieval bridge to the right of the modern one) the road winds its way northwest in the Gerakari direction. As the **war memorials** testify, the area was deeply scarred at the tail end of the German occupation, in August 1944, when villages were burnt and 164 locals shot. There may have been an element of revenge in the action, but according to historians this was a move to cow the guerrillas and ensure an orderly withdrawal of the occupying force.

Beyond Kardaki (Καρδάκι; *map p. 429, C3*), the ruined **church of Aghios Ioannis Theologos** is all that remains of the monastery at Photi. The frescoes are almost gone, but the architecture, with an unusual dome in the narthex, is worth a stop, especially since in its present state, it will not have a lock. The old stone road can still be made out behind it.

At **Gerakari** (Γερακάρι; *map p. 429, B2*), a village named after the Duke of Candia, Tomaso Geracari, the road crosses the E4: it is 12km to Spili and about 25 back to Rethymnon by the main road. For more churches and an alternative way back, take the Thronos direction. At **Elenes** (Ελένες; *map p. 429, B2*) the double-naved church of Aghios Nikolaos has 13th-century frescoes in a conservative, backward-looking style.

Three kilometres on at **Meronas** (Μέρωνας; *map p. 429, B2*), the three-aisled basilica church of the Panaghia stands at the end of the village to the right. The architectural details show Venetian influence but the church belonged to the Kallergis, a Cretan family with strong Byzantine connections. Their coat of arms appears twice: carved on the outside and painted on the inside. The frescoes are dated stylistically to the mid-14th century, with some unusual elements. Of particular interest are the scenes from the life of the Virgin at the west end, belonging to the Akathist Hymn to Mary, a part of the Orthodox Church's Lenten liturgy. The cycle, preserved complete at Roustika (*see p. 316*), is otherwise quite rare on the island.

PRACTICAL INFORMATION

GETTING AROUND

• **By car:** From Rethymnon the Amari Valley is only accessible at the turning signed 'Αμάρι' from the bypass. The road goes over a pass and then the valley opens up. The road is reasonable, though it does get narrow and winding. However, traffic is limited and there is time to admire the scenery.

The road to the Myli Gorge and Chromonastiri from Rethymnon is easier to find because it is well signed.

• **By bus:** From Rethymnon there is only a limited bus service to Amari and Chromonastiri. Map of services on www.bus-service-crete-ktel.com/maps4reth.html.

WHERE TO STAY & EAT

Accommodation is the Amari Valley is very limited. Few people seem to go there, not even the Cretans themselves.

Gerakari (*map p. 429, B2*)
€ **Despina**. At the beginning of the village coming up from the south on the right hand side. *T: 28330 51013; mobile 6978 110588.*
Phourphouras (*map p. 429, C3*)

€ **Windy Place**. Rooms and taverna on the roadside before the village. Ask Dina for *loukoumiades. T: 28330 41366; mobile 9638 056847.*
Thronos (*map p. 429, B2*)
€ **Aravanes**. Rooms and taverna. Some of the rooms are above the modern restaurant, others are in town in renovated old houses. The owner (who firmly believes that the water at Thronos is the best in Crete) makes his own wine and raki and guests can join in the fun and press the grapes if they come at the right season. *T: 28330 22760; mobile 6973 889036; info@aravanes.gr.*

LOCAL SPECIALITIES

In **Vizari**, Nikos Voskakis (*T: 28330 41061*) is a wood turner and has his workshop by the road on the edge of the village. He works olive wood, a particularly rewarding medium with a fine feel, a beautiful grain and a pleasant texture and makes boards, spoons, wine stands and turned items.

Kyria Despina at **Gerakari** runs a cottage industry with home-made Cretan delicacies including a powerful cherry brandy.

SOUTH OF RETHYMNON

Coast to coast it is barely 54km to Aghia Galini from Rethymnon on a good road, and a shorter drive (41km) to Plakias to the west, with several highlights on the way, beginning with the LM III cemetery at Armeni. Further on, a drive across the hills south of Vrysinas peak sanctuary, off the beaten track, leads to the early Christian basilica of Goulediana, 15km south of Rethymnon. The main road carries on east, on the western edge of Mt Kedros, to the popular resort of Aghia Galini. The sea is beyond yet another mountain range, with a few beaches accessible only by narrow, winding routes. Back north, 8km after Armeni, the road west leading to Plakias, the Kotsiphos Gorge and the Sphakia district beyond is signed for Selia. For Moni Preveli and the spectacular Kourtaliotikos Gorge, take the road due south 2km on.

The Minoan cemetery at Armeni

Dromos leading to one of the tombs at Armeni.

Armeni (Αρμένοι; *map p. 429, B2*) is some 8km from Rethymnon and signed to the right. (*Open Tues–Sun 8.30–3; bring a torch. A great attraction of the site is its peaceful setting in an oak wood with plenty of flowers. It is best enjoyed early in the morning before organised tours arrive with their busloads.*) It is a cemetery belonging to a settlement not yet identified. Excavations by Giannis Tzedakis began in 1969 and have so far revealed 211 rock-cut tombs of the 14th–13th centuries (the Postpalatial period). The rock itself is very hard, which makes the site an odd choice; on the other hand, this has greatly enhanced preservation. Tombs vary from simple small chambers to more elaborate structures with pillars and benches. They are approached by downward-sloping dromoi, occasionally with steps, and leading to an entrance closed in antiquity by large stone slabs. Some tombs are unfinished: only the dromos exists. A Minoan road ran through the cemetery, apparently separating smaller and larger tombs. Burials varied from plain, single inhumations with no grave goods to clay coffins (larnakes) and multiple burials with extravagant offerings, including stone vases, decorated pots, sealstones, bronze artefacts and jewellery. Of particular interest are the remains of a helmet of a type described by Homer (*Iliad X, 266*), made with 60 plates cut from boar's tusks. A quantity of broken pots (both coarse and fine ware) noted on a small paved area linked to a dromos by a channel has suggested cult practices. A selection of the larnakes, some decorated with double axes, sacred horns of consecration and scenes of ritual hunting and bulls, can be seen at Rethymnon museum. These may have been manufactured in the nearby kilns. By far the most interesting finds in the cemetery, though, are the skeletons themselves, amounting to some 500 individuals. Ongoing analysis of the remains has revealed details of their diet, which included little meat and plenty of carbohydrates, as well as an array of diseases such as bone cancer, spina bifida, arthritis, anaemia and brucellosis linked to the consumption of infected milk.

Over the hills to Goulediana

South of Armeni you have a choice. To the west is a fine Venetian fountain, to the east an early Christian basilica. The former, now dry, is at **Photinos** (Φωτεινός; *map p. 429, B2*), 4km south of Aghios Georgios, signed from the south end of Armeni, where the fine houses that Gerola admired 100 years ago are no more, on a reasonable road among oaks and olive trees. The fountain, or more precisely a spring chamber, has an ornamental column and a decoration of garlands, volutes and rosettes.

For **Goulediana** (Γουλεδιανά; *map p. 429, B2*) take the road to Kare. To the right was the site of the ancient city-state of Phalanna, birthplace of the peripatetic philosopher Phaeniades, according to Stephanos of Byzantium. Almost nothing is left above ground apart from the excavated remains of an early Christian basilica at Onythe, along a track signed from the far end of the village. The building was excavated by Platon in the 1950s. The three-aisled structure, which has been compared to North African early basilicas, with a possible baptistery to the north and an atrium to the south, is dated by its polychrome mosaic of elaborate geometric design (*covered at the time of writing*) to the 5th–6th century. A collection of bones in a pit sunk in the chancel has been interpreted as a foundation deposit, similar to the one found in Panormos (*see p. 283*).

Lambini and Spili

From Armeni the main road continues south to Spili (16km) with a recommended detour for **Lambini** (Λαμπινή; *map p. 429, B2*), to the left just before Myxorrouma, for the 14th-century church of the Panaghia, once the Episcopal church of the district of Aghios Vasileios, on a commanding position above the valley. The large building, dedicated to the Assumption of the Virgin, has a cruciform plan, unusually asymmetrical, with three aisles and a central dome decorated with blind arches also repeated on the outside at the end of the transverse vaults. Evidence for two layers of frescoes dating to the late 14th and beginning of the 15th century have been uncovered. In 1827 the church witnessed an atrocity when the Turks trapped the congregation inside and after killing the men, sold the women and children in Rethymnon.

Spili (Σπήλι; *map p. 429, B2*) is well ensconced in the centre of Crete and is an ideal base for exploring the countryside; the E4 passes through it on its way to the top of Mt Kedros to the southeast and Ida beyond. The village is well geared to the tourist trade with a choice of hotels and even a nightclub (the Rastoni, on the hill above the village to the north). The through road has been cleverly repaved so that it feels and looks like a pedestrianised area, encouraging drivers to slow down. There is no shortage of water here, as the Venetian fountain with 19 lion's-head spouts in the main square shows. Just by looking at it one feels refreshed. At the south end of Spili the cemetery church of the Sotiros Christos has the remains of 14th-century paintings, including a representation of Aghios Mamas, protector of shepherds, shown with a crook and a young goat. A short detour to **Mourne** to the west (Μουρνέ; *map p. 429, B3*) leads to another church with 14th-century frescoes featuring the martyrdom of St George.

Drimiskos and Akoumia

At Kambos Kissou go cross country (10km) for the church of the Panaghia at **Drimiskos** (Δρίμισκος; *map p. 429, B3*). The church is in the cemetery of the semi-abandoned village; inside are frescoes dated 1317 and attributed to Mikhail Veneris. The Archangel Michael on horseback is still there but the inscription that Gerola saw in the early 20th century, mentioning the Melissino family of Byzantine extraction, has vanished. From here the road continues south to the sea at Aghia Photini. Alternatively, you can return to the main road southeast along the valley between Mt Kedros (1776m) to the left and Siderondas (1177m) to the right; side roads give access to the sea at Triopetra and Aghios Pavlos. At **Akoumia** (Ακούμια; *map p. 429, B3*), before you reach the coast, the church of the Christos Sotiros is Byzantine in style, with alterations to accommodate the Latin rite. Visitors are welcomed by a 14th-century fresco by the entrance representing the donors in their Sunday best, in a clump of pomegranate trees.

Aghia Galini

Peace ends at Aghia Galini (Αγία Γαλήνη; *map p. 429, C3*) unless you come here out of season. The present village is comparatively new, having been founded in 1884 by people from Melambes up in the hills. The site, however, has a long history of occupation. In antiquity it was the port of Syvritos in the Amari Valley and was known as Soulia. The goddess Artemis had a temple here and the church of Galini Christos, belonging to the monastery of Aghios Galenos (after which the present resort is named) was built on its ruins. When Buondelmonti visited in 1415, he reported stone columns of all hues but there is nothing left now.

Aghia Galini was the first spot on the south coast to be developed as a popular holiday resort, and it shows. Accommodation (including a long-established campsite) is comparatively abundant but not enough for the crowds that descend here in the summer, and the nightlife may prove too much. Beaches are in short supply but there are daily boat trips to the Paximadia islands, Aghios Pavlos and Preveli. Out of season it is a different story: Aghia Galini is a good spot to explore the southern coast from. Phaistos is not far and on a good road. Apodoulou and the Amari Valley are only 10km to the north. Bird-watchers will find a visit to the reed beds at the river mouth very rewarding.

PLAKIAS & ENVIRONS

South of Armeni the road to Plakias runs west through Aghios Vasileios. From Aghios Ioannis it follows the **Kotsiphos Gorge** (*map p. 429, A2*), a good place for birds, though Lammergeiers may prove elusive. According to bird watchers' reports there are only four breeding pairs of Lammergeiers in the southeastern Mediterranean. Your best chance of seeing one face to face is to have a drink at the bar of the Taverna Aravanes at Thronos (*see p. 306*), but that specimen, impressive though it is, is stuffed. Rock thrushes, ravens and chukars are more likely sightings.

At **Plakias** (Πλακιάς; *map p. 429, A3*) note that the north–south direction of the valley behind it means that when the north wind (the meltemi) strikes, it can cause problems. Otherwise the place is excellent as a base, with beaches in the bay itself and to the east at Damnoni, and those of Ammoudi and Schinaria further east on the little headland. Serious walkers can use Plakias as a base to explore the empty uplands to the west, from Rodakino in the Alones direction along the E4 route. For less strenuous walking, Lance Chilton's *Walks in the Plakias Area* will be useful and inspiring. Behind Plakias there is a path to the Kotsiphos Gorge and a possible 2-hr walk to Preveli Monastery (*see below*) via Lefkogeia and Giannou, with a ferry service to get back.

On the way to Preveli, the descent of the dramatic **Kourtaliotikos Gorge** (flowers, birds, waterfalls) is highly recommended—but at the right time, avoiding holidays and weekends. The place has become too well known for its own good. The starting point is the white chapel of Aghios Nikolaos by the stream bed north of Asomatos, after the road coming from the west bends to follow the ravine. A fenced path leads to the chapel. According to a local legend, the abundance of water is due to a local saint, Nicholas the Kourtaliot. He struck the rock and was immediately rewarded with seven gushing springs creating attractive waterfalls and, lower down, large pools when the river joins the Megapotamos and reaches the sea at Preveli Beach through the lower gorge. The trip needs some planning, as is always the case when walking down gorges. There are guided tours for groups from Plakias (half-day) and from Rethymnon (whole day); alternatively, one can get to the beach by boat and ascend the gorge in its lower section along pools fringed with palm trees.

At **Asomatos** (Ασώματος; *map p. 429, B3*) Papa Mikhailis has opened his family house (*open daily 10–3*) showing a familiar collection of icons, pithoi, old pictures, war memorabilia, embroidery and the inevitable raki distillery. The old house itself, set around a pretty courtyard, is perhaps the best exhibit.

PREVELI MONASTERY

Preveli (Πρέβελη; *map p. 429, B3*) can be reached from Rethymnon by taking the south turn from the main road after about 23km in the Asomatos direction; from Plakias there is a choice of ferries or the overland route via Lefkogeia and continuing until it turns south to follow the gorge. Here the Kourtaliotis, fed by the miraculous springs (*see above*), is joined by other streams to form one of the few perennial rivers in Crete, aptly named the Megapotamos (the 'Great River'). Two kilometres on, an arched Ottoman bridge (built in the mid-19th century) comes into view, followed by the ruins of Kato Preveli.

Originally there were two monasteries on the promontory here, jutting into the Libyan Sea, both linked to the local Prevelis family. They were known as *kato monastiri* (the lower monastery, dedicated to St John the Baptist) and *piso monastiri* (the monastery behind, dedicated to St John the Evangelist). The former is now just a pile of romantic ruins. The latter, known as Moni Preveli, overlooking the equally famous palm-fringed beaches, is one of the top tourist attractions in Crete.

HISTORY OF MONI PREVELI

Rumours that the monastery is a Venetian foundation are unconfirmed, but there probably was a monastic community in the area, taking advantage of its relative isolation. Whatever there was, it was destroyed by the Turks and promptly rebuilt. The community prospered thanks to its stavropegial status (meaning they were answerable only to the Patriarchate in Constantinople) and the protection afforded by the Islamic rulers in Crete. Over time the monastery spread its influence across the whole region and became a centre of learning and of active resistance against Ottoman occupation. In 1821 Abbot Melchisedek Tsouderos led a group of insurgents in the war of independence and later, in the 1866 rebellion, the monastery played an important role in relief operations. That was just after the Arkadi episode (*see p. 282*) and supplies were flooding in to help the rebel cause: guns, ammunition and all-important boot leather (Crete's rough terrain is not kind to footwear). They landed at Preveli Beach, with the monks organising transport and the evacuation of the wounded and of some women and children. The community was cast in the same role later, in July 1941, when the retreating Allied forces had to be evacuated to Egypt. The mission had been entrusted to Lt Cdr Francis Pool, who landed by submarine at Preveli Beach. After he contacted the elderly abbot, Agathangelos Lagouvardos, the monastery became an assembly point for refugees, enabling the evacuation of British, Australian and New Zealand troops to proceed. This explains why there is a Prevelly in Western Australia. Things did not go smoothly, however, and the Germans got wind of it. As a result, the abbot had to go into hiding and was eventually evacuated to Cairo, where he swore in the new Greek government in exile. He never saw Crete again.

Kato Preveli

The site is now fenced and cannot be visited; it can only be viewed from the road (*limited parking*). Even from a distance and in its poignant, dilapidated state (though some restoration work is ongoing) the monastery has plenty of charm, probably more than its thriving counterpart.

The complex, set in a rectangular courtyard with the church of Aghios Ioannis Prodromos at the centre, had farming installations and workshops and was mainly used by younger monks and civilians, a reminder that monasteries were self sufficient, autono-

Piso Preveli: the monks' quarters.

mous communities playing also an economic role in society. At some point in 1821, there were 14,000 kg of oil stored here. We know this because it all went up in a blaze, greatly contributing to the destruction. By the north entrance, the kitchen has a monumental chimney dated 1816. The oldest remains are the animal pens and the huge stores with an olive press. Workshops were located near the southern entrance, with a long dining room opposite. After the occupying German force took away all the livestock and devastated the buildings in the Second World War, the monastery never recovered.

Piso Preveli

The monastery (*open March–May 8–7, June–Oct 8–1.30 & 3.30–6*) was built by Abbot Prevelis in the 17th century in a bid for greater security, at the back of a hill visible only from the sea but not easily accessible directly from that direction. To this site the abbot moved the library, icons and other valuables from Kato Preveli. In its present state the monastery, set in a very barren landscape, is heavily restored. Its situation on the hillside means that it is positioned at different levels on vaults and terraces. The cemetery is just outside the entrance, with an ossuary in the shape of a church. In the centre of the courtyard stands the church itself, completed in 1837 and incorporating elements of the previous building, namely the icons with scenes from the Old Testament now set in a splendidly carved iconostasis. The building has not been altered much since except for the marble door frames and the Byzantine double eagle, put in place in 1911. Opposite the church, the two-storey building in Neoclassical style was renovated in 1903 to welcome the new high commissioner for the independent Cretan state. Older buildings include the original bakery, with a reputed daily output of 800 loaves. Monks and apparently nuns as well (mainly the monks' female relatives) occupied the cells bristling with chimneys on the north side. Water was supplied by a fountain, still in use and bearing an inscription (in palindromic form) dated 15th June 1701, which translates: 'Cleanse my transgressions, not merely my face'.

The monastery's new museum is in the converted stables. It displays icons, ecclesiastical vestments in the local silk embroidery tradition, a fine painted wooden ciborium for Good Friday celebrations, vessels and other memorabilia. From the more recent past comes a pair of silver candlesticks presented in gratitude by the British government for the monastery's role in the Second World War. A commemorative plaque in the courtyard provides further tribute.

The monastery also breeds peacocks. They are kept in a fenced yard just below the museum and account for the inhuman noises occasionally piercing the air.

Preveli Beach

As a resort, Preveli Beach is quite scenic with a touch of the exotic: palm trees, oleanders in full bloom in the right season, a lagoon and the river flowing to the sandy shore. It used to be known only to the hippies, who flocked here in the '70s and lived in huts made of palm leaves. Now the hippies are gone but you will not feel alone. In the summer, boatloads come from Aghia Galini and Plakias. You can join them or choose to approach by land, and get a view from above, which is quite stunning. This involves driving to the car park before Piso Preveli and climbing down the steep steps (*about 30mins; the return uphill will be tougher*). Alternatively, to get to the sea by car from the Ottoman bridge (*see p. 310 above*), take the unmade track marked 'Preveli Limni' on the left bank of the Megapotamos, using the modern crossing next to the arched bridge north of the deserted monastery. The road crosses another bridge over a tributary and eventually, after c. 15mins, reaches a cove marked by the ugly concrete shell of a failed development. Here are some facilities as well as parking. The steps to Preveli Beach (some 10mins away) are signposted. From the beach it possible walk up to the lower reaches of the Kourtaliotis Gorge or hire a pedal boat to explore a very short stretch of the palm-fringed river up to the first pool.

PRACTICAL INFORMATION

GETTING AROUND

• **By car:** The main provincial road cuts across the landscape to Aghia Galini (50km), Plakias (36km), Preveli (24km) and Rodakino (40km) on a good tarmac road all the way.

• **By bus:** From Rethymnon there are frequent services to Spili and Aghia Galini; more limited services run to Plakias, Preveli and Rodakino. A bus connects Plakias to Chora

Sphakion via Rodakino and Frangokastello. Map of services on www.bus-service-crete-ktel.com/maps4reth.html.
• **By sea:** Boat services run in summer from Plakias and Aghia Galini to Preveli.

WHERE TO STAY

Aghia Galini (*map p. 429, C3*)
Aghia Galini offers a number of places to stay. €€ **Irini Mare** is a good holiday place (*T: 28320 91488; www.irinimare.com*). Set back from the sea at the foot of the hill is €€ **Glaros** (*T: 28320 91151; www.glaros-agiagalini. com*). Cheaper alternatives include € **Adonis**, on the quiet side of the village, with a garden (*T: 28320 91333 or 91250*) and € **Fevro**, not far from the bus terminal (*T: 28320 91275*).
Kato Rodakino (*map p. 429, A3*)
€€ **Korakas Beach Rooms**. With Vardis's special breakfast on the beach in his taverna. *Open March–Oct. T: 28320 32123; mobile 6945 523183.*
€ **Studio Akropolis**. Inland from Koraka beach, on the hillside. *T: 28320 31532 or 31473; akropolis.kreta-sun.com.*
Plakias (*map p. 429, A3*)
There is plenty of choice of places to stay in Plakias. See www.plakias-filoxenia.gr/plakias. htm.

Preveli (*map p. 429, B3*)
€€ **Villa Despina**. Between Preveli and Asomatos. Away from the sea but it does have a pool. They normally rent the whole villa, which can take up to 12 people, but are prepared to rent out rooms individually if they are free. *T: 28320 32021; www.villa-creta.gr.*
€ **Preveli Rooms**. Rooms and taverna situated five minutes' walk away from Preveli Beach at Drismiskiano Ammoudi, in a peaceful location. *T: 28310 58696 mobile 6945 704654 or 6947 523575; www.interkriti.net/ hotel/preveli/prevelirooms.*
Spili (*map p. 429, B2*)
Spili is fully set up for the tourist market and can be an excellent base to explore the region from. One option is the € **Heracles Pension**, where the owner is a geologist—which might come handy for discussing some finer points (*T: 6973 667495; www.crete-connections.com/ budget-accommodation-crete/Heracles_Pension. htm*). € **Costas Inn** (*T: 28320 22040*) and € **Green Hotel** (*T: 28320 22225*) both offer simple accommodation and good value.

BOOKS & FURTHER READING

Lance Chilton's *Walks in the Plakias Area* has 17 described itineraries.

WEST OF RETHYMNON

West of Rethymnon there is the usual choice of two roads: the new one by the coast, ideal if you want to travel quickly. If you want to linger, the old road offers fine wooded landscapes and unspoilt countryside all the way to the ancient city of Lappa.

THE COAST ROAD

This stretch is almost an uninterrupted beach all the way to Georgioupolis, though swimmers should beware of strong currents. Here and there reed beds may be of interest to bird-watchers in the right season. On the way, 6km from Rethymnon the road crosses the **Gerani bridge**. Below are a cave (*signed but not open to the public*), discovered during roadworks in 1967, and a beautiful beach. The cave was used as a sanctuary in Neolithic times: fine bone and obsidian tools are exhibited at Rethymnon museum. From the earlier Pleistocene levels, when Crete had no human occupation, came evidence of ancient fauna, including an endemic variety of the dwarf giant deer. It had short limbs and simplified antlers and occupied an ecological niche similar to today's Cretan wild goat.

ANCIENT FAUNA ON CRETE

Because of its geographic isolation, diverse ecosystems and topography, the island of Crete is home to a diverse and in some cases unique fauna, such as the Cretan Shrew and the Cretan Spiny Mouse, not to mention a whole collection of invertebrates, many of which are endemic. In earlier times, according to the fossil record, the situation was even more striking. Crete has also always had a particularly 'unbalanced' fauna with no large carnivores. This, however, did not encourage herbivores to grow very large as it did not pay to be too big and spend the whole day looking for food: the Cretan elephant, or according to recent DNA analysis the Cretan mammoth, was the size of a bullock. There was also probably a general lack of muddy rivers and lagoons: the Cretan hippo had long legs and was not aquatic. Deer were safe from predators: their bones show an adaptation to better jumping at the expense of faster running. Other species took the opposite route and feasted on the rich natural resources, producing giant rodents and insectivores.

Today they are all extinct, though the cause is still poorly understood. It has been suggested that humans hunted them to extinction, but there is no evidence of interaction between early Neolithic settlers and these indigenous species. Perhaps they were already extinct before the first settlers arrived; alternatively it was the introduction of domesticated species, coupled with the loss of habitat due to agriculture, that tilted the balance against them in an already fragile equilibrium.

THE INTERIOR

Roustika

The Old Road is worth a drive, just for the view and the flowers. The most interesting places to visit are even further inland. At the Gerani bridge a road branches south to Aghios Andreas, providing a link south to the Old Road. Two kilometres west take the direction to Roustika (Ροὐστικα; *map p. 429, A2*) via Kalonyktis for the **Monastery of Profitis Ilias**. The three-aisled domed monastery is signed from the village. A Venetian foundation, the monastery grew in power, wealth and influence during Turkish rule owing to its privileged status, which made it answerable directly to the Patriarch in Constantinople. It was involved in the struggle for independence and suffered accordingly. It still houses some fine 18th-century icons. The bellcote is dated 1644 and bears the name of the abbot Metrofanio Vlasto Markomanopoulo. The three bronze bells are decorated with images of the Virgin and of St George and the nameplate of Santino de Regis, who manufactured them in Milan between 1634 and 1636.

In the village the double-naved **church of the Panaghia and the Sotiros Christos** will be of interest to specialists for its frescoes, dated by donor inscription to 1381–82. The iconographical arrangement shows strong Western influence. Note on the triumphal arch above the sanctuary the scene of the Throne of Mercy, where God the Father, represented as an older man, holds the crucified Son with the Holy Ghost represented as a dove between them. (Traditionally in Byzantine churches the Trinity is represented by a scene of the Feast of Abraham, a reference to God's visit to Abraham at Mamre. The text (*Genesis 18, 1–8*) states that the Lord came, but Abraham saw three men. Christians take this a revelation of the Trinity.) Other aspects of the church decoration are more strictly within the Byzantine tradition. There is, for instance, a rendition of the complete cycle of the Hymn to Mary, the great 24-stanza Akathist Hymn (*see also p. 306*), so named (*a–kathisis*; 'without a seat') because the faithful were required to stand while reciting it.

Aghios Konstantinos

From Roustika a minor road leads to Argyroupolis via Aghios Georgios and Zouridi. On the way you drive across the fief of the Barozzi family, who had their country villa (which is no more) in **Aghios Konstantinos** (Άγιος Κωνσταντίνος; *map p. 429, A2*). However, 2km out of the village, at Boutzonaria, it is still possible to see the **Barozzi Fountain**, set in the midst of luscious greenery and up to the recent past a choice place for village picnics. When he visited in the 19th century, Robert Pashley was able to read the Latin inscription of 1509 stating that the fountain had been erected by a Francesco Barozzi 'for the enjoyment of his family and friends'.

Another member of the same family, also by the name of Francesco, came to prominence later in the 16th century as the founder, in 1562, of the Accademia dei Vivi in Rethymnon, an association to promote learning and self improvement, one of three in the island. A man of letters, he was well known for his scholarship (he was already lecturing in philosophy, mathematics and astronomy at Padua University at the tender age of 22) and for his huge private library. He lived at Aghios Konstantinos between 1560 and 1590. In 1587 he was investigated by the Inquisition and found guilty of black magic and witchcraft. Extracts of the proceedings show that he had confessed to seeing ghosts, mingling with local witches, trying to become invisible and consorting with the Devil to improve rainfall. Though none of his magic appeared to be working very well, and one of his mills was actually damaged by too much rain, he was still fined 50 gold ducats to be paid the bishopric of Crete and another 50 to the bishop of Rethymnon.

ARGYROUPOLIS & ANCIENT LAPPA

The settlement of Argyroupolis (Αργυρούπολη; *map p. 429, A2*) developed on top of Lappa, a Doric city-state. Situated in a valley controlling access to the White Mountains and yet with good communications to the north coast, Lappa, founded according to tradition by Agamemnon, flourished in Hellenistic times. It is credited with two harbours: Amphimalla, near modern Georgioupolis to the north, and Phoinix, west of Sphakia to the south. The *polis* was destroyed by the invading Roman army in 68 BC, but recovered a few decades later when it elected to back Octavian over Mark Anthony in the civil war and was appropriately rewarded after the Battle of Actium. Lappa prospered, becoming a bishopric in 457, one of the earliest in Crete. It was sacked by the Arabs in the 9th century and when it was resettled was simply called Polis, becoming Argyroupolis—a reference to the silver mines in the area—in 1822. The chief attraction of the place these days is the abundant water: a perennial spring emerges from a cliff, with a main outlet through a cave chapel. In the past it fed the Roman baths and a string of mills; today it supplies about a quarter of Rethymnon's water. Visitors come here from all over Crete to enjoy the cool, the lush greenery and the local trout. Tavernas have sprung up in the river valley where once the mills operated.

The upper village

Argyroupolis is set on a precipitous slope roughly on three levels, all separately accessible by car. Locals cheerfully drive between them but this is not a wise bet for an outsider: it is better to explore on foot. You can park in the plateia of the upper village, where there are vestigial remains of **Roman Lappa**. Very little survives above ground because modern Argyroupolis sits on top of it. Moreover, much building material was reused and can be seen as spolia in later buildings. In the upper village, a fine 3rd-century mosaic is on display under a canopy. The shop nearby under an archway, selling local herb and avocado products, doubles as an information centre and provides a free a plan of the village. After the archway is a rather derelict part of town, a collection of dwellings that once clustered around **Villa Clodio** (an alternative setting, according to some commentators, for the Alikianos feud; *see p. 360*). The villa itself, built on Roman remains, still retains a fine portal with polygonal columns and Gothic capitals. The lintel bears the inscription 'Omnia mundi fumus et umbra' (the world is but smoke and shadow).

The **Zografaki Folklore Museum** (*open daily 10–7*), near the rooms of the same name (past the church in the upper plateia) is set out in the private house of the Zografaki family. The museum is a treasure trove of traditional Cretan artefacts, tools and household equipment. It has an interesting collection of clothing and embroidered soft furnishings. The owner, who runs the taverna and the rooms nearby, will be only too happy to give you a guided tour in English.

The lower village

A maze of steps and narrow alleys eventually leads to the lower level where the restaurants are. When in doubt, follow the noise of the water. If you are going by car, look for signs to Asi Gonia.

Traditionally mills were built in pairs, with two presses and a shared catering and accommodation block for mill hands. A 16th-century grinding and fulling mill can be seen, but not visited, near Phaistos. In Argyroupolis, the **Palaios Mylos restaurant** incorporates the remains of such an arrangement, though inside only one olive press can be seen (the other was damaged beyond repair). Here the olives, in a woven sack, would be pressed for oil, the residue was used for animal feed and fuel. The water was brought to the mill via a conduit made of interlocking stone rings. One of these can be seen set upright in the restaurant's garden, looking like a piece of modern sculpture.

Waterfall at Argyroupolis, in the lower village, where the grinding and fulling mills once stood.

Below the restaurant, a chapel has marble capitals and columns which have been attributed to a temple to Poseidon. The building next to it is a crumbling Venetian fulling mill. Fulling was used to close the weave in woollen cloth to make it thick and waterproof and suitable for shepherds' cloaks in order to afford protection in any environment. Normally the cloth would shrink by about a third, becoming quite heavy and dense. This was achieved by soaking the cloth in an appropriate mixture to remove any grease and oils and then pounding it with wooden hammers. Here you can see the hammers and part of the mechanism. At the Zografaki folklore museum (*see above*) you can see and feel the cloth. Higher up on the left are very overgrown remains of the **Roman baths**.

Chapel of the Five Virgins

The area around Argyroupolis is dotted with rock tombs. Of particular interest is the cluster around the

Rock-cut tombs at the Chapel of the Five Virgins.

chapel of the Five Holy Virgins on the *kalderimi* off the road (*right; signed* 'Προς ι.ν. πέντε παρθένων') towards Kato Poros. Down the first hill the road crosses a *kalderimi* following the old Roman road. Leave the car and follow it downhill to the necropolis. The chapel is surrounded by tombs cut in the flat, even limestone. Lower down by an old plane tree, believed to be one of the most ancient in the island, is an idyllic picnic spot with a gushing fountain. On the first Tuesday after Easter the chapel is the scene of an ancient festival connected to the moving of the flocks to the high summer pastures. Starting about mid-morning, the sheep arrive; they are milked and blessed by the *papas*, while another *papas* officiates in the chapel. The faithful bring a special sweet-tasting bread with a topping of seeds and almonds while the milk is boiled, curdled and turned into soft cheese. At the end of the service, sometimes in the early afternoon, when all the sheep have been milked and there is no more gossip to go round, the fresh cheese is shared.

MYRIOKEPHALA & ASI GONIA

The uplands to the south are very much off the beaten track and sparsely populated: they will certainly reward bird-watchers and botanists. Walkers can cross them via the E4 from Kato Poros all the way to Rodakino, past Alones. By car, an excursion (10km) to **Myriokephala** (Μυριοκέφαλα; *map p. 429, A2*) is recommended. The former monastic church of the Panaghia, signed downhill from the village, is one of many foundations by Aghios Ioannis Xenos, the Cretan Evangelist (*see p. 166*). According to the *Typika*, the document relating to the rules and foundation of this monastery, he erected it on top of a Greek building and brought the furnishings for it all the way from Byzantium. The domed cruciform structure, dated to the 11th century, has frescoes from the Second Byzantine period that are among the earliest on the island. The dome, the sanctuary and the south cross-arm still have fragments of frescoes contemporary with the building. Later works include four scenes from the Passion of Christ (in the west cross-arm) and a remarkable *Entry into Jerusalem*, presented as a triumphal scene. The date is the end of the 12th century, and the linear style shows no Venetian influence.

Asi Gonia

The best way out of Myriokephala is through a fine stretch of panoramic winding road which follows the E4 trail on the edge of the White Mountains for 13km north to Asi Gonia (Ασή Γωνιά; *map p. 429, A2*). The town, just across the border in Chania province, has a special place in the history of Cretan resistance—to any occupier. It is said that at the time of Ottoman domination, no Turk ever lived here; the locals were always in control of the gorge, the only access to the village. The 1867 revolution was declared here. Asi Gonia is also the hometown of George Psychoundakis, an emblematic figure of Cretan resistance to German occupation. Originally a shepherd, he turned messenger, liaising between the British and the Cretan resistance. *The Cretan Runner*, translated by Patrick Leigh Fermor, is a colourful account of his adventures.

With independence and freedom now secured, Asi Gonia today concentrates on its other favourite occupation: sheep. If you happen to visit on St George's Day, here St George Galatas, 'St George the Milkman' (April 23rd unless it falls in Holy Week), you will be treated to a splendid 'Blessing of the Sheep' involving the arrival of several hundreds of animals, with their owners dressed in their Sunday best and the ladies in traditional costume. A session of 'speed milking' follows to musical accompaniment. The milk is offered to visitors and after the blessing, the flocks move on to their summer pastures on the White Mountains, amid a symphony of jangling bells.

PRACTICAL INFORMATION

GETTING AROUND

• **By car:** The E75 offers a quick getaway from Rethymnon along the coast to the west; there is not much to see, so there is no point in lingering. The inland road is winding and slow but gives you more opportunity to enjoy the countryside. For Argyroupolis, take the south turn at Episkopi. When you get there you have the choice of sticking to the low road and continuing to Asi Gonia (this takes you past the turning for the old mills) or taking the climb for the upper village and parking in the plateia. Argyroupolis stretches between the two roads on the hillside.

• **By bus:** From Rethymnon there are frequent services on the coastal road. Limited service inland to Argyroupolis, Roustika and Myriokephala. Map of services on www.bus-service-crete-ktel.com/maps4reth.html.

WHERE TO STAY

Argyroupolis (*map p. 429, A2*)
€€ **Villa Enatha**. Accommodation with a touch of luxury in a renovated old house. *T: 28310 81361 or 28979; mobile 6947 328687; villaenatha@greekhotel.com.*
€ **Zografakis Family Rooms**. Rooms to rent in the house of the owner of the folklore museum, with unreliable hot water but an excellent breakfast. The taverna serves good wholesome traditional Cretan food made by Kyria Zografakis herself—and she likes to please her guests. *T: 28310 81269; www.ezografakis.gr.*
€ **Argyroupoli Rent Rooms**. On the low road on the way to Asi Gonia. *Seasonal opening. T: 28310 81148; mobile 6974 308995.*
Roustika (*map p. 429, A2*)
€€ **Abelos**. Traditional hotel occupying two restored old houses, with pool, in a pretty village in an area that is otherwise short of accommodation. *T: 28310 91404; www.abelos.gr.*

WHERE TO EAT

Argyroupolis (*map p. 429, A2*)
There are a number of tavernas in the upper village serving traditional Cretan food; for trout try the places low down on the way to Asi Gonia.
€ **Palaios Mylos**. The 'Old Mill' combines an interesting setting beside a boisterous waterfall and mill stream, with special dishes like wild goat. Simple *mezedes* also available. An excellent place for lunch on a fine day. *T: 28310 81209; restaurantcrete.tripod.com.*

BOOKS & FURTHER READING

The Cretan Runner by George Psychoundakis (translated and with an introduction by Patrick Leigh Fermor) tells one man's story of his experiences during the German occupation of the island in the Second World War. Psychoundakis was born at Asi Gonia.

CHANIA PROVINCE

Chania province, on the west shores of Crete, offers a variety of contrasting land-scapes, with the highest massif in the island, the White Mountains, snow-capped half the year, often dominating the view from a distance. On the north coast, next to the Akrotiri peninsula which closes the immense anchorage of Souda Bay, Chania town is a bustling, sophisticated place, an excellent base for getting around. Beyond the mountains in the rugged west, mass tourism gently peters out and visitors will be rewarded with unspoiled landscapes. On the White Mountains tourists congregate in the National Samaria Park, plying the trek down to the Libyan Sea, though this is by no means the only gorge on offer. The Imbros Gorge to the east may be shorter but is no less dramatic and is as good a place for birds and flora.

In the southwest the district of Selinos (an old Venetian name) is an area of wooded valleys with plane and sweet chestnut trees; to the east of it, the district of Sphakia is still a self-contained community hemmed in by the White Mountains to the north and the Libyan Sea to the south. There is a road up the valley but it is a comparatively recent de-velopment and at the time of writing it was in pretty bad shape. For a long time the best form of communication along the south coast was the sea. And so it is still, with a ferry service linking resorts from Chora Sphakion all the way to the island of Elaphonisi.

Alternative bases for exploring the countryside and the antiquities (Byzantine church-es and monasteries, not so many Minoan remains but plenty of Greek and Roman ones) include Kissamos on the north coast and Sphakia and Palaiochora in the south.

The whole province is ideal for ramblers. The E4 walking route starts in the ferry harbour west of Kissamos; it then winds its way along the west and south coasts ex-ploring landscapes and places not always accessible to drivers. A route meanders in-land to pick up the Samaria Gorge descent from the *xyloscalo* and continues east into Rethymnon province. Side branches enable experienced and well-equipped walkers to explore the high desert on the White Mountains.

CHANIA

Chania (Χανιά; *map p. 428, C1–C2*), or more correctly in the plural, Ta Chania, also written Hania and Khania, is Crete's second city and offers visitors a graceful blend of Venetian, Turkish and Neoclassical architecture in spite of the ravages inflicted on it at the time of the Battle of Crete. The centre of the old town is lively and attractive: it makes a superb place to base oneself, though perhaps not in the height of summer. Besides the architecture, the city offers a clutch of excellent museums, some of them, like the archaeological and the folklore museums, housed in fine old buildings. For a swim, one must go out of town to Akrotiri or aim for the beaches on the west coast. Souda Bay to the east is a military zone and access is restricted.

HISTORY OF CHANIA

Present Chania, anciently Kydonia, began as Minoan settlement. The place name Ku-do-ni-ja appears in a Linear B tablet from Knossos and may be a tribute to the local quinces (*kydoni* = quince) or a derivation from a Persian word meaning 'guesthouse' (an alternative, somewhat unkind, explanation suggests that the name owes something to the Greek work for a cabbage patch). Excavations in Plateia Aghias Aikaterinis on Kastelli Hill east of the port, conducted since 1967 by a team of Swedish and Greek archaeologists, have uncovered occupation going back to the late Neolithic. Urbanism was already present in the early LM I period. Remains of four or five houses set around a large square were found in the area. These had several rooms, some with frescoes, flagstone paving and traces of a monumental entrance. Evidence of LM I occupation was ascertained in neighbouring areas and the discovery of a very large cache of Linear A tablets in Odos Katre prompted speculation that there may have been a palace there. Evidence of a palatial building was also uncovered in Splantzia at Odos Daskalogianni, where six rooms with a lustral basin, stone-slab floors and frescoes imitating marble came to light.

After the catastrophe of c.1450 BC the town was rebuilt and it peaked in LM III. Chania's products are recognised at Knossos, on Santorini, and as far away as Cyprus. The cemetery expanded considerably around the settlement. The subsequent history of the town is difficult to map as there are very few architectural remains and only the odd representation, such as the frieze in the local archaeological museum showing the façade of a temple and the statue of a goddess surrounded by archers. The abundance of ceramics and the testimonies of ancient writers, however, show that life and prosperity continued well into the Roman period. In 69 BC the Roman consul Metellus defeated the Cretans and conquered Chania (then called Cydonia), to which he granted the privileges of an independent city-state. Cydonia minted its own coins until the 3rd century. The First Byzantine period and the Arab rule that followed are poorly documented archaeologically. During the former, Christianity spread and the town was the seat of a bishop. During the latter, the Christian population was persecuted and moved to the mountains. The Byzantine Empire retook the city in 961 and held it until 1204. The Byzantines began to fortify it against another Arab invasion using materials from the ancient buildings of the area.

After the Venetian takeover of the island, the city was briefly in the hands of the Genoese, but when the Venetians reasserted control Chania was chosen as the seat of the rector (local administrator) and flourished as the commercial centre of a fertile agricultural region. The town was divided into 90 *cavallerie*, allocated to Venetian colonists with the specific obligation to rebuild the town. The walls of Kastelli (the hill was known by then as Castelvecchio, the 'Old Castle') were repaired. A rector's palace and a cathedral were built within the walls while the harbour with the arsenals, the loggia and the Jewish quarter remained outside. Chania developed into the second town of the Kingdom of Candia.

In the mid-16th century, in response to the raids of the pirate Kheir ed-Din Barbarossa, the town was fortified according to plans by Michele Sanmicheli, the architect and military engineer from Verona who also worked at Rethymnon and Herakleion. Operations began in 1538 and were completed by the end of the century, although with numerous imperfections. The Roman theatre, still in existence in 1583 (Onorio Belli saw it), was demolished to provide building material for the fortifications. The new wall followed the contemporary defensive principles of bastioned fortifications and formed a quadrangle parallel to the shore enclosing the harbour but had no sea wall. The total area of the town was greatly enlarged and the population now numbered some 8,000. The old fort of Kastelli fell into disuse; walls and towers were gradually built over as the need for residential space increased. Work was also carried out to improve the harbour and reinforce the breakwater. Seventeen dockyards (*arsenali*) were built to service shipping, while the water supply system was improved by the construction of reservoirs and the extension of the aqueduct. Under Venetian influence the town acquired a new name, La Canea, and to some it was the 'Venice of the Orient'. The community prospered both materially (the number of palaces in the old town in 1610 totalled an impressive 97) and culturally, with a gradual spreading of European influence. This was particularly true of icon painters, some of whom in the early 17th century were aware of the work of Flemish engravers and incorporated it into the traditions of the Cretan School (*see box overleaf*). When the Venetians were driven from the island many of these artists emigrated either to Venice or the Venice-dominated Ionian islands.

In August 1645 the Turks seized Chania after a siege of two short months, showing that the defences left much to be desired. Indeed the ditches were too narrow, there were many unprotected stretches and the bastions were the wrong shape. The town became the seat of the Turkish pasha and a number of churches were converted into mosques. The church of the Aghii Anargyri became the seat of an Orthodox bishop. When Pashley visited in 1834 he found the place very peaceful. The locals had adapted to the new situation and three quarters of them had converted to Islam, an expedient way of paying lower taxes and generally being allowed to get on with their lives. Cretan cities converted more readily than the countryside, where the Orthodox faith endured.

With the end of Turkish occupation in 1898, Chania became the capital of the semi-autonomous Cretan State with Prince George of Greece in residence as High Commissioner. Eventually Crete became part of the Kingdom of Greece. On 1st December 1913 the Greek flag was raised from the Firkas Tower at the entrance of the harbour, in the presence of King Constantine and Eleftherios Venizelos, a native of nearby Mournies. During the Second World War violent battles took place on the outskirts of town, leading to the final fall of Chania after a siege of 10 days. Chania was bombed and the old town suffered much damage. In 1971 the capital of the island was transferred from Chania to Herakleion.

A SHORT WALK AROUND OLD CHANIA

West of the Outer Harbour

The **Outer Harbour** is fringed with bars and cafés, mainly modern in style (traditional tavernas cluster around the Inner Harbour). At its eastern end stands the **Mosque of the**

Chania: the Inner Harbour waterfront with the Mosque of the Janissaries.

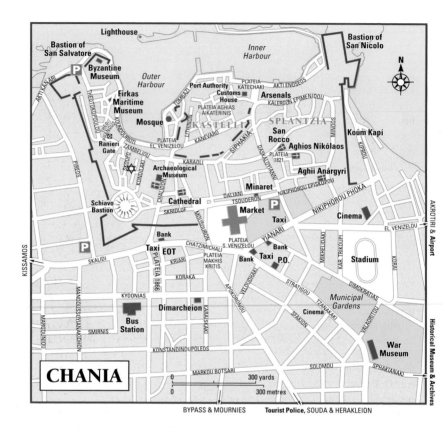

CHANIA

Janissaries, now used for exhibitions. It was built in 1645, the year that the Turks captured Chania from the Venetians. The janissaries were the household troops of the Ottoman sultans, recruited from the sons of Christian families under the *devşirme* system. At the west end of the harbour curve is the **Firkas Tower**, from where a chain stretched across to the lighthouse to close the port entrance. The parade ground is through the arch of the Maritime Museum (*see p. 333*). The old barracks were built in 1620.

Continuing north you come to the **Byzantine Museum** (*closed at the time of writing*), with icons, wall paintings and a beautiful mosaic pavement from Kissamos. It is housed in the remains of the Monastery of San Salvatore. The church, belonging to a Franciscan friary and damaged during the Second World War, is believed to date from the 15th century, with later additions and extensions. It was certainly there in 1609 when the Scotsman William Lithgow sought sanctuary in it after helping a slave escape from the Venetian galleys. The Turks turned it into a mosque. Opposite is the munitions magazine **Top Hane** (a Turkish word meaning just that), a four-sided, heavy vaulted building with only a few openings, which gives its name to the whole district.

CRETAN ICONS

As the Church marked its approval of religious images as objects of veneration and a useful visual aid to worship, a market for Byzantine icons developed in Europe. The first portable icons documented in Crete (in 1205) show that the demand was first met by artists in Byzantium, with Crete playing a secondary role. However, there is evidence for artists travelling in both directions before Byzantium fell to the Turks in 1453. Cretan artists flourished at the end of the 15th century, filling the vacuum left by the Fall of Byzantium and capitalising on their Western contacts through the Venetian hegemony. They specialised in portable icons painted on wood. In a church these would have been placed on the templon, marking the transition to the inner sanctum; in the home they would have been objects of veneration and tokens of divine protection. Outstanding, monumental examples of the former can be found in a number of monasteries on Mount Athos, where Theophanes Strelitzas worked in the 16th century. Portable icons for private use, on the other hand, were produced almost in bulk and were traded as far as Flanders. Documents dating from the very end of the 15th century are quite revealing. One set of three contracts between Venetian dealers and three Cretan workshops covers 700 icons with specific requirements in terms of style, the colour of the Virgin's garments and the use of gold on 470 of them on the brocade and in the background. The deadline is 42 days, suggesting the use of cartoons and an army of helpers, at least to apply the gold leaf. The styles specified were *'forma greca'* (strictly Byzantine) and *'forma latina'* (a fusion of the former with Western influences). Examples of *'forma latina'* show a less aloof and distant Virgin as well as the introduction of the three-quarters view and of different saints such as St Peter (symbolising the West) paired with St Paul, mainly active in the East and closely linked to St Titus, Crete's patron saint. Backgrounds become more elaborate, with an interest in landscapes, castles, lakes and distant camel riders in Oriental garb.

By 1498 there was a Greek confraternity of painters operating in Venice, though still signing their works 'de Candia'. Some settled; others, like Mikhail Damaskinos (*see p. 50*), commuted; others still sought their fortune farther afield, the most famous example being Domenikos Theotokopoulos, better known as El Greco.

In spite of this diaspora, Crete remained a centre for icon production well into the mid-17th century. Artists were trained in both styles, producing traditional icons for the Orthodox Church on Crete itself, in Cyprus, the Ionian islands and the Balkans, and in the new style for Western Europe. At some point there were as many as 125 painters on the island, all vying for a share of the market. Some did well, like the one who bequeathed 'two large houses and four small ones' to his widow. In the West, however, while their work was popular, it failed to gain intellectual approval. Vasari was dismissive of all Byzantine art, branding it a low point in the history of painting.

Examples of Venetian and Turkish architecture, often side by side, can be seen along **Odos Theotokopoulou**: Turkish wooden balconies, carved marble fountains, Venetian coats of arms, wrought-iron grilles and carved details. The alleys running to the east from Odos Theotokopoulou towards Parados lead to picturesque back streets behind the harbour. The buildings of the Contessa, Amphora, Porto del Colombo and Casa Delfino hotels are a suggestive image of what Chania must have looked like during the Venetian period. The **Casa Delfino** on Theofanous, with its wide steps, courtyard and palace buildings, was once the home of the Delfino family and of the rector of Chania. On the same street, the **Contessa Hotel**, originally a Venetian building, was converted under Turkish ownership so that the upper floors jut out across the street. From the gateway of the Casa Delfino, turning left and passing under an archway, is a courtyard to the right (now a taverna), with the tallest and oldest palm tree in Chania. Next to it is a tiny chapel belonging once to the Ranieri (or Renieri) family.

East of the Ranieri Gate

Walking though the **Ranieri Gate**, an archway in rustic work, which once belonged to the palace of the same name, note the inscription that reads in translation 'Our sweet father suffered, achieved and studied much, and toiled and perspired. May eternal peace cover him. 1608. Ides of January' (a quote from the Latin poet Horace). From the Ranieri Gate steps lead to Zambeliou. A little way along it, **Tamam**, a restaurant below street level, is housed in what was once the old plunge pool of the Turkish bath. Further along another restaurant (Tsikoudadiko) makes a creative use of a ruin: only the façade and the coat of arms are left of the old palace.

The **Etz Hayyim Synagogue** (*open Mon, Tues, Thur, Fri 10–5; Wed 10–2*), is sign-posted to the right from Kondilaki. Jews lived in Chania for centuries, many of them in a ghetto built by the Venetians. The community had two synagogues, Etz Hayyim, the Romaniot synagogue, and Beth Shalom for the Sephardic community (lost in the bombardment of the city). On 29th June 1944 the Jewish community was rounded up by the German occupying army and eventually put in a ship bound for Athens, possibly also with some Italian and Greek war prisoners. The boat received a hit from a submarine and sank with all hands. The truth only emerged in 1995, when the British Second World War archives became public: the British had sunk the boat in the belief that it was carrying weapons. For decades after the war Etz Hayyim lay in ruins. Eventually Nikos Stavroulakis, the founder of the Jewish Museum of Greece and a Jew of local descent, gathered worldwide support for its restoration. Etz Hayyim was rededicated in October 2000. In the course of the restoration work some of the past history of the site has come to light. Excavations have shown that the core of the building dates to around the late 15th century. It had been damaged in the attack by the corsair Barbarossa in 1538 and had lain in ruins for many decades before the Jewish community acquired it.

At the end of Zambeliou is **Plateia Venizelou**, the Venetian main square. The inscription mentioning Pasquale Cicogna is in lieu of a statue. Cicogna was due to have a monument here at the end of his term as rector, but as he moved on to become doge in Venice, he modestly declined the honour.

Interior of the Etz Hayyim Synagogue.

Kastelli and the Inner Harbour

From Plateia Venizelou, walk up Kanevaro (formerly the Venetian Corso), from where you can see the **excavations of Minoan Kydonia**. This is the centre of the hill of Kastelli, the original nucleus of the town, with traces of Hellenistic defences. Here once stood the Venetian duomo, built on the site of an Early Christian church and the palace of the rector. The latter is no more, although features of it have been incorporated into later buildings. The Turkish pasha ruled from the same spot. His elaborate wooden residence went up in flames in 1897. At the end of **Lithinon**, a side street leading north, the coat of arms of the Venetian archives has been preserved and an inscription dated 1624 records its construction. The remains of the **convent of Santa Maria dei Miracoli**, founded in 1615, are at the eastern end. Part of the covered passageway, with the arcade and cells on the ground floor and upper storey, still survives. The nunnery was badly damaged in 1941. Note the steps used by donkeys in Venetian times. All the treads are double in width so that the animal can get all four hooves onto one tread before moving on. This is the very last surviving medieval staircase in town. Taking the right turn at the bottom of the steps takes you to the **Inner Harbour**. This houses an active local fishing fleet and a modern marina. Here seven of the **Arsenals** have been restored as a conference centre. In one of them is an interesting display on the *Minoa*, a reconstructed Minoan ship.

Splantzia

From the arsenals heading southeast is **Splantzia**. This was the old Turkish quarter before the great population exchanges of the 19th and 20th centuries. A number of interesting churches are concentrated here, including **San Rocco**, a Venetian building with a Latin inscription dated 1630, and the 14th-century **Aghios Nikolaos**, with a minaret on one side, a church tower on the other and a grand view of the White Mountains behind. Under the Venetians it was the church of a Dominican priory. It was converted into the Imperial Mosque of Sultan Ibrahim to house a magic sword—which is still there. In front of it is **Plateia 1821**, the centre of the district. A plaque records that an Orthodox bishop was hanged from a plane tree here in 1821, during the pro-independence uprising.

Further south is the church of the **Aghii Anargyri**, the only Orthodox church to function in Chania during the Venetian and Turkish occupations. It has a fine icon-ostasis (1837–41) incorporating a work depicting Aghios Charalambos (with three martyrdom scenes in the lower register) signed 'by the hand of Viktoros', a 17th-century painter. There are also two icons, a *Dormition of the Virgin* and a *Last Judgement*, executed in 1625 by Ambrosios Embaros, a local priest-monk whose work shows the influence of Flemish engravers.

To the east of here, beyond the city walls, is the now fashionable quarter of **Koum Kapi** ('Sand Gate'), named after the Venetian Porta Sabbionara, pulled down by French occupying forces at the end of the 19th century. It was once home to Halikoutes bedouins from North Africa, who settled there in the last years of the Turkish occupation.

Chalidon and Skridlof

Chalidon, the Venetian Ruga Magistra, is now the main tourist street, together with Skridlof, which leads off it, leading to Tsouderon with the covered market (*see p. 338*). About halfway up Chalidon is Chania's **cathedral** (Trimartiri), a building dated 1860, occupying the site of an earlier church dedicated to the Presentation of the Virgin. The original church was converted into a soap factory owned by Mustapha Pasha Giritli (the Cretan), a Turkish official. In the 1850s he donated the site and the money to build the church to the Christian population. The multi-domed structure next to it was a Turkish bathhouse, formerly the Venetian convent of St Clare. Opposite the cathedral is the Archaeological Museum (*see below*), the former Venetian church of St Francis, the only surviving element of the monastery of the Franciscans.

ARCHAEOLOGICAL MUSEUM

The former church of St Francis, with its wide vaulted nave and narrow aisles, makes a good home for Chania's archaeological collection (*open Mon–Sat 10–6, Sun 11–6; T: 28210 90334*). Bianca Saracena, the wife of Onorio Belli (*see p. 34*), is buried here. The church became a mosque during the Ottoman occupation: the small garden to the north retains the base of the minaret and a pretty octagonal fountain for ritual ablutions.

The main body of the collection covers the development of western Crete up to Roman times. Labelling is erratic and explanatory notes minimal. Artefacts from the Prehistoric period (Late Neolithic and Bronze Age) take up the space nearest the entrance.

Late Neolithic: The collection, with hand axes, stone vases and obsidian blades, originates from cave sites and indicates contacts with the Cyclades.

Bronze Age: A large part of the display concentrates on finds from the LM III cemetery of Chania (note the burial of a new-born dog). Much of the pottery was produced in a local workshop, as shown by the fine distinctive clay and slip. One of the outstanding products of this workshop is the **pyxis with a man playing a lyre in a landscape with birds**. It was found in a chamber tomb near the Kiliares River below Aptera. Pottery from this same workshop has been found as far away as Cyprus and Sardinia, showing extensive trading activities between western Crete and the Mediterranean world in the Postpalatial period. The finds from the Phylaki Apokorona tholos of the same period include inlays in hippopotamus ivory for a casket with figures of helmeted soldiers showing Mycenaean influence, as wells as a collection of seals and seal impressions and jewellery.

The main **Minoan site of Kydonia**, on Kastelli Hill, destroyed by fire c.

Ottoman fountain in the museum garden.

The famous clay sealing known as the Master Impression.

1450 BC, is well represented with a display of the Linear A archive fired in the blaze that consumed the palace. In the central case a seal impression (known as the **Master Impression**) shows a young god or a ruler holding a staff and standing on the top of a large building topped with horns of consecration. Set in a rocky landscape by the sea, the scene has been interpreted as the representation of a city, a palace or a sanctuary. The discovery in 1989 of Linear B tablets at the Kastelli site confirmed that the settlement went on to prosper during the Postpalatial period, at least to the 13th century BC.

Hellenistic and Roman: Hellenistic Kydonia is represented with gold necklaces (inlaid and filigree), gold earrings, coiled hair ornaments, remains of a bronze gilded wreath and gold thread woven into a garment.

From the eparchy of Selinos comes a collection of **painted bull figurines** (a substitute for a sacrifice) from the sanctuary of Poseidon at Tsiskiana (4th century BC–2nd century AD). Some have very lifelike dewlaps; one has its tongue out. More finds from the area are in the north aisle. Note the glass ingot from Tarra and the marble vases and gold burial ornaments from Elyros.

The top end of the museum is dedicated to a **Roman floor mosaics** uncovered during building works in modern Chania and to **Roman and Hellenistic statuary** and stelae. These include an *Asclepios* from Lisos, a representation of the goddess Diktynna with hound from the Diktynnaion sanctuary on Cape Spatha (*see p. 385*) and the *Philosopher of Elyros*, a Roman copy of a Greek statue, reconstructed from fragments. The south aisle is taken up by finds from cemeteries of the Geometric period and later material (Archaic to Roman).

The Mitzotakis Collection

It has taken a long time for this collection to be exhibited to the public. It was originally offered to the Greek state by former prime minister Konstantinos Mitzotakis in 1993 only to become the centre of a heated altercation with the then Minister of Culture, the late Melina Mercouri. Mitzotakis had assembled his huge collection of antiquities (over 1,000 items) on the basis of an old Greek law intended to prevent foreigners from stripping Greece of its archaeological heritage. It permitted licensed Greek collectors to declare their collections to the authorities without specifying provenance. Mitzotakis always maintained that he acquired the objects 'from peasants and on the antiquities market'. Mercouri suspected he had enlarged his holdings by encouraging illegal excavations while he was in office. Now Mr Mitzotakis, a native of Chania, has had his wish and a selection of the collection is displayed in a purpose-built wing.

Roman mosaic pavement from Kydonia (3rd century AD) showing Dionysus and Ariadne.

Some of the objects are really stunning, such as the dagger with the gold hilt in Case 15 and the Protogeometric askos in the shape of a bird in Case 12. There are some general explanations in Greek and in English (mainly based on the lavish publication of the collection by Metaxia Tsipopoulou) introducing classes of materials, but the dating is very loose and none of the objects is closely provenanced.

OTHER MUSEUMS

The more recent history of Chania is illustrated for in a couple of museums situated in the 19th-century development of the town, on Sphakianaki, south of the Municipal Gardens. The **Historical Museum and Archives of Crete** (*open Mon–Sat 9–2; T: 28210 52606*) has memorabilia relating to Crete's struggle for independence with particular emphasis on Eleftherios Venizelos, the local politician who played a leading part in the process. On the upper floor, past a 16th-century cupboard carved with hunting scenes (a rare survival of quality Venetian furniture), is a collection of maps, pictures and engravings of old Chania. The **War Museum** (*closed at the time of writing*) is housed in the old Italian barracks. It covers the Cretan involvement in the struggle against the Turks at home and in the Balkans up to the Second World War, when Cretan soldiers posted in the north of Greece to contain the Germans were unable to join in the defence of their own homeland.

The Maritime Museum

The museum (*open daily 9–4*), in a restored building by the Firkas Tower, is set out on two floors and covers the history of seafaring from the Bronze Age to modern times. The excellent explanatory notes in Greek and in English, complemented by diagrams, make the visit a very pleasant and informative experience. The period of Venetian occupation is well represented in Room 2, with a model of Venetian Chania showing buildings and fortifications, and a large collection of maps. The revolving light in the corner is the original from the lighthouse at Cape Drepano, east of Chania. The rest of the ground floor is taken up by exhibits on maritime warfare, with photos and flags, Bronze Age ship models (including the inner workings of a trireme) and maquettes of famous battles. By the stairs do not miss the quaint representation of Cretan life as seen by the 19th-century occupying powers.

The upper floor is entirely devoted to more recent history, with memorabilia from the Battle of Crete well in evidence. The display is complemented with pictures and models and uplifting piped music. The item not to miss is the wedding dress made of knitted silk cord from a German parachute, probably the height of fashion in 1942.

The Folklore Museum

The museum (*Mon–Sat 9–3 & 6–9; T: 28210 90806*) is housed in a beautiful mansion in the same courtyard as the Roman Catholic church on Akti Koundourioti, on the Outer Harbour. It has a fine collection of embroideries, musical instruments and traditional dresses.

THE AKROTIRI PENINSULA

The Akrotiri peninsula is exactly what the word means in Greek, a promontory, closing the north end of Souda Bay. In antiquity it was known as Kiamon and the Byzantines called it Charaka. Part of it is now taken up by the airport, but there is still plenty to visit. Major attractions are obviously the beaches at Kalathas, Tersanas and Stavros on the north coast and at Marathi to the south, tucked in and protected against the meltemi (though windsurfers out in the open sea will welcome a gust of good wind). In the past its seclusion made it ideal for ascetics and monks, hence the many monasteries. Akrotiri is also known for Zorba's Cliff at Stavros, which provided the backdrop to Anthony Quinn's *syrtaki* in *Zorba the Greek*. The area was occupied in Neolithic times, as attested by the finds in the cave of Lera up the same cliff. Finds now in Chania show evidence of cult activity from the Bronze Age through to the Hellenistic period.

THE MONASTERIES OF AKROTIRI

To the monastery of Aghia Triada there is a choice of two routes from Chania (20km). The more direct route follows the signs to the airport until the runway comes into view, then turns to the north (left). The monastery is 2km away. A cross-country route will take you past the **tomb of Eleftherios Venizelos** and that of his son Sophoklis (also a prominent Greek politician), situated at Profitis Ilias (*map p. 428, C1*) on the main road to the airport. Eleftherios Venizelos, the architect of Cretan independence and of the modern Greek state, was born at Mournies near Chania in 1864. Here, on the hill where he now lies buried, in February 1897, he led a band of insurgents intent on dislodging the Turks. Eventually the Greek flag was raised, provoking a sharp reaction from Allied warships: they did not hesitate to shell the flag itself. The occupying force was there to calm things between the local population and the Ottomans; Cretan union with Greece was not part of their plan. Venizelos, however, had different ideas. Less than ten years later, in 1908, the union was proclaimed in Chania.

From the graves, take the side road to Kounoupidiana and Kambani; from there the monastery is signed.

The Monastery of Aghia Triada

The monastery buildings (Μονή Αγίας Τριάδας; *map p. 428, C1; officially closed between 2 and 5*) date from the 17th century, when two monks, the brothers Jeremiah and Laurentio Giancarolo from Venice, who had adopted the Orthodox faith, built the present church (consecrated in 1634) over an earlier foundation possibly linked to the powerful Murtaro family, who owned much of the surrounding land. Though one of the brothers had studied Byzantine church architecture on Mt Athos, the present church, with its engaged columns, reflects Venetian influence. It has three domes, the central one completed much later. Note on either side of the of the main west entrance two plaques bearing the same text in Latin and Greek, representing the mixed backgrounds of the founders. The church in its present state is the result of restoration work in 1827,

Detail from the façade of Gouverneto.

after damage sustained in the 1821 revolt and later refurbishments. The monastery was an important theological school in the 19th century; today it is still a wealthy and influential foundation with a fine library. The few remaining monks have taken up organic farming. The church stands in a courtyard surrounded by monastic buildings, including an 18th-century domed olive press. Below are the cisterns to collect rainwater as there are no springs. The small museum has a number of valuable icons by Imanouil Skordilis, a 17th-century priest from Chania.

Gouverneto Monastery

Gouverneto monastery (Μονή Γουβερνέτου; *map p. 428, C1; officially closed 12.30–4.30*) is more isolated, some 4km onwards along a track to the north. It is thought that this foundation, dating to the very beginning of the Venetian occupation, represents a retreat inland from an older position lower down at Katholiko (*see below*). The name derives from a nearby settlement, long vanished.

The monastery consists of a compound modelled like a fortress with towers at the corners. Above the entrance is a Greek inscription dated 1573. The cruciform **church**, dedicated to Our Lady of the Angels (Kyria ton Angelon), celebrating the feast of the Presentation of the Virgin, was begun in 1548 and never fully completed. Its present appearance dates to the 19th century after restoration work due to damage sustained in the 1821 rebellion. The church has a number of side chapels. One is dedicated to Aghii Deka, the Holy Ten, persecuted by the Roman emperor Decius in 250; another commemorates a revered Cretan saint, Aghios Ioannis Xenos (*see p. 166*), also known Ermitis, the Hermit, because according to tradition he died secluded from the world in a cave down at Katholiko. His feast is on 7th October and is the cause of great celebrations here and in western Crete generally.

Katholiko

The walk to Katholiko is steep in a harsh, wild landscape that will be of interest to botanists. It takes about one hour, down a path from the memorial on a rise beyond the monastery. After 10mins on the left is the **cave of the Panaghia Arkoudiotissa**, with a chapel at the entrance. The cave, with a stalactite in the shape of a bear (hence the name; *arkoudi* = bear), is believed in antiquity to have been a cult centre of Artemis, venerated in that guise towards the end of winter, just as the feast of the Panaghia Arkoudiotissa is now celebrated on February 2nd. The later legend centres on the cult of the Virgin, credited here with turning a bear to stone to stop it drinking the water

View of the ruins of Katholiko.

the inhabitants of this arid region needed so much. One hundred and forty rock-cut steps below the cave are the ruins of Katholiko, now much overgrown with fig trees, on either side of a bridge across a dried-up stream bed. A rock-cut chapel marks the entrance to a passage leading to the cave chosen for the burial of Aghios Ioannis Xenos, killed according to tradition by the arrow of a hunter who mistook him for an animal.

Katholiko is an old foundation, one of the oldest on the island, possibly linked to the general movement of re-Christianisation spearheaded by Aghios Ioannis following the lapses of the Arab interlude. The monastery was abandoned in favour of Gouverneto in the 15th century because of pirate attacks. A 10-min walk down the riverbed leads to the shore; it is possible to see the moorings the monks used and to have a swim from an ancient slipway cut in the rock.

PRACTICAL INFORMATION

GETTING AROUND

• **By air:** Chania's airport, Giannis Daska-

logiannis (*T: 28210 63171 or 63264*) is at Sternes on Akrotiri. It handles internal and international flights. There are four bus serv-

ices a day between the airport and the town.
• **By car:** From the airport there is a choice
of ways. For the centre of town follow the
exit road from the airport turning right at the
T-junction. Five kilometres on, after Pithari,
keep right at the fork. It is another 6km to
the centre of Chania's market, a building that
looks cruciform from the air but is more readily recognisable by its cream colour and mock
Neoclassical façade. For any other directions
take the left turn at the fork after Pithari. The
road joins the New National Road after 7km
past Souda. Turn left for Rethymnon and
right to bypass Chania towards Kastelli.

Approaching Chania from the east on the
E75, ignore the sign to Souda ferries and
the Old Road and stay on the bypass. After
6km take the slip road to Chania and at the
end turn left, following signs to the centre.
The road ends in front of the market. Approaching from the west on the Old Road,
just carry on. If you are on the New National
Road come off at the Vamvakopoulo junction
where the Omalos road joins. Following the
one-way system you will end up on Plateia
1866 at the edge of the old city.

Parking is very limited. There is an underground car park at the west end of Skalidi
where the road turns north into Pireos. From
there it is a short walk into the old town by
the round Turkish bastion. A car is of no use
in the old town.

• **By bus:** For city buses (blue), the station (*T: 28210 27044*) is on Plateia 1866 on
the west side of town; main-line buses are
green and the station is south of Kydonias
around the corner (*T: 28210 93306 or 93305
or 93052*). www.bus-service-crete-ktel.com/
maps3han.html shows a clear map of all
destinations from Chania. There are frequent
services to Rethymnon and Herakleion and to
Kissamos to the west. For beach expeditions,
use buses to Kalavaki and Galata and for the

airport and Akrotiri uses buses to Chordaki,
Aghia Triada, Stavros and Sternes.
• **By sea:** Daily overnight car ferries from Piraeus dock at Souda (6km east), from where
buses run into town, arriving in front of the
market. Taxis also meet the boat.
Ferries operate from Kythira, Gythion and
Kalamata (ANEN Lines, *T: 28210 24147 or
27500*) and from Piraeus (ANEK Lines, *T:
28210 27500 or 89856*; Hellenic Seaways: *T:
28210 75444 or 89065*).

TOURIST INFORMATION

Taxis: Chania taxis are dark blue and white.
   Ranks on east side of Plateia 1866 on Irak-
   liou near the police station and in Plateia
   Eleftherias (*T: 28210 98700 or 98701 and
   28210 98770 or 94144 or 94300*).
Post office: At the top end of Stratigou
   Tzanakaki, not far from the covered market.
Tourist Information: Kydonias 29–31 (*T:
   28210 36155 or 92943*).
Port Authority Chania: T: 28210 98888.
Port Authority Souda: T: 28210 89240.
Ambulance: T: 166.
Police: T: 28210 25850.
Tourist Police: On Irakliou on the road out to
   Souda (*T: 28210 53333 or 25930*).
Hospital: In Mournies, T: 28210 22000.
Road assistance: T: 104 and 28210 97177.

WHERE TO STAY

A lot of tourist accommodation, both rent
rooms and restored Venetian mansions, is
concentrated around and behind the old
harbour (www.chaniarooms.gr has a list). The
trouble is that it can be noisy because that is
where the nightlife is. € **Casa de l'Amore** (*T:
28210 64895; mobile 6977 065993; wwwcasad-
elamore.com*) has rooms to rent in the heart of
the old town.

€€€ **Casa Delfino.** ■ Rooms and suites in an old Venetian palazzo, luxuriously restored with marble floor and marble-clad bathrooms. Bedrooms are simply and elegantly furnished. Delightful old cobbled courtyard. *Odos Theophanous 9, T: 28210 87400, www. casadelfino.com.*

€€ **Amphora**. On Theotokopoulou at the north end of the old harbour, with a fine view of the lighthouse. *T: 28210 93224 or 93226; www.amphora.gr.*

€€ **Doma Boutique Hotel**. Located in a Neoclassical building, formerly the Austrian consulate, east of the old town. *Venizelou 124, T: 28210 51772/3; www.hotel-doma.gr.*

€€ **Domenico Guesthouse**. On Zambeliou, with a terrace overlooking the south end of the Outer Harbour. *T: 28210 75647; www. domenico.gr.*

€€ **Halepa**. An Italianate villa with terrace, garden and parking. *Venizelou 164, T: 28210 28440, www.halepa.com.*

€€ **Ontas**. On Epimenidou and Ikarou at the eastern end of the Inner Harbour, not far from the Venetian arsenals. A small hotel with plenty of character. *T: 28210 27691, mobile 6976 928693, www.ontas.gr.*

€€ **Porto del Colombo**. Stylish accommodation at the corner of Theophanou and Moshon. *T: 28210 70945 or 98466.*

€€ **Rodon**. Standard modern hotel on the way to the airport. *Akrotiriou 92, T: 28210 58317/8, www.rodon-hotel.gr.*

WHERE TO EAT

Akrotiri *(map p. 428, C1)*
€€ **Bahar**. At Chorafakia in the western part of the peninsula, for spectacular sunsets and an international menu. *T: 28210 39410.*
Chania *(map p. 428, C1–C2)*
€€ **Thalassino Ageri**. A good fish restaurant in the suburb of Chalepa, east of the city, with

a fine view of the sea. *T: 28210 51136.*

€€ **Apostolis**. On Akti Enoseos at the east end of the Inner Harbour, with a long-standing reputation for its high-quality fish cuisine. *T: 28210 43470, mobile 6936 956302.*

€ **Antigoni**. On Akti Enoseos, another popular choice for fish. *T: 28210 45236.*

€ **Tamam**. ■ Friendly, lively, popular restaurant serving good Cretan food, in what was once the plunge pool of a Turkish bath. When that fills up, there are also tables in the building across the road. *Zambeliou 49, T: 28210 96080.*

WALKING

For mountain climbing and walking the Greek Alpine Club (EOS) at Tzanakaki 90 (*T: 28210 24647; www.geocities.com/Colosseum/2252/hania*) provides information about climbing in the White Mountains and takes reservations for the Kallergis refuge near the Samaria Gorge.

SHOPPING & SPECIALITIES

The cross-shaped **covered market** in Chania has an excellent selection of traditional Cretan delicacies with preserves, honey, olives and cheeses. For **books**, Mediterraneo on the old harbour has a choice of books, guides and maps. Pelekanakis at Chalidon 89 and Petrakis on Chatzimichali are also excellent bookshops in Chania.

   Aghia Triada monastery on Akrotiri produces organic olive oil, thyme honey, balsamic vinegar, soap and wine. The vines are trained on stakes of chestnut wood from Mt Athos. Their products are available either from the monastery shop or at delicatessens.

EAST OF CHANIA

The area covered by this chapter lies east of Chania towards Lake Kournas, south of Georgioupolis. It is served by the E75 and the Old Road running more or less in parallel. The whole region was deeply marked by the events during the Battle of Crete. The Commonwealth War Cemetery and the German War Cemetery at Maleme (*see p. 383*) are a poignant testimony.

AROUND SOUDA BAY

Souda Bay is an immense natural harbour, one of the largest and deepest in the Mediterranean, sheltered from the north wind by the Akrotiri peninsula. Geologically it is a depression between two faults. It can be viewed from the south shore, but visitors should be aware that this is a military zone. Notices forbidding photography must be taken seriously.

Over time several plans to control the huge bay and its access were discussed in Venice. One included the building of a massive tower in the sea at the western end of the bay to defend Souda port. The idea was abandoned because of technical difficulties and lack of money. The strengthening of the northern approach to the bay was also considered and fortification work was carried out on the island in front of Marathi. No amount of ingenuity, however, could prevent the island from being overlooked from Akrotiri. Eventually efforts concentrated on the island of Fraronisi, so named after the friary of Aghios Nikolaos. The Souda fortifications were planned to take some 3,000 soldiers and to comprise a large circuit with bastions protecting churches, a loggia, residences, depots, a hospital, a jail, mills, water cisterns and an exercise ground. It was an ambitious undertaking and indeed the work was still in progress when the Turks began their conquest of the Crete from the west in 1645. The fortress held out until 1715, when the 800-strong garrison was allowed to leave. The fortress is only accessible by private boat from the nearby military base.

The Commonwealth War Cemetery

The cemetery (*map p. 428, C2*) is on the westernmost shore of Souda Bay on a turning off the old road signed to the airport. In May 1941, a month after 25,000 Allied troops, with a large contingent of New Zealand and Australian soldiers, had retreated from the Greek mainland to Crete, the Germans launched Operation Merkur, heralding the German occupation that lasted until 1945; the Allies retreated south and were later evacuated to Egypt. The Commonwealth War Cemetery, designed by architect Louis de Soissons, is the largest Allied cemetery on Crete. It is the final resting place of 1,527 men killed in the last ten days of May during the Battle of Crete. A number of them are not named, because soldiers' identities were lost when their remains were moved from their original graves by the German occupying force. All the Commonwealth soldiers who lost their lives in the operations are remembered in the Phaleron War Cemetery in Athens.

John Pendlebury (1904–41)

Grave 10E13 is that of John Pendlebury, an archaeologist whose life was deeply intertwined with Crete past and present. A Cambridge graduate, he first came to Crete in 1929, becoming involved in the excavations at Knossos. He inaugurated a holistic approach to Cretan archaeology by looking at whole landscapes and their developments within broad chronological periods. His travels on foot, criss-crossing the island and exploring its wildest reaches, became legendary and resulted in a seminal book: *The Archaeology of Crete* (1939). His name is linked to excavation at Karphi and Trapeza Cave. At the outbreak of the war he joined the Intelligence Service and was in Crete to organise its defence, using his extensive knowledge of the terrain, of the Greek language and Cretan dialects. He was shot by the Germans in mysterious circumstances in 1941, during the Battle of Crete.

The monastery of Chrysopigi

Leaving Chania on the Old National Road, take the fork signed Malaxa (Μαλάξα) and keep right. It will lead you along an avenue of eucalyptus to Chrysopigi (due south of Chania between the old and the new roads; *open 8–12 & 4–6*), an old foundation with an interesting history. The founder, Ioannis Kartofilaka, was a doctor at the end of the 16th century; his family crest is on the entrance arch. The monastery prospered until 1645, when the Turks began the siege of Candia. Like many other religious foundations on the island, it put up a fierce resistance to the invaders. According to written sources, among the fighters was a monk, Philotheos Skosuphos, an excellent icon painter. In the end the defence was lost and the authorities opted to burn the convent in order to deny it to the enemy. Today it is a much quieter place. It is a nunnery with some 30 nuns busy in different pursuits ranging from icon painting to organic agriculture. The art collection is of interest. It includes a number of icons from surrounding churches, gathered here for safety.

The Minoan excavations at Nerokourou

The village of Nerokourou (Νεροκούρου; *map p. 428, C2*) is south of the E75 on a side road between Mournies and Souda. The excavation north of the village is fenced but usually accessible. Lying in a fertile plain in view of Souda Bay, in an area showing Neolithic occupation, a MM III building believed to have been a wattle and daub construction on stone foundations was excavated by a joint Italian and Greek team in 1977–80. Although the remains had been badly damaged, especially in the north section, the excavators were able to establish the high-status quality of the architecture, which included pier-and-door partitions, light-wells, dressed limestone for column bases and door jambs, coloured slabs for paving and a possible second storey. This made it comparable to contemporary town houses in Knossos. The building was destroyed in LM

IB but immediately beforehand it had undergone a number of alterations suggesting a change of use or a decline in status. Living quarters were turned into workshops and storage areas, and access was restricted, possibly indicating concerns over security, a trend noted in other buildings across the island. Finds now in Chania indicate contacts with Lasithi and with the southeastern Aegean region.

The excavations are best viewed from the south, in other words with your back to the mountains. The area immediately in front of you was an open space in the first phase. It has a stone-lined cistern to the left. A large hall opened to the north with an entrance flanked by columns. The pillars (note the bases along the right-hand wall) suggest a possible balcony. Evidence for at least one polythyron is beyond in the damaged section. In the second phase the area was walled, either to create a diminutive court or a light-well. The access between the columns was blocked and the outside space was adapted for storage, before complete destruction c. 1450 BC.

APTERA

The ruins of the city-state of Aptera (Ἀπτέρα; *map p. 428, C2*) are on the eastern end of Souda Bay, signed from the E75. The road through Metochi passes the rescue excavations of a cemetery in use from the Geometric to the Roman periods. The name of the city-state means 'wingless', and has been explained by the myth of the Muses, who defeated the sirens in a music contest and cut their wings, so that when the sirens tried to fly they fell into the water and became islands. An alternative explanation links the name to Pteras, the mythical builder of the second temple at Delphi.

Aptera: view across the ruins to the White Mountains beyond.

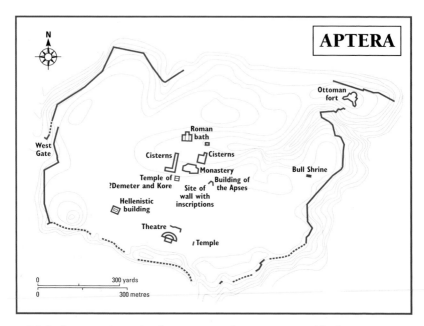

While the name Aptera has been recognised on a Linear B tablet from Knossos, it is not sure that it refers to this settlement, where there is no sign of occupation earlier than the 8th century BC. The town flourished in Hellenistic times, developing far-flung connections, minting its own coins and controlling access to the bay with two harbours either side of the strait. In the Roman period it was at the centre of a prosperous rural community and flourished until the 7th century AD, when it suffered earthquake damage followed by the Arab invasion in 823. The much-restored monastery in the middle of the site, dedicated to Aghios Ioannis Theologos, dates from the 11th century, the Second Byzantine period. It was a foundation of monks from the Dodecanese island of Patmos, a move dictated by the need to spread the Gospel in Crete after over a century of Arab occupation.

The site

The large site has not as yet been fully investigated: it is very much 'work in progress', and much remains still to be revealed. At the time of writing it was closed to the public and very effectively fenced. Some structures (cisterns, monastery) can be viewed from outside the fence. The trip, though, is not wasted. There is a fine view from the top of the plateau, and Souda Bay can be photographed legally.

Aptera stands on a plateau overlooking Souda Bay and is defined by a **wall circuit** almost 4km in length with towers and parapets, part of which is dated to the 4th century BC. A Ministry of Culture notice marks the **West Gate** to the right on the way up. It is set within two overlapping walls of polygonal masonry protected by two square bastions at either end. The funerary monuments have been restored. The guardian's hut and the fenced part of the excavations are at the centre of the site. Here, next to the monastery, German archaeologists conducted a two-week excavation in July 1942, revealing a **temple** in clamped ashlar blocks dedicated to a pair divinities, possibly Demeter and her daughter Kore. They dated it to the 4th–5th century BC, though later this was revised to the 2nd century BC. Remains of a couple of public buildings have been traced nearby: the so-called **Building of the Apses**, constructed in a technique that suggests a Roman date, and a wall with inscriptions, which Pashley recorded in 1834 and is unfortunately no more. The wall, presumed to belong to a Hellenistic building, was cleared in the 1860s and by the end of the century the blocks could not be traced.

The **cisterns** are impressive, particularly, to the north, the one with two partitions of stone-built pillars and huge vaults. They were probably originally Hellenistic with Roman rebuilding. To the south is the site of a small **theatre**: not much is left of it, but it is known that its construction date precedes the Roman conquest. To the west, recent work has uncovered a **Hellenistic building** arranged around a peristyle court; it was altered in Roman times and eventually destroyed in an earthquake. Two more temples have been recorded. One, investigated by the Germans during the Second World War, is to the east near a well-preserved stretch of town wall. It is called the **Bull Shrine** on account of the figurines found nearby. The other one was near the theatre.

THE FOOTHILLS OF THE WHITE MOUNTAINS

Inland from Aptera, a track winds its way up onto the foothills of the White Mountains towards Stylos (6km). Before the modern village at Sternaki (*map p. 428, C2*) a well-preserved **tholos tomb** with a deep, long, stone-lined dromos and a vaulted circular chamber dated to the end of the LM III is signed to the left in an olive grove. Excavations in the area by Nikolaos Platon and Kostis Davaras have uncovered a Minoan settlement with a long occupation, from Early Minoan times to the end of LM III, a possible precursor to the Iron Age site of Aptera (in which case the Linear B tablet from Knossos, mentioned above, would refer to this settlement). A path leads uphill to a kiln (now roofed) dated to the 14th–13th centuries BC.

Stylos

The church of the **Panaghia Serviotissa** is just short of Stylos (*map p. 428, C2*), on a side road to the left, 2km from the tomb. Before the bridge that crosses the river bed, take the left turn. The partly ruined church is all that remains of the monastery of Aghios Ioannis, also, like the monastery at Aptera, a foundation by monks from the island of Patmos. It is dated to 1088. The plan is a typical cross-in-square with arms of equal length and a dome on an octagonal drum resting on four pillars. The outside is decorated with blind arches and brickwork.

In **Stylos** itself (Στύλος), at the near edge of the village, the small double-nave church of Aghios Ioannis has remains of early frescoes (1271–80) in the north aisle. The austere style is in sharp contrast with the early 15th-century paintings in the south aisle, which have an aristocratic elegance. For access to the church try the *kafeneion* at Samonas (Σαμωνάς; 6km).

Kyriakoselia

If you decide to come this far, you might also like to persuade the guardian to accompany you south to Kyriakoselia (Κυριακοσέλια; *map p. 428, C2*), in a remote wooded valley (3km) to visit the **church of Aghios Nikolaos**, considered by some to be one of the most beautiful Byzantine churches in Crete. It has a single nave with three bays and was built in the late 11th–early 12th century. The chapel at the west end is a 20th-century addition. The central bay is raised to support a dome lit by slender windows. The interior is covered with frescoes dated 1230–36. These were the early years of Venetian domination, which brought with it Western influence in art, but not to this remote part of the island. Here, the strictest traditions of the Byzantine style and iconography, under the influence of the aristocratic Comnenian style from Byzantium, are still adhered to. The church is dedicated to Nicholas, the 4th-century bishop of Myra, near modern Antalya in Turkey. He was never officially canonised, but his reputation as a miracle-worker has ensured enduring veneration among the faithful, and indeed he is still venerated today as Santa Claus. In the church in Kyriakoselia, the cycle of his life begins on the walls of the central bay under the dome, and continues on the same level in the western bay. Aghios Nikolaos also figures among the Hierarchs or Fathers of the Church in the south apse.

In Venetian times the village had an important stronghold, large enough to house the population of the surrounding area as well as a garrison in troubled times. After the Venetians left, the building was used as an assembly point by shepherds at the time of the seasonal transhumance. Not much is left of the fortification walls. Inside are two churches, **Aghia Paraskevi** and **Aghios Mamas**, by the spring; the dwellings, of wood or dry stone, have disappeared.

From here the road goes no further than Kares (500m) into the White Mountains.

THE APOKORONA DISTRICT

The largest island commanding the entrance to the Souda Bay (Fraronisi; *see p. 339*) was part of a Venetian system of controlled access, together with outposts on the mainland. The new ruling power built the castle of Bicorna (which gave its name to the Venetian *castellania*) on a promontory by the sea at Kalami. By 1303 it had been destroyed in an earthquake. Repairs were almost futile as the place was exposed to piracy; indeed Kheir ed-Din Barbarossa attacked it in 1538 and the Turks besieged it in 1645. When they entered, however, they found it empty. The Venetians, sensing defeat, had already abandoned it, and the Ottomans were left speculating about booby traps and clever stratagems. Now nothing survives of the castle, though Gerola was able to photograph remains of a wall and of the tower in the early 1900s. In the same strategic area, the much-restored surviving building on the coast east of Megala Chorafia is **Itzedin Castle** (*map p. 428, C2*), named after the Egyptian pasha who rebuilt it in the 18th century after it had sustained much damage from pirates and Turks alike. It stands on an earlier Byzantine fort, which in turn overlies an Archaic theatre. The fort was used as a prison, notoriously so under the rule of the Colonels (1967–74), before becoming a tourist attraction.

Both Kalyves and **Almyrida** have good beaches (but beware of currents) and places to eat. Almyrida (Αλμυρίδα; *map p. 428, D2*) also boasts a large, three-aisled 6th-century Christian basilica with an impressive mosaic floor, well in view by the roadside at the west end of the beach. The hinterland is good walking country; bird-watchers will find it rewarding. This stretch of coast is probably more interesting to sightseers after Kalyves, where both main roads dip to the south. From there on only a track continues east in a landscape of *phrygana*, rich in aromatic dwarf shrubs and the occasional orchid, all the way to Cape Drepano, but short of the lighthouse.

Gavalochori

South of Almyrida, the village of Gavalochori (Γαβαλοχώρι; *map p. 428, D2*) has plenty of character. It boasts a Roman cemetery and some **Venetian ruins** and wells. Follow the blue sign to 'Enetiki Tholoi' ('Venetian Arches') and discover a building with double barrel vaulting and a reconstructed traditional olive press with associated feeding structure. The centrepiece, however, is the **Folklore Museum** (*open April–Oct Mon–Fri 9–8, Sat 9–7, Sun 10–1.30 & 5–8; T: 28250 23222*), located in a beautifully restored Venetian building with later Ottoman additions, namely the mezzanine floor. It offers the chance to see how a *kamara* house works and to learn more about traditional crafts, including the Cretan *kopaneli* silk lace, a technique that takes its name from the bobbins around which the thread is woven (*kopanelia*). A women's cooperative is reviving it here, where it must have been practised at least since Turkish times, judging by the old mulberry trees growing around the village (today, however, the silk worms are imported from China and Japan). The technique is based on interweaving threads wound on bobbins, normally 14, to create braids.

Around Vamos and Lake Kournas

The Apokorona district, ignored by both main roads, is historically an underpopulated area: it is stony, water is scarce and agricultural productivity limited. Tourism has come late here, in the wake of discerning foreigners who have bought old houses and done them up. In the village of **Vamos** (Βάμος; *map p. 428, D2*) at the centre of the promontory, a development agency was established in 1995 to foster tourism but in a way compatible with the local character. Tourists are welcomed in a network of renovated old houses (25 in Vamos itself and 10 in the surrounding area; *see p. 348*). As a result the village has prospered, exodus has been halted and the local character has been preserved. The scheme has been highly successful, though it is finding it difficult to expand, as suitable properties at the right price are increasingly hard to find. There has been a proposal to include the long, steep, rocky coastline in Natura 2000, the EU environmental programme.

South of Vamos, the New and the Old Road run side by side. Where they cross and the Old Road runs beneath the highway, east of Vryses, a **bridge of Hellenistic date**, known as *Helleniki Kamara*, is hidden behind a chapel. The area also has interesting churches at Maza and Alikambos.

Maza and Alikambos

At the Vryses junction the north–south road comes up from Sphakia. Along that road, 2km south of Vryses, a side road east leads to **Maza** (Μάζα; *map p. 428, D2*) for the first of two churches with work by Ioannis Pagomenos, a painter active in Crete in the period 1314–47, especially in the southwest of the island, inland from Palaiochora, where most of his work can be viewed. At Maza, Aghios Nikolaos is in the square and it is normally open. The church is small and completely decorated with well-preserved frescoes dated by inscription to 1326. The deësis in the sanctuary shows Christ flanked by the patron saint. The nave has scenes from the life of the Saviour and of St Nicholas (in the lower register). Specialists will note that Pagomenos places the Feast of Abraham, signifying the Holy Trinity in Orthodox iconography, in the eastern bay rather than, as is customary, on the triumphal arch above the sanctuary. Here instead we find the scene of the Mandylion, with Christ's image imprinted on a cloth.

Before **Alikambos** (Αλίκαμπος; *map p. 428, D2*), 3km south of Maza, signed right opposite a Venetian fountain, a path leads to the church of the Panaghia, with a pretty façade and decorated with a fine series of frescoes in the nave by Pagomenos, dated by inscription to 1316. On the north wall of the nave is the *Virgin and Child* (Hodighitria), with a Baptism scene above. Saints Dimitrios and George are shown on horseback, with the emperor Constantine the Great and his mother Helen opposite. Rather indistinct on the upper register of the vault (south side) is a fine *Nativity*. Donor and inscription are on the west wall. The work in the sanctuary shows a different hand and is slightly later. The key to the church is in the village with the *papas*, who is happy to show visitors around in an interesting mix of languages.

Georgioupolis

On the approach to Georgioupolis (Γεωργιούπολη; *map p. 428, D2*) from the west, birdwatchers should use the Old Road. It follows the river valley and passes an area known as *almyro*, the Greek for salt marshes. The town itself is named after Prince George, the High Commissioner in the last years of the Ottoman occupation, who had a shooting lodge here where three rivers meet creating a harbour. It used to be a quiet fishing village in a bay protected against the excesses of the north wind. But the beach is simply too long (9km) and there is also the only natural freshwater lake in Crete nearby (*see below*). Tourism has taken over, epitomised by the miniature train connecting the resorts and Lake Kournas, and by the pedal boats up the river. That said, it is still a walkers' paradise, either inland towards the hills around Argyroupolis or in the Apokorona district to the north, in the direction of Amphimalla, possibly one of Lappa's two harbours. Lance Chilton's *Six Walks in the Georgioupolis Area* or the more recent *Walks in Rethymnon and Georgioupolis*, will come handy.

Lake Kournas

The body of water (*map p. 428, D3*) is the result of a geological accident which allows the waters percolating from the White Mountains to collect in a natural depression lined with impermeable rock. The lake is also fed by the Amati spring near its southeast edge and drained by the Delfinas river. As lakes go it is not very big (880m across, 50m deep) but it is the only natural lake in the Greek islands and has a charm of its own, with the White Mountains reflected in its smooth surface; it is good for bird watching. Lear found it inspiring and painted a view in 1864 pronouncing the lake 'very fine and Cumberlandish'. Reputedly full of eels, it is now more full of tourists, especially in the summer, when they camp around it as the water recedes and exposes the muddy shore.

In antiquity it was known as Koresia and there may have been a temple on the shores dedicated to Athena Koresia. The present name is thought to derive from the Turkish word for the marble basins found in hamams.

Southeast of the lake, the village of the same name, **Kournas** (Κουρνάς; *map p. 428, D3*; 4km), has a church made of four dissimilar chapels laid side by side (Aghios Georgios; *signed from the main square*). It was originally lavishly decorated with frescoes throughout, in the style of the Second Byzantine period, when influence from Byzantium was prevalent in religious art in Crete. What remains, the *Communion of the Apostles* and a portrait of the patron saint, is still well worth seeing. On the way back to the main road at **Phylaki** (Φυλάκη; *map p. 428, D3*), the church of Aghia Anna has a fine Renaissance tomb of the Kallergis family with a profusion of eagles.

PRACTICAL INFORMATION

GETTING AROUND

• **By car:** The New and Old Roads run parallel from Kalyves to Georgioupolis, giving a wide berth to the Drepano peninsula, also known as Apokorona, an area well worth exploring, with good scenic roads and interesting villages.

• **By bus:** The main bus route, with frequent services between Chania and Rethymnon, follows the E75. To explore the Drepano peninsula from Chania, there are limited services to Almyrida, Gavalochori, Vamos, Kefalas and Plaka. For Kournas there is a limited service from Georgioupolis. See www.bus-service-crete-ktel.com/maps3han.html.

TOURIST INFORMATION

Police Souda: T: 28210 89316.
Police Vamos: T: 28250 22218.
Vamos Health Centre: T: 28250 22580.

WHERE TO STAY

The coastal tourist development starts at Kalami, west of Kalyves at the mouth of Souda Bay, and continues to Almyrida nearby. It picks up again at Georgioupolis, with an immensely long sandy beach and plenty of accommodation, and inland around lake Kournas (see www.bus-service-crete-ktel.com/hlist).

Inland Vryses used to be a pretty village, and though it has lost some of its charm, it is still a good base to explore the region from.

Almyrida (*map p. 428, D2*)
€€ **Dimitra**. Situated just off from the beach with a view of the sea and of the White Mountains. Recently renovated. *T: 28250 31956 or 32062; www.dimitra-hotel.com.*
Gavalochori (*map p. 428, D2*)
€€€ **Apokoron Luxury Villas**. Modern stone-built accommodation on the hill overlooking the village. *T: 6974 839879, www. eladin.gr.*
Kalyves (*map p. 428, D2*)
€€ **Kalyves Beach**. A modern hotel by the seaside at the mouth of the river Xydas. *T: 28250 31285 or 31881; www.kalyvesbeach.com.*
Plaka (*map p. 428, D2*)
€ **Bicorna**. Friendly, family-run hotel. *T: 28250 32073; www.bicorna.gr.*
Vamos (*map p. 428, D2*)
€€ **Vamos Cooperative**. The association, now in its 13th year, is part of a local movement to impart new life to the village without changing its character. The accommodation is exclusively in old stone houses, in the village and surrounding countryside, which have been lovingly and tastefully renovated. The cooperative also organises visits to local farmers as well as concerts of modern and traditional Greek music, art exhibitions, walking tours and Cretan cookery lessons. The movement has been highly successful in revitalising the village and in promoting Apokorona as a holiday destination. *T: 28250 23251; www.vamossa.gr.*

WHERE TO EAT

Souda (*map p. 428, C2*)
€€€ **Nykterida**. A venerable institution established in 1933 with a strong reputation.

This is an expensive place: you pay both for the view over Souda Bay, for the food (which is excellent), and for the history (which runs deep; it is all on the website—don't be put off by the bats). It offers a large selection of traditional Cretan cuisine from *kaltsounia* with fennel and wild greens to ice cream flavoured with honey and saffron. *T: 28210 64215, www. nykterida.gr.*
Vamos (*map p. 428, D2*)
€ **Bloumosiphis Taverna**. Near the cooperative's office in the middle of the village and recognisable by the huge plane tree. The place is well known for its selection of Cretan traditional dishes and cheeses.

LOCAL SPECIALITIES

Chrysopigi monastery has professional copies of traditional Byzantine icons. The Vamos cooperative runs the **Mirovolon traditional shop** in an old building near the Bloumosiphis taverna. It sells a variety of locally-produced Cretan delicacies including raki, honey and cheese.

FESTIVALS & EVENTS

In April **Vamos** holds the Chochlidovradia, a festival of edible snails (a celebrated Cretan speciality) and in early August hosts the Vamos Festival with musicians and exhibitions of popular art, crafts and folklore. In late June at **Souda** there is Naval Week, with some fine fireworks. At the beginning of Sept, **Gavalochori** celebrates its Folklore Festival.

BOOKS & FURTHER READING

Lance Chilton has two books of walks in the area: *Six Walks in the Georgioupolis Area* and *Walks in Rethymnon and Georgioupolis*.

THE SPHAKIA REGION

The area described in this chapter lies close to the north–south road connecting Vryses to Chora Sphakion (40km) crossing the area east of the White Mountains, altogether almost devoid of settlement. At the watershed near Ammoudari on the Askiphou plateau, a track strikes west to join one of the many branches of the E4 walking route across the White Mountains. On the coast there are a number of settlements on either side of Chora Sphakion, linked by the E4, which here incorporates part of the old road system of the region: to the west this peters out shortly after Aradaina. The only alternative in many cases is the boat service, which links various resorts.

Chora Sphakion itself makes an excellent base for exploring this unique region, in which geography plays an important role. Sphakia is rugged country, an extreme example of altitudinal compression, climbing to 2400m in barely 16km from the palm-tree lined coast. It has minimum arable land and is sharply dissected by gorges, as many as 15 running parallel in an area 35km across, the result of tectonic cracking later enlarged by erosion. The inhabitants have a reputation for being wild, picturesque and violent and above all averse to any form of domination. Shepherds roamed free in the *madares*, the high pastures of the White Mountains, an environment that only they could tame. The Turks never fully established themselves here, a fact which is illustrated by the minimal population exchange in the 1920s and the absence of mosques.

Today things have changed considerably. EU money has moved in to stem population exodus and promote tourism, a better bet for future development than cheese production alone.

FROM VRYSES TO ASKIPHOU

Vryses (Βρύσες; *map p. 428, D2*) is known for its thick creamy yoghurt, and though the village has now grown too big to be particularly attractive, it might still be worth a stop for this famous product. The road south from here branches east for Maza and Alikambos (*see p. 346*). Shortly after the turning, a detour west leads in 3km to **Embrosneros** (Εμπρόσνερος; *map p. 428, D2*). The village belonged to the patriarch of Constantinople in 1355. In the 18th century it became the fief of a local overlord, variously described as a pasha or a janissary. Ibrahim Alidakis was probably neither, just a wealthy farmer with estates on the northern slopes of the White Mountains. On the outskirts of the present village he built himself a complex with a tower (*being restored at the time of writing*). He was killed after the Daskalogiannis revolt by the Sphakiot rebel Manousakas, in a dispute over grazing rights. The main south road climbs steadily past the Krapi plateau and by the time you have reached Kares, you are in Sphakian country.

The Askiphou plateau

The Askiphou plateau (730m; *map p. 428, D3*) is a chequerboard of fields growing cereals and vines, watered by wells made possible by the shallow water table. As in Lasithi the villages, four in all, with a total population of c. 400, are grouped around the plateau's edge. On a conical hill to the east, a ruined Turkish castle (one of two) dominates the view.

Askiphou figures frequently in Cretan folklore as a place where Turks, Egyptians and Germans have all come up against the locals at one time or another. It has its own War Museum (*open daily 9–9; T: 28250 95289; limited parking*), marked with a bright yellow sign. This is a private enterprise started in 1941 by a local collector, Georgios Hatzidakis, who turned his own house at Kares over to a motley assortment of memorabilia dating from the resistance to Turkish domination to the Second World War and beyond. The place is now run by his granddaughter. The earliest exhibit dates from 1770, the latest is a gun left behind by the Americans when they vacated Souda Bay in 1960. Traditionally Askiphou was at the crossroads on the route from coast to coast. *Kalderimia* climbed west to the White Mountains and east to Asi Gonia into the higher pastures. Some of these have now been improved for the benefit of motorised shepherds. Walkers and bird-watchers will find them rewarding for the flowers, the solitude and the empty space. The left turning to Asphendou takes you onto a very scenic road to Asi Gonia, with fine views of the Libyan Sea.

After Askiphou the road south deteriorates considerably. It becomes narrow and is littered with potholes. It does not help that there are frequent buses and cars towing boats. There is evidence (in the guise of machinery and heaps of gravel on the wayside) of road works going on, but it is a huge undertaking. Prepare for a slow drive all the way to Chora Sphakion.

A WALK DOWN THE IMBROS GORGE

The Imbros Gorge (*map p. 428, C3*), also referred to as Nimbros, from elision of the preposition *stin*, in or at, may not be as grand as Samaria, but it is still well worth seeing. It is shorter and easier, which means no guide is needed and you can walk it in just two and a half hours. It is also passable all year round except in heavy snow or rain. Modern visitors will be able to appreciate the natural beauty of the surroundings, compared by Evelyn Waugh to a 17th-century Baroque landscape, and the heady scent of the aromatic plants. Back in May 1941, when the road was not completed, some 12,000 Allied soldiers retreated down the gorge in a four-day march to Komitades, with German Messerschmitts circling above; they probably missed all these niceties. The official entrance is well signed at the south end of the village with room to park (you can return here by bus or taxi from Komitades). The modern road follows the twists and turns of the gorge, in a barren landscape; after a precipitous descent of 850m both eventually emerge high above the Libyan Sea with the island of Gavdos (the southernmost inhabited point in Europe) in the distance, due south.

THE SPHAKIA SURVEY

From 1986–99 the Sphakia region was the subject of a survey run by Oxford University which combined environmental, archaeological, documentary and ethnographic evidence. It investigated landscape and human interaction over an area of 472km square, with a very varied topography ranging from the height of the White Mountains to the depths of twelve or so gorges, over a period spanning 5,000 years to the end of the Turkish occupation. It found evidence for Late Neolithic/early Bronze Age occupation all over the area, including high up in the summer pastures, as well as two large Middle/Late Minoan sites in the plain of Frangokastello. The Hellenistic period is represented by the four *poleis* and a hierarchical settlement pattern which became egalitarian in Byzantine times and from then on changed relatively little. Cult activity at the Agiasmatsi cave in the area north of Frangokastello was further investigated and shown to have begun in prehistory and flourished in the Hellenistic and Roman periods. Land exploitation in the different regions (the coast, the immediate hinterland and the high mountains) and over the different periods was studied, with particular emphasis on vernacular architecture and the *mitata*, the shepherds' huts in the *madares*, the summer pastures.

CHORA SPHAKION & THE COAST

The picturesque harbour village of **Chora Sphakion** (Χώρα Σφακίων; *map p. 428, C3*) is the main centre of the region. These days it lives off tourists (famously dubbed here 'sheep without bells') and in the summer welcomes hosts of foreign visitors arriving by road or by boat. Things were different in the past, when coastal settlement was not the norm: according to Rackham and Moody in *The Making of the Cretan Landscape*, settlement along the south coast only became firmly established in the 1930s. That said, in Venetian times, owing to the tall timber stands available locally, there was a thriving ship-building industry here, the only one Crete ever had in modern times (the arsenals in Chania and Herakleion were for repairs only and often the wood was shipped from Venice). Otherwise settlement was inland, on slightly higher ground away from the humid coast, with pleasant summer breezes and a reduced exposure to the winter elements and pirate raids. The move to the seashore is recent, dating only from the 1970s, prompted both by the tourist market and by the building of a motorable road to Anopolis. The *kalderimi* leading directly inland to Mouri and Georgitsi has long fallen out of use.

In the 18th century Chora Sphakion was a substantial town. It was guarded by a fort, now in ruins and very overgrown, overlooking the harbour, with the church of Aghii Apostoli, a cruciform building with a dome, next to it. The fort is of no great antiquity; it did not exist when Buondelmonti visited in 1419. According to Gerola it was built on the cheap and with inferior material, like Castel Selino (*see p. 378*), and was already in need of repair in 1526 when Venice turned down a request for financial help.

The Venetians had considerable trouble with the Sphakiots, who were well placed in their inaccessible country to maintain a form of quasi-independence. When Crete came to terms with Venetian domination in the 16th century, the Sphakiots had to be bought off with exemption from galley service and corvées.

The great rebellion in 1770, led by Ioannis Daskalogiannis from Anopolis, resulted in a savage repression by the Turks, from which the local economy never fully recovered. During the Second World War the harbour played a vital part in the evacuation of the defeated Allied troops, both from here and from Ilingas beach 2km west. A plaque on the way to the ferry commemorates the operation in which 10,000 or so men, exhausted by the battle on the north coast and the retreat over the mountains, were ferried to Alexandria over four days. It makes no mention of all the other troops who made the same journey but were left behind on the shore. On the approach to the village from the east, another memorial with an ossuary completes the story by honouring the Cretans who gave their lives to support the operation.

A SPHAKIAN WAY WITH SHEEP SHOULDER BLADES

Scapulimancy is the art of divination from the inspection of animal scapulae or other flat bones (tortoise shells are another example). It is divided into two main types: one involves scorching the bone and then interpreting the colour, veins, burns and cracks; the other involves no processing, the oracle simply interprets the morphology of the bone itself. Both forms originated in the Far East around the 2nd millennium BC. In North America, native Indians practiced pyro-scapulimancy, the first of the two methods, to find game. Apyro-scapulimancy (the method without fire) slowly found its way through the Asian steppes (Attila the Hun was a firm believer) to the shores of the Mediterranean. It is first documented in Europe in Wales in the 12th century, probably brought from Flanders where it had been introduced by returning Crusaders. It was still practised in Albania in the early 20th century. In the Sphakia region it has survived as a traditional male art, used to check on one's wife's fidelity and to read signs of imminent death.

WEST OF CHORA SPHAKION

Anopolis

A good asphalt road with many hairpin bends and a scenic view leads west to Anopolis (Ανώπολη; *map p. 428, C3*). Unfortunately, after a most promising start, the road deteriorates considerably and becomes a track. While the road lasts, the Sweetwater Beach (*access on foot only; see below*) is well marked and it is possible to get a very good view of Chora Sphakion and its twin harbours. Anopolis was once a powerful city, known in Hellenistic times and flourishing in the Roman and Byzantine periods. After that it ceased to prosper. Pashley, who visited in 1834, commented on the devastation he saw all around—and this was certainly not the first time that the town had so suffered. In Anopolis, resistance to occupation was something akin to a national sport. It began in 1365, against the Venetians; in the 18th century the village produced Ioannis Daskalogiannis, who led the 'great rebellion' of 1770; later the villagers took part in the disturbances of 1867. Each time Anopolis was flattened and the community dispersed. Pashley had met some refugees on Milos in 1833. Small wonder that there is very little left of old Anopolis today, apart from a section of the massive fortification walls by the church of Aghia Aikaterini, south of the modern village (*20mins on foot with a fine view of Loutro below; the temptation to embark on the steep descent to the coast, about 90mins, must be weighed against the prospect of the very stiff climb back*).

From Anopolis the road due north to Limnia soon becomes unsuitable for ordinary vehicles. It continues for 18km into the White Mountains and is one of the approaches to the summit of Mt Pachnes (2454m).

Aradaina and Aghios Ioannis

About 2km on **Aradaina** (Αράδαινα; *map p. 428, C3*) comes into view, with the 14th-century church of Mikhail Archangelos poised on the edge of one of Crete's most dramatic gorges. For centuries travellers had to scramble down the gorge and up the other side: since 1986 there has been a bridge, courtesy of the Vardinogiannis family, originally from Aghios Ioannis further on. As well as ensuring the future of the isolated community, the bridge has provided access to the high mountain pastures to shepherds' trucks and is regularly used by bungee jumpers from all over the island. The domed cruciform church of Aghios Mikhailis (*usually locked*), Byzantine in date, was built into the central nave and apse of an Early Christian basilica. The frescoes are from the mid-14th century and depict the saint and the donor, a lady clad in a white embroidered dress. Aradaina itself is now deserted, apparently abandoned after a vendetta in the 1940s. Remains of the Graeco-Roman *polis* of Araden, which include a necropolis, are south of the road and have not yet been investigated.

Through the **Aradaina Gorge** it is three to four hours to reach the coast and then another hour to get to Loutro. A degree of agility and experience is required. The access to the gorge is via a path off the main road, 500m before the bridge. Botanists should look out for the local variety of tulip (*Tulipa saxatilis*, with pink petals and a golden centre).

The road carries on to **Aghios Ioannis** (Άγιος Ιωάννης; *map p. 428, C3*; 6km), in a wooded landscape dominated by the Cretan pine (*Pinus brutia*), a species from the East that has colonised the Mediterranean as far as Calabria in southern Italy. At the beginning of the village there are two Byzantine churches (Aghios Ioannis and a Panaghia) with 14th-century frescoes. For the keys enquire at the local taverna.

Loutro

The settlement of Loutro (Λουτρό; *map p. 428, C3*) stands on a hammerhead peninsula with a harbour at either side, which in the Hellenistic and Roman periods, when Loutro was known as Phoinix, provided safe shelter for ships in the winter. It was the port of Anopolis. St Paul's ship made it here for safety from Kali Limenes, but then ended in Malta after clearing Gavdos (*see p. 160*).

After the great tectonic upheavals of late antiquity, the west harbour was raised 3–4m which made it too shallow for use. Loutro went into decline as traffic moved to Chora Sphakion—though what is left does remain the only safe winter anchorage on the south coast. In the 18th century it was still operating as Chora Sphakion's winter harbour and was the home of vessels sailing as far as Smyrna (modern Izmir) and Alexandria. The archaeology of the promontory has not yet been systematically investigated.

A few decades ago Loutro was virtually deserted, but tourism moved in when word began to spread about this inaccessible paradise. Everything is now on offer here, from residential creative writing and poetry courses, to nudist beaches. Glyka Nera, literally 'Sweet Waters', is a beach known for the freshwater springs bubbling up from the stony surface. It is midway between Loutro and Chora Sphakion on the coastal path but can also be reached by boat. The cove is at the foot of a tall cliff and is a favourite hunt of nudists and campers.

Loutro can be reached by ferry, on foot from Anopolis (*see above*) or via the coastal path from Chora Sphakion (2hrs). The E4 path is reasonably well maintained but caution is required in bad weather because of falling rocks.

EAST OF CHORA SPHAKION

The coast road and the E4 coastal path run side by side up to Kato Rodakino in Rethymnon province, from where the former route continues to Sellia (32km) and the latter strikes inland into the empty reaches of the Alones plateau. One well-known attraction on the way is Frangokastello and its fine beaches; the rest of the road east, on the way to Rodakino, offers a very scenic, cool drive with access to the sea.

The churches of the Panaghia and Aghios Georgios

From Chora Sphakion before Komitades, just after the inland turning to Vryses, the **church of the Panaghia** is all that remains of Thymiani monastery, a 16th-century foundation where, on 29th May 1821, Sphakiots gathered to proclaim a revolt against the Turks. Although the Greek mainland was successful in its bid for independence, Crete was crushed. Further on, below the village of Komitades (Κομιτάδες; *map p. 428, C3*), the church of **Aghios Georgios**, on a spur overlooking the sea, has instances of work by Ioannis Pagomenos, in fact his earliest, dated by inscription to 1313 (unfortunately not in a very good state). The church is signed from the village church (*10mins on foot*). Leave the car there and take the path downhill past a white chapel (right); turn left on a side path and watch for the doorway half hidden to the left. After Komitades, the road crosses a number of gorges. At Aghios Nektarios a walk up the **Asphendou Gorge** (2hrs; *map p. 428, D3*) may be good for birds and rare flora.

Frangokastello

Up until the 1970s the Frangokastello (Φραγκοκάστελλο; *map p. 428, D3*) area was de-

View of the fortress of Frangokastello.

serted and the castle stood in splendid isolation, an outpost in the never-ending battle against pirate raids and attacks by the neighbouring Sphakiots. The fortress never had a settlement around it. According to Moody and Rackham in *The Making of the Cretan Landscape*, discernible field systems show that the area was farmed in post-Roman times, but not later.

Built in 1371 by the Venetians in a bid to strengthen security on the coast, the **fortress** was first named after the nearby chapel of Aghios Nikitas (*see overleaf*), acquiring its present denomination over the years ('Frankish' was a generic term for Western European). In 1770 the Sphakian leader Ioannis Daskalogiannis surrendered to the Turks here and was in due course executed in Chania. The surrounding plain later witnessed one of the bloodiest battles of the 1821–30 uprising. Early in 1828, Hatzi Mikhalis Dalianis, a freedom fighter from Epirus, landed at Gramvousa (a Turkish stronghold in the northwest of the island; *see p. 396*) with a force of 700 men. By March he had captured Frangokastello but his attempts to spread the rebellion failed. In May the Turkish governor advanced on the fort with 8,000 men. Rather than retreat to the safety of the mountains, Dalianis stood firm, dying the death of a martyr with his outnumbered troops. Ever since, according to legend, on or around the anniversary of the battle, during the last ten days of May, the souls of the dead men can be seen marching away from the castle in the soft light of dawn. The occurrence has been scientifically investigated and is believed to be an optical phenomenon akin to a mirage; local opinion firmly prefers its '*drossoulites*' or 'dew men'.

View across the Frangokastello plain to the White Mountains, with the village of Patsianos.

The castle today is an impressive rectangular shell with square corner towers. Its current aspect is the result of a last rebuilding by the Turks, after the fortification had been completely destroyed at the time of the Ottoman invasion (the Venetians had defended it side by side with the Sphakiots). It still looks remarkably similar to a drawing of 1631 by Monanni. The southwest tower is the largest, with a guardhouse adorned with the Lion of St Mark and the Venetian coats of arms of Dolfin and Querini, rectors in La Canea (Chania). There is nothing left of the original buildings in the interior.

The **sandy beach** nearby, with a majestic mountain backdrop, is on rocky ledge which means that the water is knee deep for 100m or so and is quite warm, ideal for children. Northeast of the fort, the **chapel of Aghios Nikitas** stands by the track leading directly back to the main road, 400m away. It was built over an Early Christian basilica, the smallest known so far, with a polychrome mosaic floor.

The island of Gavdos

Gavdos (Γάβδος; *see map on inside front cover*; Claudos in antiquity), the southernmost inhabited point in Europe (Africa is only 270km away), can be reached by ferry from Chora Sphakion or from Palaiochora; the former is a shorter run, just over an hour.

Gavdos is the only Cretan island with a permanent population, who live in four small settlements. Fishing and tourism are the main industries. Agriculture is almost no more and the island is now more wooded than it ever was. Archaeological evidence for occupation dates to the Neolithic period; in Graeco-Roman times it was a dependence of Gortyn, with a flourishing community which led to over-exploitation

View of the Omalos plateau in early spring.

ing route should be well prepared. April is also the time when the rare wild tulip, *Tulipa bakerii*, is in flower all over the plateau. Most of the seasonal shepherd's dwellings are abandoned and in ruins today, though this has happened only in this generation. Outside many of them you can still clearly see the outlines of circular threshing floors.

THE SAMARIA GORGE

Reputedly the longest canyon in Europe, the gorge of Samaria (*map p. 428, C3*) is now a national park. Eighteen kilometres long, it is still two short of the Verdon Gorge in France; that said its rare fauna and flora amply make up for the missing length. Together with the neighbouring gorges of Klados, Eligas and Trypiti, Samaria is one of the few remaining refuges on the island for the Cretan Goat, known as Kri-kri or *agrimi*. Other interesting fauna include the Cretan varieties of badger, marten, spiny mouse and weasel, and a number of birds such as eagles, buzzards, vultures and Lammergeiers soaring in the thermals. Plants include cliff-loving species (cremnophytes and chasmophytes) that have taken to the heights to escape browsing animals, indigenous varieties of aromatics, flowering shrubs and flowers as well as the *Zelkova cretica*, a tree whose wood is traditionally used to make shepherds' crooks.

Planning a visit

A trek trough the gorge requires some planning. Taking the car to the starting point at Omalos only works if you are prepared to climb all the way back up. The arrival point at

Nea Aghia Roumeli is only served by ferry to Chora Sphakion, Soughia and Palaiochora, from where buses run to Chania. Overnight stay in the gorge is prohibited. One option is to take an all-inclusive round-trip conducted tour (they come here from as far as Aghios Nikolaos). Alternatively there is an early bus from Chania or a hotel in Omalos, though the transfer to the starting point some 5km away still remains to be taken care of. Physically the descent can be taxing; the need for good footwear, a reasonable degree of fitness and adequate sun protection cannot be emphasised too strongly. Aghia Roumeli (Αγία Ρουμέλι; *map p. 428, C3*) has a beach and rooms to rent; it may be a good way to unwind, but accommodation does need to be booked in advance. Equally the ferry tickets should be purchased immediately upon arrival at the coast. Tour operators also advertise a 'Samaria, the Lazy Way' for the less fit. It tackles the gorge the other way round, up from Aghia Roumeli to the Sideroportes (about 1hr), but it is far less interesting.

THE CRETAN WILD GOAT

Familiarly known as 'Kri-kri' a name which only dates from after the Second World War, the *agrimi* (*Capra aegagrus cretica*; pl. *agrimia*) is a geographical variation, not a true sub-species, of a kind of goat with a habitat stretching from Turkey to Pakistan. It was introduced into the island by man c. 7000 BC (the earliest bones are from Late Neolithic Phaistos) and has done well, mainly because of the absence of large carnivores. In antiquity as now, the *agrimi* was the one of largest wild animals in Crete; only the auroch would have been bigger. It is also more than likely that in Minoan times they were larger beasts altogether, an inescapable conclusion drawn from representations of them pulling carts laden with people. Pierre Belon, the 16th-century French naturalist, was the first to describe the *agrimi*, and set it apart from the ibex, with which it is often confused. Pashley later identified it from three pairs of horns he brought back in 1836.

The invention of firearms caused a great reduction in numbers. *Agrimia* are now confined to specific areas: some 500 in the White Mountains, including the Samaria Gorge, and the rest on islands (about 300 on Dia and far fewer on Aghii Pandes and Theodorou).

The male is reddish in colour with seasonal white markings which ensure that the buck is well visible in the breeding season. Body mass is in the region of 30–40 kg (females are about half or a third of that). The male's horns can grow above 80cm. They curve backwards, have a D section and are quite broad at the base. Along their length are knobs from which it is possible to tell the age of the animal. If you get close enough—and that will not be easy as *agrimia* are both shy and very agile—you will be able to see the black elongated pupil with its true demonic look, the black beard and the forked tail.

The Sideroportes section of the Samaria Gorge.

Walking the gorge

The gorge, beginning at an altitude of 1250m and stretching to almost sea level, is open to the public from the beginning of May to the end of October. Plans to start the season earlier in the spring have so far come to nothing because of safety considerations. The area is subject to flash floods and accidents have happened. Only 3,000 people are allowed in per day and it is advisable to come as early as possible before the busloads arrive and the heat sets in. The best season is the spring: it is cooler (there is little ventilation where the gorge narrows) and the vegetation is more interesting.

Guards are posted along the route to enforce the rules, which include a ban on alcohol, singing and loud noise (which might dislodge loose stones). A full list of dos and don'ts is provided with your entry ticket. On the back of it, a map shows the location of water points, first aid facilities and toilets.

It takes about five to eight hours to walk to Aghia Roumeli along the *xyloscalo*, the stone path with wooden railings. At the start the scenery is dominated by the rock-face of **Gingilos** to the right, and an abundance of scented Cretan pine (*Pinus brutia*). The path descends to an area of deciduous trees to join the stream bed of a seasonal watercourse, the Tarraios. The spectacular **waterfall** at the chapel of Aghios Nikolaos comes from a tributary. It is a good spot for the *Paeonia clusii*, with its white flowers occasionally flushed with pink.

The village of Samaria is now deserted; the inhabitants were relocated to the coast in 1962 after the establishment of the national park. The Byzantine **chapel of Osia Maria of Egypt** (which eventually contracted into 'Samaria', giving the location its name) is all that remains of it. It had some wall paintings but is now used as the guardians' station and picnic ground. Later on rise the **Sideroportes** ('Iron Gates'), a very narrow gap with sheer vertiginous faces about 3.5m wide and over 600m high in places. For centuries it afforded protection from the north to the inhabitants of the village of **Palaia Aghia Roumeli**. In the disturbances of 1866, many rebels took refuge in the gorge or congregated on the shore in the hope of gaining a passage to the mainland. The Turks sent 4,000 men and though they did not manage to gain access to the gorge, they burnt the village. A crumbling Turkish fort, a ruined Venetian church and a few derelict houses are all that remains. Palaia Aghia Roumeli was badly damaged by flooding in 1954, and was eventually abandoned when the gorge became a national park. Archaeological investigations have shown activity in the area dating to the Late Minoan period (a stone column with a double axe is in Chania museum). Palaia Aghia Roumeli stands on the site of the **city-state of Tarra**, presently 2km inland from the sea and not visible from it. It rose to importance in the Roman period, minting its own coins (with a wild goat, a bee and an arrow), acting as a staging post to Egypt and trading in timber. Glass slag and a glass ingot, now in Chania museum, suggest local glass manufacturing but conclusive evidence has proved elusive. The city's decline set in during Late Antiquity with the change of trade route patterns in the east Mediterranean. The church of the Panaghia was built within the walls of a 5th–6th century basilica of isodomic construction and with a mosaic floor. German excavations during the Second World War revealed an earlier pebble mosaic showing the head of Apollo. He apparently hid here to escape wrath of Zeus after slaying the Python at Delphi. A Hellenistic temple dedicated to Apollo Tarraios, described by Buondelmonti in 1415, may therefore have predated the basilica.

The walk ends by the sea at **Aghia Roumeli**: this village is completely new. There was nothing here until the late 1970s.

PRACTICAL INFORMATION

GETTING AROUND

• **By car:** The way to the Theriso Gorge is signed off the New National Road from Vamvakopoulo (direction Garipa). The Omalos road is clearly indicated. The loop from Theriso to Zourva and Meskla is particularly recommended but it is slow driving.

• **By bus:** Services from Chania go to Omalos (45mins). Limited services from Soughia, Kissamos (and the holiday resorts on the way) and Palaiochora, though this is long and probably not a good plan. See www.bus-service-crete-ktel.com/maps3han.html. Theriso has a limited service from Chania as does Meskla (the alternative is to get off at Phournes on the Omalos bus and walk 5km). Travel agencies organise trips to the Samaria Gorge.

• **By sea:** See ferry information on p. 357 and www.sfakia-crete.com/sfakia-crete/ferries.html. Ferry times advertised on the website are subject to change and it is always advisable to check. Anendyk Maritime S.A, Aghia Roumeli (*T: 28250 91251*). It is best to book ferry tickets from Aghia Roumeli in advance or immediately upon arrival.

WHERE TO STAY & EAT

Aghia Roumeli (*map p. 428, C3*)
A day or so in Aghia Roumeli is highly rec-

ommended, rather than making a dash for the ferryboat upon arrival. The place does die down in the evening and has a charm of its own. The village is not short of accommodation, but with the numbers trekking the gorge it must be booked in advance. Options include € **Sweet Corner Mashalis Apartments** (*mobile 6974 631029; minimum stay; www.greekhotel.com/crete/chania/mashalis/home.htm*), € **Aghia Roumeli Hotel** (*T: 28250 91241 or 91232*) and € **Tara Calypso** (*T: 28250 91231*).

Omalos (*map p. 428, B3*)
€€ **Neos Omalos Hotel and Restaurant**. The hotel is open all year round and at that altitude (1050m), snow is to be expected. It caters for mountaineers, wildlife and flower enthusiasts and provides information on walks and activities in the area. *T: 28210 67269 or 96735 or 67590, www.neos-omalos.gr*.
€€ **To Exari Hotel and Restaurant**. The hotel is open all year round and offers a minibus service to the *xyloscalo* and other departing points for hikes. *T: 28210 67180, www.exari.gr*.
Theriso (*map p. 428, C2*)
Chaniots come here for day trips; accommodation is limited to a few rooms to rent. Food is more plentiful: **O Lebentis** (*T: 28210 77102*) and **Melintaou** (*T: 28210 77292*) have a good reputation. Alternatively, drive to Zourva to **Emilia's** (*T: 28210 67470 or 67060*).

SELINOS

EASTERN SELINOS

The Venetians called the rugged southeastern part of Crete Selino (a Greek name), and its main city (now Palaiochora) was Castel Selino. Eastern Selinos covers the part of Chania province that is edged by the Aghia Eirini Gorge to the east and to the west by the main road to the Libyan Sea from Floria. Mount Apopigadi (1331m) rises to the north and settlement is on the slopes, tucked away in a maze of winding roads following the folds of the valleys. It becomes scarcer towards the coast, which is quite empty. The coastline is only accessible by sea or on foot along the E4 walking route, reaching Elaphonisi to the west and Frangokastello in the east, before striking inland towards Alones.

INLAND TOWARDS AGHIA EIRINI & THE COAST

From Chania set off in the Omalos direction and at Phournes (15km) take the right turn towards Skines. This is citrus country, but the landscape soon changes and the orange groves disappear as the road gains height towards the wooded foothills of the White Mountains, in the direction of Nea Roumata past Chliaro. **Nea Roumata** (Νέα Ρούματα; *map p. 428, B2*), now set in a land of sheep and fruit trees, is at the top of a valley with good communications to the north coast. There is evidence of early occupation in the area from the late 4th millennium, the beginning of the Prepalatial period. In the 1980s, two small tholos tombs made of river pebbles were excavated and traces

Small Early Minoan tholos tomb near Nea Roumata.

of settlement have been located in the surroundings. The tombs, the westernmost in Crete for that period, are quite small and yielded very plain grave goods. Their nearest parallel should not be sought in the more imposing tholos tombs of the Mesara (*see pp. 146–47*), which were communal (at Nea Roumata the grave was for a single occupant), but further north in the Cyclades.

After Prases take the left turn at Seliana towards Omalos (13km). This is a reasonable road, with fine views but still requiring careful driving. It leads to the western pass onto the plateau, marked by the chapel of Aghios Theodoros. West of the pass, the **Aghia Eirini Gorge** stretches all the way to the sea at Soughia. It may not be as long as Samaria but Aghia Eirini (now a nature reserve) attracts its fair share of devotees as it is equally beautiful and less crowded. The entrance can be reached from Chania by bus (trust the driver) and there are a few facilities. It may well be advisable to walk the gorge now, before everyone finds out about it. The entry is south of Aghia Eirini village (Αγία Ειρήνη; *map p. 428, B3*) and the beach is four hours away. For the final two hours the gorge follows the road and the best of the walk is already behind you. There is nothing lost at this point in trying to hitch a ride to Soughia.

Soughia

Modern Soughia (Σούγια; *map p. 428, B3*) is, like many resorts on the southwest coast, a comparatively recent development sprung up to cater for tourism; however, unlike Aghia Roumeli, it is accessible by car, which means that it can form part of a day trip from Chania. But it would be a pity to spend so little time here. The place merits more than a fleeting visit, and in fact makes an excellent base for walkers and sightseers alike. The town stands on the site of the ancient harbour of Syia, which was one of the ports of Elyros (*see p. 374*), in the days before piracy made coastal settlement insecure. Pashley saw some ruins when he visited, and **Roman remains** can be spotted east of the river bed (look for tile- or stone-faced concrete remains). Sea level was higher in antiquity and the harbour was on the west side of the river mouth, protected by a mole. It is possible to make out the old waterline on the cliff-face several metres up and to discern wave notches to the right of it. On the raised beach at the near end of the village a modern church was built into the foundations of a **6th-century basilica**, the only feature that has so far been excavated. Its polychrome mosaic has now been removed to Chania museum for safety: it is held to be among the finest of this date on the island (comparable to the one in Thronos; *see p. 301*). Designs include a kantharos with tendrils and ivy leaves with deer and peacocks. Early Christianity adopted the peacock as a symbol of immortality (*see box overleaf*).

Occupation at Syia came to an end with the Arab conquest. The assonance of the name with the ancient Greek word for pigs prompted suggestions that its prosperity had come from pig-rearing, taking advantage of the abundant oaks and acorns on the hilly slopes. There is no evidence for that. Presently the eastern end of the beach is known as the 'Bay of Pigs', but that may be an unkind comment on the nudists who have taken a shine to it.

PEACOCKS IN ANCIENT ICONOGRAPHY

Originally from India, the peacock with its stunning plumage became a symbol of power early in antiquity in spite of its ugly feet and its even uglier voice. Peacocks decorated the thrones of ancient Babylon and Persia. In Classical Greece they were associated with the chief female deity. What the eagle was to Zeus, the peacock was to Hera, who was reputedly responsible for the design of the bird's tail feathers with the hundred 'eyes' in memory of the faithful Argus, the giant whom she had entrusted with watching over Io, one of her priestesses, when her wayward husband Zeus fell in love with her. Peacocks transferred well into the Roman world, maintaining their privileged position as the totem of Juno (Ovid, *Metamorphoses 1, 721*) and developing a reputation for having something immortal about them, with incorruptible flesh and ever-regenerating plumage. They therefore became associated with the apotheosis of emperors when, upon their deaths, they joined the ranks of the gods. Images of peacocks began to appear on tomb walls and on funeral lamps, and at the same time we also find them on coins, such as those of Faustina the Younger, wife of Marcus Aurelius, in the second half of the 2nd century AD. A facing pair of peacocks pecking grapes or flanking the Tree of Life is not rare in Roman mosaics of the late empire in Rome and in Antioch. The theme makes a much earlier appearance beyond the Alps, however, on pottery of the 1st century AD. As there were no peacocks in these northern countries, it is thought that craftsmen took their inspiration from images woven into textiles imported from the East.

With the advent of Christianity the peacock's incorruptible flesh came to symbolise resurrection and the immortality of the soul. The very same scene described above, with the two facing peacocks still pecking grapes or drinking from a chalice, is frequently found in Christian mosaics, where it became the representation of the soul in paradise, while the hundred 'eyes' on their tails were the symbol of the ever-watchful Church.

The present association of peacocks with vanity and pride appears to be a comparatively recent development, though even in the past not everyone can have been convinced by the quasi-divine status bestowed on this bird. The Renaissance cookery book *Il Cuoco Napoletano* contains a recipe for roasted peacock. The bird was skinned, roasted on a spit and brought to the table clad in all its fine feathers looking alive and breathing fire through its beak.

Lisos

From Soughia the coastal path and the ferry go to Aghia Roumeli. For Lisos (Λισός; *map p. 428, B3*) there is a choice: by boat, if you can arrange for a local to take you, or on foot.

There are three ways to walk to Lisos, either along the coastal path (from Soughia or Palaiochora) or from the north. The two shorter routes, from Soughia and from the north, are detailed here.

View of the south coastline near Lisos.

The **walk from Soughia** (90mins), a marked stretch of the E4, starts at the west end of the pebbly beach where a narrow gorge leads into the mountains. After 30mins and past a smooth cliff, watch out for a left turn uphill (it is marked and there is a cairn). The path climbs through some heavily scented pines to a treeless plateau with a good view. After 10mins Lisos is below you and the descent arrives near the sanctuary of Asclepios.

The **walk from the north** is longer (about 2hrs), but with splendid views of the coast and of Gavdos, and magnificent flowers (including a profusion of the spectacular *Arum purpureospathum*, in full bloom in April–May) and birds of prey circling overhead. The walk starts at Prodromi (Προδρόμι; *map p. 428, B3*), east of Palaiochora, on a very good and scenic road. At the very beginning of the village of Prodromi, park by the tiny roadside chapel on the left (the other landmark is a cube-shaped white building with a blue door on the opposite side of the road). The path to Lisos starts on the south side of the road immediately facing the roadside chapel. The path is unmarked, with branches serving a number of agricultural plots. The best way not to get lost is to aim straight for the sea, which comes into view pretty soon. At that point there is only one path anyway. When you reach the brow of the hill, with the road zig-zagging below you, look out to the right for the remains of circular stone structures. These have been interpreted as watch-towers (*vigle*), though without excavation the date cannot be determined. With the sea in view follow the road to the plain, always keeping left of the twin peaks edging it to the right. On the plain you will meet the E4 coming in from Palaiochora. The road continues east and eventually comes to an abrupt stop. Look below and there is Lisos.

Two chapels are useful landmarks. The **Panaghia** is near the shore and incorporates Roman marble blocks and other spolia, including a fragment of a sarcophagus from Asia with a Medusa head. **Aghios Kyriakos**, with interesting frescoes, stands at the apex of the triangular valley thought once to have been Lisos' harbour. The expanse is now a beautiful emerald green pasture. The descent is a bit of a scramble, though there are some splashes of paint marking the path (they are more visible on the way back).

The location now known as Aghios Kyriakos was in antiquity an important coastal settlement with occupation attested from the Hellenistic through to the late Byzantine periods. It was abandoned during the 9th-century Arab occupation; the silting up of the harbour may have played a part in the decline. In antiquity Lisos functioned mainly as a port serving the towns of Elyros and Hyrtakina (*see overleaf*) and as a fishing and trading centre with a powerful navy. In the 3rd century BC it was allied to Carthage, a member of the league of the Orei (the mountain people) and minted its own coins with images of Artemis and a dolphin. However, ancient Lisos' real fame came from its healing spring, which made its fortune.

The shrine that grew up around the spring, the **Asclepieion**, was known throughout the region and pilgrims flocked to it, anxious for a cure to their ills. Although the location of ancient Lisos was roughly known (Robert Pashley had visited in 1834), serious investigation only began in 1957, when the Asclepieion, a small Doric temple of Hellenistic construction with a double dedication to Asclepios, god of healing, and his daughter Hygieia, was accidentally discovered by a local while digging for a well. Statues were unearthed and Nikolaos Platon was called in to excavate the structure and its fine mosaics. In the remains of the temple, built in isodomic ashlar blocks except for the east wall, which may represent an earlier phase, the excavators identified a cella opening to the south with a marble podium for cult statues inside at the north end, and a low kerb all around the floor mosaic. The pit on the stepped bench in the northwest corner has been interpreted as a libation channel or the place of Hygieia's sacred snake. The temple's fountain, piping the spring water on the east slope near the temple, is past the forecourt to the south down a flight of steps.

As well as the Asclepieion there are **Roman remains**. On the western slope is the necropolis, its rock-cut graves (over 100 have been identified) a reduced version of the arcosolium type, with barrel vaults and niches, comparatively rare in Crete. Similar tombs are known in Soughia and Lasaia in the bay of Kali Limenes. Dotted around are the remains of public baths, the foundations of houses, traces of an aqueduct and theatre, as well as the remains of port installations, possibly the old harbour mole (the 150cm-wide wall, now a good 150m inland after tectonic displacement, northwest of the present beach).

Evidence shows desecration of the site by early Christians. In the Asclepieion it seems that the cult statues were defaced and then buried in a pit dug through the mosaic floor, with scant regard to its geometric design and animal figures. After the temple collapsed in the 2nd century, Christian zealots appear to have completed its destruction. Excavations at Lisos were never completed and the site has since been left untended, which means that the ruins are not easy to find, being covered with vegetation. Nevertheless, this is a site to be savoured, as rarely these days can one can enjoy archaeological remains in the wild with a stunning view to boot. Take your time—as well as your own food and water as there are no shops—and simply look around.

THE HINTERLAND: FROM AGHIA EIRINI TO KAVALLARIANA

The village of **Aghia Eirini** (Αγία Ειρήνη; *map p. 428, B3*) is a good example of the local pattern of land use. For centuries the inhabitants have grown vegetables on the Omalos plateau and grazed their flocks on the high pastures in the summer. Beyond Prines, the road drops down to **Tsiskiana** (Τσισκιανά; *map p. 428, B3*), where excavations in the 1980s uncovered a rural sanctuary dedicated to Poseidon, in use from the 4th century BC to the 2nd century AD. A large collection of well-preserved terracotta figurines of oxen (now in Chania museum) were recovered. From Kambanos the south road leads to **Moni** (Μονή; *map p. 428, B3*) for the church of Aghios Nikolaos, with frescoes by Ioannis Pagomenos dated 1315. One of the first houses, just beyond a fountain on the left, keeps the key. The church is also on the left, hidden by trees in summer, but otherwise marked by a distinctive free-standing bell-tower, believed to be contemporary with the building. You can drive down a track from the turn-off, 800m back around the curve, or walk down a footpath (10mins) from the custodian's house. The single-nave church has an annexe across its west end which, surprisingly, could not be entered via the nave. Pagomenos painted the frescoes of the original church with stories from the life of Christ and an impressive scene of St Nicholas being consecrated bishop of Myra, in Cilicia. The frescoes in the annexe are by a different hand.

Two kilometres south a minor road sets off east in the direction of the summer pastures of Mt Achlada. The last village, **Koustogerako** (Κουστογέρακο; *map p. 428, B3*), together with Livada and Moni, suffered extensively during the German occupation because of the involvement of the menfolk with the resistance movement organised by 'Kiwi' Perkins. In September 1943 a German detachment was preparing to execute the local women and children in the main square of Koustogerako, having failed to find the men. These were hidden on a bluff above, from where, at a distance of 400m, a well-aimed shot felled the German machine gunner. In the eventual reprisal the three villages were burnt. All three have subsequently recovered. This is not the first time that Koustogerako has risen from its own ashes. In the 16th century it was destroyed by the Venetians (*see p. 360*)

Elyros and Hyrtakina

For the site of **ancient Elyros** (*map p. 428, B3*), take the right turn south of Kambanos. The location of this Graeco-Roman *polis* is on a promontory overlooking the Libyan Sea and its harbours (three, according to the latest count: Lisos, Syia and Poikilasos, though the latter, at the end of Trypiti Gorge, seems unlikely). The site has never been excavated and is mainly known from surface finds (including the '*Philosopher of Elyros*', a large Roman statue now in Chania museum). Pashley was the first to identify the location from ancient topographical references, and the French antiquary Thenon found an inscription mentioning the citizens of Elyros in the mid-19th century. Pausanias included Elyros in his *Guide to Greece* and mentioned its connection with Tarra and the cult of Apollo. The city prospered under the Romans and into the Christian era: it had a bishop in the First Byzantine period but did not survive the Arab conquest. Remains of a theatre, cisterns, a 6th-century basilica (underlying the modern church of the Panaghia) and of a wall circuit have been traced.

Pashley also identified **Hyrtakina** (*map p. 428, B3*), signed up on a hill to the southwest past Maza and Rodovani, 5km on. He visited the acropolis, noting the commanding view to Palaiochora and beyond to Cape Krios, and reported finding a fortified enceinte with polygonal masonry, scattered pottery and the remains of a cemetery. Limited excavations have uncovered remains of houses and of a Hellenistic sanctuary to Pan. A 1st-century AD statue of the god is in Chania museum. In the church of the Panaghia at **Rodovani** (Ροδοβάνι; *map p. 428, B3*), the same Kantanoleon who brought about the destruction of Koustogerako (*see p. 360*) features as a donor in a fresco to the left of the iconostasis.

Temenia

A little way south of Temenia (Τεμένια; *map p. 428, B3*; a village that is reinventing itself as the soft drink centre of Crete), before the junction for the Soughia–Palaiochora roads, a left turn points to the **church of the Sotiros Christos**, formerly part of a monastery, which sits conspicuously on a hill. It is well worth a visit because of its unusual plan. The original single-nave chapel (tentatively dated to the 13th century) has a miniature version of a cross-domed church, probably dating from the 14th century, added to its west end. It is reached by shallow steps and takes the place of the conventional narthex. The frescoes are late (17th century) and only preserved in the original nave. They include an unusual theme for Crete, namely *Christ Before Pilate*, in one panel on the north side of the vault (western bay, lower register) and again on the west wall (below the *Entry into Jerusalem*). The unexpected figure behind Christ has been interpreted as Pilate's wife.

Anisaraki

About 7km north of Temenia, at Anisaraki (Ανισαράκι; *map p. 428, B3*), four chapels (*usually open during the day*) are all signed from the road. The first two, the Panaghia and Aghia Paraskevi next to it, are to the right. The **Panaghia**, on a terrace immediately above the road, shows strong Venetian influence. Note the original doorway in the south wall and the 1614 graffito, which may be associated with alterations. The late 14th-century frescoes are particularly well preserved. In the apse is the *Communion of the Apostles* below the *Virgin and Child* (*Platytera*) while the barrel vaulting is densely painted with scenes from the life of Christ. The frescoes in **Aghia Paraskevi**, on the adjacent, higher terrace, are also in the 14th-century style and include an image of St Barbara.

Aghios Georgios, with late 13th–14th-century frescoes, is signed (right) further on. The track leads to a group of houses and beyond them, after a 5-min walk, the little church is straight ahead. The frescoes include scenes from the life of the saint on the south side of the vault (martyrdom on the north side) while on the south wall he is represented on horseback between the Virgin (left) and Aghia Marina.

The church of **Aghia Anna** is at the end of the village to the right. Judging by the column fragments, it was probably built on top of an earlier basilica of the First Byzantine period. The frescoes are dated 1462 and include scenes from the life of St Anne. Nine donors of the Petro family can be admired for the details of their colourful attire at either side of the entrance. A rare feature is the painted stone iconostasis. The side facing the sanctuary has images of bishops while the other has panels with Christ Pantocrator and St Anne holding the infant Mary.

Kavallariana

From Anisaraki the road loops abruptly west, to Kavallariana (Καβαλλαριανά; *map p. 428, B3*), where the frescoes in the cemetery church of **Mikhail Archangelos** were traditionally attributed to Pagomenos, on the basis of the signature 'Ioannis' and the date (1327–28). Recent re-examination by Angeliki Lymberopoulou has cast doubt on this conclusion. Stylistically she sees a different hand at work and also detects evidence of the incipient hybridisation of the Cretan and Venetian liturgical heritage, the Orthodox and the Latin, both in the choice of the saints and scenes represented and in the profusion of donors, 14 of them, including children, all portrayed in colourful medieval costume. Among the figures represented are St Titus, Crete's first bishop (south wall of the apse), and the emperor Constantine (south wall of the nave, next to the inscription with the date 1327–28). Below the inscription, on either side of the window, are the archangels Michael (left) and Raphael (right); below them four more figures in a donor panel. The Cretan evangelist Aghios Ioannis Xenos (*see p. 166*) is between the two blind arches. On the north wall the archangel Michael appears twice more: in the eastern blind arch and above a donor panel representing the head of the family, his wife, a small child and two grown up children with their respective wives. The inscription above the small window makes a rare reference to the Venetian dominion in Crete. Normally at this time the hegemonic authority as far as the Church was concerned would have been Byzantium.

WESTERN SELINOS

The western part of the Selinos district is sparsely populated. Settlement is mainly inland, away from the dangers of an unwelcoming coastline, concentrated around the scarce patches of arable land and mainly on either side of the principal line of communication with the rest of the island, namely the road to Palaiochora, which branches off from the north coastal road at Tavronitis. The coastline is a great attraction to walkers, with the E4 walking route hugging the sea to Elaphonisi and beyond, to Moni Chrysoskalitissa. For visitors interested in Byzantine churches, the stretch between Kandanos and Kadros is particularly rich.

Kandanos

The area suffered heavily during German occupation, being close in its northern reaches to the main battleground of the Battle of Crete (*see p. 22*). This explains why Kandanos (Κάντανος; *map p. 428, B3*) looks so new. In spring 1941, in the immediate aftermath of the battle, as the British were evacuating south, the Germans, counting the heavy price of victory, were anxious to nip Cretan resistance in the bud. A harsh declaration promising severe reprisals was issued on 31st May. Three days later, Kandanos was one of the first villages to pay the price for resisting the advance of German forces, a motorcycle detachment to the south coast. The action was led by the local *papas*, Father Stylianos Frantzeskakis, who after assembling volunteers to the sound of church bells marched them to meet the Germans and held them for two days. Afterwards, in retaliation for the death of 25 German soldiers, Kandanos was utterly destroyed. As a deterrent to the general population, the occupying forces put up a sign saying: 'For the bestial murder of German paratroopers, mountain troops and pioneers by men, women and children together with the priest, and also because they mounted resistance to the Great German Reich, on 3.4.41 KANDANOS was razed to the ground never to be rebuilt'. The village has now been rebuilt and is flourishing. The sign can still be seen as part of the war memorial. The modern waterworks were donated by a German group as an act of reconciliation.

Skoudiana, Plemeniana and Kakodiki

Evidence of ancient occupation can be seen just north of Kandanos at **Skoudiana** (Σκουδιανά). The small church of the Panaghia is very pretty with its bell suspended between two external columns. All around are spolia, possibly from an early Christian basilica. Three kilometres south of Kandanos, at **Plemeniana** (Πλεμενιανά; *map p. 428, B3*), the church of Aghios Georgios is signed immediately below the road. The frescoes, dated 1409–10, show one of the archangels triumphant on horseback as well as a more gruesome scene of St George's martyrdom, strapped onto a cartwheel.

On the other side of the valley at **Kakodiki** (Κακοδίκι; *map p. 428, B3*) the churches are high up on a side road where the old village used to be, and signed. The *papas* with the keys, technically in the house 200m uphill beyond the church, is more difficult to track down. The church of Mikhail Archangelos is the smaller one next to the modern church of Aghia Triada. Dated to the 14th century, it has a single nave divided unusually into four bays by pilasters, and a fine wooden iconostasis. The fresco decoration was damaged as a result of Venetian alterations to the original Byzantine chapel, when a door and a window were inserted in the south wall. Scenes include the *Communion of* *the Apostles* below the Pantocrator in the apse and a rendition of St Michael on horseback. The church of the Panaghia has frescoes by Ioannis Pagomenos, dated 1332 and now in need of some attention. The *papas* is sure to tell you the story of the stolen icon returned by the thief himself after experiencing a string of troubles.

Tzinaliana and Kadros

For a rare sight in Crete, scenes of the life and works of St Isidore of Chios, go to **Tzinaliana** (Τζιναλιανά; *map p. 428, B3*), on the east side of the main road, taking the left turn for Kallithea (a name probably inspired by the fine view overlooking the river valley—and beautiful it is indeed). Isidore was martyred for his faith at the time of the 3rd-century emperor Decius, who during a reign of only two years earned a lasting reputation as a persecutor of Christians. At Tzinaliana, in the church dedicated to the martyr, the Isidore scenes are in two groups: Baptism, Imprisonment and Beheading; and opposite these his Confession of his faith to Numerius, the commander of the Roman fleet under whom Isidore was serving as an officer, and the ensuing Punishment (being dragged by two horses).

At **Kadros** (Κάδρος; *map p. 428, B3*), still on the minor road south of Tzinaliana, the church of the Panaghia, with frescoes dated to the second half of the 14th century, is downhill at the end of the strung-out village. The key is held in the house nearby. In the apse Mary is portrayed as the *Panaghia Eleousa* (the 'Virgin of Mercy'); the *Dormition* is on the west wall while the nave has scenes from the life of Christ. The ruins on a conical hill south of Kadros, at the end of a narrow winding road signed off the main road, have been interpreted as the **remains of ancient Kantanos**, though not everyone accepts the attribution. Excavations before the Second World War uncovered a large building with mosaics of Roman date and the base of a statue of Septimius Severus. Kantanos, which figures in the *Tabula Peutingeriana*, became a bishopric and, according to written sources, survived to the Second Byzantine period. After leaving your car where the track ends a 10-min walk leads to the site (*fenced*) in an idyllic setting. Some ruins can be seen, but of more interest is the strategic position overlooking the Libyan Sea and valley below.

Back on the main road to Palaiochora, at **Kalamos** (Κάλαμος; *map p. 428, B3*), note the small church of Aghios Ioannis, a rare instance of a church frescoed on the outside, on the entrance arch.

PALAIOCHORA

The town

The **castle platform** of Palaiochora (Παλαιόχωρα; *map p. 428, B3*) stands quite empty and ruinous today, between the modern town and its ferry port. Its general contour can be made out by following the remains of the perimeter wall. It is possible to climb on top following a path at the very south end, first leading to a chicken shed and eventually to the platform where the fortress once proudly stood. The best way, though, to appreciate the general topography of Palaiochora, is to drive a short distance east on the road to Anydri and look back. Then fort, town and sea all come together in a coherent picture.

Location is the secret of Palaiochora's success as a holiday resort. It is reasonably well equipped for tourists, with fine beaches on either side of the promontory: the **pebble beach** (Chalikia) to the east, where the old fishing harbour is, and a **sandy beach** (Pachia Ammos) to the west. It also offers a choice of water sports, from canoeing to scuba diving, and a ferry service east and west and down to Gavdos. Walkers will find the E4 trail—which here hugs the coastline—rewarding for wild flowers in the spring. On the west coast, past the sandy Grammeno beach, serious walkers can get as far as Elaphonisi (*see p. 380*), though it is wise to check on the state of the road first. Along the way, you will encounter another of Crete's geological oddities: at Cape Krios the water temperature is lowered by freshwater springs out in the sea.

Palaiochora is best visited in the height of the season, when visitors bring the town to life. In the summer evenings the main thoroughfare, Venizelou, is closed to traffic, brightly illuminated and filled with the overflow from tavernas and bars. In low season the place is very quiet, but can still be a suitable base for committed walkers and enthusiastic botanists.

HISTORY OF PALAIOCHORA

Possibly built on the site of the ancient Dorian town of Kalamydi, Palaiochora sits on a narrow promontory jutting into the Libyan Sea, on which the Venetian governor Marino Gradenigo built a small garrison fort (Castel Selino) in 1279. Shortly afterwards, the stronghold fell into the hands of rebels and was destroyed. In 1325 Venice rebuilt the castle using local labour. The labourers were promised their freedom when the work was completed, and settlement around the castle was encouraged by granting various exemptions. Even so, the castle was never much of a defence. The corsair Barbarossa did serious damage in 1539, and pirates raided again in 1579. They blew up the gate and found the locals cowering in the cistern. After this the castle was deserted and left to the elements. In 1595 the rector of La Canea (Chania) had some repair works done and was able to report to the senate in Venice that Castel Selino had a door that shut properly, and a garrison. In 1653 the Turks trained a cannon on it from the mainland. What they did not destroy they later demolished, and over time they built their own small fort on the site. Today nothing can be made out of the original shape of the Venetian fort, which was square with four towers, though the cistern is still there.

ENVIRONS OF PALAIOCHORA

Anydri and Prodromi

From Palaiochora a secondary road runs east along Chalikia beach before climbing 6km inland to **Anydri** (Ανύδροι; *map p. 428, B3*) along a beautiful wooded gorge. The church of Aghios Georgios is signed from the middle of the village, below the road to the right.

The frescoes, dated 1323, have been attributed to Ioannis Pagomenos. The decoration includes scenes from the lives of Christ and the patron saint in the north aisle, with the saint's martyrdom vividly portrayed: the tearing of his flesh, laceration on the wheel, the lime pit, the flagellation, the cauldron and the decapitation. Note the long dedication which suggests that practically the whole village had contributed. The frescoes in the other aisle, dedicated to Aghios Nikolaos, are the work of a different artist.

Prodromi (Προδρόμι; *map p. 428, B3*) is another 7km on. The track right before the village leads to Lisos (*see p. 370*). In Prodromi the church of the Panagha Skaphidia, dedicated to the Presentation of the Virgin, is high up to the left at the north end of the village beyond the modern church. It is a small building, with a single nave and distinctive zig-zag plaster moulding on the exterior of the apse. The frescoes have been carefully restored and are dated by an inscription on the west wall to 1347. The artist, named as Joachim, shows the influence of Pagomenos.

Azogyres

Another minor road explores the hinterland at a turn north of Palaiochora, before Lygia (3km). Azogyres (Αζογυρές; *map p. 428, B3*) is a diminutive village that became popular in the 1970s and '80s when hippies flocked to it from Matala. The Alpha coffee house-cum-restaurant and museum (*open all year*), with Cretan, Turkish and Venetian memorabilia, dates roughly from that time. The hippies have now departed but the beautiful landscape is still here and Azogyres is rightly a very a popular venue for walks. The locality is riddled with caves. One of them, signed right on the way to the village, comes suitably supplied with legends concerning no fewer than 99 holy fathers who, in the 14th century, came to this cave from Egypt, Cyprus and Attalia (present-day Antalya on the south coast of Turkey) via Gavdos, and lived in it before founding a monastery. This and other manifestations, like the evergreen plane tree that makes the sign of the Cross with its branches, have bestowed on Azogyres a reputation of deep spirituality. Believers and sceptics alike should at any rate sample the delicious 'Sophia's omelette' at the Alpha restaurant. From Azogyres, past Strati, a good road climbs on to Temenia and Elyros (*see p. 374*), exploring the high ground overlooking the Libyan Sea.

The Pelekaniotikos Valley

To explore the area inland from Palaiochora, where there are some interesting churches and fine landscapes, take the secondary road parallel to the main road and to the west of it, and follow it to Kondokinigi (8km), continuing north for 3km to **Sarakina** (Σαρακήνα; *map p. 428, A3–B3*). The church of Mikhail Archangelos, with frescoes dated stylistically to the second half of the 14th century and a fine rendition of Christ and of the *Panaghia Eleousa* (the 'Virgin of Mercy') on the stone iconostasis, is signed before the village, to the right along a paved footpath. The keys should be with the *kafeneion* in the village. The modern monument on the way commemorates an incident in 1897, the last year of Turkish occupation, when 150 Turks withdrawing to the coast in order to leave the area were massacred by Christian forces. In the village itself, the church of Aghios Ioannis has remains of frescoes dated 1341–49.

For the Pelekaniotikos Valley proper, return to Kondokinigi and turn left for Voutas, bearing left at the river crossing. Note the old bridge to the right of the modern one. The area, which suffered devastating floods in 2000, is dotted with churches with 13th–14th-century frescoes, of interest to the specialist. Watch for a left turn in Voutas to **Chasi** (Χασί; *map p. 428, A3*) for the church of Aghios Ioannis Chrysostomos on the outskirts of the village, with frescoes of the mid-14th century; another **Azogyres** (Αζογυρές) for Aghios Georgios (late 13th century); and **Kityros** (Κίτυρος; *map p. 428, A3*) for Aghia Paraskevi, with a fine rendition of sinners in Hell and their punishment; frescoes dated to the second half of the 13th century on the east wall, and to the 14th century.

Sklavopoula

Sklavopoula (Σκλαβοπούλα; *map p. 428, A3*), 21km from Palaiokhora, is high enough (650m) to afford a view of the sea across the cultivated hillside. The name is said to indicate that the original settlers were of Slav origin, possibly mercenaries left behind by Nicephorus Phocas after he defeated the Arabs in 961. Alternatively it could have been a city peopled by slaves, a recurrent theme in antiquity. A cluster of ruins to the north is called Doulopolis, and there the slave connection is quite clear (from *doulevo*; 'work'), but the site has not yet been investigated. Sklavopoula has three frescoed churches. At the entrance next to a school playground, is **Aghios Georgios** (*the key should be with Pedros in the house behind the school*). The architecture belongs to two different phases, as do the wall paintings. The earlier work in the sanctuary is dated by an inscription above the window to 1290–91. The later frescoes, dated stylistically to the 14th century, depict the life and martyrdom of the patron saint on the north wall (upper register). Below, from left to right, are St Theodore and the archangel Michael flanking St George on horseback. The two other churches are in the old village below. From the main square (where the modern church is), turn left down a *kalderimi* about 400m and then left again. The guardian lives in the house near the partly ruined Venetian tower. The churches are on the left, above the *kalderimi* just after the last houses. The first one is dedicated to the **Sotiros Christos**, with fragmentary scenes of the life of Christ. On the north wall it is possible to make out the donor (Partzalis) in a bucolic setting with the church in the background (traces of an earlier phase of frescoes can be identified). The south wall has remains of military saints on horseback and two graffiti (1422 and 1514). In the **church of the Panaghia**, immediately above on the hillside, the extensive fresco decoration is in much better condition. Stylistically the paintings belong to the late 15th–early16th centuries (graffito of 1518). Art historians see them as transitional towards the Cretan School of painting. In the apse the Fathers of the Church are shown with the sacrificial Lamb on an altar and the instruments of the Passion foreshadowing the event. The vault has Gospel scenes; on the north wall the donor is shown with a model of the church.

THE WEST COAST

Elaphonisi

Long regarded as one of the most idyllic spots in Crete, the island of Elaphonisi

(Ελαφονήσι; *map p. 428, A3*) is experiencing increasing tourist pressure since the road to the north was upgraded. The height of summer, with its boatloads and busloads of visitors, is probably best avoided. Out of season, however, on an overcast day with the low windswept vegetation and that 'end of the world' look, it does look desolately striking.

The island is connected to the mainland by a shallow causeway no deeper than a metre, which can be crossed when the sea is calm. There are tavernas on the mainland (with rooms to rent in high season) and plenty of space to camp. Apart from the swimming off the sandy beaches, which is excellent, there is the promise of rare flora, of exclusive frogs, snakes and lizards. The sea turtle uses the beaches as a breeding ground, while fishermen have reported sightings of the Mediterranean seal (*Monachus monachus*). Bird-watchers will recognise it as a good spot: the last stop before Africa.

Moni Chrysoskalitissa

Situated at the south end of Stomio Bay, named after the now deserted village of the same name whose fate was tied to the coastal trade, the monastery of the Chrysoska-litissa (*map p. 428, A3*) is of no great architectural value; nevertheless, its unique position, on top of a rock jutting into the sea and battered by wind and waves in a landscape of Mediterranean scrub and *phrygana* and the occasional palm tree, is stunning and inspiring. There are no secure dates for the history of the foundation, but there was certainly something here by 1639 because it is mentioned in written sources. The name itself (Chrysoskalitissa; 'of the golden stair') has no ready explanation, or one too many. It is variously attributed to a venerated icon of the Virgin, or to a golden step, which, so the legend has it, only true believers can see. The monastery cannot be visited but do climb on top of the rock for the view and note on the way, before the entrance, the reproduction of an icon commemorating an event in 1824 when the Turks are said to have come up from Elaphonisi to destroy the monastery (empty at the time) only to be repelled by a swarm of furious bees. The view from below, from the vegetable plot off the car park, is also recommended, to get an idea of the effects of wind erosion.

PRACTICAL INFORMATION

GETTING AROUND

• **By car:** The main through road to Palaio-chora heads south from Tavronitis. An alternative route from Kissamos involves driving south to Mathiana and then going cross country via Strovles. The Selinos road network, including the secondary roads, is reasonable but sometimes short on signs.

• **By bus:** Services run from Chania to Soughia and Palaiochora (see www.bus-serv-ice-crete-ktel.com/maps3han.html for a map of services). The same website hosts information on services from Kissamos, but it is inconsistent. It shows routes but no relevant timetable. Check on the spot. Buses also run from Palaiochora to Koundoura, on the coast to the west, and from Chania to the entrance to the Aghia Eirini Gorge.

• **By sea** See information on the south coast ferry service on p. 357 and www.sfakia-crete.com/sfakia-crete/ferries.html. Port Authority of Palaiochora, T: 28230 41214. Reduced service in winter. Ferries run between Palaiochora and Elaphonisi (5km from Moni Chrysoskalitissa). Elaphonisi can be a day trip from Palaiochora using the bus and returning by ferry.

TOURIST INFORMATION

Palaiochora
Tourist office in a cabin on the pebble beach to the east (*T: 28230 41507; open Wed–Mon 10–1 & 6–9 in holiday season only*).
Bus station on Venizelou, opposite the filling station.
Post Office on the sandy beach to the west.
Tourist police T: 171.

WHERE TO STAY & EAT

Azogyres (*map p. 428, B3*)
€ **Alpha Rooms and Restaurant**. Enjoy excellent wholesome food in a café that doubles up as a museum, then retire to a room with a sea view. The place runs all sorts of activities (of late they have done a 'Sheep-Shearing Olympics') including yoga and tai-chi and can advise on walks in the area. *T: 28230 41620 or 41388; azogires-alpha.blogspot.com.*
Chrysososkalitissa (*map p. 428, A3*)
€€ **Glykeria**. Taverna and apartments with pool, very close to the monastery. *Open mid-April–end Oct; out of season by arrangement. T: 28220 61292; mobile 6947 949614; www.glykeria.com.*
Elaphonisi (*map p. 428, A3*)
Elaphonisi is only alive in high season (April–Oct). Accommodation is not plentiful and comparatively pricey. One good choice is €€

Elafonisos Rooms (*T: 28220 61548*), with a taverna and a view of the island.
Kandanos (*map p. 428, B3*)
€ **Apopigadi**. *T: 28230 22566.*
Palaiochora (*map p. 428, B3*)
Palaiochora offers a fair amount of choice. The €€ **Megim** (*T: 28230 41656 or 41690; www.megimhotel.com*) is 2km west of town. The €€ **Lisos** (*T: 28230 41122; www.lisos-hotel.gr*) is a small family hotel with a travel agency inside and a garden. Cheaper options include the € **Aris** (*T: 28230 41502; www.aris-hotel.gr*) on the southern edge of the original village, with a garden and some sea views; the € **Glaros** (*T: 28230 41635 or 41613; www.hotelglaros.gr*) right in the centre; and the € **On the Rocks Hotel** (*T: 28230 41735 or 42302*) below the castle wall, with a sea view.
Soughia (*map p. 428, B3*)
Soughia is purely a holiday resort, so tends to look a bit dead out of season. Accommodation includes rooms, studios and apartments (*http://www.soughia.info*).

FESTIVALS & EVENTS

Each year **Palaiochora** hosts a long summer festival with puppet theatre, traditional music and dance, classical music recitals and art exhibitions. At **Azogyres** on Easter Eve a midnight vigil is celebrated in the tiny chapel of the Holy Fathers followed by the burning of an effigy of Judas stuffed with fireworks.

BOOKS & FURTHER READING

Vasili: The Lion of Crete. The story of Dudley 'Kiwi' Perkins, reconstructed from documents and interviews by fellow New Zealander Murray Elliott.

Nicolaos Pyrovolakis: *Paleochora (A Look Back into the Past)*, sometimes available at the tourist office in Palaiochora.

THE FAR NORTHWEST

The northwest end of Chania province has been, up until quite recently, comparatively isolated. Kastelli Kisamou (officially renamed Kissamos but still known locally as Kastelli) is the commercial and administrative centre of the area. The economy
used to be based on agriculture and fishing but, with improved communications, tourism now holds more promise. Kissamos is only 40km from Chania and has a fast
connection along the new national road, called here the E65, all the way to Trachilos,
its ferry port. Improved ferry communications from the harbour connecting western
Crete to the Peloponnese have also helped. Kissamos works well as a base to explore
the wild countryside up the two peninsulas forming the Gulf of Kissamos, the rugged
hinterland with the remains of Polyrrhenia and the area along the empty coast that was
once the preserve of the city state of Phalasarna.

The coastal plain immediately west of Chania witnessed the crucial moments of the
Battle of Crete in May 1941, initiated by a German airborne attack from bases in Attica using parachute troopers and gliders (Operation Merkur). The prize was the vital
airfield of Maleme, now the site of the German War Cemetery (*see below*). The coast
has changed considerably since those days: the old and the new roads running parallel
have fostered a haphazard and unsightly tourist development.

Maleme and Tavronitis

The **German War Cemetery**, signed left to the west of Maleme (Μάλεμε; *map p. 428,
B1*), stands on a hill 2km inland. Over 6,000 Germans (the figure includes those lost
at sea), died in the operation. Here are the graves of 4,465 of them, remembered in
the stark simplicity of flat headstones. George Psychoundakis, the freedom fighter and
author of *The Cretan Runner* (*see p. 320*), spent his final years tending the graves. In
1966 a **Late Minoan IIIB chamber tomb** was excavated in the vicinity of the modern
cemetery (*signed*). The tomb has a very long dromos leading to a rectangular roofed
chamber. Note the doorway, designed with a relieving triangle behind the upright slab
above the heavy lintel. The tomb had been robbed but two interesting seals are recorded: one in bronze, perhaps originally covered with gold leaf, showed a cow suckling
her calf; the other in agate was carved with *agrimia*.

The cemetery lies at the north end of a ridge running out from the White Mountains:
this was Hill 107, a vital position in the battle. Prison Valley, which bore the brunt of
the German landing and along which the defeated Allied forces began their retreat to
the south coast, runs from Chania in a southwesterly direction to Alikianos. The area
today will appeal to bird-watchers. Eleonora's falcon (*see p. 262*) breeds on some of the
offshore islands (Theodorou, opposite Aghia Marina, is also an *agrimi* reserve). Further
west at **Tavronitis** (Ταβρωνίτης; *map p. 428, B1*), where the road from Palaiochora joins
the coastal road, the Tavronitis river has some promising reed beds. When the river is
fed by the melting snows of the White Mountains, it forms a small lagoon at its mouth

that offers shelter to wading birds on migration. The best spot used to be the old Tavronitis bridge but there is now a lot of builders' rubble on the banks. It is best to walk or drive for about 1km along the west bank to the shore.

THE RODOPOS PENINSULA

Stretching out into the Mediterranean for 16km to Cape Spatha at the top, the Rodopos peninsula (*map p. 428, B1*), known as Tityros in antiquity, is rough country, with steep shores, no water, no cultivable land and just a few goatherds and shepherds. It was not made to sustain settlement; human habitation huddled at the southern end, where a clutch of small villages (Astratigos, Aspra Nera, Ravdoucha, Rodopos and Afrata) used to eke out a meagre living from fruit trees and olive oil. In the distant past settlement might have spread a bit further, as shown by the finds in the cave north of Afrata, where evidence for both habitation and burial dating to Neolithic times was recorded (it is one of the few places showing occupation that early in western Crete). Beyond, the pure wilderness and emptiness of the landscape have made this an ideal setting for communion with the gods. The sanctuary to the goddess Diktynna, high on the cliffs above Menies cove, was renowned throughout antiquity. Though not much remains of its former glories, the crystal clear water of the cove, sheltered from the north wind, makes it a choice spot for a memorable swim.

There are three ways of exploring the peninsula, which is served by a single unsurfaced track along its spine from Rodopos village all the way to Menies Bay. For the average hire car with its low undercarriage clearance, the track is not suitable much beyond Rodopos. Walking, however, is a possibility, with superb views of the mountain and of the sea and the added bonus of a possible visit to the site of the **cave of Ellinospilios** (follow the sign to the left to the church of Aghios Konstantinos after Afrata; proper exploration of the cave, though, is only for specialists). Inland, in the village of **Rodopos** itself (Ροδωπός; *map p. 428, B1*), a 16th-century Venetian villa is being restored. It is much in the style of the Villa Trevisan (*see p. 387*), with the entrance on the first floor.

The peninsula can be walked in a single day. That, after all, is the way the pilgrims did it in antiquity, and they had to walk barefoot to keep in close contact with the earth: indeed at the very end of the peninsula, before the roads descends east to Menies, stretches of the original 6m-wide paved **Roman road to the Sanctuary of Diktynna** can be made out. If you elect to walk, do bear in mind that the terrain is very exposed and there is no water.

Gonia Monastery

Gonia Monastery or Moni Gonias (*map p. 428, B1; open Mon–Sat 8–12.30 & 4–7, Sun 4–7*) is situated at the base of the Rodopos peninsula on a minor road c. 1km from the centre of Kolymbari (23km from Chania). It has a good snorkelling beach below it with a fine view all around.

The monastery is traditionally associated with the Zangaroli family, Venetians who adopted the Orthodox faith and whose name metamorphosed from Giancarolo to Zangaroli (*see p. 334*). The foundation is dated to 1618, although another version purports that it is much older, dating to the 9th century, and that it was originally located at the tip of the peninsula at Menies, near the ruins of the sanctuary of Diktynna (*see below*). It was then dedicated to Aghios Georgios, but for greater security it moved here and was rededicated to the Panaghia Odighitria (the 'Virgin as Guide'). Yet barely 11 years after the first cruciform church was completed, it was severely damaged when Turkish forces chose this spot to begin their conquest of Crete in 1645. The monastery however, was able to secure stavropegial status, which put it under direct protection of the Patriarch of Constantinople. The church was rebuilt in 1662, and the monastery also ran a school which played an important part in the preservation of Greek culture, collecting an important library in the process. This was almost completely lost in the 1866 disturbances; a 17th-century codex survived. In 1821 the monastery served as a hospital and, as a wise precaution, temporarily dispersed its icon collection: they were later returned.

Visiting the monastery

The **church of the Odighitria**, now restored after damage during the German occupation, is at the seaward end of the courtyard. The **refectory** in the northeast corner has a Classical doorway in marble with Baroque volutes. The **cannonball** in the wall of the south apse is a relic of the Turkish bombardment. The monastery has a fine **collection of icons**, some of which are displayed in the small museum together with other ecclesiastical items. The icons include a triptych of the *Last Supper–Nativity–Ecce Homo* by Dimitrios Sgouros (1622) and a *Crucifixion* by Konstantinos Palaiokapas (1634), which in the treatment of the background, with buildings in a landscape and a realistic anatomy, betrays the influence of Italian art. Of particular interest is a tomb stele of the 3rd century BC, originating from the ancient Diktynnaion (*see below*). It bears a relief representation of Aphrodite with a ship and Britomartis with an *agrimi*.

Outside the west gate, a **fountain** (1708) bears an inscription translating as 'Most delicious Spring of water bubbling up for me; Water for all creation, the sweetest element of Life'. The ruins up the steep path belong to a **13th-century chapel** with traces of frescoes (*for access ask at the museum*). The modern complex above the shore beyond the monastery is the Orthodox Academy of Crete.

The Diktynnaion

The Sanctuary of Diktynna or Diktynnaion (*map p. 428, B1*) was the most prestigious sanctuary in western Crete in Roman times. Control over it was a matter of fierce rivalry among the cities of the area, especially Kydonia (Chania) and Polyrrhenia.

The Diktynnaion can be reached by vehicle (four-wheel drive recommended), but it is a much more appealing idea to approach it as the ancients would have done, either on foot, or by sea. For the latter option, it is possible rent something privately in Kolymbari, though it will be expensive.

The present remains date from the time of Hadrian and his purported visit to the island (c. AD 122–23), and incorporate earlier structures. The temple is located on either side of the water course that runs into the cove where the excursion boats land. There are remains of Roman buildings on the north side of the beach; a head of Hadrian (now in Chania museum) was discovered in one of them in 1913; on the south side are traces of a bridge which may also have served as an aqueduct.

THE CULT OF DIKTYNNA

The cult of the Greek goddess Diktynna, related to that of Britomartis (meaning 'Sweet Maiden'), was linked by Hellenistic writers to hunting and fishing. A temple built in the late 6th century BC is mentioned by Herodotus (*III, 59*) and it may not have been the first one. A possible survival of the Minoan mother goddess, Diktynna developed over time into a deity of nature, of the wild countryside and mountains, a local variant of Artemis with whom, according to the poet Callimachus, she spent much time. Diktynna was venerated in several sanctuaries (in Athens, in the Peloponnese and at Marseilles) but the focus of her cult was always western Crete, and this temple was her most important. According to tradition it was guarded by hounds as fierce as bears.

The great temple stood on the promontory to the south of the cove: it would have been visible in its stark whiteness from a great distance. The Germans carried out excavations here in 1942 and concluded that the site had been extensively looted and robbed in antiquity. They uncovered a platform belonging to a temple built in limestone with columns in blue and white marble. It stood in a court paved in marble with a stoa on three sides. This was tentatively dated to the 2nd century AD; earlier remains to the west point to occupation from around the 7th–6th centuries BC. South of the terrace are four cisterns of Roman date, with a total capacity of c. 400 cubic metres. Between the temple and the cisterns stood a stepped altar of white marble, while at the southwest corner of the temple was a circular building, a possible treasury. The statue of Diktynna with hound, now at Chania museum, was found here in 1913.

INLAND TO THE MESAVLIA GORGE

A short detour inland south of Kolymbari leads through beautiful countryside to interesting Byzantine churches and the beautiful Mesavlia Gorge.

Spilia and Episkopi

The church of the Panaghia at **Spilia** (Σπηλιά; *map p. 428, B2*), signed to the right at the far end of the village on a wooded hill, has frescoes dated stylistically to the 14th century with a 1401 graffito cited as an early example of the Cretan School. The name of the location suggests the presence of a cave, and indeed there is one at Marathokephala above the village. The chapel inside the cave is dedicated to Aghios Ioannis Xenos (*see p. 166*). Two kilometres further south, on the way to Episkopi, **Aghios Stephanos**, a tiny

10th-century frescoed church, is signed to the right, 150m away, surrounded by plane trees beside a ravine. After Drakona take the right fork for **Episkopi** (Επισκοπή; *map p. 428, B2*) and the church of Mikhail Archangelos, situated on the slopes of a wooded valley before the village. The settlement was the seat of the bishopric of Kissamos in the Second Byzantine period. Architecturally it is unique in Crete: the only comparable building in Greece is Aghios Georgios in Thessaloniki. Essentially it is a rotunda with an apse, the whole enclosed in a rectangular building. The rotunda rises to a stepped dome consisting of five concentric rings. Evidence for a mosaic floor dating to the 6th century suggests that the present structure was built over the foundations of an early Christian basilica. Recent investigations have uncovered graves and pushed the date back even further, making this possibly the earliest church in Crete, of which the rotunda itself may be the relic. Three different phases of wall painting have been identified, dated from the 10th–12th centuries. The elliptical baptismal font with two semicircles at the ends has a ready comparandum in Venice in the church of San Giacomo dell'Orio.

Deliana, the Mesavlia Gorge and Palaia Roumata

The church of Aghios Ioannis at **Deliana** (Δελιανά; *map p. 428, B2*) has an attractive façade with putti, lions and peacocks, all originally part of a sarcophagus belonging to the Vernier family, of Venetian extraction as the family crest testifies. Still deeper in-land, 5km on towards Mouriziana, is the **Mesavlia Gorge** (*signed*), 6km long and still a well-guarded secret, superb for flowers and aromatic plants. Indeed this whole area is particularly beautiful, and was much favoured by the Venetians for rural pursuits. At **Palaia Roumata** (Παλαιά Ρούματα; *map p. 428, B2*; take the right turn to Daskaliana, 11km from Voukolies) is a Villa Ranieri, nicknamed '*kamares*' because of the arches (*kamara* = arch). It is still lived in but you can climb the outer staircase to the main entrance to see a fine doorway with the Ranieri crest. Another 10km south from Kako-petros, on the main road at Floria, take the turning to Sasalos for **Kato Floria** (Κάτω Φλώρια; *map p. 428, B2*). The church of Aghios Georgios is in the cemetery beyond the little bridge. Well-preserved frescoes by Ioannis Provatopoulos, dated 1497, show the donor and a number of saints. Of interest is the inscription above the head of the donor stating the bequest of one Alvise Cocco, a descendant of the very first Venetian settlers, of 20 goats 10 beehives and a tract of land with house and vineyard in 1462.

The Villa Trevisan

Back on the coast at Drapanias, Villa Trevisan or Travasiana, between the old and new roads at Kokkino Metochi (*map p. 428, B2*), is still an impressive sight, though it is much in need of restoration. The 15th-century Venetian country house overlooking the bay is signed up a narrow path after the Koleni exit on the main road. It is in true Venetian Cinquecento style. The shell of the building in worked stone survives to the first floor, accessible by two flights of steps supported by arches on the east and south façades. The ground floor is taken up by vaulted structures used for storage and supporting the living quarters on the *piano nobile*, which would have been cooler as a result. It is the same strategy that Arthur Evans adopted for his Villa Ariadne. Above the main entrance is the emblem of the Trevisan family. A certain degree of opulence can be seen in the surviving stone door frames and window cornices and the traces of plain fresco decoration. The villa is surrounded by a number of ancillary buildings, all stylistically contemporary. An EU programme is apparently set to carry out restoration work, but at present Villa Trevisan sits in a state of genteel abandonment.

KISSAMOS & ENVIRONS

Officially Kissamos (Κίσσαμος; *map p. 428, A2*), the town known locally as Kastelli Kisamou or just Kastelli, is an eccentric sort of place but it is served by a good road network and can be an excellent base for local exploration. It has good beaches: several on the western coast and one long one all the way to the base of the Rodopos peninsula.

HISTORY OF KISSAMOS

The traditional place name refers to the castle built by the Genoese buccaneer Enrico Pescatore, who challenged Venetian claims to the island in the early 13th century. The town is first mentioned in written sources in 1262 in connection with a revolt by the Byzantine Chortatzis and Skordilis families. The rebels were let down by the Byzantines and were crushed by Alexios Kallergis, the initiator of the 'Pax Kallergi' (*see p. 18*). In antiquity this was the site of Kisamos, a maritime and commercial centre and one of Polyrrhenia's ports. Over time it became an independent city, eventually superseding Polyrrhenia itself. In Roman times, with the demise of Phalasarna, it became the main port of western Crete, but suffered extensively in the earthquake of AD 365. Kissamos was the seat of a bishop until the Arab conquest in the 9th century and flourished under the Venetians.

The castle and the surrounding villages were restored by order of the Venetian Senate in 1334 but suffered from a pirate raid in 1554. The castle was left in disrepair for a time while different plans were being considered. In 1632, the authorities decided on a limited restoration, to be financed by the inhabitants. The plaque above the gate, dated 1635, commemorates the operation but overlooks the bad quality of the repairs: already by 1637 some of the walls were giving way. The Turks conquered it with little difficulty in 1646 and later reworked it, giving it an irregular pentagonal shape.

By the 19th century, Kissamos was a backwater. The 1866 drawing from the *Illustrated London News* in the museum shows a castle surrounded by a few shacks.

The town

Although early travellers speak of impressive remains (Onorio Belli mentions a theatre and an amphitheatre), archaeological investigations are not easy: the new town sits on top of the old one and excavations are linked to ongoing building programmes. With the development of good road communications, the town is expanding fast as a tourist resort, as reflected by the haphazard mix of holiday flats and the dwindling evidence of the traditional activities of agriculture and fishing. Sheep and goat pens, chicken coops and vegetable plots sit side by side with mushrooming hypermarkets. Kissamos at the moment is a construction site; indeed building supplies outlets are much in evidence. As the building works progress, however, and the Greek Archaeological Service gets a chance to excavate, a picture of the old town is beginning to emerge. Some old remains are signposted in the town, but the best place to gain an understanding of them is the Archaeological Museum.

The Archaeological Museum

The museum (*open Tues–Sun 8.30–3; T: 28220 83308*), which opened in 2001, is one of the very best in Crete. It is housed in an old public building used in turn by the Venetian and the Ottoman authorities. It was originally outside the castle enceinte but became incorporated in the fortifications when the defences were extended by the Turks. The museum is in the centre of the town, in Plateia Stratigou Tzanakaki.

The display, complemented with maps and explanations in Greek and English, is organised on two floors. Downstairs the exhibit deals mainly with finds from the area, while the upstairs space is devoted to the town itself.

Ground floor

Room 1 displays material from the site of Troullia, near Drapanias, where a Minoan settlement covering the period EM II–LM III has been excavated. Some of the finds, such as scuttles and fire boxes, are usefully presented with pictures of frescoes from Thera showing them in use, while a whole block of conical cups and fragments of rhyta found in a pit (possibly the result of a ritual practice) is presented 'as found'. The settlement was reoccupied from the 5th century BC to the First Byzantine period. Pashley identified it with Mythimna but there is no evidence to support the hypothesis.

Room 2 is mainly devoted to Phalasarna and Polyrrhenia, the two most important city-states in western Crete. Phalasarna (*see p. 394*) was destroyed by the Romans in 67 BC and eventually put out of use by the rising of the shoreline. It is well represented, with finds both from the harbour and the necropolis. Note the board for a game of *enneada*, still played around the Mediterranean. Polyrrhenia (*see p. 392*), a powerful city-state south of Kissamos, with influence and land possibly extending to the south coast, had a longer history, continuing into the Byzantine period. The panel on city-states puts the two settlements in context, charting their development into oligarchies consumed by infighting, followed by the establishment of the *Koinon Kriton* (the Cretan Federation) under Knossos or Gortyn and the end of independence with the arrival of Rome. Tylipho's stele (a stone now lost, here a picture) from Gramvousa island's Sanctuary of Aiakos belonging to Phalasarna, sets out the terms of the alliance between Polyrrhenia and Phalasarna. It specifies military responsibilities and the allocation of booty and reconfirms borders. A similar stone would have been set up for Polyrrhenia in the Sanctuary of Diktynna at Menies.

RHYTA

Wide opening

Narrow opening

Unlike most vessels, rhyta were not meant to hold or store their contents. Indeed, the word rhyton derives from the Greek verb meaning to flow. Rhyta had two openings and judging by the diminutive size of the secondary one, they were designed to handle liquids (water, wine, oils, perfumes and even blood).

While waiting for organic residue analysis to shed light on the question, archaeologists have turned their attention to the morphology of the vessels to work out how they were used. Rhyta come in two main groups: they either have a narrow main opening that can easily be stopped with a finger, or they have a wide mouth. The first type could be filled by immersion, very much like a 'toddy lifter', an 18th-century glass device for decanting punch into glasses. The advantage is that in the process the sediment would not be disturbed and the collected liquid would be pure. The operation of course relies on blocking the main opening with a thumb when lifting, thus creating a vacuum inside, preventing the liquid from escaping. This is not possible with wide-mouthed vessels, which archaeologists interpret as strainers, with wads of wool used as filters. Rhyta therefore played a part both in purifying liquids or adding flavour to them with spices, honey and herbs.

The earliest examples, from around the 3rd millennium BC, come from the Mesara and are mainly in the shape of animals. This makes the rhyton a Cretan invention, which was eventually exported to Egypt, the Middle East, mainland Greece, Cyprus and even Italy. Over time rhyta developed into a variety of regular shapes, though animals (pigs, beetles, hedgehogs, birds, tortoises, bulls, rams and lions) appear to have remained firm favourites. Materials range from pottery to metal, stone, rock crystal and, in the case of the Minoan levels at Akrotiri on Santorini, ostrich eggshell with faïence fittings.

Rhyta are found in Crete from Prepalatial levels onwards in settings such as tombs, foundation deposits or peak sanctuaries, for which a ritual purpose can be surmised. They are normally more associated with males, which has prompted speculation that they were also used by priests in libations at important social events. There is probably some truth in this, as in Crete rhyta disappear with the collapse of the palatial society, of which the priests were an expression.

Room 3 has finds from the minor Hellenistic centres. Of particular interest are the black-painted ribbed vases with twisted handles and relief decoration. The inspiration is Ptolemaic and the main centre of production was Alexandria, though a number of these *Plakettenvasen* were made in local workshops. The rest of the room is taken up by Roman sculpture, with local copies of Hellenistic prototypes. Some came from the baths, others may have been in the theatre or other public buildings. A number of fragments were reused in the Venetian castle and have come to light with its gradual disintegration. By the lift to the upper floor, note the part of a Roman bathhouse *in situ*. It was found during renovations.

Upper floor

The entire upper floor is dedicated to the Hellenistic and Roman town. It is well worth taking time to look at the panel at the top of the stairs. It shows the modern town superimposed over the Roman Hippodamian grid, with the locations of the excavations. Even more interestingly it shows the old coastline, which in antiquity only reached as far as the castle; the old harbour was to the west but quite a way back. Indeed the ancient cement moles are now on dry land.

Room 4 brings home the lavish lifestyle of the upper classes in Roman Kissamos. Excavations have shown that dwellings could be quite large, sometimes occupying a whole *insula*. They had peristyles, atria, frescoes and mosaics. The examples here are particularly striking. The Dionysiac mosaic dated to the second half of the 2nd century, with the sacred hunt and putti pressing wine, is from a tablinum (a reception room connecting the atrium to the garden) and would originally have been larger, with the addition of a wide border on three sides. The mosaic of the Hours (in the middle) and the Seasons (in the corners; note the particularly good rendition of Winter), part of a larger composition, belonged to the triclinium of the same mansion.

Room 5 covers the town's economy with a well-documented display of amphorae.

Room 6 focuses on daily life in Roman and Hellenistic Kissamos, with some interesting pictures of the destruction layer connected to the earthquake of 365.

Room 7 deals with the world of the dead. Kissamos's necropoleis chart the continuity from the Hellenistic through the Roman to the early Christian eras, showing that life continued after the calamitous events of AD 365 and that by the 5th century Christianity had arrived in western Crete.

Environs of Kissamos

South of Kastelli the main road makes a wide loop around a massif that rises to above 1000m. This is chestnut country, with an annual festival at Elos (*map p. 428, A2*) in October. Going clockwise south of Kastelli on a narrow road, at Kaloudiana take the road right to Potamida for **Kalathenes** (Καλάθενες; *map p. 428, A2*; 10km) for the Rotonda, a 16th-century Venetian villa with barrel-vaulted ceilings (which probably gave it its name) and original fireplaces. It now houses a spinning and weaving cooperative. At **Topolia** (Τοπόλια; *map p. 428, B2*) the gorge of the river Typhlos is very dramatic, with high sheer sides dotted with numerous caves. Aghia Sophia cave, signed from the village (*15mins climb*), is known for its spectacular stalagmites and tiny chapel. Investigations have shown signs of Neolithic to Roman occupation. The village itself, in a pretty natural setting, has an interesting Byzantine church, Aghia Paraskevi, signed from the main street. High up on the gorge but only accessible from the secondary road (*signed Vlatos*) 6km to the right, the village of **Milia** (Μηλιά; *map p. 428, A2*) offers the ultimate 'away from it all' residential experience (*see p. 398*).

The road continues towards the coast skirting around the high ground. **Kefali** (Κεφάλι; *map p. 428, A2*), 24km from Kissamos, high up on a wooded valley, looks out to the distant sea. At the southern edge of the village, the church of the Metamorphosis has wall paintings dated to 1320. For the church of Aghios Athanasios, enquire in the village. It is a 20-min walk down a narrow path into the valley. The frescoes are the main attraction. On the south wall are the portraits of the donors, two women of the Venetian period, Anna and Moscanna, in their very best outfits. At the left turn to Moni Chrysoskalitissa (*see p. 381*), the village of **Vathi** (Βάθη; *map p. 428, A2*) has two frescoed churches. Aghios Georgios in the village (*signed right from the main square*) has paintings dated by inscription to 1254. In the fields immediately below the road, a few minutes south of the village, the church of Aghios Mikhail Archangelos has early 14th-century frescoes, notably the *Fall of Jericho* and the *Presentation in the Temple*. The paintings in the apse are slightly later. Ask for the keys at the café. The village used to be called Kouneni, and according to some it may have been the Roman town of Inachorium.

The west coast road closely follows the E4 path, with occasional side roads leading to the sea for a swim at Batisiana, Plaghia and Sfinari. This is a lovely, empty stretch of coast, served by a winding road in a wild landscape with olive trees and oleanders. The road itself, recently upgraded and completely asphalted, is not to be driven in a hurry. In spring this is a good place for wild flowers, always bearing in mind that the relatively damp, cool, west-coast climate may keep the season two weeks behind the rest of the island. At Zachariana a road turns inland along the E4 path to Polyrrhenia. Drivers may prefer to come straight from Kissamos (7km). Less then 2km on, before Platanos, a left turn leads to Phalasarna (6km).

POLYRRHENIA

The ruins of the ancient hilltop stronghold of Polyrrhenia, situated just north of the modern village (Πολυρρηνία; *map p. 428, A2*), are a recommended excursion. Park by the fountain in the village and take the path that skirts the acropolis on the south side. It leads through the picturesque old village to remains (marked) of the Hellenistic walls and higher up to the Roman cisterns. The path is overgrown but full of flowers and bees and not too difficult to follow. The north end of the acropolis is accessible by car. The ancient city lay spread out on the slopes with the acropolis high up with rock-cut cisterns. Water for the rest of the settlement was fed through a tunnel linking it to the abundant springs still operating in the village. The site, believed to extend over at least 30 hectares, has not yet been fully investigated. Halbherr visited in 1893. Since then Greek archaeologists have worked here intermittently.

HISTORY OF POLYRRHENIA

Originally an Archaic *polis*, founded, according to Strabo, by settlers from Laconia, Polyrrhenia flourished in Hellenistic times as a land-based power with a territory possibly extending as far as the south coast. Its name, according to the 6th-century grammarian Stephanos of Byzantium, is connected to its wealth in sheep (*rhenea*).

Polyrrhenia positively welcomed the Roman invasion and even erected a statue to Quintus Metellus Creticus, 'Saviour of the City'. This may explain its continuing prosperity. It declined, however, in late Antiquity, to be reoccupied by the Byzantines in the 10th century and used as a stronghold by the Venetians. Its strategic position on top of a hill defended by ravines made it almost impregnable. Even so, it was also walled and the fortifications, a mix of Byzantine and Venetian built on top of Hellenistic walls repaired in Roman times, reflect its chequered history.

The site

After leaving your car, the track leads to the church of Aghii Pateres (the 'Holy Fathers'), built on top of a large Hellenistic building, probably a temple, and incorporating spolia. Polyrrhenia's houses, cut in the rock with built façades, have not survived. The view from the church, taking in the whole gulf, explains the continuing appeal of the location. The Byzantine bastioned wall circuit is on the skyline to the right. Below the church a path leads to the Byzantine fortification, with some remains of the Hellenistic walls en route. These are marked in places and in any case are clearly different. The Byzantine walls are made of large boulders, the Hellenistic ones of carefully worked blocks.

Polyrrhenia's Hellenistic necropolis (finds in Kissamos museum) is signed below on the road to Lousakies. The chamber tombs can be seen from above—which is just as well since the directions are none too clear. It is a lovely walk among some very old and gnarled olive trees.

PHALASARNA

The site of ancient Phalasarna (Φαλάσαρνα; *map p. 428, A2*), on the western edge of the Gramvousa peninsula, lies below Cape Koutri, the rocky promontory at the north end of the bay of Livadi. The sandy beach is one of the finest on the island. In Venetian times it was surrounded by a defensive system. In the early years of the last century, Gerola was able to photograph a tower in the village of Kavousi to the south that was still standing to the second storey. Now the structure has been subsumed by a newly-built holiday home but its isodomic masonry can still be made out.

The site is at the end of an unmade road by the seaside, north of the modern settlement, past the last hothouses. On the way you see a **rock-cut 'throne'** which has given rise to much speculation. One suggestion is that it served as a speaker's podium. From the white chapel of Aghios Georgios, a footpath left leads to the site.

HISTORY OF PHALASARNA

Although already occupied since Minoan times, Phalasarna became an important naval and commercial hub in the Hellenistic period, when for a time it was the west-coast harbour of Polyrrhenia. What really set it apart from other coastal cities was its fortified enclosed harbour, spoken of in admiration in antiquity from as early as the 3rd century BC. Known as a '*kothon*', this kind of arrangement has Phoenician antecedents and parallels in Motya in western Sicily and in Carthage.

The sea entrance to the complex arrangement was via a purpose-built channel connecting the harbour to the water. The harbour was surrounded by walls and fortified by towers. The city maintained trade contacts with the Greek mainland and Egypt as well as with the rest of Crete; it minted its own coins.

The city was ultimately attacked and probably sacked by its rival Kydonia (modern Chania). Its final undoing, though, was a combination of events resulting from geological factors (rising sea levels) and historical events (Roman expansion). Phalasarna had already lost 1,500 of its men when it unwisely backed Macedonia in its wars against the Romans in 168 BC. Hard times may have encouraged it to turn to piracy, which attracted Rome's attention. According to the excavators, the defensive, quasi-military style of the port installation leaves little room for commercial enterprise. The destruction of Phalasarna can be dated to 69 BC when the Romans attacked, blocked the channel and destroyed the fortifications (several catapult stones weighing 6kg were recovered; they can be seen in Kissamos museum). By that time anyway Phalasarna was experiencing problems of land subsidence. This is confirmed by the archaeological record, which shows a series of makeshift structures built on top of the grand Hellenistic harbour in an attempt to keep it open.

After the Roman destruction, Phalasarna was no more. Nor was that the end of its geological troubles. In late antiquity tectonic displacement raised the coast several metres. In the mid-19th century Captain Spratt was the first to realise that owing to a change in the sea level, the enclosed harbour was high and dry 100m inland. Spratt also left an invaluable record of the upstanding remains.

Excavations began in the 1960s. Since then a mixed team of American and Greek archaeologists has been working at Phalasarna.

The harbour basin

The site, in a windy landscape of low, spiny vegetation, is always open and should be explored with some care and a good pair of shoes. The artificially excavated **har-**

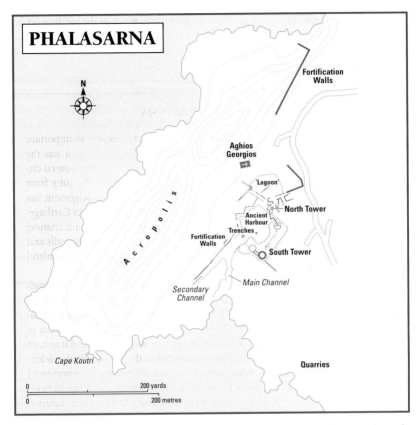

PHALASARNA

N

Fortification Walls

Aghios Georgios

'Lagoon'

North Tower

Ancient Harbour

Trenches

Fortification Walls

South Tower

Secondary Channel

Main Channel

A c r o p o l i s

Cape Koutri

Quarries

| 0 | 200 yards |
| 0 | 200 metres |

bour basin, roughly rectangular in shape (100m by 75m) is now filled with earth, but originally it would have been connected to the sea via a **channel** 10–12m wide. Investigations have shown that it had been deliberately obstructed with huge blocks. It is presumed that the Romans did this to stop the harbour being used for warships. A shallower **secondary channel** has been interpreted as a desilting device or as a dock for smaller boats. The harbour had a system of stepped quays in limestone and sandstone. It was defended by a stretch of the city wall with four towers. Early 20th-century reports mention large metal rings still attached to these towers: they would have been used to secure the ships docked in the harbour. The **south tower**, dated to the second half of the 4th century BC, was circular with massive foundations built in blocks of ashlar sandstone, isodomic in style, without mortar and strengthened inside by an arrangement of quadrants deliberately filled with rubble. In one part the tower is preserved to a height of over 4m. To the west, two parallel walls separated by a moat have been interpreted as a protective sea wall. A cistern (now covered) was bonded into the northwest side of the tower; its interior was plastered and then treated with black paint.

The rectangular **north tower** was reconstructed in late Hellenistic times. In antiquity there was a second basin to the north of this tower: its function remains uncertain.

The acropolis and walls

The **acropolis** (*not accessible*) on Cape Koutri is now in poor condition; it has the remains of two temples as well as cisterns and wells. The promontory was crossed in Hellenistic times by a fortification wall. It is possible to follow this all the way to the next cove north of the acropolis. On the way note the basins (under cover) looking like sit-up baths. These are Late Hellenistic and were used in industrial installations for washing ore and clay. A walk to the south on the limestone outcrop that sits on top of the conglomerate shows where the building stone came from. The **cemeteries** were on the rising ground inland.

THE GRAMVOUSA PENINSULA

The Gramvousa peninsula (*map p. 428, A1*) is named after the cape at its northern tip. It is a barren stretch of land reaching out due north into the Aegean. From its far end Antikythera can be made out in the distance to the northwest: it is only 64km away. Control of the channel was vital to the Venetians and prompted the building of a fortress to guard it.

The main attractions of the peninsula are the barrenness itself, the sandy lagoon at Balos and the fort on the island to the north. The area has unique flora and is protected as part of the Natura 2000 programme; fauna includes rare birds (98 species have been recorded), the Mediterranean seal (*Monachus monachus*) and even a herd of wild donkeys.

Access is by boat or on foot. Ferries run in the summer from the harbour east of Kissamos and proceed anti-clockwise along the coastline, with a visit to the fortress, ending the day with a swim in the green waters of Balos Bay. On foot it is a 21km round trip along a barren and very exposed path from Kalyviani at the base of the peninsula (it is possible to drive the first 3km). The path keeps to the eastern side of the peninsula, gaining height gradually to pass above several water courses. Long stretches are across bare hillside but a little over halfway a conspicuous clump of oleanders marks a welcome spring and conceals the weathered blocks of the old Aghia Eirini fountain. From the top of the plateau bear left, cutting off the narrow tip of the peninsula to Balos Bay. The cove is sheltered by the Tigani headland, connected to the shore by a sandy spit. The Venetian fort is on the island immediately north.

The Venetian fort

The fort, with a single access point and sheer cliffs all around, can only be visited as part of a boat trip. Building began in 1579, and because of the lack of local manpower, the workforce included prisoners, pressed labourers and volunteers, the only ones who were paid a wage. In a way the work was never completed. Its utility was questioned and, as always, Venice ran out of money. The fort suffered major damage in 1588 when the munitions stores were struck by lightning. It was rebuilt in 1630; in 1669 Francesco

Morosini hung on to it together with Souda and Spinalonga in a bid to secure Venetian trade routes in spite of the loss of Crete to the Turks. The defences were strengthened, it had huge water cisterns and even space reserved for cultivation. Even so Gramvousa was lost in 1715, when the Turks made their way in after bribing the garrison. In 1825, it was liberated by Cretan nationalists, who proceeded to use its strategic position for a spot of piracy, prompting an intervention by the French and the British. They posted a garrison here in 1828 with the consent of the newly-formed Greek state.

PRACTICAL INFORMATION

GETTING AROUND

• **By car:** On the New National Road (the E65 on this stretch) it is 22km from Chania to Kolymbari and another 12km to Kissamos. The Old Road runs closer to the sea and to the beaches up to Kolymbari and serves a ribbon development of holiday resorts. A very reasonable road loops south from Kissamos to Elos and Amygdalokephali, then turns north on a very winding, narrow coastal road hugging the hillside to Trachilos. This is part of the E4 and there will be walkers. The roads within the loop are of variable quality. Both peninsulas have very limited road access.
• **By bus:** Regular services run from Chania to Kissamos via Kolymbari (see www.bus-service-crete-ktel.com/maps3han.html. This gives a general idea, but it is inconsistent and tends to show routes but no timetables. It is always best to check on the spot). The bus station at Kissamos (*T: 28220 22035*) is in the centre, next to the Archaeological Museum.
• **By sea:** Kissamos' harbour is at Trachilos, 3km to the west. Summer ferries operated by ANEN Lines go to Kythera, Antikythera, the Peloponnese and Piraeus (*T: 28220 22655, www.anen.gr*). Summer day trips operated by Gramvousa Balos Cruises (*T: 28220 24344 or 83311, www.gramvousa.com*) go to Gramvousa

and Balos.
Kissamos Port Authority: T: 28220 22024.

TOURIST INFORMATION

Kissamos Police: T: 28220 22115.
Kissamos Health Centre: T: 28220 22222.

WHERE TO STAY & EAT

Kambos (*map p. 428, A2*)
€ **Sun-Set**. Rooms and taverna by the wayside in a forlorn spot overlooking the rugged west coast. *T: 28220 41128; mobile 6977 476551; info@sunset-crete.gr.*
Katsomatados (*map p. 428, A2–B2*)
€ **Panorama**. Rooms and taverna in the Topolia Gorge, on the main road with a very fine view. *T: 28220 51163.*
€ **Archondas**. Rooms and taverna south of the Topolia Gorge where the valley opens up. A good place for walks. *T: 28220 51531 or 24131; mobile 6946 577164.*
Kissamos (*map p. 428, A2*)
€€€ **Balos Beach Hotel**. Rooms, suites and apartments on the edge of the sea in a complex with its own beach and pools. *T: 28220 24106/7; www.balos.gr.*
  Other hotels include the €€ **Elena Beach** (*T: 28220 23300; open April–Oct*), next to

the beach as the name implies; and the €€ **Hermes** (*T: 28220 24109; www.hotelhermes. info*), also next to the beach, with a pool.

Two good-value choices are the € **Hotel Peli** (*T: 28220 23223 or 23654*), set in a garden with a pool. The owner, Mr Pateromichelakis, will be pleased to introduce you to his home-produced raki and wine. The € **Kissamos Hotel** (*T: 28220 22086; www.hotelkissamos.gr; open April–Oct*), with pool, is in the centre of town.

In Kissamos the better **eating places** are outside the centre. For fish try the two tavernas 1km to the west at Limni (**Captain**, *T: 28220 22195*, and **Gerotsengas**). On the way, next to the Hotel Aphrodite at Mavros Molos beach, **Stelios and Katina** (*T: 28220 23166; www.stelioskatina.com.gr*) offer typical Cretan food and local wine.

Kolymbari (*map p. 428, B1*)
The **Taverna tis Eftychias** (*T: 28240 22540 or 22777*) is acclaimed for its *Chaniotiki tourta* (a meat and cheese pie).

Milia (*map p. 428, A2*)
€€ **Milia Traditional Settlement and Organic Restaurant**. The 17th-century settlement of Milia (a name derived either from the wealth of apples in the region or the powerful echo of the surrounding mountains) lived and died without any interference from either Venetians or Turks. A look at the approach road (7km of it) and you know why. Now the stone houses have been restored as guesthouses powered by solar panels. Milia is an eco-adventure where guests can reconnect with nature by walking, hiking or simply by being there and enjoying the peace. Taxis will take you from Kissamos and Chania and the management runs a pick-up service off the main road if you come by bus. *T: 28210 46774, www.milia.gr.*

Phalasarna (*map p. 428, A2*)
The place has limited accommodation and only comes to life in season. The € **Sunset** (*T: 28220 41204 or 41440; mobile 6932 363374*)

has rooms and a taverna next to the site.
Platanias (*map p. 428, B1*)
Mylos tou Kerata. Situated in an old Venetian mill with both and Cretan and Mediterranean cuisine on offer, this is a good place to try the Chania *borek* (layers of vegetables and cheese covered in pastry). *T: 28210 68578; www.mylos-tou-kerata.gr.*

FESTIVALS & EVENTS

Culture festival at **Vathi**, last three days in July. **Vlatos** holds a Festival of Nature (first 10 days of Aug). The Feast of the Assumption (Analipsis; 15 Aug) is lavishly celebrated at **Gonia Monastery**. **Elos** holds a chestnut festival (around 21 Aug). The **Voukolies** raki festival is held in the first week of Nov. On the Tues after Easter at **Topolia** there is a grand feast in the cave of Aghia Sophia. **Rodopos** celebrates the feast of St John (28–29 Aug) at Aghios Ioannis Gionas, 15km to the north of the village in the direction of Cape Spatha and in the village itself.

WALKING

The **Forest of Peace** (*www.interkriti.org/visits/ kissamos/vlatos.htm*) around Vlatos (*map p. 428, A2*) covers an area of a million square metres and is part of a larger programme whereby 20km square have been reforested. Paths lead north to Milia and south to Rogdia.

LOCAL SPECIALITIES

In the village of **Voulgaro**, take time to visit Andonia Korkidakis's workshops (signed from the road) where she manufactures leather sandals (*T: 28220 51348*). In **Elos** Argyro Pantelantonaki (*T: 28220 24592*) runs a shop in the village and a stall by the wayside with local honey, wax, oil, herbs and raki.

PRACTICAL INFORMATION

GETTING AROUND

By public transport

Public transport on Crete began in 1927, with horse-drawn omnibuses. There is not, nor ever has been, a railway. The island now boasts an extensive bus network, based on the main towns, which is cheap, comfortable, efficient and reliable up to a point. On weekdays services are fairly frequent, becoming very restricted at weekends, often with only a single bus on Sundays. It is important to check on the spot, especially if you are intending to travel on public holidays. Buses are a good way to get around the main centres, but there are obvious limitations. The website www.cretetravel.com/Bus_schedules/index.htm provides an overview of services. Skeleton information with relevant links is provided in the Practical Information sections of each chapter.

By sea

Until the Ottomans began to develop the road network in the 19th century, water was the fastest and safest way to travel from port to port. While the north coast now has a fast road, the south-coast villages are still best served by boat. Ferries also operate on a number of popular routes, for example to the castle of Spinalonga north of Aghios Nikolaos. Where relevant, information about boats and boat trips is given in the individual chapters.

By road

Until the 1930s the Cretan road system consisted mainly of a dense network of mule tracks known as *kalderimia* (singular *kalderimi*). The word has a curious history. It is originally Greek (*kalos dromos*, meaning 'good road') and as such was exported east. The Turks contracted it and incorporated it into their own language, introducing it back to Greece in its new form. The routes of the *kalderimia* are probably very ancient: some may follow Roman or even older roads. Stretches of Minoan roads paved with small stones have been identified. *Kalderimia* were designed with a gradient or with steps that could accommodate beasts of burden and a drover on foot; they were not intended for wheeled traffic, though Minoan representations of carts pulled by *agrimia* are known. In the busy Cretan landscape, people walked (or were possibly carried by litter), which explains why the island was an importer of leather up until the 19th century, especially the heavy variety for the soles of boots. Walkers will find stretches of *kalderimia* incorporated into the E4 walking route. Cargo traffic was by sea, primarily along the north coast where the main cities were.

The first asphalt road was built by the Ottomans in the second half of the 19th century. The Old Road, as it is now called, runs east–west connecting towns and villages and often diving inland and meandering through beautiful landscapes. Some stretches have escaped widening and 'improvements', which makes motoring slow at times, but extremely pleasant and scenic. To accommodate the growth of traffic, a new highway was built in the 1970s. It has evolved into the New National Road, officially the E75, which can give the unwary tourist the mistaken impression of driving on a motorway (*see below*). Communication with the interior of the island and with the south coast is assured by a good road network running north–south. There is no continuous road along the south coast.

To explore much of the island, you do need to hire a car. Few Cretan hire cars are very robust; specify that you want a jeep or four-wheel drive if you plan to go much into the hinterland or the mountain areas.

Driving in Crete

Newcomers to driving in Crete will find themselves on a steep learning curve. Here are a few tips:

Maps and roads: It is possible to buy detailed maps of 1:100,000. That does not mean that all the information about roads is up to date, as these are routinely upgraded. Sometimes you will get a brand new road, but often the upgrading is still in progress: be prepared for heaps of gravel and heavy machinery by the roadside. The south portion of the road to Chora Sphakion from Imbros was, at the time of writing, precisely at that stage. It makes driving a challenge, especially when the road is already narrow, winding and busy. Alternatively the resurfacing peters out but the next stretch has already been dug up and made impassable for the average hire car.

The E75: This is not a motorway. Drivers should expect walkers, cyclists, slow farm machinery as well as stray dogs, sheep and pigs. Not all incoming roads have slipways. Be alert to possible crossing traffic.

Speed limits: On the E75 the limit is 70 or 90km/h, depending on whether it is single or dual carriageway, and 40km/h on the slipways. On the other roads the speed limit is variable and marked. At-

tempts to abide by speed limits on any road can be frustrating for other motorists. Tourists are expected to retire to the hard shoulder or take a break in lay-bys to allow the faster traffic to move on.

Petrol: There is no problem filling up in towns and along main roads. However, when venturing onto minor roads it is better to start with a full tank. There will be nothing in the villages. Petrol is not self-service and stations can normally only accept cash.

Tapping local knowledge: Cretans are only too happy to assist. The only problem can be linguistic, though a good map and a dose of body language will overcome it. Misunderstandings can arise as to the state of roads. What is a passable road for a tractor or pickup truck is probably not suitable for the average hire car.

Directions. Directions are normally well marked on main roads, not always so on minor ones. Tourist signs are not yet standardised. Be prepared for a variety of shapes and hues (mainly brown or blue) and, north of Elounda, for an elegant but tiny script scarcely legible from a safe distance.

Traffic signs: Most are immediately recognisable; some are written only in Greek, to no international format. Προσοχή! (Caution!) is the one to learn fast.

Parking: Parking can be a problem, especially in town centres. Be alert to the system of alternating parking, when you can park on some days of the month and not others: the sign looks like a blue and red no-parking sign with a I (for uneven days) or II (for even days). The local police are known to resort to dire measures to enforce the rules (for anyone, tourists included), including unscrewing number plates, which the hapless motorist then has to retrieve from the police station.

Going cross-country: The layout of Crete's road network is dictated by its geology and geography. Apart from the north coast, nothing is in a straight line. It can be futile to embark on minor roads in the hope of finding a more direct route. When in a hurry, make for the nearest main road. Going cross-country means slow driving along minor, winding, narrow roads with unpredictable surfaces. That said, in the right circumstances it will be extremely enjoyable and rewarding.

ACCOMMODATION & FOOD

The provision of accommodation reflects the history of tourist development. It is particularly abundant along the north coast, sometimes in an unsightly ribbon development, and in the main towns. This guide has paid particular attention to accommodation in the interior, not necessarily luxurious, but located off the beaten track in small centres, and aiming to provide a truly 'Cretan' experience. Note that these may not be open all year round and that prices may be based on multi-occupancy or a minimum stay. Many places are open only from Easter–October.

Crete has experienced many waves of destruction in its long history, both by man and by earthquakes. A lot of the accommodation might seem to be plain and functional, in modern buildings of little outward charm. Do not be deterred. The welcome you receive will almost always be warm and your stay will be made as comfortable as possible. Cretans are extremely hospitable.

Many hotels lack a website. Most are small and family-run and the telephone number will often be the mobile number of the owner. A number of booking agencies exist. CreteTravel (www.cretetravel.com) is one good example.

Price guides

Accommodation
(double room per night in high season)

€€€ (€150 or over)
€€ (€100–150)
€ (under €100).

Restaurants and tavernas
(per person, with a glass of local wine)

€€€ (over €25)
€€ (€15–25)
€ (€15 or under).

BLUE GUIDES RECOMMENDED

Hotels, restaurants and tavernas that are particularly good choices in their category—in terms of excellence, location, charm, value for money or the quality of the experience they provide—carry the Blue Guides Recommended sign: ■. All these establishments have been visited and selected by our authors, editors or contributors as places they have particularly enjoyed and would be happy to recommend to others. To keep our entries up-to-date, reader feedback is essential: please do not hesitate to contact us (www.blueguides.com) with any views, corrections or suggestions, or join our online discussion forum.

CRETAN FOOD

Lying in the centre of the east Mediterranean, Crete has developed a style of cuisine that reflects a variety of culinary influences. The quality of the raw ingredients (meat vegetables and olive oil) is also excellent. To sample this godsend, short of being asked into a Cretan home, the best strategy when looking for a taverna is to ask the locals where they go themselves.

Formal restaurants are few and are restricted to towns. They can be good, but they will be pricey. On the whole their menus tend to focus on 'international' cuisine, not always convincingly executed, and totally foreign to Crete. For the real thing, you need to find a village taverna with a good crowd of noisy locals, the television at full volume and the owner's wife in charge of the food. For much of the year it will be possible to eat at tables placed outside, and watch village life unfolding.

You can choose to have a light meal made up of *mezedes*, which are snacks of a bewildering variety including cheese, *dolmades* (stuffed vine leaves), *tzatziki*, *keftethakia* (little meat balls) and delicious deep fried zucchini balls, to name only a few. A more substantial meal will involve fish (at the *psarotaverna*) or meat, with roast lamb or kid, or *stifado* (a stew that still retains its Venetian name). Cheese has always been an important part of the Cretan diet, as an efficient way of preserving surplus milk. It has spawned a whole family of pies (*pites*, *bourekia*, *kaltsounia*), some sweet and some savoury, which show just what one can do with some fresh cheese, pastry and a lot of imagination and skill. These can be found at tavernas but also at the *fournos*, the village bakery. Finally, for those lucky enough to be in the right place at the right time, there will be the festival breads that combine gastronomy and religious symbolism and are a pleasure to behold. Easter is the time of renewal, fertility and the promise of plenty that the return of the spring brings. Hence the housewife will not stint on butter and eggs when preparing a *tsoureki*, and she will decorated it lavishly. At Christmas the *Christopsoma* ('Christ breads') are full of nuts, dried fruits and spices, as is traditional everywhere when nature takes a rest and there is no fresh fruit available.

OTHER INFORMATION

When to go

Crete enjoys a typical Mediterranean climate, meaning hot, dry summers and wet winters, with the added bonus of snow in the high mountains. The best seasons for travelling are spring and autumn. In the summer the coast will be very hot (the meltemi wind might help to cool the temperatures, but will make sitting on a sandy beach an unpleasant experience). In addition, not all accommodation has air conditioning and in some hotels it is an added charge. Locations in the interior will be cooler.

The sea on the north coast is warm enough for swimming by May. The south coast has higher temperatures and the Libyan Sea offers a more extended season.

For bird-watchers April is a good time for the spring migration. Botanists will be able to explore the lowlands from March and climb to higher altitudes as the season progresses and the snow recedes. Bear in mind, however, that early in the year the weather can be very unpredictable, with sudden changes and very cold nights. May is best for walking holidays, though with the risk of rain in the western part of the island, and the high mountains may still be snow-capped. Autumn can be good too, but the water supplied by the melting snow will have dried up and the landscape will have suffered as a consequence.

The winter season is very quiet, with a number resort hotels closing towards the end of October. There will still be accommodation in the main towns and in some inland locations high up if you fancy snow.

Maps

Good maps of Crete are published by Anavasi and Road Editions. Road Editions' 1:100,000 maps called *Eastern Crete* and *Western Crete* are excellent touring maps. Anavasi also has detailed walking maps. GPS data is being improved all the time, but some of the remoter areas will still show up blank on the screen.

On the maps in this book, places covered in detail in the text appear in black. Places mentioned for the purposes of orientation, road directions or for accommodation and tavernas appear in grey.

Telephones

The international dialling code for Greece is 30.

Opening times

Where possible we have given opening times for museums and archaeological sites. These should be treated as a guideline only. Opening times on Crete are always subject to change and can be very erratic, particularly outside the main tourist season. Village churches and chapels in the countryside are kept locked. The local *kafeneion* sometimes keeps the key; in other cases you need to track down the *papas* (priest). Wherever you are, don't hesitate to ask. Local people are always happy to help. When taking possession of a key, you will sometimes be asked to leave your passport as security.

GLOSSARY

Abacus (pl. *abaci*), flat block above the capital of a column, on which the horizontal architrave linking the columns rests

Aceramic, though pottery is normally present in the archaeological record from the Neolithic period onwards, there were phases known as aceramic in which alternative solutions (leather, wood or stone) were used for the same domestic functions normally performed by ceramic containers

Acrolithic, statue where the head and extremities are of stone while the rest is made of wood and covered by drapery

Aghii Anargyri, literally the 'penniless saints', Cosmas and Damian

Aghios, (*m.*), aghia (*f.*), aghii (*m.pl.*), aghies (*f.pl.*), saint(s), holy

Agora, public square or market place of an ancient city

Agrimi (pl. *agrimia*), wild goat (*see p. 365*)

Alabaster, soft sedimentary stone, sometimes translucent, pearly or banded in a variety of shades; gypsum, in a Minoan context, refers to the opaque variety. Much used in Minoan architecture for building blocks, though it quickly loses its finish on contact with water

Alabastron, small vase in alabaster, glass or clay, used for oils and perfumes (*see illustration on p. 411*)

Amphora (pl. *amphorae*), large two-handled vase for the storage and transport of both liquids and solids (*see illustration on p. 411*)

Amphoriskos (pl. *amphoriskoi*), a small amphora

Analipsis, the Assumption of the Virgin (the ascent of the Virgin to Heaven)

Andreion, public building or hall where men and youths ate communal meals

Apotropaic, said of objects or procedures intended to ward off evil spirits or bad luck (from the Greek meaning 'to turn away')

Apse, vaulted semicircular end wall of a basilica (*qv*) or church

Archaic, of sculpture, denotes a style from before the Classical era (*see Chronology, p. 412*), characterised by large eyes, a stiff smile, and stylised posture (*see picture on p. 182*)

Archontopouloi, traditionally the twelve aristocratic families sent to Crete from Byzantium to strengthen the Christian ruling class around the 12th century

Arcosolium (pl. *arcosolia*), a tomb where the sarcophagus or funerary bed is in a recessed niche surmounted by an arch

Ares, the Greek god of war, equivalent of the Roman Mars

Arsenali, Venetian shipyards

Ashlar, masonry consisting of blocks of stone precisely cut with even faces and square edges, laid in regular courses

Asclepieion, a sanctuary dedicated to the healing god Asclepios, where patients would seek cures

Askos (pl. *askoi*), squat, spouted pouring vessel for oil, often used for refilling lamps (*see illustration on p. 411*)

Backfilling, process whereby a trench is filled up again to the level of the surrounding soil at the end of an excavation or between periods of excavation. It is done as a safety measure but also to protect structures that are left *in situ*. Backfilling, however, does not stop the process of degradation, which starts as soon as excavation begins because excavation inevitably disrupts the delicate equilibrium that has ensured preservation

Basilica, originally a Roman hall used for public administration; in Christian architecture a three-aisled church with apse(s), the nave separated from the aisles by columns supporting the central raised roof

Bothros, a pit used in sacrifices and libations

Bouleuterion, a public building where the council of citizens (*boule*) met

Boustrophedon, a system of writing that involves alternating lines of left-to-right and right-to-left, like an ox ploughing a field (the derivation of the term); intended to avoid interpolations

Bucranium (pl. *bucrania*), originally an ox skull, sometime covered in plaster and used for ritual purpose. Later a sculpted ornament representing an ox skull

Carinated, pottery shape whereby a vessel with sides slanting outward is fused to an upper part with sides tending inwards. The joining line is often ridged (*see illustration on p. 411*)

Caryatid, female figure used as supporting column

Castellania (pron. '*castellania*'), a Venetian denomination for the subdivision of a province in Crete, normally controlled by a castle

Cavalleria, a Venetian denomination for an urban district in Crete

Cavea, the seating area of a theatre, named from the semicircular hollow dug out (exCAVated) from a hillside

Cella, enclosed interior part of a temple, also known in Greece as the naos

Chryselephantine, describes a statue or figurine in which ivory is used for the flesh parts and gold leaf (from the Greek *chrysos*, gold) is used for garments and armour. Other materials ranging from glass to precious stones were used for the eyes, jewellery and weapons

Ciborium, casket or tabernacle containing the Host (the Communion bread or wafer)

Cippus, an inscribed stone pillar used as a grave marker or as a boundary stone

Cloisonné, a metalworking technique in which objects are decorated with areas of multicoloured enamel partitioned by thin strips of metal

Codex, a medieval manuscript bound in book form

Corbelling, building system which gives support by the superimposition of projecting courses, each bearing the load of the next; used in tholos tomb vaulting

Corinthian, an order of architecture characterised by a capital with the shape of an inverted bell decorated with two or more rows of acanthus leaves sprouting scrolls at the top, and surmounted by an abacus (*qv*) with concave sides (*see illustration on p. 409*)

Corvées, a form of forced labour whereby a feudal lord may compel his subjects to perform unpaid work

Cross-domed, Byzantine church type in which a square central bay, with four arms of equal length (Greek Cross), is surmounted by a dome

Cross-in-square, a form of Byzantine church architecture consisting of intersecting barrel-vaulted naves of equal length (Greek Cross). The central section is surmounted by a dome, with smaller domes in each of the four corners

Cyclopean, a type of masonry composed of huge blocks, so large that they appear to have been laid in place by giants (the Cyclopes)

Daidalic, sculpture of the Bronze Age and Archaic period characterised by large, staring eyes, wig-like hair and stiff drapery. The term derives from Daedalus the mythical Bronze Age craftsman, builder of the Labyrinth

Deësis, iconographical composition of petition or intercession with Christ between the Virgin Mary and (usually) St John the Baptist

Dendrochronology, dating system involving the study of tree rings

Devşirme, system under the Ottoman Empire whereby Christian boys were recruited (even abducted) at an early age and trained as janissaries

Dimarcheion, the Greek word for a town hall

Dormition, the 'falling asleep', in other words death, of the Virgin Mary

Double axe (*see Labrys*)

Dressed stone, stone worked to a surface finish

Dromos (pl. *dromoi*), literally 'road', used to denote the entrance passage to a tomb

Eisodia, literally 'entry', used in a theological context to denote the entry of the Virgin into the Temple, known in the West as the Presentation

Enosis, a Greek word meaning 'union', which came to symbolise the will of the people of Crete to be united to the mainland after Greece became independent in 1832

Eteocretan, refers both to the descendants of the original inhabitants of Crete and to the language they spoke, which is unrelated to Greek

Evangelists, the writers of the four Gospels, Matthew, Mark, Luke and John, often represented in Christian art by their symbols, respectively a man, a lion, a bull and an eagle

Exedra, semicircular or rectangular recessed area, often with seats

Ex-voto, votive offering left at a temple, shrine or other holy place

Faïence, in antiquity a non-clay ceramic material made of crushed quartz or sand coated with an alkaline glaze, frequently of a characteristic blue-green colour due to the presence of copper

Firman, a decree from the Ottoman government

Fresco, wall painting executed while the plaster is still wet

Graffito, scratched design or date on a wall

Gypsum, (*see Alabaster*)

Hierarchs, the three pre-eminent Doctors of the Eastern Church, St Basil the Great, St John Chrysostom and St Gregory of Nazianzus

Hippodamian, refers to the regular grid plan for city streets named after the 5th-century BC town planner Hippodamus of Miletus

Hodighitria (*also written Hodeghetria, Odighitria*), icon type representing the Virgin with the Child seated on her lap. It functions as a 'guide', presenting the infant Christ as 'the way'. Traditionally based on the prototype said to have been painted by St Luke

Horns of consecration, stylised ox skull only showing the horns, a Minoan cult symbol

Hyksos, people from Asia who invaded and ruled northern Egypt in the 17th–16th centuries BC. Their capital was at Avaris on the Nile Delta

Iconostasis, screen holding icons in a Byzantine church, separating the sanctuary from the laity

In situ, denotes an object or work of art that has been left in its original position. Archaeological remains found *in situ* are those found upon excavation in their final place of (ancient) deposition

Insula, the basic unit of the Hippodamian system; a block of housing

Ioannis Prodromos, St John the Baptist

Ioannis Theologos, St John the Evangelist

Isodomic, masonry made up of blocks of

TYPES OF MASONRY

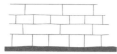

Isodomic

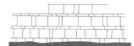

Pseudo-Isodomic

Polygonal

identical size with the vertical joins coming in the centre of the block below. The variant known as pseudo-isodomic has alternating taller and lower courses (*see illustration on p. 406*)

Kalathos, a vase in the shape of a basket with handles.

Kale, a Turkish word meaning castle or acropolis

Kalderimi (pl. *kalderimia*), a paved road dating from before the modern era

Kamara house, a type of vernacular architecture in Crete in which the room is divided lengthways by an arch defining four separate areas in the corners (*see illustration on p. 161*)

Kentis house, a single-room dwelling in which the beam supporting the roof rests on a forked post

Keraton, a stone box filled with the horns of young goats

Kernos (pl. *kernoi*), a cult object in stone or clay with several hollow receptacles (*see illustration on p. 123*). No firm interpretation exists. Some scholars have suggested that they may have been gaming boards; others believe they were for ritual offerings

Koimisis tis Theotokou, Dormition of the Virgin (*qv*)

Koinon, the loose alliance of Cretan city-states in the Archaic and Classical periods

Kore (pl. *korai*), from the Greek word for young girl, used to describe a standing female figure in Archaic style (*qv*). It is also a name for Persephone

Kouros (pl. *kouroi*), from the Greek word for young man, used to describe a standing nude male figure in Archaic style (*qv*)

Krater, large, wide-mouthed vessel used for mixing wine and water (*see illustrations on p. 411*)

Labrys, an artefact with two blades similar to those of an axe set on either side of a central shaft; a tool, but in a Minoan context a cult symbol

Larnax (pl. *larnakes*), chest or rectangular tub, normally in fired clay, used as a coffin

Lustral basin, a small, sunken room found in Minoan palaces and high-status buildings, of controversial purpose (*see p. 26*)

Madares, the high summer pastures, typically of the White Mountains

Mandylion, holy relic consisting of a piece of cloth on which the face of Christ is imprinted

Marine Style, style of Postpalatial pottery decoration which makes use of motifs of sea creatures, particularly octopuses

Martyrion (pl. *martyria*), building or chapel commemorating the death of a saint or martyr, or built over his or her tomb

Mastaba, in ancient Egypt a rectangular funerary structure made of mud brick, with sloping sides and a flat roof

Megaron, a large rectangular hall, typically the chief building of a Mycenaean city, with a roofed entrance lobby at one end

Meltemi, the north wind

Metamorphosis (tou Sotirou), the Transfiguration (of the Saviour)

Metope, square ornamental relief on a Doric frieze, alternating with triglyphs (*qv*); (*see illustration on p. 409*)

Mihrab, prayer niche in the wall of a mosque, indicating the direction of Mecca

Mitata, shepherds' stone huts in the high mountain pastures

Moni (pron. 'moni'), the Greek word for monastery or convent

Narthex, vestibule of a church or basilica stretching across the façade before the west entrance to the nave

Naumachia (pl. *naumachiae*), mock sea battle as staged in amphitheatres; also, by association, the area that was flooded for such a mock battle to take place

Nomarcheion, in a Greek town, the seat of the district government or prefecture

Nymphaeum, in the Greek and Roman world, originally a grotto filled with streams and springs considered the habitat of the nymphs. It came later to designate buildings or a room in a villa with fountains, plants and flowers and statuary

Obsidian, a natural glass occurring in volcanic areas when lava comes into contact with water. When hard it flakes much like flint, and was used for tools from early antiquity

Odeion, small theatre, occasionally roofed, typically used for musical performances

Opus sectile, geometrically patterned floor or wall covering made of coloured pieces (larger than mosaic tesserae) of marble or glass

Orientalising, decorative style originating in the Near East that swept through the Aegean from the second half of the 8th century BC, eventually reaching Etruria in Italy, and exercising a profound influence on the figurative arts and the development of mythology. It is characterised by an almost baroque exuberance, contrasting with the home-grown, more austere Geometric style

Orthostat, large stone slab set vertically in the lower part of a wall

Ostrakon (pl. *ostraka*), a potsherd used in antiquity as a writing medium

Palindromic, denotes a text whose letters form the same word or phrase when read either backwards or forwards

Panaghia, the 'All Holy' Virgin

Pantocrator, literary 'He who Controls All', a representation of Christ in Majesty traditionally featured in the central dome of Orthodox churches and in the main apse of an Early Christian basilica

Peak sanctuary, a Minoan cult place in an elevated position, thought to protect the settlement or settlements it overlooks

Pendentive, one of four concave spandrels (triangular spaces) descending from the 'corners' of a dome, in Christian architecture decorated with images or symbols of the Evangelists (*qv*)

Peristyle, colonnade surrounding all four sides of a courtyard or a building

Phrygana, type of scrubland that occurs on limestone soils around the Mediterranean as a result of woodland degradation, with an interesting population of aromatic bushes

Phi figurines, Mycenaean clay statuettes where the body bulges in such a way that the whole figure resembles the Greek letter *phi* (Φ)

Pier-and-door partition, (*see Polythyron*)

Pitharakia, smaller pithoi

Pithos (pl. *pithoi*), large ceramic container used for storage, often taller than a man

Platytera, representation of the Virgin and Child as a symbol of the Incarnation. The Christ Child is placed in the centre of the Virgin's lap or abdomen. She holds her hands out wide. The full name of the icon type is '*Platytera ton Ouranon*', wider than the heavens. It illustrates the paradox that the Virgin's womb yielded space to the godhead, creator of the Universe

Polygonal, a style of masonry in which blocks of irregular shape are roughly hewn to fit (*see illustration on p. 406*)

Polythyron (pl. *polythyra*), Greek for 'many doors', a way to articulate space and divide rooms in a high-status Minoan dwelling by slotting removable partitions between posts (piers)

Pronaos, vestibule at the entrance of a temple, preceding the naos (cella) or temple proper

Protogeometric, pottery style with simple, non-figurative decoration (1050–900 BC)

Prytaneion, a public building in which the governors of the city conducted their business and took their meals

Pseudo-isodomic (*see Isodomic*)

Psi figurines, Mycenaean clay statuettes where the stylised arms are held aloft so that, with arms and head together, the figure resembles the Greek letter *psi* (Ψ)

Pyxis (pl. *pyxides*), small, round, lidded box

TYPES OF COLUMN

Below: Typical Minoan column, tapering from top to bottom. The columns were made out of cypress tree trunks, placed upside down to prevent sprouting. All have perished,

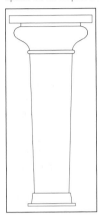

but their shape is known from surviving clay models of buildings. The columns at Knossos are concrete reconstructions.

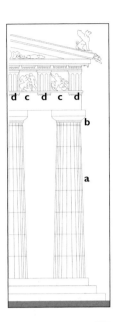

Right: Section of a temple portico in the Doric order. The column shaft **(a)** is quite stout, made of fluted stone rings placed one upon another. They stand directly on the temple platform, with no base. The capital **(b)** is plain. Above it, the entablature is made up of carved metopes **(c)** separated by triglyphs **(d)**.

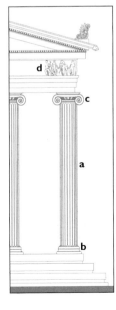

Right: Section of a temple portico in the Ionic order. The column shaft **(a)** is slender and fluted and stands on a base **(b)**. The capital **(c)** is distinguished by its scrolls, known as volutes. Above a stepped architrave, the entablature is made up of a continuous carved frieze **(d)** (*only a portion of it illustrated*).

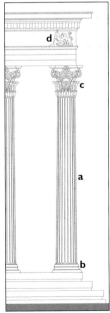

Far right: Section of a temple portico in the Corinthian order. The column shaft **(a)** is very tall and fluted, and stands on a base **(b)**. The capital **(c)** is distinguished by its decoration of acanthus leaves. There is a continuous frieze **(d)**, as in the Ionic order.

made in pottery, stone, ivory, metal or wood (*see illustration opposite*)

Quadriga, a two-wheeled chariot drawn by four horses

Refuge site, a site often in an unhospitable location, difficult of access, where, after the destruction of the palaces, the vestiges of the Minoan population are thought to have retreated and clung on to their way of life

Relieving triangle, three-cornered empty space above a lintel, designed to lessen the load that it has to bear. It is a characteristic feature of tholos tombs (*qv*)

Repoussé, a metalworking technique in which metal is shaped by hammering on the reverse side, 'pushing out' the design

Rotunda, a building with a circular plan, often covered by a dome

Rhyton (pl. *rhyta*), vessel made of clay or metal, sometimes moulded at one end in the shape of an animal head, with an opening for the liquid to run through when making libations (*see p. 390 and illustrations opposite*)

Scarab, a dung beetle; by association, a beetle-shaped seal

Sealing, impression left by a seal stone or a seal ring showing at times, on the reverse, traces of the cloth or the string onto which the clay was applied

Serenissima, the Most Serene Republic (of Venice)

Sima, the upturned edge of a roof acting as a gutter; made of fired clay or stone, it may be continuous or broken by spouts

Sistrum (pl. *sistra*), a percussion instrument like a rattle (*see illustration on p. 43*)

Snake tube, hollow ceramic artefact open at both ends with sinuous appliqué decoration. Used as a pot stand

Sphyrelaton, a metalworking technique meaning 'hammer driven', invented in Egypt in the 3rd millennium BC. In it elements of a figure were made separately by hammering unheated metal sheets over wooden forms; the sheets were then held together with rivets and worked with incisions

Spolia, building material reused from an earlier ruined or demolished structure

Stavropegial status, a term derived from the Greek word '*stavropegion*', referring to the cross fixed by the bishop to the side of a new church. Institutions enjoying stavropegial status owed canonical allegiance directly to the Patriarch of Constantinople

Stele (pl. *stelae*), upright stone slab sometimes decorated and used as a grave marker

Stirrup jar, a pottery vessel with stirrup-shaped handles from shoulder to false neck and the spout on the shoulder (*see illustration opposite*)

Stoa, a covered, free-standing colonnaded portico, often with a row of shops under the arcade

Stratigraphy, refers in archaeology to the study of the layers defining different deposits, with the topmost generally being the most recent

Stylobate, the solid base on which a row of columns stands in a church or ancient temple

Tabula Peutingeriana, the medieval copy of a Roman road map covering the whole Roman Empire and named after the Peutinger family, who owned the document in the early 18th century

Temenos, a sacred precinct

Templon, a partition separating the faithful from the officiating clergy in an Orthodox church

Tholos tomb, circular funerary building, roofed in a domed, 'beehive' shape either by stone corbelling or by an organic structure

Threnos, in the Classical world, a poem or speech of lamentations, normally for the dead. In Christianity it dwells on the sufferings of Christ

Triclinium, in a Roman house, specifically a room with three couches; by association, the 'dining room'

Triglyph, a small decorative panel on a Doric frieze carved with three vertical channels (*see illustration on previous page*)

Vitex, a purple-flowered shrub native to the Mediterranean region (full name *Vitex agnus-castus*)

Xoanon (pl. *xoana*), from the Greek word for carving and scraping, it refers to a cult image in wood

Xyloscalo, a path with a wooden railing

Zoödochos Pigi, popular church dedication to the Virgin as the 'Fount of Life'

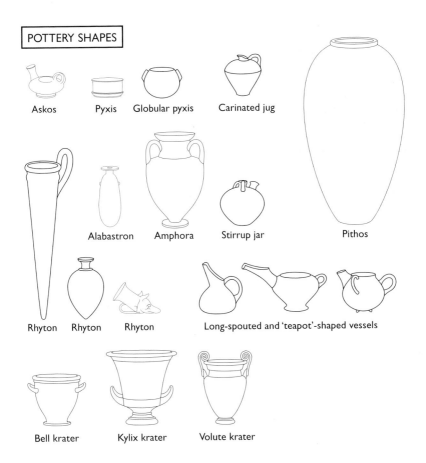

POTTERY SHAPES

Askos

Pyxis

Globular pyxis

Carinated jug

Alabastron

Amphora

Stirrup jar

Pithos

Rhyton   Rhyton   Rhyton

Long-spouted and 'teapot'-shaped vessels

Bell krater

Kylix krater

Volute krater

CHRONOLOGY

Pre-pottery Neolithic and Neolithic
(7000–3400 BC)

The first permanent settlers introduce cereal cultivation and domesticated cattle across the island. Spinning and weaving, contacts with the Cyclades.

Bronze Age
(3400–970 BC)

Prepalatial (3400–1900 BC)
The climate becomes drier and overseas contacts increase. Bronze working introduced; settlements become larger. Vasiliki ware. Communal burials with rich offerings (Mesara tombs) show the beginnings of a stratified society not yet mirrored in settlements. Peak sanctuaries.

Old Palace/Protopalatial Period (1900–1700 BC)
First palaces built in Knossos, Malia, Zakros and Phaistos, plus high-status villas. Emergence of elites able to control food production and distribution. Settlement expands. Evidence for writing (Hieroglyphs and Linear A). Kamares ware and new metalworking techniques. Fresco painting. First terrace walls to expand agricultural land.
c. 1600: General destruction (earthquake or fire, possibly both).

New Palace/Neopalatial Period (1700–1370 BC)
Palaces rebuilt but with a different focus: more cult areas, reduced storage and an accent on production of luxury goods. Religion is concentrated here, at the expense of the peak sanctuaries, which go into decline. Reduced contacts between palace and surrounding settlement. More villas with increased storage capacity. Wide-ranging foreign contacts.
c. 1600: Santorini eruption: contrary to persistent rumours, Crete is little or not affected.
c. 1450: Troubled times, with decreased settlement and trade followed by general destruction by fire, probably the result of fighting.
Early 14th century: Knossos's revival at the hands of the Mycenaeans. Linear B. Warrior graves (individual).

Postpalatial Period (1370–1070 BC)
Chania peaks. On the south coast, Kommos flourishes and builds gigantic shipsheds.
End 13th century: Mycenaean dominance in the Mediterranean comes to an end. Crete eases itself out of the Minoan period, fills cemeteries with larnakes, and stops writing.

Subminoan Period
Minoan diehards take to mountain refuges while new arrivals from the Greek mainland mark a turning point in Crete's destiny.

Iron Age
(970–630 BC)

The time of the city-states (as many as 90 according to Homer) with new burial practices (cremation), new technologies (iron metallurgy) and a pottery style (Geometric) imported from the Greek mainland.
Late 7th century: First inscriptions in Greek on Cretan soil.

Archaic Period
(630–480 BC)

Crete contributes to the emergence of Greek sculpture with the Eleftherna Kore.

Classical and Hellenistic periods
(480–67 BC)

Crete is a backwater, leaving the limelight to Athens. The island is preoccupied with internal warfare. However, the Gortyn Law Code does emerge. Alexander the Great opens up new trade routes and new opportunities for piracy.

146: Rome conquers mainland Greece. Crete follows not long after.

Roman Period
(67 BC–AD 330)

Crete twinned with Cyrenaica for administrative purposes, settles down for a long period of peace, expanding settlement up to the coast, where pirates are no longer a danger. Agricultural production picks up and so do exports. Cretan city-states turn into model Roman towns. Knossos becomes a Roman colony, Gortyn is the new capital.

First Byzantine Period
(330–824)

The time of the Christian basilicas, some 70 of them, large buildings with mosaics showing a degree of wealth. Decline sets in towards the 7th century, when Knossos is no more and Byzantium can no longer ensure Crete's protection against external attacks.

21st July 395: The Byzantine Paroxysm, an enormous earthquake. Crete's geography is irrevocably altered.

Arab Period
(824–961)

Saracen conquest of Crete. Rabdh el-Khandak (later Herakleion) operates as a slave market.

Second Byzantine Period
(961–1204)

Crete is re-evangelised; new churches are built but on a reduced scale. Rabdh el-Khandak, renamed Khandakas, is made the new capital, after an unsuccessful attempt at finding an inland location. Venice now emerges as a power in the eastern Mediterranean and threatens Byzantium, which it sacks in 1204. Crete is transferred to Venice as part of the ensuing settlement.

Venetian Period
(1204–1669)

Venice takes control of Crete as its first overseas colony and establishes a dominion known as the Regno di Candia. Khandakas becomes Candia. Increased contacts with the West and with the ideas of the Italian Renaissance affect the cultural and artistic life of the island.

1211: First revolt led by the ruling Byzantine families followed by the Pax Kallergi, an agreement intended to buy them off.

1360s: St Titus Revolt led by the Venetian settlers themselves against the excessive demands of the motherland. Lasithi is cleared out, settlement is banned.

1453: Fall of Byzantium to the Ottomans. Crete is now the easternmost Christian outpost in the Mediterranean.

1514: Lasithi is repopulated and drained. Agriculture expands but not on the coast, where settlement is in retreat because of pirate attacks.

c. 1567: Domenico Theotokopoulos (El Greco) moves to Venice on his way to Spain.

1583: Onorio Belli comes to Crete and spends the next 16 years recording Roman remains.

1645: The Turks land at Gonia (in west Crete, at the foot of the Rodopos peninsula).

1669: The Ottoman conquest of Crete is completed with the end of the siege of Candia.

Ottoman Period
(1669–1898)

The Turkish occupation spells almost the end of pirate attacks and settlement expands accordingly. Herakleion (now called Megalokastro) is still the capital. While churches are turned into mosques in the towns, a proportion of the urban population converts to the new faith. In the late 19th century archaeologists flock from west Europe and America to Crete, tempted by the amazing surface finds all over the island.

1770: Daskalogiannis revolt.

1832: Greek independence.

1837: Robert Pashley travels all over the island and records ethnographical and archaeological observations.

1866: The Great Uprising. The Ottomans grant equal rights to Muslims and Christians, but the Cretans now have *enosis* (the union with Greece) firmly in their minds.

1878–79: Minos Kalokairinos's excavations on Kephala Hill (Knossos).

1898: Intervention of the Great Powers (Britain, France, Russia and Italy), followed by the departure of the Ottomans.

Independence to the present

Crete becomes independent under a High Commissioner. The capital is Chania.

23rd March 1900: Sir Arthur Evans starts excavating at Kephala Hill (Knossos).

1913: Union with Greece.

1923: The great population exchange: Turks leave and are replaced by Greek and Armenian refugees expelled from Turkey.

1941–45: The Battle of Crete.

1960s: Mass tourism comes to Crete bringing about important social changes.

1971: Herakleion becomes the capital.

INDEX

Numbers in italics are picture references. Where many pages are listed, references to those where the main content or information about a subject appears are given in bold. Names in brackets after a reference, where there is more than one place with the same name listed, indicate the province or nearest town.

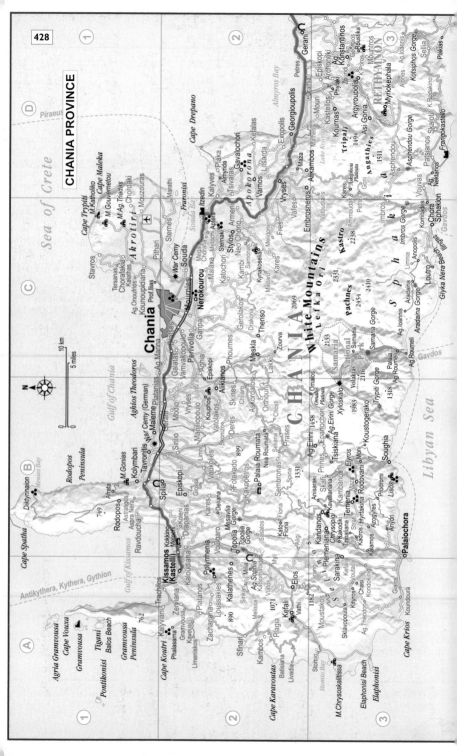

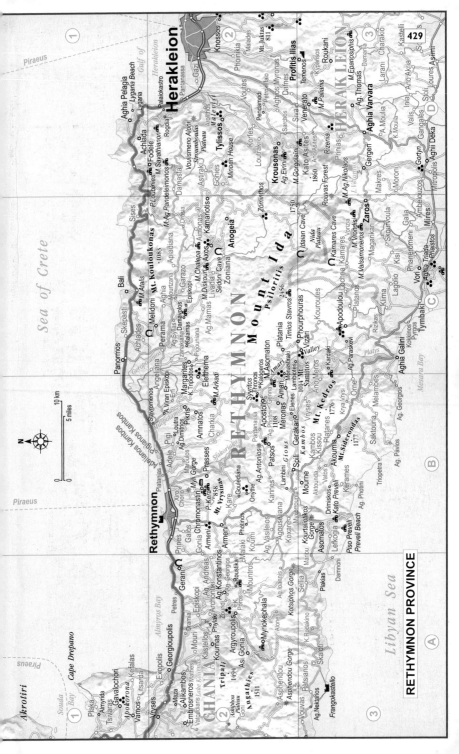

RETHYMNON PROVINCE

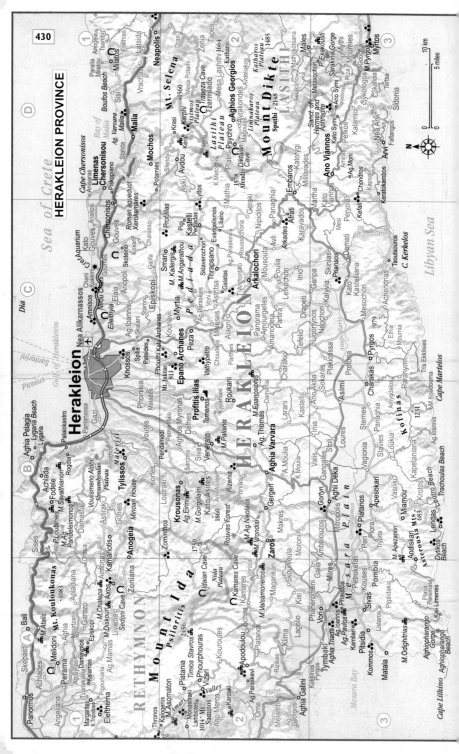

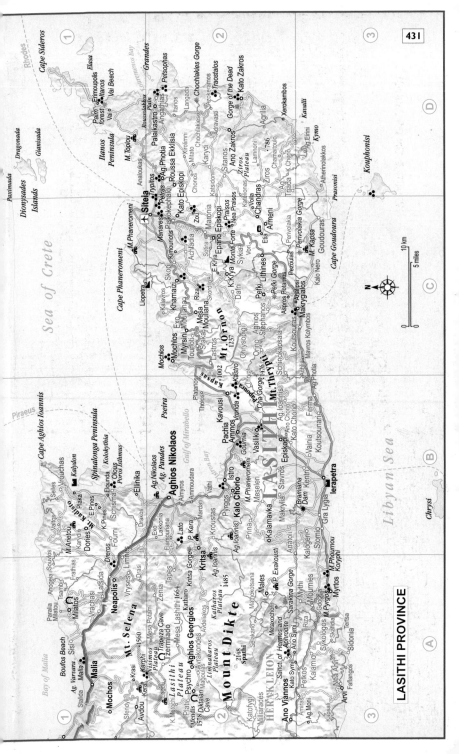

LASITHI PROVINCE

Sea of Crete

Libyan Sea

Gulf of Mirabello

Mirabello Bay

10 km
5 miles

Mount Dikte

Mt. Selena

Mt. Oreon

Mt. Thripti

HERAK LEION

Rhodes

Cape Sideros

Paximada

Dionysades
Islands

Dragonada

Gianisada

Grandes

Enimoupolis
Plain

Palm
forest

Vai Beach

Vai

Itanos

Ianos
Peninsula

M.Toplou

Roussolakkos

Palaikastro

Ag. Photia

Angathias

Petsophas

Chochlakies Gorge

Zakros
Gorge of the Dead

Kato Zakros

Ano Zakros

Ziros
Plateau

Xerokambos

Agnia

Kouphonisi

Karoulli

Prasonisi

Goudouras

Kalo Nero

M. Kapsa

Pervolakia Gorge

Cape Goudouras

Pezoulas

Makrygialos

Analoukas

Sitanos

Katsidoni

Chamaitoulo

Lamnoni

786

Chonos

Xiroliimni

Karydi

Mitato

Chochlakies

Adravasti

Zakatheros

Traostalos

Langadh

Sitela

Praisos
Nea Praisos

Epano Episkopi

Forte
Monte

Voni

Etia

Ziros

Ag.
Tigada
Jiada

Ananolakkos

Ag.Eirini

Kymo

Lithines

Pefki Gorge

Pefki

Orino

Chandras

Sykia

Maronia

E. Krya

K. Krya

Datmi

Schinokapsala

Aspros Potamos

Koutsouras

Mavros Kolymbos

Agios
Stephanos

Ornio

Chrysopigi

Agios
Ioannis

Lastros

Stavrochori

Ag. Pholia

Pervolakia Gorge

Ferma

Koutsounari

Gra Lygia

Stomio

Kato Chorio

Vainia

Bramiana
Dam Kent?

Ierapetra

Makrylia?

Meseleri

Anatoli

Kalogero

Mythi

Males

Riza

Sykologos

M.Pyrgos

Mournies

Gdochia

Myrtos

Tertsa

Sidonia

M.Phoumou
Konphi

Kalamafki

Kato Symi

Sanct. of Hermes and
Aphrodite

Pefkos

Kalamio

Ano Symi

Metaxochori

Sarakina Gorge

Ano Viannos

Ag. Moni

Nea Ana?

Amira

Kassli

Fafangos

Milliarades

Katofygi

Sikala

Selakano

Mattokotsana

Matokotsana

Exakousti

Kalamafka

Ag.Ioannis

Pyrgos

Kalo Chorio

Prina

Istro

Kalamaka

Gournia

Vasiliki

Episkopi

Pachia
Ammos

Mardati

Kroustas

Ag.Ioannis

Vathi

Ammoudara

Aghios Nikolaos

Ag.Nikolaos

Ag. Pandes

Lato

P. Kera

Kritsa

Kritsa Gorge

Dreros

Exo
Lakonia

Flamouriana

Ellinika

Olous

Poros Isthmus

Kolokythia

Elounda

Spinalonga Peninsula

Cape Aghios Ioannis

Schisma

K.Pines

E. Pines

Vrachasi

Milatos

Neapolis

Paralia
Milatou

Sisi

Boufos Beach

Ag. Varvara

Slatia

Malia

Mochos

Krasi

Kera

Karphi

Nisimos
Plateau

Trapeza Cave

Tzermiado

Lasithi
Plateau

Psychro

Diktaian
Cave

Avrakondes

Magoula

K.Metochi
Cave

Mendis

Platit
Plateau

Mesa Lasithi 1664

Katharo
Plateau

1578

Plati
Plateau

Limnakaros
Plateau

Katharos
Plateau 1485

Aghios Georgios

Kaminaki

Ag.Charalambos

Zenia

Gonies

Vrysses

Latsida

Limnes

Drasi

Tapes

1002

Kapsas

Kavousi

Vronda

Meseleri

Pseira

Platanos
Tholos

Mochlos

Myrsini

Exo
Mouliana

Mesa
Mouliana

Stavrod?

Touditoi

Skopi

Piskokephalo

Manares

Petras

Tripitos

Kimoundis

Roussa Eklisia

Kato Episkopi

Zou

Achladia

Sotra

Chonos

Sitanos

Prina?

Kalavros

Khamaizi

Riza

Exo

Vori

Epano Episkopi

Ziros

Forte

Vola

Armeni

Ag. Ioannis

Chamalevri

Cape Phaneromeni

M. Phaneromeni

Lioperta

M.Phaneromeni

Kalo
Chorio

N

Chryssi

Kato Symi

Spathi
2148

Vrouchas

Kalydon

Selles

Valtos

Souloi

Anogeia

Tsambi

Frathsi

Karydi

Dories

M.Aretou
1560

M. Kaisou

Karfi

Kefo

Avdou

Sfendyli

Slatia

Kroustallenia

Livada

Piraeus

786

contd. from p. 4

Editor: Annabel Barber

Regional maps: Dimap Bt and Kartext; Site plans: ©Blue Guides and Imre Bába
Watercolours: Edit Nagy

Photo research, editing and pre-press: Hadley Kincade
Photographs by Phil Robinson: pp. 42, 51, 65, 72, 92, 147, 179, 181, 183, 273, 276, 325, 329, 331, 332; Paola Pugsley: pp. 96, 105, 135, 146, 251, 307, 312, 331; Tom Howells: pp. 74, 90, 181, 182, 216; Annabel Barber: pp. 30, 70, 78, 80, 91, 116, 121, 123, 131, 177, 182, 183, 192, 198, 199, 203, 218, 248, 277, 284, 286, 290, 318, 319, 363; Roger Barber: p. 213; Gábor Bodó: p. 73; Ian Swindale: pp. 87, 368; ©Samuel Magal/Sites & Photos: pp. 157, 193, 195, 209, 237, 264; The Art Archive/Herakleion Museum/Gianni dagli Orti: pp. 44, 127; ©1990. Photo Scala, Florence, courtesy of the Ministero per i Beni e Atti. Culturali: p. 53; ©dk/Alamy/ Red Dot: p. 170; courtesy of Minerva Magazine (www.minervamagazine.com): p. 153; Sezione di Storia ed Epigrafia del Dipartimento di Scienze storiche, archeologiche ed antropologiche dell'antichità, Università 'La Sapienza', Roma: p. 141; ©Walter Bibikow/Corbis/Red Dot: p. 188; ©istockphoto.com/rainmax: p. 260; ©istockphoto.com/Jean Bienvenu: p. 336; ©istockphoto. com/Paul Cowan: pp. 355, 371; ©istockphoto.com/Tobias Jo: p. 356; ©istockphoto.com/fe- linda: p. 364; Shutterstock: p. 266; ©Vick Fisher/Alamy/Red Dot: p. 335; ©Eyebyte/Alamy/Red Dot: p. 341; ©Istituto Veneto di Scienze, Lettere ed Arti: pp. 36, 39, 47, 54.

Cover photographs:
Top: *Tulipa bakerii*, endemic in western Crete (photo: Nature Picture Library/Alamy/Red Dot)
Bottom: Tigani beach and the islet of Agria, Gramvousa peninsula (photo: © Robert Harding Picture Library Ltd/Alamy/Red Dot)
Frontispiece and spine: Details of the Knossos frescoes *Prince of the Lilies* and *Ladies in Blue*.

Line drawings pp. 390, 406, 409, 411: Gabriella Juhász & Michael Mansell RIBA; pp. 27, 256: Annabel Barber; p. 45: Edit Nagy.

The author wishes to thank Cambridge University Library, Yorgos Brokalakis, Hilary and Phil Dawson, Don Evely, Oliver Rackham and Carlo Urbani. Thanks from the editor also to Nikos Stavroulakis.

Material prepared for press by Anikó Kuzmich, Printed in Hungary by Dürer Nyomda Kft, Gyula.

ISBN 978-1-905131-29-7